Xavier Herbert was born in Port Hedland, Western Australia, in 1901. He was educated there and in Fremantle, qualifying as a pharmacist. After the First World War he travelled in Australia, reaching Darwin in 1927. There he worked as a railway fettler and visited the south Pacific, experiences that went towards his first novel, *Capricornia*. He continued to travel, both overseas and within Australia, until, in 1946, he settled near Cairns with his wife Sadie Norden. He combined writing with a variety of casual occupations.

Capricornia was first published in 1938 and won the Sesquicentenary literary competition in the same year. He won the Miles Franklin award for *Poor Fellow My Country* which was published in 1975. His other work includes *Seven Emus* (1959), *Soldiers' Women* (1961), *Larger Than Life* (1963) and *Disturbing Element* (1963).

Xavier Herbert died in 1984.

AN ANGUS & ROBERTSON BOOK

First published by Publicist Publishing Company, Sydney in 1938
The second Australian edition was published
by Angus & Robertson, also in 1938
First published in the United Kingdom
by Angus & Robertson in 1939
Subsequent Australian editions in
either hard-bound or paperback form
were published by Angus & Robertson in
1939, 1941, 1943, 1945, 1946, 1947, 1949,
1956, 1959, 1963 (twice), 1969, 1970, 1973,
1974, 1975 (twice), 1977, 1979, 1981, 1985, 1989
This Imprint Classics edition published in Australia in 1990 by
Collins/Angus & Robertson Publishers Australia

Collins/Angus & Robertson Publishers Australia
A division of HarperCollins Publishers (Australia) Pty Ltd
Unit 4, Eden Park, 31 Waterloo Road, North Ryde
NSW 2113, Australia
William Collins Publishers Ltd
31 View Road, Glenfield, Auckland 10, New Zealand
Angus & Robertson (UK)
16 Golden Square, London W1R 4BN, United Kingdom

National Library of Australia
Cataloguing-in-Publication data:

Herbert, Xavier, 1901-1984.
    Capricornia.
    ISBN 0 207 17024 X.
    I. Title
A823.2

Cover painting: Margaret Preston
                   Australia 1875-1963

                   Aboriginal Art
                   colour stencil on paper
                   21.8 x 30.2 cm

                   Collection: Australian National Gallery, Canberra

Printed in Australia by Griffin Press

6   5   4   3   2   1
95 94 93 92 91 90

IMPRINT CLASSICS

CAPRICORNIA

XAVIER HERBERT

Introduced by
Mudrooroo Nyoongah

A division of HarperCollins*Publishers*

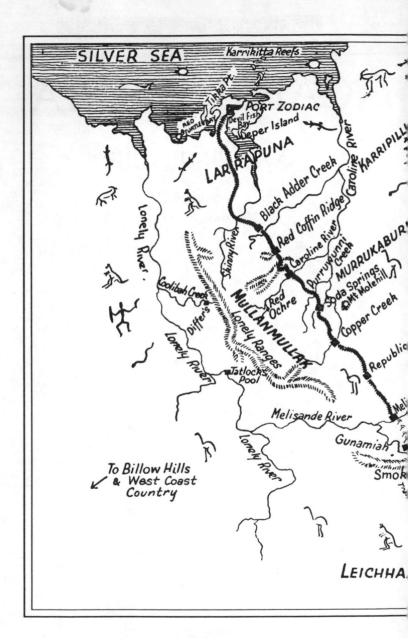

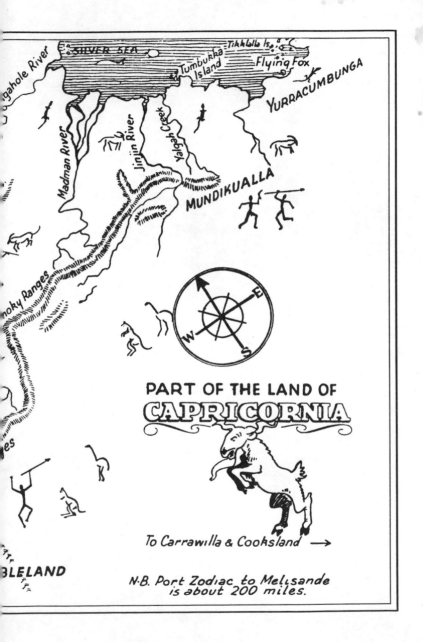

PART OF THE LAND OF

CAPRICORNIA

To Carrawilla & Cooksland →

N.B. Port Zodiac to Melisande
is about 200 miles.

INTRODUCTION

Vast and sprawling, of almost epic dimensions in that theme
and counter-theme battle for dominance, *Capricornia*
reflects Australia in its failure to create an alternative to
the society depicted in its pages. It is a rich Australian
cultural archive. Herbert labours over the wide brown plains
of the colony of Capricornia and finds characters who are
readily identifiable as Australian types. There is an unpre-
tentiousness of style which is often appealing; but an
Aboriginal reader may find the narrative painful in its
seeming historical objectivity. He or she begins to read the
novel and finds scenes of devastation and heartbreak as
the newcomers, the 'dingoes' of the text, destroy Black
culture without a qualm. These 'dingoes' are depicted as
a terrifying almost elemental force, an aspect of 'natural
selection', which destroys the old in a process of 'evolution'
towards a new 'synthesis'.

But this scientific theory, which provides ontological
thrust to the novel, is weakened by a counter-theme of
'Fate'. Few, if any of the characters possess the gift of
analytical thought, or question their place in the universe,
and I use 'universe' deliberately as Herbert (and critics)
has stressed that his narrative is concerned with universal
themes. Thus events are seen not as random occurrences
but as contradictions between theme and counter-theme:
natural selection and Fate. The dominance of Fate in the
opening pages of the novel is alarming. Events begin to
unfold from the very beginning of white settlement and
the arrival of what passes for civilisation in a territory on
the outskirts of the British Empire. Capricornia is founded
in the heyday of that Empire, in the late nineteenth century,

and from inauspicious beginnings it stagnates into the first decades of the twentieth century. This period was not at all a good time for the natives of the colonies. The Indian mutiny of 1857 underlined the problem of the 'native', and Capricornia too has its 'native problem'. By the time we reach the end of the long narrative, the problem has still not been resolved. The natives and a newly engendered 'Coloured' race persist in a system from which there seems to be no future relief.

Capricornia is a work of great length. The original editor P. R. Stephenson claimed co-authorship on the basis of his editorial work, and perhaps the underlying sternness of the text owes something to him. Stephenson was a complex character searching for a novel in which to be featured. His politics were bizarre though they seemed not to have alarmed any of his associates. Did they listen avidly or painfully as he espoused neo-Nazism, berated the Jews and accepted the importance of Japan in the world in which the red of the British Empire blooded much of the globe? Also a strong nationalist, he sought for things Australian and found the Australian Aborigines. He declared them essential to Australian nationalism. His position in this matter is quite interesting and from it extends a bridge to those racists in the Northern Territory—the 'Capricornia' of the novel—who trade in Aboriginal art and artefacts and acknowledge the Aborigines as essential to their economic well-being while treating the artists with disrespect. But then Australian nationalism has always been a fragile thing of, of . . . Perhaps someone will find a word and put it here for me. I cannot locate a singular word of worth, though I might write 'defiance'. Stephenson is indicative of the complex and contradictory ways in which Aboriginality is presented and articulated in this wide brown land, a great swath of which is 'Capricornia'.

First published in 1938, *Capricornia* was with affectionate irony called 'that old botch', but it was popular from the day of its publication and has remained in print to this day. It is a bit 'blotchy' and if not for the sternness of its vision, I might read it as a Picaresque Romance detailing life in the distant colony of Capricornia under conditions which are barbaric to say the least. Much of the novel is taken up with the plight of the rapidly increasing mixed race. A representative of 'the Coloureds' is the sympathetic main character 'Norman'. The emphasis placed on this new 'racial' type, who is seen as being more noble than either White or Black, reveals a mythology which uses oppositional symbolism to stress the theme and counter-theme of the novel.

In many ways, *Capricornia* finds a mate in the much later Maurice Chauvel film, *Jedda* (1955), even to the construction of characters who often seem flat and, writing from the present, slightly absurd. *Jedda* could also be called a Picaresque Romance, though placing them under the same label glosses over the very contradictions which the novel proposes to explore. Additionally, the underlying seriousness of *Capricornia* separates it from the somewhat simplistic realist film of Chauvel. Both, however, have endings which reveal the pessimism Europeans seem to get from exposure to an Australia so markedly different from Europe.

Capricornia is massive and might have become an epic in which two races with opposing cultures meet, battle it out, sink into each other's arms and create the new Australian race, a mixture of good points from the opposing cultures; but this synthesis never occurs. Vincent Buckley writes, 'The total impression of the book is one of great creative energy battling against a universe of appalling waste'. The vision of a 'new race' being created in the colony is at odds with the strong emphasis placed on Fate which plays 'dingo to all men'—black and white. (Does this 'Dingo of Fate' equate with the Giant Devil Dingo of Aboriginal mythology, which devours humankind?) It is an all-compelling deity bringing to nought man and his works, including the promised new race. The novel ends on a note of pessimism. Things will continue as they are fated to do, and as I have argued before, this is a strong trait of the Australian character. Even the very metaphors applied to the land reflect this pessimism: Ancient, arid, the dead heart, flood-ridden, drought-infested, 'one bloody thing after another'. Man is caught in the twister of Fate and goes around and around. This is stressed in the novel and there is absent a sense of control which the concept of a 'new race' might have been able to supply. If I read the novel correctly, the 'new race' in the process of being formed would eventually be able to direct its own fate. Unfortunately the vision falters and, instead of exploring any political and cultural possibilities inherent in the 'new race', Herbert resolves his novel by the acceptance of an overarching Fate against which mankind strives in vain.

I use 'man' and 'mankind' because I find Herbert's novel hard and masculine. The style is close to the bald prose of reportage. Thus, the wide brown land may also be used as a metaphor to a text which is close to the popular best seller. Characters are not so much developed as created in a nutshell, that is, in a name. Thus 'Norman' may equal No-man or New-man, a Coloured who is a representative of the new race. Norman is a product of what Thomas Keneally in *The Chant of Jimmy Blacksmith* has called 'the white phallus' (which may also be equated with white shame). He is the bastard son of the grazier Mark Shillings-worth and an unknown black woman. Norman is also the protagonist in the novel, and it is through him that the 'new race' is shown and a transformation attempted.

Sexual need and sexual shame mark the colonisation of Capricornia. And it is this sexual need and the resultant shame that Herbert seeks to exorcise, or transform. The sins of the Colonisers can be no sins, if the result is a New Race of Capricornians. It is not individual sexual need which is at issue; but the very 'fact' of natural selection. The novel represents sexual need and shame, not from the position of colonial dominance; but through the workings of the Darwinian theory of Natural Selection as applied to races. In trying to do this, Herbert begins his narrative with a wry description of the founding of the main settlements on the coast and moves on to the eventual subjugation of the whole territory of Capricornia. The novel is similar to those by Wilbur Smith which detail the founding and development of the colony of Rhodesia and its revolution into the sovereign state of Zimbabwe; but unlike these postwar novels which are firmly slotted into the genre of romantic adventure, Herbert has a more serious intent in writing the history of his colony. In truth, it is a sad colony and not one man of the stature of Cecil Rhodes appears. It is a 'universe of appalling waste'; but one in which the promise of the 'New Man' is seeded. The promise is there, but remains only a promise. The New Man is confronted by Giant Devil Dingo Fate, and goes under as the crows cry dismally. Herbert's characters are under the control of this 'Fate' and develop towards an acceptance of it as the overarching Law of the universe.

Uncle Oscar gives Norman an education and then property. Norman becomes a man of substance, one able to take his place in what passes for society in Capricornia. But, after journeying South for an education, he returns to find he is still a 'half-caste'. Initially, he is shocked to discover that he does indeed belong to both races; but then he comes to the realisation that he is their heir. It is at this point that Herbert's vision falters and Norman suffers a personal tragedy which prevents him from taking his rightful place. The Giant Devil Dingo Fate intervenes on the side of the 'status quo'.

Herbert peoples the colony of Capricornia with a rich cast of characters, some of whom marry the native women they keep as mistresses. An important minor character is Peter Differ. Peter 'I beg to differ' is a failed poet and has been considered Xavier Herbert's mouthpiece. He is a sympathetic character, and in his obligatory discourse on race relations he takes the side of the emerging 'Coloureds'. He has helped in the creation of this race; but unlike most other white men, he elects to marry his Black woman. He begs to differ and refuses to accept the syndrome of need and shame under which many men of the colony suffer. He seeks to place himself on the side of the scientific theory of natural selection. But the matrimonial act means little to his fellow colonists; merely a shift in shame. Now he suffers the shame of a white father whose children are treated no differently from illegitimate half-castes.

Herbert reveals, though he does not state, that a colonial society works by exclusion. Effectively, it is made up of many settler factions, each with some degree of power or influence, which find unity only in defending their privileged position against the colonised. This state of affairs is recognised in the novel, though Herbert does not give an analysis of the political situation in the Territory. In 1937, the year before the novel was published, state representatives of Aboriginal Authorities met in Canberra. Each state representative gave an account of Native Affairs in his respective state. Most favoured the assimilation of the Aborigine into the wider society. This position was endorsed by the representative from the Northern Territory who in his address expressed alarm at the rapidly increasing mixed population that, growing up bitter and unfranchised, might in time take over the whole territory.

Thus, at the same time the novel was being written there was a fear in the Northern Territory that the white minority population might lose its place of dominance and be replaced by a 'Coloured' majority. Xavier Herbert, active in Aboriginal Affairs, would have been aware of this concern, and he addresses it in his novel. He shows us the formation of this race, but none of its political ambitions. His 'New Race', coming into being through natural selection and destined to succeed both black and white, is set up in opposition to 'Fate'; and eventually 'Fate' wins. In his narrative, it is the 'Coloureds' that suffer the most and who exist in the most precarious social position. They are more victims than victors, and this may be what Herbert had in mind when raising the idea, or vision, of a superior mixed race. Politically, they have no power and no status, except in the set speeches of 'well-meaning' white characters. What happens to them may be seen in the case of the character Constance, who after being seduced and made pregnant by a Protector of Aborigines, Humbolt Lace, is then wedded to the Coloured Peter Pan in order to hide his need and shame. Although this might be seen as an example of natural selection, the end of the novel is symbolic of the Coloureds' dilemma. The Giant Devil Dingo Fate rules and the crows salute him.

Herbert uses symbols and simple oppositions to structure his novel. In Chapter One, the heading 'The Coming of the Dingoes' underlines the then generally accepted civilisation/primitive opposition which is given in the lines:

When dingoes come to a waterhole, the ancient kangaroos, not having teeth or ferocity enough to defend their heritage, must relinquish it, or die.

This sets the theme of the coming into being of a 'New Race' through natural selection. Herbert is using the theory correctly though simply, and if we accept it at face value, he is not talking about Social Darwinism at all, but about natural selection in which one species succeeds another, not one society another. He is not describing the replacement of Aboriginal culture and society by the stronger British 'civilisation'; but by a 'new' society emerging from the amalgamation of the two. The opposition of primitivism and civilisation engages in an ironic dialectic, and the synthesis of the dialectic is the 'new' race; but the potentialities of this 'new' race are not 'realised'.

Herbert introduces a counter-theme in which natural selection is opposed to Fate. Fate is both antithesis and synthesis. A transcendent force which rules Black, Coloured and White. There is no escape from it and the dialectic collapses into confusion. Fate excludes any attempt at transformation, or social mediation, and stymies any movement towards resolution. What we may finally decide is that we are reading a good yarn, filled with conflict and tension, which are aspects of life and from which there is no escape. It is then that we accept the notion of a 'universe of appalling waste' which may only be mitigated through irony and good humour.

Incidents such as Tom O'Cannon's death on Christmas Day, Joe Ballast's death and Nick's 'seeming death', are humorously presented so that the bitterness of Man's Fate is lessened, though not diminished. Apart from this there is the Dickensian caricature which operates throughout the book. Names of the characters O'Crimmell, O'Theef, Paddy Pickhandle, McCrook, Nibbleson, Thumscough, Ponderosass; Shouter Rightit, Major Luffmay and so on, although enjoyable and pointing towards the great Aussie yarn with its emphasis on good humour and irony, may be felt to be too heavy-handed. But it does make for a structural opposition between seriousness and irony which adds to the complexity of the novel. I find the roots of Herbert's style in the Aussie Yarn. In fact *Capricornia* might be considered 'The Great Aussie Yarn' in that it goes on and on like a river flowing towards the mythical inland sea, which in reality turns out to be a desert of ill-promise.

In summing up my comments on Herbert's novel, I stress that the theme of *Capricornia* is the producing of a 'new' race from the mixture of Aboriginal and European stock. This is a product of natural selection. Against this is opposed a counter-theme of man at the mercy of Fate. Man proposes, Fate deposes. As natural selection is considered a rigid scientific principle, Fate is considered a rigid metaphysical principle. This opposition results in pessimism. The cawing of the crows at the end of the novel stresses this. By resolving his narrative in this way, Herbert has, I believe, revealed an important aspect of the Australian character. A fatalistic attitude which, instead of stressing change for the betterment, argues for stasis. Thus we have 'accords' and 'consensus' and calls for unity and conformity as against experiment in difference. It was perhaps Herbert's knowledge of the Australian character which prevented him from giving us a more optimistic ending in which the two races in Capricornia unite to produce a 'new' national type. It is said that an author is only as good as his material allows him to be, and so Herbert has only been able to produce a text which reflects Australia and Australians. It is here that the value of his narrative lies and the reason it has remained a perennial best seller. *Capricornia* is about what makes Australians Australian.

Mudrooroo Nyoongah
May 1990

CONTENTS

PRINCIPAL CHARACTERS

A

AINTEE, DOCTOR. Protector of aborigines.
ANGEL. *See* **BLACK ANGEL.**
ANNA. *See* **FAT ANNA.**

B

BALLEST, JOE. Railway Ganger.
BICYCLE. Aboriginal stockman, of Red Ochre cattle station. A member of the Mullanmullak tribe.
BIGHTIT, CAESAR ("THE SHOUTER"). An eminent lawyer.
BLACK ANGEL. An aboriginal woman, of the Mullanmullak tribe; a midwife.
BLAIZE, MRS VIOLA. Postmistress at Soda Springs.
BLEETER, REV. SIMON. A missionary.
BLOSSOM. *See* **O'CANNON, BLOSSOM.**
BOOTPOLISH. Aboriginal stockman, of Red Ochre station. A member of the Mullanmullak tribe.
BORTELLS, EDWIN. A pharmacist, friend of Norman Shillingsworth.
BOYLES, DR BIANCO. Government Medical Officer.
BURYWELL, JACK. Grazier, a purchaser of Red Ochre station.

C

CALLOW, CEDRIC. A grazier, of Agate Bar station.
CHARLIE WING SING. A Chinaman. Cousin of Blossom O'Cannon.
CHIN LING SOO. A Chinese. Father of Mrs Cho See Kee.

CHO SEE KEE. A Chinese. Storekeeper at Port Zodiac.
CHO SEE KEE, MRS. Wife of Cho See Kee.
CHO SEK CHING. A Chinese cook, brother of Cho See Kee.
CHOOK. *See* **HENN, ALBERT.**
CHRISTOBEL. An aboriginal halfcastle girl, friend of Tocky.
COCKERELL ("COCKY"). A fettler.
CON THE GREEK. Constandino Kyrozopolis, a Dago cook.
CONNIE. *See* **DIFFER, CONSTANCE.**
CROWE, JOE. Undertaker and cabman of Port Zodiac.

D

DIANA. Black quadroon girl, daughter of Yeller Jewty (q.v.).
DIFFER, CONSTANCE. Aboriginal halfcaste girl, daughter of Peter Differ. *See also* **PAN, PETER.**
DIFFER, PETER. A settler and author, of Coolibah Creek.
DINGO JOE. An aboriginal halfcaste, employed by Oscar.
DRIVER, JOCK. A Pommy. Grazier, of Gunamiah station, Melisande River.

E

ELBERT ("YELLER ELBERT"). An aboriginal halfcaste, an assassin.

F

FAT ANNA. A laundress, and woman of independent means, living on the Port Zodiac waterfront. Classified

PRINCIPAL CHARACTERS

as an aboriginal, though daughter of a Japanese. Foster-mother, for a time, of Norman Shillingsworth.

FLIEGELTAUB, KARL. A German, settler, of Caroline River.

FLUTE, COLONEL PLAYFAIR. Resident Commissioner of Capricornia.

G

GIGNEY, SIDNEY. A railway construction engineer.

GINGER. Aboriginal, of the Mullanmullak tribe. A police tracker.

GOMEZ, EMILIO. A Spaniard. Captain of S.S. *Cucaracha*.

H

HEATHER. *See* **POUNDAMORE, HEATHER.**

HENN, ALBERT ("CHOOK"). Locomotive engineer, bosom friend of Mark Shillingsworth.

HOLLOWER, REV. THEODORE. A missionary.

HUGHES, MORRIS. *See* **MORRIS HUGHES.**

J

JASMINE. *See* **POUNDAMORE, JASMINE.**

JEWTY ("YELLER JEWTY"). Aboriginal halfcaste woman, daughter of Edward Krater (q.v.). One of Mark Shillingsworth's wives.

JOCK. *See* **JOCK DRIVER.**

K

KET, CHARLES. Grandson of a Chinaman.

KEYES, PADDY. Head Guard of Red Turtle Bay Jail.

KLINKER, CHARLIE. A locomotive fireman.

KRATER, EDWARD. Scotsman. Empire-builder. Pioneer of civilization at Flying Fox Island. Also known as Munichillu, "The Man of Fire".

KURRINUA. An aboriginal savage, headman of the Yurracumbunga tribe, original owners of Flying Fox Island.

L

LACE, HUMBOLT. Superintendent of the Government Agricultural Experimental Station at Red Coffin Ridge. A protector of aborigines.

LACE, TOCKY. White quadroon girl, daughter of Humbolt Lace and Connie Differ (q.v.). A waif, also known as Tocky Pan, or Tocky O'Cannon.

LARSNEY, PADDY. Magistrate, of Port Zodiac.

LAVINDICATIF, FROGGY. A Frenchman. Settler.

LEDDER, JACOB. A fettler.

LOW FAT. Chinese family. Settlers.

M

McCROOK. Police trooper, of Melisande River.

McLASH, FRANK ("THE LOCOMOTIVE LOONEY"). Only son of Mrs Pansy McLash.

McLASH, MRS PANSY. Postmistress and storekeeper at Caroline River.

McRANDY, ANDY. Grazier, of Gunamiah station.

MARIGOLD. *See* **SHILLINGSWORTH, MARIGOLD.**

MARK. *See* **SHILLINGSWORTH, MARK.**

MAROWALLUA. Aboriginal woman,

PRINCIPAL CHARACTERS

of the Yurracumbunga tribe, of Flying Fox Island. The mother of Norman Shillingsworth.

MOOCH, JOE. A nomad, friend of Mark Shillingsworth.

MORRIS HUGHES. Aboriginal rouseabout, of Red Ochre station. A member of the Mullanmullak tribe.

MUTTONHEAD. An aboriginal stockman, of Red Ochre station. A member of the Mullanmullak tribe.

N

NAWRATT, ALEXANDER. A lawyer, of Port Zodiac.

NIBBLESOM, HANNIBAL. A lawyer, of Port Zodiac.

NORMAN ("NAWNIM"). *See* **SHILLINGSWORTH, NORMAN.**

NORSE, IAN. Railway superintendent.

O

O'CANNON, BLOSSOM ("THE BLOODY PARAKEET"). Daughter of a Chinese father and an aboriginal mother. Consort of Tim O'Cannon, and mother of the O'Cannon family.

O'CANNON, TIM. Railway ganger, of Black Adder Creek.

O'CRIMNELL. Police trooper, of Soda Springs.

O'HAY, PAT. Grazier, of Tatlock's Pool.

O'PICK, MICK. Irishman. Fettler, of Caroline River.

O'THEEF. Police trooper, at Soda Springs.

OPAL. Aboriginal woman, of the Mullanmullak tribe.

OSCAR. *See* **SHILLINGSWORTH, OSCAR.**

P

PAN, PETER. Halfcaste aboriginal. Legal husband of Connie Differ.

PICKANDLE, PADDY. Railway roadmaster.

PONDROSASS. A judge, of the Capricornian Court.

PONTO. A halfcaste Philippino, assistant to Joe Crowe.

POUNDAMORE SISTERS. Two in number, viz.: (1) Jasmine, who became wife of Oscar Shillingsworth, and mother of Roger and Marigold; (2) Heather, the younger sister, who became closely interested in the welfare of Mark Shillingsworth.

POUNDAMORE, JOE. Grazier, of Poundamore Downs, Cooksland. Brother of Jasmine and Heather.

PRAYTER, REV. GORDON. A clergyman, of Port Zodiac.

PRINCESS. Aboriginal woman, cook at Red Ochre station.

Q

QUONG HO LING. A Chinese settler.

R

RALPH. *See* **SHILLINGSWORTH, RALPH.**

RAMBLE, JACK. A nomad, friend of Mark Shillingsworth.

RANDTER, REVEREND. Clergyman, of Port Zodiac.

ROBBREY. Police trooper, of Port Zodiac.

ROTGUTT, JERRY. A publican.

S

SETTAROGE, CAPTAIN. Police superintendent, of Port Zodiac.

SHAY, MRS DAISY. Proprietress of the

PRINCIPAL CHARACTERS

Princess Alice Hotel, Port Zodiac. A friend of Heather Poundamore.

SHAY, WALLY. Son of Mrs Daisy Shay.

SHILLINGSWORTH BROTHERS. Three in number, viz: (1) Oscar, owner of Red Ochre station, husband of Jasmine, father of Marigold and Roger; (2) Mark, a nomad, the father of Norman ("Nawnim"); (3) Ralph, a city-dweller Down South.

SHILLINGSWORTH, MAUD. Sister of the Shillingsworth brothers; married to Ambrose: a city-dweller.

SHILLINGSWORTH CHILDREN. Three in number, viz: (1) Marigold and (2) Roger, the children of Oscar and Jasmine; (3) Norman ("Nawnim"), a halfcaste aboriginal, the sone of Mark and of the lubra Marowallua (q.v.).

SNIGGER, SAM. A foreman at Red Ochre.

STEEN, JOE. Settler, of Caroline River. Sweetheart of Mrs McLash.

STEGGLES, STANLEY. Railway bridge engineer.

T

THUMSCROUGH. State Prosecutor of Capricornia.

TITMUSS, GEORGE. Station master, Port Zodiac.

TOCATCHWON. Sergeant of Police, Port Zodiac.

TOCKY. *See* LACE, TOCKY.

W

WHITELY, SAXON. Postmaster at Republic Reef.

Y

YELLER ELBERT. *See* ELBERT.

YELLER JEWTY. *See* JEWTY.

All characters is this story are fictitious.

THE COMING OF THE DINGOES

ALTHOUGH that northern part of the Continent of Australia which is called Capricornia was pioneered long after the southern parts, its unofficial early history was even more bloody than that of the others. One probable reason for this is that the pioneers had already had experience in subduing Aborigines in the South and hence were impatient of wasting time with people who they knew were determined to take no immigrants. Another reason is that the Aborigines were there more numerous than in the South and more hostile because used to resisting casual invaders from the near East Indies. A third reason is that the pioneers had difficulty in establishing permanent settlements, having several times to abandon ground they had won with slaughter and go slaughtering again to secure more. This abandoning of ground was due not to the hostility of the natives, hostile enough though they were, but to the violence of the climate, which was not to be withstood even by men so well equipped with lethal weapons and belief in the decency of their purpose as Anglo-Saxon builders of Empire.

The first white settlement in Capricornia was that of Treachery Bay — afterwards called New Westminster — which was set up on what was perhaps the most fertile and pleasant part of the coast and on the bones of half the Karrapillua Tribe. It was the resentment of the Karrapilluas to what probably seemed to them an inexcusable intrusion that was responsible for the choice of the name of Treachery Bay. After having been driven off several times with firearms, the Tribe came up smiling, to all appearances unarmed and intending to surrender, but dragging their spears along the ground with their toes. The result of this strategy was havoc. The Karrapilluas were practically exterminated by uncomprehending neighbours into whose domains they were driven. The tribes lived in strict isolation that was rarely broken except in the cause of war. Primitive people that they were, they regarded their territorial rights as sacred.

When New Westminster was for the third time swept into the Silver Sea by the floods of the generous Wet

Season, the pioneers abandoned the site to the crocodiles and jabiroos and devil-crabs, and went in search of a better. Next they founded the settlement of Princetown, on the mouth of what came to be called the Caroline River. In Wet Season the river drove them into barren hills in which it was impossible to live during the harsh Dry Season through lack of water. Later the settlements of Britannia and Port Leroy were founded. All were eventually swept into the Silver Sea. During Wet Season, which normally lasted for five months, beginning in November and slowly developing till the Summer Solstice, from when it raged till the Equinox, a good eighty inches of rain fell in such fertile places on the coast as had been chosen, and did so at the rate of from two to eight inches at a fall. As all these fertile places were low-lying, it was obviously impossible to settle on them permanently. In fact, as the first settlers saw it, the whole vast territory seemed never to be anything for long but either a swamp during Wet Season or a hard-baked desert during the Dry. During the seven months of a normal Dry Season never did a drop of rain fall and rarely did a cloud appear. Fierce suns and harsh hot winds soon dried up the lavished moisture.

It was beginning to look as though the land itself was hostile to anyone but the carefree nomads to whom the Lord gave it, when a man named Brittins Willnot found the site of what came to be the town of Port Zodiac, the only settlement of any size that ever stood permanently on all the long coastline, indeed the only one worthy of the name of Town ever to be set up in the whole vast territory. Capricornia covered an area of about half a million square miles. This site of Willnot's was elevated, and situated in a pleasantly unfertile region where the annual rainfall was only about forty inches. Moreover, it had the advantage of standing as a promontory on a fair-sized navigable harbour and of being directly connected with what came to be called Willnot Plateau, a wide strip of highland that ran right back to the Interior. When gold was found on the Plateau, Port Zodiac became a town.

The site of Port Zodiac was a Corroboree Ground of the Larrapuna Tribe, who left the bones of most of their number to manure it. They called it Mailunga, or the Birth Place, believing it to be a sort of Garden of Eden and apparently revering it. The war they waged to retain possession of this barren spot was perhaps the most desperate that whitemen ever had to engage in with an Australian tribe. Although utterly routed in the first encounter, they continued to harass the pioneers for months, exercising cunning that increased with their desperation. Then someone, discovering that they were hard-put for food since the warring had scared the game from their domains, conceived the idea of making friends with them and giving them several bags of flour spiced with arsenic. Nature is cruel. When dingoes come to a waterhole, the ancient kangaroos, not having teeth or ferocity sharp enough to defend their heritage, must relinquish it or die.

Thus Civilisation was at last planted permanently. However, it spread slowly, and did not take permanent root elsewhere than on the safe ground of the Plateau. Even the low-lying mangrove-cluttered further shores of Zodiac Harbour remained untrodden by the feet of whitemen for many a year. It was the same with the whole maritime region, most of which, although surveyed from the sea and in parts penetrated and occupied for a while by explorers, remained in much the same state as always. Some of the inhabitants were perhaps amazed and demoralized, but still went on living in the way of old, quite unaware of the presumably enormous fact that they had become subjects of the British Crown.

That part of the coast called Yurracumbunga by the Aborigines, which lay about one hundred and fifty miles to the east of Port Zodiac, was first visited by a whiteman in the year 1885. By that time the inhabitants, having only heard tell of the invaders from survivors of the neighbouring tribe of Karrapillua, were come to regard whitemen rather as creatures of legend, or perhaps more rightly as monsters of legend, since they had heard enough about them to fear them greatly. When one of the monsters, in the shape of Captain Edward Krater, a trepang-fisher, suddenly materialised for them, they thought he was a devil come from the sun, because they first saw him in the ruddy light of dawn and he was carroty. Krater was a man of fine physique, and not quietly carroty as a man might be in these days of clean-shaved faces and close-clipped heads, but blazingly, that being a period when manliness was expressed with hair. When the Yurracumbungas discovered that he was mortal, they dubbed him Munichillu, or The Man of Fire.

Ned Krater wished to establish a base for his trepang-fishing on a certain little island belonging to the Yurracumbungas and called by them Arrikitarriyah, or the Gift of the Sea. This island lay within rifle-shot of the mainland and was well watered and wooded and stocked with game and sheltered from the roll of the ocean by the Tikkalalla Islands, which lay in an extensive group along the northern horizon. The tribe used the island at certain times as a Corroboree Ground. Krater had already visited it before he came into contact with the owners. They first saw him when, waking one morning from heavy sleep following a wild night of corroboree, they found his lugger drifting up the salt-water creek on which they were camped. He was standing on the deck in all his golden glory. They snatched up their arms and flew to cover. One of Krater's crew, who were natives of the Tikkalalla Islands and old enemies of the Yurracumbungas, told the ambuscade at the top of his voice who Krater was and what would happen if it was with hostile intent that they hid, then took up a rifle and with a volley of shots set the echoes ringing and the cockatoos yelling and the hearts of the Yurracumbungas quaking. Krater then went ashore. After spending some hours sneaking about and peeping and listening to and occasionally answering the assurances shouted from time to time by Krater's men, the Tribe came back shyly to their gunyahs, among which the Man of Fire had pitched a tent.

Thenceforth till a misunderstanding arose, the Yurracumbungas stayed in the camp, staring at Krater and his strange possessions, and learning from his men all they could tell about whitemen, who were, it seemed, not mere raiders like the brownmen who used sometimes to come to them from the North, but supermen who had come to stay and rule. And they learnt a little about shooting with rifles and catching fish with nets and dynamite and making fires by magic, and came to understand why witnessing such things had disorganised and demoralised the vanquished tribes of whom the islanders spoke. As the islanders said — How could one ever boast again of prowess with spear and kylie after having seen what could be done with rifle and dynamite? Far from hating the invader, the Yurracumbungas welcomed him, thinking that he would become one of them and teach them his magic arts.

The tribes of the locality were divided into family sections, or hordes. When a man or men of one horde visited another, it was the custom to allow them temporary use of such of the womenfolk as they were entitled to call Wife by their system of marriage. Because they regarded Krater as a guest and a qualified person, the Yurracumbungas did not mind his asking for the comeliest of their lubras, though they did not offer him one, perhaps because they thought him above wanting one. But they objected strongly when his black crew asked for the same privilege. The islanders were definitely unqualified according to the laws. The granting of such a privilege to them would mean violation of the traditions, the weakening of their system, the demoralisation of their youth. Thus the Yurracumbungas argued. The islanders said that the old order had passed; and to prove it, one of them seized a lubra and ravaged her. The violent quarrel that resulted was settled by Krater, who hurled himself into the mob, bellowing and firing his revolver. Then Krater ordered the Yurracumbungas to give his men what they wanted.

The Yurracumbungas were struck dumb, appalled by their impotence. Night fell. They sat by their fires, staring at Krater and his men. They stared long after Krater had retired to his tent, long after they had relaxed to their own mattresses of bark. Hours passed. All of Krater's men, except two who dozed over rifles before the tent, fell asleep, gorged on a great meal of fish.

The headman of the horde was Kurrinua. He had argued fiercely against violation of the laws. He was a man as big and hairy as Krater. In the middle of the night he nudged the man next to him and whispered. His neighbour passed the whisper on. Before long the whole camp knew of his intention. No-one stirred till the tip of the old moon appeared above the bush and splashed the inky creek with silver. Then the man next Kurrinua crawled without a sound across the clearing to the scrub.

A tiny casuarina nut, shot out of the scrub, struck one of the dozing guards and roused him. He looked about. The camp was silent but for snores and the sigh of the wind in the trees. Then a slight sound in the scrub drew the guard's attention. He listened intently. Again he heard it. Tiny crackling as of a foot treading stealthily on leaves. He rose, and with the movement roused his mate, who whispered. Both listened, heard a peculiar pattering sound, and went rifle in hand, with backs turned to the camp, to investigate. Louder crackling. Kurrinua and young Impalui rose with stones in hands and sped towards the guards like shadows. The guards were knocked senseless without a sound. The horde rose to knees, women and children and ancients ready to fly, warriors in arms. Kurrinua and Impalui snatched up the rifles, crept to the tent. Kurrinua was crouching at the flap of the tent with rifle raised when — BANG! — a bullet tore through his body, through the tent, crashed into the fire. Impalui had fired accidentally. Kurrinua fell into the tent.

Uproar! Spears whizzed. Rifles crashed. Men roared
and howled. The horde rushed, fought fiercely for a
moment, wavered, turned and fled. A few of the islanders
rushed to the tent, which was collapsed and sprawling about
like a landed devil-fish. They pounced on it and dragged
it clear of the men beneath, dragged Kurrinua free of
Krater's grip.

Kurrinua rolled over and over like a sea-urchin in a gale,
got free of clutching hands and kicking feet, rose, and
with blood spurting from his back and belly, plunged into
the scrub, followed by a hail of bullets. His pursuers lost
him. They spread, passed within a yard of where he lay
with thigh-bone snapped by a bullet. He crawled towards
the isthmus that lay between the creek and sea, bent on
reaching the canoes. He heard cries and shots as other
fugitives were found. He was in sandy hillocks out of the
shelter of the scrub when the hunters, now carrying torches,
rushed on to the beach. He rolled into a hollow and buried
himself to the neck.

The night passed, slowly for the hunters, all too swiftly
for the hunted. No hope now of escaping by canoe. The
hunters had dragged the vessels high. But Kurrinua might
swim if he could not walk, swim by way of the sea to the
passage and the mainland. Surely he had less to fear from
crocodiles than from Munichillu and his men. Still he
dared not leave the hollow while the hunters prowled the
beach, because they would find the wide track of his
crawling before he could reach the creek. They splashed
along the water's edge, crashed through the scrub, crept
among the hillocks, never went far away.

The dark creek silvered. The hunters' torches paled.
Birds stirred in the bush. A jabiroo flew in from the sea
on great creaking wings, swerved with a swish and a croak
at sight of the hunters. Jabiroos were gathering at the
Ya-impitulli Billabong for the nesting. The Nesting of the
Storks. It was the time of the great Corroboree of the
Circumcision, for which the men of Yurracumbunga were
gathering.

Swiftly the sky lost its stars and the scrub found individ-
uality. Footsteps. A shout when they found the blood and
the track of crawling. Footsteps pattering. Kurrinua
looked his last at the gilded skyline. Another shout. They
danced around him, pointing, kicking sand in his eyes.
Soon Munichillu came, and with him the light of day, as
though that too belonged to the like of him. At his appearance the east flamed suddenly, so that the sand was gilded

and fire flashed in his beard. He looked at the face in the
sand, grunted, raised his revolver.

Kurrinua's heart beat painfully. His eyes grew hot. The
pain of his wounds, which he had kept in check for hours
by the power he was bred to use, began to throb. But he
did not move a hair. He had been trained to look upon
death fearlessly. To do so was to prove oneself a warrior
worthy of having lived. His mind sang the Death Corroboree — Ee-yah, ee-yah, ee-tullyai — O mungallinni wur-
rigai — ee-tukkawunni —

BANG! Kurrinua gasped, heaved out of the sand, writh-
ed, shuddered, died. Ned Krater spat. In his opinion he
had done no wrong. He did not know why the savages
had attacked him. He thought only of their treachery,
which to such as he was intolerable as it was natural to
such as they.

PSYCHOLOGICAL EFFECT OF A SOLAR TOPEE

So slow was the settling of the Port Zodiac district that
in the year 1904 the non-native population numbered no
more than three thousand, a good half of which was
Asiatic, and the settled area measured but three or four
square miles. But the civilizing was so complete that the
survivors of the original inhabitants numbered seven, of
whom two were dying of consumption in the Native Compound, three confined in the Native Lazaret with leprosy,
the rest, a man and a woman, living in a gunyah at the
remote end of Devilfish Bay, subsisting on what food they
could get from the bush and the sea and what they could
buy with the pennies the man earned by doing odd jobs
and the woman by prostitution. The lot of these last was
not easy. Fish and game were scarce; and large numbers
of natives of other tribes were available as odd-jobbers
and prostitutes; and it was made still harder by the fact
that they had to dodge the police to keep it, their one lawful place of abode in the land the Lord God gave them
being now the Native Compound.

Such was the advanced state of Civilization in Port
Zodiac when the brothers Oscar and Mark Shillingsworth
arrived there. They were clerks, quite simple men, who

B

came to join the Capricornian Government Service from a city of the South that, had it been the custom to name Australian cities after those who suffered the hardships of pioneering instead of after the merely grand who ruled the land from afar, might have been called Batman, as for convenience it will be called here.

Hopeful as the Shillingsworth brothers were of improving their lot by coming so far from home, they had no idea of what opportunities were offering in this new sphere till they landed. In the ignorance of conditions of life in Capricornia, they came clad in serge suits and bowlers, which made them feel not only uncomfortable in a land but ten degrees from the Equator, but conspicuous and rather ridiculous among the crowd clad in khaki and white linen and wideawake hats and solar topees that met their steamer at the jetty. Nor were they awkward only in their dress. Their bearing was that of simple clerks, not Potentates, as it was their right that it should be as Capricornian Government Officers. When they learnt how high was the standing of Government Officers in the community, especially in that section composed of the gentlemen themselves, as they did within an hour or two of landing, their bearing changed. Within a dozen hours of landing they were wearing topees. Within two dozen hours they were closeted with Chinese tailors. Within a hundred hours they came forth in all the glory of starched white linen clothes. Gone was their simplicity for ever.

Since no normal humble man can help but feel magnificent in a brand-new suit of clothes, it is not surprising that those who don a fresh suit of bright white linen every day should feel magnificent always. Nor is it surprising that a normal humble head should swell beneath a solar topee, since a topee is more a badge of authority than a hat, as is the hat of a soldier.

Carried away by this magnificence, Oscar added a walking-stick to his outfit, though he had till lately been of the opinion that the use of such a thing was pure affectation. Mark still thought it affectation, but did not criticise, first because he feared his brother, and then because his opinions generally had been considerably shaken. Both were changed so utterly in a matter of days by their new condition as to be scarcely recognisable as the simple fellows who came. They dropped the slangy speech that had pleased them formerly, and took to mincing like their new acquaintances, and raised the status of their people when families were talked about, and when the subject was education, made vague reference to some sort of college, while in fact they were products of a State School. Their father, who was dead, had been a humble mechanic in a railway workshop. They described him as a Mechanical Engineer. Their brother Ralph, who was second engineer or third officer on a tiny cargo-steamer, they spoke of as though he were a captain of a liner. They did not lie boldly, nor for lying's sake. They felt the necessity forced on them by the superiority of their friends. In fact it was Oscar who lied. Mark merely backed him up, not unaware of the likelihood that those to whom they lied might also be liars. But he did not dare even in his mind to question the wisdom of his brother who was by so many years his senior. Oscar was about thirty, and grave in his years when in the company of Mark. Mark was about twenty-two.

Within a week of arrival they knew all the best people in Town, including the Flutes of the Residency, head of which house was Colonel Playfair Flute, the Resident Commissioner, first gentleman of the land. As Oscar said gravely, they were Getting On. He appeared to be deeply impressed. Not so Mark, although he took part in the Getting On at first quite as well as Oscar, in fact even better, because he was a youth of more attractive personality. But he was urged mainly by the unusual notice Oscar was taking of him at the time. Previously Oscar had practically ignored him as a very young and rather foolish youth. In fact, but for their mother's wish that they should be together, Oscar would have prevented Mark from joining him in applying for posts in Capricornia. Their mother was living in the city of Batman with their married sister Maud.

Oscar was soon moved to consider quitting the rather poor bachelor-quarters in which they had been placed and taking a bungalow such as married officers occupied, with a view not nearly so much to making himself more comfortable as to advancing himself socially and in the Service by getting into a position in which he could entertain his superiors as they now condescended to entertain him. Chief cause of this ambitiousness was the fact that through being employed in the Medical Department he had come into contact with the nurses of the Government hospital whose ladylike and professional airs made him feel sensitive as never before of his deficiencies. Mark agreed to share the bungalow willingly, thinking only of comfort.

The Shillingsworths were young men of good taste, as

they showed in the style in which they furnished and decorated their new home. Though forced by jealous superiors to take an inferior kind of house, they made of it the prettiest in the town. Mark, who was inventive, fitted up on the wide front veranda a punkah of both beautiful and ingenious design, which worked automatically when the wind blew, that is when its working was not required. Oscar took a smelly native from the Compound and converted him into a piece of bright furniture that made up for the defects of Mark's machine and called him the Punkah Wallah. This Wallah fellow also waited at table and did odd jobs; and his lubra worked as housemaid. The services of this pair cost the Shillingsworths five shillings a week in cash and scraps of food, and added inestimably to the value they now set upon themselves. Most of their own food they had sent in from a Chinese restaurant.

They had not been living in the bungalow long, when one night they held a party that was honoured by the presence of Colonel Playfair Flute. Then Oscar said gravely to Mark, while watching the temporary Chinese butler at work, "By cripes we're getting on!" Mark only smiled, too deeply touched by his brother's pleasure for answer. Within a month of that party Oscar was raised to the post of Assistant Secretary of his Department. He considered that he had become Professional.

Just as Oscar was affected by the atmosphere in which he worked, so was Mark, but with results quite different. Mark was troubled by the fact that while employed in the Railway Department, which pleased him greatly, he was as far removed from the rails and cars and locomotives, connection with which was responsible for his pleasure in his job, as Oscar from the lepers in the Lazaret he dealt with in his ledgers. The work of his hands was merely to record with pen and ink what other hands accomplished with the actual oily parts of that interesting machine the railway. He breathed the mustiness of an office, while the owners of those other hands breathed the smells of locomotives, brakevans, and the flying wilderness. He was a musty clerk, while they were hefty men. When he attempted to discuss what troubled him with Oscar he was told not to be Silly. When he put it to his office-mates he was stared at. When he came out with it one day down in the railway-yards before the station-master and the engineer of the mail-train that ran once a fortnight between Port Zodiac and Copper Creek, he was laughed at and told he was a queer fellow for One of the Heads. The

frank contempt of these two last for those they spoke of
as The Heads filled him with desire to prove that he was
really not one of them but rather one of their hefty selves
by telling the truth about his railwayman father. It was
only loyalty to Oscar that checked him. Soon he came to
detest the perpetual gentility in which he lived as One
of the Heads and to wish for nothing better than to be dis-
rated to the company of the hefty fellows of the Yards.

No-one in the railway-yards wanted anything to do with
The Heads. When Mark went there in pursuance of his
duties, as he did much more often than necessary, eyes that
regarded him plainly said, "Here's a pimp!" He would
sooner have lost his job than he would have informed on
them for whatever they felt guilty about, as for weeks
he tried to prove to them. He won regard at last by taking
beer along with his official papers and by betraying secrets
of the office.

He fawned particularly on George Tittmuss, the station-
master, a giant of a man who awed him with his physique,
hefty enough youth though he was himself, and Albert
Henn, or Chook Henn as his friends called him, the engineer of the mail-train, a jovial little fellow who was
rather kind to him. These men were very popular among
workingmen, were what are called Booze Artists, fellows
who can drink continuously without getting drunk, or
at least not as drunk as youthful Mark got on a single
bottle of beer, and very amusing yarn-spinners and music-
ians and singers. The parties they held in the house they
shared were the joy of the railwaymen. By dint of sheer
truckling, Mark at last won an invitation to the house to
hear Chook Henn play his concertina, or Make it Talk, as
his friends said. Soon he began to attend their parties
regularly, though furtively. Soon he began to drink in a
manner that to him was excessive. Soon he replaced his
topee with a grubby panama, and took to rolling his cigarettes and going about the town without a coat. But there
were times when a reproachful word from Oscar, who for
a long while remarked nothing more than the slovenliness
of dress, made Mark feel that he was not the remarkably
adaptable fellow he mostly thought himself, but a poor
thing of common clay who was weakly retrogressing. When
he felt like that he kept away from the railwaymen, resumed coat and topee, and took a spell of gentility.

One night in Henn's house he told the truth about his
father. Forthwith he was accepted as a brother. But even
as he staggered home that night arm in arm with Chook

Henn and Tittmuss, his conscience scolded his tipsy ego
for its folly in having betrayed that best of all men his
brother. Next morning, while he lay in that state of
stagnant calm which precedes the drunkard's storm of suffering, Oscar came to him and growled. Oscar was not
a teetotaller; indeed he had often drunk with Mark of late;
but he carried his liquor like a gentleman, or a Booze
Artist, and with dominance forced Mark to do the same.
At any other time he would have made a joke of Mark's
condition. But that morning he knew, as half the Town
did, that Mark had staggered up Killarney Street in Low
Company. In a quiet, dry, relentless voice that Mark
knew well and dreaded, Oscar called him a fool, a waster, a
disgrace, and ordered him to mend his ways. Then he
went off, erect, cool, clean, sober, sane, a gentleman, everything that Mark was not. Envying him, loving him, loath-
ing himself, Mark choked, swallowed the scum in his
mouth, rose hastily, rushed out to vomit. Oscar at breakfast heard him, rose grimacing, slammed a door.

Mark forsook his railway friends for some time. He
did not remain virtuous for long, but made the acquaintance of old Ned Krater, whose tales of life on the Silver
Sea made the railwaymen seem almost as musty as himself.
Then he began to see Port Zodiac as not a mere place of
business but a tarrying-place on highroads leading to adventure. He really learnt to drink through being taken
up by Krater. Drink! He began to consider himself a
finished Booze Artist, not knowing how he carried his
grog, since he often carried so much, nor suffering the
aftermaths so badly, since he learnt the trick of taking
a hair of the dog. In fact he carried it so ill that the
friends he made through associating with Krater often had
to carry him home. Hair-of-the-dog made him proof
against the criticism of his brother.

And through associating with Krater, he began to take
an interest in native women, or Black Velvet as they
were called collectively, affairs with whom seemed to be
the chief diversion of the common herd. He had heard
much about Black Velvet from his railway friends, but had
not taken their confessions of weakness for it seriously
because they had always waxed ribald when making them.
And he heard of it from Government Officers, who also
jested about it, but at the same time gave it to be understood that they considered the men who sought the love
of lubras — such men were called Comboes — unspeak-
ably low. Although he had often eyed the black house-

maid with desire, he had been of the same opinion as his brother Officers till he came in contact with Ned Krater. Krater evidently lived for Black Velvet. He waxed eloquent when he talked about it. He said that it was actually the black lubras who had pioneered the land, since pursuit of them had drawn explorers into the wilderness and love of them had encouraged settlers to stay. He said that a national monument should be set up in their honour. Mark believed him, but could not bring himself to woo the housemaid.

After living on whiskey for three or four weeks he collapsed. He was sent to the hospital by the doctor, who, being himself a drunkard, listed him as suffering from gastritis and neurasthenia. But Oscar's friends the nurses were not drunkards. Mark suffered much from their contemptuous eyes, especially from those of Sister Jasmine Poundamore, who was Oscar's sweetheart. Oscar often came to the hospital while he was there, but never to see him.

Once again he was turned back to the path of virtue. But now he trod it only because he knew he needed change of scene, having no illusions about whither it would lead him, nor any desire to be led elsewhere than to adventure on the Silver Sea. He did not return to the social whirl; instead he spent most of his leisure in prowling round the back parts of the town, observing how the bulk of his fellow-citizens lived. What he saw surprised and delighted him. He had not realised how multifarious the population was and for the most part how strange.

When he met Krater again he learnt that he was on the eve of returning to his camp on the island of Gift of the Sea, or, as he had renamed it, Flying Fox. Krater invited Mark to accompany him, offering to bring him back to Town within a couple of weeks if necessary. There was a reason for the kindness. Krater liked Mark, but did not want his company so much as his help to finance his trepang-fishing business. Mark did not guess the reason, though Krater had fished for his help before; but if he had would not have accepted the invitation less eagerly than he did, nor have suffered keener disappointment than he did to learn that, accept or not, he could not go. He applied to the Resident Commissioner for a fortnight's special leave. He was not only refused it, but in a quiet way rebuked. His Honour apparently knew more about his private life than he supposed. Along with a polite letter of refusal he sent a copy of *Rules and Regulations for the Conduct of Of-*

ficers, in which red-ink marks drew attention to the facts
that Indulgence in Drunkenness and Low Company were
offences and that an officer was entitled at the end of
every three years of Faithful Service to three months' leave
on full pay with a first-class passage home. Evidently His
Honour regarded Port Zodiac purely as a business-centre.
So Krater's lugger, which was called the *Maniya* — after
a lubra, some said —, sailed without Mark. Mark watched
her go. And his heart went with her, out over the sparkling
harbour, out on to the Silver Sea, leaving him with nothing
in his breast but bitter disappointment.

Some quiet weeks passed. Then Wet Season came with
its extremes of heat and humidity and depraving influences
on the minds of corruptible men. Even Oscar began to
drink to excess. But he never bawled and pranced and
wallowed in mud and came home in the arms of shouting
larrikins. He always came home as steadily as he went
out, though perhaps a little more jauntily, and ended ex-
cesses by simply dipping his head in cold water and
swallowing an aspirin and a liver pill or two, not by groping for the bottle and subsisting on it for a week. The converse of his conduct was his brother's.

During Wet Season most work was suspended, neces-
sarily or not. So common was the saying *Leave it till
after the Wet*, and so often used while the season was still
a long way off by people with difficult tasks to do, that it
seemed as though the respect for the violence of the ele-
ments was largely a matter of convenience or convention.
However, the necessity for suspension could never be gain-
said in view of the experiences of the early settlers, which
were never forgotten by good Capricornians.

When the town became crowded with idlers just before
Christmas, Mark, who had in him all the makings of a
good Capricornian, chafed because his job went on. He
was in this mood when the good Capricornian Krater came
back to Town to idle and began again to try to interest him
in trepang-fishing. A few days before Christmas, Krater
asked him if he would like to go out to Flying Fox for a
few days during the week of vacation. Mark accepted the
offer eagerly. This time he said nothing about it to anyone but his bosom friend Chook Henn, whom he asked to
join him in the excursion, and the Wallah fellow, whom he
told at the last minute, instructing him to pass the news on
to Oscar. He sailed into the Silver Sea aboard the *Maniya*
at sundown on Christmas Eve, drunk, and roaring *Black*

Alice with Chook and Krater, accompanied by Chook's concertina.

Oh don't you remember Black Alice, Ben Bolt,
Black Alice so dusky and dark,
That Warrego gin with a stick through her nose,
And teeth like a Moreton Bay shark,
The villainous sheep-wash tobacco she smoked
In the gunyah down by the lake,
The bardees she gathered, the snakes that she stewed,
And the damper you taught her to bake —

§

As the *Maniya* drifted before a dying breeze into the creek up which she had stolen with Civilization years before, the sun was sinking. The creek lay like a mirror, fleckless but for chasings here and there where fishes stirred. Rich red gold was splashing on the waters of the reaches to the west, flowing to the sea in dazzling streams down gently-rolling troughs. The sun sank swiftly. Purple shade of night came creeping in. The red gold faded to the hard yellow gold of coins, to the soft gold of flowers, to silver-gilt, to silver, to purple pewter chased with filaments of starlight. The changes passed with the minutes.

"Leggo!" bellowed Krater. The anchor splashed. The chain snarled through the hawse. The echoes clattered across the darkening creek to stir the silence of the brooding bush.

A cry from the shore — "Oy-ee-ee-ee — yah-a!"

Fire leapt in the clearing above the beach, illuminating mighty tree-trunks and the forms of naked men, sending great shadows lurching, splashing the creek with gold. High the fire leapt — higher — higher — blazed like great joy, then checked, fell back, and died.

Again the cry. It was answered only by the echoes. The lugger's crew, harassed by snarling Krater, were all engaged in snugging ship. The fire leapt again. Ragged patches were snatched from it and carried to the beach. Torches blazed for a minute or two over the launching of canoes. Soon the splash of paddles was heard. Then ghostly shapes shot into the wheel of light shed by Krater's lantern.

"Itunguri!" cried a voice.

"Inta muni — it-ung-ur-ee-ee-ee — yah!" cried the crew.

"Kiatulli!" shouted Krater. "Shut y' blunny row!"

Somewhere out of the lamplight a voice cried shrilly, "Munichillu!" The cry went back to the shore, "Munichillu, Munichillu, Munichillu-ee-ee-ee — yah!" Krater raised the lantern, so that his hair looked like a silver halo round his head, and glared across the water.

The canoes came up to the lugger, their crews looking like grey bright-eyed ghosts. A crowd scrambled aboard to help with the snugging and to get the dunnage. Krater told Mark and Chook to go ashore and wait for him. Chook was shaving hastily in the cabin. Mark looked in at him, laughed at his occupation and said a word or two, then dropped into a canoe alone and went ashore with a smelly, peeping, whispering, jostling crowd.

Mark stepped into the lukewarm water where it broke as into fragments of fire on the lip of the beach, and went up to the native camp, chuckling and distributing sticks of niki-niki, or trade tobacco, to a score of black snatching hands. He stopped to stare at two old men who sat beside the fire, naked and daubed with red and white ochre and adorned about arms and legs and breasts with elaborate systems of cicatrix. They grinned at him and spoke a few words he did not understand. On the other side of the fire, attending to a huge green turtle roasting upturned in its shell, squatted a withered white-haired old woman who wore nothing but a tiny skirt of paper-bark and a stick or bone through the septum of her nose. She also grinned at him, and cackled something in the native tongue that roused a laugh. Feeling self-conscious, Mark clumsily gave her tobacco and lounged away to examine a pile of arms and accoutrements, fine pieces of work, elaborately shaped and carved and painted, wrought presumably with primitive tools and the coarse pigments of the earth. And there were other handsome articles lying about, some in wraps of paper-bark, finely woven dilly-bags and slings and belts and corroboree-regalia of strikingly intricate and beautiful design. He was surprised, having been taught to regard his black compatriots as extremely low creatures, the very rag-tag of humanity, scarcely more intelligent and handy than the apes.

He beckoned a young man standing near, tall and well built as himself, and asked him would he exchange some article for tobacco. Having but a poor grip of the lingua franca called Beche-de-mer or Pidjin, he could not make himself understood. "I want a spear," he said. "A spe—ar or something. Savvy?"

"Lubra?" asked the man, pointing with fleshy lips to some women squatting by a gunyah.

Mark experienced a shock. Apparently at a sign from the man, a young lubra wearing nothing but a naga of paper-bark rose and came forward shyly. She was not more shy than Mark, who dropped his eyes from her and said to the man simply out of politeness, "Belong you?"

"Coo — wah," said the man. "You wantim?"

The girl was comely, Mark thought, a different creature from the half-starved housemaid. But his thoughts were at the moment as turbulent as his heart. A true combo would have thought her even beautiful. One who was observant and æsthetic would have gloated over the perfect symmetry expressed in the curves of the wide mobile nostrils and arched septum of her fleshy nose, would have delighted in her peculiar pouting mouth with thick puckered lips of colour reddish black like withered rose, in the lustrous irises and fleckless white-of-egg-white whites of her large black slightly-tilted eyes, in her long luxuriant bronzy lashes, in the curves of her neck and back, in the coppery black colour of her velvet skin and its fascinating musky odour, and might have kept her talking in order to delight in her slow, deep, husky voice, or laughing in order to delight in the flash of her perfect teeth and gums and the lazy movements of her eyes.

Mark was trying to excuse himself for seeing beauty in a creature of a type he had been taught to look upon as a travesty of normal humanity. He was thinking — would the Lord God who put some kind of beauty into the faces of every other kind of woman utterly ignore this one?

"You wantim?" asked the man again.

"Garn!" gasped Mark, digging bare toes in the sand.

"Nungata kita kunitoa," said the man.

"N-no s-savvy," gasped Mark.

"Givvim one bag flour, Mister?"

Mark did not heed. He was staring at the lubra's feet which were digging as his were. Then he looked at the man, hating him for a procurer, knowing nothing of the customs of the people nor realising that the man was only doing what he thought had been asked of him, what he had learnt to expect to be asked of him by every whiteman with whom he had ever come in contact, and what he was shrewd enough to expect to be asked by the momentarily scrupulous Mark. Nor did Mark realise that the man and his kind might love their womenfolk just as much as whitemen do, even though they were not so jealous of their conjugal rights. At the moment he considered the man un-utterably base. He said to him huskily, "You're a dirty dog, old man. Let the lady do her courting for herself."

§

In spite of the contempt in which he had held authority
when he left town, Mark was still careful enough to return before the vacation ended. He arrived back in the
morning of New Year's Eve. But he did not go home at
once. In wandering drinking round the town with Chook,
he came to a disreputable bar where he made the acquaintance of a half-caste Philippino named Ponto, who was employed by Joe Crowe the undertaker, with whom he said
he was that afternoon going to bury a destitute Chinaman.
The idea of taking part in the simple funeral appealed to
Mark. He went off with the corpse and Chook and the
undertakers and a bag of bottled beer.

That night the Government Service Club held a New
Year dance. Mark attended, dressed appropriately, but
drunk and filled with his experience of the afternoon. Several times he buttonholed acquaintances, saying such things
as, "Now warrer y'think — buried a Chow 'safternoon —
me'n Joe Crowe —." The interest of the person buttonholed
would draw a group, to whom he would repeat the introduction, then continue, "N'yorter heard the hot clods
clompin' on the coffing — hot clods — n'im stone cold.
Course he couldn't feel 'em — but I did — for him. Planted
him. Then we sat'n his grave and waked him with beer.
Gawd'll I ever forget them clompin' clods! Clamped down
with a ton of hot clods! Gawd! D'y'know — shperiences
is the milestonesh of life ——"

Oscar joined a group and heard, then led him outside,
smiling, telling him that he had a bottle hidden out on the
back veranda. In the darkness he fell on him, dragged
him to the back gate, and flung him out neck-and-crop. Mark
fell in mud. He got up blinking and gasping, to stand
waist-deep in dripping grass till Oscar went back into the
noisy brilliant hall. Then he turned away, striking at fireflies and mosquitoes that flashed and droned about him,
making for the road, sniffing and snivelling, hurt not by
the manhandling but by the fact that the manhandler was
that best of all men his elder brother.

He wandered into the middle of the town for the double
purpose of getting more drink and showing himself in
rumpled and muddy dress-clothes. He met Ponto in the
disreputable bar again, and through him again found unusual entertainment. Ponto took him to a party at a Philippino house in the district called The Paddock. He was
the only whiteman in the company, the only person wearing
a coat, one of the few in shoes. Because the company in

general were afraid of whitemen, his appearance checked the revelry till Ponto, speaking Malayan, the language of the district, made it known that he was an associate of wild blacks and a burier of destitute Chinamen and generally a hefty fellow, who was come to them as one of them, bringing six bottles of whiskey and a bag of beer. He was acclaimed. Soon he was out of his mess-jacket and boiled shirt. Before long he shed his shoes. He spent half the night trying to woo a starry-eyed Philippino girl who played a guitar.

The party went on till peep of day, when by some mischance that no-one stopped to investigate, it suddenly ended in a battle-royal that raged till the coming of the first sun of the year and half the police-force. Most of the rioters were taken to the lock-up. Mark, though found in the thick of the fight, was taken to the hospital, primarily because he was white and of respectable standing. secondarily because the lover of the starry-eyed girl had vented long-restrained jealousy by cracking a bottle on his head.

Mark spent three terrible days in hospital, tortured by a monster headache, a frightful thirst, a vast craving for hair-of-the-dog, and an overpowering sense of shame. From hour to hour he was visited by noisy bands of half-breed Philippinoes and Malays, who, because they showed no regard for the prescribed hours of visiting, were frequently descended upon and ejected by the tight-lipped nursing staff. He saw Sister Jasmine Poundamore but once. She was now engaged to Oscar. At sight of her he hid his head.

The first respectable person to discuss the escapade with him was that most respectable of Capricornians, His Honour Colonel Flute. What he said to him when he summoned him upon return to duty Mark did not plainly repeat, though he talked bravely enough of what he had said in reply. Oscar cut his boasting short by telling him in the presence of other officers that but for his own friendship with the Colonel he should have been dismissed.

His Honour and Oscar had intended to put Mark in his place. They succeeded, and more, showed him exactly what was his place. He learnt that he was a slave, in spite of all the petty airs he might assume, a slave shackled to a yoke, to be scolded when he lagged, flogged when he rebelled with the sjambok of the modern driver, Threat of the Sack. The dogs! thought he. They had learnt their business in the stony-hearted cities of the South, into which

it was imported from those slave-camps the cities of
Europe. But they could not wield their whips to terrify
in this true Australia Felix, Capricornia. No — because
the sack meant here not misery and hunger, but freedom
to go adventuring in the wilderness or on the Silver Sea.

He decided to become a waster. But to become a waster
in the face of the hard ambitious world, he found, is a
strong man's job, like going down a stair up which a great
discourteous crowd is climbing; and he was far from
strong; moreover, he was struggling with inhibitions. Sometimes he lived virtuously, more often not, though more
through weakness than through wilfulness. Twice again
during that Wet Season he was reprimanded by His
Honour. Throughout that period Oscar mostly ignored
him. Still he was at the head of the stair.

Wet Season passed. The Shillingsworths completed their
first year of service in Capricornia. Then, one day in May,
Oscar passed a remark over lunch — or Tiffin, as he called
it — that led to Mark's divining that a plot had been hatch-
ed by the Medical and Railway Departments to effect the
dismissal of Chook Henn. Oscar did not intend to dis-
close the plot. He said what he did merely with intent to
sting the disreputable Chook Henn's bosom friend. And
Mark would not have divined it had he not known that
such a plot was to be expected. Chook was off duty on
the spree. Previous attempts by his superiors to catch
him had failed because the doctor they had sent to prove
his condition had been loath to report the facts. But
another doctor had been added to the staff, an officious
fellow who did not drink. Mark made a few cunning in-
quiries at his office that afternoon. As soon as possible
he slipped away to warn Chook, who should have been
marshalling his train for the trip to Copper Creek.

Next morning the new doctor had to go to the Yards
to find Chook, who was on his engine, shaky of hand and
ill of temper. The doctor came with the Loco-Foreman,
who ordered Chook to come down from the cab so that the
doctor might see if he were fit to do his duty. Chook was
prepared. At sight of them he had sent his fireman away
to see about coal. He produced a copy of *Rules and
Regulations* and showed the Foreman and the doctor that
he was forbidden either to leave his· engine unattended or
to allow anyone not taking part in his work to enter the
cab. He then became abusive. Doctor and Foreman went
away amid derisive laughter of a crowd of low fellows.

Unfortunately for Mark, or perhaps fortunately, Chook in his fuddled state had made known the fact that he had been warned. An Enquiry was held. It was a simple matter to trace the betrayal to Oscar. His Honour sat in judgment. Oscar was accused of that worst of all offences in Civil Service — Blabbing. He looked so bemused and miserable that Mark was smitten to the heart. Mark took the blame, and more, told the Cabinet that he had discovered their paltry plot unaided, that Oscar was the best man in the Service, and the only honest, decent, and intelligent one, and that the faithful service he gave was pearl cast before mean, gutless, brainless, up-jumped swine, chief of which was His Blunny Honour. Mark worked himself into a towering rage. He was still expressing his opinion of his superiors when there was no-one left in His Honour's sanctum to hear but Oscar and himself. Oscar gripped his hand and said huskily, "Thanks Son, you're a man." For less than that, romantic Mark would have gladly gone to jail.

Mark and Chook were dismissed on the same day. They celebrated by getting drunk with Krater and a man named Harold Howell on some of the £25 that Mark was given to pay his passage home. A few days later Mark and Chook between them bought a twenty-ton auxiliary lugger for £500, and with great festivity named it the *Spirit of the Land*. About a week afterward they sailed in company with Krater's lugger to Flying Fox, taking with them Harold Howell and another young man named Skinn, to help Ned Krater make of trepang-fishing the most important industry of the land.

Trepang, the great sea-slug, prized by wealthy Chinamen as a delicacy and aphrodisiac!

SIGNIFICANCE OF A BURNT CORK

IF MARK and his companions had had the energy to execute the plans with which they went to Flying Fox they might have turned the fair place into a township and themselves into bumbles. They planned to build houses, stores, curing-sheds for the trepang they intended to bring in by the ship-load, and a jetty, and a tramway, and a reservoir, and —

this was inventive Mark's idea — a dam across the mouth
of the saltwater creek and a plant connected with it for
drawing electric power from the tide. They did nothing
much more in the way of building than to erect a number
of crazy humpies of such materials as bark and kerosene-
cans, into which they retired with lubras to keep house
for them. Mark built for himself by far the best house,
and furnished it very neatly. The lubra he selected was
a young girl named Marowallua, who, after he had wasted
much time in trying to teach her to keep house to suit his
finicking taste, he found was with child. He sent her away,
refusing to believe that the child was his, and took another
girl. It was Krater who caused him to disbelieve Marowallua. Krater said that several times he himself had been
tricked into coddling lubras in belief that they were carrying children of his, to find at last that he had been made
cuckold by blackfellows. Marowallua went off to the mainland with her people.

The humpies were set up on the isthmus between the
creek and the sea, among a grove of fine old mango trees
and skinny coconuts that Krater had planted. In these
trees lived a multitude of the great black bats called flying
foxes, the coming of which when the mangoes began to
bear was responsible for the renaming of the island. Back
some little distance from the settlement lay a large billabong, screened by a jungle of pandanuses and other palms
and giant paper-barks and native fig trees. The billabong
provided much of the food of the inhabitants. Yams and
lily-roots grew there in abundance; and it was the haunt of
duck and geese, and a drinking-place of the marsupials
with which, thanks to Krater's good sense in helping the
natives to preserve the game, the island abounded. More
food was to be got from the mainland, where now there
were to be found wild hog and water-buffalo, beasts
descended from imported stock that had escaped from
domesticity. And still more food was to be got from the
sea, which abounded in turtle and dugong and fish. The
whitemen left the hunting to the natives. It was not long
before the settlement became self-supporting in the matter
of its supplies of alcoholic liquor as well, thanks to Chook
Henn, who discovered that a pleasant and potent spirit
could be distilled from a compound of yams and mangoes.

The months passed, while still the trepanging-industry
remained in much the same state as it had throughout all
the years of Krater's careless handling of it. It was not
long before Krater showed that he resented the intrusion

of the others. Thereafter, Mark and Chook and the other young men fished for themselves.

Wet Season came. The Yurracumbungas returned in force to their Gift of the Sea. Wet Season was drawing to a close, when one violent night the lubra Marowallua gave birth to her child. A storm of the type called Cockeye Bob in Capricornia, which had been threatening from sundown, burst over Flying Fox in the middle of the night, beginning with a lusty gust of wind that ravaged the sea and sent sand hissing through the trees. Then lightning, like a mighty skinny quivering hand, shot out of the black heavens and struck the earth — CRASH! The wind became a hurricane. Grass was crushed flat. Leaves were stripped from trees in sheets. Palms bent like wire. Flash fell upon flash and crash upon crash, blinding, deafening. Out of nothing the settlement leapt and lived for a second at a time like a vision of madness. Misshapen houses reeled among vegetation that lay on the ground with great leaves waving like frantically supplicating hands. Rain stretched down like silver wires from heaven of pitch to earth of seething mud. Rain poured through the roof of Mark's house and spilled on him. He rose from his damp bed, donned a loin-cloth, and went to the open door.

As suddenly as it had come the storm was over. The full moon, rain-washed and brilliant, struggled out of a net of cloud, and stared at the dripping world as though in curiosity. The air was sweet. For a while the ravaged earth was silent. Then gradually the things that lived, goannas, flying foxes, snakes, men, frogs, and trees, revived, began to stir, to murmur, to resume the interrupted business of the night. From a gunyah in the native camp came the plaint of one whose business had only just begun.

Mark returned to bed. He was not feeling well. Of late he had been drinking too much of Chook's potent grog. He lay behind the musty-smelling mosquito-net, smoking, and listening idly to a medley of sounds. Water was dripping from the roof; a gecko lizard was crying in the kitchen; mosquitoes were droning round the net; frogs were singing a happy chorus on the back veranda.

The silhouette of a human form appeared in the doorway. It was a lubra. Another joined her. Two for sure, since two is dear company at night in a land of devil-devils. They stood whispering. Mark thought that they were come to sell their favours for tobacco or grog. When one stole in to him he growled, "Get to hell!"

The lubra bent over, plucked at the net, said softly, "Marowallua bin droppim piccanin, Boss."

After a pause Mark breathed as he slowly raised himself, "Eh?"

"Piccanin, Boss — lil boy."

He asked quickly, "What name — blackfeller?"

"No-more — lil yeller-feller — belonga you, Boss."

Mark sat staring. The lubra murmured something, then turned away. He sat staring for minutes. Then hastily he searched the bed for his loin-cloth, found it, donned it, and slipped out. At the door he stopped. What was he doing? Was the child his? Should he ignore it? Better see. But first put on trousers. A whiteman must keep up his dignity.

He went back for his trousers. Now his hands were trembling. Holy Smoke! A father? Surely not! He felt half ashamed, half elated. What should he do? What should he do? What if people found out? What if Oscar — ? A halfcaste — a yeller-feller! But — gosh! Must tell Chook and the others. Old Ned — old Ned would be jealous. He had been trying to beget yeller-fellers for years. Not that he had not been successful in the past — according to his boasts. Boasts? Yes — they all boasted if they could beget a yeller-feller ——

He fumbled for the lantern, lit it, then got out a bottle that was roughly labelled *Henn's Ambrosia*, and drank a peg — and then another — consuming excitement! Gosh! A father!

He took up the lantern and hurried out.

He found Marowallua in a gunyah, lying on bark and shivering as with cold. But for her he had no eyes. On a downy sheet of paper-bark beside her lay a tiny bit of squealing squirming honey-coloured flesh. Flesh of his own flesh. He set down the lantern, bent over his son. Flesh of his own flesh — exquisite thing! He knelt. He touched the tiny heaving belly with a fore-finger. Oh keenest sensibility of touch!

After a while he whispered, "Lil man — lil man!"

He prodded the tiny belly very gently. The flesh of it was the colour of the cigarette-stain on his finger. But flesh of his own flesh — squirming in life apart from him — Oh most exquisite thing!

Smiling foolishly, he said with gentle passion, "Oh my lil man!"

The two lubras who had called him stood at the open end of the gunyah. Beside Marowallua, fanning her with a goose-wing, watching Mark with glittering beady eyes, sat the midwife, whose hair was as white as the sand beneath her and skin as wrinkled as the bark above. Mark remembered them, looked up, eyed each one coldly. He believed that lubras sometimes killed their halfcaste babies. He might have guessed that they did not do it very often in Capricornia, where the halfcaste population was easily three times greater than the white. The thought that harm might come to his son caused him a twinge of apprehension. He looked at Marowallua and said sharply, "Now look here, you, Mary Alice — you no-more humbug longa this one piccanin. You look out him all right. I'll give you plenty tucker, plenty bacca, plenty everything." She dropped her tired eyes. He went on, "S'pose you gottim longa head for killim — by cripes you look out!" Then he addressed the women generally, saying, "S'pose some feller hurtim belong me piccanin, I'll kill every blunny nigger in the camp. Savvy?"

They stared without expression.

He turned to his flesh again, and smiled and chuckled over it till he found the courage to take it in his arms. Then in a rush of excitement he carried it away to show his friends.

In spite of the lateness of the hour, the whitemen rose from their beds and gathered in Mark's house to view the baby. At first Mark was shy; but when the grog began to flow he became bold and boasted of the child's physique and pointed out the features he considered had been inherited from him; and while it squealed and squirmed in the awkward arms of Chook, its Godfather, he dipped a finger in a glass of grog and signed its wrinkled brow with the Cross and solemnly christened it after himself, Mark Anthony. When the party became uproarious, a lubra slipped in and stole the child away.

The christening-party went on till noon of next day, when it ended in horseplay during which Mark fell over a box and broke an arm. His comrades were incapable of attending him. Chook wept over him. He drank frantically to ease his pain — drank — drank — till he was babbling in delirium tremens. Natives found him next morning in the mangroves of the creek, splashing about knee-deep in mud, fleeing from monsters of hallucination, while scaring devil-crabs and crocodiles he could not see. His comrades trussed him up and took him in to Town.

§

Mark returned to sanity to find himself lying a physical wreck in hospital, exhausted from the strain of raving for days in delirium tremens, tortured by his broken arm, and otherwise distressed by cirrhosis of the liver and the utter contempt of the nurses, to the point of wishing he had never regained his sanity at all.

His first sane act was to ask his one kind nurse, Chook Henn, if he had talked in his madness about the halfcaste piccaninny. His next was to question the drunken doctor warily to prove the worth of Chook's assurances. His next was to bury his head in the pillows as the result of learning that he had thrice chased lubras working in the hospital garden, and to swear that henceforth he would live decently or die. He drove Howell and Skinn away when they came to visit him, but not before securing their solemn word that they would never tell a soul about the piccaninny. He quarrelled with the drunken doctor because the amiable fellow persistently spoke of his condition as though it were a brave achievement, not a loathsome visitation as it was to himself. He told Chook to keep at a distance so as not to fan him with his alcoholic breath, and asked him to visit him less often and never unless shaved and neatly dressed and sober. And he sent a message to the matron, apologising for any trouble he might have caused. The doctor and the others humoured him; the matron ignored him.

He learnt with great grief that Sister Jasmine Poundamore was no longer on the staff. Then he was hurt to learn that the lady no longer went under that name. She had become Mrs. Oscar Shillingsworth some three months before and as such had been till lately honeymooning in Malaya and the Philippines. He was not hurt because Jasmine had become his sister-in-law, but because he had not been invited to witness the event of her becoming so, nor even told when the event was likely to take place, although he had been in Town and talked to Oscar not a month before it did. He was also hurt because Oscar ignored his presence in the hospital. But was he worthy of the notice of decent people? Oh God! As soon as he could leave the hospital he would leave the country for ever!

Thus stricken in body and soul he lay in hospital for about a fortnight. Then swiftly he began to recover. He withdrew his head from ostrich-hiding in the pillows and took an interest in the world. The purpose of the stream of sugar-ants that flowed along the veranda past his bed on ceaseless errands to and from the kitchen seemed less irritatingly futile than before. Without realizing as much, he decided that the Trade Wind was not roaring across the harbour and bellowing in the trees and frolicking in his bedclothes simply to annoy him, and that this was not the purpose of the halfcaste girls who sang all day in the Leper Lazaret, nor of the possums that romped all night on the roof, nor of the windmill whose wheels were always squealing. He began, without realizing as much, to think of these things as pleasant things, parts of the pleasant world of which it was good to be a functioning part. He began to walk about and read and talk and even take some pleasure in bawdy jesting with his fellow patients. The doctor said that he was recovering from the cirrhosis.

One day, about a month after his admission to hospital, while in town for an hour or two on furlough, he met Oscar. The meeting took place on the front veranda of the Princess Alice Hotel, where Mark was sitting, resting and drinking ginger-ale. Oscar was about to enter the hotel. "Hello!" he said, smiling. "Quite a stranger."

"Hello!" returned Mark weakly, and rose, and extended his grubby right hand. He was disconcerted. He had planned to avoid Oscar if he should meet him, or, if unable to avoid him, to assume a pose of haughtiness to punish him for having so long ignored him. First of all he was ashamed of his appearance. He was clad in a shabby khaki-drill suit and grubby panama and sandshoes, and wore neither socks nor shirt, and was unshaven. The slovenliness of his appearance was mainly due to the fact that he had the use of only one hand.

Oscar was brilliant in whites and topee. He looked at the grubby sling in which Mark's left arm hung, and at the sandshoes, and at the hint of hairy chest to be seen through the buttons of the high-necked khaki tunic. Mark looked at the ebony walking-stick and the patent-leather shoes.

"They tell me you've been knocking yourself about," said Oscar, twisting his moustache.

Mark searched the calm brown face for feeling. He saw no more than he could have expected to see in the face of a casual acquaintance. He was filled with bitterness; but he answered with a weak grin, "Yes — a bit."

"Getting right again?"

"Close up."

Mark dropped his eyes. While Oscar was so calm and

cool and handsome, he felt flustered and sweaty and un-couth.

"Heard you were in the hospital," said Oscar. "I'd've come out and had a look at you, only I've been pretty busy fixing up the new joint."

Mark felt relieved. So Oscar had not been shunning him deliberately! He cast about for something to say. At length he said lamely, "Heard from home lately?"

"Yes, of course. Haven't you?"

"Not for months. Reckon they must be shot of me."

"Rot! If you don't write to 'em regular, you must expect 'em to do the same to you."

Mark was of the opinion that his people were ignoring him because Oscar, who had shown strong disapproval of the trepang-fishing, had black-balled him when writing home.

A pause, during which Oscar destroyed a hornet's nest in the low roof of the verandah with his stick. Then Mark said suddenly, and with so much feeling that he almost gasped it, causing Oscar to look at him with raised brows, "They — they tell me you're married."

Oscar's brows fell. He smiled and answered, "What — you only just found out?"

Mark choked. He was on the point of retorting passion-ately; but he merely said, "Y — es — since I came in."

"Been married four months," said Oscar airily, whirling his stick.

Mark mouthed another passionate retort. He swallowed it, said weakly, "How d'you like it?"

Oscar grinned and shrugged. "We had a great trip round the East," he said. "Going to have another soon — a run down home this time."

After a pause, during which Mark searched Oscar's face for signs of what he felt, he asked huskily, "How's your wife?"

He meant it for a thrust. Oscar answered it with a chuckle, saying, "What about coming down and learning to call her by her name?"

Mark flushed deeply and replied, "Sure I'm wanted?"

Oscar's face was expressionless. "Don't be silly," he said. After a pause he added, "We've got young Heather Poundamore staying with us just now — Jasmine's sister. Nice kid. She'd like to meet you, she said. We live down by the Residency now —"

"So I heard."

Oscar looked genuinely surprised. He asked, "Well why the blazes haven't you been down?"

Mark was bewildered. What could one make of the man? He was on the point of unburdening himself when Oscar said, "Well, I'll have to be getting along, Mark. I've got a date with a feller inside. See you later." He touched Mark lightly on the shoulder and added, "Don't forget to come down."

Mark flushed and stammered, stepped awkwardly down to the gravelled footpath, and went off shuffling, with eyes cast down. Oscar looked after him as he entered the hotel. Mark did not see. He walked for many yards without seeing anything. He was insensible to everything but a keen sense of dismay in his heart. So the best of all men had come to treat him as a casual acquaintance!

He wandered down to a street called The Esplanade, which traversed the edge of the promontory on which the town stood. Directly below the point where he stopped lay the *Spirit of the Land*, careened on the beach of Larrapuna Bay. Chook Henn and a blackfellow were painting her hull. Mark merely glanced at that, then looked over the wind-swept harbour and over the miles of mangrove-swamps of the further shore and over the leagues of violet bush beyond to a blue range of hills that stood on the dust-reddened horizon. He stared at the hills as he often had when he lived in what he had called Slavery, but stared now with no such yearning for the wilderness as then, because at the moment the world was a wilderness in which he stood alone. For minutes he stared. Then suddenly he shrugged and swore.

He looked down the road. An old Chinaman clad in the costume of his race was shuffling along under a yoke from which hung two tin cans of water. He disappeared into an iron shop, one of a group, above the verandas of which stood vertical, bright-coloured Chinese trading-signs A waggon drawn by a pair of lazy buffaloes and driven by a dozing halfcaste was slowly lumbering along. High in the blazing blue sky two kites were wheeling slowly, searching the town with microscopic eyes for scraps. Somewhere in the distance a mean volley of Chinese devil-crackers broke the stillness. Mark sighed. He was thinking that the charm of the town was its difference from the state it would have been in had it been peopled entirely by people like Oscar. Then the scent of whiskey came to his nostrils. He sniffed. He had merely remembered it. He swallowed. He was Low, he decided. He found himself glorying in the fact. He turned to the sea, looked at the ship, saw Chook pounce on the blackboy and cuff him. He grinned. After a moment he went to the steps that led to the beach and descended.

"Hello Chook!" he shouted as he neared the lugger.

Chook looked round, stared for a moment, then answered, "Gawdstrewth! Ow are ya?"

"Fine. What — painting, eh? Where'd you get the paint? Aint got money, have you?"

"Pinched it. There's a ton of it in a shed down in the Yards near Fat Anna's. But I've got a bit of cash too, if you want it."

"Yes? Where'd you get it?"

"Won it in a two-up school yesterd'y. I've been hangin' on to it to pay the debts. Want it?"

"I could do with a drink."

"No!"

"Dinkum."

"But what about your guts and things?"

"Oh they're all right now."

"Well ——" said Chook, beaming, "that's fine! I could do with a drink meself. Aint had one for two days." Then he turned to the blackboy with a scowl and said, "Here boy — me-feller go walkabout. You go on paintim all-same — or by cripes I'll break y' neck." He turned to Mark beaming, and said, "Good-o, son. Just wait'll I get the paint off."

§

Although Mark's digression did not last long it was thorough. He returned to the hospital just twenty-four hours after leaving it, not on foot and alone as when he left, but in Joe Crowe's cab with Chook and a policeman. The nurses already knew that he was drunk. The police had sent word to the hospital by telephone. The sister in charge met him at the front steps and handed him his belongings in a parcel and told him to go to the devil. He was too drunk to understand and too ill to obey if he had understood. The policeman left him, saying that he would not take responsibility for the care of a man with a broken arm. He was left on the steps where he slept soundly with his head on the parcel till the drunken doctor came. The doctor pacified the sister and put him to bed himself.

Mark woke to find the glory faded from his lowness and the ants returned to their maddeningly purposeless pursuits and the Trade Wind more annoying than before.

Thus he lay for several days, renewing his avowals to the pillows.

This time he recovered health and wilfulness in a week. But while the debauch had affected him thus slightly in person, it took more serious effect on him in another way. This he discovered when he sent for tobacco to a store from which he had dealt for many months, and received nothing but a note that stated in uncertain characters inscribed with a Chinese writing-brush: *Carn do. More better first you pay up big money you owe.*

He sent for Chook, who, he learnt, was suffering a similar boycott. The next evidence of the displeasure with which the business people of the town regarded the debauch came in the form of a lawyer's letter from the one European store, demanding the settlement of a bill for £28 7s. 8d., under threat of legal action.

Mark would not have been worried about debts had he been entirely without means. A creditor could do nothing worse to an incapable debtor than have him sent to live very comfortably for a month or two at the State's expense in the Calaboose at Red Turtle Bay. Because whitemen were treated so well in the Calaboose that few objected to imprisonment for a reasonable length of time and many took pains to be sent there when desirous of taking a spell from the struggle for existence, creditors usually took to court only such debtors as they feared might leave the country. Once a man was judged a defaulting debtor by the law, he could not leave Capricornia till he regained his solvency or died. Mark was not in the happy state of bankruptcy enjoyed by the majority of his fellow citizens. He had a half-share in a ship worth £500. If one creditor should sue him the rest would follow suit, and would sue Chook too, with the result that they would have to sell the *Spirit of the Land.* Whatever the change in his moral condition since learning what freedom cost, Mark still dreamt of adventures on the Silver Sea. He loved the *Spirit of the Land.* Therefore he decided to ask Oscar for assistance, to ask him first for money and then for help to get a lowly kind of job in the Government for the purpose of repaying the loan. Oscar was now employed in the Department of Public Works, and hence would be able to get him a job as a labourer.

One day, about a fortnight after the meeting, Mark called on Oscar. On this occasion he was dressed in whites he had borrowed from a friend. He was first of all abashed by being met at the door by the Philippino girl on whose account he had been struck with the bottle. She was Oscar's maid. He was on the point of flight when Oscar came out and greeted him. He was next abashed by the gentility of his relatives, whom he found taking afternoon-tea in a style quite foreign to him. At first he thought that they were drinking beer, because their beverage was brown and was served with ice in glasses. It was tea. And he found to his discomfort that a strange combination knife-fork was given him with which to eat cakes so small that he could have put six in his mouth at once. Such an instrument should have been welcomed by one crippled as he was; but it did anything but please him, because in using it he had to expose his grubby-nailed hand more often and for far longer periods than he wished. He sweated and fumbled and blushed.

He was further abashed by the treatment he received. Since Oscar and Jasmine had become engaged and it had become evident that he was a waster, their attitude towards him while together in his company had always been one of strained politeness. Now Oscar received him heartily; and Jasmine was gushing. He was pleased till it dawned on him that they were treating him just as they would an ordinary visitor. Then he turned bitter and tried to strike back by calling Jasmine sometimes Miss Poundamore and some-times Mrs. Shillingsworth. His intent was lost on Oscar and Jasmine, who seemed to regard his stiffness as a joke. But evidently it was not lost on Heather. When Mark persisted in calling her Miss Poundamore in spite of her calling him by his first name, she came to blushing and avoiding his eyes.

Heather was about nineteen, and rather too good-looking and self-possessed for the liking of vain, sensitive Mark. He went out of his way to slight her. When she attempted to question him about his ship and the life he led, he told her that such things could not be of interest to such a person as she. After that the talking was mostly done by Oscar and Jasmine, and mostly concerned the City of Singapore, paradise of affected people. Their sojourn there had had a marked effect on them. Their house was furnished, their food was cooked, their speech was spoken, according to the fashionable style of Singapore.

It occurred to Mark at length that Oscar had changed greatly since his marriage, and that the indifference in his attitude towards him was the result of that change, and that the cause of the change was that Oscar was no longer the fellow he had been but the husband of Jasmine. He observed how thoroughly Oscar had become Jasmine's husband when he learnt that he intended to resign from the Government after another year of service and take up a cattle-station called Red Ochre in the Caroline River Country. Jasmine's family, the Poundamores of Poundamore Downs, in the Barkalinda Country, State of Cooksland, were graziers born and bred. Oscar's interest in bovine beasts had never before gone beyond the beef he ate. Joe Poundamore, one of Jasmine's many brothers, and Archie Poundamore, one of her multitudinous cousins, would be coming up to Capricornia with Jasmine and Oscar when they returned from the trip to the South that they intended to take when Oscar left the Service. Joe was coming to act as manager of Red Ochre and to teach Oscar the grazing business. Archie would go on to Manila to make arrangements for shipping Oscar's cattle to the Philippines. Oscar and Jasmine had already had dealings with influential people in Manila while they were there on their honeymoon. Knowing that Oscar had never met these young men, Mark was amazed to hear him speak of them with affection. This evidence of his having become absorbed into the Poundamore family made him feel that Oscar must now regard him as a stranger and put him off the object of his visit. He went away without asking for the loan.

But the loan must be raised if the *Spirit of the Land* were not to fall into the hands of Chinamen. Mark plucked up courage a few days later and went to Oscar's house again.

The consequences of the second visit were such as to put him off the subject again, indeed to put him in a position in which he came to regard the saving of the lugger as of secondary importance, since they even threatened to make him a Poundamore of Poundamore Downs as well. For he called at the house to find young Heather in sole occupation, to be befriended by her, and to be charmed as he had never been by a woman before. Heather impressed him first with her frankness. Without much delay she asked him why he had sneered at her and the others. He told her. Then she impressed him with her astuteness by telling him something of what she understood of his character. Before long he produced his hand from hiding and explained why it was not clean. She called him a silly boy for behaving so shyly before one who was virtually his sister, and got hot water and soap and a manicure-set and put the matter right. The intimacy of the operation caused both of them feelings that were certainly not fraternal. Then she impressed him with her desire to learn about ships and the sea and the

wilderness. Over a manly sort of afternoon-tea he told her
a good deal about his life, some of which was true and none
discreditable. She told him that she had come to love Capricornia already and would give much to be able to see the wild
parts of it as he had. He had it in his heart to say that
he would like to show it to her. Instead of waiting for
Oscar, he took her down to the beach and showed her the
lugger and stayed with her till sundown. That night he was
haunted by thoughts of his halfcaste son.

Later on, after she had made several short trips in the
lugger and heard many tales about the Silver Sea, Heather
told Mark that she would love to live all her life in Capricornia and that she hated the thought of having soon to return to dull Poundamore Downs. She said it with a sigh.
Mark looked at her as though he understood her thoughts,
but suggested nothing to help her, although he had the suggestion in his heart together with the horrible knowledge
that he was the father of a halfcaste.

Thus a match was made by fate. Mark tried to keep it
secret, because, while taking it seriously himself, he realized
that his cronies would take it as a joke. But such a thing
could not be kept secret for long in a community as small
and curious as Port Zodiac. The news of it spread rapidly.
Oscar and Jasmine smiled over it and said that it was the
best thing that ever could have happened to these two restless
youngsters. The nurses at the hospital, moved by feminine
love of romance, on account of it gave Mark as much furlough as he wished and for once treated him as a fellow
creature. Other women chattered about it, some in Heather's presence and not without dropping a hint or two about
the little they knew of Mark's character. His cronies roared
over it, all except Chook, who fretted over it as news of
an impending bereavement.

Talk of Mark's bad character was by no means new to
Heather. She had heard much about him from Jasmine.
But she was not concerned about his reputation then, not
realizing how bad it really was. She gave all her attention
to studying the effect her presence had on him and to
enjoying the profound effect that his had on herself. Although Mark was unaware of it, he had overwhelmed her.

In this innocent stage the affair lasted for a fortnight. It
almost reached the kissing-stage, which, indeed, it might
have reached before but for Mark's mixed feelings of reluctance to commit himself and fear of giving offence and
terror that later she might discover his monstrous disgrace.
Heather had been ready to be kissed all along.

Fate was jesting for the time. One afternoon while the couple were leaving the jetty in the lugger, setting out on a short fishing-cruise that in the minds of both of them seemed likely to end with kissing, Harold Howell, who, with Skinn and another of Mark's cronies, had followed Mark down to the house from the town and had been running about and chuckling ever since, came rushing down the jetty, shouting and waving a small brown-paper parcel. Mark sent the blackboy, who was the third person on the ship, to attend to the engine, and took the wheel himself and turned the vessel back. "What's up?" he shouted at Howell.

"Something you forgot," answered Howell.

"Me? I didn't forget anything."

"Oh yes you did!"

"What is it?"

"Dunno. Feller up town gave it to me. Said you'd forgotten it. Something for the lady, I think. Catch."

Howell tossed the parcel and skipped back out of sight. It fell on the deck near Heather, who picked it up. Mark turned the ship back to sea, shouted to the blackboy, then went to Heather. "Something for you?" he asked.

"For you isn't it?"

"He said for the lady."

"Yes — but something you'd forgotten. Shall I open it?"

"Yes — wonder what it is?"

After unwrapping many layers of brown paper, Heather came to a small cylindrical object screwed up in tissue paper. Mark was leaning over her shoulder, pleasantly near her hair. She unscrewed the tissue and revealed a charred beer-bottle cork. She looked up at Mark in surprise, to be still more surprised by the sight of him. His face was crimson, his eyes glazed. After a moment she asked, "Why — what is it?"

Mark grinned feebly, and answered, "Oh — er — a — er —— just a bit of a joke."

"Joke?" she murmured, staring.

He chuckled weakly and took the cork and tossed it overboard, foolishly to windward, so that it flew back and fouled his white shirt and lodged in the sling of his arm. He picked it out and flung it to leeward, hard. But there was no escape from the memory of it. There were corks by the score in the sea, and on the beach where they landed, and in the bottles of soft-stuff they had for their picnic. For the rest of the afternoon Mark behaved quite guiltily. There was no kissing.

That night Heather called on a knowing acquaintance of

hers, Mrs. Daisy Shay, proprietress of the Princess Alice Hotel. In the course of conversation she carefully asked what jocular significance could be found in a burnt cork. It was not specially to ask the question that she called on Mrs. Shay; she called by prearrangement; but she went filled with curiosity and not a little foreboding about the incident of the afternoon. She learnt to her horror that the men of Capricornia said that once a man went combo he could never again look with pleasure on a white woman unless he blacked her face. And she learnt much more that horrified her, some of it about Mark, who owed money to Mrs. Shay.

Next day she did not go up Murphy Street as usual to meet Mark coming in from the hospital, but went for a walk round Devilfish Bay that kept her out till sundown. Next afternoon she went for another long walk, and again the next, after which there seemed to be no further need to avoid Mark. Instead of calling at the house on the third afternoon, Mark went to the First and Last Hotel and got drunk. Next day he had to leave the hospital.

It was Mark who did the avoiding subsequently. He guessed what had happened, and realized that the dream was ended, knowing that while white women might forgive a man any amount of ordinary philandering they are blindly intolerant of weakness for Black Velvet. For a while he felt bereft. He cursed Heather, not knowing that he had caused her much weeping. Then he shrugged off the yearning for her company and sought that of the delighted Chook instead. When he met Howell he tried to quarrel with him. Howell persisted in arguing that he had done him a good turn, saying that any fool could get married, that it was the strong man who did not.

About a week later he got the promise of a job in the railway-yards. By making this known, he was able to quiet his creditors. As soon as his arm was healed he went to work as an Inspector of Rolling-stock. His duty was to examine and oil the wheels of rolling-stock. It was not at all laborious. The rolling-stock of the Capricornian Government was limited, and little of it ever rolled.

WHEN Mark and the other men left Flying Fox, Ned
Krater stayed behind, congratulating himself on having got
rid of a set of pests. The pests had been gone about a
month when, taking advantage of the mild weather following the Equinox and the end of the Wet, he set out in his
lugger, accompanied by six natives, to fish for trepang
among coral reefs that lay some twenty miles to the east
of the Tikkalalla Islands. One still starry night, while the
Maniya, with captain and crew sound asleep aboard, lay
at anchor among the reefs, a cockeye bob, as violent as un-
seasonable, roared down from the north. Before her crew
could bear a hand she snapped her cable. In a moment she
was engulfed in mighty seas and whirled away like an
empty box and smashed to pieces on a projecting reef.

Four of the natives were lost. The others and Krater
had the doubtful fortune to be hurled high on to the reef
and saved from drowning at the expense of being terribly
maimed. One blackboy sustained such severe injuries to the
head that, though he remained unconscious, it was not long
before he was raving mad. The other boy had his right
arm broken, his left ear torn off, and a great slab of flesh
stripped from his left thigh. Krater was lacerated all over
and had half his starboard ribs stove in.

Thus these favourites of doubtful fortune found each
other in the peaceful dawn, objects of interest to a horde
of crabs and a flock of seagulls. The boys had lain down
to die, as it was the custom of their race to do when life
seemed not worth living. But Krater, in spite of his more
than sixty years and the fact that, when he breathed, blood
gurgled in his chest, rose and took stock of things. He
found the dinghy cast up, battered and waterlogged, but
evidently seaworthy; and he found as well the lugger's jib
and a sweep and a tangled mass of rigging. He thereupon
decided to have the dinghy floated and rigged with sail.
Being unable to shout at his dying comrades, he attacked
them with a piece of wreckage and convinced them that
they were still alive and living with a whiteman.

They were unable to move the dinghy until the tide fell
at noon. But Krater permitted no idling, because he guessed
that the others were dying and desired to use whatever life
they still possessed. He never thought that he might die
himself. He felt immortal. First he had them bind his

chest with rope in order to restrict his breathing and so ease
the pain in his lacerated lung; then he had them help him
fashion a mast from the sweep and attach wire stays to it
and tear the jib to the shape he desired and make a bailer
from canvas and wire and bent wood. The boy who was
becoming mad was valuable because he had two sound
hands that could be forced to hold things. When Krater
was done with him he tied him to the coral to prevent him
from making himself sick by drinking of the sea. He wanted
his assistance in the task of moving the dinghy, and hoped
to be able to make further use of him during the voyage
to the Tikkalalla Group. Thus while the day advanced,
cloudless, windless, burning hot.

The dinghy was moved and emptied. It was badly sprung,
but not so badly as to daunt Ned Krater in his purpose. He
stopped the springs with rags torn from the jib and with
plugs of wood, thus occupying himself for half the afternoon, while the boy with the broken arm lay in the hot
water watching, and the other, now quite mad, lay lashed
to the coral howling.

In the middle of the afternoon the madman's raving and
struggling to get at the water became intolerable. Krater
went to him, and after studying him for a while, released
him. He uttered a joyful yell and scuttled into the water
like a crab. While he was drinking, Krater took up a heavy
piece of wood and crept on him and struck him on the head
with all his might. The boy rolled over in the water,
struggling violently. Then he gained his knees and turned
on Krater. Krater struck at him again. He jerked his head
aside and took the blow on a shoulder. He did not make
a sound. He gaped, as though surprised.

"I'm only puttin' y'outer mis'ry, me lad," gasped Krater.
"Gawdsake keep still."

When the club was raised again, the madman squealed
and dived at Krater's legs. Krater hit him — hit him —
till flakes of brains spattered out of his broken head.

Krater dropped the club, spat out a mouthful of blood,
then signalled to the other boy to come and help him throw
the body into deeper water. The other would not come,
though Krater scowled at him horribly, doubtless because
he thought he was to be put out of misery too. Krater left
the body to the crabs and gulls.

The rest of the afternoon was spent in silence. Krater
sat in the dinghy watching for the first breath of the breeze
he expected to spring up from the east. His companion lay

in the water, now with a sharp-edged rock in his hand. He
wished to die, but not by another man's hand.

At nightfall they set out for the Group, steering by stars.
Krater sat in the stern, the boy amidships bailing. They
rarely spoke. They were tired and racked to the point of
death. They reached Chineri Island late in the following
morning. Here they abandoned the dinghy for want of wind
and continued their way down the burning beach, heading
for a native camp. A thousand flies went with them to suck
their suppurating sores. Time and again they fell by the
way exhausted, and would have died there but for Krater's
Anglo-Saxon will, which could not realise that it was inextricably in the grip of death and hence flogged the wretched
body on to unnecessary misery. On they went and on and
on, Stone-Age Man and Anglo-Saxon, clinging to each
other for support, blending the matter of their sores.

It was dark when they reached their destination. Krater
asked the natives to take them to Flying Fox at once. They
demurred, saying that the sea between was a haunt of
terrible devils after dark. But they might as well face the
devils as defy the Man of Fire. He could only command
in whispers; but he made up for weakness of voice with
terrible gestures and violence with a stick. They obeyed
him. By now he was almost delirious. His old heart was
galloping to death. He did not know it. He thought only
of the need to reach home as quickly as possible, and hoped
that at home he would find the pests.

He reached his home, and lived long enough to hear the
natives wailing in a Death Corroboree over his late comrade. He knew what the wailing was about. At first he
chuckled, considering the cause of it proof of his superiority. But after a while the corroboreeing drove him mad.
He shouted to the mourners to stop their row and come and
open his doors and windows that he might not suffocate.
They did not hear him. What he thought was shouting
was mere gasping. And his doors and windows were open
as it was. At length, unable to tolerate the wailing longer,
he leapt up and rushed out to the mourners with a mighty
club and laid about him, cracking heads like eggs and limbs
like carrots. But he did not stop the corroboree even then.
His violence and the fragility of his victims were only
fancies of his dying mind.

When the natives found that he was dying, they forgot
their dead brother and came and peeped at him, while he
grovelled on the floor fighting for his breath. Long after
he fell back dead they peeped, amazed to find that the

c

mighty Munichillu was merely mortal. For many hours they were afraid to touch him, lest they should discover to their cost that they were taking a liberty. So the ants got at him first. The natives buried him in a shallow grave in the hillocks of the isthmus where he had shot Kurrinua, then looted his house, then staged another Death Corroboree in which they sang of Kurrinua and Retribution. Then, in accordance with their custom, they left the island for the time required for the laying of his ghost or devil. The crocodiles, being respecters neither of persons nor of devils, came and rooted him out and devoured him as soon as they discovered where he lay.

§

Ned Krater had been dead about nine months when Mark and Chook returned to Flying Fox. They had heard that Krater was dead from a friend of his who had gone out to visit him some time before. They found the island deserted. The natives had gone to the mainland. Mark was in a way relieved. It was disinclination to set eyes on his halfcaste son that had kept him away from the island so long. He came only because he wished to get some things he had left there. Yet he felt curious to know how the child was progressing, so much so that instead of staying only as long as it took him to get what he wanted, as he had intended, he stayed for several days in the hope that natives might come who could tell him where the child was. No-one came. At length he and Chook departed. Soon afterwards they secured a contract for transporting cypress pine in the lugger from a mill that had been set up on an island near Port Zodiac.

Another year passed. Then Mark and Chook returned to Flying Fox with intent to take up trepang-fishing in earnest. By now Mark had got over the shame of being the father of a halfcaste. In fact for some time he had been thinking that most likely the child was dead. This time the natives were in occupation; and with them was young Mark Anthony Shillingsworth, or, as the natives called him, Naw-nim, which was their way of saying No-name. The child's baptismal name had not got beyond the witnesses to his baptism. The name No-name was one usually given by the natives to dogs for which they had no love but had not the heart to kill or lose. It was often given to halfcastes as well. Little Naw-nim's mother was dead.

When Mark first saw the child he was playing in sand with a skinny dog. He scampered into the scrub when

Mark approached. It was with difficulty that he was caught. Mark picked him up gingerly, not because he was afraid of hurting, but was afraid of being soiled by him. He was unutterably filthy. Matter clogged his little eyes and nose; his knees and back and downy head were festered; dirt was so thick on his scaly skin that it was impossible to judge his true colour; and he stank.

For all his former callousness and the timidity with which he had come to see the child when he learnt that he was there, Mark was revolted and enraged by the sight of him. With the lump of squealing squirming filth in his arms he passionately reviled the natives for their foul neglect. Then he gave it to a lubra to scrub. He went back to his house spitting and grimacing and brushing contamination from his hands. It occurred to him soon afterwards that most of the responsibility for the foul neglect rested on himself. He was smitten with remorse. That night little Nawnim slept on a blanket beside his father's bed, now as clean as a little prince and smelling sweetly of Life Buoy Soap, and, though chafed almost raw, quite happy. His father had given him a large bowl of milk porridge to which was added a dash of rum.

Being bathed became a daily experience in Nawnim's life. At first he objected to it strongly, but soon became used to it, as he did to wearing the quaint costumes his father made him and to eating whiteman's food. The food he ate was often strong far beyond the alimentary powers of a child as young as he, but evidently not for one whose system had been hardened with food snatched from dogs and salted with sand and ants. His distended belly soon subsided when more than air was given it to digest; and otherwise he took on more comely shape, as his father observed with great interest. His brassy yellow skin became sleek and firm. His eyes lost their hunted-animal look and shone like polished black stones over which golden water flows. Soon he became fat and bold and beautiful. Mark loved him, and in nursing him wasted scores of hours that should have been occupied elsewhere. Often when there was no-one near to see, stirred by the beauty of the delicate little features, he would kiss him passionately and address him from the depths of his heart in terms that made him burn with shame when recalled in moments less emotional. But for Chook, who refused to take his affection for the child seriously, he might have adopted him frankly.

Several months passed. Then Mark and Chook decided to make a voyage to the Dutch East Indies Mark left

Nawnim in the care of his lubra, who looked after him dili-
gently till it seemed as though his father did not intend to
return, when she abandoned him to his old friends the dogs.
Mark was away for about a year. When he returned he
renewed his attention to Nawnim, but did not keep it up
with anything like his former interest, because he took as
mistress a halfcaste girl named Jewty, who would not have
the child in the house if his father were not there to protect him. Jewty was one of Ned Krater's children, a wilful, spiteful, jealous creature. Under her influence and that
of Chook and by reason of the fact that he spent most of
his time away from the island, Mark eventually lost interest
in Nawnim almost completely. And the occasions when he
was forced to take notice of the child did anything but
rouse paternal love in him, because they were usually in
consequence of some foul childish ailment or of the boy's
escapades in theft. Nawnim, associate of niggers' dogs, had
learned to steal as he learned to use his limbs. His father
was his chief victim.

The years passed, as the years will, even in places like
Flying Fox, where their passage may go long unnoticed.
Mark passed from youth into manhood, while spending half
his time at Flying Fox and the rest in Port Zodiac and
other easy-going places, and so without acquiring much
more understanding of moral values than he had ever had,
which was perhaps no less than that possessed by most
folks. His son spent all his time roaming with the Yurracumbungas, growing up half in the style of the Tribe and
half in that of their dogs.

HEIR TO ALL THE AGES

THE Shillingsworth family in Capricornia had increased in
the eight years of Mark's and Oscar's residence to the number of six, Mark's halfcaste bastard being included, though
perhaps not rightly, as well as Oscar's two legitimates and
himself and his wife, all of whom, though bearing the name,
were perhaps more rightly Poundamores. The younger generation were Oscar's children, Marigold and Roger, and
Mark's Nawnim. In the year of the census, 1910, Mark
was thirty. Oscar's age was now indeterminate, he having

reached the doldrums of life, the period between thirty-five and forty-five, in which a man, not knowing whether to forge ahead and pretend to be a hoary elder or to slink back and pretend to be a youth, just drifts and lets his age be known as the — er — thirties.

The year of census was an eventful one for the whole family. The first to whom adventure came was Roger, aged one year. His adventure was the greatest one can experience. He died, or, as Oscar stated on his tombstone, was Called Home. Measles had a voice in the calling.

Bitter trouble in Oscar's home followed the death of Roger. Just prior to it, Jasmine, who was in the unhappy state into which many handsome potent women fall in the early thirties through too closely considering the dulness of the future against the brightness of the past, had been neglecting her home at Red Ochre for what was a frantic endeavour to enjoy the dregs of her almost exhausted youth in the social whirl in Town. Oscar had long since dropped out of the social whirl. He would have liked Jasmine to do the same, as he often hinted. But when he accused her of neglecting her child and so having been to a degree responsible for its death he did not really mean what he said. He was not speaking his mind but the craziness that the death of the potential perpetuator of his name had induced in him.

Jasmine sprang out of mourning perhaps bitterer than his and spat at him all that over which she had been ruminating for years. He learnt that he was a thing of wood, a thing of the gutter sprung from stock of the gutter (distorted reference to disreputable Brother Mark), risen by chance to be — what? — to be a bumptious fool whose god was property, not property in vast estates such as a true man might worship, but in paltry roods. Bah! His very greed was paltry. He dreamt of the pennies he could coin from cattle-dung! (Poor Oscar! He had always resisted her urging him to secure more land and buy more stock, because, not being a grazier born like the Poundamores who controlled vast Poundamore Downs on account of which they were born and buried in debt, he realised that cattle-raising was a business, not a religion, and that as it was he held more country and ran more stock than was warranted by the mean trade he could do. And once he had said quite idly that he wished there were a sale for the cattle-dung that ·lay about the run in tons.) And she spat at him something that would not have hurt him a few years earlier or later, namely that he was already old and flaccid, while she, who was by eight years his junior, was young—

yes — young! Young — and Oh God — aflame with life!

Stung to malice, Oscar jeered at her for a faded flower blind to its own wilting through pitiful conceit. She fled from him weeping. Poor blundering ass, quickly stricken with remorse, he went after her and begged forgiveness, and thus only made himself more hateful to her by being weak and her more desirable to himself by causing her to be inexorable. They were never reconciled. A few weeks after the scene, she eloped to the Philippines with the captain of the cattle-steamer *Cucaracha*, accompanied by a cargo of Oscar's beeves. Oscar was shocked, firstly by having lost her, secondly by having lost her in a manner so unseemly, thirdly by having lost her to a man he had regarded as a friend. He had taken Captain Emilio Gomez into his house as a Spanish gentleman. The fellow had turned out to be nothing but a Dirty Dago.

There was ample justification for believing that Oscar and his family should not rightly be numbered as Shillingsworths. At the time of the census Red Ochre was bidding fair to become another Poundamore Downs, there being resident in the place eight persons of whom no less than seven were Poundamores of the blood. Oscar himself was the outsider. The seven were Jasmine and her children, and Joe Poundamore and his wife and child, and Heather. Joe had never left the place since coming up to show Oscar how to run it five years before. Heather had been there since having returned with Jasmine when that lady came home from Poundamore Downs where she had gone to bear her baby Roger as a true Poundamore.

Heather was then twenty-five, still unmarried, and not yet completely recovered from having been overwhelmed by Mark, though disposed to think of him less harshly than she had for a long while after the incident of the burnt cork. She had not seen Mark since her return, not because she had taken pains to avoid doing so, but because he had. Indeed her main reason for returning to Capricornia was to see Mark again. But he was not to be seen in Port Zodiac much in these days. He had visited Red Ochre only once, when his mother and sister Maud came up to stay there for a while about eighteen months before the return of Heather. After that, in spite of the success of the family reunion, he had not set eyes on Oscar for a whole year; and then the circumstances that brought them together was no less than the news of their mother's death. After Heather returned, Mark did not see Oscar again till after Jasmine deserted.

The Poundamore stronghold in Capricornia collapsed when Jasmine deserted. Soon after she left, Oscar quarrelled with Joe, not for the first time by any means, but for the first time with any courage. He told Joe to go to hell, and advised Heather to go with him. Joe went back to Poundamore Downs, taking his wife and child, and offering to take the motherless Marigold to give her into the care of her grandparents. Oscar declined the offer, but paid the steamer-fares for which Joe was fishing when he made the offer. Heather, whose love for Capricornia was genuine, did not go home. To the annoyance of Oscar, who would sooner have supported her than see a relative engaged in what he considered a disreputable calling, and to the disconcertment of Mark, whose favourite drinking-place the Princess Alice Hotel was, she got a job as barmaid at the Princess Alice with her old friend Mrs. Daisy Shay.

Oscar ceased to be a Poundamore with the fall of the stronghold. This Mark discovered when next they met. The discovery caused him great astonishment, because the evidence of the fact was Oscar's quite unexpected brotherly act of coming to the Calaboose and offering to effect his — Mark's — release. At the time Mark was serving a term of six week's imprisonment for having failed to pay a debt of £30 that had been owing for forty months. It was his fifth sojourn in the Calaboose. He had long been legally insolvent, having made himself so by deeding his property to Chook, who carefully kept out of debt himself and lived on Mark's credit. When Mark went to jail, as he now did at least once a year, Chook usually found temporary employment in the town and lived as meanly as possible, saving money against the time of Mark's release; if unable to find employment, he always got drunk and assaulted the person responsible for Mark's imprisonment, and thus got sent to jail himself, at once to be with Mark and to save the cost of living.

Oscar was appraised of the fact that Mark was in jail by Chook, whom he found working in the railway-yards. He also learnt that the pair still owned the lugger and the rest of the trepang-fishing plant, all of which could be turned into money. Oscar was in need of money at the time. His need was largely responsible for his sudden show of magnanimity. He decided that it would be a good idea to get Mark to turn his share of the lugger and other property into cash and then to take him as a partner in his own business. He told Mark that if he would accept the offer of

partnership he would settle the debt on account of which
Mark was imprisoned.

Mark accepted the offer eagerly, but not honestly.
Strangely enough, though always eager for Oscar's friendship when it was difficult to secure, he valued it lightly then.
He had no intention of becoming Oscar's partner. He only
wished to get out of jail. When he did get out he played
with Oscar, accompanied him to Red Ochre, and spent a
month with him, pretending that he was considering how
best he could dispose of his property, while in fact he was
making plans to take up pearl-fishing and waiting for Chook
to earn more money. At last he told Oscar that he would
like to try his hand at pearl-fishing first, and vowed that if
he made a profit he would invest it in Red Ochre. On the
strength of that Mark tried to sell Oscar the hydro-electric
power plant that he had erected at much expense and for
little purpose at Flying Fox. Oscar would not buy, in spite
of the attractive picture, which imaginative Mark drew for
him, of Red Ochre electrified free of cost by the waters of
the Caroline River. However, when Mark was leaving,
Oscar lent him £20 and refrained from mentioning the
£30 Mark owed him on account of the debt.

§

Mark was tired of Flying Fox and trepang. It was his
plan to set up a new camp on Chineri Island in the Tikkalalla Group and to fish for pearl-shell on the shallow banks
that lay between there and the Dutch East Indies. This was
the result of his having lately made the acquaintance of
Japanese pearlers from the Van Diemen Islands, from
whom he had learnt something of the art of diving, which
had brought him to believe that the Silver Sea was floored
with mother-o'-pearl. It was for the purpose of raising
money to buy a diving-outfit that he was trying to sell the
electric power plant.

He was beginning to despair of ever being able to sell the
plant, when he met a man named Jock Driver, who owned
a cattle-station called Gunamiah, situated on the Melisande
River. Jock Driver was a North-country Englishman and
very mean. His reason for being interested in the machine,
as he confessed, was only that he hated to see the waters
of the Melisande running to waste. He was deeply interested in the machine from the moment he heard of it, but
did not show that he was more than casually so, because he
wished to make a bargain of the purchase. An ordinary
Australian of the locality would have taken Mark's word

for what he said about the machine, and would have said Yes or No to the price asked, and, as a preliminary to doing business, would have stood the needy seller treat. Mark had to stand treat himself, and had to take Jock out to inspect the plant.

Thus it happened that one quiet afternoon in the early part of the Wet Season of that eventful year, little Nawnim, now aged six, while playing in Mark's house, taking advantage of Mark's absence in Town and Yeller Jewty's in the native camp, heard the splash of the anchor and the rattle of a chain. For a moment he stood bewildered, then crept to the front door and peeped out, to be confronted with the sight of Mark and Chook and Jock landing from the dinghy. They had set out for the shore before the ship dropped anchor.

Nawnim ran to the back door, intending to flee. But flight was put out of the question by the sight of heavy-handed Jewty running home. For a moment he hesitated, gathering his little wits, then drew back, and, after making a wild survey of his surroundings, rushed into hiding in the bedroom. Jewty was rushing home to get her infant daughter Diana, whom she had left asleep on Mark's white-sheeted bed. Diana was a black quadroon, her father being a blackfellow. Mark forbade Jewty to have the child in the house.

Mark's house consisted of one large room, with a kitchen built under the back veranda and connected with the room by a curtained doorway. The room itself was large and high. Two-thirds of it served as a living-room, the rest, screened off by canvas curtains prettily stencilled by the finicking hand of Mark, as the bedroom. Nawnim rushed into the bedroom so precipitately that he nearly crashed into the bed. He woke Diana. She was naked like himself, but chocolate-coloured, not copperish as he was. She did not see him. He darted under the bed.

The whitemen came up the beach, roaring *Black Alice*. Jewty flew in through the back door, took a peep from the front. The whitemen were within a few yards now. She drew back, hesitated for a moment, then darted into the bedroom.

Nawnim could see into the living-room through a gap in the loose-drawn curtain. He saw the whitemen enter, as did Jewty, who was crouching by the gap. The whitemen stopped in the middle of the room and shouted their song to conclusion, then laughed, hugged each other, and sat down. Jock asked for a drink. Mark said that they must wait till the crew brought the things from the ship. Then

Chook said that he would like Jock to try his *Ambrosia*, and rose and went off to his house to get some. Soon Mark rose, went to the front door and looked to see what the crew were doing, then, seeing that the boys were idling, went out to hurry them.

Jock rose and walked about the neatly-appointed room, examining it. Nawnim could see his face, which was one such as he had never seen before. It frightened him. Jock was, in fact, quite a good-looking fellow. What troubled Nawnim was his colouring. His mouth was as red as fresh raw meat, and thick-lipped and wide and constantly writhing. Nawnim was used to lean-faced, brown-faced, thin-lipped, small-eyed whitemen. Jock's face was as red as a boiled crayfish, even redder than it usually was in this climate in which it was as foreign as a gumtree would be in his native fogs, because it had lately been put under the blood-rousing influences of salt-wind and grog. The redness of his face set off the blueness of his bulging English eyes and the blackness of his hair and the whiteness of his large prominent teeth. His teeth looked like a shark's to Nawnim, his eyes like a crab's. When he approached the bedroom Nawnim turned sick with fright. Jewty must have been given a turn too. She rushed to the bed and snatched up her baby and trod on Nawnim's little hand. Nawnim yelped, heaved away, struck his head on the underneath of the bed, and rolled into view bawling. Diana screamed and clutched at her mother's hair.

Jock looked in. The children's cries died in their mouths. All three stared at him. "Hellaw!" he cried. "What's this — the fahmily, eh?"

Still the trio stared. Jock looked them over, grinning, then said to Jewty, "You Mark's missus?"

She blinked.

"Eh?" he asked.

"Yu-i," she muttered.

"These his piccanins?"

She nodded to Nawnim and muttered, "Dat one belong Mark."

"Not this one?" he asked, stepping up to look at Diana.

Jewty shrank back, with Diana shrinking in her arms.

"Eh?" asked Jock.

"Him belong him blackfella," she muttered; then, as Jock put out a hand to touch the child, she cried sharply, "Nomore!" and struck his hand back with her own.

Jock's eyes blazed. "You bitch!" he hissed.

Jewty stood rigid, with hand upraised to strike again.

Then Mark and Chook came in. Jock turned, looked round the curtain, and said to Mark with a grin, "Joost introdoocin' meself to your fahmily. I didn't knaw ye had one."

"Eh?" murmured Mark, approaching. He stopped at the doorway and gaped. Nawnim shrank back to the wall.

Jock chuckled. Mark swallowed, looked from one to another of the group, then said thickly to Jewty, "What the hell you doin' here with those brats?"

She frowned, hugged Diana to her, and answered sulkily, "Him two-fella come himself."

After a moment Mark grunted, "Get out!"

She slunk past him, eyeing him sideways. Nawnim still shrank against the wall. Mark growled at him, "Come out of that — come on now!" Nawnim shrank more.

"That your kid, eh?" said Jock with a grin.

Mark glanced at him sourly.

"The lassie tawl me he wuz," said Jock, and chuckled deeply.

Mark stepped up to Nawnim. As he put out a hand to seize him, Nawnim shot from the wall, collided with the bed, stumbled, dashed to the door. Jock grabbed him. He shrieked, fought furiously, wriggled free, and darted to the back door. Jewty was on the veranda. As Nawnim bounded past her she dealt him a cuff that sent him sprawling on his face in the sand. In an instant he was up and flying, shrieking, to the bush.

Jock laughed heartily, slapped scowling Mark on the back. As they were sitting down to drink, he said to Mark, "Fine stahmp of laddie, that. What ye goin' to do wi' him?"

Mark answered with a grunt that was intended to give the impression that he did not wish to discuss the matter.

"Ye leavin' him behind here when ye gaw awee?" asked Jock.

Mark looked at him, and after a moment, said, "Well — as a matter of fact I was thinkin' of sendin' him to the Compound. He — he's not really mine, you know. I — I found him in the bush."

"In the bulrushes, eh?" asked Jock, and winked at Chook.

Mark blinked, fingered his glass.

It was true that he had thought of sending Nawnim to the Native Compound in Port Zodiac. He had thought of doing so for years whenever his conscience was pricked by the thought of the boy's growing up as a savage. He had been prevented by fear that the Protector of Aborigines might discover that he was the father of the child and charge him with the cost of his maintenance. He did not know that the cost of maintaining a child in the Compound Halfcaste's Home — indeed of maintaining any inmate of the Compound — was, even there where the necessities of life were expensive, only fourpence per day. Had he known it, he surely would not have been troubled by the thought of his son's growing up as a half-starved savage.

"I could do wi' him if ye dawn't wawnt him," said Jock. "There in't many yeller-fellers doon my way." He chuckled, and added, "I in't been there long enough yet. I've got one yeller-feller meself. Boot it's a bluidy gurrl. I wawnt boys." He laughed.

He went on, "I wawnt yeller kids to train as foremen. The Government cawn't mairk a bloke pay wages to his own soons — see?"

"What — you raisin' a herd of yeller-fellers?" asked Chook.

Jock swallowed a mouthful of *Ambrosia*, gasped, blinked. "Gawd!" he breathed. "Wha's thaht — kerosene?"

Chook frowned.

Mark grinned, and said, "Yeah — you can have the kid if you want him, Jock. But don't go tellin' anyone where you got him. Dinkum, he's not mine —"

"Aw I wawn't say nawthin'," said Jock.

"Give's your word on it," said Mark. "And give's your word you'll treat him decent."

"Right!" said Jock, and grasped his hand. "There's me worrd. You can rely on me to bring him up like he wuz me awn soon, cos then I wawn't have to pay him wages — see?"

Mark thought that a mean motive, but was satisfied that by reason of it Nawnim would be well treated for the rest of his life.

Jock's station was about two hundred miles inland from Port Zodiac. It covered some two or three thousand square miles. Such a holding was not thought vast in Capricornia, where there were some of even more than ten thousand square miles. Such land was put out to lease at a purely nominal rent, the Government considering itself under obligation to the lessees for their courage in developing the country; indeed so deep was the Government's sense of obligation that it exempted the lessees from taxation on the profits — often vast profits — of their business. The joke of it was that by no means all the lessees were settlers like Jock. A good number, among whom were included practically all those who controlled the large stations, were English or other foreign companies, who had never seen the land they controlled, but put men on it to work it for them who had to pay taxes out of meagre wages. Indeed many of these big companies controlled similar properties in other countries that were Australia's rivals in the meat-trade of the world. Thus they were never troubled by competition.

Jock intended to place Nawnim in a stock-camp, in which he would grow up to learn the ways of horses and cattle as the business of his life. He would take to the saddle as soon as possible and work with native stockriders as one of them till he became a man, when, should he prove to be more intelligent, or rather, perhaps, more selfish and purposeful, than a native, he would be made a foreman. By growing up thus he would save Jock the expense of employing a whiteman. The natives made the best of stockriders, but could not be relied upon to remain at work. Jock often had to track his black staff down and bring them back to work at the point of a gun. Nawnim's status and pay would never be much better than a native's. The pay of Jock's natives was tobacco and food and clothes of a sort, their status not that of his horses. He and the many graziers like him excused their meanness by saying that it was useless giving the natives money when they did not understand the value of it. They took pains to see that the natives were never taught it.

Jock had no difficulty in securing native-labour, for all his meanness. On the contrary, he secured it easily. For, when his cattle came, the native game was scared away, or if not scared then starved away, because, during the lean times of Dry Season, the cattle, themselves hard put for succour, would take possession of all permanent grazing. This state of things would greatly affect the natives whose country the Government had leased to Jock, so that they, who, unlike their game, were prevented by tribal laws from wandering out of their domain, would be put to the alternatives of starving or eating Jock's cattle or going to work for him. The second would be their choice till the police came and shot them. All over the land were bone-piled spots where lazy Aborigines were taught not to steal a whiteman's bullocks. For natives who were unable to work there was the fourpenny Compound. But for some reason or other that institution was not popular. Most Aborigines who had been born in freedom preferred to do their starving in the bush. And all the while the Nation was boasting to the world of its Freedom and Manliness and Honesty. Australia Felix!

§

Flying Fox was washed by a vigorous tide, which was capable of rising during spring period to a height of some twenty-five feet. Hence the mouth of the salt-water creek was usually surging like a mill-race, but wasting its power — or so it had been — on transporting such things as jelly-fish, leaves, and crocodiles. This waste had been the cause of great irritation to Mark, who, though careless of most forms of ineconomy, could not bear to see the wasting of natural force. Therefore, after years of irritation, at the cost of much study and money on his own part and great labour on the part of the men of Yurracumbunga, he had dammed the mouth of the creek and cut a culvert through the isthmus, causing the water to flow through a quaint-looking machine that sucked out kinetic energy and churned it into electric power. The machine was ingeniously constructed, consisting of an old centrifugal pump of brass, a flywheel of concrete, a dynamo of antiquated type, and an elaborate system of gears comprised mainly of bicycle parts, which was capable of reversing action at the turn of the tide without interfering with the running of the dynamo. Although of rather Heath-Robinsonian design, the machine was quite effective, and when the tide was running, kept the settlement ablaze with electric light. Unfortunately, owing to the perversity of Nature, the tide was usually not running when the light was most required.

There were many electrically-operated gadgets about the place. Jock studied them with interest, wishing to learn how they were made so that he might not have to buy them. And he listened with interest to Mark's confiding that the building of the machine had given him more pleasure than any job he had ever undertaken in his life, and that therefore it pained him to have to do that which he would not do but for his urgent neediness, namely, part with it for money. Jock thought this an extraordinarily cunning method of bargaining, and therefore responded warily, praising the damming and sluicing and other parts of the contrivance that he would not have to buy, and saying with reference to them that Mark would have made a clever engineer, but cruelly criticizing the machine itself, although secretly delighted with its efficacy, in order that Mark might not be led into forming an exaggerated idea of its value.

Simple Mark was hurt by the criticisms, thinking them genuine, and was influenced by them and other subtle methods of Jock's to make a mighty reduction in his price. He began by asking for £150, which was, he said, £50 less than the machine had cost, and was about the same amount as Jock would have paid had his bargaining not succeeded. He ended, exhausted by hours of merciless wrangling on Jock's part, by agreeing to take £48 10s. For some hours after the settling of the deal Mark wandered at a distance up the beach, struggling, as he confided to Chook, to keep his hands from choking the life out of a Lousy, Bloody, Pop-eyed Pommy.

Jock's stay at Flying Fox was brief. As soon as the machine was packed and stowed, he responded to Mark's hints about the likelihood of their meeting with bad weather if the return were delayed for long, and said that he was ready to go. Nawnim was captured and taken yelling aboard the lugger.

Mark's forecast of the weather proved truer than he had realized. The lugger sailed right into bad weather and was buffeted for days. Five days were spent at sea, nearly every hour of which Jock spent in the cabin, sick. Mark was pleased, and wasted many an hour in letting the ship drift broadside to the sea. Through Jock's confinement, little Nawnim had no need to cower in the chains as he had during the first hour or two; and because of Jock's lack of appetite Nawnim got most of his helping of food.

At last the end of the voyage came in sight. The *Spirit of the Land* passed into Zodiac Harbour and went slowly towards the town, revealing to Nawnim one by one the wonders of Civilization. First wonder was an automobile, a high-wheeled waggon of the type called Motor Buggy, the forerunner of the modern motor-truck. As the ship was making her way under sail alone, Nawnim heard the strange thing roaring in the bush long before he saw it, and saw the cloud of red dust it was raising. Mark noticed his interest and forthwith ordered the helmsman to hug the shore. The buggy — it was just a Thing to Nawnim — rushed from the bush, swung into the beach-road, ran parallel with the lugger's course. Nawnim had never seen a wheeled vehicle before. He was amazed, and still more amazed when his father waved to the Thing and received an answer.

They crept past the Calaboose. Nawnim stared in wonder at the buildings on the hill and at a gang of black felons working on the road and at a gang of white ones fishing from the cliff. They passed the great Meat-works, which was still more amazing because painted black, whereas the

Calaboose was white. They coasted Mailunga Beach, which was an almost exact miniature of the ocean-beach at Flying Fox; but it was rendered incomparably more interesting by the fact that two men were pedalling bicycles through the grove of coconuts. Nawnim hopped with excitement and clapped his yellow hands.

Then Jock, who had been asleep, became aware of the fact that the ship was running in smooth water, and leapt up and poked his crimson face from the hatchway, saw what there was to see, and said fervently, "Thahnk gawd!"

Nawnim started, edged away.

Then came into view the Compound, the Nation's Pride, a miniature city of whitewashed hovels crowded on a barren hill above the sea. Then they passed the hospital, then the Cable Station, then the Residency, then a cluster of neat white houses standing amid ponciana trees that blazed like torches under masses of scarlet blooms. Nawnim's attention was then snatched away from the shore to the jetty, which suddenly appeared from behind a point, standing with red piles high above the fallen water, looking like a crowded flock of long-legged jabiroos. But even that amazing sight did not hold his attention for long. At the end of the jetty lay an utterly astounding Thing. He gaped, too young and too amazed to think. A blackboy near him said in the Yurracumbunga tongue, "That's a steamer."

When at length the steamer was hidden behind a headland, Nawnim, who had been staring at it, wrapt, became aware of bustling aboard. He dodged among scrambling legs, concentrated on not being pushed too close to those devil-devilish creatures the whitemen, till a pair of black hands whisked him out of the way and dropped him in the middle of a high coil of rope. He heard the anchor fall, then struggled out of the coil to see that the lugger was lying among several other vessels of similar type, which were peopled with squat quaint-visaged human creatures of a breed he had never seen before. While he was staring at these objects he was seized again, lifted high in the air, lowered with sickening rapidity into the dinghy. He found himself so close to his foster-father that he could smell the sickening whiteman smell of him. For once he was glad when the hands of his true father at length took hold of him, because they lifted him out of that terrible red presence and bore him to the wide wide shore. He was about to fly when Mark seized him again and carried him, protesting uproariously, towards what he was convinced was something frightful. He was left in a humpy on Devil-fish Bay in the care of a halfcaste woman named Fat Anna.

§

To Nawnim a deserted house was a delightful playground, but an occupied house a place to be avoided like a reputed lair of debil-debils. Therefore his first few hours' residence in Fat Anna's house were not at all comfortable; indeed they were hours of incarceration rather than residence, because it was necessary to restrain him owing to his determination to escape. Anna chased him through mud and mangroves and brought him home thrice before it occurred to her that he was what she called a Myall, a wild creature. The chasing upset her, because she was very fat; but she was also very good-natured and did not thrash him as another person might, nor even reproach him, nor do anything more unfriendly than to hug him to her ample breast and pant a few laughing protests while bathing him with the scent of sweets. It was with her sweets that she eventually dispelled his mistrust of her. She made these herself of butter and sugar and essences in her kitchen. It was with these that she had made most of her mass of flesh.

Having tamed him with sweets, she washed him, performing the operation with such delicacy of touch that he, engaged with a sugar-filled pawpaw, scarcely realized what was going on below his chin. Then she dressed his sores and cropped his hair and put him into his first pair of breeches, which she had made from an old blouse of spotted blue print during his period of intractability. Not even one so misanthropical as Nawnim could long resist the motherliness of Anna. Before many days were out he was snuggling up to her in sheer love.

Anna was of a lower caste than Nawnim. Her father was a Japanese. Therefore, according to the Law of the Land, which recognized no diluent for Aboriginal blood but that of a white race, she was a full-blooded blackgin and not entitled to franchise as Nawnim theoretically would be when he came of age. But Anna did not care. She had small dealings with franchised people, and lived in her own style, untroubled by the formalities that bound the rest of the band to which she legally belonged, because the police seemed to realize that, at least as far as she was concerned, the law they served was an ass. She earned her living by washing clothes for the richer members of the Asiatic crews of the pearling-fleet and by giving her favours to those of them she liked. These were the creatures Nawnim had been amazed to see about him on the day of his arrival. When he inquired about them, Anna told him they were Japs an' Chows.

She took him for walks through the railway-yards, and down round the pearling-stations, and up the jetty, but never through the town. The Yards were quiet just then, that being the 'tween-trains period; and the jetty was not nearly so interesting when viewed from above and without its steamer; and the town was forbidden ground for one who was a Ward of the State as well as a whiteman's shame. But Nawnim saw countless interesting things that Anna did her best to explain to him. There was, however, nothing that interested him so much as Anna's large naked feet. He never tired of watching these, whether they were in action or at rest. She often let him play with them while resting, and made them cut capers to amuse him, or rather suffered them to do so, since it was a fact that more often than not they got out of her control at his touch; for when he touched he tickled, which was always more than she could bear; usually his attention was diverted from her feet by her shrieks of laughter and the astounding involutions of her huge brown-yellow frame.

One day he wandered into the railway-yards, and, becoming tired, sought rest and shelter from the sun beneath a cattle-car that stood in a silent rake. He lay on a cool steel sleeper, unconcerned about the grime he gathered and the reek he breathed, amusing himself with slaughtering with a rusty bolt the meat-ants that ran about him. Then he heard a distant sound and sat up listening. The cause of the sound was approaching rapidly, so rapidly that he leapt up to flee and struck his head against the dung-encrusted undercarriage with such force as to knock him flat. The sound was now a thundering. The very earth quaked. He dug fingers into earth and steel, about to dart into sunshine and safety, when, with a frightful grinding roar and a belching of scalding vapour in his face, a Thing of horribleness unutterable dashed across his path. His shriek was as feeble as the plaint of a grass-stalk in a storm.

He recovered his wits to find himself lying with throat on a rail and hands outstretched clutching gravel and teeth clenched on oily grass. He looked up, dazed. There was nothing terrible before him — nothing, indeed, but the roof of Anna's humpy smiling at him through the tops of palms. He crawled out warily. Nothing in sight to right or left. When he looked at Anna's again his heart ached with love

for her. He slowly rose, and rising glanced to right to see
— Horror! — the Thing rushing down on him — black
hair trailing and white whiskers billowing about its pounding flanks.

He tripped over a rail. The Thing yelled at him. He
echoed it with all his might, shot to his feet, raced to the
embankment, pitched headlong down,·fell in a heap, shot
up again, crashed through the scrub, tearing his flesh and
scuttling crabs and birds, rushed into the humpy, and shrieking, flung himself into the outstretched arms of Anna.

"Whazzer madder liddel man?" she crooned. "Aw wazzer madder wid de liddle myall now?"

She hugged him close and kissed his distorted face and
nursed him and petted him till he could find the voice to
speak.

"Oh trice!" he moaned. "Dibil-dibil — dibil-dibil ——
Oh jeezon trice!"

THE COPPER CREEK TRAIN

THE life of an infant is like a passage over a gigantic strip
of carpet that rolls out ahead and up behind as one goes
on, hiding the future and obliterating the past. While living with Fat Anna little Nawnim was aware of no other
state of existence. Flying Fox and its associations had
faded from his mind. The world was the region visible from
the humpy, its people the crabs and snipe and occasional
crocodile that haunted the shores of Devilfish Bay, and
Anna herself, and her Japs an' Chows, and the devil-devil
of the railway-yards, and the few brave whitemen who
worked there.

He spent with Anna what seemed to him a lifetime, but
was in fact tén days. Then one night Jock and Mark and
Chook came, appearing to him like monsters materialized
out of a forgotten nightmare. That was the day before the
mail-train's fortnightly trip to Copper Creek. Next morning Anna woke him early, washed and fed and dressed him
with more than usual care, then carried him up to and
through the Yards to a whitewashed iron shed that bore on
a board in great black letters the name PORT ZODIAC.
He himself carried a newspaper-parcel containing a paw-

paw and a huge beef-sandwich and a lump of toffee. He knew he was going somewhere, having been told so repeatedly by Anna, but cared about it not at all, supposing that she was going with him.

A noisy crowd of people of all the primary colours of humanity and of most of the tints obtainable by miscegenation was gathered about the train, moving freely, with neither platforms nor officials to impede it. Somewhat to Nawnim's consternation, Anna shouldered through the crowds, chatting with people as she went, and pushed about till she found Mark and Chook and Jock Driver. While she was talking to these monsters, each vainly tried his hand at petting Nawnim, who would not take from any hand but Anna's even the large bag of lollies Mark had brought him. At length Jock gave Anna some money and a pinch on the rump. Then she went off with Nawnim, past the three coaches provided for superior passengers, to the trucks at the front, where the crowd was entirely black. She squeezed him for a while, and kissed and petted him, then passed him to a blackboy. Before he was properly aware of his transfer, he was swung into the air. His heart stopped. A momentary glimpse of the jostling crowd, a last sight of Anna's face; then he was dropped into an open truck.

Sense of desolation smote him. He would have bawled and hammered on the wall before him had he not suddenly become aware of the presence of three black naked piccaninnies and a large mangy mongrel dog, all of whom stared at him so hard that he forgot his forming purpose in staring back. Then the dog attacked him, writhing with friendliness, knocked him down, licked him, tore open his parcel, gobbled his bread-and-beef. The piccaninnies pounced on the rolling pawpaw. He had the wits to grab the sweets.

He had no time to recall the desolation. Scarcely had he recovered from the welcome when the locomotive came. It came horribly, rumbling and grumbling and clanking and hissing, all the more horribly because it could not be seen. All the piccaninnies stiffened. Their faces became blank. Their eyes widened and assumed expressions of sightlessness that told of full sensory powers flung into the one of tense audition. The locomotive stopped, so close that its hot breath choked the listeners and its frightful noises entered their very hearts.

A terrible voice —— "Good-o —— ease-up!"
Hsssssssssssss!
The voice —— "Wha ——ho there!"
Crash! The couplings clanked throughout the train. The

children fell. The black ones howled at top of lungs. Nawnim was silent, clinging desperately to the struggling dog. They rose together, to stand huddled like yarded sheep. Hiss and bubble and clatter and chatter and bunkerlunk behind them and around.

Then to the sudden great delight of the black ones, their parents climbed over the side. Nawnim turned from watching wild embracings to look for Anna. He was watching when a bell clanged. One of the children shrieked, as though the brazen tongue had struck on flesh. Nawnim gasped.

The voice —— "Aller — bo —ud!"

Sounds waxed louder, reached a climax, suddenly stilled. Then *pheeeeeeeep!* And the voice —— "Rightaway Fitz — ledder go!"

Dead silence — silence presaging a dire event. Nawnim's knees knocked.

Then a *Shriek* —— a *Hssss* —— then *Snort! Snort! Snort!* The truck leapt under Nawnim's feet. He reeled, clutching at the wall. Then the engine shrieked again, and hissed and raged and roared and filled the truck with smoke and steam and cinders.

Nawnim fell on the dog, which yelped and snapped. Chaos raged in the undercarriage. Wheels groaned and squealed and thumped. Chains and drawbars rattled and crashed. No piccaninny shrieked louder then than Nawnim. He thought it was The End.

A few sound whacks from a hard black hand soon told him that he was alive and with his kind. The black hand lifted him from the floor and dumped him in a sitting posture by the wall. Overhead reeled black and white clouds in a sapphire sky, and rocky walls and grass and trees, all dancing madly.

After a while his terror subsided. Rain poured down and proved his condition earthly at least. Rain roared and raged down. The truck would have been filled to the top but for the gaping holes in its bottom. Then the sun beat down and charged the soaking truck with steam and the stench of sweating flesh. By now little Nawnim had found a crack in the wall he leant against. He examined it carefully to be assured that it was no inlet for danger, then set an eye to it, to see a world of trees go spinning by in a wild arboreal corroboree. A red wall leapt at him. He gasped and hastily withdrew. But nothing happened; so he peeped again, and stared and stared and was amazed.

The train roared over culverts rocking, clattered over bridges shuddering, panted up inclines clanking, raged down declivities rattling as though falling to pieces. Swollen creeks flew underneath; jungles flashed by; stony hills leapt out of grassy plains and plunged into forests; flocks of geese swept up from swamps; a herd of buffalo charged into the bush; while little Nawnim stared and stared and was amazed.

Back from the engine with the din and smoke and soot and steam were flung the chink of glass and the sound of whitemen's voices raised in song; and similar sounds joined the whirlwind that followed the van; for the progress of the train to Copper Creek was not so much a business as a pleasure, not so much a journey as a locomotive picnic for the passengers and crew.

Sometimes the engine stopped for water, or to drop stores at fettlers' camps, or to accumulate the steam to take it up a heavy grade. It was an old machine and badly strained and prodigal of its vitality. On account of the prodigality, stops were sometimes made to give the fireman a rest and a chance to damp with something from a bottle the fire he stoked within himself while feeding the greedy furnace. And at least two stops were made while the engineer went back with water to extinguish fires that had broken out in axle-boxes missed by the Inspector of Rolling-Stock. When the train was stopped, the clinking and singing could be heard to better advantage by the people in the trucks, who looked towards the source and licked their sooty lips.

So the hours passed. Little Nawnim, worn out in body and mind by buffetings and sights and sounds, at length fell asleep with head on the weary dog. And while he slept the niggers ate his sweets.

§

At two o'clock in the afternoon the train bowled over the Caroline River Bridge and rolled into the 80-Mile Siding, just as Mrs Pansy McLash, the keeper of the Siding House, was flogging a herd of goats from her garden. The goats surged on to the railway, intent on escaping the stockwhip whistling behind; and Mrs McLash went after them, intent on teaching them the lesson of their lives. The small crowd waiting before the Siding House yelled at the woman and the goats. The woman turned and saw the train, tripped on a rail and fell. The crowd, among which was Oscar, rushed to her assistance.

Finding that the chase had ceased, the goats drew up and looked to see what had happened. The track was packed

with them. Mrs McLash screamed as she was raised, "My
God — my goats!"

"Goats!" yelled the fireman to the engineer.

The engineer looked, then shot a hand to a valve and
released a mighty jet of steam. The goats looked interested, but did not move. The engineer laid hold of reversing-
gear. Fireman and passengers rushed to the hand-brakes.
The locked wheels raged against the strain. Every bolt and
plate of the engine rattled. Coal crashed out of the tender.
Water shot out of the tank. The engine halted in an atmosphere of goats. The goats themselves were well on the
way to Copper Creek.

Mrs McLash came up to the engine fuming, vowing to
report the engineer for neglecting to whistle on the bridge.
He promptly silenced her by presenting her with two wet
bottles of beer, saying winningly, "Tchsss! Off the ice in
Town, Ma, and all the way up in the water bag. All chilly
and bubbly and liquidy — and all for you, my heart."

She swallowed, and staring at the bottles muttered, "Don't
try to blarney me ——"

"Now who'd do that!" cried the engineer. "But where's
young Frank? Ah! There he is." He looked at a figure,
clad in khaki pants and sleeveless cotton singlet, bent over
the driving-mechanism. It was Frank, son of the widow
McLash, or her Pride and Joy as she called him. He was
a low-browed youth of about twenty, very big for his age,
swarthy as a Greek, and shaped rather like a kewpie doll,
having a rotund pendulous paunch and a distinctly egg-
shaped head. He looked around.

"Good-o Frank," said the engineer. "Water her up and
have a look see what's knockin' back of the steam-chest
there. There's a couple of waggons to come off. Charlie'll
tell you."

Mrs McLash's anger was gone completely, douched not
nearly so much by the beer as by this attention to her son.
She loved alcoholic liquor next to her Pride and Joy, but
would have gone and lived for ever on salt-bush and dew in
a desert for his sake. Indeed she had done something like
that by coming to live in Capricornia, because she had for-
saken a cosy little shop she had owned in her native city of
Flinders and friends of a lifetime and a perpetual supply
of cheap liquor, to save him from a life of crime. His last
place of residence in Flinders was the Spring Hill Reform-
atory, where he was sent for the second time in his young
life for committing burglary. His mother had secured his
release by swearing to take him away to what they called

down there *The Land of Opportunity.* She had done well.
Two years before it had been his ambition to become a first-
class criminal; now it was to become the engineer of the
Copper Creek train.

People who had come to hear the siding-mistress assail
the engineer, turned with the pair and followed them to the
house. Oscar was not one of them. He had been at the
brakevan getting his stores and the district mail. He met
the others on the veranda.

When Jock Driver saw Oscar he shouldered his way to
him. He and Oscar had lately quarrelled over a mixed-up
train-load of imported breeding bulls. He bawled at Oscar,
"Why — there's the big Mister Shillingsworth —— hey
there, I wanner word wi' you!"

Oscar looked and scowled. Jock was drunk. He tripped
on the mat at the dining-room door, and staggering, crashed
into the iron wall. After sprawling against the wall for a
second or two, he stood erect and bawled at Oscar, "By
jees Orscar — j'know you'n me's relairted?"

Again Oscar scowled.

"Aye," cried Jock. "S'blunny fact. I'm fawster fawther
y' lil nevvy No-name —— so'm fawster brither t'you —
aint it? Ha! Ha! Ha! You'n me ——gawstrewth —
n'y'dunno it — Ha! Ha! Ha!"

He reeled against Oscar, who flung him off crying,
"What's wrong with you — gone mad?"

Jock laughed till he wept, and while doing so staggered
to the wall. "Uncle Orscar," he gasped. "Gawd — thaht's it
— Uncle Orscar! Hey guard — hey Chawlie — where's lil
yeller bawstid — lil No-name — bring'm lennim see's grea'
big gennelmally Uncle Orscar — Ha! Ha! Ho!"

"Shut your meaty moosh or I'll shut it for you," cried
Oscar.

Jock stopped laughing and glared, then lurched into a
fighting attitude and bawled, "I'll crack ye — big flash coo!"

Oscar blew out his big moustache contemptuously,
snapped, "Rat of a Pommy!" and picked up the mail-bag
and walked down the veranda to the little room at the end
called the Post-Office.

In the dining room Jock attempted to make more trouble,
choosing as his victim the halfcaste waiter Elbert, a
mottled-brown-faced youth of about the same age as Frank
McLash, though of nothing like the same physique, as could
be seen at once, because he wore a ragged khaki shirt and
trousers that betrayed by extraordinary looseness at the
waist the fact that they had belonged to Frank.

"Yeller scoom!" bawled Jock, making a rush at him. "By jees ——"

Mrs McLash pushed Elbert into the kitchen and stepped in front of Jock and drove him protesting to a seat.

"Him!" bawled Jock. "Why thaht's the yeller bawstid ——"

"I know what he done, my good man. He pinched his wife back off you who pinched her off of him. I'm surprised at you. Sit down'n eat your dinner and leave the poor skelington thing alone. He never had a decent feed in his life till he come here."

"I tell you ——"

"Shut up or I'll kick you out!"

Jock obeyed. For a while he mouthed about Elbert, then remembered Oscar and began to mouth about him, explaining why he had called him Uncle Oscar, while giving the impression that Mark had several halfcaste children. His audience could listen with ease, because Oscar had gone off with his little daughter Marigold to avoid further contact with Jock. While Jock was talking, Oscar and Marigold were watching Frank McLash shunting trucks.

Just before the train left, while passengers were leaving the dining-room and Mrs McLash was occupied with collecting the money, Jock slipped into the kitchen and caught Yeller Elbert unawares. Mrs McLash came to the rescue with a broom.

"I'll dawg him," shouted Jock, struggling with the woman, "I'll dawg thaht moongrel bawstid off face yearth I will — lemme at him ——"

"Get on the train!" screeched Mrs McLash. "Think I want a thing like you on me hands for a fortnight? Get out or I'll brain you — Hey! — Hey! —stop, you cheat, you aint paid me for your dinner!"

For some time after the train had gone Oscar stood on the track conversing with members of the fettling gang, while Marigold sat on the Siding House veranda on the knee of Mrs McLash, innocently listening to a low-spoken discussion of her Uncle Mark and Cousin No-Name. Mrs McLash's companions were her son, Joe Steen, a settler of the neighbourhood, who was reputed to be her lover, and Peter Differ, who was employed by Oscar. While they talked they kept their eyes on Oscar, delighted to have the laugh on one they hated for his superiority. He stood there with the shabby grubby fettlers, tall and erect and neat and clean as ever. It was not clothes that made him so. He would have looked superior as a swagman. He wore a battered wideawake hat, faded blue tunic-shirt, rusty black neckerchief, grubby white moleskin pants, and spurred top-boots that were colourless with dust. Nor was it means that made him so. Any of the fettlers were better off in respect of ready-money than he was.

The discussion stopped abruptly when Oscar left the gang and came across. All looked at him with something like respect, except young Frank, who looked at the land-scape and snickered. Oscar glanced at Frank distrustfully. They were not friends, these two, having become rather too well acquainted as master and man in the early days of Frank's residence in the district.

Mrs McLash began to talk at once of a piece of news that had come up with the train. There followed a pause, during which Oscar, leaning against a veranda post, rolled a cigarette, and Frank, lolling on haunches near him, bombarded an ant with spittle. Then Frank said in a thin drawl-ing voice, "Eh Oscar—you hear about your yeller nephew?"

Oscar looked at him while licking the cigarette.

"That kid Jock Driver was tellin' you about."

Out of the corner of his eye Oscar saw Frank's mother shake her head and glare. He asked, "What's that?"

Gazing afar again, Frank said, "Jock had one of Marks halfcaste kids with him on the train."

"Don't be a fool," muttered his mother.

Frank looked at her and said, "'S fact — you's been talkin' about it last half hour yourself."

She flushed and snapped, "Garn — bag y'r 'ead!"

Oscar flushed too, and said to Peter Differ in a rather strained voice, "What is it Peter?"

Differ, who had been studying the ground, looked up and for a moment held Oscar's eye. He was himself the father of a halfcaste, for which he knew Oscar despised him. Therefore he was pleased to tell the truth. He spoke quietly, in a rather cultured voice, saying, "Your brother Mark gave Jock one of his halfcaste piccaninnies for a stock-boy. Jock had him on the train."

Oscar looked astonished. After a moment he said huskily, "Bosh! Mark hasn't got a — a halfcaste."

"Well that's what Jock said," answered Differ.

"He said Mark's got two yeller-fellers at Flyin' Fox," said Frank, "and plenty more in the bush."

Oscar carefully lit his cigarette, then said, "You can't be-lieve a drunken fool like Pommy Driver."

"Jock's a decent coot," snapped Frank, "even if he is a Pommy."

"May suit you," said Oscar coldly; then he turned to Differ and said in an employer's tone, "Got everything ready?"

"On the buckboard," said Differ in the tone of a Capricornian employee.

"Good-o. Then let's get going. Come on Marry."

Marigold slipped from Mrs McLash's knee, stood for a moment to be kissed, then went to her father. Mrs McLash then assumed an amazingly childish expression of goodwill and admiration and said, "Goodbye Mister Shillingsworth. I'm sorry for what Frank said. Goodbye loveyducks — tatta pretty dear. Please don't take no notice of poor Frank, Mister Shillingsworth. I'm afraid he's not all there."

"Oh that's all right Ma," said Oscar. "Hooray."

"Let Frank do his own polgizin," Frank growled as Oscar went away.

His mother showed her few teeth at him and said with terrible emphasis, "You fool! Your mouth's bigger'n your brains."

"Where'd I get me mouth — and me brains too?"

"Not off me you poor galoot. And don't you start young man."

"Well you stop then."

"My gawd — to think I ever took the trouble to raise it!"

"Who asked you to?"

"Damn you boy ——"

"Shut up, Frank," cried Joe Steen. "Don't go upsettin' your Ma or I'll dong you one."

"Try it!" yelled Frank, then rose because his mother rose, and fled.

§

Train-day was a special day to people living on the railway, particularly to the fettlers, to whom the train brought not only mail and stores and news from civilization in the form of gossip, but wages for the past fortnight's work and liquor for the next fortnight's drinking. At least in the Caroline River Gang's camp the night of the day was always one of carousal.

It was the habit of Joe Ballest, ganger of the Caroline Camp, to invite his men to his house to drink beer on trainday nights. He was one who liked company with his beer so much that although these parties always ended in a brawl he persistently gave them. And he was one who loved beer so much that, not having means to buy it in quantity sufficient for his needs, since beer cost two-and-six a pint and he could consume four pints for every working-hour of a day while he earned but three-and-six, he brewed his own. He was not particular about the taste of beer so long as it was strongly alcoholic and hopsy. He brewed with hops and sugar and yeast and mashed potatoes and any other likely ingredient he happened to have in hand, and fortified with a liberal dosing of overproof rum. Owing to the climate it fermented well and quickly; indeed it often frothed right out of the barrel, especially at night, since then it could work without interference, when it would even creep into the brewer's bed and cause him pleasant dreams. In such a climate the use of preservatives in brewing was imperative; but Joe Ballest would use none but O.P. rum; he belonged to that backward school of drinkers which regards scientifically-preservatized liquors as All Chemicals and therefore harmful; hence his beer always turned out to be all clots and ropes and bacteria.

Ballest held his usual party this train-day night. His guests were his mate, Mick O'Pick, and the ordinary fettlers, Funnigan and Cockerell and Smelly. In and about the doorway leading to the back veranda lounged the lubras of the men, and behind them a crowd of natives from the local camp. Now and again a pannikin of beer would be handed to the lubras, who sometimes gave a sip to those behind.

When the party waxed lively the lubras came in and took seats, and the others took the doorway. When it became boisterous the lubras took liberties with their men, and the others sometimes slipped inside and snatched. Frank McLash came later, then Sam Snigger and Karl Fliegeltaub, who both lived across the bridge. The party was uproarious when Cockerell crept up to Mick O'Pick, who was laying down the law about politics, and poured a glass of beer over his head. All but old Mick and Ballest laughed loudly. Ballest shouted angrily about wilful waste. Mick gasped and groped till he regained his sight, when he leapt up bellowing, snatched up a large kerosene-lamp that stood on the table beside him, and dashed it at the iron wall. Flames shot up to the roof.

Everyone rushed out but Ballest and Mick. Ballest was sitting on his lounge when the lamp was smashed. He had risen and was shouting. Mick rushed at him and hit him on the jaw, sent him flying. Funnigan and two blackfellows rushed in with sodden sacks and tackled the flames. Cockerell and Frank tackled Mick.

Mick bellowed, "Strike an old man — strike an old man — hooligans — cowards!" and fled.

Thus the party ended, as usual.

An hour passed. The camp was silent save for clicking of music-sticks in the distant native camp and the drone of voices of Frank and Smelly and Cockerell in the house of the last-named and the incessant muttering of Ballest in his house — "Drink a man's beer and murder him — ungrateful unsociable ill-bred 'ounds!" Old Mick was sitting on a chopping-block by his back veranda with a young lubra smoking at his feet, watching the moon rise over the bush and crooning an Irish folk-song.

Suddenly a wailing-cry rang out. Mick's lubra turned her half-naked body quickly to the right. Mick turned too, listened for a while, then said, "An' what was that m' dear?"

The girl, with cigarette hanging from her lips and chin advanced, clicked her tongue for silence. A pause. Then the cry again, long and mournful. And again, this time in a different key.

"Dingo," said Mick.

"No-more," said the lubra. "Two-fella. One-fella dog no-more dingo, one-fella piccanin." She rose, adding, "Go look see."

She went off towards the railway with Mick at her heels.

Again the cry, this time accompanied by faint thumping sounds. "Him dere," said the lubra, pointing to a rake of cars and trucks. She cooee'd, was answered at once by a burst of joyful barking.

They found that the sound came from one of the trucks. The lubra climbed in and found Nawnim and the dog he had travelled with. Nawnim rushed into her arms, thinking she was Anna. The dog whined and rubbed against her legs. She kicked it away. She lifted Nawnim and called to Mick and lowered the child to him, then picked up the dog and tossed it into the night. Back on the ground she took Nawnim from Mick and examined him, then said contemptuously, "Yeller-feller," and gave him back.

Mick took Nawnim to Ballest, bawling as he entered the house, "Hey Joe — look't I got!"

Ballest sat up on his bed and stared for a while, then said in a surly tone, "Where'd you get that?"

Smiling broadly Mick replied, "I found the little divil in a thruck."

Ballest snorted, said, "Tell that to the marines!"

"Look at him!" cried Mick, excited. "Lil yeller-feller.

Look at his pants — like blue chicken-pox. I found him in
a thruck with a dawg ——"

"Bah — found it in the bulrushes!"

"In a thruck I said."

"In the bulrushes! Take it away man, take it away. You
can't unload your brats on me."

CLOTHES MAKE A MAN

OSCAR held dominion over six hundred square miles of
country, which extended east and west from the railway to
the summit of the Lonely Ranges, and north and south from
the horizons, it might be said, since there was nothing to
show where the boundaries lay in those directions.

Jasmine had said that he worshipped property. It was
true. But he did not value Red Ochre simply as a grazing-
lease. At times it was to him six hundred square miles
where grazing grew and brolgas danced in the painted sunset and emus ran to the silver dawn — square miles of
jungle where cool deep billabongs made watering for stock
and nests for shouting nuttagul geese — of grassy valleys
and stony hills, useless for grazing, but good to think about
as haunts of great goannas and rock-pythons — of swamps
where cattle bogged and died, but wild hog and buffalo
wallowed in happiness — of virgin forests where poison
weed lay in wait for stock, but where possums and kangaroos and multitudes of gorgeous birds dwelt as from time
immemorial. At times he loved Red Ochre.

At times he loved it best in Wet Season — when the
creeks were running and the swamps were full — when the
multi-coloured schisty rocks split golden waterfalls — when
the scarlet plains were under water, green with wild rice,
swarming with Siberian snipe — when the billabongs were
brimming and the water-lilies blooming and the nuttaguls
shouting loudest — when bull-grass towered ten feet high,
clothing hills and choking gullies — when every tree was
flowering and most were draped with crimson mistletoe and
droning with humming-birds and native bees — when cattle
wandered a land of plenty, fat and sleek, till the buffalo-
flies and marsh-flies came and drove them mad, so that they
ran and ran to leanness, often to their death — when mos-

quitoes and a hundred other breeds of maddening insects were there to test a man's endurance — when from hour to hour luke-warm showers drenched the steaming earth, till one was sodden to the bone and mildewed to the marrow and moved to pray, as Oscar always was when he had had enough of it, for that which formerly he had cursed — the Dry! the good old Dry — when the grasses yellowed, browned, dried to tinder, burst into spontaneous flame — when harsh winds rioted with choking dust and the billabongs became mere muddy holes where cattle pawed for water — when gaunt drought loafed about a desert and exhausted cattle staggered searching dust for food and drink, till they fell down and died and became neat piles of bones for the wind to whistle through and the gaunt-ribbed dingo to mourn — then one prayed for the Wet again, or if one's heart was small, packed up and left this Capricornia that fools down South called the Land of Opportunity, and went back and said that nothing was done by halves up there except the works of puny man.

Red Ochre was so named because an abundance of red ochre was to be found in the locality. Not far from the homestead was a cleft hillock of which the face was composed entirely of red ochre that was scored by the implements of men of the Mullanmullak Tribe who had gathered the pigment there for ages. From the hillock a score of red paths diverged as black ones do from a colliery, one of them leading to the homestead itself, trodden, so it was said, by Tobias Batty, founder of the Station, who went mad and took to painting his body after the fashion of the blacks.

Red Ochre was founded twenty years or more before Oscar settled there. His predecessor, who succeeded the mad Batty, was a man named Wellington Boots, formerly a Cockney grocer, who had a young wife whom he worked like a horse and five young children whom he kept perpetually in a state of virtual imprisonment. It was said that he used to weigh out the rations of his native riders in niggardly quantities on loaded scales. He was killed by a bull on the plain to the south and eaten by ants and crows and kites till buried in a sack by his wife.

The homestead stood in these days just as Batty had built it. It was of corrugated iron on an angle-iron frame. In the dwelling the materials even of the doors were such as could not be destroyed by termites. The windows had been sheet-iron shutters till Oscar glazed them. But in spite of the materials, the house was airy and cool; for the walls stopped short of meeting the sprawling roof by a foot or two, leaving a wide well-ventilated space between the iron itself and the ceiling of paper-bark, the entry of possums and snakes and other pests being prevented by wire netting. The walls were lined with paper-bark, pipe-clayed and panelled with polished bloodwood. The floor was of ant-bed, the stuff of the termites', or white-ants' nests, which when crushed and wetted and beaten hard makes serviceable cement. Mrs Boots was responsible for most of the interior fittings. Oscar had improved on them. Carpets and marsupial skins lay about the floors; bright pictures and hunting trophies such as tusks of boars and horns of buffaloes adorned the walls. Broad verandas surrounded the house, each screened with iron lattice covered with potato-creeper, and decorated with palms and ferns and furnished with punkahs and rustic furniture made by Oscar.

The homestead was about twenty miles from the railway. It stood on the brow of a hill about which the Caroline River, hidden from view by a belt of scrub and giant trees, flowed in a semi-circle. It was the northern side of the house that faced the river, a side that was raised on a high stone foundation because of the rapid slope. The veranda on that side was the part of the house most used in dry weather. On the eastern veranda were the snowy mosquito-netted beds of the family, which now unhappily numbered only two. Peter Differ and his halfcaste daughter Constance lived in a little house of their own at the rear. Differ worked on the run as foreman. Constance, who was aged about eleven, worked in the house as a sort of maid. The eastern veranda was sheltered by two great mangoes, part of a grove that led down to the river. On the opposite side were ponciana trees and cassias and frangi-panis and many other tropical growths that made the place very brilliant and fragrant in Wet Season.

§

One afternoon a few days after that of the incidents at the Siding, Oscar was sitting on the front veranda with his daughter Marigold, watching an approaching storm, when the child pointed to the scrub by the river and said, "Look Daddy — dere's a niggah wit sumpin on his back."

Oscar looked and saw a blackfellow in a red naga toiling up the flood-bank with a strangely clad halfcaste child on his back. The man came to the veranda steps, panting and sweating profusely, and set his burden down. "What name you want?" asked Oscar. For answer the blackfellow stooped and took from the waist-band of the spotted blue breeches of his burden what proved to be a crumpled letter. He gave it to Oscar, who opened it and read:

Dear Oscar,
    Herewith my nigger Muttonhead. I sent him acrost you with little ½ carst boy belong to your brother Mark his names No Name and belongs to Jock Driver of the Melisande Ma McLash reckons you knows all about it he got lef here in a truck we found him and trid keep for Jock nex train but carnt do it because hees too much damn trouble here Oscar hees gone bush 3 times allready and wats kwonskwence we friten for sponsbility to lose him plese you keep him there for Jock I will tell him if I heres from him hees good kid No Name and got good sense for yeler feler but too damn cunin like a dingo be a long way corse if hees look after I reckon heel be O.K. corse you see we gotter go out to work and Ma McLash wont have no truck with him and no good of putin him with nigers seen hees your nefew and seen as how hees one for goan bush like he does. Plese you give my niger Muttonhead a feed and a stick of tobaco or he wont do nuthen more hees cheeky swine thet Muttonhead belt him if he givs you trouble excuse pensl and hast hoppen to find you as it leves me at present. I remain

                        Your obediant servent
                        Joe Ballest
                        Ganger 80-Mile.

Oscar raised a flushed face and looked at Nawnim, who was standing with hands clasped behind him and dirty yellow-brown face elevated and black eyes staring intently at Marigold. In a moment Nawnim became aware of Oscar's gaze and lowered his face slightly and regarded him slantwise, assuming an expression almost baleful that reminded Oscar of Ballest's reference to a dingo.

Then a stream of white lightning poured from the heavens. The dead air stirred. Nawnim started, looked at Muttonhead. Thunder crashed, and monster echoes pealed through valleys and caverns of the mountainous clouds. Nawnim thrust his head into Muttonhead's belly. Again the white lightning poured; the thunder crashed; a blast of cool wind struck the trees and whisked a few leaves on to the veranda. Then rain came rushing across the river —

D

humming drumming rain — and up the hill and over the house — hissing roaring rain.

"Round the back," yelled Oscar, pointing. Muttonhead took Nawnim's hand and ran.

Oscar and Marigold went into the house and through and out to the back veranda, from which through the teeming rain they saw Muttonhead and Nawnim crouched under the eaves by the wall of the detached kitchen. In spite of what Ballest had said about Muttonhead, he was evidently too well-aware of his humbleness to enter a whiteman's shelter uninvited. Oscar had meant that they should go to the back veranda. Seeing that they were fairly well sheltered where they were, he let them stay.

Oscar bent to Marigold when he heard her reedy voice.

"Is dat a lil boy Daddy?" she cried in his ear.

He nodded and smiled weakly; and, because the wind had changed and was blowing the rain in on them, he led her inside to the dining-room, where he sat and held her between his knees.

"Dat not a lil niggah boy, Daddy?" she asked.

"No."

"What kind lil boy is he den Daddy?"

"Little halfcaste."

"Like Conny Differ?"

He nodded, began to roll a cigarette.

"Is dat Mister Differ's lil boy Daddy?"

Unpleasant subject. He frowned and said, "Now don't start asking silly questions."

She fell silent, and gazing through the back door at the rain, turned over in her mind a mass of thoughts about this boy, who, since he did not look like one of those prohibited Dirty Little Niggahs, might make a playmate. She was allowed to play with Constance, which was very pleasant, although Constance was more than twice her age and evidently not as eager to play as she herself. Carried away by her thoughts she asked, "Daddy — who dat lil boy's farver?"

The question came as a shock, because it interrupted thoughts of Mark. He looked at her almost suspiciously, then said, "Go and play with your toys and don't worry me."

He went outside and lounged about, occupying himself alternately with looking for leaks in the roof and studying his crouching nephew, till the rain stopped; then he went into the yard. After looking at Nawnim for a while as best he could — Nawnim slunk behind Muttonhead at his approach — he said to the blackfellow, "You takim picca-nin back longa you boss."

"Wha' name?" asked Muttonhead, shaking Nawnim from a leg.

"Takim back longa Mister Ballest. Me no wantim. Him no-more belong me."

Muttonhead gaped for a moment, then said, "Carn do it."

Oscar frowned and snapped, "Don't be cheeky or I'll crack you."

Muttonhead cringed and said, "Mist Ballest him say, 'Takim dat one pic longa Boss Chilnsik — him belong him brudder.' "

"I don't give a damn what he said. Takim back. Here's some baccy — now then — what say?"

"Tahng you very mush Boss," said Muttonhead, placing a stick of tobacco behind each ear. Two sticks of tobacco valued at tuppence each were perhaps small reward for a forty-mile walk with a child on his back, but no more than he expected. But he continued to protest, saying, "Carn do it, Boss. Me no-more go back longa railer line lo—ng time. Me go foot-walk longa Lonely River country for lookim up Ol' People." He jerked his thick lips in the opposite direction to that in which he had come.

"Then take the brat with you," snapped Oscar, and walk-ed off.

Muttonhead turned out to be quite as bad as Ballest said. Oscar found that out some hours after dismissing him. He was superintending a job in the smithy when he heard a commotion in the kitchen and went to investigate and found Nawnim being belaboured by the lubra cook. The lubra turned an angry face when he entered the kit-chen. Nawnim's howls died in his gaping mouth.

"What's the matter?" demanded Oscar.

"Him come sinikin longa brett," cried the lubra, pointing to bread-tins that stood on the table ready for the oven. Nawnim tried to get behind her. She seized him, flung him back into exposure. He yelled.

"Shut up!" shouted Oscar.

There was dough on Nawnim's face and hands, and on a leg of the table. Oscar stepped up and grabbed one of his skinny arms and demanded, "What name you no-more go away all-same me talk?" Nawnim blubbered and shrank away. "Which way Muttonhead?" demanded Oscar of the cook.

"Him go longa Lonely River, Boss."

"Blast him!" cried Oscar. "Left me with the brat after all!" He looked at his captive, stared at him sourly for a while, then sighed and said, "Well I don't know what I'm going to do with you, poor hungry little devil. God help you! Oh give him some tucker, Princess, and don't hurt him. Get someone to wash him — he stinks."

Nawnim spent his first night at Red Ochre in the quarters of the native servants. It was not the servants' choice, nor a particularly good one of their master's, since the place was not so far away from the house as to leave the occupants unaware of what was going on there when the going-on was as loud as Nawnim's. He wailed all night, set the dogs barking in the camp on the river and the dingoes howling in the bush and the pigs squealing in the sty and the horses snorting in the yards. The servants could pinch and punch and smother him into periods of silence, but could not still the external racket he had raised, which seemed to be worse when he was silent and to his ears quite devilish, so that before long he would be moved to start again. The red day dawned on a red-eyed household and on a halfcaste brat who was covered with red wales and regarded with general malignity.

Oscar gave him into the care of Constance Differ. All went well throughout the day, because he slept. When he woke at sundown he set up a worse wailing than ever, and tried to escape, so that Constance had to lock him in. He would neither sit nor lie, but stood in a corner with hands clasped behind, watching Constance and venting his incessant tearless grief. Constance was gentle and patient as noone he had ever known but Anna. But she looked rather too much like Yeller Jewty. Differ tried his hand with him, first with food, then with dancing and singing and playing tricks, finally with a strap. At last Oscar rushed in and spanked by hand, and because the matter had become much worse, took Nawnim by the scruff of the neck and threw him at a blackfellow for removal to the camp. There was some peace in the homestead that night, but none on the river.

Three days passed, during which the people of Red Ochre adapted themselves to broken sleep and kept away from the native camp. Oscar sent a message to the Siding to learn whether Jock had inquired after his uncoveted property, and learnt that he had not. He settled down to wait for word, hoping that Jock might not be drinking at

Copper Creek and that he might not go on his way forgetting his responsibilities.

On the afternoon of the fourth day Oscar was wakened from his siesta on the front veranda by sound of cat-like moaning in the yard below, and, rising to investigate, saw little Nawnim standing in the reddish shadow of a ponciana near the steps. Nawnim stopped moaning for about five seconds when Oscar's head appeared, then resumed. Oscar stared in astonishment. It was obvious from the way in which the child was studying him that the moaning did not interfere with his ability to take an interest in things about him. In fact he was not so much weeping as expressing a vague sense of misery he had felt ever since parting with Fat Anna. He stood in his usual attitude of hands behind back and eyes glancing sideways. When Oscar came to the head of the steps the moaning rose a note higher; but the moaner did not move. Oscar saw Marigold peeping from the hall and told her to go inside, then went down the steps, muttering. Nawnim did not move till Oscar reached the ground, when he retired slowly, walking sideways, watching with one eye and gouging the other with a grubby fist.

"Come here," said Oscar.

The moan rose by another note. Nawnim continued to retire. Oscar hurried. Nawnim yelled and ran. Oscar stopped. So did Nawnim, and dropped his voice to the moan.

"Blast you!" cried Oscar. "Shut up!"

Steady moan.

"Shut up!" roared Oscar, and moved. Nawnim moved. Oscar snatched up a stick and rushed. Nawnim fled howling, to fall shrieking when Oscar caught him a sound whack on the seat of the spotted blue pants. Oscar pounced on him shouting, "Shut up — shut up — shut up!"

Gritting his teeth with rage, Oscar picked him up and carried him down to the camp, prepared to ease his feelings on those he considered he could flog without stooping to cowardice, the delinquent natives. But they were not there. Nawnim had worn their patience to rags. They had taken their belongings and gone bush. He had been driven to the homestead by hunger and loneliness.

As Oscar's precepts would not allow him to copy the wisdom of the natives, he had to carry Nawnim back to the house. He dumped him under the scarlet tree where he had found him, and left him bawling, to go find Constance. Constance was away on the run with her father.

Oscar came back fuming, to find to his surprise that Nawnim was as quiet as a mouse, standing in his usual attitude,
staring at Marigold. When he saw Oscar he prepared for
flight. Oscar was too wise to go near him. He crept back
to his chair.

"Can I play with the lil boy Daddy?" asked Marigold.

"No — stay where you are."

"But I wanna play."

"Stay where you are."

"But Daddy —" she said, coming towards him.

The instant she passed out of Nawnim's sight was announced by a long-drawn moan. Realising at once what
was the cause of the good behaviour, Oscar said quickly,
"Go back to the edge and stay there."

"But can't I play?"

"No — go back — for heaven's sake go back!"

The moaning stopped. But Marigold did not stop en-
treating. "Why can't I play wid him Daddy?" she begged.
"He's not a lil niggah."

"He is. Now be quiet. Throw him that doll — anything
— everything if you like — but stay where he can see you.
Let me have a moment's peace for heaven's sake. There's
been no peace in the place since that brat came near it."

There was peace that night and thenceforth. Nawnim
went to sleep on a lounge on the back veranda within sound
of the last sleepy words of Marigold. Next day he spent
under the ponciana tree, playing with a doll and watching
Marigold, seeing her not merely as a desirable playmate as
she saw him, but, since she was so different from any
creature he had seen and clad in garments that amazed
him, rather as a human monstrosity like Anna's Japs an'
Chows.

After a while he lost his distrust of Constance and could
be placed in Differ's house. He slept there in the cot that
had been bought for his cousin Roger. Constance taught
him to use a knife and fork and spoon, discouraged him
from the practice of voiding urine indiscriminately, and
made him a laughable suit of clothes.

But Oscar's troubles were far from done. The child was
still his nephew. He believed that in his heart though he
would not admit it. The sight of him was a constant reminder of terrible disgrace. And Marigold made matters
worse by pestering him for permission to play with the
child, taking advantage of a situation he had created by
frequent sentimental talks about Dear Mumma and the
loneliness to which that faithless one had left them both,

backing up her petitions with such heart-rending statements
as, "Oh dear I am such a lonely lil girl Daddy — no mumma an' no nobody even to play wiv — Oh Oh, I am so
lonely lonely!"

When Oscar and Marigold next went to meet the mail-
train, Nawnim went with them, not for a treat as he and
she supposed, but for the purpose of being disposed of
should a chance occur. Oscar had lately learnt that Jock
had left Copper Creek for home, not by the usual route
that would take him past the Melisande telegraph-station,
but by one that lay far to westward, being forced to go out
of his way because the Melisande River was in flood. And
according to the report the fellow had gone on his way
blind drunk. Oscar's hope was that there might be someone on the train going out Jock's way to whom he could
give Nawnim. It turned out to be a vain one.

At the Siding he left Nawnim in the buckboard with a
black boy and well out of sight of the house, and studiously
avoided any form of conversation with the people there
that might lead to questions concerning him. He felt sure
that they were laughing at him. When Mrs McLash told
him that some unknown person had sent her a box of unwanted kittens up from Town last train he frowned and
left her.

It happened that the people at the Siding had no need
to ask questions about Nawnim. Differ had been in a couple
of times for grog since the child's arrival at Red Ochre
and had talked; and Frank McLash had been out there for
beef when the rioting was at its height. As a matter of
fact the story of Nawnim's doings since his coming into
the district was known to nearly everyone on the one hundred and fifty-seven miles of railway. Mrs McLash had
gossiped about it over the telephone to Mrs Blaize of Soda
Springs; and since all the railway telephones were connected to the same line and all the bells rang together and
all the operators made a practice of listening to every conversation whether the signal-rings told them it was intended
for their ears or not and then passed on what they heard,
such gossip, in that country where all news was good because it was scarce, could travel quick and far.

Oscar learnt from passengers that Mark was still in
Town and staying at the Princess Alice. It did not strike
him as strange that he should be staying there, not knowing that he had been avoiding Heather previously. As a
matter of fact Mark and Heather had lately come together

again. Mark had got bold through having got rid of his shame. Heather was going to help him with his pearling.

Oscar did not think of Heather at all. He was thinking of how annoying it was that he could not telephone Mark and ask if there were truth in Jock's assertions without telling his business to the world. Before he left he wrote Mark a letter.

Thus Nawnim's ride to the Siding turned out to be a treat after all. He went back to Red Ochre sitting high on the stores in the carrier of the buckboard, listening to Marigold's and Oscar's singing, and loving them with all his little heart.

That night Differ came to Oscar to see the papers that had come by the monthly mail from South. Oscar was glad to see that he was sober, even if reeking with drink. Differ was a drunkard; train-days were his weak-days; but lately he had been drinking less through having been threatened with dismissal if he continued in the old sottish way.

"Well," said Differ, after learning of the failure to dispose of Nawnim, "and what're you going to do with him now?"

"Think I'll send him up to the Compound on Friday's train," said Oscar.

"Eh ?— Oh that's a hell of a place. He'd be better with the black Binghis."

"What else can I do with him? I won't be able to get in touch with Driver for months."

"Why not keep him yourself?"

"He's no good to me. Binghis are as good as halfcastes any day, and give less trouble."

"Other men find good use for 'em," said Differ dryly.

Oscar looked him in the eye and said "Yes?" It was meant as a thrust. Differ used Constance as a drudge.

It seemed lost on Differ, who went on, "You can do as much good with a halfcaste as a white. There's my little Connie to prove it." Differ, who was an educated man, had schooled his daughter well.

"She's young yet," said Oscar. "Wait'll she gets out on her own away from your influence."

"She won't do that if I can help it. I want to take her South out of this colour-mad hole."

"No matter where she is, the stigma of the Binghi blood'll always be on her."

Differ smiled as he answered, "Ah no — I'll pretend she's a halfcaste of another race — Javanese or some such race that the mob doesn't know much about and therefore'll respect. She could pass for a halfcaste Javanese. She could pass for a Javanese princess, in fact. Then she could marry well and mix with the best society."

Oscar wondered whether Differ were not drunk after all. He asked after a pause, "You mean that?"

"Yes — to an extent. I mean I'm going to do all I can to make up for the crime of begetting her. Certainly I can't let her stay here and live for ever regarded as an Aboriginal. And she'd be regarded the same down South if I didn't say she was a halfcaste of another breed."

"But that's cruel — making her live a lie."

"How's she going to live otherwise and be happy as she ought to be? You've got to lie to fools — or they'll crush you for not being to their liking."

"Halfcastes should be left in their place — with the Binghis. That's the kindest way to treat 'em. If they don't know they've got rights they won't want 'em. What the eye doesn't see, you know."

Differ smiled and stroked his chin, then said, "But why left with the Binghis?"

"Because they're half that."

"What about the other half — the white?"

"That's submerged."

Differ smiled again, and after a while said smoothly, "You look on Binghis as animals. They're not really. They've got a different code to ours, that's all — but one no more different in its way than a Chinaman's. As a matter of fact their code of simple brotherhood is the true Christian one. Retarding sort of thing, of course, when considered in the light of our own barbarous ways, still, the recognized ethical one of civilization, whether practised or no. Civilized people are still too raw and greedy to be true Christians. The Binghis are a very ancient race who've had the advantage of living in small numbers in a land that supplied their every need. Of course they had to limit their population and guard their game to make the advantage a permanent one. At any rate, they were able to overcome the sheer animal greed that is the chief character of the average creature of the races of the Northern Hemisphere. The Binghis are really highly intelligent. Apart from their own very wise practices, which naturally look ridiculous when judged beside our entirely different ones, see how eager they are to learn anything a whiteman'll teach 'em. Trouble is whitemen won't teach 'em anything that might raise 'em a bit —"

"Go on! You can't teach 'em. I've tried."

"Oh? Give's an instance?"

"Well — Oh I've tried lots of things — for instance I've tried to teach 'em about the cattle-market — commerce generally — in a very rough way, of course, so's they won't think the Government's my father and keeps me for love, as they do with their communistic ideas — so's they won't pole and waste. I put it to 'em very simple. Just as you would to a child. Oh, but they haven't any idea to this day what I meant."

"What language did you use?"

"Why — Pidgin, of course."

"Ah! Now suppose I tried to explain to you in Pidgin how a locomotive works —" Oscar looked thoughtful. Differ went on, "If Binghis were taught English properly, sent to school like other people, instead of being excluded as they are —"

"That may be so. But they're filthy cows. No get away from that. Look at their quarters here."

"What about the slums of highly civilized cities? Why are teams of sanitary inspectors employed if the human race is naturally clean? Cleanliness as we know it, Oscar, is something we've learnt through living in crowds where it's dangerous to be dirty. Binghis are clean enough in their camps. If they were properly taught they'd be clean elsewhere. Send 'em to school as infants."

"But would they go?"

"Not they! Would anyone of us go if we could get out of it? I said send 'em, same as we're sent as kids. Keep at it for generation after generation. Don't look for immediate results. Consider how long it took to civilize our own race. Our condition is the result not of a mere ten years or so of schooling, but of ages. See that the Binghis get the same."

After a pause Oscar said, "Well it's not much use worrying about 'em now. They're dying out."

"What — with thousands upon thousands of 'em still in this country and many yet never seen a whiteman? Why, do you know that even as far as can be judged there are more more-or-less wild Binghis in this country than there are white people in India? Ah!—what you have just said, Oscar, was said twenty — fifty years ago too. If only the Nation'd give a little time to trying to understand the Binghi, they'd find he isn't such a low fellow after all. All sorts of evil breeds — the sex-mad Hindoos, the voodooing Africans, the cannibals of Oceania, all dirty, diseased, slaving, and enslaving races — are being helped to decent civilized manhood by the thoughtful white people of the world, while we of this country, the richest in the world, just stand by and see our black compatriots wiped out. They'll be like the Noble Redman someday — noble when gone! They put up as good a fight for their rights as the Redman, and without the guns of Frenchmen to help them. Why, the kids of this country honour the Redman in their games! What do they think of that just-as-good-if-not-better tracker and hunter and fighter the Binghi? And how was the Redman any better than the Binghi but in that he wore more clothes and rode a horse? You don't need clothes in this country, and you can't ride kangaroos. And look at the Maoris. They have seats in Parliament these days, go to the best schools, even receive knighthoods. They were as basely treated as the Binghis at first. How did they win honour? Why — someone put them in the way of handling firearms, sold them firearms as trade! And then one of them was taken to England, where he was given so many presents that he came back as a rich man able to buy enough firearms to start a great war against the whiteman. Matter of luck in getting hold of the firearms to show the whiteman they were as good as he. Poor Binghi missed it. Study the Binghi, Oscar, and you'll find he's a different man from you in many ways, but in all ways quite as good. Study him, and you'll discover that dominant half of the inheritance of the halfcaste you despise."

Oscar pondered for a while, then said, "Oh, but halfcastes don't seem to be any good at all. All the men here are loafers and bludgers, the women practically all whores —"

"Do the men get a chance to work like whitemen? Look, the only halfcastes of all the thousands in this country who are regularly employed are those who work on the nightcart in Town. Occasionally others get a casual labouring job. When it peters out they have to go back to the Old People for a feed. They get no schooling —"

"There's a school in the Halfcastes' Home."

"Bah! A kindergarten. A hundred children of all ages crowded into one small room and taught by an unqualified person. I'll tell you something. Once I had a look at that school, hoping to get the job of running it, knowing that the teacher barely taught 'em more than A.B.C. and the fact that they're base inferiors. The teacher there then —

a woman — thought I was a visitor from South or somewhere. She led off by telling me not to get false notions
into my head about her pupils' unhappy lot. With a smile
she told me they were Only Niggers. So ignorant of her job
was she that one quarter-caste kiddie I pointed out she
said was a halfcaste, and to prove it called the child out
and asked her, as one'd speak to a prisoner in jail, wasn't
her mother a lubra. As it happens I was right. A cruel ugly
business. Of course the kiddie took it calmly, not knowing
any other kind of treatment. Just think of it — when those
kids leave that lousy school they have no-one to go to but
the Binghis; and so they forget even the little they learn.
The language of Compounds and Aboriginal reserves is
Pidgin. A few score of words. No wonder such people come
to think like animals! You said the women were whores.
What chance have they to be anything else? Moral sense is
something taught. It's not taught to halfcaste girls. They're
looked upon from birth as part of the great dirty joke Black
Velvet. What decent whiteman would woo and marry one
honestly? It wouldn't pay him. He'd be looked upon as a
combo. Look at Ganger O'Cannon of Black Adder Creek,
with his halfcaste wife and quadroon kids, a downright
family man — yet looked on as as much a combo as if he
lived in a blacks' camp. Isn't that so?"

"Oh I don't see much difference between a black lubra
and a yeller one. Anyway, Tim O'Cannon's lubra's father
was a Chow, which makes her a full-blood and his kids halfcaste. But this is a distasteful subject. I don't like this
Black Velvet business. It makes me sick."

"You're like the majority of people in Australia. You
hide from this very real and terrifically important thing,
and hide it, and come to think after a while that it don't
exist. But it does! It does! Why are there twenty thousand
halfcastes in the country? Why are they never heard of?
Oh my God! Do you know that if you dare write a word
on the subject to a paper or a magazine you get your work
almost chucked back at you?"

"I wouldn't be surprised. Why shouldn't such a disgraceful thing be kept dark? Is that what you're writing about
in this book of yours?"

"No fear! I've learnt long ago that I'm expected to write
about the brave pioneers and — Oh bah! this dissembling
makes my guts bleed! But talking about Tim O'Cannon,
Oscar — most of the men in this district go combo, mainly
on the sly. How can they help it? There are no white
women. Would moralists prefer that those who pioneer

should be sexual perverts? Well, if there are any kids as the result of these quite natural flutters they are just ignored. The casual comboes are respected, while men like O'Cannon and myself, who rear their kids, are utterly despised. Take the case of your brother Mark for instance. A popular fellow —"

"All this talk about Mark has got to be proved."

"There's plenty more examples — popular and respected men, their shortcomings laughed over, while Tim O'Cannon's been trying for years to get a teacher sent down to Black Adder for a couple of days a month to get his kids schooled a bit. The Government tells him again and again to send them to the Compound School —"

"Well, if he's so keen on getting 'em schooled —"

"Better have 'em ignorant than taught humility, the chief subject on the curriculum of the Compound. But O'Cannon's a taxpayer. He pays his whack towards the upkeep of the State School up in Town —"

"Can't he send 'em there?"

"Who'd look after 'em if he did? Who'd protect 'em from the contempt of the white kids? All he wants is a teacher sent down once a month to stay the couple of days while the train's down the road. They won't do it."

A long pause fell. Both men smoked, and stared into the black breathless night. At length Differ said earnestly, "Don't send the kid to the Compound, Oscar. It'll mean the ruin of him. He'll grow up to learn nothing but humility. And after all the Government will only send him out to work for some brainless cruel fool like Driver. My friend, any person who can adopt a halfcaste as his own and doesn't, will surely burn in Hell, if there is such a place. Think of the life before the kid — like Yeller Elbert's — worse — like poor savage Peter Pan's. Life-long humiliation. Neither a whiteman nor a black. A drifting nothing. Keep the boy a while, Oscar, teach him just a bit to test what I've said. You're a good-hearted man I know. I'm sure you'll see the good in him when it begins to show, in spite of the prejudices bred in you and drummed into you by Australian papers and magazines that use the Binghi as something to joke about. Remember that though his skin is dark and there is Aboriginal in his blood, half his flesh and blood is the same as your own."

Oscar turned on him angrily and cried, "I told you that's still got to be proved!"

§

Oscar let Nawnim play with Marigold, just for an hour
or so now and again. Then Nawnim began to change, not
in his own little body, but in Oscar's idea of him, and came
to be not so much a family disgrace as a personal problem,
a fascinating terrible problem. If he were to grow up to be
a cringing drudge like Yeller Elbert or a pariah like Peter
Pan, how would fare the half of him that was proud
Shillingsworth? Oscar began to think about him more than
anything else that concerned him just then, and came at
length to the decision that if it were proved that he was
the son of Mark, he would see to it that Mark took care
of him and would himself advise Mark how best to do so.

Another fortnight passed. Then Oscar went in to meet
the train, fully expecting to get a letter of denial or con-
trite confession from Mark, and half expecting to see the
fellow himself, since during the fortnight of changing and
softening opinions he had forgotten how harsh was the
letter he had sent him. Neither Mark nor letter came.

Oscar was annoyed. Much of the new softness hardened
in a matter of minutes. He thought for a while, then telephoned the Princess Alice Hotel and learnt that Mark was
still there. He spoke to Heather, but did not say who he
was. She went to get Mark, and, in Oscar's opinion, returned with him, because, although she said that she had
been unable to find him, her manner of asking who was
speaking and what his business was gave him the idea that
she was repeating what someone near was whispering. He
told her nothing but that he wished to speak to Mark concerning a matter of great importance and would be obliged
if she would see to it that he was at hand when he would
ring again at five.

Oscar came out of Mrs McLash's little post-office
prickling with heat and anger. As he did so, Mrs McLash
crept out of her bedroom smirking. She had been listening.
She guessed that it all had something to do with Nawnim,
as she told Mrs Blaize of Soda Springs when she telephoned to learn what had been said by the other party.

At five o'clock Oscar rang the Princess Alice again. This
time he would have no dealings with Heather when she
said that Mark was still away. He asked for Mrs Shay,
who addressed him by name and told him just what Heather
had before. All his softness was callousness now. He went
home vowing to teach Mark a lesson.

Two days later Oscar came to the Siding again, this time

dressed for travelling and bringing with him a portmanteau and laughably-clad Nawnim. That was return-train day. As soon as Mrs McLash saw him she said to people sitting with her that she would bet her bottom dollar that he was taking Nawnim up to Town to throw him at Mark's head. Sure enough, Oscar asked if he might use the telephone, and rang up the Princess Alice. She heard him tell someone that he required Mark to meet him at the train in Town, that Mark must be got if getting him necessitated calling in the help of the police.

As soon as the train left the Caroline, Mrs McLash rang up Mrs Shay, as it was usual for her to do, to tell her how many passengers were likely to require lodging at her hotel. She also told why Oscar was coming. Mrs Shay had no love for Mark and did not know that Heather had much; when she returned to the dining-room whence she had been called, she passed on what she had heard. Thus, while the train was still in the Caroline Hills, most of Mrs Shay's lodgers knew that Mark was going to have a halfcaste piccaninny thrown at his head that night. That was the first that most of the lodgers knew of the existence of a child of Mark's. Indeed it was news to Mrs Shay herself. To Heather it was a thunderbolt. While landlady and lodgers laughed over the news, Heather stole up to her room and wept. Mark was down at the beach at work on his ship.

The people who heard the tale from Mrs Shay took it down to the station when they went to meet the train that evening and passed it on to the crowd. Before long it was generally known, so that as much attention was given to watching for Mark as for the train.

True to the tale, a sullen-faced Oscar arrived with a halfcaste brat. But no Mark was there to have it thrown at his head. Mark was gone, sailing out into the Silver Sea. For Heather had gone to him to learn the truth and had told him everything. He denied Nawnim, but declined to prove himself by facing Oscar. She left him, telling him that she never wanted to see his face again. In two or three hours he completed arrangements for his pearling-expedition that otherwise he might have dallied over for weeks. He was not fleeing from responsibility for Nawnim, but from the shame of exposure before the Town.

Oscar was infuriated. His reason for wanting Mark to meet him was mainly that he wished to save himself the embarrassment of having to carry the child through the town and hand him over to Mark in a public place. He never dreamt that Mark could be warned and would flee.

As it was, he had to carry Nawnim to the Princess Alice and show him to Mrs Shay. The lady seemed amazed. He cursed himself for having trusted to the telephone, but not nearly so vigorously as he cursed Mark for deserting and Mrs McLash for tattling. That night Nawnim slept in his arms in the best room in the hotel. He had to be held in arms because, distrustful as he was of the strange surroundings and the noises of the bar, he was disposed to wail. Oscar was glad of the room to hide in.

Next morning after a quiet breakfast in the room, Oscar took Nawnim to the Aborigines Department and handed him over to the Protector, confessing with malicious pleasure that he was uncle to the child. He confessed because he wished the Government to take action against Mark. It was a mistake. Just then the Compound was being closed owing to an outbreak of measles among its people, on account of which the Protector could not admit Nawnim without endangering his life. The Protector said that Aborigines were particularly prone to die of the disease, and suggested that Oscar, as the child's uncle, should continue to take care of him till the danger was past. Oscar dreaded measles since the death of his infant son, and was loth to expose Nawnim to it, but resented being expected to act charitably on account of a relationship he did not recognise. He became angry and told the Protector to place the child in some other institution. The Protector responded to his anger and told him that the measles was everywhere, and that he considered it extremely mean of him to avoid a trifling inconvenience that might be the means of saving the child's life. Oscar went off in a rage, with the prospect of having to keep Nawnim with him in the town during the eleven days till next train-day.

Before returning to the hotel he took Nawnim to a Chinese store and bought him a tusser-silk suit and sandals and a sailor hat. A mighty improvement was effected in the child's appearance. Oscar did not slink back to the hotel nearly as shyly as he had slunk away from it. Mrs Shay called Heather to look at Nawnim, little knowing that Heather's eyes could scarcely see anything for tears of which Nawnim was the innocent cause. Heather came for fear that a refusal might set her mistress off suspecting what was the cause of the headache that had kept her out of company these many hours. The result of her coming was a further improvement in Nawnim's appearance; for in spite of the pain his existence caused her, she was touched by the sight of him; she saw faults in his dress that were invisible to Oscar and a Chinaman, and therefore took him back to the store and had his suit changed, and at Oscar's expense bought him more clothes and a Teddy Bear she found him staring at and a huge bag of lollies. Then she took him back to the hotel and bathed him, and had a cot fitted up for him on the veranda outside her own quiet bedroom. Oscar was grateful, but reluctant to let a Poundamore make free with a Shillingsworth disgrace.

For three rather miserable days Oscar lounged about the town, trailing or carrying Nawnim, since Heather was usually too busy to mind him and he would not suffer the company of others. Then the problem of disposing of the burden suddenly appeared to solve itself. Freddie Radato, the halfcaste Philippino barber, while shaving Oscar one morning and talking about Nawnim, who sat near, offered to take care of him for thirty shillings a week till Mark returned. Oscar jumped at the offer. He left Nawnim in the saloon. But he did not experience the feeling of relief he had expected. He left Nawnim howling, and, because Radato's house was near the hotel, heard him howling for hours afterwards. And he felt distinctly mean about abandoning him. Next morning at breakfast, to the sound of Nawnim's howls, he confessed to Heather that he had come to like him.

When three days later the doctor came and told him that he must take Nawnim away from Radato's at once because one of the Radato children had contracted measles, Oscar was not really dismayed. That night he took him to Tommy Tai Yun's open-air picture-show and showed him his first moving pictures. Next day he took him aboard the mail-boat and showed him the wonders it contained, including the captain's monkey, which he was even moved to try to buy for him. The days that followed were by no means miserable. There were more pictures — free pictures this time, because the last performance had been interrupted in the middle by a thunderstorm —, and motor-rides out to Tikatika Point, and a fishing expedition down the jetty. Oscar came to find pleasure in watching Nawnim's delight in these simple entertainments, and in teaching him to speak English properly. And he came to feel that it would be pleasant to introduce him to the mighty world as he had dreamt of introducing Roger. But at the same time he did not entirely give up trying to dispose of him nor forget to write to Mark a stinging letter in which he stated that if he refused to accept his responsibilities he would see that an action for affiliation was brought against him.

At length the day of the return journey came. Nawnim went down to the train with Oscar in Joe Crowe's cab, clad in a neat little khaki suit and khaki topee. The rest of his belongings were packed away in Oscar's bag, together with pencils and pads and slates and primers and picture-books. Oscar led him through the crowd with little of the shame he had felt when last he trod that ground with him. And Nawnim, holding the big brown hand he had come to love, felt none of the fear he had felt there only six weeks before.

Just as the train was moving out, a yellow face, round as the moon at full and wide-eyed and open-mouthed, came bobbing through the crowd towards the open window of the coach where Oscar and Nawnim stood, screaming, "Nawnee — Nawnee!" He recognised it. His eyes brightened. His body tensed.

"Nawnee — Nawnee! Hello lil manee — which way you walkim?"

"Who's that?" asked Oscar, leaning out to stare — to stare back as the train passed on.

It was Fat Anna. But Nawnim did not know her name, nor much about her beyond the fact that she was something pleasant come suddenly out of the misty past. She was soon lost to view. Thus Oscar never realised how close he came to solving the problem completely.

They returned to Red Ochre. And as though it were true that clothes make a man, before many weeks were out, little Nawnim, under the respectable name of Norman, came to live in the Shillingsworth household as a Shillingsworth of the blood.

MARS AND VENUS IN ASCENDANCY

MARK's pearling-expedition took him far. He made the acquaintance of most of the islands of the Silver Sea, Australian, Dutch, and Portuguese, and many of the Coral Sea as well. He might never have returned had he not been forced to do so when, towards the end of 1914, Freedom of the Seas suddenly ceased to be. The *Spirit of the Land* was dogged from island to island by gunboats, like a city loafer by police, received with suspicion at every port, sent on her way again and again, till at last she fell in with a particularly officious gunboat that escorted her home.

Oscar had almost forgotten Mark. The first he heard of his return was when he was disputing over the telephone with a Chinese storekeeper in Town concerning £30 worth of stores he had not bought. The Chinaman told him that Mark had bought the stores in his name. Mark was at the time away on the Christmas Banks, pearl-fishing. He had bought the stores to go there, believing that he would be back with means to pay the bill before it was presented. Oscar had to pay to avoid the cost and inconvenience of having to face the legal action with which the Chinaman threatened him. He was furious. For a while he contemplated proceeding against Mark as he had not long before against Peter Differ for a similar imposition. It was only the thought of the severe lesson he had learnt in Differ's case that restrained him.

Differ had long since drunk himself out of Oscar's employ. He had taken up land on Coolibah Creek, a tributary of the Lonely River, where, with Government assistance, he had planted peanuts. He was also reluctantly assisted by Oscar to the tune of some £50 while preparing his plantation. In spite of this, one time while in Town he bought £20 worth of stores in Oscar's name from a storekeeper who thought that he was still employed by Oscar. He did so in belief that he would be able to pay the bill, before it was presented, out of the profits from the sales of his first crop of nuts, the harvesting of which was about to begin, considering himself forced to adopt such means, because no storekeeper would give credit to one who must hand over his crop for marketing to his principal creditor, the Government. Unfortunately the price of peanuts was not nearly as high when the Government sold his crop as it was when he made bold to impose on Oscar. There was just enough profit to meet the Government's demands.

The Differ affair happened at a time when Oscar was deeply worried by his own affairs. The cattle-market was dead as far as Capricornia was concerned. The cruel part of it was that the trade was elsewhere very much alive. According to reports from South, Australian beef was being exported as fast as butchered at prices high and in quantities large as never before. Butchery was the order of the day just then. A great war had broken out in Europe. Yet not a pound of meat went out of Capricornia.

The Port Zodiac meatworks, which was flourishing at the
time of Oscar's entry into grazing, had been closed for
some years. The loss of this trade had not been felt so
much, because, as it had slowly declined, the trade in cattle
on the hoof with the Philippines, incipient at the time of
Oscar's entry, had increased in a manner more than com-
pensatory. Now the Philippines' market had also failed,
had suddenly collapsed, indeed, owing to the very thing responsible for the great prosperity of grazing in the South
— the European War.

It happened thus. The cattle-steamer *Cucaracha*, already
a vehicle of trouble for Oscar, had been arrested for traf-
ficking with a German raiding-cruiser prowling about the
Silver Sea. Her people were American citizens of Spanish
and Philippino origin and hence in no way bound to favour
any party in the hostilities; but the rights of Neutrals were
not receiving much reverence anywhere at the time from
those maintaining Freedom of the Seas; she was locked up
in some sort of nautical prison while a lengthy argument
on International Law went on. A complicated business. A
diabolic business it was to Oscar, the devil behind it that
Damned Dago Gomez, and the design of it another cowardly blow at himself. So he thought, although he knew
that Captain Gomez had changed his ship immediately after
helping Jasmine to change her affections. He hoped that
the fellow might have been taken as a traitor and shot.

The *S.S. Cucaracha* was not replaced; nor did she return
to the Capricornian trade for many a year. Such a comparatively unremunerative occupation as that of carrying a
few score head of cattle six times a year from Port Zodiac
to Port Marivelles was not worth a ship-owner's thought
at a time when half the world's shipping was locked up by
blockade and a good half of what was free lay in Jones's
Locker and the rest was being paid any price its owner demanded to carry cargoes into the zone of war.

Exciting times were those for the world in general, but
dull in far-off Capricornia; good times for the graziers of
the Southern States with the multitudinous railways and
easy distances from stations to abattoirs and ships, hard
times for the graziers of that distant land which was divided from such happy outlets by a wilderness of which the
width was not reckoned in mere hundreds of miles but
thousands.

Differ was well aware of this state of affairs and how
it affected Oscar. Therefore Oscar, who disregarded the
fact that the man had done what he had in honest belief

that he could rectify it, thought the imposture particularly mean. But at the outset he wished to deal with Differ leniently. He went out to Coolibah Creek and told him what he thought of him, which was even less than he had thought when he set out, because he found the fellow drunk and living in utter squalor, with his Javan Princess more than ever his drudge. Oscar went too far with expressing his opinion. From cringing, Differ flew into a rage, took up a gun, drove him off his property. Oscar went for the police.

Differ was arrested on the charge of having obtained goods by false pretence. He was sentenced to six months' imprisonment, one of which he spent in jail, the rest, because it was found that he was suffering from an internal growth, in hospital. Far from treating Oscar as one he had wronged or who had wronged him, he honoured him by sending him Constance to take care of. He sent her with a letter describing her as "a tender flower at a dangerous age, who must be shielded from the evil world." She was then thirteen. Oscar could do nothing but take her.

Differ came out of hospital about a month before Mark's return. He did not go straight home. He went to Red Ochre, where he stayed a long while convalescing, whiling the time with teaching Marigold and Norman and behaving as one who had been irreparably injured by a faithless friend. By the time he went back to Coolibah Creek his crime had cost Oscar a good hundred pounds.

§

The people of Capricornia took little interest in the European War at first. Not only were they about as far removed from the seat of it as it was possible for anyone to be and almost utterly ignorant of the cause of it and virtually unconcerned in the issues, but they were out of range of the propaganda of those who would have had them become as frenzied as most of the rest of the world was at that time. There was but one newspaper in the country, THE TRUE COMMONWEALTH, which was published in Port Zodiac once a week and, lacking means to deal with telegraphic news, devoted to local topics and the strongly anti-imperialistic views of the man who ran it. Such references as THE TRUE COMMONWEALTH made to the war did anything but lead the populace to think the affair any business of theirs. And the news and propaganda in imperialistic papers imported once a month by the mail-boat from the South lacked power because it lacked continuity and was stale. Even such slave-minded people as the Government Officers in Town were for a long while of opinion that it would make no difference to Australia who won the war so long as Australia kept out of it.

Then a war-monger, or Sooler, as such people were called in the locality, made his voice heard in the land. He was Timothy O'Cannon, ganger of the railway, a soldier born, his birth-place being the garrison at Southern Cross Island in Cooksland, where his father had been a sergeant-major and he himself had served some little time. His own attention to the vastness of the war was drawn by chance when once, while on a visit to Town, he found in the hotel where he was staying an English magazine containing photographs taken in the war-zone. As an artilleryman he was particularly interested in the great guns that were being used. He wrote to a newsagent in the city of Flinders asking for a regular supply of this magazine and of a certain strongly imperialistic local daily. Thus he became an agent of the Propagandists. He spoke of the Belgian Atrocities as though he had witnessed them. When he had read and digested and succumbed to these journals he passed them on.

If ever a man made a true unselfish voluntary sacrifice in that European War it was the same Tim O'Cannon. He sacrificed the chance to take a soldier's part in it, which to him meant the chance to attain to paramount glory. Countless times he all but sooled himself into khaki. But much as he loved that cloth he loved his children more. He was the father of four quadroons who were regarded as halfcastes because the lighter part of their mother's blood was Asiatic; and he was only too well aware of what their future would be should he desert them. So he had to satisfy his lust for homicide with passing on the urges of the Propagandists and sooling the able-bodied off to war and hounding pacifists and enemies into retirement. Thus for a while. Then he conceived the glorious idea of growing cotton to feed the thundering guns. He imported cotton-seed from Cooksland, where cotton-growing for the war had already begun, and planted it on the little cattle-station to which he had previously given his spare time.

People scoffed at O'Cannon's cotton, saying at first that it would never see the Wet through, then that it would never live through the Dry. It flourished and bore well. The price he got for his crop was grand. Then Capricornia went cotton mad. The Government imported seed by the ton and gave it away, and set up a great experimental culture-station at Red Coffin Ridge, a place on the railway

between the Caroline and Black Adder Creek. It was Tim
O'Cannon who suggested the building of the station. As the
instigator of the madness he should have been given the post
of Superintendent. He was not. His character was against
him. He was regarded as a combo. The job was given to
Humbolt Lace, a Government clerk, who claimed to be an
amateur botanist.

Oscar planted cotton at Red Ochre. Differ planted cotton
at Coolibah Creek and considered the future of his Javan
Princess assured. The people of the Caroline Siding, except Karl Fliegeltaub, whom O'Cannon had hounded into
retirement, banded together and established the biggest
cotton-plantation in the country. Patriotism for profit! The
very pursuit in which the Propagandists themselves were
occupied! Thus Capricornia, freest and happiest land on
earth, was dragged into a war between kings and queens
and plutocrats and slaves and homicidal half-wits, which
was being waged in a land in another Hemisphere, thirteen
thousand miles away.

Nature was against it. The wholesale planting was begun at the end of the Wet Season in 1916. The following
Wet was the heaviest for many a year. Every plantation
was washed bare. Karl Fliegeltaub and Mick O'Pick got
drunk on the strength of it. The cotton-boom collapsed.

So it came to seem as though there were something in
the enemy's boast of *Gott Mit Uns*. People began to listen
to O'Cannon, who went round hounding mercilessly. Then
news came that Australian troops were now being sent to
Europe and were having the time of their lives, and that
owing to the great depletion of the manhood of the Southern States, harvests of all kinds were going begging for
reapers. An exodus began. Oscar decided to join it, to be
one of the number going to Keep the Home Fires Burning in a good soft job, because, on account of his responsibility to Norman and Marigold, and on account of his now
determinate age, he considered himself ineligible for more
dangerous service. He decided to sell his stock and sub-let
his lease and go home for the Duration.

§

In the middle of the Dry Season that followed the collapse of the cotton-boom, one day while Oscar was in the
midst of drafting an account of Red Ochre's stock-in-trade
for presenting to a man named Burywell who was contemplating taking on the lease, a naked blackfellow brought him
a message from Differ.

Messages from Differ were by no means rare just then. The man was ill again and poorer than ever, and, knowing that Oscar was going away, was desperately snatching at whatever crumbs of charity remained. He had lately become an utter pest to Oscar. First Oscar had been forced to take care of Constance again while he returned to the hospital for an operation. Fortunately his treatment cost nothing. As it was, other expenses he incurred cost Oscar a pretty penny. It was impossible to refuse him. He made Oscar feel that he would have a death on his conscience if he did not help him. After all, the operation did him more harm than good. He returned to say that it had been decided that he must undergo special treatment necessitating his going to a hospital in the South, in order to do which he asked Oscar for the loan of £150. He offered as security the manuscript of a novel and a stack of poems and short stories he had written, which, according to him, were worth a fortune. Oscar did not discredit the man's literary ability; in fact he considered him a very clever fellow in an unpractical way; but he had little faith in the value of literary ability in Australia, having been thoroughly taught by Differ himself that Australian editors and publishers did not know what literary ability was; so he suggested that Differ should cash the securities himself. Poor Differ had tried that long ago. They were dog's-eared by the hands of many a publisher's-reader and postman. Next Differ asked for £100 without security, and when that was refused asked for £50, and finally £33 10s. — the bare second-class fare for two to Flinders. Oscar refused.

Still Differ was not silenced. When he learnt that Oscar was contemplating going South he begged to be allowed to manage the Station, first asking a small salary for his services, finally offering them for the mere right to live in a comfortable home and eat free beef. That would have suited Oscar admirably at the time, because it had looked as though he could not find anyone fool enough to take the place off his hands; but last of all the careless caretakers he could easily have found would he have chosen drunken Differ; while the wretched man was pleading he was thinking how his cattle would be butchered wholesale for hides that Chinese storekeepers would take in exchange for a few shillings' worth of grog.

At length Differ gave up begging favours for himself and concentrated on begging for Constance. Already up to the time of his last message he had four times begged Oscar to take Constance with him down to Batman, where he desired to have her placed in a convent. This latter line of begging was done by means of flowery letters that said much about Oscar's unparalleled kindness to Norman and stated that the writer was at death's door. Thrice Oscar sent back apologetic refusals. The fourth time he gave the messenger a stick of tobacco and told him to go to hell.

When the naked blackfellow handed him the latest letter, Oscar snorted with anger, pitched the missive into the litter of papers on his table, and went on with the drafting. He was working in the dining-room. He looked up but once during the next half-hour, and then only to bawl at the blackfellow for lounging on the back veranda near the door. At last he picked up the letter. It consisted of five sheets of rough brown paper rolled into a cylinder and tied with string. The writing had been done with a wet ink-pencil by a shaky hand. It was scarcely readable. As Differ usually wrote with care, Oscar at once assumed that he had written shakily to lend colour to the cause he surely would be pleading. He sneered as he smoothed out the paper. Yes — sure enough Differ was dying again. Pity that wolf would not come!

The letter ran:

Dear Friend, I am dying. My course is run. For God's sake help me. The hæmorrhage I told you about is much worse. I've scarcely any blood left in my miserable body.

I've been a burden to you for years. Forgive me for a poor weak fool. Soon you'll be freed of me for ever. I ask but one more favour, friend of years, my only friend. Take my child with you to the convent. You can't refuse me. On your charity, think of my little girl and what will happen to her when I am gone. The Compound, humiliation, prostitution, at last a place by the camp-fire in the bush, and always the unutterable debasement of being coloured and an outcast.

It will cost you so little to do this — £16, and a few shillings for clothing. At present she's in rags. Oh my darling, my sweet sweet child, just budding into beautiful womanhood, my Javan Princess — in rags!

My friend, come to me at once so that I might not have to die alone. I can't come to you. I'm too weak to ride. I'd have to ride, because for one thing the white-ants have eaten the wheels of my buckboard, and my one cart-horse has gone bush with the brumbies. Laughable, isn't it! I feel I can laugh now, even in the shadow of death. I am happy. For I know you won't fail me. Oh you can't — you can't — Heaven would surely strike you if you did — And I — I would die mocking you for your meanness.

Forgive me, my friend. Understand my anguish. Please come at once with the buckboard and take me to the rail. If I can make the journey I'll go up to the hospital. Oh I don't care about dying. I've suffered enough. Really I think I'd be disappointed if I recovered.

If I should die before you come, I shall send Constance across to you. I bequeath her innocence to your care. And I bequeath to you my literary work. Useless though these might be commercially, they are the attar-drops distilled from the long and futile ebullience of my life.

Consider my darling's peril, Oscar. It is real — so terribly real. Her peril, from which no hand but yours can save her. Then, on your charity, come to me.

Yours,

PETER.

For some minutes Oscar stared before him, seeing Differ dying, and while dying striving to write what he called the Perfect Phrase — poor devil! And seeing Constance, the ragged Javan Princess, the sweet bud of womanhood. And seeing the rubbish-heap on to which the flower would be cast if his hand were not put out to help. And thinking that if he did not help he would be a fiend.

Then suddenly he remembered something Differ had often talked about, what he called the Suggestive Power of the Written Word, the making, by means of arrangement of word and phrase, of mesmeric passes as it were before the reader's mind in order to convince — that was Differ's word, Convince! — Convince Against All Reason. Ah! — here was Differ trying to mesmerise him with an ink-pencil — and succeeding! He shuddered, searched among the papers for his pipe. Was Differ mad, or extremely cunning? he wondered. Cunning. Yes — he had been using him for years. He had never been anything but an Old Man of the Sea. And he had got pretty nearly everything he had ever wanted from him. Mesmerism — yes!

He picked up the letter and read it again, then again. With each reading it lost its power. No, he decided, the wolf had not come; and Constance was not a Javan Princess; nor would he be a fiend if he left her to her fate, which would surely not be as bad as Differ said. And Differ? Well, perhaps he would abandon beggary when there was no poor fool about to beg from.

He rose and went outside. The naked blackfellow was leaning against a veranda post, watching Marigold and Norman playing with their toys. He noticed for the first time that the fellow was naked. He had taken little notice of him in the darkened room, and afterwards had seen him only through the fly-wire door. He snapped at him, "You dirty myall — what name you no-more gottim trouser?"

The blackfellow grinned and said, "Me number-one poorman, Boss."

Oscar stepped up and pushed him, crying angrily, "Go catchim flour-bag — dirty cow standing front of children like that!"

The blackfellow stood and stared. "You dopey cow!" roared Oscar. "Get to the devil out of it!" He rushed. The blackfellow fled. Then Oscar went inside, and wrote to Differ thus:

Dear Peter, Your strange letter to hand. No I'm sorry I can do nothing in re Constance. I've told you often enough how matters stand with me. Money's tight. And I might not be going right to Batman yet. If I can get a job in Flinders I might stay there. What could I do with Constance then? Really I wouldn't like the responsibility of having to take care of her. Norman is different. He's a boy. And then again — what say they won't take her in this convent in Batman you speak of? I've heard that a girl has to be of good parentage before she can become a nun. Perhaps they'd put her in an orphanage. Then I reckon she'd be better off in the Compound, because girls out there have at least the good clean bush to go to if things go wrong, but girls out of an orphanage have only the streets.

Now I suggest you take her over to Red Coffin Ridge. Lace is a deputy protector of Aborigines and therefore bound to take care of her. But this is my main reason for suggesting it. Mrs. Lace is going down South next boat to have a baby, and I know she'd like to have someone to look after her, because Lace told me so, and she might take Conny with her as a maid, and you never know might fix her up somewhere down there. A woman can do more in that line than a man. Then you could go to hospital. I'm sure you'd be all right if you'd leave the booze alone.

If you like this suggestion you'd better hurry over to Red Coffin, because Mrs Lace will be going up next train. Even if she doesn't want Conny on the trip it's pretty certain she'll want someone to help her with the baby when she returns, so Lace might keep her there.

Well, Peter, I'm sorry I can't get over for a while. I'm expecting Jack Burywell up tomorrow to show him over the joint. I'll come when he's gone and run you over to the rail. I promise that if you send Constance over to Lace I'll keep an eye on her while I'm still about. But look here now, Peter, don't send her over here. Not under any circumstances. If you do I'll send her straight to the Compound. And another thing, make that nigger of yours wear something when he comes here. It's not decent for the children.

Yours ever.

OSCAR.

§

The wolf had come to Differ. His cries of its nearness had never been exaggerated much. He had been convinced for months past that his days were numbered.

Lying helpless in his bed, which was a blanket-covered buffalo-hide strung to a sapling frame, behind a mouldy mosquito-net that swarmed with flies, he read Oscar's letter. At first he groaned; and while he stared at the stained calico canopy of the net, tears oozed from the corners of his sunken eyes. Constance was sitting on a box beside him, fanning him with a goose-wing. She saw the tears, but took little notice of them. He often wept.

After many minutes of silent weeping he breathed deeply; then his scraggy grey-streaked beard parted in a smile as he turned to his daughter. His blue eyes met her velvet brown ones. He whispered, "Love —" and put out a skinny hand to meet the small brown one that came creeping under the net.

"Love," he went on in a whisper, "God knows what's to become of you in the meantime, but rest assured one day you'll die and be at peace. Princess or prostitute, you'll die. Strange there are fools who kid themselves they'll live again. Who would want to who has really lived already? Oh my little one, I've given you a lot of trouble in your little life, worrying you about your future. What's it matter what happens to you after all? The aim of the world in general is to live happily ever after, to exist like the beasts of the field, wanting nothing but good pasture and quiet mating and the right to moo a bit."

A pause. It was broken by Constance, who looked up from the letter lying on his breast and asked, "Is Mister Shillingsworth coming, Daddy?"

He searched her face for a while, then answered, "No darling, not now."

She blinked and looked down.

After a while he asked, "Do you want to go to Batman very much, dear?"

"Yes," she whispered, looking up quickly.

"You'd give anything?"

"Yes Daddy."

"If I had to die today to let you go?"

She looked down.

"Answer truly dear, like my own truthful Conny. If I were to die today and Shillingsworth were to come to take you, would you stop crying?"

"No Daddy — I could never stop."

He smiled. After a while he said, "My dear one! But I reckon you'd nearly stop. But honey, would it break your heart to know you couldn't go?"

She stared for a moment, then said, "But Daddy — you said he'd come for sure. Isn't he going to take me?"

"Yes dear. He'll take you. He'll have to. His heart can't be stone. When he realizes he will."

"Isn't he — can't I go now Daddy?"

"Yes dear. But he's busy just now. We'll have to go over to Missus Lace first."

"Not Mister Shillingsworth?"

"Of course he'll take you in any case. But Missus Lace might take you first. Anyway, we'll see. We'll have to go soon so's not to miss her. What's today?"

"Wednesday."

"Train-day. We'll have to go tomorrow. Get Bootpolish to catch two horses — old Walleye for me."

"But you're too sick to get up Daddy."

"I'll have to talk to Missus Lace about you."

"But you can't ride a horse."

"I can ride old Walleye."

"But he's got the swamp-cancer. He's dying, Daddy. He's nearly dead."

Differ smiled as he said, "All the better. Dying horses for dying men."

She stared.

"You don't think I'm dying, do you?" he asked.

"No," she whispered.

He smiled and whispered, "Well I am — strange as it may seem."

In the red dawn of the following day the naked Boot-polish carried his master out of the house and set him in the saddle. Differ scarcely knew what was happening. During the night he had vomited blood till it seemed there could be none left in his body. His skin was as white and limp and dry as paper-bark; bloody froth oozed from his lips. Bootpolish fixed a blanket on the horse's bony withers, and laid his master forward. Walleye staggered under the puny weight and groaned. Oh wretched horse! He could scarcely hold up his head. His breast was eaten almost to the bone by a frightful sore. It was merciless to load him; but he was the only quiet horse that Differ owned.

They set out. Constance rode ahead, holding in her own impatient mount and leading Walleye. Bootpolish walked beside Differ and held one of his flaccid arms. Thus they travelled towards the railway, following a short-cut through the sterile stony hills. In the red evening they came within sight of the white roofs of the Experimental Station. Constance saw it first and cried out joyfully. Bootpolish looked up from weary feet and told his master, and getting no response, tugged at the arm and said, "Close-up Boss — look see." Still Differ did not answer. Bootpolish tugged harder, and to his astonishment, and the horror of Constance, tugged him out of the saddle. Differ fell like a bag of sand.

Constance cried out. Bootpolish bent over Differ and took his outflung hand. Constance dismounted and came running. She found her father staring. She fell to knees and said anxiously, "Daddy!" Still he stared, rather malevolently, and without winking a lid. "Daddy!" she said. "Oh Daddy don't look at me like that! What's the matter?"

A pause.

Constance looked wide-eyed at Bootpolish, who turned away and spat. She turned back to her father and clutched his thin shoulders and whispered hoarsely, "Daddy — Daddy." Her voice rose high and shrill. "Oh Daddy if you look like that — I — Oh Daddy don't be dead — Oh don't you — I — I — Oh Daddy dear — my Daddy!"

§

Mrs Humbolt Lace was gone. She was hundreds of miles

away. The steamer from Singapore, always erratic in her movements, and especially so just then when more than reefs might lurk to do her harm in the lonely Silver Sea, had arrived in Port on Tuesday night instead of Friday as expected, and had departed at noon next day.

Mrs Lace had rushed up to Town on Tim O'Cannon's motor-trolley. Her spouse had stayed at home. Because the lady took much baggage, there was neither room nor power left in the vehicle for the conveyance of another passenger. Her spouse was glad, having had too much of the lady's going as it was, it being rather like the coming of a myall cow to the Station's stockyard branding-ramp, a panting, stamping, straining, goggle-eyed business. Lace thought in such terms these days, having become the State Stock Expert since the collapse of the cotton-boom, and therefore being in daily contact with bovine beasts.

Mrs Lace was quite a young woman, bride of only a year, but no longer the sprightly heifer that her spouse had wooed. She was a grown cow now, and a cow in calf at that, than which there is no more irritatingly irrational creature on the earth. Not that Lace did not respect her nor feel concerned about the burden that so angrily she often told him he had thrust upon her; far from it; he thought a great deal of her, even supposed he still loved her; but of late she had become extremely tiresome.

She had not voluntarily parted thus hurriedly from Humbolt. To her it seemed indecent that a pregnant woman of her standing (Government Service) should have to board the steamer without a husband to go with her and dispute about her accommodation and whisper anxiously to the doctor and stewardess — almost as indecent as a Government Service woman's having her baby in the hospital in Port Zodiac with the wives of workingmen and Greeks. She had tried hard to induce Tim O'Cannon to give up the driving-seat to Humbolt. Tim said that to do so would be a breach of *Rules and Regulations,* for which, in military style, he was a stickler.

Lace had at the back of his mind a desire to go combo. He had had it ever since he came in contact with the comely lubras of the district. But at first it had been kept in check by what he called his Sense of Decency. Not that he was a prude. Apparently he was only colour-proud. Then he had met Miss Carrie Oats, holidaying niece of the Government Secretary, promise of conjugality with whom had made thoughts of going combo baser still. Then the realisation of the promise had ousted such thoughts completely; or al-

most completely; for when the joys of wedlock began to
pall, he found that the roots remained. The roots began to
put forth their weeds again when in his flaccidity he observed how potent bulls could be with a variety of wives.
Still he dared not try to emulate the bulls while Carrie
was about.

Such was the man to whom came Constance the Javan
Princess, exotic enough to spice desiring her with the bar-
barity of comboing, ordinary enough to save the spice
from the suspicion of being poison. But it was not as a
Princess that she came to him. She came as a distracted
child leading a dying horse on which lay her limp dead
father. As such Lace saw her first, and as such regarded
her for some time to come, except in moments when without wishing it his eyes enjoyed her curves and sturdiness.

He was very kind to her. He telephoned to the police in
Town and with their permission buried Differ, and of his
own accord, and being a man who respected Religion, read
over him the Burial Service, consigning him to Eternal
Life. Then he sent for Oscar and heard with genuine
sympathy the story of Constance's life and hopes. So kind
was he that he did not directly tell her that her hopes were
dashed, but said that though it seemed unlikely that Mr
Shillingsworth would be able to take her down to Flinders,
it was not unlikely that some day Mrs Lace might do so
when she found it became necessary for her to make the
trip again. It was his intention to send her to the Compound, not hurriedly and harshly, but bit by bit as it were,
by carefully talking to her about it and trying as a Protector of Aborigines to prepare the way for her. She made
him sorry for the halfcaste race, so much so that he determined to draw the attention of the people of the South
to their plight some day, and began his good work with a
practical expression, by buying her some expensive clothes
to replace her rags, though it pleased him to catch a glimpse
of her pretty body that the rags made possible.

Constance liked him. He was about thirty, twice her age,
but younger by far than any whiteman she had ever spok-
en to but ugly Frank McLash. And he was handsome. She
liked his curly brownish hair and kind blue eyes. He was
like the men in magazines, whom one always saw with women
in their arms, crying passionately, "I love you." How well
she knew that phrase! Pleasant tales were those of the
magazines, telling of a world in which she lived in dreams.
No world that of weary open spaces and inevitable Wets
and Drys and snakes and ants and kangaroos and eternal

trees and cancered horses. She had lately read a tale called *The Hybiscus Flower,* which dealt with a halfcaste girl of the Oceanic Isles whom a young man like Lace wooed delightfully at first, then gave a baby to and treated badly. Constance, associate of lubras, was not nearly as innocent as her father had believed. And then the hero of the story, after many adventures in which he acted with meanness that would seem unforgivable to anyone less simple than Constance and the author and publisher of the tale, fell back into love with the girl, and, defying all the principles that at first had worried him, married her in a mission-church and settled down to make her happy ever after.

At first she slept in a little hut not far from the station house, in which had dwelt a bevy of young lubras who had drifted in as soon as Mrs Lace was gone. After a few days' residence there she was allowed to sleep in a real bed under the elevated house in a little cane-screened room that Lace had had rigged up for himself when he tired of the bridal bower. She was glad to have the pretty little room, and therefore did not deny what Lace said about the danger of her being molested by niggers if she remained in the hut, though she did not think the danger existed.

Thus many days passed quietly. Constance stopped grieving for her father. Lace began to be troubled in his mind, or rather in that part of it where what he called his Decency held sway, because that part of it where the desire to go combo lurked was prompting him to stop thinking about sending her to the Compound. Gradually they became more friendly. Once he asked her if she were sorry he was married, and argued till she said Yes to please him, then told her that if he were not he would marry a girl like herself. She was pleased. Later she was puzzled by his begging her to forget what he had said. And she was puzzled by his conduct in the matter of her drinking whiskey. He forced her several times against her will to drink it, then scolded himself for having done so, saying *It Isn't Right.*

Then one night while she was undressing by the light of a candle, she heard a noise outside the little room, and thinking that it was some prowling animal, rushed half-dressed to the curtain to see what the creature was. It was poor peeping Lace.

He rose as though his backbone had been turned to lead. She was much too astonished to retreat. After a moment he gasped, "You all r-right?"

She simply stared.

"I-I-I thought I heard you c-call."

Still she stared.

"Afraid?" he gasped.

"No," she murmured, and becoming aware of her nakedness began to retreat.

He held up the curtain and blinked, murmuring, "Th-
thought I heard y-you sing out."

She snatched up her nightdress and donned it hastily,
then said, "I thought it was a dingo."

He chuckled weakly, then said, "Nice night, isn't it. You
not in bed yet, eh?"

"Just going."

A pause. No sound in the night but the very distant yelling of cockatoos that something had disturbed. Lace stood
till the nightdress, which was one of Carrie's and rather
large, slipped from her shoulder and exposed her breast. He
stumbled forward as she raised a hand to draw the dress
back, and gasped, "Lemme do it." He did it without permission, and roughly, with lingering contact of fingers with
her flesh that startled her.

For a moment he devoured her with his eyes, then turned to blink about the room as though he thought that God
was watching him. After a while he looked at her and said
mildly, "You comfy?"

"Oh yes," she answered, smiling, watching his face.

He smiled too, eagerly, then reached and took her hand.
His was cool and trembling, not unpleasant to her touch.
"You're hot," he murmured.

"Hot night," she murmured in reply. And she began to
tremble with him and to feel afraid.

A moment. Then he muttered, "Gi's a — gi's a kiss,"
and took her in his arms. No question of giving. He devoured her lips, crushed her, till God roared at him. He relinquished her as suddenly as he had seized her, and blurt-
ed in her astonished face, "It isn't right!"

She stared. It was somewhat in the style of such first behaviour that the *Hybiscus Flower* girl was wooed and won.
Exciting even if rather terrifying. She felt a sense of disappointment when he laid a trembling hand on her shoulder as quietly as her father might and said with a sickly
smile, "My dear, I'm sorry. Forgive me — please. Now off
to bed — it's late."

Humbolt Laee found himself battling with that uncon-
scionable part of him that he had planned to give rein to.
He won that bout; but found little joy in the victory. And

he won a few more bouts with it later. But finally it beat him. Thus he was saved from going utterly combo and having to prepare burnt corks against the day of reunion with Carrie.

FE FI FO FUM

A FEW days before Christmas, the Shillingsworths, driven by the new lessee of Red Ochre, Jack Burywell, set out in the buckboard on the first stage of their long journey to the South. A pack-team driven by natives followed with their baggage.

Many more people than usual were waiting for the returning mail-train, most of them to travel up to Town for a Christmas spree. Among the crowd, though not one of the intending travellers, was Humbolt Lace of Red Coffin Ridge, come down on business. Another of the people, though not one of the crowd at the Siding House, was old Karl Fliegeltaub, benign, bespectacled, square-headed old outcast, who waited with his only friends, the blacks, near the goods-shed. He was waiting for a bottle of Christmas cheer from Soda Springs, expensive liquor on which Mrs Blaize put a tax on account of the sinking of the *Lusitania* and the prestige she lost through dealing with him. Mrs Blaize had no rivals in her trade with Fliegeltaub. Mrs McLash had refused to serve him since having become involved in the war through her son's decision to enlist; indeed she had threatened to run him through with a bread-knife if he came near her. Frank had not yet enlisted. As a matter of fact he was making the steam of the train for which the crowd was waiting, being now fireman of the mail-train, well on the way to realise his great ambition. His rapid advancement was due to the fact that many of the railwaymen had gone to the war. But this was his last day's work as a civilian. He would be sailing for the South on the same steamer as the Shillingsworths.

Oscar spoke to Lace and learnt that he was the father of a son whom he would see when his wife came home on the steamer after next. Then, as though divining the thought in Lace's mind — thought of the return of Carrie as it concerned the pregnancy of halfcaste Constance, which of late had caused the man much worry —, he asked after Constance, and learnt to his surprise that she was about to marry Mrs McLash's halfcaste rouseabout, Yeller Elbert.

Lace looked uncomfortable when Oscar stared at him. Oscar said, "But the kid's so young — only fifteen or so!"

"Elbert's young too," said Lace to the ground. "Only about twenty-three or four. And he's a good sort of coot for a yeller (he remembered Norman's presence) — er — halfcaste."

"I mean she's too young to get married," said Oscar. "Doesn't know she's alive yet — like calfing a weaner."

"I feel that way about it too," said Lace. "But you see she picked up with Elbert when he came up my place for eggs and things for Ma McLash — and — well I'm going to see him stick by her. That's the size of it."

"You don't mean to say she was carrying on with Elbert?"

"Yes."

"Well I'm hanged. How long's this been going on?"

"Can't say exactly. Pretty well from the time she came, I think, to judge by her condition. Of course I've got to see the girl protected."

"Well I'd never have thought that of her. Always a good kid, and well brought up."

Lace said with a smile, "With a drunken combo."

Oscar felt nettled. He said rather brusquely, "Differ was a good father to her, whatever his faults. He taught her well. It's a damn shame if she's got to go back to the Binghis."

"Elbert's not a Binghi."

"He's damn near it."

Lace tried to spit. The fluid simply fell from his lips and fell on his khaki breast. Cleansing himself with a handkerchief, he slowly said, "Well it's no fault of mine she's got into trouble. I trusted her same's you'd've done yourself. Couldn't watch her day and night. I've reported the matter to the Protector."

"I wasn't meaning anything against you," said Oscar. "Only it's a pity she never got the chance to marry white."

"She'd never get that. And that's just the reason I want to see her settled down with Elbert. There isn't a yel — er — halfcaste in the country better than he is since he's been working for old Ma McLash. I'll see he looks after her. I've leased See Ghoon's old peanut farm down the river here. That's 't brings me here today. I'm going to set 'em up as farmers."

Oscar cocked his head, rather surprised to hear that this nincompoop was capable of arranging anything so wise.

"I've bought seed for 'em," said Lace. That was a lie; he had taken the seed from the station-store, together with tools and many other things. "And I'll place a tenner for 'em with Ma McLash, so's they can draw on her for a bit of tucker till they get on their feet."

"Who's paying?" asked Oscar. "Abo Department?"

"Oh no," said Lace lightly. "I'm doing it on my pat."

Oscar felt embarassed. Here was a good fellow to be sure, going to all this trouble to help a child he hardly knew, while he himself, who had known her half her life, had done nothing, had indeed treated her rather meanly, as he sometimes thought. He said with feeling, "That's very decent of you Lace."

Lace smiled, and kicked the gravel, and made much clinking with his spurs. Oscar went on, "I'll put in a few quid too. Can't do much with things as they are; but later on if there's money needed I might be able to help. Just ask Jack Burywell. He'll know my address. I told Peter I'd keep an eye on her. Afraid I've been too busy. But it don't seem necessary with you about, anyway. Most protectors are only that in name. Very decent of you, very decent."

"Don't mention it," murmured Lace.

"When's the wedding?"

"Day after New Year's Day, up at my place. The Protector will send a parson down."

"That's the stuff. Do it properly. I wish I could be there. Look, I'll give you seven quid — a fiver for the farm, two for wedding-presents. Give 'em a treat. Poor kids haven't had many in their lives. Yes — by golly, I wish I was round about to keep an eye on 'em with you."

They were talking about halfcastes, very quietly so that Marigold and Norman might not hear, when someone in the crowd cried, "Here she comes!" Every eye turned to see.

Away in green distance, in the tiny yellow-floored gap in the bush between the blue peak of Mount Packhorse and a hill of sparkling quartz that stood on Red Ochre territory, a black dot appeared, a dot surrounded by a haze of dust.

"He's hitting her up," said someone.

"So he oughter," said another, "seein' he's three hours late."

"My Frankie's drivin', I'll be bound," said Mrs McLash with a gulp.

No grass grew under a train when the engineer let Fire-man McLash take the throttle. Frank was one of those creatures that have become so common since his day, a speed-maniac. The Capricornian Railway had great need of such as he.

The train came in grinding and shuddering, with coal and water spilling from the engine.

"She'll run through," said Mick O'Pick.

"Not if my Frankie's pullin' her tail," said Mrs McLash.

It was no uncommon sight to see a train overshoot a stopping-place. The causes were several. First, the engineers of the service were not always properly trained men and hence not expert in judging speed in relation to distance and load and braking-power as they should have been; then they were not always sober; then their trains were not equipped with automatic braking systems such as are used on more up-to-date railways. When an engineer wished to stop a swiftly-moving train he had first to whistle to the guard requesting him to apply the hand-brake of the van, and then apply the hand-brake of the engine. Guards did not always hear. Sudden stopping, which could be effected easily by sanding the rails and reversing the driving-gear, was dangerous, because the train might telescope and overwhelm the engine. Locomotive crews on duty lived like rats on leaky ships, always ready to leap overboard. However, Frank McLash was an expert driver. Rarely did a train play tricks with him. As his mother guessed, he had control of the mail-train that day. The engine stopped dead at the water-hydrant. A bolt or bar or some such thing was seen to fly from out the off-side bogey and sail over the stockyard.

Looking for all the world like more parts of the train detached through the jar of the sudden stopping, the passengers dropped off, most of them heavily, many to stagger and fall. This was a specially festive journey. Not only were all the passengers coming up for a Christmas spree, but many were also going to the European War. No — not all were coming for a spree; for there were chained in a stinking cattle-car eight Aboriginal prisoners who were coming up to jail; according to what their fellow passengers said with laughter they were not so much felons as excuses for outback policemen's holidays. The cattle-car was near the engine, and thus within sound of the gushing hydrant, which was music in the chain-gang's ears. While their sodden fellows staggered past on the way to the Siding House, they rattled their chains and cried out miserably, and in vain, "Water — water!"

"Damn," growled Oscar. "Here's that cow Jock Driver."

There was Jock in the middle of the crowd, waving his wideawake and shouting. He was going to the war. That was what he was shouting about. When he saw old Fliegeltaub he hooted, "Bluidy awl' Boche, wait'll we get B'lin and see't we do to bluidy awl Koyser — wait'll we get Potsdam — and Rotterdam and Amsterdam and Tinker's Dam — Remem'er Belgium, ye rottendamn stinkin' bluidy awl' Hoon." And he burst into song, in which others joined him, a song that went to the tune of The Marseillaise:

There is a spot in Germany where we Aussies soon
    will be;
We'll get to Berlin if it costs us our lives,
We'll kill all the Fritzers and pinch all their wives.
Tar-ra-rah, tar-ra-rah, tar-ra-rah —

"Ugh!" grunted Mick O'Pick. "Remimb'rin' Bilgi'm wit' a vingince!"

Oscar hastily took the hands of the children and led them through the house to the back veranda. He was joined there soon by Lace and Burywell, and later by three passengers who could not find seats inside. It was with dismay that he learnt that Jock was going to the war, since it meant that his obnoxious company must be suffered all the way down South. There would surely be unpleasantness if Jock came into contact with Norman. As Oscar had observed when several times he had met Jock in the past four years, the fellow regarded the adoption of Norman as a great joke. The boy had not yet been exposed to his ribaldry. Oscar was particularly anxious that he should not be exposed to it now, wishing to get him away from Capricornia in the same state of ignorance of his origin as he had succeeded in keeping him in so long. His wish was partly for Norman's sake, partly for his own. Because he was not looking forward to the task of having to explain the boy's true origin to his relatives in Batman, he had it in mind to adopt Differ's idea and say he was Javanese.

Norman was then a little over ten, and had not the slightest notion of who and what his parents were. Nor had he thought about them with any penetration, not having come into contact with anyone who would have or could have encouraged him to do so. He knew that Oscar was his uncle, but called him Dad as Marigold did, and felt as she did towards him. Such questions as he naturally asked about himself were always tactfully sidetracked.

There was little hope of avoiding Jock even on the train. Surely passengers would tell him that Norman was about and he would come to see. As it was, the three passengers eating with them were taking a livelier interest in the boy than was pleasant, and annoying Oscar by asking him a question that in recent years had become quite common to his ears — "What d'you think you're going to do with that kid?" Rarely was it simply, "What are you going to do with him?" It seemed as though most who asked it were pretty certain that whatever he had in mind would prove a failure. As yet Oscar had nothing in mind. He clung to Norman because he had come to regard him as a son, but had never quite decided to keep him always, never quite got over his shame of him in fact. After lunch he took the children to the train and placed them in a coach, forbidding them to look out of near-side windows.

The people in the dining-room took three-quarters of an hour to eat and drink their dinner. They might have taken longer but for Frank McLash's eagerness to be getting along on his journey to the war, which would amount, by the route he must take, to one of more than sixteen thousand miles. He dragged the guard and engineer out. The passengers followed, picking their teeth, dropping their money into Mrs McLash's tray, all of them careless of how much they paid her except Jock, who, in spite of her contemptuous smile, waited for his change.

Mrs McLash was dressed for travelling. She wore a black lustre skirt that just exposed her broken button-boots, a white blouse topped heavily with moth-eaten lace, a long coat of well-worn tusser, and a purplish black silk hat that looked like a wreath stained with sun and gravel of a grave; and she wore stays, as anyone with half an eye could see by the cut of her at a hundred yards, and as anyone not deaf could hear at ten; she creaked. And she was out of breath with flurry and grog and woe. She was going up to Town to see her Pride and Joy go off to war. Her bulging dress-basket lay with Frank's tin-trunk on the veranda.

"Carry your traps out Ma?" asked one of the passengers.

"Thanks, Jerry," she said as she stuffed the last of the money into her bag. "My boy Elbert'll do it." She called, "Elbert — El — bert — where are ya?"

Elbert's mottled face popped out of the door near the

post-office. He was looking for Jock, who had been worrying him during the meal.

"El — bert — dammit!"

"Coming Missus," cried Elbert, running.

Jock was standing with other passengers, hidden from Elbert by creeper-grown lattice, actually within a few feet of Mrs McLash, but not on the veranda.

"Get a move on," said Mrs McLash. "Basket in front coach, trunk in van — mind — mind — be careful!"

Elbert staggered under the weight of the trunk, nearly let it fall as he stepped off the veranda, and had to stop to heave it up again on to his shoulder. He heaved it high and wide, and struck Jock in the mouth with a corner of it, then trotted off, labouring under the load, all unconscious of what he had done.

Jock hung in the creeper for a moment, dazed. He recovered with a jerk, howled with rage, rushed after Elbert, and with a violent push sent him flying. Although the trunk fell on his head and he on his face, Elbert was more amazed than hurt. His face was so comical as he rose to his knees that a laugh was roused. When he saw Jock he leapt to his feet, but not quick enough to dodge the mouthful of blood Jock spat at him.

"Yah!" he yelled, wiping his face.

"Bawstid!" hooted Jock, and spat again.

"Ow wow — woffor?" cried Elbert.

"I'll show you woffor," hooted Jock, aiming a blow at him.

Elbert, enraged, thinking that he was being set upon for nothing, retaliated, but not with fists as, being a member of the Anglo-Saxon community, he must if he wished to be regarded by the crowd as worthy of fair treatment. Not having been trained in the niceties he was supposed to observe, he kicked Jock in the shins, made him hoot, then tried to kick him in the abdomen, and drew a hoot from the crowd. Jock caught the treacherous foot, twisted it sharply, and kicked its owner's backside hard. The crowd made no comment. Such kicking was in accordance with the niceties; indeed it was a clever piece of work.

Elbert rushed at Jock again, kicking like a footballer, yelling like a savage. He knocked Jock down with a splendid kick to the heart, then fled. Jock's heart was of stone; he was up again in an instant and in pursuit; and, whereas Elbert had to cleave his way through an unsympathetic crowd, Jock had not; he came within reach of him at the dining-room door and struck him a terrific blow on the back of the head. Elbert's head was as solid as Jock's heart; he was not hurt much, but knocked off his balance; he fell over a table, bringing it down with a mighty crash of ware. Jock caught him as he lay. Whether he kept to the rules in kicking him no-one could say, since there were no witnesses. When the crowd rushed in the pair were on the floor, rolling among the wreckage, fighting as though they intended the combat to be mortal. The crowd was on them, trying to part them, when Jock, who was at the moment sitting on Elbert's legs and twisting one of his feet off, suddenly screamed, released the foot, and shot to his knees. The crowd gasped. The yellow handle of a table-knife was projecting from his back. Mrs McLash's knives were as old as she and worn by use to the sharpness of her tongue.

A second of goggling. Then Jock groaned horribly, groped frantically for the handle of the knife, and fell on his face in the debris.

"Stabbed!"

"What they done — the fools?" cried the distant voice of Mrs McLash.

Elbert gained his knees as hands grabbed at him.

"Knife — knife — look out!"

He had another knife. His eyes were wide, teeth bared. He was an infuriated savage. The crowd fell back. They had rushed in bargaining only for the safe and simple niceties.

"Drop it!" cried someone. "Chair him!" cried another. "Look out!" they all cried, and fled when Elbert rushed. Mad with rage, he passed men he could have disembowelled. One of these lucky fellows hurled a chair and nearly brained him. He crashed into the sideboard, senseless, fell with mouth gaping, hands outflung. A second. Then the crowd piled on him, vieing with each other to overpower him.

When the excitement passed it was found that Jock was stabbed right through the body. The point of the knife could be seen as a purplish knob between the second and third ribs from the bottom on the left. Someone said he was stabbed through the heart. That could not be so, since he was still living. Even one so hard of heart as he could not have lived with a table-knife in his heart.

The advisability of withdrawing the knife was debated. Some said that if it was withdrawn he would bleed to death, others that it would poison him if left there. Then they argued whether it would be better or not to give him brandy, to lie him on his face or side. With a woman's practical wisdom, Mrs McLash suggested that they should ring up Town and ask the doctor.

There were three police-troopers among the passengers. While one of them went to the telephone, the others and some of the crowd carried Elbert to the cattle-car, where the native prisoners lay, and cuffed him to the chain. One of the troopers said, "We'll have to bring the barsted round. Get a bucket of water." Luckily he recovered before he was douched. Thus the other prisoners got the drink for which they had been crying all day.

The doctor's orders were that the knife was to be withdrawn, iodine liberally applied to the puncture, and this to be plugged with sterile cotton, the patient to be given no stimulants, and brought to Town as soon as possible lying on his face with trunk raised slightly above the hinder parts, head hanging slightly down, left side raised a little above the right. This the trooper read out bit by bit from a slip of paper, seeing one order obeyed before he gave another, as one reciting a recipe for making pudding.

At the direction of the guard, who was occupied with holding Jock's trunk a little above the hinder parts preparatory to the last and most important task of withdrawing the knife, someone ran to the brakevan to get the ambulance-kit. The knife was found to be wedged like an axe in springy timber. At last it came out, scraping over bone, and followed by a fountain of blood.

"Artery!" cried Oscar.

The leading trooper snatched up Jock's shirt and applied it to the wound, saying to the guard, "What you do for artery in the back?"

"Wait'll the book comes," said the guard. "Might be this'n's round the front."

"Betcha it's coming from his heart," said someone.

The trooper looked up contemptuously.

Then a panting man ran in with a black box on which a red cross was painted, crying importantly, "Gangway — gangway!"

The box was set down, the stiff buckles of its mildewed straps tackled by a dozen thumby hands, the lid hurled back. To the staring crowd there was revealed a broken shunting-lamp, two greasy magazines, an axe-head, and a pair of boots.

"Cripes!" murmured the guard.

"Where's the kit?" cried the trooper. "Man'll bleed to death. That your kit, George?"

"Never used it yet," murmured the guard.

"Nothing much use there," said another policeman grave-ly.

"Joe!" cried the guard to Ganger Ballest. "You got a amb'lance-kit."

Ballest blinked and gaped, too drunk to understand. O'Pick answered for him, saying, "Aw —taint no good."

The leading trooper snapped, "Go'n get it."

"Taint no good, I says."

"Get it and we'll see," barked the trooper.

"I know't I'm talkin' about," snapped O'Pick. "The white-ants've et the box."

"What about the contents?"

"Contints too. They love that there waddin'. They've et the stuffin' outer me bed before today."

"Bah!" snapped the trooper. "See things want tightenin' up round here."

Then Mrs McLash, with woman's wisdom, came rushing from her bedroom with cotton-wool and bandages and iodine and chlorodyne and carron-oil. Soon afterwards Jock was carried out on a table to the train. Then Oscar went back to the children, thankful in his heart for having been relieved of the company of a pest, but too conventional to admit his feelings even to himself.

The engine whistled urgently. The guard yelled at pass-engers, "Get a move on there. Don't get jiggerin' about. This's a matter of life and death." Oscar climbed on to the platform of his coach. He was just about to go inside when he heard his name called, and looking back saw Lace on the ground below. "Ah — Lace," he said, stepping back to shake hands. "So long old man. Forgot you in the excite-ment." Then he noticed Lace's haggard face and added, "Hello —what's wrong?"

"Oscar —," said Lace, taking his hand.

The train began to move. Lace walked with it, holding a stanchion.

"Well — Merry Christmas," said Oscar. "Best of luck."

"Same to you," said Lace. "Er — Oscar —" he stepped on to the bottom step and continued, "Is that yeller-feller Peter Pan still out Tatlock's Pool way?"

"Peter Pan? No — he's down the river here in the big camp below Fliegeltaub's I think. He was there a month or so ago, anyway."

"Thanks," said Lace. "Good-o." He lowered his foot

preparatory to alighting, adding, "Best luck, Oscar. Hope see you again. Pleasant voyage."

Then it dawned on Oscar why the question was asked. He said quickly, "Hey — not thinking of marrying Conny to Peter, now —?"

Lace cast him one haggard glance, then stepped to the ground and disappeared.

Oscar leapt to the bottom step, looked back and shouted, "Can't do that — Peter Pan worse'n nigger — Hey!"

Lace smiled wanly and raised a hand.

"Can't do it!" Oscar bawled. His voice was drowned in the din of wheels. "Damnation — fool — God! I do b'lieve you got the kid in trouble 'self — see by your face — you swine — I'll tell the Protector!"

Lace smiled and waved again. The coach rattled past the trolley-shed, lurched and clattered over points. The children were at the near-side windows now and craning out to see. Natives from Red Ochre, forgotten by Oscar, were running with the coach yelling, "Mummuk Mist Chilnsik — mummuk chillen — goo'luck —plenn foyitch — mummuk — mummuk — goo'bye!"

Oscar remembered the packet of tobacco and sixpences he had for them. He tossed it out, waved, shouted with the children, "Mummuk!"

The natives were left behind. The train was running swiftly. The bridge was crossed, the Siding lost to view. Oscar looked up at the black and white and azure sky, and out upon the bright green countryside towards Red Ochre, where a silver mist of rain hung over the hills.

Goodbye Red Ochre — home of sweet and bitter memories, of hate and love, of hope and disappointment — goodbye for years, perhaps for ever, mummuk, mummuk, goodbye!

§

At the Princess Alice Heather took the children from Oscar and led them away to eat with her in private. Oscar let them go reluctantly, and only because the dining-room was too full and riotous for him to take them in to eat with him. Since the children had grown old enough to understand, he had always taken care to keep them away from Heather if he were not about to guard them, notwithstanding the assurance she had given that she would not speak to them about their parents. She was quite reliable. In fact she had not even let them know she was related to them.

After dinner Oscar met George Tittmuss, the station-master. He asked him if he had heard of Mark lately, and was told that he was in Town, that he had but recently come out of Calaboose, where he had been serving a term for debt, and was living with Henn in his own house in The Paddock. He might have learnt as much from Heather had he cared to discuss another Shillingsworth disgrace with a Poundamore, and knew he might, having long since learnt that Mark was Heather's lover. However, the pair were not on good terms just then, which was why Mark had had to go to Calaboose. Heather had refused to help him as she usually did because he wished to go to the war.

Oscar talked to Tittmuss till he asked what he thought he was going to do with the Yeller Kid, when he answered curtly, "Teach him to mind his own business for a start," and went off.

On a side veranda he stopped to look into a lounge-bar at six officers from a Japanese cruiser that lay in the harbour as the country's defence. They were drinking wine and playing dominoes, and were quite alone, because they were regarded by those they were defending as inferiors. Oscar was attracted by their child-like laughter and animation. While he watched, young Wally Shay, who worked as bar-man for his mother, thrust a head through the little serving-window, and addressing the group collectively, said, "How you gettin' along yous Charlies — all-i?"

"Thank you very mush," replied all the Charlies bowing.

Oscar turned to the garden, smiling. The moon was bursting from a mass of clouds, its light sweeping through the shadows, silvering leaves, flooding the wet and fragrant earth. With his eye on the moon he considered the Colour Question. No doubt, thought he, the Japanese despised Malays, Malays despised Papuans, Papuans despised the black Australians. It was good to be in a position to despise them all. But was it good-natured? Was it even good-sense? Was not colour-consciousness merely a form of class-consciousness, of snobbery? he demanded of the moon.

The moon, tired these million years of the arguments of men, ducked into another bank of cloud. Oscar went off for a stroll to the jetty to see the *S.S. Malagoro,* the ship that was to bear him away to the half-forgotten city of his birth. While he walked he thought about Constance, and about Lace, who he now felt sure had seduced the child, and about what he would tell the Protector next morning.

The mail-boat was bathed in the light of her loading-lamps. Her winches wheezed and clattered and clanked.

Great shadows sprawled about the jetty, shadows of masts and derricks and labouring men and moving loads. The ship was Camouflaged, and had in the bow a gun. Peaceful old *Malagoro,* whose normal business it was to lounge across deserted tropic seas disturbing flying-fish and dugongs and ghosts of long-dead buccaneers, armed for war! The world was gone mad! But how much more interesting in utter madness than in the usual semi-sanity! Was the cause of war then, Oscar wondered, simply a desire in men to stir things up?

A path of light led from the steamer's bow to the Japanese cruiser, which lay at anchor in midstream, a huge black mass against the starry southern sky, raking the Southern Cross down with her alien rigging. Shadows of war reared in a land that had lain in what Oscar, forgetful of the bloody skirmishes of pioneering-days, considered peace for all time. Many thousands of miles away as the southern crow would fly should he wish to travel to another hemisphere, the earth and heavens were being rent with violence scarce imaginable, and men were being smothered, burnt, and torn to death, while here, in spite of the machinations of murderous propagandists in a foreign land, the tide was whispering to the ancient shore, snipe were playing on the beaches, humming birds were sipping honey from the hearts of flowers. What a world it was in the hands of men! Guns in the bows of ships, the widow McLash weeping her heart out in a pillow while her Pride and Joy got drunk with strangers, ragtime and laughter in hotel bars, Jock Driver lying on his death-bed, Yeller Elbert snivelling in a cell, while the eternal Southern Cross —

"Hello Oscar!" said a voice. Oscar turned and saw the nuggety figure and smiling brown face of Chook Henn.

"Hello!" said Oscar, and looked in search of Mark.

"Heard you's up," said Chook. "George Tittmuss told me you's goin' South this boat."

"Yes. Where's Mark?"

"Out home — The Paddick — bit crook."

"Booze, eh? And I hear you're still in debt."

Chook grinned and said, "George tell you, eh?"

"Yes — he said you'd lose the lugger this time sure."

"Aw I dunno. We've nearly lost her so many times, what with shoals and sharks, I don't think we ever will. We're tryin' to get away. If we can, we're goin' to have a crack at the war. Can't, of course, till the debts are paid."

"Yes you can. The Government will fix that for you."

"Not 'less you've passed the doctor and got your papers for goin' down to a recruitin'-station. We tried it long ago. But Mark couldn't pass. That noo quack says he's got a crook heart. Bosh, aint it? This here quack's too damn strict. You know Sam Stiff? Well he's got miner's complaint he got down in the West so bad he can hardly talk. Course they wouldn't look at him here. So he went down South and got away right off and got killed. Shows what you can do if you can only get down South."

"Can't you make a break in the lugger — to Southern Cross, say?"

"Can't. Got no stores, no ammunition. And we'd want kerosene for the injin this weather. Can't go far east sailin' this time of year."

"Why not sell her and pay your debts?"

"Debts worth more than she is."

"Strewth! How much d'you owe then?"

"Better ask Mark that. He's the 'countant of the firm. What about comin' out? He'd love to see you 'fore you goes. Thinks a lot of you, you know, just quietly. We was only just talkin' about you 's afternoon. Heard you'd sold out to Burywell."

"Bit far out there tonight. Might come tomorrow."

"I'll take you round in the dinghy. Just goin' home meself. Dinghy's here at the landin'. Won't take fifteen minutes from here."

"What — all that way in a dinghy?"

"Sure — we got a outboard motor in her now. Bought it for pearlin'."

"Motor, eh? Flash, aint you, for burdened debtors?"

"Aw that's one of the blunny burdens. Aint paid for the paint on it yet."

Oscar looked at him squarely, guessing that he was not being asked to go for nothing. Chook looked away to hide his eagerness. As a matter of fact he had been rushing home to tell Mark that Oscar was in Town and to urge him to go and see him and raise a loan. Oscar was thinking of Mark as when last he saw him — Mark defying him when he attacked him on account of that £30 worth of stores. Chook broke in on his thoughts by saying softly, "We wanter go to this 'ere war awful bad. It's the chance of a life-time to Aussies. 'Sides, men's wanted terrible bad they reckon. The blunny Fritzes seem to be winnin' hands down."

Oscar bit his lip. Shadow of War had fallen even on his little brother. Perhaps Mark would go, perhaps be killed, reckless fool that he was. He looked at Chook and said, "Good-o. I'll come now."

The Paddock was a sort of reserve for people who wished to live and build houses after styles not prescribed by the Town Council and to build on ground they need not buy or rent. The houses of the district were arranged in no order, but scattered about like boxes, mostly hidden from each other by scrub. It was the home of scores of children of almost any colour one might wish to see, and of a multitude of mongrel dogs, and of a medley of weird sounds — laughter and chatter of strange people, tinkle and boom and wail of outlandish musical instruments, and, at night when yellow lights were twinkling through the scrub, squealing of flying foxes, purring of possums, dismal cry of kwiluks.

Mark's house was in the heart of The Paddock, reached from the landing on Devilfish Bay by a track that wound like a maze. It was a queer-looking hovel, built of galvanised iron and kerosene-cans and bark and saplings and bamboo, according to no definite plan, and obviously, to knowing eyes, by one of those masters of the craft of jerry-building — Chinamen. Chook led Oscar to the door and drew back to let him enter.

The door was open. Mark was lying on a broken-backed stretcher reading, clad only in ragged pyjama pants, with dirty feet hanging over the side. He was the only dirty thing in the rough but tidy little house. Oscar paused. Even at a distance he could see that Mark was ill. His unshaven face was lined and hollow, purplish white like the skin of pickled pork. Beside him on a brightly painted box stood a jar containing ponciana and laburnum blossoms, and a bottle and a dipper and a pannikin.

"What-o," said Oscar.

Mark got up gasping.

Oscar came to him and took his hand, saying, "Not well, eh?"

"Not so bad," said Mark. "Take a seat."

Oscar chose another painted box, though Chook was bringing him an upholstered chair made from a barrel. For a while he kept his eyes on the hand he had just released. It was as thin as rag and shiny with sweat. Mark was sweating profusely. Sweat streamed down his face, down his neck, through the hair of his chest; he blew drops of it from his nose. During the scrutiny he scrutinised Oscar, noting that the bald patch and grey hairs had increased. Observing Oscar's criticism at length, he smiled as though to confess that he was a wreck, and said, "They tell me you've sold out."

"No — just sold the beasts and leased the rest. I might come back if things improve."

"They all come back. Anyone't spends five years here always comes back to leave his bones. So you'll have a bit of an income?"

"Not really. Only a few bob a week. Can't get much of a price while the market's like it is. Lucky to get anything at all."

At that moment Chook clicked his tongue, and when Mark looked, tossed him the black cotton shirt he had doffed behind Oscar's back. Mark donned the shirt, and Chook a wreck of a khaki coat.

Talk went on smoothly. Norman was discussed, and Mark's finances, and his hope of going to the war. Mark confessed that he was in debt to the tune of nearly £700. Chook worked himself into a frenzy signalling him to ask Oscar for a loan. Mark kept on telling Oscar that he would get out of his difficulties somehow.

At last Oscar said he must be going, and rose. "Don't forget to look me up if you come down South," he said. "I'll be stopping with Maud for a while, I dare say. She'll put you on to me if I'm not there when you come."

They shook hands, and walked to the door together almost arm in arm, with Chook sidling ahead of them looking forlorn. At the door Oscar stopped and unbuttoned a pocket of his starched white shirt and took out a roll of notes. He handed the notes to Mark without looking at them, saying, "There you are son. Don't waste it. It's hard enough to get. Use it to go to the war. It's not a loan or a gift. It's my bit of service. So long."

For a moment Mark was overcome. He squeezed Oscar's arm and muttered inaudibly. Oscar grunted gravely and withdrew.

"Oh Chook!" Mark called as Chook and Oscar were moving off. "Half a tick." He drew back from the door to count the notes. "Fifteen," he said to Chook. "Not so bad. Here Chook, take it and buy some tucker and kero. Bust the lot. Get Oscar to do the buying so's not to arouse suspicion that we're off. He'll do it. And slip along and tell Heather that I'll drop in to see her about midnight. And while you're there get a case of whiskey off Wally. No — better get George Tittmuss to get it. Course don't say a word to Heather we're going. She'd stop us. Shake it up before the stores close. Dump the stuff at the stone landing near Fat Anna's. Joe Crowe 'll cart it and won't say nothing, seeing we don't owe him anything. Gosh boy — we're off after all!"

"When?"

"Daybreak. Better get away while this quiet spell lasts. Don't take the engine out of the dinghy. We'll want to leave here soon's you come back. I'll have everything ready."

"Good-o," said Chook, and withdrew.

§

While packing his few belongings, Mark thought with growing anger of a neighbour of his, a Chinese storekeeper named Cho See Kee, who, in his opinion, owed him money. Some months before, this Cho See Kee had employed him in a smuggling venture, sending him with the lugger to the Karrikita Reefs to pick up a case, presumably of opium, thrown overboard from a mail-boat coming in from Singapore. Mark had brought the case in badly damaged, having had his task made difficult by a heavy sea that washed the case among the rocks. He was to have received £20 for the job. Cho gave him £10, saying that half the contents had been spoilt by water. Mark had argued, bullied, threatened violence and exposure, without avail. He had been dunning Cho ever since.

Damn the old joss! he muttered as he packed. He should have taken his dues by force. What could the old dog say if he did? Nothing. Damn and blast the filthy rogue! Damn and blast his weak-kneed self for allowing a jiggering Chow to beat him!

Done packing, he poured out a stiff drink of rum and drank. Barefaced blunny robbery! He ought to have gone dunning the old cheat with a club. Ought to go to him now and snatch it. Poor weak fool to let a Chow bluff him! He drank again, more liberally. Next day he would be going off for good, going to serve his country, to help defend the likes of that filthy thieving old hound, who would go on spinning money while he himself suffered, perhaps died. To defend him and the other thieving hounds on whose account he had to steal away like a thief himself to do his honourable duty. Damn and blast and curse them all! Be a man — a whiteman — go take the money now!

He drank again, stood staring through the doorway at the night, seeing Cho See Kee among his money-bags, in which was that ten pounds. He stood for minutes, glowering, breathing hard, then muttered, "And be jees I will!"

He drank again. A few minutes later he discarded his pyjamas and donned khaki trousers and sandshoes. After some
hesitance he went out.

Cho See Kee's store lay about a hundred yards from
Mark's place. It differed only from the humpies round
about in that it was larger and had glazed windows in the
front and a Chinese trading-sign above the veranda. The
shop itself was small, or seemed so, being crammed with
merchandise. It was lit by one large oil-lamp hanging from
the roof among all manner of Chinese and European wares.
Two Chinamen were there when Mark arrived, talking with
Cho, who lounged behind the laden counter. Mark stopped
at the step of the veranda, and, unseen by those within,
stood for a while watching, then retired to a tree and lounged there waiting for the customers to go. On each side of
the doorway joss-sticks glowed in clusters, guarding the
house from evil. Soon evil tip-toed in on rubber-soled
sandshoes.

When Mark entered, Cho was sitting at a little wood-
barred desk at the end of the counter, perched on a stool
and computing on an abacus. At his elbow lay a large
brown leather bag, so well filled with silver that a heap
of coins had oozed from its gaping mouth. Mark saw
everything before he was seen, was actually standing looking through the bars when Cho became aware of him. Cho
looked up and started.

"Hello old ruggerlugs!" said Mark.

Cho did not answer, but hastily scraped the money into
the bag and tied the thongs.

"Don't put it away," said Mark. "I've come for my
tenner."

"What you want?" asked Cho, tucking the bag under his
arm and blinking.

"My ten pound, of course."

Cho said mildly, "Go way."

"Not without my money."

"Go way."

"Not without my cash, I said. I've come to get it. And
by jees I will. S'pose you no-more pay up tonight, old joss-
face, I'll kick your blunny guts in and smashim up your
shop and makim big-feller fire. No-more gammon. I'm in
dead earnest. Had just enough of you, you blunny lousy
old cheat you. Now come on, gimme my ten pound before
I make roast piggee-pig of you."

"Go way."

Mark exhaled heavily. Cho sat like a wooden god. But Mark was not discouraged. He had seen enough of Chinamen in his time to believe that one might easily be quaking with fear for all his apparent calmness, not because able to control his features, but because he did not express emotion with them in the way a European does. "Carm on!" he snapped. "You owe me money. Pay up."

"Carn do it," said Cho.

"You got fifty pound in that bag if you got a deener. I want ten of it. It's mine. Now come on Cho, or I'll makim big-feller trouble. Fair dinkum."

"Go way."

"No-more humbug. I'm proper wild tonight."

"Hi callim pleeceeman Mist Chilnsik."

"You would! And what wouldn't I tell pleeceeman about your opium and your smuggling halfcaste girls to Java!"

"Go way."

"Will you pay up my ten pound?"

"Carn do."

"Then by jees I'll take it," snapped Mark; and with that he stepped to the right and vaulted the counter.

"Hey!" shouted Cho. "Whaffor?"

"Shut your trap and give me my money."

"No-more no-more no-more!" cried Cho, hugging the bag.

"Give it to me or I'll belt heck out of you," hissed Mark, grabbing.

Cho heaved the bag up to his chest. Mark caught hold of an empty corner of it, and tugged, hissing angrily. He dragged him off the stool; and when Cho, through tugging desperately, fell on his back, he fell on top of him. Cho yelled and seized Mark's ear, forcing him to fight desperately to get free, when he had been on the point of giving up the struggle. Mark let go the bag and seized the wrist of the hand that was screwing off his ear, and twisted it till it cracked. Cho let the bag fall. Mark snatched it up, rose, blundered over the fallen stool, fell heavily. Cho leapt up and pounced on him. Mark shook himself free, lifted the bag to arm's height, and brought it down with all his strength on Cho's bald head. Cho grunted and collapsed.

Mark stood swaying. He saw Cho shudder, saw a trickle of blood leave the corner of his gaping mouth. Then he heard a sound behind, turned, saw a pantalooned Chinese woman, Cho See's wife, and the curtain leading to the dwelling flapping behind her. She had been asleep, was not

yet properly awake. She gaped at Mark. Then her eyes
dropped to her husband, out of whose mouth, unseen by
Mark, the blood was now gushing. Then her eyes, popping
like black cherries, flew back to Mark. Slowly her mouth
opened. Mark rushed at her, struck with the bag a glancing
blow above the ear, and felled her.

For a moment he stood over the woman, saw that she
was senseless, then glanced at Cho, but did not see how
bad it was with him. Then he looked at the money-bag,
then at the door, then, still with the bag, vaulted the counter
and ran out. In the scrub not far from the store he collided with an aged Chinaman and sent him flying. He did not
stop till he got home, where he found Chook sitting on
the bed.

"Wha's up?" murmured Chook, staring.

Mark was pumping for his breath.

"What you done?" murmured Chook, rising, staring at
the bag.

"Robbed — Cho — See — Kee."

"Gawdstrewth!"

"And — knocked him — Quick — let's do — a bunk!"

IN THE MIDST OF LIFE WE ARE IN DEATH

To say that the citizens of Port Zodiac were delighted with
the bloodshed would be true but perhaps unfair, since like
folk of any Anglo-Saxon community they preferred to appear doleful in the presence of human death, to say of it
How Sad! when they meant How Interesting!

The pity of it was that the murder of Cho See Kee happened on top of the assassination of Jock Driver, so that
the citizens had gone to bed with the pleasure of one and
risen to that of the other, which meant that both must be
enjoyed together — a waste, since such excitement was not
so common there that citizens would wish to heap it. As it
was, they were unable to discuss the details severally as
they would have done had murder not become thus wholesale. They were overwhelmed, could only say, "Gosh —
what's the old joint coming to!"

So it happened that Jock Driver, over whom a crowd
would have set a death-watch, whose every failing pulse

would have been noted by the doctor and police, whose death-rattle would have crashed like thunder in the ears of Town, died alone. For at the time of his death the nursing-staff were taking morning tea, half the police-force were watching the doctor do an autopsy on the corpse of Cho See Kee, the other half were out searching for Mark and Chook; and Jock's friends, being friends of Mark's and Chook's and better friends, because, after all, poor Jock was only a Pommy, were far more interested in the business of the living.

Poor Jock! That meaty mouth would curse no more, stuffed as it was now with cotton-wool and cramped with bandages. His big blue eyes were obliterated, sturdy limbs lashed here and there, hands folded in a pious attitude, the whole of his British Bulldog Being hidden forever in a shroud. Thus in a canvas stretcher, in which he sagged pitifully and looked so weak and small, he went to the mortuary, borne by native orderlies who jiggled him about and made game of him.

When the mortuary was reached, a hitch occurred in Jock's ordered movements as a corpse. The place, built to meet the requirements of normal times, was fitted with but one table, which was occupied by Cho See Kee. The orderlies, only too well aware of the niceties of the colour-conscious system that prevailed, debated, then sent one of their number to ask the matron what should be done. The matron said that Cho must give precedence. He was laid on the concrete floor.

Later in the day, when the Coroner came to look at Jock, so many officials and witnesses and morbids accompanied him that, since the mortuary measured only ten by twelve and it was unconventional to stand on the body of even a dead Chinaman, Cho had to be moved again. He was taken to a whitewashed iron shed called the Asiatic Ward and placed on the bed of a compatriot who was at the moment absent.

When the Coroner had done with Jock, Joe Crowe, who had been hovering about the hospital for hours, fell upon him and measured him for his last raiment. That night when people passed Joe's house in Murphy Street they heard the merry tap-tap-tapping in the shed behind, and said to each other gravely, "That's for Jock." Later, had they paused and sniffed while passing, they might have caught among the scents of flowers and sodden grass and earth the smell of the varnish with which Joe converted simple pine into expensive rosewood, and later still, by listening intently,

might have heard the whisper of shears as he cut silver
emblems from kerosene-cans. Joe Crowe did not believe
in wasting good material on the dead, though it was for
that he charged.

Jock's funeral was arranged for the morning of the day
after his demise. For that reason half the white population
wore white coats and black ties at breakfast. But as though
the heavens were mourning him, seven inches of rain fell
that day, in one long roaring shower. Therefore Jock lay
in the mortuary, peeped at by the native orderlies and the
lubras that worked in the laundry and yard, and coveted by
ants that could not pass the doctored vaseline with which the
table-legs were smeared.

The grief of the heavens was overdone. Next day was
worse. During the morning the rain roared down at the
rate of an inch an hour. The man at the Post Office who
gauged the rain did so with a bucket. But since it was desired that Jock should be buried with respect, as he could
not be if followed to his grave by flies, delay could go no
further. Joe Crowe sent word around that the funeral would
start at noon.

Only a quarter of the white population attended, and
that clad in khaki and oil-skins. Cars and covered buggies
and Joe Crowe's cab gathered in the hospital grounds. On
the veranda, watching not with indecent frankness but from
behind the creepered lattice, were the white patients and
the staff. Watching from the kitchen, all-seeing but unseen,
were the orderlies and the halfcaste maids and the cook,
who was a Greek. The hearse had not yet come.

All eyes were fixed on the mortuary. The mourners all
looked mournful. Some whispered. Some smoked, though
rather guiltily, like schoolboys behind a fence. Mrs Shay
and Heather were the only women present. The nurses
whispered about them, saying that women's attendance at
funerals was Not the Thing. But Mrs Shay and Heather
lived rather more like men than women. They knew every
whiteman in the country, how much he was worth, how
much liquor he could hold without bringing discredit on
themselves, how much he could pay for; and they knew
every swear-word in the dialect, and often used them. Indeed Mrs Shay was one of the few people in the world
who would be poorer for the death of Jock; for while he
had paid his household bills before winding up the business
of his station, he had left his large liquor bill for settling
with expense he had intended to incur during his last brief
stay in Town. She had throttled down the chagrin the loss

had caused her, observant of conventions, leaving it until decay had robbed the debtor of the right to the respect that must be given those that are Lying Dead.

Heather was not thinking of the dead, but of the incorrigible living, of him whom she had striven hard, not with tears and common female wiles but with comradely devotion, to save from his worst enemy, himself. She had helped him out of countless tangles, weaned him off the drink, wheedled him into loving her unselfishly and hence into coming almost to know himself. He had always backslid. Lately she had let him go, wanting him to lose those curses of his life, the *Spirit of the Land* and vile spaniel Chook. He had been begging her to let him go to war. The fool! As though she had done all she had, to lose him altogether. Better perhaps if she had let him go, as things had happened. For then he might have come back, someday. Now he was lost to her as utterly as Jock was to the world. Dear Mark, dear laughing handsome dirty boy. A murderer, a fugitive for ever!

Above the roar of rain the mourners heard the sound of wheels, and turned with one accord and stared to right. Soon into view a shaggy horse trudged, hauling a vehicle that was just a box on wheels, a black box shaped like a coffin and little bigger, with large unglazed portholes in the sides. Joe Crowe was perched in the driving-seat, clad in oil-skins and sou'-wester, crouched in the rain, clutching two iron buckets. The hearse rolled past the Lazaret, crashed over a roaring drain, barked a pawpaw tree with the hub of a wheel, stopped when a clothes-line of the laundry hurled Joe flat.

Joe got down and backed the hearse to the mortuary door, then climbed up and got the buckets. Pall-bearers left their vehicle and came splashing, bringing glass-covered artificial wreaths, and followed Joe into the mortuary, to stand behind him while he drew from his coat a brace and bit and bored eight holes in the coffin-lid. Joe bored with care, so as not to betray the fact that rosewood might produce white shavings and not to bore eight holes in that which lay beneath.

The cortege set out, wound mournfully through the sheeting rain down the Mailunga Road. The gates of the Cemetery were open. The grave was open too, sheltered by a huge tarpaulin sheet to which the mourners rushed, stumbling apologetically over other graves, blasphemously over ruts and gutters. A clay ridge built about the grave to stem the flood had given way, so that the grave was brimming. Joe Crowe brought a shovel and a coil of rope from the tool-shed, and under the gaze of solemn eyes set to work to repair the ridge. Then he took up one of the buckets; and one of the mourners took the other; and they set to work to bail the grave. All the male mourners took a hand either at bailing or repairing the ridge or dragging back the sheet when it tried to blow away or restraining the hearse-horse when it tried to wander; all, that is, except the Rev. Gordon Prayter, who, being the officiating clergyman, perhaps could not be called exactly male or mourner; he just watched.

Joe's pipe slipped from his belt and fell into the grave. Work was stopped while he solemnly dipped for it. Still the rain roared down. For every bucketful of water bailed a half poured in. Still the solemn ones worked on, not daring to stop till the water was reduced below the level of the eye, lest the burial should look indecently like a drowning. Joe called a halt when the water was down three feet. When the coffin was lifted from the hearse three blow-flies shot out of the holes in the lid and dashed off guiltily.

Mr Prayter's work began. With sou'-wester under arm, and oil-skin open so that God might see the stole and know that there was no deception, he chanted from a prayer-book in a tone exactly like that of a blackfellow devil-dovvening:

"I knawt my redeem livtan ateel stan ladday pon yearth — tutairk unnerself sawlvar dear brothah heah deported, we tharfore committees bardy tuther groon, earth tearth, ash tash, dusser duss, in shore unsartin hawper razraction tarnal laif awmen."

He stopped and took up a handful of mullock. The stones clattered on the coffin; the mud remained in his hand. He put away his book, wiped his fingers on his streaming coat, then turned away with most of the other mourners. Only the workers and the indecently curious could stay to see the sinking of the stone-weighted coffin, to hear the hiss and gurgle of the bubbles rushing from the vents. The others went back to the carriages, back to Town, to dry clothes and the shelter of bars and houses and liquor in which to drown the sorrows they had never felt, quite at a loss to know which was the worst offence, frank indifference or pretence.

About an hour after the burial of Jock, a cockeye bob roared out of the north and tore the front veranda from the First and Last, blew two Chinese children right across

Killarney Street from their father's doorstep to that of a Greek who had lately tried to take their father's life, wrecked one of the mail-boat's derricks, blew a few trees down, and was gone, taking the rain-clouds with it. The sun blazed down as bright and hot as vaporizing silver. As though Heaven's grief were like the grief of Man — an hour or two of weeping, then back to laughter and the workaday.

§

That afternoon the mail-boat sailed, bearing away the bright-eyed Shillingsworth children and their brooding guardian. Oscar had looked forward to departure, anticipating much. But it was spoilt by the monstrous calamity of Mark.

The police had talked freely about the murder of Cho See Kee as soon as it had come to their knowledge. They were as keen gossips as any in the town. Thus Oscar had learnt that no-one had seen the *Spirit of the Land* depart. He was a witness at the inquest. He gave his evidence with lips that trembled because they did not honour the oath he had declared. He said that he had met his brother at nine o'clock that night by arrangement made a couple of weeks before. He knew his brother contemplated flying from his creditors. In fact he had himself advised him to do that, and was not ashamed to say so, since even if a few Chinese would suffer by his flight, his country and the Allies would gain. The Coroner commended him for his patriotism, and told the Court that he himself would gladly go to war but for his — er — responsibilities. Oscar was heartened then to lie with strength. He went on to say that he had gone aboard the lugger, which had lain in Devilfish Bay, with Mark and Henn, and then at half-past ten or thereabout had come back to Town with the latter, as a dozen witnesses could prove, to make certain purchases. His brother had stayed behind preparing the vessel for the voyage, which was to be made on the tide in order that advantage might be taken of the weather. He had himself returned to the stone landing in Joe Crowe's cab. Henn went out to the lugger in the dinghy and brought Mark back. His brother could not have left the lugger during their absence unless he had swum. Unfortunately the cabman had not stayed long enough to see Mark come. Mark came merely to say Goodbye. He himself stayed on the landing till he saw the lights of the lugger pass out of sight.

No-one but Oscar had seen the lugger depart. However, several residents of the shores of Devilfish Bay testified to having heard the engine of the dinghy at about the time Oscar said it was running to and from the lugger. Oscar explained why Mark could not buy the stores for himself, and said that though he was deep in debt he had no need of money, since he (Oscar) had given him a hundred pounds. Heather swore that she had spoken to Mark at eleven o'clock for a minute or two near the stone landing. In fact she was broken-hearted because he had not come near her at all.

Thus in spite of the damning evidence given by Mrs Cho See Kee, and that of her father, Ching Ling Soo, who said that Mark collided with him in the scrub at about eleven o'clock, the Coroner had adjourned the inquest pending receipt of news of Mark's arrival at Southern Cross Island, and had told the police that they had been too hasty in gathering their bit of evidence, and ordered them to go find more. But whatever the Coroner's opinion, Mark had little to fear. Of the two or three vessels that could be used to pursue him, none was more fast nor more seaworthy than his own; and the routes he might take were countless.

Although Oscar was the only person to give much evidence in Mark's favour, he was one of the few who after the inquest had no doubt about his guilt. However, he regarded him not as a cold-blooded miscreant, but as an unfortunate fool who had allowed a rogue to make an assassin of him, the rogue being Cho See Kee. He had never felt more love for Mark before. At Southern Cross Island he received a telegram from his sister Maud, to whom he had telegraphed, but without mentioning the calamity, before he sailed. Maud knew of it. She had seen a meagre report of it in a newspaper in Batman. She asked him to telegraph details to a post-office address, warning him that she wished to keep it secret from her husband and children.

The calamity also marred the joy of homecoming that Oscar had anticipated. Maud, distraught with feelings like his own and absurd fears that the hideous thing might ruin her respectable family, met him at the train on which he travelled down from Flinders, took a fearful affectionate grip on him, and kept it on him for days, allowing him in her private presence to think and talk of nothing else but Mark. Maud, bright little sister of boyhood days, had become a sort of milch cow, mother of five blaring calves. Oscar found it difficult to regard her with love, and was heartily thankful for having introduced Norman as the son of Mark's high-caste Javanese wife, since it saved him from suffering more tears and talk of the folly of their little brother. He told her that Mark had only lately brought the boy to Capricornia and confessed that he was married. She never doubted. And he told her and Ambrose, her husband, that Mark's wife was dead, and that he had adopted Norman because Mark could not take proper care of him while working at his pearling and because he did not wish to see him brought up as a heathen by his princely Javan grandfather. He told Ambrose that Mark had gone to the war. Later on he said that he feared Mark had been killed, since he had not heard from him for a long while. At first it worried him greatly to have to lie to such an extent. Soon, however, coming to despise Maud and Ambrose, he found it easy, even amusing; and at length he saw it as a duty; for Ambrose, who was a Government draftsman, said he believed that Norman had in him the makings of a draftsman and proceeded to cultivate them, which, as Oscar could plainly see, he would not have done had he known that the boy was the son of a murderer and a blackgin. Norman himself, and Marigold too, learnt his history from Oscar's lies.

A CROCODILE CRIES

WHEN Mark failed to show up at any of the places to which he would have gone had his going been as innocent as his brother had said, the Coroner declared that Cho See Kee had been wilfully murdered by Mark Anthony Shillingsworth, and ordered the man's arrest.

A search-party was organised, but with difficulty, because few policemen could be spared from regular duty at a time when half the force was at the war, and few citizens cared to debase themselves by acting as policemen. The party set out. Nothing was heard of it for about three months, when a second party went out to find it. The second party was easily organised and fully manned, since the task in hand was only that of tracking down the contemptible mantrackers. The first was found at Flying Fox, camped with lubras. Neither party had seen the *Spirit of the Land* nor heard of it; and both were of the opinion that no-one within a thousand miles of Port Zodiac ever would again. The Government, already thinking that too much money had been spent on account of a Chinaman, gave up searching actively and contented itself with sending descriptions of the lugger and Mark and Chook to the few places on the Silver Sea where there were policemen. The Kai Yoh Tang, the Chinese Society to which Cho See Kee had belonged, offered £100 for Mark's arrest; but that was not inducement enough to make a self-respecting law-despising Capricornian take the trouble to look for the wanted men under his bed. Mark had little to fear from the law.

§

While this futile business was in the initial stage, the case of Yeller Elbert was being tried. He was brought before the Criminal Court within three weeks of committing his crime. The charge was Felonious Slaying, commuted from the one of Murder for the convenience of the law. The penalty for murder in Capricornia was death. But no jury of Capricornians could ever be brought to seal the doom of a person with whom they must be acquainted if not actually friendly. And even were it possible to secure a conviction, there was no means of exacting the penalty. There was a gallows at the Calaboose; but there was no-one to operate it. Juries had been known occasionally to declare convictions in murder trials in which the principal was a coloured man; but the Sheriff, whose duty it was to carry out the executions, had always resigned his office before he could be made to perform it. The gallows at Red Turtle Bay had been used but once, when the hangman was imported. The determination to satisfy the law on that occasion cost the Judge and Resident Commissioner who engineered the hanging their billets. Moreover, the satisfaction was very costly. In addition to fees and travelling-expenses, the hangman secured compensation from the Government for the rough handling he got from indignant citizens. It was impossible for Jack Ketch to move anonymously in Capricornia.

However, the Law of the Land kept up the pretence, and perhaps even the belief, that it could hang murderers if moved to do so. At any rate, it always put the fear of execution into every person arrested for murder by first charging him as a murderer.

Yeller Elbert's Judge was offended by the fact that the prisoner possessed no surname, and ordered a search of his history to be made in order to find him one. It was suggested that his father was Trooper McMerder, late of Bannidillu, on the McHaggis River, a settlement about nine hundred miles from Port Zodiac. The only ground of this suggestion appeared to be the fact that Elbert's mother, who was the wife of one of McMerder's native trackers, had acquired the nickname of Mrs McMerder. The trooper was now stationed in Port Zodiac. He stoutly denied the suggestion.

Elbert was born in a native camp on the McHaggis River, where he lived as a native till he was about eight, when he was given employment by Billy Boyle, the Bannidillu store-keeper. He worked for Boyle as a sort of slave till aged about fourteen, when he was transferred to Arthur Grunter, the district mail-man. His association with Grunter was not happy. He complained that the man had starved him and had beaten him almost daily. Grunter happened to be in Town. He came forward and said that Elbert was a liar; he admitted that he had flogged him a few times, but declared that it had always been for the fellow's own good; and he had fed him according to the amount of work he did, which was never very much.

The rest of Elbert's history was known to the police. According to his own statement, at about the age of seventeen, as the result of having been flogged by Grunter with a hobble-chain (Grunter denied having flogged him, saying that he had merely thrown the chain at him a few times to punish him for having put a stick of niki-niki in his tea), he crept on him one night and battered him with a nullah-nullah, leaving him for dead. Grunter recovered and went for the police. Elbert was found near the scene of his crime, crippled with beri-beri, the result of malnutrition. He was taken to Port Zodiac and convicted on a charge of Attempted Murder and sent to the Calaboose for two years. He was released after six months through the efforts of a missionary who had argued that he was under prison age. Subsequently he went to the Melisande River. Trouble seemed to travel with him. There he quarrelled with Jock Driver over a halfcaste girl, his so-called wife, whom he had lent to Driver. He said that Driver had failed not only to pay him the promised fee but to return the girl upon demand. So he had taken her away by stealth. Driver tracked him down, thrashed him, and took the girl back and kept her till he stole her again. The second time Elbert sent the girl off with a party of natives who could hide their tracks, and himself took the road to Copper Creek. Subsequently he met Driver in many places and was always thrashed or in some way harassed. The trooper stationed on the Melisande, who was one of those who arrested Elbert at the Caroline, said that he had once arrested him in his own district for attempting to shoot Jock Driver. Being unable to bring him up to Town because the river was in flood at the time, he had given him a good hiding and sent him bush.

No surname was found for all this probing. The one of McMerder was out of the question, since the adoption of it would bring ridicule on the officers of the law. Still the Judge would not let the matter pass. He said he did not mind trying a nameless prisoner if he were an Aboriginal, but strongly objected to trying a nameless man who was possessed of the State Franchise, and would not regard him as an Aboriginal as both Prosecution and Defence suggested.

The Judge was in one of his argumentative moods. Counsel (Defence was employed by the Aborigines Department) muttered behind hands. The Prosecutor at length made bold to suggest that since Elbert was likely to go to jail he would very soon lose the Franchise for a good while, so why not assume that he did not possess it and treat him as Aboriginal? The Judge talked at length about the Law of the Land, which was so constituted that an accused person was considered innocent till proved guilty, no matter what hopes a State Prosecutor might have of securing conviction; then he scolded the Prosecutor for having split an infinitive and fused a participle, and talked at length about English Usage. The Prosecutor shrank. Then Defence suggested that perhaps the prisoner knew nothing about the Franchise, in which case, seeing that he was aged about twenty-four, he could be considered *non compos mentis,* which would turn the case into one of *ne plus ultra.*

The Judge seemed impressed. He turned to the Prisoner and said, "Prisoner at the bar — do you know what the Franchise is?"

Elbert gaped.

"Franchise," said the Judge. "The State Franchise —"

"Yeah," said Elbert, brightening suddenly. "Me savvy, Boss."

"Well, what is it?"

"Belong him Missus McLash boy — him go longa war — Franchish McLash."

All laughed heartily except the Judge, who frowned.

At length the Judge asked, "Are you on the Electoral Roll?"

"No-more," said Elbert readily.

"You savvy that, then?"

"Aw yeah."

"Well — what is it?"

Elbert pointed to the chandelier that hung from the roof, and said, "Makim light. Big-fella injin — tuff! tuff! tuff! — belongim Mister McCamfrage, for makim lectral light."

Laughter and more frowns.

After some more argument in which the Judge took keener and keener pleasure as he observed the increasing anger of Counsel, it was decided that the prisoner should be called Elbert Smith. Under that name he faced his trial.

Prosecution with one intent talked at great length about Prisoner's history. Defence did the same with another intent. Judge in his address said that perhaps Prisoner was something of a blackguard, but certainly one no worse than those who had reared and ill-treated him; no doubt he had committed with malice aforethought the crime upon which he was arraigned, which was what was required to be proved or disproved; the fact that he had been moved to commit it through an accidental occurrence was subordinate; but what amazed himself was the fact that, considering the provocation to slay he had suffered from his infancy, he should be arraigned on such a charge so late in life.

Jury retired, to return before long with a verdict of Guilty, tempered with a strong recommendation for mercy on account of the provocation. Judge, after saying that Prisoner would be better off in jail than out, sentenced him to five years' imprisonment in the Native Division, which was the sentence he had decided on after reading the details of the Coroner's inquest in the TRUE COMMONWEALTH. No-one knew he read newspapers but himself. Indeed he pretended he never knew what was going on outside his head.

§

The Rev. Gordon Prayter soon had another ceremony to perform, one he would have described as Happier. It was a wedding, the wedding of Constance Differ to Peter Pan.

This took place two weeks after the conclusion of Elbert's trial, for the results of which the Protector had waited before he would give Humbolt Lace permission to transfer Constance's affections to Peter. Not that the Protector cared a hoot whom Constance married; but he did not wish to have his neat records spoilt by unnecessary alteration.

Had Elbert been acquitted, as the Protector had half expected he would be, it was Elbert and no-one else who should have married Constance, since that was the arrangement made by Lace six weeks before. Oscar had forgotten to report what he had suspected, the troubles of Constance having been clean swept from his mind by the Calamity. So the Devil looks after his own.

Thus it happened that one day Mr Prayter, all unwittingly an instrument for carrying out his Enemy's designs, had cause the other passengers just melted away, not rudely, not because the Aborigines Department had reserved a car for him, nor because he shunned common company, but because to board the Copper Creek train. H travelled alone, quite gently indeed, so that by the time the train drew up at the Two-Mile he was surprised to find that he had the whole grimy coach to himself. He was too new to the country to understand that the height of incongruity, there, was a cleric riding on the Copper Creek train. Consequently he was a little hurt.

Lace was waiting at Red Coffin Ridge. Brilliant Lace decked out for the solemnization in bright blue shirt and spotless yellow corduroys and bright tan elastic-sides and velour wideawake. Mr Prayter leant from a window as the train drew in, and waved. He also had the opportunity to wave as the train ran past; for the guard had forgotten him and therefore had not heeded the engine's whistling for brakes.

Mr Prayter's coach stopped at a point about two hundred yards beyond the siding. He saw the engineer lean out and look back and the guard lean out and look forward. They waved to each other. The guard put fingers to his nose. Then all the passengers looked out. Silence reigned for a minute, spell of sweet peace after the din of travelling. Then a voice shouted, "Hey there — shake it up!"

Prayter turned from contemplating the singing bush, saw the guard standing on the caboose steps and waving. "Aint you gettin' off here?" the guard shouted.

Prayter blinked, looked past the guard at the distant figure of Lace, then back to the guard, and answered with a laugh, "Aren't you going to take me back?"

"No time."

"But it's too far — must be a quarter of a mile — and I've a portmanteau to carry."

Heads turned from guard to parson as each spoke.

"Garn!" shouted the guard. "Taint ten chain. Lace's got

niggers back there with him. Leave your gear side of the road."

Prayter stared for a moment, then muttered "Bother!" and withdrew his head. He alighted with his portmanteau. The train began to move at once. As the next coach passed him, Prayter said with a smile to the faces looking down, "Rilly — this train's a joke, isn't it!"

A wag yelled, "Yes — a smutty one!"

With raucous laughter in his ears, the parson turned and looked for Lace, feeling rather lonely.

Lace and Prayter were old friends. Prayter it was who had wedded Lace to his lawful spouse. They greeted each other warmly. Prayter pinched the other's arm and said he looked well, then drew a deep breath and added, "As you surely ought up heah in this bracing claimate." As though himself, come jaded from the Metropolis where three thousand people jostled in a mere three or four square miles surrounded by the wilderness, were feeling the tonic effects of the clean air of this settlement of but one white inhabitant. Lace answered that indeed he was not feeling very bright, that he thought he could do with a holiday. Prayter looked at the bright red ridge after which the place was named, and across the verdant wilderness and violet hills and vales, across the wastes of experimental station where experiment was paid for still but done no more, and murmured, "Yes? — a holiday? — well well!"

Lace went back to get a parcel that was tossed out by the guard when he believed his train was an express. It was a parcel from a Chinese store, containing one calico print dress, one woman's straw hat, one tobacco pipe, one pound of niki-niki, one khaki shirt, one pair of khaki pants, and one wedding-ring, all of quality in accordance with the stipulation Lace had made in ordering, Suitable for Aborigines. Lace would not have been so mean had he not known that generosity would have been wasted on the bridegroom.

On the way to the homestead Lace described the bride and groom, and told how he had made arrangements for their future. Prayter beamed. He said that he had heard that Peter Pan was something of a myall. Lace said that Peter was not half so bad as people said, and certainly not a trouble-monger like that Yeller Elbert. He said he was thankful to Providence that Elbert's trouble had occurred before it could affect Constance. That was a lie. He still regarded Elbert's trouble as an act of Providence to spite his sinful self. Mean Providence to choose poor Elbert for the scapegoat! But it was the sort of talk that pleased the parson, who said that halfcastes would be happier if other people thought the same.

Near the homestead they came upon Peter sitting on the shaft of a jinker, crooning a corroboree song and gazing so intently at the coffin-like ridge that he did not see them.

"What does he see there?" asked Prayter, beaming.

Lace smiled, privately thinking that Peter could not see past his nose. He said a little brusquely, "Peter!"

Peter turned. He was tall and thin, sharp-featured and tight-lipped in spite of his fleshy-faced inheritance. But as though to compensate for so much unmerited rise above the ragtag of Humanity, his skin was darker than the average halfcaste's, and one of his eyes was wally, a condition common among the natives of the land. He certainly did not look attractive. He would have looked worse, however, had he been seen as he was upon arrival at the Station a day or two before, clad in a filthy naga and a shirt that once had been a sugar-bag. Just then he wore a brand-new singlet and khaki trousers; and he was washed and clipped and shaved.

"Well Peter," said Prayter, holding out a hand and beaming. "How are you?"

Peter stared at the hand, never having in his thirty years or so of life seen such a pretty one nor had a whiteman offer to shake with him.

"Come on man," said Prayter.

Peter eyed him suspiciously and asked, "Wha' name?"

"Shake hands," said Prayter, and to save further embarrassment he reached and took the hand. Peter was afraid to desist; but he snatched his hand away as soon as it was freed.

Still beaming, Prayter spoke about the Happy Event, but failed to rouse enthusiasm in Peter, who either stared blankly, gaping, or watched his chocolate-coloured toes digging in the steaming earth. At length Prayter patted his shoulder, and left him, saying with a kindly smile, "You mustn't be afraid, my boy. You're as good a man as any. Get that into your silly noddle. Be a man — like Mister Lace — like me — like anyone you fancy!"

"A pity," he continued as they walked towards the house, "that a grown man should be like that. Tcht! Tcht! Not even like a blackfellow — like a blackfellow's dog!"

"It's only because he's shy of you," said Lace. "I've studied him. There's good in him. With a good wife and independence he'll do well, I'm sure. I'll keep my eye on him."

"But I understood the Protector to say you'd be going back to the office soon?"

"Yes," said Lace. "But I can watch him from Town. I'll keep at the Protector about him. Must for Conny's sake. She's a really fine kid, considering the way she was reared."

Prayter looked at him and said, "Humbolt, you're splendid!"

Lace stumbled on the stairs.

Up on the wide latticed-in veranda Lace excused himself and went downstairs again. Prayter deposited his topee on a chair and produced the marriage-papers and a prayer-book, then took out a handkerchief and mopped his streaming face and neck, and ran a hand up the back of his soaked white tunic.

"Ah!" he murmured. "Exhilarating — very!" Still mopping, he went to an open louvre and looked out across the miles of paddocks where the cotton used to grow, where now tall grass grew, green as emerald, still as stone, so high that no trace of the fences could be seen. He sniffed the thick hot scent of it, and looked across a forest to the Caroline River Hills, which stood before him variegated, violet where the sun shone, black under clouds, silver where rain was falling. In the east a pillar of cloud reared from horizon to zenith, with a kind of arm outstretched like a threatening colossus. "Wonderful!" he breathed, and blinked a tear distilled by deep emotion. "Wonderful — God is good!"

Lace returned and said, "A reviver Mister Prayter? Whiskey — or a drop of wine? Sorry we got no ice out here in the wilds. But it's cool enough. I keep it down the well."

"With the frogs?" said Prayter, smiling. "Good idea! But — er — one usually associates the cup that cheers with creatures less benign — snakes, eh? — alligators — Ha! Ha! Ha! Thanks offly — a little waine. My word man — what a gorgeous view you have!"

They went downstairs to see Constance in the kitchen. Now she was living in the hut again. Prayter shook hands and beamed and said all that which Peter would not hear about the Happy Event. He was very merry, a veritable Old King Cole. She loved him, giggled all the while. Back on the veranda he said to Lace gravely, " I do believe that poor child's in the family way."

Lace, tracing the pattern of the matting with his boot, husked, and murmured, "Yes — I think so."

Prayter uttered sounds of disapproval, said, "Is it Peter — or that Elbert?"

Lace husked again. His face was burning, his eyes filled with shame. But Prayter, innocent fellow, though he saw the signs, did not understand them. He thought that Lace was foolishly embarrassed by the subject. People were rarely ever frank about distasteful matters in his presence, often to his annoyance.

"It's hard to say," muttered Lace at length. "Halfcastes are hard to understand."

Prayter turned the statement over, absently trying to get the meaning of it. He was well used to doing that. People usually talked such nonsense to him. At length he said, "But rilly, if it was Elbert — er — what does Peter think?"

Lace forced himself to look up, his conscience urging that the parson must suspect him if he could not meet his eye. For one horrible second he obeyed. He felt sure that he had betrayed himself. He cursed himself for not having shown Constance in the darkness of her hut. Oh cursed delay of his plans! How it had made him suffer! He saw the accusation in the parson's eye, heard his wife's hard voice accusing, even thought of flight to a recruiting-station and the war. All in one horrible second. Then fear dragged down his eyes. He muttered, "It — it mighter been Peter. He — he's been hanging round a lot — before — Elbert."

He waited bowed for the denunciation. Prayter said mildly, "Well well. I dare say it's all raight. It's a mercy, anyway, that's she getting married. Splendid of you to do what you have, Humbolt — splendid!"

Lace sighed quietly. When the house stopped spinning he went off to see about the lunch.

Lunch was a well-cooked dainty meal of goat-flesh and pumpkin and beet-root and sweet potatoes, the work of Constance's hands. Mr Prayter was a thorough-going cleric in the way of eating. He ate till there was nothing left. Peter and Constance ate similar food in rougher style in the kitchen, sitting silent at the ends of a long table, dressed in their factory-stinking wedding clothes.

At half past two the second witness came. He was Jacob Ledder of Black Adder Creek, one of Tim O'Cannon's fettlers. Tim himself, though unfriendly with Lace, had offered his services. They were rejected. Lace considered Tim objectionable under any circumstances, combo and coarse fellow that he always was, and insulting Sooler, and foul-mouthed bitter rival in the cotton-planting days, and especially objectionable under circumstances that could not stand the probing of such a notorious busybody and champion of halfcastes as he was. The rejection caused Tim great annoyance, not so much because he had been slighted by a man he despised and nowadays avoided, as because, knowing both bride and groom, he was of opinion that the wedding was a very bad job; and it was his habit to think that bad jobs could be made better by his interference. He had known all along that Constance was at the Station, but had never feared for her safety there, because, like most other people of the neighbourhood, he knew from having questioned natives that Lace was not a combo, and believed that he was not likely to become one while yet a newlywed. He had learnt only a few days before that this wedding was about to take place. Lace himself had told him, saying that previously Peter had taken Constance off into the bush and that he had gone after them and brought them back. That sounded reasonable to him, since he knew that Peter had been living in the district for the past two or three weeks, while knowing nothing of Lace's intentions regarding Elbert. He sent over a wedding present of a parcel of household accessories robbed from his own kitchen.

Soon after Jake Ledder's arrival the ceremony took place. It was conducted under the house near the little cane-screened room. Only one hitch occurred, and that when Peter refused to say *I Will*. When Prayter gently urged him he became angry, turned his one black eye on the kindly man, and with body tense and stringy chocolate hands clenched tightly and thrust down stiffly by his sides, demanded, "What's blunny matter all-time humbug? Me no savvy."

Prayter smiled, closed his book on the ring, and said gently, "Now when I ask you — er — that is to say — time me-fellow talk 'Wilt thou take this woman to be thy lawful wedded waife, to live togethah after Gard's ordinance in the hawly state of matrimony?', that mean all-same 'You wantim this one girl for belong you properly Government waife for look out him good for keeps?' — see? All raight. Then you talk back 'I will' — all-same 'Good-o'. Quaite simple. Now —"

Peter uttered an obscene word. Fear was the cause of his anger, fear engendered by frequent mention of that awful concern the Government. Had he done wrong to agree to marry Constance for what Lace had promised to give? he was wondering.

"Now now!" said Prayter rather sternly. "Bad talk no good here."

"What name?" demanded Peter. "Mist Leash bin talk before 'Spose you marryim dis one gal I give you —' "

Lace paled. Prayter saved him by saying, "Yes, yes, yes. We know all that. But listen —"

"Woffor all-time talk — talk — talk?" demanded Peter. " 'You wantim dis one gal, you wantim dis one gal, you wantim waife, guvmin, guvmin, guvmin' — woffor? Me no-more bad man. Me no-more Yeller Elbert. Guvmin no want for catchim me. Course I want dat one gal. Me bin talk longa Mist Leash all-same — aint it?" he asked of Lace.

Lace tried with all his might to join the smiling of the parson and Jake.

At length the ceremony was performed. The couple were congratulated by the witnesses and their uniter, the three of whom drank their health. They themselves could not drink, since the Law of the Land, which was sacred like the Name of God in Prayter's presence, forbade it. Then they went off to prepare for the journey to the bridal bower on the Caroline, Constance strangling sobs, Peter filling his sixpenny pipe with tuppenny tobacco. Peter went off spitting — spitting, spitting, because that pipe drew furnace-hot — to where two saddled horses, gifts from Lace, formerly property of the State, were waiting in the stockyard. Constance went to the hut.

Up to the moment of departure Constance had smiled. To her the wedding was only a trick to hide from the uncomprehending world that which her dear lover desired to be kept a secret. To have babies was to her a very natural and simple business. Lubras had them anywhere and anyhow. But from what dear Humbolt — Hummy as she called him — said and what she had read in magazines, it appeared to be a far from simple business among white people. He had told her that to save him from disgrace so terrible that he would run away rather than face it, she must marry someone and go away somewhere till she bore her baby. Afterwards he would send her down to Flinders. She could leave her baby with the blacks. Perhaps he would come to her in Flinders later on. If not, she would not miss him much with all the fine friends she would soon have there. But no-one must ever discover that the baby was his. Peter believed it was Elbert's. Other people would wonder, perhaps, but would never guess whose it was unless she told. Peter would do her no harm. He had his own lubra. There was nothing to fear from the future, she felt sure. Still she felt it hard to leave the place where she had known so much happiness. For some minutes she stood with her bundle of belongings in hand, looking through the window at the house and muttering to herself, "Oh I don't wanner go!" Then Peter rode up to the hut, cracked his fine Government stockwhip loudly, and bawled, "Y'ready?"

Mr and Mrs Pan rode away. Away over the grassy paddocks, away and away towards the violet and black and silver hills. Lace and Prayter watched them.

Prayter saw Lace's face working, saw him swallow, and muttered to himself, "How sad!" Lace turned a haggard face to him. Prayter thought he understood the cause of it, and pulled a wry face to show he did, and said, "Poor children!" Lace turned abruptly, walked down the veranda.

Prayter looked after the Pans again and said aloud, "And so they go, poorest children in the world, out into the mystery of laife. How hard it all seems! May Gard have mercy on you my dears, may Gard have mercy!"

Lace at the end of the veranda was watching too. His hands gripped the rail as though to break it. His teeth bit deep into trembling lip. He shut his eyes and whispered into scalding darkness, "Oh God forgive me — and help her — help her — I am too miserably weak!"

§

That Divinity with which Messrs Lace and Prayter were on such- familiar terms was apparently not so much at their beck and call as from their utterances it would seem. No blessings fell on the Halfcaste Pans. Far from it.

Misfortune went home with them and camped with them for the rest of their lives.

On the second night after the wedding, a great storm burst over the Caroline district and washed away the big native camp near the railway bridge, causing all those natives who were relatives of Peter's, a good score of them and their dogs, to go seek his charity. Being a Binghi bred, he did not turn the homeless ones away; he simply ordered a lot more food from Mrs McLash; he knew how hard it was to hunt near the whiteman's railway.

Mrs McLash was very angry, not because she objected to doing business on a wholesale scale, but because Peter and Constance had not waited a decent length of time before setting to work to bankrupt themselves, as bankrupt themselves she had predicted they would from the moment of being entrusted with their capital. She said to Joe Steen after the second or third wholesale purchase had been made, "There's yeller-fellers for you for a caution. About as much idea of bein' 'conomical as my old Bikehandles." Bikehandles was a well-horned billy-goat. "Waste of good money, wilful waste. I told Lace so right away. Interferin' fool to want to marry the girl off. Why couldn't he've sent her to the Compound? They'll be in the camp with the niggers before the Wet's out, mark my words. Anyway, I aint gunner help 'em keep that lazy gang. I've started givin' 'em short weight and chargin' 'em extra. That aint dishonest — so you needn't look boss-eyed at me, Joe Steen. It might's well be in my pocket as in a loafin' nigger's guts. Tcht! Tcht! It's damn well sickenin'."

So what with one thing and another, the Pan's capital was soon exhausted. Luckily there were the seed peanuts to fall back on when food could no longer be got from Mrs McLash. They and their relatives ate peanuts till they were covered in nettle-rash. After that there were the horses and the harness, which Jack Burywell of Red Ochre bought from them for twenty-seven shillings. And then there were Tim O'Cannon's presents, for which Karl Fliegeltaub paid two-and-six. Then there were their clothes, what few Constance had prevented Peter from using as stakes for gambling.

Clothes were regarded by the natives of the district more as convertible stock than garments, and were usually worn only between the games of poker to which the natives were madly addicted. Anything in the camp could be bought for clothes; and the moneyed people, who lived by prostituting to the fettlers and passengers of trains, would always cash clothes if the owners wished to buy from Mrs McLash. Since the Caroline camp was composed of several tribes, the natural communism had been ousted by commerce caused by rivalry.

Peter was an incurable gambler and unlucky. He lost all his own clothes within a day or two of coming home and had to return to his valueless sugar-bag shirt. Constance would not let him try his luck with hers. Though this was all very objectionable to her, she suffered it bravely, believing that she would not have to suffer it long. The thorough apprenticeship to hardship she had suffered with her father stood her in good stead.

With advent of hard times, Peter's relatives, having tried

in vain to find enough food in the rather poor country that surrounded the plantation, returned to the new native camp. Peter's lubra stayed behind to minister to him. He did nothing but gamble and corroboree and sleep. At the end of the Wet, Constance decided that they had better start planting peanuts or at least some kinds of vegetable that might be used as food. Therefore she sent Peter over to the Experimental Station to ask for seeds, and at the same time for more clothes and money. She would rather have gone herself, but did not wish to disobey Lace's order that she must not come without his permission. Apparently Lace had meant that order to apply to Peter too; for as soon as he saw him he told him to go to hell; and when Peter began to argue he shouted to his wife to bring the gun. Constance was hurt to hear of this, but convinced that the ogre Carrie and the fool Peter were more responsible for it than dear Hummy.

A week or so later, when Peter had reasoned out the fact that it was better to live in a native camp where there was little food than on one's own plantation where there was none, that careless fellow and his lubra and his wife filled a gunny-bag with their possessions and followed in the track of their relatives. Constance was made very welcome at the camp. There she found her black grandmother, whom she had never known, and whom, out of politeness, she joined in a day of wailing for her mother, who had died in the Compound of tuberculosis some three years before.

Then, in the middle of June, the midwives of the camp took Constance away to a place in the hills, where, in a cave, hidden from men and devils, she bore her baby. It was a girl, a tiny fragile thing, so white that the lubras, all of whom had believed that the father was Elbert, exclaimed as soon as they set eyes on it, "Ah — Mist Leash!"

Constance was unaware of the baby's sex for many days. She called it Hummy. The lubras took the child from her; for she was at first demented, and more, was beginning to develop the terrible cough that the Aboriginal people take so quickly from the whiteman; moreover, since the building of the railway, food was always too scarce in Dry Season to allow of feeding a woman and a cough and a baby all in one. The lubras hid Constance from the prying eyes of whitemen, having come to regard her as a sister and preferring to see a sister rot rather than be dragged away to the Compound. Never could they understand that the Government was their friend and the Compound their refuge, simple, simple creatures that they were.

Lace left Red Coffin Ridge. The Experimental Station was shut down. Constance knew that before the baby was born, but was not dismayed, since Lace had told her he might soon return to Town. She regained her sanity. She regained a little of her strength. Then, in order to keep the dingo from the door till the coming of either Hummy or Wet Season, she joined her black sisters in prostituting to the fettlers and the passengers of trains.

DAWN OF A NEW ERA

A FEW words spoken in a railway car in France, spoken ever so softly, because these history-makers are as jealous of their business as stingy schoolboys of correct results of sums, were overheard by pressmen, gossips of the world, who rushed off shouting, shouting till the world was ringing with the news.

The news was translated into code. The code was translated into impulses of electric force. In that form the news sped southward, through the tangled settlements of Europe, across the wastes of Persia, through the steam and stench of India, on and on with lightning speed, down through the roaring jungles of Malay, the paddy-fields of Java, into the Silver Sea among the coral and the pearls, up Capricornia's lonely shore, through Port Zodiac, away and along the singing Transcontinental Telegraph Line, over the Caroline River, into the ever-open ears of Mrs McLash.

The Great War was ended.

Kneel World! Kneel and give thanks for deliverance from Armageddon unto Him that visited it upon thee, kneel! Kneel and give praise, mad World. Shout thyself hoarse with hosannas. Seize upon thine enemies; embrace them; bathe them with the tears of joyous brotherhood; make thine enemies thy friends; then by way of change make thy friends thine enemies; forget the mistakes of the past and press on to the greater follies of the future — Crazy World!

Mrs McLash collapsed. She did not hear whether peace was the result of victory or defeat, nor care to hear, since the end of the war simply meant to her the end of anxiety for the life of her Pride and Joy. As she had often said

before she got mixed up in the mad business, it was not her
war, nor Frank's. It did not occur to her for an hour or
more that others might wish to hear the news. During that
time she sat communing with tearful joy with a bottle of
rum and a photograph of a grinning soldier. Then she roused herself, called her houseboy, Morris Hughes, and sent
him off to tell the fettlers.

Morris said quite casually, "B'long me missus talk for
tellim big-fella war him finis." He knew his masters were
interested in some kind of protracted brawl that was going
on somewhere between factions of their civilised breed, and
little more. He was surprised when the fettlers dashed off
to the Siding House as though they had been told it was
afire.

That night there was great rejoicing on the Caroline.
Messages had been sent to everyone around, including old
Karl Fliegeltaub, on whom all suddenly took pity. The
gang from Soda Springs came up on trollies, trikes, and
pump-cars, bringing with them Mrs Blaize and a load of
her liquor, Charlie O'Theef, the district trooper, and Bandy
Coots from the Republic. Down from Black Adder came
Tim O'Cannon and his gang, pumping a pump-car for all
they were worth, trailing behind them a flat-top trolley
packed with Tim's Blossom and his six quadroons.

Many old enemies met in that joyous gathering, but none
with enmity. Joe Ballest apologized to Bandy Coots for
having stolen a lubra from him years before, and Bandy to
Joe for the calumnies that he had spread in consequence.
Tim O'Cannon apologized to Cocky Cockerell for having
called him a Slimy Slacker, and Cocky to Tim for having
called him a Soolin' Sod. Mrs McLash and Mrs Blaize
settled some old score in whispers. All shook hands with
Fliegeltaub, who beamed, convinced again of what he had
come convinced of and begun to doubt when he saw how
gay the party was — that Deutschland was indeed Uber
Alles and that the vanquished had called him in to do him
homage. But no-one thought of apologizing to Blossom
O'Cannon for a single one of the scores of times they had
slighted her, nor even invited her or her children into the
house to join the revelry, nor, in some cases, even spoke to
her. The Great War was ended; foe was embracing foe;
but the Ethiopian had not changed his skin, and therefore
was still contemptible.

Tim was hurt. His family was as keenly interested in
the war as any in Australia. He had conducted his house
as a sort of garrison throughout the war. His children knew

more about the map of Europe than they did of their own
country. The elder ones had helped to feed the guns with
cotton. If what he said was true, the younger ones were
begotten simply to provide the guns with that other kind
of fodder if the Nation's need went on. And all were trained to make the Last Stand that at times had seemed immin-
ent during the latter stages of the war. This was known
to everyone in Capricornia. Hence he had thought his family might not be scorned for once. He was hurt, deeply,
but not for long. The occasion was too great to allow of
waste of feeling on petty battling. He found a place for the
humble ones on the back veranda, from which they could
see what went on inside; then, with the Federal Flag he
had bought to fly at the Last Stand, he went within, and
soon, for all his love of them, forgot them.

As a rule Tim did not drink, being a thorough family
man and independent of outside company, and a thrifty one
who spent all his leisure and savings on developing the
little property intended to provide for his family when he
was gone. But that night he was nothing more or less than
a Sergeant Major who had helped to win the war. None in
the gathering was so drunk as he. Waving the Federal Flag,
he drowned Mrs McLash's piano and the roaring crowd,
singing:

Rally round the Starry Banner of your country,
Take the field with brothers o'er the foam;
On land or sea, wherever you be,
Keep your eye on Ger-her-many;
Old England, France and Belgium, have no cause to
     fe — ar,
For 'Stralia will be the — ah — Australia will be
     there!

Karl Fliegeltaub, sitting in a corner watching, began to
doubt again. When last he had heard news of the war, which
was early in the year, he had been led to believe by his in-
formant, Mick O'Pick, that his side was winning easily,
that England was in ruins and the English whimpering for
peace, that the French, what few remained alive, were fleeing — Ha! Ha! Hoch! — like bandicoots before a bush
fire. And that this happy state of things was no mere fig-
ment of an Irishman's imagination, was proved shortly
afterwards when Froggie Lavindicatif of the Melisande had
yelled at him while passing in the train, "Dog of a Boche
— peeg of a Hun — yah — I speetze on you!" And he had
spat, which was iust what one would expect of a defeated

Frenchman. When Morris Hughes came with the news he merely said, "Big fella war him finis, Boss. Missus him say you come longa house for makim friend." So Karl had thought it was Der Tag and had come quietly hocking, prepared to boast a little of the superiority of his breed, but determined to treat the vanquished very kindly.

Old Karl was at last disillusioned by the same tongue as had caused him to be misled. Old Mick O'Pick, who had chuckled over the prospect of the extermination of the race of Cromwell, shouted the truth at Karl when asked for it, shouted the news of the Cromwellians' victory as though he loved the breed, as indeed he did just then, being a man of very warm heart for all the relentlessness of his memory. Old Karl rose quietly and crept away.

O'Pick, the man who had laughed over the bombing of England, saying that it was something in return for the Atrocity of the Boyne, who had countered the cry Remember Belgium with Don't Forget Old Ireland, who had proudly gone to jail not long before for having in a public place, to wit the bar of the First and Last, exposed a picture of a certain British Personage framed in a privy-seat, roared in that gathering at the Siding House till he drowned Trooper O'Theef's concertina and all but drowned O'Cannon's voice: "Rule Britannyer, Britannyer Rule the Wavesh!"

So this gathering of people at the end of the earth echoed the joy with which the earth was ringing. And so while the swift-winged hours sped towards the dawn of a day that was to be the first of a New Era, the era in which men blamed that European War for all their subsequent stupidity.

At the peep of day Blossom O'Cannon roused her man. He was lying on the table with head pillowed on the broken concertina and body sheltered with the Federal Flag, looking like a martial corpse. He did not wake properly till Blossom dragged him to the tap outside and turned the water on him. He drank as a camel does, dipped head in the drip-tub, let the stream gush down his spine, set the drunken sleepers licking crusted lips and dreaming they were lost in the Great Salt Desert.

Blossom roused him because a special train was coming down that day and he must run the length before it on his section. It was a train bringing material for the extension of the road from Copper Creek to the Melisande, which was under construction. "Wha' shpecial train?" groaned

Tim. "Jigger blunny trainsh! Lemme lone woman — Oh — Ah — I'm dyin'."

Later he tried to rouse his gang. Being in no fit state to fight them, he went off alone with his family, and, watched by The Day's red baleful eye, pumped the pump-car homeward, pausing at the summit of every bank to drink with greed from the water-bag and nurse his head.

The other revellers did not wake till noon, when, having no-one to remind them of special trains, they got out hair-of-the-dog. Soon they were in a fair way to continue the rejoicings. Then at about one o'clock it occurred to Joe Ballest that he was neglecting an important duty. He tried to rack his memory, but did no more than tickle it and send it reeling about and singing 'Stralia Will Be There and P-hic Up Y' Troublesh N'y'ole K-hic Bag. He asked O'Pick what it was he was trying to remember. Mick embraced him and sang Black Alice. Thus for a time the necessity to run the length remained forgotten.

At about half past one the sense of dereliction again took hold of Ballest. After some irritable minutes of trying to get rid of it he ordered his gang out to work. They protested. Loudest of all in protest was O'Pick. He became downright insulting. Ballest threw a chair at him.

Unfortunately, it was always on such occasions that Ballest, who was usually the most easy-going ganger on the road, chose to assert his authority. Or so it seemed to his men. It may have been that under the influence of liquor he was more conscientious than usual, or more officious, or simply that on such occasions his authority attracted more attention. At any rate, the fact that trouble always arose was not so much his fault as his men's, and not so much the men's generally as O'Pick's. He and O'Pick had worked together for years, and were in their hearts the best of friends; still, whenever it was possible for them to annoy each other they did so. Every quarrel that arose between ganger and men concluded as one between Ballest and O'Pick. It was so on this occasion. O'Pick returned the chair to Ballest, who replied to it with a bottle. They came to grips. Mrs McLash drove them out with the broom. They fought in the yard till Ballest collapsed, when O'Pick picked him up and flung him into the goat-yard.

When Ballest regained his breath he told Mick O'Pick through the goat-yard fence that he was suspended from duty, that his complete dismissal from the Service would be engineered, that he had a face like a black baboon, and that he was many things so unutterable that some of the on-lookers cried out for moderation for the sake of the none-too-particular ladies in the house. Mick was not lost for answers.

Then Ballest summoned up what dignity he could and marched out of the yard by a gate remote from Mick, then ran for his life to his house with Mick bellowing behind him. Mick raged and ramped at the barred door till his voice failed, while Ballest bravely raged within and fired shots from a shotgun into the door. The few of their companions who had been able or inclined to stagger so far stood by and cheered. Such behaviour on the part of the ganger and his mate, while by no means uncommon, was always entertaining; and there was always the attraction in it of the exciting possibility that Ballest's well-peppered door might someday prove to be not as effective a shield as he and Mick believed.

Mick went off at last to his own house, hoarsely delivering himself of opinions about Informers and Scabs and Bosses' Men, and dressed himself in his best. It was his intention to go up to Town to report Ballest to the Road-master before he could do the same to him. Ballest would have to wait four days for the mail-train before he could deliver his report. He nearly always suspended Mick when thrashed by him, and reported him in his official memorandum as having been guilty of insubordination and drunkenness and riotous behaviour and assaulting a superior officer and any other breach of the numerous *Rules and Regulations for the Conduct of Officers* he could think of. And nearly always Mick, not having an official memorandum in which to express himself, set out on a tricycle for Town. Both old fools were always in dead earnest. But Mick never carried his intentions further than the summit of the steep 75-Mile bank, where he always stopped to rest, fell asleep on his machine, and woke with a burning thirst, an urgent memory of the liquor left behind, a saner understanding of the seventy-five miles of hills and dales before him, and a much better opinion of the ganger. He would return. Not long after his return the voice of Ballest would bellow across the road, "Hey there Mick! Com'n have a spot o' beer." The result of the inevitable acceptance of the invitation would be another entry in the memorandum carefully scored out.

While Mick was dressing on this occasion, Ballest got out his memorandum and began to write the offences already committed, then sat waiting to hear the sounds of

Mick's departure. He heard the door of the trolley-shed flung open with a crash, then the clatter that attended the railing of the tricycle. He took out his watch and held it for a minute or so, when, upon hearing the creak of mechanism and the click of wheels, all amid the steady foul-mouthed bellowing of Mick, he thrust the watch into his pocket, took up his pencil, and added to the list of offences: *Unorthrized usn trike on main road 2.56 pm this day.* The clatter and bellowing of Mick passed rapidly out of hearing.

The writing of *2.56 pm* reminded Ballest of that dereliction. He whipped out his watch, stared at it for just ten seconds, then started. He rose and grabbed his working-shirt from the wall, and took from the breast-pocket his note-book. Hastily he turned the leaves till he came to the entry he had made when called to the telephone soon after he went to the Siding House to celebrate. He had to read twice before his addled brains could grasp the meaning of the scrawl: *Speshul leves Town 7.30 am tomorrer doo 80-Mile 12.03 aprox.*

"Gawd!" he whispered. "Forgot it!" He looked at his watch again. A train coming, already more than two hours overdue; and there was that old fool, blind as a bat and drunk as a jigger and silly as a cut snake, riding out to meet it! He rushed out. Mick was at the foot of the bridge, about ten chains from the siding. He shouted, "Mick — Mick — Mick!"

Above the clatter of the trike Mick could not have heard a sound less loud than a dynamite-blast at a distance greater than a dozen yards. The men who were about came up to Ballest and asked what was the matter. In whimpering tones he said, "A special's comin'. I forgot. Old fool's goin' out to get killed. Gi's hand with motor. Goin' after him."

"Special?" asked one of the Soda Springs gang. "We aint heard of no special."

Ballest ran off with Cockerell to get the motor-trolley from the shed. Other hands flew to help them. The railing of the machine was an intricate job, since it had to be run up and carefully turned on a table, and a difficult one just then, since the heads that guided the hands were in no fit state to deal with intricacies. Precious moments were lost through bungling. Mick passed on to the bridge and out of sight. Owing to a curve in the road between the siding and bridge the latter presented a slanting side-view to eyes surveying it from the former. There was a similar curve beyond.

For the third time the trolley was railed and derailed. All were cursing, Ballest in a thin sobbing voice. Then someone shouted, "Here she is!" All looked, to see above the trees beyond the bridge a moving plume of smoke. Mick would not see it yet.

The hands on the trolley relaxed, letting the machine roll back to the shed. All eyes were on the bridge, seeing nothing, but visualizing the narrow iron road between the girders, just two rails laid on transomes on the naked iron of the bridge. No footway there but a narrow plank that ran between the rails; and the rails were only three-feet-six apart and each only two-feet-six from the girders. Above the azure sky, below green river, ahead black iron rushing death, behind — regrets. A death-trap. Even if Mick could cross before the train rushed down he would have small chance of getting off the road in time. The curve ahead would hide the danger.

The road was all curves — curves and cuttings and towering scrub. Damnation! Locomotives rarely whistled. Perhaps their crews had rarely steam to spare. Still, they seemed to care just about as much for the lives of fettlers as for those of the foolish kangaroos that thought it easier to travel along the railway than through the bush — to care only for the lives of such great beasts as buffaloes, collision with which might wreck a train. A death-trap every chain of it. A man took his life in his hands every time he rode it on a trolley or a trike. Yet the soft-handed nincompoops who sat in offices controlling it begrudged the fettlers their pay. The lightness of the traffic that the nincompoops argued about as a reason for cutting down the pay or increasing the section-lengths was the very danger of the job; a man never knew where the light traffic was till he saw it. Ballest had been unlucky enough to forget this train, but lucky enough to be about when its coming was announced to Mrs McLash. Damnation! Many a time the coming of a special train was announced to Mrs McLash while the gang was out at work. They learnt it was coming when it came.

Ballest cried out in a mad voice, "It'll get him — it'll get him! Oh Mick — my old mate Mick!"

"He might get across," said someone soberly.

"Stop him!" Ballest suddenly shrieked. "Stop him! Gawd — I let him go. I oughter known — Oh I've killed my old mate Mick!"

"Steady," said Cockerell, taking his arm. "Steady on, Joe."

Ballest snatched his arm away and ran up the road. At

the cattle-trap he tripped and fell, because he was intent on the bridge. He was up in an instant, rushing on, shouting, "Mick — Mick — Oh Mick for gawd-sake stop!" The others raced after him.

The train turned the further curve. The sky was filled with smoke. Oh that train had never sped like that before! In a moment it was on the bridge. Joe Ballest stopped, to stand with hands upraised and mouth agape, transfixed as when he had been shouting, all wits flung into bulging eyes and straining ears.

There was no sound on earth but the roar of wheels on the bridge. Roar of wheels! Then out from the girders on the western side flew the body of Mick and fragments of his tricycle, like rubbish flung from the porthole of a ship, to hang for a dreadful instant above the trees, then disappear, plunge into the river a hundred feet below. Then to Ballest's ears came a compact *clop!* — like the sound of the deviltry of a far-off axe. Then the devil itself burst from the bridge, came down raging, belching smoke and spitting steam. From the cowcatcher hung the outrigger of the tricycle, leaping about as though in the grip of death itself, beating against the iron that had shattered it, striking the road, sending the gravel flying.

A head popped out of the left side of the engine's cab and craned to see what was causing the hail of gravel. Another popped out of the other side. Then the whistle screamed at Ballest for obstructing the permanent way.

Ballest's companions dragged him clear, and held him, because without support he would have fallen. He was mad, reeling about and gesticulating at the rushing train, and champing and gurgling like a lunatic.

The train roared up, grinding and shuddering under the strain of brakes. Engineer and fireman were staring, guessing that something was amiss. The hands of the fettlers shot up to wave, their mouths opened wide to shout — then mad Joe Ballest shrieked, leapt out of hands and on to the road, and rushed at the engine with fists raised. Hands and mouths were paralysed. Eyes — nothing but eyes -- eyes — bulging and horrified!

The cowcatcher struck him in the shins, hurled him backward through the air a dozen feet or more, then caught him as he fell on back with smashed legs flying like a pair of empty socks, and scooped him up and rolled him over as he were nothing but a bag of rags, engulfed his legs, his hips, and with snout dug in the pit of his stomach ploughed up the gravel and grass with him all the way to the cattle-trap, where it dropped him for the wheels.

The engine stopped at the trolley-shed. Half the coal was out of the tender, half the fire out of the box, half the trucks were off the track, so violent was the stopping. The crowd rushed up. Ashen-faced engineer and fireman dropped down and came running. They met at the blood-drenched trap. They dropped to knees. Oh God the sight! That horror tangled in the wheels! And meat-ants swarming! The fireman rose and shuffled back, leant against a truck and vomited.

"Who is it?" whispered the engineer. Someone whispered a reply. After a pause he whispered again, "It wasn't my fault — so help me God!"

"Wazzer burry matter?" cried the guard, staggering up and rudely thrusting in. "Half blunny train off, four hot boxes, three hours late — Christ! Oh Christ! Ugh! Ugh!" He vomited.

The engineer rose, mopping face with greasy waste. Cockerell like an accusing demon rose beside him, muttering, "You killed old Mick O'Pick as well."

The engineer's haggard eyes grew wide. Cockerell blinked and said again, "You killed old Mick O'Pick as well."

"Liar!" gasped the engineer.

Cockerell was trembling. Suddenly his face convulsed. He yelled, "You killed him on the bridge!"

The engineer goggled at him.

Tears blinded Cockerell. He said with an effort, "Careless — murderin' — barsteds!"

"Steady Cock," said someone, taking his arm.

The engineer remembered the thud on the bridge. He drew a deep breath. Someone said to him, "You'll have to get the jacks to get him out."

He turned away — turned away to see beside the train some distance off old Mick coming up, smothered in mud and trailing river-weeds, waving and cursing. He clutched an arm beside him, caused a man to turn and stare and cry, "Mick — here's Mick!"

Mick came up cursing. "Run a man down and murder him!" he roared. "I'll fight the mob of yez. Where's the ganger? I'll start on him. Ganger — ganger — where are yez, you dirty informin' old sod?"

Cockerell seized him and cried, "He's dead — he's dead!"

"Who's dead?"

"Joe — poor Joe — he's under there Mick — under there !"

"What — old Joe?" demanded Mick, then laughed deeply and added, "That'll taich the damned informin' old hound it will. Suspind me, would he? Come outer that Ballest and suspind me to me fairce !"

"Shh, Mick!" whispered Cockerell. "He's dead. They run him down."

"He jumped on the road himself." croaked the engineer.

Mick went to look, saw, gasped, goggled. When the truck was lifted and the crumpled mass freed from wheels and springs and rails and laid on a blanket on the cess-path, he bent over it, kissed its shattered head, wept over it like a mother over a dead baby, crying again and again, "Oh Joe, man dear! — Oh wirrah man wirrah! — Oh whoy did ye do it! — Oh whoy did ye doye so harrd?"

§

Four days later, while riding up to Town on the trike to report certain visions of delirium tremens to the Roadmaster, Mick was struck by the mail-train while he rested as usual at the top of the 75-Mile bank, was run over and cut to pieces.

So the Great War ended; and the weary nations knelt before the Throne of God and bespoke God as though they never expected to have trouble with Him again.

§

A few months after the Armistice, a soldier in uniform, a tall stout fellow, somewhat like a war-time kewpie doll in appearance and in condition rather the worse for drink, suddenly appeared to people waiting for the mail-train at the Caroline. He climbed down from the engine. The people stared at him. None of them had ever seen a real live soldier before, at least not in the happy land of Capricornia.

Tim O'Cannon was one of the people. He was then ganger of the district, for the Caroline length had been linked to that of Black Adder by the economical nincompoops as the result of the tragic reduction of the local gang. He stared at the soldier with eyes fairly popping from his head. To him the sight of a soldier meant as much as that of an angel to an evangelist. But the soldier was not a bit like those to be seen in imported magazines. His feathered hat was on the back of his head, held by the chin-strap, which was on his brow; his tunic was wide open showing a naked hairy belly and chest; and each of his big side pockets held

a bottle; and while he walked his feet kept forming fours.
"It's Frank!" cried Tim.
"My God!" cried Mrs McLash. "My boy!"
When Frank saw that he was recognised he shouted,
"What cheer Mum!" and came forming fours at the double.
The crowd rushed him. His mother fell into his arms.
"What cheer!" he cried, "Gawdstrewth what cheer, what
cheer!"
"My darling, oh my darling little boy!" cried Mrs McLash.
"My precious one, my Pride and Joy — Oh I've got him
back again! Thank God — thank God! Lambkin, you're
not wounded are you?"
He looked down at her, said laughing, "Na —ow! I'm
jakerloo."
"You're what?" she demanded, looking scared.
"Jakerloo Mum, jakerloo."
"What — not a disease, my darling?"
"Na—ow — that's French for 'I'm good-o'."
"Oh!" said everyone.
"And what's that you's singing out?" asked Tim. "Wot-
chee, wotchee, or sumpen?"
"What cheer? Oh that's Pommy-talk — English for
'How's it cobbers?'"
"By cripes," said Tim, "you been pickin' up furrin lingoes
all right."
"Oh I'm sure you're wounded somewhere," moaned Mrs
McLash. "You must be — cos how'd you get back so soon?
Bill Boakes, what lost his left arm and's got a toob put in
him, told me you'd be munce and munce gettin' demopol-
ished — unless you was wounded, he says. Let me look at
you. Let me feel you —"
"Hey — edge it Mum! Ow — y' ticklin'! I tell you I'm
jake. Never better in me life. I didn't wait for no demobbin'.
I sold out and snuck home."
"Snuck home?"
"My oath. Come back Singapore way — first-class and
cabin-dee-luxe — the proper bonn tonn. I kep' it dark so's
I'd give you a surprise."
"But — but where'd you get the money to go doin' that?"
asked his mother, ever afraid of the criminal in him. "Last
time you writ you says you's down on your bone."
"Oh I come up on it lovely. Me'n me cobber Bluey broke
the bank in a big two-up school in France and won twenty
thousand francs — French money."
"Gawd!" gasped Tim O'Cannon.

"Oh that aint so much," said Frank. "Them Froggies use cheap sorter money so's it sounds a lot when they count it. They love money — the cows. But gawd, I'm dingo hungry. What you got to eat Mum? Some the old kangaroo you used to kid 'em was beef, eh? Gawdstrewth how I've longed for a bit of old Capricornian 'roo! There's no place like home, Mum. Have me head read if ever I leave this gawd's own lovely land again. You dunno what a lovely land it is till you've seen them other crowded, foggy, frozen, furrin holes. I got a case of beer in the van, and six kit-bags. Some you boys get 'em?"

His mother, again suspicious, asked, "Six kit-bags? What you been bringin' home?"

"You wait'n see. For a start I got some dresses for you, Mum. The dinkum oil from Gay Paree. I bought 'em there meself. I'll take you up to Town in 'em next time the mail-boat's in. They'll strike the mob there blind. Oh gi's a kiss Mum. Strike me — I missed you too!"

It turned out that Frank had brought home a fair amount of the debris of the battlefield, together with some articles of value he had stolen here and there. Tim O'Cannon did no work that afternoon; he sat on the floor of the veranda of the Siding House with Frank and all the other people of the district, fingering the souvenirs and asking scores of questions about modern warfare, saying as he got his answers, "Marvellous — marvellous!"

That night Tim got drunk again and fought in the war with Frank, and so again the next night, and the next; and for the first time in all the years that he had been a father he did not go home for the week-end. But when in the middle of the next week he did go home, he took on his trike a good two-thirds of Frank's souvenirs, which he had bought at no small cost to stock the O'Cannon Garrison. Each souvenir was marked with a number; and for each number there was written in a note-book a few words of the story Frank had told about that particular thing. But the story Frank told, tall though it might have been, was nothing compared with that retold by imaginative Sergeant-Major O'Cannon. Night after night his children went to bed with shell-shock.

Tim pumped Frank dry in no time, so dry indeed that after a day or two Frank would not let his information flow about the war unless he was first primed with whiskey. Tim bought a case of priming from the Mesdames Shay, that is from old Mrs Daisy Shay and her daughter-in-law

Heather, widow of Wally Shay, whom she had married on the eve of his fatal departure for the war.

On the whole Frank rather disappointed Tim. It seemed as though he had fought most of his battles in the back lanes of Montmartre and Shoreditch against military police, as though the only captures he had made were among the Mademoiselles and Tarts, as though he had been more often "shot" than shot at. His talk of life in the zone of war dealt mainly with rats and lice and mud and evil sanitation and fun with comrades. And it seemed as though he had hated the French and British far more than he had the Hun. Tim was annoyed. He felt that a marvellous adventure had been wasted on a fool. Frank was also annoyed by this incessant questioning about a subject he wished to forget. The moment the priming gave out he told Tim to go to jiggery. Tim gave him up in disgust. However, Tim learnt enough about modern warfare to be able to make revolutionary changes in the old Southern Cross Island system under which the O'Cannon Garrison had always been run.

A SHOTGUN WEDDING

IF their father was to be believed, the two younger children of the O'Cannon family owed their existence solely to the fact that at the time they were begotten the Nation badly needed men. They were girls, however. When they were born their father was greatly disappointed, but not nearly so much on the Nation's account, nor even on his, as on their own, because he knew that the lot of a coloured female in Capricornia was even harder than that of a coloured male.

There was but one coloured male in the family. He was Thomas, the youngest of the pre-war children. But the household was no less a garrison for being overstocked with females. The three elder girls made even smarter soldiers than the boy. The younger ones were still too small for active soldiering, but were soldiers none the less. That Federal Flag of Tim's, the only privately-owned flag in the country, was broken at the head of a tall staff at his homestead every Sunday and holiday morning of the year in the presence of the entire Garrison standing in order and at attention. Tim himself ran up the flag, and having done so, played on a key-bugle first *Reveille* then *Lift Up The Five-Starred Flag*. At sundown the flag was dropped as reverently as a field-marshal to the grave; then Tim played *Last Post* and *What's The Matter With Father*.

Nor did sex interfere with the rank of the O'Cannon soldiers. Tim himself was Commandant simply because an old soldier. Maud, aged fifteen at the end of the war, was Colonel. Next to her was Margaret, aged twelve, then Kitty, aged eleven, then Tommy, aged nine, then the babies Bridie and Mollie, aged four and three. Last and least of all was Blossom, who was merely a conscripted cook.

Tim despised Blossom, first because it was she who was responsible for his children's colour, secondly because she was, in his opinion, crassly stupid. Why — for years he had been telling her that the earth spun round in the light of the sun; and still she went on believing that a new sun was made every night by devils over Skinny River way, who pitched it into the sky at about half past six each morning so that it landed in the Copper Creek country at about half past six at night. And she would never speak English properly, or rather, not as properly as he and the children did. And she was hopelessly vain in her person and addicted to wearing brilliant clothes and making herself look with reds and greens and yellows like what he called a Bloody Parakeet. And she had that damnable habit of producing female children. And then, because she believed with the natives of the district that if a woman killed a snake she would give birth to a monster, she took pains to leave the pests alone, so that the house, being in a region over-run with snakes, was often like a reptilarium. And she chattered in her sleep at full of the moon, and always got meals ready an hour early or an hour late, and was so docile that he could get no pleasure from bombarding her with acerbity. But she was devoted to him and the children, for which he tolerated her.

At the end of the war, Blossom was about thirty-five, Tim's junior by a good ten years, a handsome creature, remarkably so, with features so symmetrical — this a heritage from the two symmetrically-featured races she was sprung from, Aboriginal and Chinese — that a micrometer gauge could scarcely find a disproportion in her smooth and broad mahogany-coloured face. Finding disproportion in her body, however, was a job for a tape-line rather than a gauge; she was, as Tim said, as big as Kaptilist, his mule;

though she was grown to be so from a slip of a girl. Her eyes were as black and lustrous as well-used engine-oil, wide because her mother was a lubra, slanting because her father was a Chow. And her hair was as glossy black as a dry tar-brush.

Tim had good features too. He had been quite good-looking in his day. Now his dark-brown hair was greying and falling out; and his ginger cavalry moustache, so proud and fierce a feature in days gone by, looked as though the rats had been at it; and round his smiling bright blue eyes and laughing mouth a multitude of lines were gathering. Compared with Blossom he was, as he said himself, but a bit blown off a man. He was descended from pure Southern Irish stock, another symmetrically-featured breed. Thus symmetry of features was the main factor in the O'Cannon children's inheritance. But what sources of inheritance! Irish, salt of earth — Chinese, stuff of heaven — Aboriginal Australian, ragtag of humanity.

They were a queer brood, like neither parent except in that their hair was Blossom's tar-brush stuff and their imaginativeness their father's. They were all small of stature, and as active and perky and dainty as birds. Their exquisitely-moulded faces were the colour of wheatmeal porridge slightly browned, with numerous freckles as the bran. Sickly-looking little faces really, if one paid much attention to the skin. But one could hardly do that for gazing at their laughing mouths and into the dark brown depths of their oily almost almond eyes.

A stranger quite familiar with the faces of Chinese people might have guessed that there was blood of that race in the O'Cannon children; but no-one would ever have guessed at the quarter that was black. However, it was not necessary to guess about their blood. Should a stranger suppose that they were white, he would soon be told that they were half-caste. Should one doubt it, as passing strangers sometimes did, the children would be seized if unprotected and have the whites of their eyes and bases of their finger-nails searched for that bluishness which is supposed to be the evidence of black blood. The evidence was always found. As Tim said, if those who looked for the bluishness would look as keenly at their own nails and eyes they would see it there as well as any other bloody colour they desired.

The children were regarded by the law as halfcaste. Tim had long since ceased to argue that they were white quadroons and had concentrated on a far more practical way of whitewashing them than with his tongue, namely by en-

riching them, making them owners of a huge combination cattle-station and cotton and peanut plantation, a
hive of industry and centre of envy that he hoped to have
built up at Black Adder Creek before he should die. "Rich
people have no colour," he used to say. "Look at them fine
gentlemen the Hinjun Rajahs beside them dirty niggers the
coolie Indoos!"

He was in a measure glad of the incorporation of the
Black Adder Length with that of the Caroline, since it
brought about the removal of the fettlers' camp, which he
had always feared might prove to be an influence on his
children most certainly humiliating and perhaps malign.
Moreover, he had a pretty scheme in mind, which was that
in a few years' time he would find some healthy, handsome,
and moderately clean-living youth whom he would make his
work-mate, whom he would cunningly interest in the possibilities of Black Adder Creek, and whom he would finally
introduce to Maud. His sons-in-law must be white and of
good breed. He had pictures of them in mind pretty often
now that Maud was adolescent, fine pictures, much too good
to be true, like those of Black Adder as a sort of market-
garden in the midst of an unconquerable wilderness. Having
settled Maud, as the years went by he would bring in another and another youth, till at last the Garrison was fully
manned, was packed with troops of the good O'Cannon
breed yet of a type such as even old fools like Mrs McLash
and Joe Steen could not call coloured.

It was impossible to carry out that scheme if the fettlers'
camp was at the 58-Mile, right at the Garrison door, since
then the necessary cunning moves would be apparent, and
being so would surely be cruelled by the mean old-timers of
the gang, who would jeer at the chosen youths for falling for
coloured wenches. Then again the glory of Black Adder
and the beauty of the girls might not appeal so well to
youths who saw them every day. And yet again, it was not
unlikely that with handsome young fellows hanging round
the Garrison day and night, familiarity might breed not
only contempt but little recruits without producing sons-in-
law. Tim loved his daughters as dearly as ever a father did,
but had no illusions about their human nature. He used
to say that he had studied human nature on his cattle-run.

So he was in a measure glad of the change the nincompoops effected to cut down expenses and have their own
pay raised, although it meant his having to be absent from
home for five days of the week, because the gang must now

camp at the Caroline. During his absence he left the Garrison in charge of Colonel Maud.

§

Too late did Tim discover, for all his knowledge of human nature, that breeches may disguise a woman but never change her sex, that Joans may be relied upon to lead an army into battle but never may be trusted not to betray it for the sake of love. Far from being the Garrison's strength, Colonel Maud turned out to be its very weakness.

Nearly a year had passed since the Armistice, another Wet Season was on the way, when Cedric Callow came to Black Adder Creek. Maud was then sixteen. Cedric was twenty-five, of medium height and graceful form, and had the face of a romantic hero of the screen. He was quite a man, however, and knew as much about horned cattle as Tim did. Why — when Tim told him that no-one on earth could ride the old myall horse Misanthropy but himself, he asked if he might have a crack at it, and proved that Tim was wrong. Riding Misanthropy was test of manhood enough for Tim. What if the fellow cleaned his teeth and reamed his nails and wore side-lever whiskers? From regarding him with good-natured contempt, Tim came within a few short hours to admire him greatly, to note the languid movements of his dark-blue eyes and the curl of his perfect lips and the lines of his slender body with almost as much pleasure as Maud did, and with far more frankness. But he never thought of him as a possible son-in-law. That lovely creature was not made for coloured trash.

Cedric said that he and his brother owned a cattle-station near Agate Bar in the West Coast Country. That was the truth, as Tim subsequently learnt by inquiry. He said he had been up to Java for a trip and had come to look at Capricornia on the way home, part of which he intended to travel overland in order to see the great stations of the Leichhardt Tableland and study their methods.

He called at Black Adder one Friday afternoon when Tim happened to be at home, seeking the hospitality that all in Capricornia except the Government Officers and the most jealous of the comboes were always eager to extend to travellers, and to learn something of the way ahead. Tim kept him for the whole week-end, and on the Monday morning delayed his own departure for several hours in order to see him off and put him on the track to Red Ochre, through which he must pass to go to the Tableland.

Cedric went. So handsome in his black silk shirt and

faun-coloured moleskins and bright brown top-boots and high-crowned wideawake. So smooth of face, so fine of eye, so much a beautiful part of his beautiful chestnut prad. He went with Tim's good wishes and with pack-bags bulging with Tim's good food and with so much of Tim's heart too that he left him empty. Tim watched him right out of sight, then turned to the homestead sighing.

Young Cedric's knowledge of cattle was not confined to the horned variety. Those languid eyes had paid much less attention to the old bull Tim than to the soft-eyed heifers of the herd, particularly to Maud, whose heart he saw in her eyes. After breakfast that Monday morning, while Tim was fussing with his horses, he had found an opportunity to slip into the kitchen and catch Maud washing-up alone. For a second he had stood at her elbow looking into her eyes, then had whispered, "Come down to the old dam 's afternoon. I'll be waitin'." Face burning, eyes wide, lips parted, she had looked up at him, dazed. He had gently grasped her soft plump creamy arm above the elbow. His breath had fanned her fluffy inky hair. After a pause he had gone on, "I'm not goin' right away. I'll hang about. Camp up the creek somewhere no-one'll see me. Will you come 's afternoon — tonight if you can't get away? To the old dam. I'll be waitin'." Still she was dazed. Another pause. Then he had bent and kissed her parted lips, gently at first, then passionately, drawing her, dishclout and suds and all, into his strong brown arms. A moment. Then he had relaxed, gasping, "Gawd — I love you!" A step on the back veranda. He had looked at the veranda door, stood for a second with Maud in loose embrace, then released her, darted into the dining-room. When Bridie had entered the kitchen singing, Maud was furiously washing up.

Tim went off on his trike to the Caroline at eleven o'clock. At two in the afternoon, Maud, barefooted as usual and wearing the clothes of workaday, slipped from the house, looked about, then sauntered over to the water-tanks. She carried her best straw hat and louis-heeled shoes rolled up in an old rag hat. From behind the pawpaws and bananas that grew about the tank she surveyed the house. It was dead. The family was dozing in siesta. The native camp in the timber by the creek was silent. The sun beat fiercely; but Maud did not feel it; she did not even feel the strangled beating of her heart. After a moment of surveying, she turned and ran to the home-paddock fence, slipped through and into the scrub, turned once again, stared for a moment, then went on as in a dream.

Days passed, or rather nights, since after the first clandestine meeting it was always night when the lovers met and to them the daylight hours meant naught but hours of waiting. It was easy for Maud to slip away unseen at night, and easy to make up lost sleep in siesta. While Tim was away the family usually went to bed with the crows.

Cedric would come up on horseback to meet her, ride off with her behind him, bring her home. The dogs were witnesses to his prowling, but knowing and liking him, never barked. And the natives soon found out what was afoot, but kept it to themselves, considering it natural and amusing and nothing to do with them. Another knowing creature was Blossom, who had known of it from the start, having discovered that Maud went out that afternoon and then divined from her behaviour where she had gone. Maud's absent eyes, her burning cheeks, her unusual care in washing and dressing, her happy listlessness of mornings, her burning exuberance of nights, her staring up-creek from the kitchen window, her secret smiles, her sighs, all this and more told the rest of the tale to Blossom. One night Blossom spied. Hearing a faint sound in the house, she slipped from bed and stole to the back veranda, to see a wraith-like figure flit across the yard. She stood staring at the bush long after Maud had gone, then with a sigh crept back to bed.

Thus for five nights of a waxing moon.

Maud was not at home when Tim returned on Saturday afternoon. He inquired about her and learnt that she had ridden out early in the morning to look for her favourite horse, which had strayed. Then he inquired innocently about Cedric, whom he had been thinking might have returned, having learnt from Jack Burywell, whom he had met at the Caroline on train-day, that Cedric had not passed through Red Ochre. He was puzzled about Cedric, but not suspicious, thinking nothing of Blossom's strained replies. He spent the rest of the day away from the house, and did not think of Maud again till he returned to tea and found that she was absent still, when, becoming anxious, he questioned Blossom thoroughly. Very soon he saw the guilt in her face, and demanded, "What you hidin' from me?"

Blossom wrung her yellow hands.

"Out with it!" cried Tim. "Where's that girl? What's she done? I can see be your face there's sumpen wrong. Is she hurt?"

"Oh Tim!" she gasped, and began to blubber.

"Cut that out!" he cried. "Tell me. Come on — quick!"

"Oh I dunno — rilly truly Tim — I dunno nuthen. She just say she go look for Fleabag, an' kiss me an' go way. I go look in her room and see clotheses gone —"

"What — her clothes gone? What you mean?"

"Rilly truly Tim, she tell me nuthen."

"But dammit you looked to see if her clothes was gone! Come on and tell me or I'll kill you. Where's that girl? What's she done?" He seized her by a wrist and twisted it.

Blubbering she told him.

For a while he was struck dumb. Then he panted, "What — what — you monster, you knoo all the time and did nuthen?"

"Oh Tim!" she moaned, "What good stop her after she go first time? She love dat pretty boy too much. Oh love is strong strong ting for woman, Tim. I know. Dat lovely boy! Poor lil Maudie no get a boy lika dat for marry. Only colour boy or white rubbitch —"

"Shut your foul mouth you barsted!"

"Oh listen Tim — you no onnerstand. If Maudie lose dat lovely boy must her heart break —"

"You lunatic — d'you think he'll stick to her?"

"No — but if her heart can live happy lil while no matter die. Cos she have pick de flower, Tim. No matter flower die if she have pick an' love it for a lil while, dear Tim —"

"Shut up you filthy bitch! He'll chuck her away like rubbish when he's done with her. She'll finish in a nigger's camp. Oh my Maudie — my little girl!"

"She come back, Tim, she come back to mumma," Blossom sobbed. "More better losim man when he get tired. More better she go with him time he love her. What chance she got, poor pretty dear, for gettim good hubin, Tim? Before I tink dat Cedric he gittim tired two t'ree day an' go away. I not tink he wanner take her wid him. So I let her go to pick de flower, Tim — Oh!"

Tim silenced her with a blow on the mouth, shouting, "Shut your dirty mouth, you barsted. Call yourself a mother, call yourself a woman, call yourself a human critter? Artch!" He spat in her bleeding face. "You nigger thing — you barsted — you — Oh Gawd Almighty you — Oh Christ you fiend!"

He flung her away shouting, "But by Gawd there'll be a weddin', if it's gotter be a shotgun one! I'll bring that barsted back to marry her, or leave his stinkin' carcass for the crows."

He turned to the door, brushing the whimpering children from his path, and shouted to natives who were eating on the back veranda. "Here you — catchim three-feller horse —and saddle-up — and God damn you move!"

With that he went to his room. Some minutes later he came back with a lantern and a revolver-belt. He set down the lantern, took the revolver from the holster and examined it, then replaced it and donned the belt, watched by his trembling family, to whom his harsh lined face was utterly strange. When he took up the lantern he turned to Blossom and said in a low strained voice, "I won't come back without her. But if I don't come back with that dolled-up barsted too, you better take to the bush — where you belong, you nigger!" He strode out in the gathering dusk to the horseyard.

Early on Monday morning, after a long and exhausting search through rain, Tim and his blackboys, drawn to the place by the neighing of horses, came upon a tent pitched in a jungle-glade, not on the track to the Tableland, but on the Skinny River. They knew their search was at an end when they saw the hobbled horses.

Tim dismounted, and with face wearing an expression such as his boys had never seen on whiteman's face before, went quietly to the tent. His face was as white as paper and furrowed with great vertical lines and bristling with greying whiskers. His eyes were red and blazing, his scant hair flying in the wind, his broken black teeth bared like a snarling dog's. He drew back the flap of the tent and peered inside. There in a bed of blankets on a heap of leaves, curtained and made to look more beautiful even than they were by a mosquito-net, lay Maud and Cedric, naked, he with a slim arm round her shoulders, she with face pillowed on his smooth white breast, sleeping like innocent children.

Tim stared. Slowly his lips relaxed, slowly the lines were smoothed from his cheeks, slowly the trembling of his limbs ceased. For a minute or more he stared. Then he stooped and entered.

He lifted the net and gently touched Maud's head. She woke, blinked, started up, and starting woke her lover. Cedric did not move.

"What you doin' here?" Tim asked them gruffly.

Cedric swallowed. His left hand groped for something with which to hide his beauty.

Tim looked deep into Maud's eyes and said sternly, "Are

you happy child?" She swallowed. "Tell me," he said. She nodded.

Tim looked at Cedric, studied him for a while, said, "All right. Well I'll go out while you get up. I wanner talk to you."

The lovers took so long to come that Tim was moved three times to call them, in a voice that was kindlier each time. At last he cried, "Hey there! Come on. This aint the Palace Hotel."

By the time they appeared the fire was burning brightly and the billy on the boil and the tucker out of packs and spread for breakfast. And by that time Tim had done so much thinking that he could say with a genuine smile, "Goo' mornin' Mister and Missus Noolywed. The weddin' break-fus' is now hon."

They could not return his smile. Nor could they join him in eating a hearty breakfast. He chatted to them easily, or so it seemed to them, about the rain that had fallen and the district they were in. They had nothing to say but an occasional shy Yes or No. When the meal was over he took the tobacco-pouch from Cedric's breast-pocket without invitation and rolled himself a cigarette. Cedric followed his example with trembling hands.

"Well," said Tim, breaking a silence that fell upon a short dissertation on the merits of the various kinds of tobacco, "I'm glad to see yous two young people's took up together. Yous emmigrantly suited. Howdever, it'd've saved a lot of bother if you'd've talked straight about it. I've lost a coupler stone lookin' for you. And most prob'ly I'll have to take me holid'ys now to fix up the noopshals which'll be follerin' as a matter of conskwence."

A long pause fell. A little lizard popped out of a crack in a log on the fire and ran to the cooler end. All watched it for a while. Then Tim looked at Maud and smiled till she smiled shyly, then said, "You like this boy a lot, don't you Maudie dear?"

She answered timidly, "Yes father."

"And I reckon he must like you a heap of a lot too," said Tim, "or he wouldn't've run off with you like he did — eh?" He turned to Cedric.

Cedric looked away.

"Well I don't mind tellin' you," said Tim, "that I'll be glad t'ave you's a son-in-law. And that's talkin' straight. It's to be hoped the feelin's mootyal."

Cedric concentrated on the lizard. So did they all. Tim

addressed it, saying, "Now you lil idjit, don't try runnin' out'n that part, cos the underneath of it's burnin'. Stop where y'are. You shouldn't've got y'self into wood that'd get afire." The lizard took his advice.

Then Tim said to Cedric, "Yeah — there's gonner be a weddin' at Black Adder Creek. The first. Who'd've thought it a week ago! We'll make a bonzer shivoo of it too. Booze — dancin' — all the people in the country there. You a Catholic? No? Good-o — we'll have a parson then. Priests ask too many barrassin' questions. How's that strike you?"

Maud returned his smile; but Cedric kept his eyes on the lizard, which ran about madly and shed a bit of its tail.

"I don't see you laughin' for joy, young feller," said Tim after a pause.

Cedric heard the steel in the voice, looked up and smiled weakly.

"You keen on goin' back to Agate Bar?" asked Tim.

"Yes," said Cedric huskily.

"You can make your home with us, you know. One these days when things is hummin' round this way you'll want to. Sure you wanner go home?"

"I — I've gotter help me brother."

"Please yourself. Course you's takin' Maudie with you. That's a foregone conclusion. It'll do her good too. Aint never been away from home yet. Would you like a honeymoon in a steamer, dear — first-class cabin-dee-luxe down the West Coast on the *Kinanna*?"

Maud smiled brightly.

Tim spat in the fire and said to the lizard, "Don't go beltin' about like that or you'll fall in. Stay quiet and save your bref. You won't have it much longer — 'less you's a young dragging." Then to Cedric he said, "You know this here young Maudie's been pretty well brought up. You's had the hopportoonity to see that for yourself. But she can look after herself too, take it f'm me. She'll write to me every mail and keep me posted how she's makin' along with you. I'd like you to know I'm a hard old hoss for the road. By cripes you dunno't a wicked old jigger I am when I get rousted. And there aint nuthen rousts me like some'n hurtin' my kids. By golly I'm worse'n a lion-ess in that respec'. You dunno. Take me tip and don't try to find out. Cos — my God Ceddie! — it wouldn't pay you. I like you a lot, and that's a fact. I think you's a marvellous good-lookin' kid all over. But be jees, if I found you workin' the teeniest bit of dirt on this here Maud of mine, I'd — with-

out the slightest zaggeration Ceddie — I'd take the keenest
delight in pluggin' you full of holes. See? I mean it. Would
I care about goin' to the Calabush? Not a scrap! Why —
me'n old Paddy O'Keyes, the Head Guard there, was workin' on the railway here in charge of coolie Chows when it
was bein' built. He'd give me his best cell. And anyway, I
know they wouldn't send me to jail for it. I know. And
anyway, married women has their rights to protect 'em's
well as their old dads — aint that so?"

Their blue eyes met. Cedric smiled wanly, then looked
away to the lizard, which was now quite frantic, having
through folly got itself into a very confined space.

Tim sighed and shifted from one haunch to the other
and said, "Well that's that. I've quite enjoyed this little
chat. Sorter brings us together. And now I don't mind tellin' you I'm right down glad of the whole business. You'll
make the bonzerest couple ever seen this side the Tropic.
You got nuthen to worry about, neither. I'm at the back
of you. I'm not a rich man yet be any means; but I prog-
noshticate the day aint too far distant when I will be. And
then I want yous two back here at Black Adder to get the
benefit."

For a while he watched the lizard, which was very near
the end of life. Then he looked at Cedric and said, "D'you
reckon you can make her happy, son?"

Cedric blinked, and after a while said, "Well — as a
matter of fact — I — I — I can't — I —"

He saw Tim's jaw move.

"Eh?" said Tim sharply.

Cedric looked down, licked his lips, said slowly, "Well
— yes — I reckon I can, Mister O'Cannon."

Tim smiled and said, "Good-o!" He seized Cedric's hand
and shook it, adding, "But cut out the Mister. I'm Dad
to you from now on." He smiled broadly, clapped Cedric
on the back, nearly knocked him into the fire.

The couple smiled sheepishly.

"Oh well," he said, rising, "we better get off home.
There'll be plenty to do arrangin' these here noopshals —
aw, poor lil cow, he's gone! Well he should have had the
guts to take a flyin' leap out of it before the fire got too
hot."

§

By far the most successful civilized social event that ever
took place in Capricornia was the Callow-O'Cannon wed-

ding. But the success of it was only achieved with great expense and effort on the part of the bride's father.

Tim fixed a date for the wedding and had invitation-cards printed and sent to every man employed on the railway and many others. Out of the one hundred and eighteen guests invited only twelve sent back the desired acknowledgement. He brooded over the failure for a week. Then he conceived a brilliant notion, and as the result of it telegraphed to a brewery in the city of Bullimba to ascertain the price of beer by the hogshead. Despite the fact that the reply was staggering, after a few hours of calculating he wired an order for eight hogsheads, together with orders for a large parcel of goods from a great departmental store of the same city whose catalogue he had, the whole to be sent at once to Port Magnetic to catch the mail-boat already on the way to the North. Three days later another one hundred and eighteen invitations were sent out, these not mere cards, but large printed sheets that contained the following information:

Mr & Mrs Tim O'Cannon of Black Adder Creek cordially extend to you an invitation to attend the festival that will take place on the 18th November on the occasion of the marriage of their eldest daughter Maud to Mr Cedric Callow of Agate Bar. The solemnization will be performed by the Rev. Gordon Prayter, and the festival will last three days, viz. Saturday, Sunday, and Monday, the last a public holiday.

Guests living down-road from the 58-Mile may come on Friday by the returning mail-train and travel at excursion-rates. Railwaymen may travel by free pass by applying to the Roadmaster. All may return to their homes by the material-train that will pass through the 58 on Tuesday morning. Up-road guests may come by special train (run by special courtesy of the Superintendent), at excursion rates, that will leave Port Zodiac 3.30 p.m. Saturday and remain at Black Adder till 10 p.m. Monday, when it will return. There is no fixed time for those who wish to come by horse or trike. Just roll up when you like. You will be welcome.

The following entertainments are promised in addition to the nuptials:

Horse-racing: Guests may bring their mounts. Prizes will be decided. *Buckjumping*: A jewelled lever watch will be presented to anyone not Aboriginal who can stick the famous Misanthropy for 5 mins. *Foot-racing*: Tim O'Cannon challenges all-comers over 35 to purse of £5. *Boxing*: Chance to settle old scores and make money same time. *Tug-o'-war*: Permanent-way v Loco for case of beer. *Putting-the-shot. Dancing. Music.* Trooper O'Theef of Soda Springs with his famous concertina, and Pat O'Hay of Tatlock's Pool with his heart-rending fiddle, and the Ponto Bros of Port Zodiac with their renowned guitar orchestra. *Impromptu Concerts. Decorations. Fireworks. Tons of Southern Fruit. Tucker & Lollies in Abundance.* And last but not least —

                420 IMPERIAL GALLONS OF BEER!
                            R.S.V.P.

The response was wonderful. Out of the one hundred and eighteen guests invited three hundred and seventeen arrived, most of them, fortunately for the happiness of all, bringing some food and liquor. Frank McLash, now second-engineer of the Service, drove the special down from Town, and drove so hard that thrice he broke his couplings and left behind the cattle-cars in which his passengers rode, and drove so rough that on the Skinny River bridge his engine shed a driving-rod, which might have been utterly lost had not Frank seen it fall and dived straight after it; and Frank, that valuable speed-maniac, who had already won the nickname of Mad Mack the Locomotive Loony, might have been utterly lost to the Service through his recklessness but for the Providence that watches over drunken men; for had he struck the shallow river with narrow head instead of his broad back he would have been killed. But more haste less speed. His train did not reach Black Adder till Saturday midnight.

The program was enriched with many impromptu events, of which the most entertaining was the quarrel that followed Mrs McLash's sneering because the bride and groom occupied the same bed on the night before their marriage, as indeed they had been doing since the night of their betrothal. Mrs McLash told this to Mr Prayter, who merely smiled, stroked his chin and murmured, "Well well — the funny dears!"

Mr Prayter's reply should have satisfied Mrs McLash. It did not. She prattled about the breach of etiquette till it reached Tim's ears. He was greatly annoyed to learn that what he had condoned as harmless and thought unnoticed should be discovered as a scandal. He tried to defend the couple by saying that all engaged couples enjoyed conjugality even though they might not be honest enough to show that they did in public. A host of married people howled him down. He took his revenge on Mrs McLash by asking her at top of his voice was it good etiquette to have Joe Steen in bed with her. A silence followed, one of those silences that presage a dire event.

Then Mrs McLash called on Steen to thrash the foul-mouthed monster. Steen replied that much as he would like to do so he was too old, and called on Frank to deputize him. Tim refused to fight the deputy because he was too young, and called on Jacob Ledder to do it for him. But Frank would not fight Jake because he had been a profess-ional weight-lifter. It was finally decided that Frank's fire-man, Charlie Klinker, should fight Jake for Mrs McLash's honour and that Jake should fight him because some mem-ber of an engine's crew had once thrown a lump of coal at him while passing. It was a grand fight. But the fight that followed it was grander, since that was all-in and any-how, the cause of it being the dispute over who was the winner of the first. Mrs McLash tackled Blossom; Mrs Blaize pulled Mrs Cracker's hair; even Mr Prayter was seen to take his coat off and glare about.

There were many such rows. But they were all of short duration, and were matters more of mettlesome hands than malicious hearts. The special train did not leave for Town on Monday night as scheduled, but on Tuesday morning, rather late because Frank McLash and Charlie Klinker had to chop up wood to start their fire, which, owing to their being in no fit state to handle instruments such as axes that did not run straight of their own accord on rails, was a difficult task. Tim and the bride were anxious, filled with the knowledge that the *S.S. Kinanna* was due to sail at dusk.

The first watery whistle of the engine brought the crowd from the house, headed by bride and groom, he in whites and topee, she in satin and veil. All were agreed that they were the Bonzerest couple ever seen. Arm in arm they walk-ed in front of Trooper O'Theef and Pat O'Hay, who play-ed the Wedding March on fiddle and concertina. They climbed into the brakevan in a blizzard of confetti and rice, and amid a hurricane of cheering from the crowd and a cyclone of whistling from the engine, were drawn away in-to the mystery of the future. Then Mrs McLash and Blos-som buried their faces in each other's fleshy necks and mingled the **attar-drops of their hearts**.

The total cost of the success to Tim, after deducting the

amount he secured for the sale of two crates of butter-dishes and one of biscuit-barrels to a Chinaman in Town, was £308 13s. 7d. He did not smoke for six or seven months.

PEREGRINATIONS OF A BUSYBODY

EARLY one Monday morning a few weeks after the wedding, Tim O'Cannon set out from home for work with his children marching before him. One child carried his tucker-tin, another his oil-skin coat, another the shotgun he always carried on the trike in case he met scrub-turkeys. He wore a homemade shirt of unbleached calico, and home-made dungarees, and a flat-topped wideawake that gleamed with varnish with which it had been waterproofed. Occasionally he barked at the children, "Left!"

The procession disbanded at the railway in orderly style to get the tricycle from its little shed and set it on the track. Then the units formed themselves in line before the Sergeant Major.

"Carmp-an-ee!" roared the Sergeant Major. "Atten-shoon!"

They sprang to it, to stare stiffly at a jungle of pandanus palms where brilliant parrots danced and mocked them.

"Numb-ah!"

"One, two, t'ree, foah, fi'!" Strength of voices decreasing with the height.

"Any complaints?"

"No, no, no, no, no."

"Good-o then — Goodbye Maggie O'Cannon, goodbye Kitty O'Cannon, goodbye Tommy O'Cannon, goodbye Bridie O'Cannon, goodbye Mollie O'Cannon."

"Goodbye father — " down the line.

"Carmp-an-ee — deezmeez!"

They rushed him. He climbed on to the trike, kissed each one and was kissed. Then he cried, "Letter go Gallagher! Off agin, on agin, away agin, Flannigan! Hurroo f'r Casey!"

They shoved him off. He pulled away steadily, looking ahead with smiling eyes till he reached a curve, then turned in his seat and waved. The children yelled. Blossom the

Parakeet, up at the house on the hill, waved a blue and red table-cloth. Tim waved, sighed, turned back to the road, passed out of his family's sight.

He trundled on, up grade and down, through dripping cuttings where golden catch-fly orchids grew in mossy nooks and tadpoles wriggled in sparkling pools, over culverts where smooth brown water sped over beds of grass, past towering walls of weeds that stretched out leaves and flowers to tickle his face and shower him with dew and touch him — as though he were a flower to be fertilised! — with blobs of pollen. He trundled on, up grade and down, keeping one eye on the permanent way, the other on the telegraph — the Transcontinental Telegraph, strand of copper linking Australia with the world, shimmering plaything of the sun and wind, live-thing humming as if to occupy itself in loneliness with repeating gossip of the hives it linked — keeping one eye on that and the other on the per-way, looking for defects, but not so sedulously as to miss any passing fancy.

A kangaroo leapt off the road and thud-thud-thudded into silence. A family of kangaroos, same number as the O'Cannons and about the same size, bounded ahead through a cutting. A buffalo dozing in Chinaman's Creek woke with a start and bolted. A shower of white cockatoos fell out of a bloodwood tree, yelling, "A man — a man — a Disturbing Element!" A large admiral lizard leapt up on a rail, stood on hind legs with fore legs raised like hands and watched for a moment that trundling Thing, then loped down the cess-path with arms swinging and iridescent frill flying out like a cape, looking for all the world like a bandy old admiral of days of Drake. Tim cried after it, "Hey — Sink me the ship, Master Gunner, sink her, split her in twain, fall into the hands of Gawd, my men, not into the hands of Spain!"

On a flooded plain through which the road ran high on an embankment a group of long-legged brolgas stood. They stared at Tim, who, as he always did, took off his hat and bowed and cried to them, "Goo' mornin' ladies — lovely day!" And they, as if in courteous reply, extended pearl-grey wings and curtsied, stared after that strange creature that neither walked nor crawled nor flew but glided so fantastically with creaking limbs.

He trundled on, up grade and down, crushing a billion ants that sped along the lightly-rusted crowns of rails, scaring humming-birds from hearts of flowers, startling more kangaroos, big red boomers and wallaroos and little does with bright-eyed joeys peeping from their apron pockets. He came within sight of the Caroline Siding, the whitewashed roofs of which gleamed as dead white against an inky horizon as faces of nuns against black hoods. He trundled on, over shadows of antheaps that dwarfed the telegraph, on and on, past Sam Snigger's place where horses were sporting, past old Karl Fliegeltaub's, a ruin of a place, like the ruins of the hopes of his kind, and so on and down to the red-girdered bridge.

In a big pool into which a torrent poured from old Karl's dam a crowd of black piccaninnies were bathing. Tim clapped on the brake and stopped to watch. The children dived and swam like seals. A yelling mob of them would plunge, and like black corks their heads would bob about in froth, and like a mass of helpless ants they would be whirled about and flung into the shallows of the river. Tim shouted. They turned to him, red mouths gaping, teeth agleam, dashing water from their eyes. He shouted a few words in a native dialect. They screamed with laughter and replied. He grimaced and shook his fist. They screamed and danced and mocked him.

His feet began to press the pedals and the trike began to move, when his eye was caught by the sight of one child in a group of smaller children playing in the shallows some little distance down — a white child, so white by contrast with the others that at first he thought it must be ochred, which it could not be while playing in the water.

He stopped again, and sat staring at the child and wondering. There were no white children to his knowledge thereabout; if there had been one it certainly would not be playing with the native children. The piccaninnies stared at him, suspicious of his interest, till he dismounted and began to come down to them, when they scampered down the river towards the camp. The natives were now back on their old camping-ground. Tim had not had much to do with them.

He ran after the children, calling on them to stop. They sped the swifter. Shrewd savages for all their immaturity, they scattered as they went. But Tim knew which one he wanted. He caught it when it bogged in mud beside the river. It was a girl of about three, a white quadroon; though Tim would not have guessed that it was anything but white had he not found it as he did. She bit and tore and kicked, yelling like a wounded cockatoo. He gripped the vicious little legs with one arm and the top part of her with the other, and so marched off with her to the camp.

"Here!" he cried to the lounging natives. "Where'd this piccanin come from?"

They stared.

"Come on!" he roared. "Tell me, or I'll belt some of you. You, Morris Hughes — what name this one?"

"Him Hummy, Boss."

"Which way him mumma?"

"I dunno."

"Now no humbug. Which way him come longa camp? — Here!" A lubra snatched the baby out of Tim's arms and ran off. "Blast you!" roared Tim. "Bring her back." The lubra stopped at safe distance.

Tim glared, then demanded of Morris Hughes, "Where you get him?"

"Findim longa bush, Boss."

"Woffor you no-more sendim longa Compound?"

"Me forget, Boss."

"Liar!" cried Tim. "I'll bet there's a yeller girl here somewhere." He strode off to inspect the gunyahs. Before they could head him off he found Constance. She was lying on a bed of leaves, clad only in a sugar bag, thin as a skeleton, black with filth and flies. He did not recognize her. Indeed, at first he thought she was an old lubra. He bent over her, stared at her scaly skin, then said, "Hello girl — where'd you spring from?"

She regarded him fearfully with great sunken eyes, drew away the skinny hand he tried to take. "Don't be frighten'," he said gently. "I won't hurt you. I'm Ganger O'Cannon. Know me?" She nodded. "What's your name?" he asked.

After some hesitation she whispered it.

He was amazed. "Conny Differ!" he cried, staring. Then he turned to look at the child, which was glaring at him from the lubra's arms close by; then he turned back to Constance and asked, "That your kid?" She nodded. "Not Peter Pan's?" he asked. She shook her head. "Then whose?"

She stared dumbly. "Come on child," he said. "Tell us. Aint a fettler, is it?"

She shook her head.

"Then whose? Now come on."

Still she stared. Then, as though he read the answer in the light that flickered in those caverns in her gaunt brown face, he said slowly, "Hummy — Humbolt Lace — was — was that him?"

She did not move.

He drew a deep breath. At last he said softly, "I oughter known — gawdstrewth I oughter known — well of all the hell-bound barsteds!"

She began to cough. She coughed till her body heaved, till dust was flying from her wretched bed, till it seemed her poor thin frame must burst into leathery fragments, till she fell back gasping, with tears streaming from her eyes, bloody spittle from her mouth. Tim took a hand that was frantically gathering leaves, and said, "You — you got an awful cough, girl."

She would tell him nothing till she learnt that Lace had long ago gone South, then told him all. At last he said, "Come with me. You can't stay here, girl. No matter how bad the Compound is, it aint as bad as this. Here, let's lift you."

The fettling-gang, sitting watching for Tim's coming from the bridge, were surprised to see him come from the bush behind his house carrying what appeared to be a half-naked lubra in his arms, followed by Morris Hughes who was carrying a white child, heading for the Siding House. They rose and went to meet him.

"Hello Tim!" said Jake Ledder. "Wha's up?"

"Sick woman."

"Give you a hand?"

"No thanks," Tim answered shortly. And on he went, marching like a soldier, though truth to tell his arms were on the point of snapping. The fettlers winked behind his back. His self-important strutting was well known. He stood on the veranda of the Siding House, and still with the burden up, shouted, "You there Missus?"

No response. He shouted thrice. Then, because he was on the verge of collapse and conscious of the grinning men behind, he kicked the iron wall and roared, "Hey Missus! Dammit — you dead?"

Frank McLash, home for a few days, flung open the refreshment-room door. He was clad only in short striped cotton drawers, and looked more like a hairy ape than the usual kewpie doll. He blinked at Tim and demanded, "Wasser burry matter?"

"Mother up?" snapped Tim.

"Wasser mat?"

"Mother up, I hasked you."

"And I hasked you what's the matter!"

"Is your mother up?"

"No she aint, Mister Blunny Sergeant Major. And don't you bark at me like that or I'll wallop you one on the regimental nose toot sweet."

"I want your mother quick!" cried Tim with passionate anger. "This woman's sick."

"What's up with her?"

"Dyin' be the looks of it — and dead for all you damn well care. Go to ruddy stinkin' flamin' jiggery!"

Tim stamped off towards the post-office. Frank winked at the fettlers and withdrew.

At the other door Tim gasped, "You there Missus?"

"What you want?" asked a muffled voice.

"I got a sick woman here I want you 'tend to."

"Eh — what woman?"

"Conny Differ — Conny Pan. I foun' her in the niggers' camp."

"What's wrong with her?"

"Sick," gasped Tim.

"And what you expec' me to do?"

Tim set Constance down with back to the wall, drew a deep breath, and asked in a strained voice, "Can I use the telephone, Missus?"

"Now don't get impatient. Think a body's gunner leap outer bed and come rushin' to — "

"Can I use the telephone, Madam?"

"Do't you ruddy well like!"

"Thanks, Madam, you're a lady."

"I am that — compared with the likes o' you. Now look here Tim O'Cannon —"

Tim went into the post-office and rang Soda Springs. He had to ring several times before Mrs Blaize answered. Meanwhile Mrs McLash talked to him through the wall.

"Hello!" he said at last to a wheezing voice. "O'Cannon here, Ma — wanner talk to the police."

"Don't call me Ma," snapped Mrs Blaize. "I've told you often enough before. And what you want the police for?"

"Mergency."

"But what's the matter? I aint gunner call the man for nuthen."

"I wouldn't ask for him for nuthen!" bawled Tim. "What's matter with yous all 's mornin' — got the keck liver or what?"

She bawled at him, "If you bawl at me I'll ring you off. Tell me what you want and have done with it."

"Good God woman, I told you minutes ago I want the jonnop. If you don't get him right away I'll report you."

"Oh you would, you informin' ol' hound!"

"Where's O'Theef?"

"Don't deafen me! The man's in his house I s'pose."

"Get him."

"Now look here Tim O'Cannon — "

"Oh for gawdsake don't go on, Missus. There's a woman here dyin'."

"Eh? What woman? Not poor Missus McLash?"

"No such luck."

"Eh? Who then? What other woman's there but that old thing?"

"Conny Pan."

"You said a woman."

"Well — dammit?"

"Don't swear at me, Sir! Conny Pan's a halfcaste — and a halfcaste's a lubra."

"Oh have it your own damn way," bawled Tim. "Have it any damn way you like. But I say there's a woman here dyin', a woman to be considered as much as any other in the land, and on behalfs that fact I want the trooper of police, and if you don't go right off and get that hofficer and he don't come at once, Madam, I'll have the greatest pleasure in puttin' the matter 'fore the proper hauthorities and reportin' yous both for derelectin' to do your lawful dooty — "

"Ah! He's run outer bref — "

"I said there's a woman *dyin'*!"

"Oh no he aint!"

"Are you goin' to — "

`Crash!` Then sound of shuffling feet. Then Saxon Whitely of Republic Reef and Mrs Quibble of the 122-Mile both said together in Tim's ear, "What's wrong with Conny Pan, Tim?" He ignored them.

Trooper O'Theef was livery too, and resented Tim's interference in the business of the police. He said he should have found Constance eventually, and told Tim to put her back in the camp so that he might do so. "No fear!" said Tim. "I'm keepin' her here. You come right up on Al Packer's trolley and take her up to Town."

"Don't you dictate to me," snapped O'Theef. "Put her back where you found her, Mister Busybody."

"I won't do nuthen of the sort, Mister Conscientious Hofficer. If you can't come, then ring up Town and tell 'em come down and get her. She's dyin', don't I tell you!"

"How long's she been sick?"

"I dunno — years."

"Then I reckon it'll be years 'fore she dies. Put her back in the camp."

"So's she can die in the years you'll be comin' to look for her — "

"Damn you O'Cannon! Why the hell can't you stick to your own job and keep your long nose outer other people's? You're a pest. Eh? Oh blast it — all right, I'll come when I can. Eh? No — I can't promise today. Might be tomorrer. I can't promise nuthen. I'm busy."

"What you busy at?"

"Mindin' me own flamin' jiggerin' blunny business."

Crash!

Tim found Mrs McLash, clad in nightdress and a blanket, bending over Constance and treating her with kindness. Without a word he picked Constance up and carried her to his own house, followed by Morris Hughes with the child. Mrs McLash sneered after him, "Gertcha — fishous ol' busybody!"

Tim sent a fettler for the trike, and set to work to make tea. When his tucker-tin arrived he laid out a meal of cold roast goat and lettuce and bread and tomato-sauce and pickles. The child ate heartily, though with one eye always on her benefactor and one hand ready to clutch her mother. Constance ate nothing but a little bread soaked in tea. After the meal Tim heated water for baths. Constance washed herself as best she could, then sat near while Tim washed the child, to convince her that she was not being murdered. Then Tim cut up a shirt and made a smock for the child and sent to Mrs McLash for a lubra's dress for Constance. Eventually he won the trust of the child by entertaining her with his alarm-clock, through doing which he came to call her Tickety-Tock.

Trooper O'Theef did not come next day, so Tim rang Soda Springs again, and learnt that, far from being on the way to the Caroline, the trooper had gone out to Mount Molehill to stop a native war. He then telegraphed to the police in Town, who told him to put Constance back in the camp and wait for O'Theef. He then tried to make friends with Mrs McLash with a view to inducing her to take his charges off his hands. She ignored him.

On the third day, which was train-day, he took Constance and Tickety-Tock up to Black Adder on the trolley when he ran the length, and left them with his family. Then he sent a letter on the train to Trooper O'Theef, saying that the Pans would be ready waiting at the 58 for the returning train, on which it was expected he would come to take them up to Town. Now that the railway had been extended to the Melisande, a distance of fifty miles beyond Copper Creek, there was a mail-train every week.

On Friday afternoon, when the coloured portion of the O'Cannon family heard the mail train in the hills near Red Coffin Ridge, they escorted Constance and Tocky, both now clad in brilliant garments of the Parakeet's make, to the railway. Constance was so weak that she could scarcely walk. The food and care she had enjoyed of late had only made her condition more acute through having roused her powers of resistance. During that short walk, leaning heavily on Blossom, she coughed incessantly. Tocky, on the other hand, was as skippy as a goat when the first green shoots of the Wet have put an end to the dull Dry-Season diet of bark and bitter leaves.

The train stopped. Out of it climbed not a khaki-clad policeman, but Ganger O'Cannon, clad in home-made dungarees, who told the waiting group at the top of his voice that as that flaming loafing jigger O'Theef had not come, he himself must take the Pans to Town, where he was going to make a lovely barney at Police Headquarters. His family stared at him. Idea of an O'Cannon's going to the Metropolis in dungarees and varnished hat was unthinkable. Tim had to bawl at Margaret to get her to run up to the house for his bankbook. Passengers craned out to stare at the strange gathering. The engineer whistled impatiently, at the risk of delaying the start for want of steam. The guard shouted, "Hey there! Don't get holdin' us up too long. We're late." As if they had never been late before!

Tim was fuming. At the risk of being left behind he abused the guard in strong language. The guard merely grinned. But Saxon Whitely, who was travelling with his wife, bawled, "Here — moderate your bl — ooming languige!"

The engineer opened the throttle as soon as flying Margaret reappeared. Tim bundled the Pans on to the platform of a coach. He did not follow at once, but walked with the moving train, giving his family instructions how to occupy themselves during his absence. Margaret, thoughtful girl, brought his best boots and hat along with the bankbook. Therefore Tim flung the varnished hat at Blossom, and as soon as he stepped aboard sat down on the step and took off his working-boots, which Tommy found later at the 57½ peg.

§

Charlie Wing Sing, the restaurant-keeper, took Tim and his charges from the station to his restaurant in a motor-truck. Tim and Tocky ate a huge meal there. Constance swallowed a mouthful of Chinese medicine that Charlie recommended and a cup of condensed milk. Then Charlie took the charges into the labyrinthine dwelling at the back of the restaurant and entertained them while Tim went off to see the doctor. Charlie was a cousin of Blossom's, her father's brother's son.

Tim found the doctor at home, and resting after a hard day's work that had included the amputation of a gangrenous leg, the delivery of a Greek woman of triplets, the vaccination of a score of Compound natives, the post-mortem examination of a long-dead Chinaman, and the dealing with a friend of his in D.T.'s. He was playing bridge and was rather annoyed at being disturbed, but quite courteous. He listened to Tim's long tale without once interrupting; or rather appeared to listen; for in fact he was thinking mostly of how he had best play those hearts he had left behind. At length he said, "You really ought've taken them to the police, you know."

"What?" cried Tim, who had explained his previous dealings with that body in detail. He began to explain again.

The doctor nodded wearily and said, "Good-o, old man. I'll attend to 'em. Take 'em to the Compound and tell the matron I sent you."

"What?" cried Tim, who had talked at length about their right to go to the hospital. "They aint niggers. The mother ought to go into the hospital, I tell you."

"There's a hospital in the Compound."

"But it's a native hospital."

"Well?"

"Aw dammit doctor — that's no blunny good!"

"Why — what you got against it?"

"It can't be any good — cos — well cos it's a native hospital, of course. Native hospital! Gawd, anyone'd think a nigger got sick different to a whiteman — sort of in the Native Fashion. And there's a native cemetery too. Gawd-

strewth, I'll bet there's colour-sections in the whiteman's
Heaven and Hell!"

"That remains to be seen."

"Aw look here, doc — this 'ere woman's dyin' with consumption. She oughter be seen to right away."

"People don't die of consumption in a few hours."

"What about gallopin' consumption? I know of a case
—"

"Keep it for the Medical Journal, old man. Now please
excuse me. I've got a case waiting inside — urgent case —
heart. Take 'em to the police or the Compound or wherever
you like. I'll see 'em in the morning. Goodnight old man."

Tim took them to the Compound in Charlie's truck. The
matron disputed with him for a while about the rightness
of her taking them without written directions from the
doctor. Then she took them away and locked them in an
iron shed.

In the afternoon of the following day he returned to the
Compound, and after more disputing with the matron, was
allowed to see Constance. He found her lying wrapped
in a ragged blanket on a bed of planks in the corner of a
dark little earth-floored hovel that stank of phenyle and
black bodies. Tocky was playing in the barren steaming
yard with black piccaninnies. The doctor, he was told, had
not yet come. This was the Native Hospital. It stood in a
corner of the Compound enclosure behind a barbed-wire
fence of its own, and consisted of a group of whitewashed
iron sheds, and looked something like the latrines of a
military camp.

Tim called again next day, which was Sunday. Failing
to get any response to his knocking at the door of the
matron's house, he went to the Compound of his own accord, and, happening to find the gate of the hospital open,
made his way to Constance. He found her as before, but
obviously weaker; and Tocky was dirtier and clad in the
dungaree uniform of the Halfcastes' Home. The doctor
had not yet called.

While Tim was talking to Constance, a whiteman suddenly appeared and roared at him, a man rather like himself in face and form, though older and white-haired. This
was the Officer in Charge of the Compound. Tim had never
met him, but knew him by name and repute.

The Officer in Charge told Tim that he was committing
an offence by being on those premises without authority,
and that it was his duty — yes, and it would be his pleas-

ure too, if Tim gave much more cheek! — to give him in charge.

Duty! roared Tim. And there and then he cast aspersions on the Officer's manner of doing his duty as it was reflected in the wretched state of his institution. He swore heartily. So did the Officer. A crowd gathered.

Tim was not a bit afraid of the Officer's threats, having heard enough about him to know that he was a good old fellow, and liking the look of him in spite of what he said. Still he could not take bullying lying down. He told the Officer that if he, the Officer, were not so old and feeble he would wipe the ground with him. Try it! bellowed the Officer. And he demanded to know Tim's name so that he might report him to the police. Tim gave it. At once the Officer's face changed. He had heard of Tim; but it was not his reputation that softened him; it was his name — Timothy Patrick O'Cannon. His own was Aloysius Furphey. During the evacuation of the hospital, which had begun with force, the raging of them both abated swiftly, so that by the time the gate was passed a blarney-contest was in progress. Furphey told Tim that it was very kind of him to have done what he had for the Pans, and fine what he had done in the way of Home Service during the war. Tim said that it was great of Furphey to say so.

At the gate that led to the road the recent war was mentioned. Mr. Furphey had seen service as a captain. Tim was delighted. And he delighted Furphey, but rather scared himself, by saying on the spur of the moment that he had seen service as a sergeant major in the Suppression Campaign in South Africa. War experiences were then discussed to the exclusion of all other subjects, boastfully by the Captain, since what he said was possibly true, modestly by the Sergeant Major, since he was only representing what he had picked up from the veteran Pat O'Hay of Tatlock's Pool.

The legs of Captain Furphey weakened long before his tongue or audience. He suggested an adjournment to his office, where he produced a bottle. Tim helped with the bottle as an old soldier should, even one who has fought his battles only in imagination. Then Furphey brought the war to an end, demobilized himself, and came home to the Compound. He said that no-one realised the wretched state of his institution better than he. But the fault was not his, he declared, nor was it the fault of the new Protector, who was one of the best men living. That man, said he, had done more for the blacks and halfcastes than all the other protectors put together, and had done it at the risk of incurring general displeasure. The fault of the state of the Compound rested on the entire Nation. At back of it was the mad pride in colour, and greed for petty exaltation, of the general public, the callousness of people who used the labour of the Aborigines, the stupidity and selfishness of both local and National Governments.

Why — it cost more to pay the Resident Commissioner's salary than to feed and clothe and doctor all the thousands of blacks and halfcastes in the land! Not a word of exaggeration. And that gentleman's salary had recently been raised to meet the increased cost of living. Still only fourpence per head per day was provided for the maintenance of the inmates of the Compound. In the bush the blacks were dying like flies of consumption and measles and leprosy and gonorrhoea for the sake of a few pounds' worth of facilities to treat them. Oh the paltriness! The foul neglect! But it was no fault of the Protector's. He had striven with all his might to get the means, and still strove though the expenses allowed him were even reduced and he was constantly reprimanded for exceeding the Estimates. Poor unproductive stock he had! Why were they so? Because they were not allowed to be anything else. Were they to flourish and be incorporated into the life of the Nation the problem of miscegenation would become great. The prudes who ruled the Nation were afraid of that. To prevent it they would rather wipe out the Aborigines — wipe out a race! That in a nutshell was the reason of the National Government's vast and almost incredible callosity. The man behind it was the President of the Commonwealth himself. How the man could sleep of nights with this monstrous thing on his soul — God knows!

Consider the callosity of these parliamentary pigs. The Government could afford to buy a £10,000 schooner for the purpose of making a search for five white people supposed to have been marooned somewhere down the coast when the S.S. Rawlinson was lost, but not a sixpenny syringe for the Compound hospital, could afford to overstaff the Government Offices with men at a minimum salary of £8 a week, but not a few sheets of iron to repair the roofs of the hovels that lay there in view, could afford to build a new quarantine station to hold people stricken with infectious diseases that had never yet broken out — people who could quite easily be placed in a camp if the need arose —, but were so poor that they could not allow people who died in the Compound even a shroud of the ragged blanket in which they died, were so poor that they had to house the hundred-odd children of the Halfcastes' Home in a building of exactly similar proportions to that in which the matron of the institution lived alone. Oh the paltriness! Wasting money on useless Commissions to investigate the problems of settling the land, which the blacks and halfcastes would have settled in no time if trained to do it, while seventy thousand blacks and twenty thousand halfcastes lived like dogs. What a Nation! If it ever got anywhere in the world there was no God!

"But O'Cannon," said Captain Furphey, "for the love of Mike, man, don't be repeatin' a word of what I'm tellin' you. I'm in the gun already with the brass-hat brigade. They're trying to dismiss me: Why? I'll tell you. Simply because I'm doin' the work I'm paid to do, and that's take care of these poor spalpeens, these God's creatures like yourself and me you see arount you. I give 'em more than the Estimates provide for, see? Bedad, man dear, they'd be gettin' sweet but-all if I didn't! They want to put a young feller in me place. He had this job temporary betwixt the time the last hog that held it died — bad cess to him! — and the time I had the good fortune to secure it. Held it temporary, the blunny black-hearted dingo, and wore out two stockwhips assertin' his authority. Bad cess to the lot of 'em, O'Cannon, me boy, bad cess to the flamin' lot!"

"Here, here!" cried Tim. "Hic! Hic!"

Captain Furphey went on to say that the doctor could not be blamed for not attending to Constance, since yesterday was Saturday and today was Sunday, and all the week the little man worked so hard. But would he neglect a sick Government Officer on a holiday? demanded Tim. And would the Protector risk his job by flying full in the face of authority to do for his charges what he was supposed to wish to do? Captain Furphey wheedled him away from that and back to the war. At last Tim staggered back to Town to spend the rest of the day asleep in his room at the First and Last.

On Monday at noon Tim called at the Compound again, to be met by the matron who refused even to discuss Constance with him unless he had a visiting-permit from the Protector. For some time he mooched round hoping to see the Officer in Charge. Women in the closely-wired venereal-diseases section of the hospital, black women and brown, young girls and hags, stared at him till he retired in embarrassment. He walked back past the matron's house, underneath which he saw two young and obviously pregnant halfcastes washing clothes, and at the same time heard the clink of glass and the sound of laughter in the house above. He clicked his tongue, as though he thought the misery of the girls below should make their mistress mournful.

The Halfcastes' Home was next to the matron's house. Sure enough it was a building of exactly similar proportions, though its residents numbered a hundred-odd. Tim stopped at the fence and watched the children, most of whom, as he could see by looking through to the back under the elevated building, were eating their penny dinner in an open-fronted shed. Some of the children were playing in a muddy gutter at the side, others in the barren yard in front. All were dressed in the dungaree uniform, with hair cropped close, so that it was impossible to tell their sex. They ranged from infants like Tocky to striplings like Tim's own Margaret. Two of those in front were quite as white as Tocky. To them Tim called and beckoned. They looked at him as cur dogs might and slunk away. He swore and spat and drifted off.

On Tuesday afternoon he came again, this time with a permit. But again he was refused admission by the matron, who said that Constance was confined in the venereal-diseases section, which none but an officer might enter. Why was she there? Because the doctor had found that she was suffering from gonorrhoea as well as the consumption. The matron added that she was not expected to live for more than a few days, and that Tocky would be placed in the Home.

Tim did not go away, but lounged about outside the Compound in the hope that the doctor might come again, as the matron had said he might, and allow him to speak to Constance, if only from a distance. The thought that he might never set eyes on her again appalled him. At sundown a car drew up at the matron's house. He hurried towards it, thinking that the doctor was come at last. It was not the doctor, but a crowd of white-clad people whom the matron greeted with squeals of joy. Soon there was in progress in the house what sounded to Tim like a party. He drifted back to the gate of the Compound, meanly begrudging the matron the right to enjoyment when one of her humble charges lay dying. He had in mind as he walked an idea that had occurred to him some hours earlier. He put it into effect when he reached the gate. He called a lubra to him, talked to her earnestly through the fence, then gave her a handful of silver, turned away and went back to Town.

Four hours later he came back to the Compound gate, passing the uproarious house of the matron with unnecessary stealth, and after carefully surveying the dark surroundings, whistled softly. After a while a lubra came, and, giggling, lifted Tocky over the fence to him. He whispered, "Now, mind — no-more tellim no-one."

"Yu-i," she whispered.

"Good-o. Mummuk."

"Mummuk," was the soft reply.

He stole away, bearing Tocky, who snuggled against his breast and murmured sleepily. At a spot some distance off he stopped and looked back. A new moon hung above the faint white blur of the Compound. He looked at it, at the blur, and said softly, "Mummuk lil Conny — mummuk and peace to you, child."

Next morning Tim left Town on the mail-train, sitting in a coach with Tocky beside him sucking lollies. She was finely dressed and very clean and pretty. Passengers talked to Tim and eyed the child, but took little notice of her, since possession of any sort of coloured brat was expected of him. Only one person eyed her closely. That was Frank McLash, who was driving the train, and who saw her when Tim walked past the engine with the child in his arms while water was being taken at the 40-Mile. Frank looked up from oiling his drivers and stared for a moment, then asked, "That yours, Tim?" Tim said, "Yes," and walked on.

At Black Adder the family was waiting. Tim dropped off into their arms, cried, "Hello!" and handed over Tocky whispering, "Here's a noo rooky for you. Look after her well — Go on, Maggie, duck up and get my old hat and boots. What — you got 'em? Good girl! Well, I must be off to work. Back on Sat'd'y. Hurroo f' Casey!"

MUCH of Tim O'Cannon's life subsequently was darkened by misfortune. Things went so badly with him that at length he became convinced that he was being dogged by a Jinx or agent of misfortune, which he suspected was that descendant of unfortunate people, Tocky.

Two months after the enlisting of Tocky in the Garrison force, Molly, aged five years, took convulsions and died in her father's arms. She was taken ill one Sunday afternoon while Tim was branding calves on the run. Margaret brought the news to him. He galloped home, riding his favourite, General Birdwood, whom he forced in exhaustion to clear the home-paddock fence and so destroyed. The horse fell and broke a leg, and, left by Tim, and utterly forgotten for hours, crawled down to the creek and drowned himself. At the time the natives were away hunting.

Tim rushed into the house, snatched the baby from the mother's arms, to have it turn up its little toes in his own. He was amazed. Death at Black Adder was something that affected only goats and horses and bullocks and niggers. He stared at Blossom. He had always suspected her of hating the child, because she had tried to abort its birth. He stared and stared till Blossom dropped her eyes and shuffled, slunk away. He put the dead child on the table, rushed at her, took her by the throat, and bawling accusations in her face, strangled her till she was senseless. He wrapped the child in a blanket and took it up to Town on the trike.

Though it was two in the morning when he reached the town, he went straight to the doctor, and, having made him prove that the child was beyond recovery, ordered him at first, then begged him, to perform an autopsy at once so that he might bring without delay a charge of murder against the fiend who slew it. The doctor was convinced that the child had died naturally. He turned Tim out, flung him out, shouted at last that if he would not go he would call the police. Tim was crazed. He went off, to roam the silent streets with his rigid burden till the dawn.

When the excitement of Molly's death was past, Tim discovered that he had left fifty calves to die of thirst in the branding yard. Then most of the next season's calves and a good third of the adult stock were drowned in a great flood that swept over the district next Wet Season.

Then Maud wrote from the settlement of Anchor Bay

on the West Coast to say that her husband had broken his back through a fall from a horse and had been sent to hospital for life, and that his brother had turned her and her baby out. Tim sent her money to come home, and made arrangements to claim her dues from Cedric's brother. His letter was returned. He telegraphed to the police of Anchor Bay, and learnt that Maud and her baby had left for Capricornia aboard a Japanese pearling lugger that had been lost in a cyclone somewhere off Point Danger.

In the following year Tommy, aged twelve, the pride and joy and hope of his father's life, the future Commandant of the Garrison, met with a terrible accident. He went down to the Caroline one time, as he often did, to spend a week with his father and take lessons in general subjects from Perfessor Brains, a new member of Tim's gang, and, while the gang was away at work one day, went into the trolley-shed to play. There he found a box of track-detonators. He knew what they were, having seen his father place them on the track to warn approaching traffic while repairs were being effected, and sometimes explode them for fun. He put four detonators in a bag and struck them with a short-handled hammer. Three fingers of his right hand were shattered, his face mutilated, his eyes blown out. He spent a year in the hospital in Town. Then, because it was found that his brain was permanently affected, his father sent him to a State asylum in Bullimba.

Not long after Tommy was sent away, Tim was suspended from the Service for a year for having left the points of the siding at the Caroline open and so caused the mail-train to collide with and destroy a rake of trucks. And he was further punished for the same offence by being prevented from working as a ganger for twelve months after reinstatement. The first year was a lean one for the O'Cannons, and one productive of no good to them, in spite of all the work they put into their property. The Dry Season of that year was extraordinarily long; and the Wet that followed it was one of the heaviest on record. What they bred and planted in that year was either burnt up or drowned. When Tim returned to work he was nearly bankrupt.

He was worried for years by the thought that Tocky was the Jinx. But he never thought of getting rid of her. She had taken the place of Molly in the house and in his heart. She was not an O'Cannon of the blood, but was of similar stuff, it seemed, in spite of her parentage. That made her valuable as well as beloved. What with the disasters that had already depleted the Garrison and those Tim feared might deplete it more and the inability of the faded Blossom to replace the losses, O'Cannons, whether of the blood or stuff, had become most precious.

He was dogged by the jinx for the conventional seven years. Then it left him suddenly, with suddenness that was frightful, but left him utterly, so that he never had another care. He never discovered what it was.

§

On the day before the Christmas Eve of 1927, a special train carrying Christmas mail and stores left Port Zodiac for the Melisande at noon, and after having travelled for thirteen hours at an average speed of six miles an hour, arrived at the Caroline. The delay was due both to mechanical defects in the train itself and the effects of the season on the crew, to one no more than the other. Such a state of affairs with the Christmas train was not unusual.

It crawled into the Caroline Siding at 1.13 a.m. on Christmas Eve. There were only three passengers aboard, who were sleeping with the guard in the caboose. The night was stormy, and so black that the trailing smoke was lost in it. And a high wind shrieked through wheels and springs, tore at loose fittings, snatched at smoke and steam, as though playing a spiteful game.

In the Siding House sat the fettlers and Ganger O'Cannon and the people of the district, including Burywell of Red Ochre and O'Hay of Tatlock's Pool. Mrs McLash was there, and Frank, and old Joe Steen, all grown much older and looking it, though not in their own eyes nor in those of each other, because they had all grown old together.

Frank was then out of a job, after having attained his ambition to become First Engineer of the Service. It was not through any delinquency of his as a locomotive-engineer that he had lost his job, but through a peculiar accident due to the moral laxity of another, George Waistbin, lately Loco-Foreman in Port Zodiac.

George Waistbin often came down the road to inspect the engines of the water-pumps that supplied the railway tanks. He used to come down on the mail-train and return on it, spending the two intervening nights with whomever lived near the engine he came to inspect. So he had come to the Caroline one time when Frank was home on holidays, and had, as usual, camped at the Siding House.

Frank found him in the middle of the night making love to his own favourite lubra. The fact that the fellow was his boss made no difference to Frank, who bawled him out. He would have left it at that had not the fellow told him, perhaps with intent to dissuade him from making common knowledge of the affair, that he knew there was a box of tools in Mrs McLash's shed that had been stolen from the Loco. Frank had been in trouble for stealing tools before, and threatened with dismissal if he got into it again. The things were of little use to him; but he loved tools; and he loved to steal. Waistbin's talk sounded like a threat to Frank. So he thrashed him. Waistbin was as big and heavy as Frank and had to be thrashed soundly to be defeated. The result was that he went back to Town with a dislocated collar-bone, a fractured jaw, three broken ribs, and a terrible desire for revenge.

Subsequently the Siding House was searched by apologetic Trooper O'Theef, who reluctantly found the tools in the piano. Frank was apologetically arrested. He swore in court that he had found the tools in a bag in the bush near the 85-mile, and produced three native witnesses to prove it. Unfortunately, just when all looked as though it were going well, one of the black witnesses, when asked by the magistrate if he understood what Truth was, stated that he had been instructed by Frank not to speak the truth. In spite of his war-service, of which he made much in court, having been led to believe through reading Southern papers that it could be used as a good excuse for committing breaches of the law, Frank was sent to Calaboose for a month and dismissed the Service. He left the dock shouting that the Soldier had been forgotten and that if there were another war he would be hanged before he would go. He was broken-hearted. There was no joy in life for him unless he was living in sight and sound and smell of locomotives. Back at home he had to resume the unremunerative practice of his boyhood days of attending to the engines of the lucky fellows who stopped to eat at his mother's.

Mrs McLash denounced Waistbin as a combo. But it was a difficult charge to prove, and proved or not, even though it was an offence to consort with lubras, would not have been punished by the law. If every man guilty of going combo in Capricornia were convicted, how worn the road to the Calaboose would be! So Mrs McLash put a curse on the man. A week or so later he won £5,000 in the Sturt State Lottery and went down South to live.

The people in the Siding House that stormy Christmas Eve were divided into groups and variously engaged. None was drinking, not because any had mended his ways, but because there was nothing in the district to drink just then but kerosene and water. It was for that more mellow beverage from the bottle that most were waiting for the Christmas train. Tim O'Cannon was not waiting for grog, but for other pleasant things connected with the season. All had been waiting since sundown, unaware of the position of the train, because there was no telephone station between the Caroline and the 20-Mile.

At the time of the train's arrival, Tim was engaged in conversation with Jack Burywell, who, though a robust fellow when he took over Red Ochre, was now a lean and faded-looking man, become so through excessive drinking and comboing and worrying about his unproductive business. They were speaking of Oscar Shillingsworth, whom Burywell had been trying for some time past to persuade to resume control. Burywell said that Oscar would do nothing but insist on payment of the money that was owing him, which, said Burywell miserably, was utterly, utterly impossible. He said many things about Oscar so comical, though said with terrible bitterness, that Tim, for all his understanding of the weight of an unproductive business, could scarcely hold his laughter.

No-one heard the train arrive, so slowly for want of steam had it crept in, and so boisterous was the night and noisy the fittings of the old building. It announced itself with a watery squeak. "The train!" cried the gathering, and ran out.

Tim climbed into the van and woke the guard, who cursed him first, then rose and embraced him, demanding to know where they were. "Goowole Timmy!" he cried when he was told. "Goowole cobber. Alls a grey yelp."

"Now lookeer Timmy," the guard went on, "I'm lil bit shicker t'night, an' I wan you t'elp me get ev'thing off proper sidin's. Ole Shoupentennan says to me, he says, 'Now lookeer Charlie, use y' nut a bit this time or you'll get the bullet — see?' an' he says, he says, 'Now lookeer Charlie, I'm 'lyin' on you t' get ev'thing off proper sidin's, not like las' Chris-hic-ass, half ev'thing off wrong sidin's, half ev'thing brought back Town,' he says. 'Use y' bit o' brains,' he says, 'an take a jerry to y' self.' An' so I wan' you t'elp me Timmy, gettin' ev'thing off proper hics!"

Tim rummaged among the packages looking for those

addressed to the Caroline, while the guard staggered round with his shunting-lamp, casting feeble beams of red and green on the dingy surroundings. The passengers, who had lain in a heap on the mail-bags, snoring, till moved by Tim, rose, got out their bottles, and sang lustily: *Chris-hic-ass comesh but wunst a year.*

The train left at 2.5 a.m., whistling merrily in the new strength it had gained from the skilful attention of Frank. It made good speed. By the time it reached Purruwunni Creek it was travelling at sixty miles an hour and mowing down sleepy kangaroos as a cyclone mows down city chimneys. By the time it reached Soda Springs all the loose fittings had fallen off, and the guard and passengers were crouching in the swaying caboose waiting for the end. It flashed through Soda Springs like a meteor, blew the hats off the waiting crowd and vanished into the night. All this by a train that had struggled for half a day at a mean six miles an hour, simply because the Locomotive Loony had taken charge.

Tim carried many packages to his house, and after putting on the billy, donned steel-rimmed spectacles and looked to see what had come. His eyes were failing; and most of his hair was gone; and what was left was paper-white, even that which bristled on his lined and sunken jaws. Thus does relentless Sergeant Major Time break the bodies of even the toughest soldiers.

He made his tea, sipped it noisily from a large enamel pannikin. He did not taste. His senses were concentrated in his shaggy eyes, which were intent upon the articles lying on the bed. Toys and clothes and many other things. Clothes for modest maidens and Bloody Parakeets; and beads and parasols and watches; and a bright new rifle, a gramophone, a brand-new Federal Flag. And on the floor was a box of three compartments in which were packed in delightful order preserved nectarines and plums and cherries. And on the table were a great plum pudding and a cake in tins. Tim gargled his tea and smiled.

When he had drunk his tea he took up the hurricane lamp and knelt and studied each thing with care. Thus he was occupied for hours. Nor was he the only late sitter in the camp that night. The houses of his men were loud with revelry. A score of times the shout rang out: "Hey Ganger — come'n have a drink!" He went to his men at last and spent some minutes with them, drank a glass and chaffed them for their foolery with their lubras. Returned to his

house, he resumed examination of those things that made
the dull old iron room so bright. The sounds of revelry
across the track reached climax at about five o'clock, then
slowly died away, so that by six, when those sun-making
devils of the Skinny River started on their job, which was
when old Tim put his billy on again, the world was silent
save for faint snoring in the houses and the chop-chop-chop
of Joe Steen's horses grazing near and stirring of birds and
insects. The storm had long since passed.

Tim went outside and sat on a stack of dewy wood to
watch the dawn. The Southern Cross was fading. The
Morning Star was glittering like a pin's head above a cush-
ion of terracotta cloud. The sky over Skinny River way
glowed with the reflection of the devils' furnace. Soon the
red was tinged with gold. Trees and palms were silhouettes,
those at close quarters faintly green. Slowly the terracotta
cloud became brick-red; and then the gold that was in its
heart melted and ran out in streams. Along the southern
horizon a chain of litmus-violet clouds appeared. A golden
beetle droned out of east and sped in pursuit of the fleeting
shadows of the night. In the west a bank of clouds reared
like a mountain of black ice and fleecy snow, in the peaks
of which played lightning. Gold spread across the scarlet
clouds. Tim's lantern flickered and flucked as though im-
ploring him to douse it before it should be shamed by
Light of Day. He ignored it, watching the brave Morning
Star, which was staying on to flash defiance at the Usurper.
For a minute the world lay golden. Then slowly the gold
was dulled — dulled, dulled — till lo! it was shimmering
silver. A wave of silver flushed the eastern sky, washed
out the Morning Star, washed the gold flecks back to the
uttermost reaches of the horizons — washed and washed
them, bleached them in a minute; but it could not reach the
peaks of the cloud-mountains of the west, where the gold
settled, to blaze extravagantly as Youth burns out its gold-
eness on mountains of experience. Two black birds flapped
slowly out to meet the day; and as though their going had
to do with it, a golden glow swelled in the east, swelled,
swelled, appearing like the halo of a mighty Christ — and
Oh! the golden golden sun burst forth and touched the
prostrate earth with trembling fingers, touched the hoary
head of Tim and blessed him. But just as golden Youth
from gentleness to harshness turns, so did the infant sun
spring up and sweep the sentimental worshipping world with
harsh white cynical light and bleach it, bleach it of the

gentle-tinted humbugs that, by eventide, itself would have adopted, and left it stark, bewildered, and distressed.

Tim rose, picked up his cringing lamp. At the veranda he stopped to look at a spider's web that stretched between two posts. It was laden with tiny drops of dew that blazed in the new-born sun as diamonds never did. A twisted rope of gems it was, more precious than all the jewels of all the queens that ever lived, Crown Jewels of Nature, Queen of Capricornia!

A minute or two before half past seven Tim went into the middle of the track and, standing with watch in hand, waited for the stroke of the half-hour. Then he raised his head and bawled in parade-ground voice, "Right-o lads — blow up!"

The lads did not answer. He waited ten seconds by the flying hand, then bawled again, louder, "Feller wage-slaves — blow up and do your dooty!"

Beside the undrunken grog they lay, Black Velvet in their arms.

Tim smiled at the silent houses and went to work alone.

Midway through the morning a fettler joined him, a young man, bleary-eyed and husky and foul with the smell of grog and lubra. Tim chaffed him about the joys of wine, women, and song. Frequently while they pottered about, the young man stole away for hair-of-the-dog. Tim let him go, because such stealings-away gave him the chance to go and peep at the precious things in his bedroom.

That night was really Christmas Eve. The camp rang with the pealing laughter of black belles. Tim took part in the revelry till it became boisterous, then slipped away and went on with the urgent task of fixing tags to the presents. He was tired out. He went to bed at eleven.

Early on Christmas Morn he rose, breakfasted with haste, put the presents in a packing-case, and carried them and the fruit and cakes to the trolley-shed. He took out the trike, lashed the case on to the outrigger, the other things on to the carrier behind. Then he went up to the Siding House, and after knocking and getting no response but the snores of Mrs McLash and Steen, went into the post-office and rang up Soda Springs. Three long, two short, a long — *Brrrrring! Brrrrring! Brrrrring! Bring-bring! Brrrrring!* He wished to know where the train was. It should have come back the night before. He hoped it was near at hand because he wished to load his trike on to it and travel home without labour.

No answer. No answer from any siding. Evidently the Christmas festivities were being generally enjoyed, by the train as well as by the sidings. He went back to the tricycle. But before he set out he looked into the houses of his men to wish them the Compliments. None was capable of accepting.

He set out down the gleaming grassy track, today not a rusty one but silver, two slender bars of silver laid on a green velvet mat. He trundled on, bearing his precious burden homeward, feeling not the weight of it on labouring arms and legs, since it was a load of love. He trundled on, caring nothing for the per-way or the T.T.L. today, because he was off duty, and nothing for the humming-birds or ants or kangaroos, seeing nothing, hearing nothing, because his thoughts were away at the 58 with his loved ones. He trundled on, through dripping cuttings, over roaring culverts, past brooding jungles, under silver hills, he trundled on and on.

From the summit of the 62-Mile bank he caught first glimpse of the white roofs of his homestead, gleaming brightly, a cluster of sails on an ocean of trees. He pulled with renewed vigour, smiling to himself, thinking of those great girls Margaret and Kitty O'Cannon, of those big-kneed youngsters, Bridie and Tocky O'Cannon, of that great ungainly Bloody Parakeet, who would all be there beside the road awaiting him, a hundred times more eagerly than ever, because today he was not merely old Ganger O'Cannon whom they loved for nothing but himself, but old Father Christmas with his swag up. Tocky, he knew, that cheeky kid, would be lying on the cess with ear to rail, listening for the rumble of the trike, which she declared she could hear in that way a distance of two hundred chains, and the rumble of a train at five hundred. Now if fettlers could listen-in to those erratic trains like that —

The smile vanished. His hair leaped under his hat. He turned — and Horror! — saw behind him dashing round a curve an engine. He yelled. He tried to jump from the trike. His foot caught in the load of love. He sprawled back helpless on the carrier. The engine was upon him.

The engine struck. The trike shot ahead. It left the rails, turned over in the middle with Tim entangled. Again the engine struck, hurling it on to a culvert where it jammed between the transomes. And struck again and smashed the thing to pieces and thundered over and away. Slowly Tim's broken body freed itself and slid through the transomes, fell into a little creek below, crumpled and dead among the scattered presents, its warm blood trickling into the tinkling stream. Oh, death of a kangaroo for a Sergeant Major!

§

The O'Cannon Garrison fell weakly before the advance of one Julius Derkouz, a German prospector whom Tim had hounded during the war. He said there was gold to be found at Black Adder, and proved there was, though without digging holes in the earth. He lived there like a lord for eighteen months without cost to himself of a penny. Not only did he eat Tim's meat and spend Tim's hard-earned savings, but despoiled his relict, and not only that, debauched his pretty Margaret. Shortly before the Garrison tumbled down, Margaret went up to the Compound to be delivered of a child, which, fortunately for itself, no doubt, died upon seeing to what it had come.

When the Government told Blossom finally and a little curtly that she could not claim compensation for the death of Tim since he had not been on duty at the time, Julius Derkouz went off to rob his mother earth. When the last goat was eaten, Kitty, the scholar of the family, wrote to the Protector an appeal for help. That gentleman replied promptly, inviting the whole family up to his Compound for as long as they cared to stay.

Thus one day it happened that the returning mail-train stopped at the 58 to pick up four ragged and gaudily attired females at whom the passengers grinned. The guard had some difficulty in lifting the largest of them on to the platform of a car, so fat was she and tearful. The gaudy ones stayed out on the platform, shy of the passengers within, and stood and stared at the old white homestead, and the grave on the hill before it, out of sight.

Goodbye Black Adder, fallen fort, mummuk, mummuk, goodbye!

PROSPERITY IS LIKE THE TIDE

As though the O'Cannon Garrison were a Jinx on the fortune of the land, Capricornia, which had lain high and dry in a state of industrial slump, was inundated with prosperity as soon as that institution fell.

H

Prosperity is like the tide, being able to flood one shore only by ebbing from another. Good times came to Capricornia when bad times went to the Argostinian Republic. The bovine beasts of Argostinia, which country had been given the trade with the Philippines that was lost to Capricornia through the misdeeds of the *S.S. Cucaracha*, were stricken with foot-and-mouth disease. Then an ill-wind blew upon the Australian States of Cooksland and Sturt, blasting their cattle with the pleura. Thus it became the business of Capricornia to supply beef not only to the Philippines, and not only to the Southern States, but, since all the great beef-exporting countries were now out of business, to a large part of the beef-eating world. Capricornians were staggered. "Where's the catch?" they gasped.

No catch was apparent. Indeed it seemed as though Fortune was bent on favouring that ill-favoured land to the utmost. Winds of such clemency blew upon it during the two years following Tim O'Cannon's death that Dry Season was scarcely distinguishable from Wet. During that happy period rain fell in moderate quantities all the year round, which, though not a unique state of things, was extraordinary enough to make the inhabitants regard it with amazement, and say, "Gosh — what's the old joint coming to!" Herbiverous inhabitants were delighted, especially those unfortunate ungulates to which the fair conditions boded anything but good.

Black Adder Creek, as soon as abandoned, became a verdant paradise. Grass grew there luxuriantly as nowhere else; or so it seemed to Mrs McLash and Frank and old Joe Steen, who stocked it with one hundred and fifty head of cattle. But for the astuteness of these people there would have been no mouths to eat the grass but those of old Misanthropy and the fat mule Kaptlist, which, because neither Derkouz nor Blossom's creditors could turn them into cash, still lingered by their master's grave.

The McLash, Son, Steen Corporation sold their herd as stores within six months of founding it, then went out of business, being unable to restock after neighbouring graziers became suspicious of the manner in which they had stocked at first. They were well content, however, the price they got being clear profit.

Then the people of the land went cattle mad. As few had means to buy stock and the Government was not on this occasion giving away seed, those who had none duffed unbranded beasts from those who had; and those robbed thus robbed others; and so on till the balance was adjusted at the expense of the great foreign-owned stations of the Leichhardt Tableland. For a while the police were kept busy chasing suspected duffers and drinking their liquor. But soon the country settled down to serious business.

In Jack Burywell's opinion, grass grew most luxuriantly at Red Ochre. He was particularly fortunate at the beginning of these prosperous times, in spite of the depredations made on his stock by the McLash, Steen Corp. and the Fliegeltaub, Snigger Coy; for he had been left two thousand head of stock by his friend O'Hay of Tatlock's Pool, who, after years of struggling, died just as the prosperous times began. And the proximity of Red Ochre to the Port — no big station was as near — added to the value of his stock. Red Ochre became a hive of industry.

Trade was so brisk in Capricornia that never a week passed unless two steamers left the Port with cattle. And railway traffic was busy as never yet. What scenes the lamps shone on at night on the jetty when the cattle-race that ran from train to ship was a cataract of tossing horns and rolling eyes, brawling amid a storm of bellowing and cursing, the lightning-crack of stockwhips, the thunder of cloven hoofs! What scenes on the railway the sun shone on, when rusty engines and dilapidated cars went forth from the scrap-heap to meet Prosperity's demands! What scenes when those trains became entangled on the loops, when they collided, derailed themselves, upset themselves, spilled bellowing cargoes into the bush! What scenes, what thrills, what spectacular disasters, when Mad Mack the Locomotive Loony got back to an engine's cab!

The Meatworks in Town, for years but a rowdy plaything for the Trade Wind, was reopened by an American Company from Argostinia; and its machines were set to work to freeze and can meat for export. Hundreds of workmen then flocked from the South and from Malaya and Java and the Philippines. Money was flung about. Publicans and lubras reaped a harvest, the latter not in cash alone.

The water of the harbour ran with blood. Sharks and crocodiles came in hundreds, though apparently only for the sake of swimming in a pleasant medium, since the Americans, who originally hailed from Chicago, a city famous for its thrifty butchers, threw away nothing from the Works but blood. And soon the monsters (the crocodiles and the sharks) were even denied that simple pleasure when the economists found use for blood and closed the sluices. In fact before long the economists were boasting that they wasted nothing of a carcass, that hoofs and hairs and bones and horns were all put through some process that converted them to use, even that they used the dying bellows of their victims to blow the furnace fires.

As a result of all this activity, Jack Burywell, who had fallen into debt so deeply during his eleven years' occupation of Red Ochre that he had long since considered that only by dying could he ever recover solvency, profited so handsomely that in a single year he was in a position to pay every penny he owed and still have something left. But the fact that he attained to that position did not mean that he paid his debts. Considering that he had been meanly treated by his creditors while times were hard, he was determined to take revenge. It was long before his creditors in Capricornia could wring their dues from him. Those not near to witness his prosperity he never paid. Oscar Shillingsworth was one of these. To him Jack Burywell owed £350 for rent and instalments on the stock and plant. He ignored Oscar utterly.

The citizens of Capricornia went cattle mad, but not all at once. Most spent six months or more in waiting for the Catch. Still prosperous month followed prosperous month, so that at length all succumbed to the madness. A year passed, eighteen months, two years, and still no Catch. By that time even the most pessimistic had forgotten that no wind, fair or foul, ever blew in Capricornia without developing into a hurricane.

Red Ochre became a hive of industry; but money-making men were not the only creatures thriving there. Among other pests there came that devilish little insect the Anopheles Mosquito.

The anopheles bred in Capricornia as in most tropical lands, but in no great numbers usually, because he needs water for his breeding, and, being particularly frail, mild weather for his peregrinations, neither of which were usually found together for long in Capricornia. When there was water on the ground in Capricornia, it was either being boiled by a blazing sun, lashed by a raging wind, or churned by a deluge. Moreover, for his capability as an infective agent, the anopheles needs a fairly thick population of malarial and healthy subjects, which he would not find normally in Capricornia.

But these were not normal times. Far from it. While Fortune blew fair winds upon the land all those conditions favourable to the anopheles prevailed. There was perennial water, mild weather, an influx of people from malarial lands. It might all have been a well-planned jest.

Business was soon disorganized. Malaria was rife before the medical officers in Town were aware of its presence. And before they could prove its presence they had to send South for a new microscope, because the old one was spotty in the lenses and apt to make more of its own disease than that of the case in hand. Scores of men died of malaria believing that they were suffering with something else. Jack Burywell was caught like that. He had been drinking heavily on the strength of his prosperity and thought the fever was the beginnings of D.T.'s. He hid himself, being a rather sensitive man and loth to let himself be seen in a state he considered disgusting. He swallowed bromide in large quantities, thereby lowering the resistance-power his body so urgently needed. His natives found him in a state of collapse and rushed him to the Siding. He died in the arms of Mrs McLash while waiting for Ganger Jacob Ledder to fish a beetle out of the magneto of the trolley on which he was to be taken up to Town.

GRANDSON OF A SULTAN

OSCAR learnt of the boom in Capricornia when the newspapers reported the outbreak of malaria. Far from considering himself lucky to be out of the place, he bewailed his folly in not having resumed control of Red Ochre when begged to do so by Burywell to secure his dues; and then news of the man's death reached him. It came in a letter from the Government of Capricornia, which asked him to make his claims on the dead man's estate. He did not reply at once, but wired to an agent in Port Zodiac to ascertain the true state of the cattle-trade. He was told that at least the Philippines' market would remain permanent. Then he opened negotiations with the Government for settling his claim by resuming control of the Station. When these were complete he went North.

Oscar was then fifty-four. He had been living in Batman for twelve years, employed as a clerk in a Government office, living in very simple style in a little home of his own with the children. The children had for five or six years attended the same State School as their fathers had, and then gone into other institutions, Marigold into a modest ladies' school to acquire some sort of polish, Norman into a State Technical College to learn his trade. The makings of a draftsman that Uncle Ambrose had seen in Norman had not been brought out, for one reason that Ambrose and Oscar had soon become bad friends, for another that Norman was not keen on the job. Engines were what interested him, not engines in the form of bloodless diagrams, but in the shining steel. He wished to be an Engine-Fitter like his white grandfather — not a sultan or something of that kind like the shadowy grandfather on the other side. Oscar had apprenticed him to the fitting-trade in the State Railways. He was nearing the end of his term when Oscar went away.

As yet the children knew little that was true and nothing that was discreditable about the Shillingsworth family, having so far been too deeply preoccupied with the absorbing things of youth to bother much about their origin. That there was something mysterious about their parents they had long been vaguely aware. Dad avoided discussion of Uncle Mark, although the man had apparently done nothing worse than die on the battlefield. Even Uncle Ralph, who sometimes visited them when home from sea, seemed unwilling to discuss his brother Mark. And why did Dad avoid the subject of Mother, when she had apparently done no worse than die while holidaying in Manila? Perhaps to prevent the opening of wounds. Then again, he shunned the subject of the high-born Javan lady and that old heathen the Sultan or Rajah or whatever he was. Both children often wondered, though never with suspicion, since they thought that he whom they called Dad was beyond reproach. Once Marigold was prompted by an idea she got from a novel to ask if Mother had eloped with Uncle Mark. That was the most pointed question either of them had ever asked. She was answered with a laugh that was not nearly so much an expression of amusement as she thought it was as of relief from the shock the word Elope had caused her father. Subsequently she was fairly well convinced that the mystery about her mother and uncle was not worth considering.

The years passed. Norman grew up among mechanics and other rough but respectable people who, generally speaking, did not bother much about his colour. He often went prowling of nights without Oscar's knowledge, whistling at street corners and venturing on excursions in buffoonery from which he learnt the mysteries of life. Marigold played the Lady in a simple way with congenial companions, making the mysteries of life still more mysterious. But neither went far from their quiet little home and their quiet half-bald white-haired old guardian. So the years passed till the death of Burywell.

When Oscar left Batman he intended to stay in Capricornia only so long as it took him to set Red Ochre in order and appoint a manager to run it. For one thing he was afraid of the malaria, for another he hoped to live the rest of his life as a beef-baron, to spend half his time in Capricornia, half in the cities of the South. It was with a promise to take the children with him next trip that he left them in some content, a promise that was not worth much, perhaps, since he went away feeling apprehensive himself of meeting people who would remind him of the infamies of Mark and Jasmine. However, he did not carry out the intention, for one thing because the malaria had been wiped out by the return of the old harsh conditions, for another because the flood of prosperity was rapidly falling. He had been away about seven months when he found that it would be necessary to sell the house in Batman to raise money. After that he could no longer refuse Marigold's incessant begging to let her join him. So Marigold went North, leaving a very disconsolate Norman to finish his apprenticeship.

Marigold left Norman with a promise to do all she could to help him follow as soon as possible. Her promise was apparently worth more than Oscar's, judging by the first few letters she wrote. She wrote telling him of all the things that one must know to travel saloon in the *S.S. Maranonga*. It was impossible for him to travel second-class as he had said he would, she declared, since no-one did so in that palatial ship but Dagoes and Chinamen and a few poor whites who appeared to be Very Rough. The Shillingsworths were well known, she said; therefore they must keep up their dignity. She instructed him in behaviour becoming in saloon-class passengers. He must not talk engines there as he was always doing at home. Saloon-class passengers were always Professional or Office People, who talked of such things as Golf and Tennis and the Stock Exchange and the Prospects of the Vacant North and the White Australia Policy. Norman had best begin by listening. Certainly he must not confess to being a mechanic. Better that he should say he was the nephew of a wealthy grazier and that he had been studying Mechanical Engineering, which was the truth after all. He must Dress for Dinner. That was a most important thing. Then he must dress in white after the ship crossed the Tropic. There were many formalities to be observed. Norman took it all quite seriously, as anyone might.

She described Capricornia to him, and Red Ochre, and sent him photographs and repetitions of her promise. Then she suddenly took to writing letters even more discouraging than those of Oscar, saying that Capricornia was a dead-and-alive hole, that the climate was hellish — why, the climate even made impossible the use of a much-needed radio-set, since one could hear nothing but cackling Static, which seemed like the mocking voice of the Spirit of the Land. She said she was sure he would hate the place. But she said nothing about leaving it herself. Norman was puzzled, but far from put off his desire to go home. He asked by every mail for permission to come as soon as his apprenticeship was finished. Oscar repeatedly told him that he must not think of coming for at least another year.

Norman was twenty-two when he finished his apprenticeship. But for Oscar he would have resigned his job at once. Instead he applied for three months' leave, and when he got it, wired to Oscar to say that he was compelled to take the holiday owing to slackness in the Loco Shops in which he worked. Oscar wired telling him to wait a while. He replied saying that he had already bought his steamer-ticket. Oscar said no more. So he went to the bank and drew his savings, got measured for an outfit of clothes, and bought a ticket.

§

When Norman went to buy his ticket he was looked at closely by the clerk with whom he dealt and asked his nationality. He answered, "Why — Australian."

"Your father?"

"Same."

"Your mother?"

"Javanese."

The clerk went off to consult the manager. When he returned Norman asked, "What's wrong?"

"Nothing," said the clerk. "Just wanted to fix up your berth. What's your occupation?"

"Oh I'm an engineering student. My uncle's a grazier up North. I'm going to visit him."

"Your uncle well known?"

"Sure. Our station's one of the biggest in the country. Six thousand square miles."

The clerk whistled, then asked, "Your uncle'll be meeting you, I suppose?"

"Course. Why — what's wrong?"

"You understand you'll be required to fill in a special form before landing, eh?"

Norman stared.

"Just to prove you're Australian-born," said the clerk. "White Australia business. I suppose your uncle'll fix all that. Just excuse me a second." He went off again. Norman saw the manager peeping at him from the glass door of his office. At length the clerk came back and allotted him a berth aboard the *S.S. Maranonga*.

A shipping company was bound to keep check on the movements of coloured passengers travelling between Australian ports; but apart from this, the running to and fro and questioning concerning Norman was done because this particular company took care when placing coloured passengers among the white ones. Although the manager and clerk might not themselves be colour-proud they were well aware of the fact that most of their clients were. As it was, Norman was given a berth in the most remote part of the saloon accommodation.

The *Maranonga* was a full ship that trip. Norman was given a cabin-mate who was a Pharmaceutical Chemist, a large, baldish, vacant-faced young man, going for a trip to Singapore, for the first sea-voyage of his life. They became friends at once. Before the ringing of the first dinner-gong they knew all about each other, Norman that the Pharmacist's father was a wealthy chemist, his brother a famous dentist, his mother a native of Barrel Flat and daughter of a gold-mining magnate, and the Pharmacist that Norman's grandfather was an Eastern Potentate, his father a Major killed in France, his uncle a Beef-Baron, himself heir to one of the biggest cattle-stations in the world. Each was much impressed.

The Pharmacist, whose name was Edwin Bortells, asked Norman about Capricornia and the Prospects of the Vacant North generally. Norman told him, and asked many things about medicine and physiology that perhaps a young man should not know. And both spoke guardedly of ships they had previously sailed in and high society they had known. Then these two youths of such enviable circumstance dressed for dinner with the utmost care, and crept into the dining-saloon, blushing and fumbling, almost clinging to each other for support, to sit cringing under the knowing eyes of the Chinese stewards, wishing in secret that they had travelled in comfortable second-class.

The two days' voyage from Batman to Flinders was very quiet. The weather was bad and as yet the passengers were very few. Norman and Mr. Bortells spent the two days' and three nights' stay in Flinders together. Norman had planned to go to the Greenfern Loco Shops to study the methods of the Sturt Railways. He could not manage it, because Mr. Bortells took him round to see the chemists' shops. Together they visited seven chemist shops, to the staffs of which Bortells made known the fact that he was a colleague by asking for medicaments by their Latin names. At first Norman thought he was using pass-words of the Pharmaceutical Society. In most cases they were invited into the dispensaries to take quite ordinary morning or afternoon tea among the measures and mortars. Norman studied the railway system of the State in half an hour by taking a flying trip to Central Station while Bortells was talking Latin in the eighth chemist shop. And while Bortells was in the ninth on the last night ashore, he managed to slip away and learn something about the local ladies, though not in a mere half-hour. Back on the ship next morning he explained to the rather indignant Bortells that he had strayed and got lost.

The S.S. Maranonga was built for aristocrats, though whether to truckle to their vanity or to exploit it, it is difficult to say. She was luxuriously appointed, and crewed with the humblest complement that could be conveniently employed. The firemen were Indians, stringy-limbed wild-looking creatures who momentarily appeared at the ringing of the watches, in the acts either of plunging into the bowels of the ship like brown ferrets or crawling out like black rats. Knowing passengers called them Lascars, with a certain contempt. Everyone was positive that they would be leaping out like rats if disaster smote the ship. Such behaviour on their part was traditional. And who could blame them for it, knowing that they worked twelve hours a day like demons for wages of one shilling a day? The sailors were Malays, who ran up rigging, perched on rails, hung over bulwarks, like brown monkeys. Yellow-brown

Norman loved to watch these humble ones and glory in his superiority over them no less than did his pale-faced fellows. The Chinese stewards were different. One knew that they also were paid but a shilling a day and were supposed to be worth only threepenny tips, but could not help suspect them of getting money by other means and of knowing how poor one really was oneself and of laughing over their knowledge up their sleeves; still one could take revenge on them by bawling at them, "Boy!" for every trivial thing one wanted done. A whiteman must keep up his dignity.

Such was the *S.S. Maranonga*. Small wonder that her first-class passengers swelled into Great White Tuans when they joined her, even though they came to her as little clerks who travelled somewhere at expense of someone else to earn their daily bread, or as little tourists temporarily out of the moil of struggling for a crust to spend the shillings they had scraped for years, or as Halfcaste-Aboriginal mechanics come from whistling in back streets.

First Gentleman of the ship that trip was Mr Percy Tappit, an operator in a cable-station somewhere in the East. A telegraphist! Ignorant persons were surprised at first and even a little resentful of the fact that a mere telegraphist should have the effrontery to strut so. He came aboard at Flinders. He was an experienced traveller. He organised the Deck-games Committee and automatically became President. A holidaying bank-clerk took on the job of Treasurer, the very one he should have dodged.

Norman was greatly surprised at the acceptance of Mr Tappit. He realised that he himself was very humble, but considered he was a cut above a mere telegraphist, having known boys at State School who had gone into post-office and railway work as messengers with a view to qualifying as telegraphists. He talked about it to Mr Bortells, though without admitting that he had known the humble boys of whom he spoke. What was the difference, he demanded, between tapping telegraph-keys in a post-office and in a cable-station? Bortells could see none, and vowed that he would have no dealings with an up-jumped postman.

But soon both changed their attitudes if not actually their opinions, upon learning that in the East a man who was elsewhere a postman could become a potentate. And they learnt that a similar if less pronounced metamorphosis could be effected in the atmosphere of Port Zodiac. For look at those clerks returning to that town from leave!

They behaved like military majors! Norman was inclined to sneer; but Bortells was carried away by thoughts of what a pharmacist might become in such magic atmospheres, and went to truckle to Percy Potentate by offering himself as a player of medicine-ball.

Mr Tappit told Bortells that Norman was a Eurasian. He spoke of the condition as of a disease. Then he told all he knew about Eurasians, nothing of which was to the race's credit. He seemed to dislike them intensely, though, to judge by his jocular digressions, he could not have regarded the mode of their origin with much disfavour. His knowledge spread throughout the ship.

Norman first observed a change in the attitude of Bortells as the ship was steaming up the Bullimba River. When he joined the fellow at the rail he was greeted with strange noises and before long left alone. When a little later he found him again, this time in the company of Tappit, he was practically ignored. Thinking he had offended him in some small way, he let him go, and went ashore alone. He had the time of his life in Bullimba, first with the grimy youths he met at the Loco Shops, next with the painted ladies to whom the youths took him in the night. Back on the ship and out at sea again he found Bortells a little more friendly, though nothing like the friend of old. He sought the company of others. Thus the first thousand miles of the journey was travelled.

Most of the first-class passengers now knew all about Eurasians. At least they had Norman to thank for giving them something new and strange to talk about, and something exciting too, suggesting lust — lust in the sun, or before the moon's hot face, amid the scent of the frangipani and the throb of heathen drums. Oh East is East and West is West, and never the twain shall meet but on such red-hot occasions as produced that tall strong handsome grandson of a sultan! Interesting subject. Norman never heard it.

Some people expressed pity for Norman, many admiration for his physique. Most of these were women, especially young girls, who stared at him hard when he was not looking, but fled with something like terror in their tender hearts if they thought he was coming after them. One man in Mr Tappit's large and perennial audience said one day that he considered a Eurasian as good as any other breed of man; and a surprisingly large number agreed with him. Mr Tappit put them out of countenance by asking would they give their daughters or sisters to such a person in marriage. They had to answer No; whereupon Mr Tappit assumed that they did not honestly regard such a creature as an equal. No-one sought Norman; but no-one was rude to him except such boors as Tappit, with whom he had no dealings; thus he continued to enjoy himself while the second thousand miles was travelled.

At Port Magnetic he again went ashore alone. He did not enjoy himself at first, because the one or two men he tried to befriend in hotel bars rebuffed him. Now he was north of Capricorn. One man addressed him as Nigger. He had often been called that before, both as boy and man, but never unless the mouth that uttered the name intended to insult him. He had generally been able to shut such mouths with his fists. But this man addressed him in a tone quite friendly. Norman glared at him and retired. Then he found a girl with yellow hair and ruby lips, and with her spent a jolly afternoon and evening. He returned with the girl to the ship a few minutes before it sailed. Two sailors had to carry him up the gangway.

Saxon Whitely, of Republic Reef, Capricornia, came aboard at Port Magnetic, and said as soon as he set eyes on Norman that he was a Yeller-Feller, the first he had ever seen aboard a ship, and surely the first that had ever sailed saloon. He wanted to know what the Shipping Company was coming to. Mr Tappit was annoyed by the intrusion of this common-class stranger who was robbing him of his Eurasian, and disputed with Whitely about Norman's race, calling on several fellow-potentates to bear him out. The dispute was settled when Whitely heard Norman's name. "What — Shillingsworth?" he cried. "Why — that must be the son of Mark who killed the Chow. Red Ochre? Yes — that's who he is. Says his mother's a Javanese, does he? Ha! Ha! Ha! Don't you believe it. She was a Capricornian gin!" The passengers were staggered, especially Bortells, who actually tried to find another berth.

Before long the only saloon-class passenger who did not know the history of the Shillingsworths in Capricornia was Norman. No-one enlightened him, supposing that he knew the truth about himself quite well and was concealing it. Many all but cut him dead. He was surprised at first, then came to the conclusion that he had brought disfavour on himself with his behaviour at Port Magnetic. So he went to the Dagoes and Roughs of second-class and won their friendship by buying them liquor and telling them how he

had been cast out by the Wonks of the saloon for being a
Man. Two low fellows took him ashore at Southern Cross
Island and at his expense showed him more than all the first-
class passengers together would have seen in a stay there
of a month. Again he was carried aboard. Thus the third
thousand miles was travelled; and the fourth was much the
same.

The *Maranonga* entered Port Zodiac Harbour and steamed past the sights that Norman had seen for the first time
sixteen years before. He did not remember. His first distinct memories were of Red Ochre. What he looked on
had not changed much in all the years. There stood the
Calaboose, no larger, and the Meatworks, back at the old
occupation of being a plaything for the wind, and the hospital, and the cable-station, and the jetty. No steamer lay
at the jetty now. The old *S.S. Cucaracha* lay at anchor in
the stream.

There was a crowd at the jetty. Norman searched it for
his relatives, seeing while he did so a number of brown-
yellow faces like his own, which set him wondering vaguely
whether the owners were halfcaste Javans like himself,
though he was certain they were no grandsons of sultans,
because not one wore boots and most were clad in rags.
Thought of these people was whipped from his mind by
sight of Oscar and Marigold, Oscar in whites and topee
and carrying a stick, Marigold in bright light silks and
carrying a sunshade. He cooee'd, caught their eyes, waved
to them eagerly. They waved and smiled. As soon as the
gangway was down he ran ashore and embraced them,
watched by many eyes.

STIRRING OF SKELETONS

Now the town of Zodiac had lately become world-famous,
not through anything its citizens had done, nor indeed by
their desire, but through the exploits of a certain aviatrix
who had chosen it as goal when making a flight from Europe
that attracted the attention of the world. Thus, fifty or
sixty years after the place was hacked out of the wilderness
by Britins Willnott, whose reward was death by a spear, it

was put on the map of the world by a slip of a girl who scarcely trod its dust.

It never rains but it pours in Capricornia. Hot on the wings of the aviatrix came a swarm of males of her species, like drones in pursuit of their queen. Some lost themselves in more or less convenient places and caused more of their kind to come in search of them. Old Capricornians were moved to say again, "Gosh — what's the old joint coming to!" but not with the pleasure they usually felt when uttering those words, because most felt that it was going to the dogs.

And then to meet this migration of birdmen, pressmen came by aeroplane from the South, and as they came took stock of the wilderness, which looked so promising when viewed from on high and at great speed that, in spite of having been insulted by all the old-timers they had questioned on the subject of settling the land, they went home and told the old tale of *Wonderful Country Going to Waste — Go North, Young Man, Go North!*

The threadbare tale roused up a section of people who, no doubt because they were interested in such a project financially, had many times declared that there was but one way to utilize the wasted Opportunities, and that by linking North and South by rail. This section clamoured in the press and got a hearing, because the National Government, undertaker of such tasks, had recently been elected and was in a lavish mood and was under the leadership of a man who was obsessed with the notion that a certain Asiatic Power was about to make war on the land. There were people who wrote to the papers deploring great waste of money when the Nation was staggering under a huge burden of debt; but such a feeble objection could scarcely be expected to discourage Senators from adding two thousand miles to the many thousand miles of railway on which they could travel free of cost with parliamentary passes. Therefore, after several Commissions had been formed and many big land-owners dined with and a great number of estimates made and remade and much money spent on what appeared to be nothing at all, it was officially stated that a railway would be built to link Port Zodiac with the Southern city of Churchton, or, to quote from a rhetorical article written on the subject in the leading paper of that city, *To bridge with steel the terrene gulf, twenty-five parallels of latitude wide, that divides the Austral Ocean from the Silver Sea*

§

At the time of Norman's arrival, a bridge was being
built over the Melisande as the first link in the rhetorician's
Bridge of Steel. The builder of the Melisande bridge was
Stanley Steggles, a young engineer, who was a close friend
of Marigold's. Mr Steggles brought Marigold and Oscar
down to meet Norman, and while they greeted him, stood
waiting to greet him himself. When the time came he
greeted him heartily. They all went up to the Princess
Alice in his car.

Norman's entry into the hall of the Princess Alice caused a stir. His appearance anywhere would have drawn attention. There, however, it was awaited. Mrs Daisy Shay
came out of her office, stared at him, said in a cracked
voice, "Lord boy, how you've grown!" Had he remembered
her he might have answered, "And how you've withered
and shrunk!" He merely smiled.

Mrs Heather Shay came out of the bar. She was somewhere about forty now, plump, as good-looking as ever,
unchanged from shoulders up, in fact, except for her hair,
which, to hide a light touch of grey, she had bleached from
brown to tawny gold. She stared at Norman without comment. When her mother-in-law said, "Spit of his father,
aint he?" she merely answered, "Yes."

Norman shook hands with Heather and, when she asked,
said that he remembered her. That was untrue; he had even
forgotten her name. She looked at Oscar, who had told
her nothing about Norman's coming, nor indeed about Marigold's. She had learnt of both from old Mrs Shay, whom
Oscar had told when booking rooms for them. And he had
not introduced her to Marigold. He avoided her eyes.

Late that afternoon, the Shillingsworths and Mr Steggles
went back to the jetty to see the *Maranonga* sail. Norman
introduced Mr Bortells to his people. Bortells was out-
wardly most gracious, while inwardly cursing himself for
having heeded the blather of a telegraphist and so lost the
chance of knowing this handsome girl and wealthy old beef-
baron better. He alone of all the first-class passengers
heeded Norman's waving as the ship drew out. Marigold
and Oscar noticed this. Norman made light of it by laughing and saying that the crowd was Tripe. They lingered on
the Jetty to watch the berthing of the *Cucaracha* and the
shunting in of the first train-load of cattle, because for one
thing Oscar was secretly interested in the ship, not having
seen her since she took away his Jasmine, because for

another Norman wished to see the cattle that, according to the labels on a couple of the cars, had come from Red Ochre.

Norman rode in front with Steggles on the return drive by car to the hotel. Steggles was most friendly with him. Marigold and Oscar were grateful, especially Marigold, who, though she did not know what Norman's breed was truly, had been greatly worried of late about his colour, and had been forced, or rather thought she had been forced, to make rather distressing explanations to her friends. After dinner that night Steggles, who had dined with the Shillingsworths, took Marigold for a run in his car. At about nine o'clock Oscar told Norman that he wished to see the cattle loaded and asked him to accompany him to the jetty. By that time Norman was yawning, tired out from having been in a state of excitement since the dawn. He said he would rather go to bed. So Oscar went off alone.

On his way in from the veranda where he had been sitting with Oscar, Norman passed through the hall, which was now deserted but for one white-haired man of great stature, who was dozing in a deep cane chair. This was George Tittmuss, station-master of bygone days. His hat was lying on the floor beside him, fallen from his knee. Norman picked it up and placed it on a table near, and in doing so upset a glass of liquor. Tittmuss woke and blinked with meaty eyes. Norman smiled and said, "Sorry — I've knocked your grog over. Let's buy you another."

Grunting and blinking, Tittmuss heaved his huge frame up from the chair, and asked in a husky voice, "Young Shillingsworth, aint you?"

"That's me," said Norman. "What you drinking?"

"Double whiskey. So you're Mark's boy, eh?"

"Yes. You know my father?"

"Know him? Course I knoo him! Who didn't know that boy and Chook Henn? Great times we had in the old days."

Smiling, Norman took the glass to the little window that communicated with the bar, and when the barman came, said, "Double whiskey for the old chap here, and beer for me."

The barman looked out at Tittmuss, then at Norman, and said, "Can't give *you* a drink, sonny."

Taking the glass, the barman glanced back into the bar, then turned to Norman, and said, "Police in the bar." Then he went off and filled the glass.

"What's up?" asked Norman when he came back. "Why can't I have a drink? I'm of age."

"Colour," said the barman. "Don't you know?"

"No," murmured Norman, surprised.

"Halfcaste," whispered the barman. "Same's the Binghis. Agin the law." He glanced into the bar again, then back to Norman and went on, "You're not allowed to drink up here. But I'll always see you get one when you want it. Not here though. Too public. Duck round into the parlour there and I'll slip you one. Beer you said?"

Norman got his beer and went back to Tittmuss feeling rather bemused. Tittmuss said to him, "What — you had to sneak to get it? Bah! Them and their blunny laws! This place's gone rank lousy with laws since the war. Only ones't got a victory outer that flamin' war was the blasted wowsers!"

Norman took a seat on the edge of the table. Tittmuss said to him, "And where's your ol' man now, sonny?"

Norman looked at him for a moment, then said, "Oh — he's dead."

"Dead? Well, well! He muster been fifteen years me junior too. What'd he die of?"

"Oh — he was killed in the war."

"Go on! So he went to the war, eh? How'd he manage to get away?"

Norman stared, said, "How d'you mean?"

Tittmuss blinked. He was on the point of asking how Mark managed to get to a recruiting-station past the police, when Heather, who for some minutes had been standing unseen at the office door, came out and said to him, "What are you gassing about, anyway?"

Tittmuss blinked at her and said, "Eh? Just talkin' the boy about his dad. Reckons he was killed in the war —"

Heather snapped at him, "Gertch — you old blowbag! You're only humming for a drink. Nick off home." And to Norman she said, "You been trying to get drink?"

"Yes," said Norman. "I didn't know it was wrong. This — this gentleman's an old friend of my father's. He was just —"

"Don't take any notice of him," said Heather. "He's the biggest shikker in Town. Now nick off, you old sponge. Chattering like a washerwoman! Go on — get out — or I'll get 'em to put knock-drops in your grog."

Struggling up, old Tittmuss showed his few teeth and

snarled, "You been doin' that for years, you bitch. And look 'ere —"

Heather drew Norman away, saying, "Don't listen to their gossip, Norman. They're all a bunch of old women." At the foot of the stairs leading up to the bedrooms she asked, "Don't know much about your father, eh?"

"No," said Norman. "Did you know him?"

She looked down smiling, answered, "Oh — quite well." Then she looked up and said, "Where's your uncle?"

"Gone down to see the cattle loaded. I was too tired. Just off to bed."

"I'll show you up to your room," she said. "Now don't you go listening to gossips."

§

Oscar at the cattle-race watched the cataract of flesh and blood go brawling from the train to the ship. Men on the roofs of cars were prodding at beasts and bellowing above their din; others on the rails of the race flogged savagely with stockwhips; others with electric goads connected with the power of the ship were prodding through the rails at atoms of the flood that caught by horns or fell. Legs and horns and ribs were broken, bodies lacerated, eyes gouged out. The sloping floor of the race was sloppy with dung and blood. On and on flowed the cataract, its atoms bellowing, slavering, mad with fear. Oh where is the carnivore that mauls its meat more savagely than man!

Oscar turned from the cattle to the steamer, stared at the lighted window of a cabin underneath the bridge, wondering if it were the same in which Captain Gomez had several times in bygone days entertained himself and Jasmine. It was nearly twenty years since he had seen the *Cucaracha*. He had known ever since his return that she was back in the local trade, but knowing also that her captain was not the Damned Dago, had not thought about her much. Her captain's name, so he had learnt, was Juan Andanak.

At length he left the race and strolled along the jetty to the ship and went aboard and stood at the rail abaft the meagre midships housing to watch the stowing of the cattle in the hold. Din rose up in waves, like the clangour of a mighty bell. The beasts ran from the jetty-race to another, a veritable maze that baffled the eye with its intricacy and seemed to lead down to the bottom of the sea. Blazing lights and dust and flies and stench and din. Amazing sight!

Descent of bovine sinners into steel and timber hell —
sinners tailed and cloven-hoofed themselves — not the
demons that tormented.

Feeling the rail he leant on quiver, Oscar turned, to see
an officer of the ship beside him, standing on a rail and
craning over the hold. As the man stepped back and turned
he glanced at Oscar, and nodded as he walked away. Oscar
turned right round. The man, short and stout and clad in
grubby white uniform and carpet-slippers, shuffled forward
towards the bridge. Oscar saw him enter a lighted cabin.

For minutes Oscar stared, then slowly followed. The
cabin the man entered was the one he knew. He got a
glimpse of the interior through the half-open door. He passed, then repassed, then took up a position from which he
might see without being seen. The man sat down before a
ledger on a desk and wrote while running brown fingers
through his thick white hair. His moustache and bushy
brows were black, striking features for a white-haired man.
His face was fat and florid, the skin about his dark eyes
deeply wrinkled. At length, as though the scrutiny of Oscar
drew him, he looked up, and seeing Oscar faintly, called
out something. Oscar's heart leapt. The voice!

For a while Oscar stared into the oily eyes from a distance, then slowly approached, stopped on the wooden mat
before the door, thrust his head in. At first the officer stared
inquiringly, then smiled and said, "Goo' night."

Oscar stood with a hand on the frame of the doorway,
the other on the handle of the door. A moment. Then he
swallowed, said huskily, "Gomez!"

The officer stared. His eyes widened; his mouth opened.
So they stared for seconds. At first the face of Gomez paled.
Slowly the blood crept back. Oscar could hear his own heart
thumping. Weak old heart these days, but only in the flesh
of it.

"Ah!" breathed Gomez at last, and slowly rose. Then
suddenly he held out his hand, smiled brilliantly, cried,
"Meest Sheelingsworth!"

Oscar did not move. Still with hand extended, Gomez
said, raising his eyebrows, "Am I mistook?"

Oscar swallowed, pushed back the door, slowly stepped
inside. "So you've come back," he muttered.

Gomez dropped his hand. After a pause he smiled again,
timidly, and answered, "Ye — es — but I come back long
time — maybe four month. Nother one captain finish."

Then he shot out his hand again, shot up his inky brows, cried eagerly, "How are you, Sir?"

Oscar frowned. Gomez dropped his hand and brows and said quite sadly, "Oh Sir — not de friend?"

"Dammit!" muttered Oscar. "Friend?"

Oh so weak it sounded after all the rehearsing given it years ago!

"Ah! But why not?" murmured Gomez.

Oscar licked his lips, swallowed, said huskily, "You dirty crawler — where's my wife?"

Gomez looked startled. He sank into his chair, shook his head vigorously, then combed his white hair frantically with fingers, while he stared at Oscar as though he were the Devil.

"Where's my wife?" demanded Oscar with a little more strength, though not with half the purpose now, because the strange behaviour of the captain was distracting his thoughts.

"Dunno," gasped Gomez, still combing and staring hard.

"Liar!" snapped Oscar.

"Oh!" gasped Gomez. "No Sir — it's too true!"

Oscar leant forward, raised a large clenched hand, and with a thrill of pride in the strength he felt, demanded, "Tell me you dirty Dago, or I'll smash you."

"Oh I dunno," said Gomez miserably. "I no see long time."

"Liar!" roared Oscar, now pleased to know by the feel of his own face and the sight of the other's that he must be looking as savage as he ought. Life in the old dog, life in the old dog yet!

"Tell me!" he roared. "Out with it or —"

Gomez leapt up, and with hands raised spinster-fashion, cried, "N-no Sir — w-w-what's up?"

Oscar was astounded. His face relaxed. He drew out his handkerchief and mopped his brow.

"I'm sorry Meest Sheelingsworth," said Gomez with a pleading gesture. "I wanner be de friend —"

Over the handkerchief Oscar said, "What — after you stole my wife and ruined me?"

"Ah no stole, Meest Sheelingsworth!" Gomez cried, lifting hands and brows together. "My God don't say such ting! No stole. Certainly not no stole. And ruin — Oh my God Sir, I am ruin two times by dat woman!"

"Bah!"

"Ah don't you say it. Cut dat out. Dat woman say she wanner do de bunk with me."

"I don't doubt it. And you did!"

"Too true I did!" moaned Gomez, and sat down slowly and went on, "She wanner do de bunk with me, and me got de wife and keeds at home. Oh she give me hell of a time dat woman. You no ruin, Sir. Don't you tink one minute. You de lucky guy — I am de mutt —" And he popped up and cried, "Oh Sir, sit down."

"No," snapped Oscar.

"Okay chief," said Gomez with a sigh.

They surveyed each other in silence, each mopping his moist old face. Then Oscar sighed, and sat down slowly in a padded chair.

"Ah!" breathed Gomez, sinking down again. But in a moment he was up and rushing to a cupboard. He came back with a large green bottle of Philippino gin and a decanter of orange juice. He set these on the desk, then rushed to get glasses and cigars. He leant over the desk and offered the cigars to Oscar, beautiful things, fragrant as roses, ornate as rajahs, the kind that only millionaires, ships' captains, and customs officers can get to smoke. Oscar coveted them, but waved them aside. Gomez sat down with a sigh.

But the man could not keep still for long. Up he popped and mixed two drinks with shaky hands. Oscar said coldly, "None for me. Tell me about my wife."

Gomez gulped the contents of a glass, then placed its mate near Oscar, then flopped back into the chair and sighed and smacked his lips and said, "It aint a pleasant story. It mek my poor heart seek to tell. First dat woman like a bebby — cry and cry and cry — den like de tiger — Brr! and Yowl!"

Oscar stared, demanded, "What on earth d'you mean?"

"Oh Sir. I mean dat woman's character. I no want her. I geeve my bloody oath for dat. She say to me, 'Emilio my goo' friend, please tek me way, cos me usbin is the number one beeg steef. He got no guts. I wanner be beeg woman; and he so ver' small. Tek me way. I am so much unhappy.' Can I refuse dat, I ask you, Sir? Can you? No — cos she cry so many tear. I forget my nasty wife and leetla keeds. I tek her way for charity, not for love, and put ashore with cattle at Port Marivelles, tell her not to come Manila for de long times, cos dere's my nasty wife. All right. I go Manila in de steamer. But oh dat woman come! She come close up in de train. Dem two women — her and my nasty wife — raise merry hell. What's kwonskwence? My wife she mek deevorce and keek me out and mek me pay beeg alimony. I am ruin. I gotter get another job for mek more money. Den bye'n bye I marry Jasmine —"

"Marry?" demanded Oscar.

"Sure. Do de properly ting. Dat's what for your Jasmine mek de trouble. Cos I gotter mek her honest woman she say —"

"But dammit man, that's bigamy. She's married to me."

"She get deevorce from you lil bits after she come Manila."

"From me?"

"Yes Sir."

"Rot! I never divorced her."

"No Sir?" cried Gomez, jumping up. "But Sir, she show me pepper!"

"What paper?"

"Lawyer pepper what you send her. I can't read him; but she say all right, dat decree nisi made here in Port Zodiac."

"You sure?"

"My God Sir, am I mad?"

"You might be."

"I tink you might be right. You not mek deevorce you say?"

"I certainly did not."

Gomez gave vent to a stream of Spanish, while his eyes popped and his hands worked frantically. At length he said, "You say so?"

"Absolutely."

"Well — well — I am mad, Sir! My godfathers! She play de treek!"

He flopped back into his chair, goggling. After a while he panted, "Bye'n bye she mek deevorce with me!"

"Who?"

"Me — meself — poor mutt Emilio! She tek me court and mekim finish conjugal rights."

"God! How many more divorces?"

"Ah, plenty deevorce Manila. Dat American country now, don't you know. American lady say, 'Marry in haste, and when love fly out de door de alimony will fly in by de winder'."

"Go on."

"Dat Jasmine she get tired of me queek. All time I work

like de horse mek money for her to spend on high society. And all time she treat me like a dog, cos I'm poor captain and she de beeg dame in de town. She 'shamed of me."

He drank the liquor he had set for Oscar, then quickly filled both glasses.

"Go on," said Oscar.

"Drink Sir."

"No — go on."

Gomez drank again, shuddered, blinked, smacked his lips, went on. "Yes Sir, bye'n bye when I, poor lonely man, mek leetla play with half-breed maid, dat Jasmine with de sharp eye she ketch me, tek me court, sue me for deevorce."

"God!" breathed Oscar.

"Yes Sir, God!" cried Gomez. "I'm with you there. She mek me proper mutt in Town, ketch me for beeg expense for court and damage to de name of high-class lady, and beeg beeg alimony. I am ruin Sir, yes, ruin two times twice!" He concluded with a violent gesture.

"My God!" breathed Oscar. "Then?"

"Ah yes, senor — and then!" cried Gomez, half risen and bent forward waving hands. "One year more — and then she marry beeg American beef-baron from de Argostinia, and go home with him to America!"

"Ha! Ha! Ha!" roared Oscar. "Well I'll be damned — what a woman!"

For a dozen seconds Gomez held his pose, staring at Oscar in amazement; then suddenly he seized the full glass, thrust it at Oscar, crying, "Drink Sir — drink my friend!" And as Oscar took the glass he added, "You and me's de two beeg mutts, Meest Sheelingsworth — but I am sorry for America!"

It was late when Oscar reached the Princess Alice. The town electric-power plant had long ceased its operations for the night. He had to rouse the yard-man to guide him through the pitch-black house to the room he was to share with Norman. He entered the room on tip-toe, collided with a chair, accidentally tore the netting from his bed, and flopped down fully clothed.

"Dad," said a quiet voice in the darkness.

Oscar struggled up and said, "Wazzit?"

"It's me — Norm."

Oscar dropped back to the pillow grunting.

"Dad," said Norman after a while, "is there anything queer about my father?"

"Hic?" was the reply.

Norman waited for a while, then said, "Dad —"
"Gusslip," murmured Oscar. "I — I'm s — hic!"

§

Oscar was ill next day, as the result, he said, of eating
Spanish victuals. Heather, who brought him a plate of
iced prunes to the breakfast table, touched his brow and
said that he should go to Leo Lariquez's cafe and take the
hair-of-the-dog cure by eating a Spanish breakfast. Norman
chuckled. Marigold looked surprised. Oscar blushed and
mumbled that he did not want to see Spanish food again.

Later in the morning Oscar felt so bad that he went with
Norman to the doctor. Then they went out to the hospital
in a Chinese hire-car to get the medicine. Norman took the
prescription in while Oscar nursed his head in the car.

Norman went into the main building of the hospital, where
he was met by a sister who addressed him brusquely and
in Pidjin and directed him to the dispensary. The dispenser
grunted at him and called him Boy and left him standing
on the front veranda. His presence caused a stir. Two young
halfcaste serving-maids peeped out of the kitchen at him.
Natives working in the yard relinquished tasks to stare. The
halfcaste girls in the Lazaret were gathered on their veranda.
After a while the leper girls began to shout to the others,
asking questions. Norman thought it was some native
tongue they used, though their words were as plain English
as he might have shouted himself. "Oozit?" shouted the
leper girls. "Weddeecumfum? Mygawdaineeflash!" The
people in the yard and kitchen took no notice of the shout-
ers, except one little halfcaste maid, who screamed, "Shur-
rup!" Then the dispenser came out and roared. The watchers vanished.

Norman was dressed in fresh whites, glossy as mother-
o'-pearl. His double-breasted coat hung open, showing a
beautiful fresh white tunic-shirt. And the creases of his
trousers were like knife-blades, his socks of finest silk, his
shoes tan patent-leather, his hat a spotless topee, his poise
imperial.

Down an iron-roofed gangway came Yeller Elbert, who
was an orderly, barefooted, clad only in holey singlet and
well-worn khaki pants. He was then aged about thirty-five,
was thin of body, sharp of face, and slightly grey. Oscar
noted the difference in the two brown-yellow faces, Norman's full and oval one, with small and soft and curving
nose. They compared as the sun and a piece of cheese. It

was not only rich attire that made Norman what he looked. He had been fed on the best of food for sixteen years, had slept on decent beds, had walked the earth like a man, not slunk like a mongrel dog with kicks to harry him. Had he stood there naked the comparison would be just the same, though no doubt the stir would have been greater.

Elbert stopped before him, and, head cocked, eyed him rudely, though not with rude intent. Norman dilated his nostrils at him, then turned away. Not understanding, Elbert said with an ingratiating smile "Goodday Joe — how's it?"

Norman turned dilated eyes on him.

"Where you come f'm?" asked Elbert, running black eyes over the marvellous sight.

Norman's eyes became contemptuous, flicked from the long nose to the calloused feet. He drawled "D'you know where you can go to, snoozer?"

"Where?" asked Elbert eagerly.

"To blunny hell!" snapped Norman, and walked away.

Elbert slunk into the kitchen, Norman heard a bustle there, and heard the Greek cook ask, "Who dat flash bloke, Elbert?"

"Dunno," said Elbert. "Proper flash, aintee!"

"Yeah — he yeller-feller?"

"Yeah — I tink so — By cripes I tink dat Mist Chilnsik belong Red Ochre sitting in dat car!"

"Oh he pretty!" cried a small female voice.

"Shut up, monkey," said the cook. "I's de pretty one for you."

The dispenser roared again.

The dispenser was quite ungracious when he gave the medicine to Norman. So Norman did not tell him that he had a friend a chemist as he had intended. The man went back to his den without so much as a Good-day.

Norman was not much troubled by this treatment, thinking that he had merely found a gathering of boors. He strutted back to the car, and completely disorganised the business of the hospital as it concerned the coloured staff. Oscar opened the door for him. He climbed in like a rajah to his throne. The hood was down. The watchers missed nothing of the sight. As the car rolled past the Lazaret and the staring girls he asked Oscar what the place was, and upon being told looked back. The girls shrieked and waved. He waved back. They danced for joy, and when the car was swallowed in red dust, turned to the mean ones in the kitchen and the yard and yelled at them, "Ya — ah — see — ee— he waved to u —us!"

Some distance down the road, Norman said to Oscar, "Eh Dad — what's a yeller-feller?"

Oscar stared ahead for a while, then asked, half-turning, "Did someone call you that?"

"No — least I heard some one say it, talking about me I think. What is it?"

Oscar studied the close-clipped head of the Chinaman at the wheel for a moment, then answered, "A halfcaste. But don't get cut up if people call you names like that. This's a rough country. People talk and act rough. But they don't mean anything, really."

"Oh I'm not cut up," said Norman lightly, and turned to grin at a string of quaintly-dressed natives past whom they sped.

At lunch in the presence of Oscar, who said he would spend the afternoon in bed, Norman asked Marigold if she would join him in a stroll. She readily agreed. But when he came to fetch her about half an hour later she refused, saying that it was too hot for walking. After some bantering he left her. She was lying in a hammock on the side veranda. As he went she moved. She nearly rose and called him back. She checked herself, relaxed, began to bite her lip. She was not troubled by the heat but by the fact that she did not wish to be seen abroad with a coloured-man, even though the man was virtually her brother and beloved by her. While with him on the previous day she had been troubled by the stares they drew. She knew why people stared. She would have stared herself, with mind if not with eyes, to see a young good-looking girl beside a coloured-man. But only since she came to Capricornia. In Batman, where people had often stared, she had not cared. Why? Perhaps because in Batman the people had not stared so hard as did the Capricornians.

Oh why had Norman come? Just as she was taking the place to which she was entitled! Daughter of a beef-baron, heiress to broad acres and multitudinous beeves, likely to be heiress to one of the greatest properties in the country if she could persuade her father to increase his lease and stock as she was trying to do. Daughter of a beef-baron, one of the most sought-after girls in the community, come to be stared at by every common loafer in the streets! Oh but how mean, how mean! She was despising him whom all her life she had known and loved as a brother, simply be-

cause it was the custom of the country to despise a coloured-
man. She must avoid it. But how unfortunate that he was
coloured! For whom? For all of them. But for whom the
most? Of course for him. She must remember that and
help him, not join with the community against him. After
all he was not staying long.

When Norman came to her at four o'clock, carrying a
tray of tea, she hailed him brightly. On the tray lay a packet of cigarettes of a kind she prized. She had told him that
she could not get them in the town. So he had been
tramping round to get them for her! Tears came to her
eyes. She took up the tray and carried it out to a strip of
lawn that she knew was under the eyes of the people on
the balcony. They talked and laughed together as of old.
When he asked again if she would join him in a stroll she
went and got her hat. But for all her good intentions, she
would not walk through the town as Norman wished to do.
She suggested a walk to the railway-yards to see the stacks
of materials for Mr Steggles' bridge. He agreed. Thus he
came to tread again the ground over which he had fled from
the devil-devil of long ago.

They went from the Yards to the shore of Devilfish Bay,
and, strolling about, came upon the crazy house of Fat
Anna, which they approached with intent to get a drink of
water. They knocked. A shrill voice answered, "Ye-ah —
what you want?" Norman shouted, "Can we have a drink
of water, please?"

Fully two minutes elapsed before anyone appeared. But
it was evident all the while that someone was coming. The
old house creaked to the movements of a ponderous body.
When Anna appeared they stared at her, surprised, not
because her face recalled the past to them, but because her
form was such as they had never set eyes on. Anna had become elephantine. She was so huge that she could scarcely
move. Her face was as round as a cheese, and as smooth
as Marigold's, in spite of the fact that her hair was as white
as Marigold's dress. She was as much surprised as they.

"Sorry to trouble you," said Norman with much politeness; "but could you oblige us with a drink of water?"

"Wotah?" she asked, eyeing them intently. "Wotah —
yeah — but might be you likim tea more bettah — eh?"

"No, just a glass of water, thanks," said Marigold.

From staring at the rajah Norman, Anna turned about
with difficulty. He touched her arm and said, "Oh please
don't trouble to get it. We'll get it ourselves."

She smiled, drew aside to let him pass, and told him where the butt was. He went inside with Marigold at his heels. They got their drink, luke-warm and saline. Then, pressed by Fat Anna's invitations and pleased with the strangeness of her den, they sat down and let her give them bread, hot and delicious from the oven, and strong goat-butter and bitter milky tea.

After some talking had been done, Anna said to Norman, "Batman belong your country, eh?"

"No," said Norman. "I belong here. Red Ochre. You savvy?"

Anna raised her brows, stared, exclaimed, "Retogger? Yeah — me savvy. What you name?"

"Shillingsworth. My uncle's Mister Oscar Shillingsworth. You know him?"

Anna's eyes popped. Leaning forward she asked breathlessly, "What name belong you?"

"Norman."

"Nawnee!" she cried, flopping back and raising great fat hands. "Goddam! You face! Yeah — me savvy — gawd now what you tink dat!" She beamed. "Oh Nawnee, Nawnee! Time you lil fella so-high you papa givvim me for look-out nursim you."

"Is that a fact?" asked Norman, reflecting her pleasure.

"Yu-i. Oh me bin makim first-time trouser belonga you." She giggled. "Oh dat long long time now. Dat time you come Fline Fockis. Dat you country — Fline Fockis — no-more Retogger."

"Eh — Fline Fockis — what's that?"

"One place. Dat you mumma bin droppim you. Wha' name — you forget?"

Norman looked at Marigold.

Anna was panting. "Longa big salt water," she said. "Fline Fockis. Dat place you papa gottim camp time catchim trepang."

"Salt water?" murmured Norman to Marigold. "Does she mean the sea?"

"Yeah," said Anna. "Sea. Longa sea. Dat lil islan'."

"Ah!" he said. "You mean Java, eh? Place long long way away longa sea?"

"Yeah Fline Fockis. Place you papa stop."

"That must be her name for Java," he said to Marigold.

"Which way you papa now?" asked Anna.

"Oh he's dead."

"Daid — dat one! Oh dat proper bad luck now. Which
way he die?"

"Oh he — " Norman hesitated, conscious of his ignorance of his father's history. "He — was killed in the big
war."

"Oh too bad! All-same Wally Shay an' Missus Blinker's
Sammy, eh? Too bad! Dat p'liceman no can catch first-
time?"

"Policeman?" murmured Norman.

"Yu-i. P'liceman first-time go chasim."

Norman stared. At length he asked, "What — policeman
chase my father?"

Anna said brightly, "Yu-i — for killim Chow."

Norman looked at Marigold, to find her gaping.

Anna prattled to some length about the murder of Cho
See Kee; but because Marigold and Norman had much
difficulty in following her speech, she conveyed little of her
knowledge to them. However, they learnt enough to decide
that there was something decidedly questionable about the
history of Uncle Mark. They left her feeling puzzled.
Norman told Marigold how Heather had interrupted George
Tittmuss the night before. She listened with interest, but
made no comment, feeling that the situation was a delicate
one. Uncle Mark had suddenly come to life out of legend.
Real or legendary he was still her uncle; but to Norman he
had never been mere uncle; one may spy upon one's
uncle's guilty past without concern, but not in the presence
of his son, even though the son might be one's virtual
brother.

Marigold dined away with friends that night. Oscar was
still suffering recovery. Norman took a tray of food to him,
and while sitting with him told him what he had learnt
from Anna and what had happened with Tittmuss. Oscar
fumbled for a while, then in a short hot speech denounced
the tattlers, then said that Mark had been involved in a
brawl in which a Chinaman was killed, that the affair had
happened on the eve of his departure for the war, and had
been investigated after he was gone and unable to defend
himself, that the trouble was nothing very serious, and that
Norman should not think of it nor listen to silly tales.
Though by no means satisfied, Norman let the matter drop.
Down in the hall he met Heather, and, filled with the subject, got her to have a glass of beer with him on the veranda and led her on to talk of Mark. She talked about

Mark till the gong called him to dinner, but told him nothing that he wished to know.

Alone at dinner he was embarrassed by the attention he received from other diners. He had been given even more at other meals, but had not noticed while in company. But soon his interest was absorbed in the halfcaste Philippino waitress who attended him, Pearl Ponto, daughter of Mark's friend of bygone days, a handsome, slight, pert, starry-eyed, brown creature, making eyes at him. She was not true halfcaste. Her halfcaste father had married a full-blood of his race. Soon Norman was familiar enough with her to ask if he might see her home that night. Giggling she consented, and told him where he might meet her.

Pearl lived in The Paddock. She did not go straight home that moonlit night, but round by the Compound and down Mailunga Beach, treading the silken silver sand beneath the grove of coconuts in which the soft wind whispered spicy tales it brought from Java. Norman was with her, arm about her waist, whispering spicy stories of his own. He left her near her home, promising to come there to a party to be held next night.

§

Next day was Saturday. Norman's first thoughts were given to planning how he might forestall any arrangement Oscar and Marigold might make for his entertainment that night and how he might go to Pearl's party without their knowing. So far they had arranged nothing but a morning of shopping preparatory to their departure for Red Ochre on a cattle-train on Monday morning, and an afternoon at a cricket-match to be played between the Government Officers and the rajahs of the Cable Station.

Soon after lunch, while the others were resting, waiting for the time to go to the match in the cool of the afternoon, Norman went out for a stroll along the road he had walked with Pearl the night before. So he came to the Compound. He knew what the place was, having had it pointed out to him by Pearl. He left the road to see more of it, going towards the gate, intending to walk right round. Natives lounging at the doors of huts sat up and stared at him, cried out to friends, brought out crowds that even included cripples. Norman saw among them youths resembling himself in face. One of these called out to him and waved. Feeling by now embarrassed by the stir he caused, he left the fence, abandoned his intention of walking round, and took the road past the Home. He felt distressed, slighted because people obviously of his own breed were living in squalor such as he had never seen before. Then sight of the children in the Home, who rushed to the fence to stare at him, increased this feeling in him. He went on hurriedly.

At length he came to a bend of the road, where he turned and followed a track through scrub, heading for the sea, which he had glimpsed, bent on exploring and occupying himself till it was time to go to the match. He came to the hospital, saw the girls in the Lazaret, who screamed and waved. He smiled and waved, went on down the wire fence through scrub till he came to the edge of a steep deep gully and was confronted with the sea. He descended. The hospital was now high above him, screened by a grove of poncianas and pandanus palms. He was standing at the water's edge, gazing at the distant western shore, when a voice, a deep-toned female voice, cried out near him, "Ow! Blast an' damn you, blunny jiggerin' cow!"

The owner of the voice was hidden from him by a tumble of schisty rocks at the base of the cliff on which the hospital stood facing the sea. He stole up and peeped, to see a small black-headed girl engaged in a duel with a devil-crab. At one moment it was the girl who attacked, striking with an iron gidgee and swearing heartily, doing damage only to the sand; at another it was the nimble crab, rushing in with claws extended, sending the opponent back with squeals. Then the crab, retreating, came within a yard or two of Norman, who rushed at it and kicked it into the air. "Oh!" cried the girl, turning black eyes on him. "Oh!" Then looking at the crab, and seeing it lying on its back and struggling to regain its legs, she withdrew her attention utterly, rushed in and settled the duel.

Norman came up and said, "What — crabbing?"

She looked him over in a glance, with tip of tongue between her teeth like a cherry.

"That's a big one," he said. "Can you eat it?"

"Course," she said in her pleasantly strange deep voice — the voice of a lubra almost — and giggled, bending to examine the crab.

Norman dropped to his calves, said, "Not poison, is it?"

She glanced at him, giggled. and said, "You Shillingsworth, aint you?"

"Yes. How'd you know?"

"I see you yes'd'y long hospital."

"Oh, you were there, eh?"

"Dere all time."

She rose, a mite compared with him, and with hands behind and body swaying, eyed him shyly. Norman smiled and looked her over. She wore a short ill-fitting smock of the dungaree-material used for dressing the children of the Halfcastes' Home, trimmed with grubby white braid. When he took out his cigarette-case she thrust out a honey-coloured hand and said, "Gimme."

He laughed and gave her a cigarette and lit it for her. "What's your name?" he asked.

"Tocky O'Cannon."

"How old are you?"

"Close-up fourteen, I tink. I dunno properly."

"When's your birthday."

"I forget."

"Garn! You're kidding."

"No-more. I no have me buffdee long time now, cos papa and mumma belong me daid."

"Oh? Where d'you live?"

"Wit' Christobel."

"Who's she?"

"Nother one harcarse girl."

"Halfcaste? You're not a halfcaste, are you?"

"Yu-i — colour-pipples all-same."

"Coloured people? Why — what colour was your mumma?"

"Harcarse — but him Chow harcarse, makim blackfella. What kind your mumma?"

"Javanese."

"Japanese?" she cried incredulously.

"No no — Jar-vanese. Don't you know those people?"

"No-more. That nother kind blackfella?"

"Oh no — not black."

"Close-up, eh?" she asked, staring frankly at his dark face.

He looked down.

"Gimme two t'ree cigarette," she said. "I wanner give Christobel."

He gave them, saying, "You talk funny. Didn't you go to school?"

"You all-same," she said.

"Me — how you mean?"

"You talk all-same whiteman."

He grimaced. "But didn't you go to school?" he asked.

"Lil bits longa Compound."

He stared at her, said, "Compound? But that's for blacks, isn't it?"

"Yu-i. Harcarse all-same."

After a pause he said, "What they teach you? Read and write?"

"Lil bits. But I bin losim head."

"You what?"

"Bin forget."

He laughed and said, "Where d'you live now?"

"Long hospital. Me'n Christobel's maid."

"Ah! Do you like the job?"

"No-more!" she cried, wrinkling a pretty nose. "All dem sister proper humbug."

"How's that?"

"All time roustin'. All time tink we go out wid boys. We no can talk boys. But dem sister proper mad long boys demself."

He chuckled, saying, "What's sauce for the chickens aint for the old hens, eh? Why don't they let you talk to boys?"

"Matron and Doctor Aintee tink might be —" She expressed herself with a frankness that made Norman gasp.

He swallowed and asked, "Who's Doctor Aintee?"

"He's Protector — Ah! — look, dere Christobel."

She pointed to the tumble of rocks, where another girl, dressed like Tocky, was watching them.   Tocky called. Christobel came shyly. She was a year or two older than Tocky, better looking, darker, a true halfcaste, and much less bold. Her shyness put an end to the animated personal conversation. She said little of what was said after her coming, occupying herself mainly with describing circles in the sand with yellow-brown toes and searching Norman's face with swift interested glances.

The conversation was suddenly interrupted by a cry from the cliff-top, "Christo — bel! Taw — kee!"

"Sister!" exclaimed Tocky.

"You gotter go?" asked Norman.

Christobel swept her dark eyes over him and nodded. He smiled at her slyly and winked the eye remote from Tocky.

"Come on quick," hissed Tocky. "De cow might come."

The girls left him. At the rocks Christobel turned and waved. Norman blew her a kiss. While they were running up the steep path through the trees Christobel said, "Oh ainee lovely!" Slapping at mosquitoes, Tocky answered, "Ainee! Must be awful richman, eh?"

"Lookout!" hissed Christobel. "Cow's on veranda."

On the veranda of the hospital, at the head of the steps leading up to the back of the kitchen, stood a woman in uniform, whose lean white face was hard with anger. "Where have you been?" she cried as the girls came panting up the steps. They tried to dash past. Christobel succeeded. Tocky was caught by an arm. Shaking her, the sister cried, "Where have you been, you monkey?"

Tocky mumbled, "On'y down de beach."

"With boys?"

"Oh, no Sister!"

"Little innocent! Now get to your work. How dare you run away when there's so much to do? Next time, Doctor Aintee comes — Look at me like that, you little beast, would you!"

Tocky bounded into the kitchen.

The sister spoke to the dispenser, who was glaring from the back door of his den, then went through his den to the front, and there, on the front veranda, encountered Constandino Kyrozopolis the cook, talking to a fellow Greek who was waiting for medicine. Constandino jumped when she appeared. She bawled at him, "What are you doing here?" He gaped. "Get to your work! Everybody idling and gossiping while there's a thousand things to do. Get back to the kitchen."

In a moment every hand was busily engaged. That afternoon there was extra work to do, because those members of the nursing-staff who were going to the cricket-match would bring home several guests for dinner. The sister was primarily annoyed because responsibility for the preparations had been left to her, while she alone of all the sisters missed the match. She glared at the humble ones, the maids and cook and black scullions, till satisfied that they were settled to their tasks, then left them, going back to her other duties with the sick. When her footsteps ceased to ring, the humble ones with one accord stopped work, and, in the manner in which they customarily replied to those that browbeat them, puckered their mouths and vented a chorus of unseemly sounds.

§

The shadow of the windmill crept across the hospital yard till it touched the front veranda of the kitchen; then it vanished. The gold that splashed the kitchen window-panes and spilled on the greasy floor became as red as the fire in the range. The nyctophobic sugar-ants abandoned foraging and fled to nests; hungry cockroaches peeped from cracks; hermit-crabs crept out from hiding; violet night came stealing. But the workers in the kitchen did not note the changes; they were engrossed in pots and pans.

During a momentary lull in the bustle, Con the cook heard a far-away sound, and cocked an ear, then looked to see if the ever-watchful leper girls were craning out. They were. So he concluded that the cars bringing the sisters and their guests were coming in, and said to his sweating comrades, "Here dey comes — de great white pipples."

A car raced through the yard, past the lazaret, round the mortuary and the Asiatic Ward, out of sight towards the nurses' quarters. Then another car, another, then a fourth. The last was lost in dust. So was the Evening Star, as though the Great White Pipples could do what they liked with it.

Con said to Tocky, "Better nick off and change yous clotheses, monkey. Here, Christy, gif dat jobs to Barney and start cuttin' dat breads."

"I aint a monkey," Tocky cried. "But you'n ol' g'rilla."

"Brrrr!" he snarled, acting the part and rushing at her. She squealed, and laughing bounced out of the kitchen and skipped away down the roofed-in gangway to an old white building where she and Christobel lived. This building had once served as the maternity section of the hospital. It could almost have served as an oven during the heat of a Dry Season day; for it was of corrugated iron built on a concrete floor; and by night and during the humid days of the Wet it could have served as an incubator. The few white women who were willing to breathe the same air as the wives of Greeks and other low-class people, were now confined in a modern building of asbestos. But the old place was not utterly disused; sometimes such halfcaste women as needed more attention in travail than could be given them in the Compound hospital were confined there; such women were often so ill that they died.

Before Tocky entered her little room at the rear she peeped round the latticed back veranda to see if Yeller Elbert was about, knowing from experience that he was not above creeping on her while she dressed. Elbert and his lubra, who was a kitchen-maid, lived, or camped, as they more aptly called their squalid state of residence, on the back veranda. Elbert was not there. So Tocky went into her room and switched on the light. The room was about fourteen feet square, terribly paint-worn, its furniture two

rusty iron beds, a wooden cupboard, three kerosene-cans, a
pickle-bottle holding a bunch of ponciana flowers, and a
footworn fibre mat.

Tocky removed her smock, exposing her light brown body
to the waist. Mosquitoes had been waiting all day for that.
They rushed her. Stamping and slapping and swearing stockrider's oaths she rushed to the cupboard and took out a
simple dress of flowered print. She dressed with haste, then
surveyed herself as best she could without a mirror. Thus
she was dressed in her best in a minute, though not so much
because she lacked the feminine desire to make a long job
of dressing as the means to exercise it. Dressed, she went
to her bed and took from a hole in the mattress a mouth-
organ. She sat on the bed, and, with shoulders dancing,
played *Waltzin' Matilda*. So she was occupied till a burst
of laughter was swept down to her from the nurses' quarters, a reminder of her duties.

At the nurses' quarters thirteen well-dressed people sat
among palms and flowers in the bright well-furnished
lounge, talking and drinking cocktails. Among them were
Marigold and Stanley Steggles.

Meanwhile, in the kitchen Con the cook was putting the
finishing touches on the meal. At last he cried "Done it!
Now let 'em come an' not keep us poor cowses waitin' half
the night. Ring de bell, young monkey. Now den you
pigses." He addressed the black scullions, who were standing by with chipped enamel dishes and a billy-can, and the
temporary workers, who chopped wood and cleaned the
yard, and who were sent from the Compound by the week
to do these jobs for nothing, and who bore nothing with
which to collect their rations but sheets of newspaper and
jam-tins. Into these receptacles Con tossed what remained
on plates and in pots and pans of the food prepared for
the patients, and several chunks of bread gone stale and
mouldy, and syrupy black tea from the patients' pots, and
handfuls of an anty mess called in the hospital Blackboys'
Sugar.

"Rubbitch!" growled one of the scullions who had eaten
better.

"Give it back den," bawled Con, and grabbed at the
growler's dish. But rubbish or no, the growler clung to it,
and took it away to eat with his comrades in their hovel
behind the closets of the Asiatic Shed or Ward. Con grimaced when their backs were turned, and said, "Poor cowses.
Taint my fault."

Then he served the domestic-staff with food of better quality. These were Tocky, Christobel, Elbert and his lubra, Margaret O'Cannon, and her halfcaste lover Blackantan Bruce. Margaret was the laundress. She had inherited the job from Blossom, who had died of heart failure in the Compound eighteen months before. Her sister Kitty was married to a Philippino and living in a camp on Devilfish Bay; and her sister Bridie was working as a coloured maid in a private house in Town. The domestic-staff sat at a table on the back veranda of the kitchen. All were barefooted and ragged, and talked in Pidgin, even Tocky and Margaret, who, through having lived for long with the people of the Compound, had forgotten the reasonably good English they had spoken in their home. And they talked quietly, afraid of the dispenser in his den. Only one voice could that gentleman not control near his dispensary — the loud voice of the Trade Wind, that hearty thing which often burst his back door in, roared through his sanctum, brought down his bottles on his head.

At last Constandino was heard to cry, "Here dey comes — de great white kings and queenses. Come on you mob an' tend to 'em. I'm off."

Tocky and Christobel and the others bolted the rest of their food, then rose and went munching into the kitchen. Con tore off his apron, hurled it into a dresser-drawer, then got out his bicycle, and just as he was, coatless, hatless, wearing nothing but a brightly-hued but filthy cotton shirt and greasy broadcloth pants and Chinese slippers, mounted and sped across the yard. As he passed the Lazaret the girls, waiting for him, screamed and danced, while he, at risk of injury, waved both hands and yelled like a madman, "Mummuk kidses — mummuk, mummuk!" The girls waved him out of sight. His coming and going was the joy of their weary lives. He came with the sun and went with it, and let scarcely an hour of the day go by without coming out to wave to them and often to shout at risk of annoying the dispenser, and never let a day go by without delighting them by smuggling some nurses' titbit into their monotonous meals. He came with the sun and went with it, leaving their small world darkened not only by the night.

So easy was it to do something to amuse those leper girls. But perhaps it should be left to low-class people like themselves. When the white people came from the quarters to the hospital dining-room they passed the Lazaret but did not see the girls. Laughing, they trooped into the dining-room, to sit at a gleaming cloth before bright silver and fragrant flowers. The matron took up a little bell in plump white hands and rang imperiously. In came brownish-handed Tocky with the soup, and soon was deftly lifting deftly setting down, speeding on bare prehensile toes, scarcely breathing for fear of giving offence, wide-eyed and watchful, open-lipped with cherry tip of tongue between her teeth. Everyone around the shaded lights that night looked beautiful, but none so beautiful as swarthy Tocky; yet no-one looked at her, no-one thanked her, no-one even realised that she was there breathing, feeling, living as they were; for she was Coloured, and hence unseeable, not even to be thought of. But she saw everything and heard, and bore it to the kitchen and related it to Christobel dishing up, crying over incidents that struck her as comical, "Oh dear, oh dear! An' den Mist Steggles an' Fatty Don't Do Dat look at Sister Hogg an' —" But always the little bell would ring and ring and call her back to work.

To the scullions waiting for the dishes from the sisters' table it seemed as though the meal would never end. They waited fretfully, cursing the white ones for their dallying. For Saturday night was picture-night. The picture-house was a mile away. The show began at eight. Oh how the minutes flew! Black Bicycle, who understood a clock, watching that in the kitchen, told his comrades, "Twen tate — quar tate — ten tate — fi tate!" And still the great ones chattered over empty plates! The meanness was not deliberate, but merely thoughtless, or perhaps more rightly brainless. The Great Ones rose at ten past eight. At half past eight they left for a house in the Government Officers' community at Fathead Point near the Compound, where a party was to be held that night.

Tocky and Christobel were not going to the pictures. They were not allowed to leave the hospital grounds unless accompanied by persons thought reliable by Dr Aintee. No doubt there were plenty of people qualified, but few who would be pleased to have the honour; and those who would were usually of such forbidding character as made the girls regard excursions with them more as punishments than pleasures. Sometimes the matron of the hospital took them to the pictures. They were always glad to go, since the occasions were not by any means so common as to make the pleasure pall. But for her kindness they called the lady Don't Do Dat. Sometimes the matron of the Compound, virtually their foster-mother, took them into Town to buy new clothes. They loved the clothes but hated the woman almost as much as they hated their foster-father, Dr Aintee, who, always to their discomfort, sometimes took them riding in his car. Yet none of these people treated them badly. Their dislike of them was something requiring greater understanding than perhaps these people could give.

Dr Aintee held no high opinion of the great black and brindle family he fathered, nor viewed their plight with sentiment, not understanding their plight nor being expected to do so by his employer, the Government. Like his employer, he regarded them merely as marsupials being routed by a pack of dingoes; and he understood that his duty was merely to protect them from undue violence during the rout. Most of the dingoes hated him for interfering with their rights as the stronger animals; the marsupials regarded him as a sort of devil-devil, and trembled at mention of his name. Thus he was loved by few; but he was well enough paid to be careless of what was thought of him; his salary amounted to about a quarter of the total expenditure on Aboriginal Affairs in Capricornia.

Just now, however, Dr Aintee was ignoring the maids in their need of entertainment, because they had lately fallen into deep discredit on account of suspicious circumstances pointing to their having dabbled in secret wickedness. Their credit for good morals was never high, since it was generally believed that they had no moral-sense. Most likely there was ground for that belief, since Dr Aintee, who was not a man to believe anything without good reason, shared it. But nothing had been proved, though a strict investigation had been made, a veritable round-up of all the coloured youths of the community who might be suspected of having dealings with them. In their state of discredit they were regarded by most virtuous people who came into contact with them as depraved and dirty little wretches. But Dr Aintee merely regarded them as mature females who could be suspected of having what he called Their Feelings and as such capable of motherhood and of increasing his unwieldy brood of halfbreeds. So Tocky and Christobel were living under a cloud. They had not been treated to an excursion of any sort for weeks.

Because they had no pleasures to fly to when the toil of the day was done, these children usually had no sympathy with those who had. In fact they often were at pains to aggravate distress caused by the lingering of the Great

Ones by further impeding the progress of their comrades of the kitchen. On picture-nights the kitchen was usually in an uproar from the time the nurses rose from the table till the infuriated scullions plunged to freedom down the hill and made a bee-line for the pictures through the scrub. For usually the maids were at their jealous aggravating. But this night there was no uproar. For some reason too delightful to be probed by the scullions, the maids not only did their own work quickly but helped the scullions with theirs. If left to themselves the kitchen-staff would always have made short work of cleaning up; but that they never were; on picture-nights the early-duty sister always came to watch with a sharper eye than ever.

At twenty past eight the work was finished. That meant that the scullions had missed the always-interesting Zet, as they called the Gazette or Newsreel Tocky and Christobel bounced off to their room. The others, just as they were. dripping suds and grease and sweat, plunged into the gully and ran for their lives. That night a hero they called Duggish Fairbung would be on the screen. They would not have missed him for a whole month's pay. They loved him, even more than they did those heroes of the blazing guns, Wimmessart and Wimmeldunkan. Strange that those children of the wilds should seek relief in make-believe. Stranger still that ones so simple, the Ragtag of Humanity, should be delighted by the self-same romances as delight the millions that consider them semi-animals.

§

As Tocky had told Norman, though no doubt she had exaggerated, the nursing-staff of the hospital was composed of women of amorous nature, which was so evident that sneering people of the town had lately come to call the institution The Harem. The path to the nurse's quarters was worn to a gutter by the feet of their lovers.

Some of the sisters even entertained their males while on duty at night, which was not at all difficult, since only one sister was on duty at a time, for a period of six hours, and at night on duty without assistant nurses. There was no question of neglecting duty about it. At night the hospital was usually as quiet as a yard of sheep. Without her friend the sister must have occupied her idle time with reading or sewing or taking naps.

The sister on duty that night, after seeing the scullions depart, went from the kitchen to her duty-room, did what

there was to do till nine, then walked through the wards to
see that the patients were comfortable and put out the
lights. Then she paid a visit to the Old Maternity and
flashed her lantern on the beds of the halfcaste maids. The
children were in bed and apparently asleep. At half past
nine the sister's lover came, drifting across the shadowy
yard like a cloud across a moonlit sky. They met at the
steps. They went with arms encircling to the back veranda,
there to sit snuggled in the moonlight, looking out upon the
placid harbour, listening to the splash of fishes, the murmur of the tide, the tiny clatter of hermit-crabs. Dear Capricornia!

At eleven the sister left her man, and after making a
quiet tour of the wards, went to the kitchen to prepare him
supper. While waiting for the tea to draw she took up her
lantern and paid another visit to the maids, it being one
of her duties to keep an eye on them, a duty that for
a while had not been rigidly observed, since it was thought
that they had been scared out of their wickedness; usually
the night-sisters each paid them only one visit, one such
as this early-duty sister had already paid, the other in
the small hours by her successor. No particular notion
prompted the sister to go to them again; she remembered
them through finding a dirty butter-dish and went to fill
in time; but afterwards she said she had been prompted
by a Feeling.

The children's beds were empty. Their dungaree smocks
were lying as before, their cheap print dresses missing.
The sister searched the empty building for them. Her footsteps clattered harshly on the concrete floor, rousing echoes
that sounded in the roof like cackling of ghosts; and shadows that her lantern roused leapt up and lunged at her, as
though they were the bitter ghosts of halfcaste women
who had died there.

The sister was shocked, knowing that the truancy could
mean but evil. And she was annoyed as well, as was her
lover when he heard, because their night of love was ended
now that she must summon Dr Aintee and the matron.
After supper her lover rose to go; but he did not go at
once; he took her in his arms, drew her close, pulled the
tail of her cap down slowly till it fell. No longer a sister
in uniform, no longer a hooded machine that worked to
rules, but a woman with hair, with heart and lips. She
clung to him. Kissing, they stood, a silent silhouette against

the moonlit silent world, seen by no eyes but those of a peeping possum in the roof.

Tocky and Christobel were breaking the rules that governed their lives by having the time of their lives at the house of the Pontos in The Paddock. Pearl's brother Enrico, a slim, sleek, mahogany-skinned youth, was wooing Tocky with a guitar and Spanish love-songs rendered in Malayan. Norman, drunk as a lord, was making love to Christobel less picturesquely but with as good effect. There were no whites at Pontos. Therefore the company could be trusted to keep the truants' secret. They were not strangers there. The company knew them well, and treated them well, understanding the hopeless dullness of their lives.

But all good things must end. Having in mind the visit of the early-morning sister, the truants left for home at one o'clock. Norman and Enrico took them home in Min Sing's hire-car. Min Sing had carried them before. He needed no telling when to douse the lights and where to run into the scrub and drop them. The girls alighted with the boys, and quietly approached the fence. Enrico did not hinder Tocky; but Norman had to be dragged away from Christobel. The girls scrambled through the fence. The boys ran off chuckling.

The girls slipped across the yard. Christobel was leading, carrying a parcel containing beads and powder and a wrist-watch that Norman had gone into Town and bought her in return for the favours she had bestowed upon him in sheer love. She tiptoed on to the veranda and disappeared, while Tocky was still in the moonlight giggling.

"Oh!" cried Christobel in darkness.

"Wha's up?" asked Tocky in a whisper.

"Where have you been?" demanded Dr Aintee. He was echoed by the ghosts of the empty house.

"Wazzer burry mat?" growled the sleepy voice of Elbert.

Tocky turned to flee. But a white thing shot out and seized her; and a firm voice said, "No you don't, you little minx."

The light in the girls' room, dim as it usually was, blazed bright and spitefully. The doctor and the matron and the white-clad sister were revealed.

"Where have you been?" thundered the doctor.

"Why be so mean?" cackled the ghosts.

"Shurrupangusslip!" growled Elbert.

The girls were dumb. Christobel's lips, which but a moment before were hot with love, froze with fear. There was not so much startled love or fear in Tocky as amazement. In freedom she had forgotten the Devil-Devil. The lips of the man and women might never have known a kiss to judge by their expressions then.

"Speak up!" thundered the doctor.

"Shut up!" cackled the ghosts.

Elbert was silent, now awake and listening eagerly.

"Where have you been? Come on. Out with it."

"N-nowhere," answered Tocky.

"Come on. I want the truth, or there'll be trouble, mark my words."

"The truth means double trouble trouble. Keep it dark," cackled the ghosts.

"W-w-we bin down de beach," said Tocky.

"Rot! Don't waste time with silly lies. You've been in a car. Where — and who with?"

The sister had seen the leper girls run out in their night attire, while she was watching from the hospital veranda, and the doctor and matron were inside. So she surmised that a car had come, and had gone to tell the others. The matron unfolded her mouth and said, "Better talk to Christobel, Doctor. This one's an awful liar. She couldn't speak the truth if she wanted to. And awful deep."

"We bin down de —" began the deep one.

"Shut up!" snapped the doctor. "I'm not talking to you. Come on Christobel — tell me."

Christobel was dumb. He shook her, but shook nothing out of her but tears. "Don't cry, my girl, for heaven's sake," he said. "Dammit, I'm not hurting you! Lord — if only I'd been in time to catch those gentlemen in the car!"

"W-w-we bin out in car," said Tocky suddenly.

"Ah!" said the doctor, drawn. "Who with?"

"Dunno name. Some spectable pipples pick us up while we go walkabout. We go lil way walk cos no can sleep for de mosquitoes. White pipples they was, pretty ladies."

"She's telling her lies," said the matron. "Better question them apart, I think, Doctor."

"All right," he said. "Please keep Tocky here, Sister. Come on Christobel."

Tocky strove so hard to hear what was said at the other end of the veranda that the sister had to push her into the room and shut the door. Afterwards the sister mentioned this as evidence of the child's renowned low cunning, not as loyalty to a friend. The questioning lasted for more than an hour. But nothing of any use was learnt. Of course the maids were suspected of gross misconduct, because their guardians knew that no man in the town would befriend them honorably; indeed they would have despised him had they known of one. At two o'clock they were taken to the Halfcastes' Home, to dream over their loves in company with a hundred snuffling children.

On the way back to the party at Fathead Point the matron, riding with the doctor in his car, said, "And what're you going to do with the little wretches now? I won't have them back, that's a certainty. They're incorrigible."

"They are just about," said the doctor. "I suppose I'll have to send 'em to the Copra Co. Who would you like in place of 'em?"

"No-one that's come out of the bush, thanks. These bush girls are all too cheeky. I want someone born in the Compound. Those ones know their place."

"I've got to place the other poor kids somewhere too."

"Leave them in the bush where they belong. Or marry them off to Philippinoes or Japs or something. I don't want them, anyway. And there's another thing. I want you to speak to Elbert. He's getting too cheeky lately. The other day I caught him giving a drink to a nigger out of one of our glasses — *nurses' glasses!*"

The doctor stopped the car before a large bright noisy bungalow. He said to the matron with a grin, "Did you have to boil it afterwards — or break it?"

She grimaced, saying, "You never take it seriously. I've got to put up with all — "

She was interrupted by a whoop. Out of the house and down the steps came a crowd in evening dress and surged about the car. One of the men lifted the matron out; others babbled invitations to the doctor to join them in a moonlight picnic out at Tikatika Point. The doctor jeered at them and drove away.

More revellers appeared, some bringing food and drink. Cars were started. Engines roared and spoilt the clean night air with the stench of gasoline. The crowd began to romp. Men and women, squealing and yelling like children, ran about while the Chief Medical Officer chased them in a baby-car. They laughed and yelled and cheered and screamed till birds left trees a hundred yards away. A child in the Home began to wail. Then another wailed, another. And dogs barked in the Compound.

WHAT Dr Aintee called the Copra Company was an institution situated on the island of Flying Fox. Time had dealt freakishly with Flying Fox. Of all places, that old sink of iniquity had been chosen as the site of the Gospelist Aboriginal Mission Station. It had become a font at which the natives of the neighbourhood were baptised into Christian Grace.

Flying Fox as Flying Fox had ceased to exist. That name was spoken only when old-timers told old tales. By the missionaries and their friends it was called what it has been called above, and by irreligious scoffers the Hallelujah Copra Co. The irreligious called it so intending to deride the fact that the missionaries did good business with the coconuts produced on the plantations worked free of cost by their converts. Jealousy was mainly responsible for the derision. The Gospelists, contemptible by reason of their virtue in the eyes of normal Capricornians, had done something that the normal ones had failed to do, that is, had developed methods of doing business successfully. No doubt the secret of the Gospelists' success was their very virtue. For since it is a sin to idle, they would not hearken to that devil's whisper Do It After The Wet, and, being thus strong in mind, were no doubt also weak in lust, and hence not greatly troubled by the lure of Black Velvet. Of course they themselves did not hew and dig and sow, as scoffers pointed out. But did Moses leading his people through the wilderness go out and gather the manna for them?

The Gospelists preached a doctrine of self-denial, which if their converts thought it good enough to accept, was worth their while to give their labour to. The Gospelists paid no wages to their labourers in cash, nor much in kind, but gave them freely of their knowledge. Civilization, even the little that had touched that part of the country yet, had robbed the Yurracumbungas and their neighbours of much of their own philosophies and left them on the way to become spiritually destitute. The Gospelists offered them spirituality for their labours, or, if that were not acceptable, at least mere labour to keep their hands in trim and their minds alive, and into the bargain taught them to read and write and think like whitemen of the kind they were themselves. Surely better pay than a pound a month and pigswill and the status of a dog, as prescribed by the Government? Gen-

erous people were those Gospelists, though terribly narrow-
minded, and therefore not as successful in their work as
otherwise they might have been. They could not be but
narrow while enslaved to a cult. For naturally to them it
was cult first and Binghis afterwards. Pity someone not enslaved had not taken on their job. But perhaps one must be
so enslaved to do as they.

Dr Aintee had checked the utter downfall of a number
of incorrigible waifs by handing them over to the Gospelists, who were glad to have them, it being their great hope
to get control of all the Aboriginal people in the land. So
it happened that a few weeks after that exciting night of
truancy, Tocky and Christobel, weeping bitterly, were set
aboard the mission-schooner *Alice Carstairs* and banished
for the good of their souls.

§

The Gospel Mission had been established many years, so
long in fact and thoroughly that the island had been changed out of recognition. Not a stick of the old settlement remained. Even the ancient mango trees and skinny coconuts had been uprooted as though they were counted as
original sins. A neat village of iron and asbestos buildings,
including a steepled church and a double-story school, stood
on the site of the humpies; and another village, this of
whitewashed iron, bark and hessian, scrupulously clean and
neatly placed, stood where the native camp had stood. This
second was the native quarter. It was drained and served
by kitchens and latrines and shower-baths, and enclosed by
a high barbed-wire fence. A grove of coconuts, comprising
a thousand or more fine palms, lined the ocean-beach from
end to end, these the virtues, as it were, supplanting the
ousted sins. Above the palms from the sea could be seen
the tip of the stack of the copra-mill and the sail of a great
windmill that pumped water from the billabong. And the
land between the billabong and the beach and creek, formerly overgrown with scrub and jungle, was laid out like a
market-garden, fenced, and scored with irrigation streams.
Birds and beasts had fled; so had the crocodiles; so no doubt
had Krater's devil.

Building the station must have been difficult, but simple
compared with the founding of the flock. Converts came of
their own accord at first, thinking the station just an ordinary whiteman's business, and the religious practices in which
they were invited to take part merely another kind of white-

man's incomprehensible amusement; they even offered their
women to the male missionaries to secure their goodwill.
But when the necessary discipline was brought to bear, most
of the converts went bush, and warned their ignorant brethren against the Mission.

This did not surprise the Rev. Theodore Hollower, lead-
er of the Mission, though he had not foreseen it. He knew
that anything was to be expected of the Prince of Evil. So
he went after the brands that had been snatched back, and
with wiles equal to His Highness's, again plucked a fair
number from the burning. And he took the schooner *Alice
Carstairs* far away and combed the islands of the Silver
Sea for converts. He even stole into the territory of the
Catholic Mission near Port Zodiac and snatched a few more
brands from there, considering the holy-water with which
they had been baptised about as effective an extinguisher
of Hell Fire as gasoline. And down the eastern coast he
went as far as Cape Nordoster, gathering converts by simply
blackbirding them. The *Alice Carstairs* made several quiet
trips like this, so that within a year or two the islands and
the coastlands were completely depopulated, though not
with so much advantage to the Mission, since at least two-
thirds of the natives had fled to avoid the *Alice Carstairs*.
Naturally a number of converts turned out to be good
Christians who could be relied upon to force their views on
others. These kept order at the Mission and prevented the
unwilling from escaping. No canoe was allowed on the
island.

It was not Mr Hollower's wish to keep a prison. He
wished only to bring his victims into contact with Chris-
tianity and keep them there till they might grasp its significance, which was something in which he had such great
faith himself that he was prepared to keep them in its
neighbourhood till they died.

Better than those of natural Christian disposition to
keep order in the Mission and prevent escapes were converts brought from lands so distant that they knew they
could not find their way home if liberated. They were more
robust that the natural Christians and harsh in their jealousy of those who knew their way home. Mr. Hollower
would do anything to outwit His Highness.

But still that Spirit worked contrarily. The old order of
things had changed in Yurracumbunga. Refugees from
islands and distant coastlands joined the tribe, so that at
length it became a mob with mixed philosophies, whose

common tongue was Pidgin, whose purpose was to harass the Mission. This mob called itself The Cowboys, a name no doubt adopted by knowing fellows who had been to Town many years before with Mark and had seen the pictures. They used to raid the Mission by night and slaughter pigs and poultry, beat the Christians who resisted them, debauch the large number of women who did not mind, and carry off as many people as they could. Usually they raided only for raiding's sake; but sometimes it was for the purpose of stealing back their lubras. For the zealous Hollower, believing that no couple had right to conjugality unless joined according to his own particular formula, did not scruple to separate pagan husband and wife; in fact he had found that an easy way to bring in converts was to catch stray lubras and keep them till their owners called for them and consented to be christened and to undergo a period of righteous living, in which event he married them to their wives and gave them freedom of the island. Consequently there was a preponderance of females at the Mission. But it was all great fun for everyone, including Mr Hollower, who never would admit it. The Christian natives thanked their new-found god for Grace and Mr Hollower, the Cowboys their ancient devils for the same good man and something for which to live.

The Missionaries did not mind the raiding as a rule, because that provided another easy means of making converts. Frequently the raiders fell into traps and were baptized; and frequently the Christians, mainly those robust ones unable to go home, assumed their right to counter-raid. Usually the violence in these affairs was limited to what was done with fists and sticks and stones, the opponent forces having no desire for bloodshed because for the most part they were brothers; but blood was spilt occasionally, as the result of which any raiders caught were sent up to Town to jail.

Several times there was serious trouble when sentries at the Mission were clubbed to death and mutilated for the fat of their kidneys. Such outrages were usually dealt with by punitive expeditions brought from Town. The fat-taking practice was introduced by refugees from the Jittabukka Country, who believed, in common with several other tribes, that if the bark of a certain tree were impregnated with the fat of an enemy's kidneys and burnt at billabongs or creeks or hunting-grounds, the devils responsible for the supply of fruit or fish or game would be more indulgent.

It was a sort of religious rite, like the burning of blessed candles. The punitive expeditions brought out to punish these outrages did little more than scare the Cowboys away for a while. The Mission natives, who were of necessity the guides of the expeditions, having respect for their own kidneys and an un-Christian belief that the fat-takers were devils, were always too scared to follow tracks with certainty. Any natives caught on the mainland on these occasions, whether associated with the fat-takers or not, were taken to Town and sent to the Calaboose for life.

This rather confused state of things was generally kept secret. However, occasionally it came to light, causing scoffers great amusement. But Mr Hollower was never daunted, convinced that someday he or his successors would establish order and win the Aborigines to Him who had created and neglected them so long. And truly, year by year the confusion was being in a measure overcome. In reply to scoffers he would merely say, "These people are human beings and children of the Lord. They must be found an honourable place among mankind and taught Salvation. Else how can we sleep of nights? Suggest a better plan to deal with them and I shall try it." No-one suggested anything but that he should mind his own business, leave the natives to go the way of old. To that he always gave the unanswerable reply, " 'Tis not my business but the Lord's."

§

At the time of the arrival of Tocky and Christobel, the Mission comprised some ninety persons, or Souls as Mr Hollower called them, of whom all but eleven were Aborigines. There were six white people, Mr Hollower and his wife, Brother Simon Bleeter and his, and two devoted spinsters, Sisters Wings and Harp. The assistants were five coloured missionaries, three Fijians and two Solomon Islanders and their wives, people of breeds that make most zealous Christians, in spite of, or perhaps on account of, the fact that they are by heritage head-hunters. These were assisted in turn by the best of the converts. And there were also eight Aboriginal halfcastes, five girls and three boys, not counting Tocky and Christobel, all of whom were nothing but pests just then, though Mr Hollower hoped to make of them evangelists to deal with the natives in the bush, to which end he was patiently instructing them in the Yurracumbunga tongue.

Mr Hollower himself brought Tocky and Christobel out. Thus in their opinion they met with the worst part of their exile first. His reward for doing everything conforming with his cult to win their regard was their whole-hearted detestation. Of all nicknames, they gave him the one of Old Lucifer, which they chose on account of his resemblance to their conception of the Prince of Evil as described to them in Compound sunday-school by the Rev. Finchley Randter. The name Lucifer was always used in teaching Aborigines about the Devil, lest they should confuse Him with the unauthentic devils of the bush. Mr Hollower was tall and thin, gaunt of face and shaggy of eye, and swarthy. He gave the maids to understand that he expected much of them, and placed them in the care of the two white sisters, who controlled the department of young unmarried lubras and halfcaste girls.

On the second night after their arrival, at an hour when the humbler Souls were in bed, Mr Hollower's attention was drawn from the subject of *God In The Silver Sea* as dealt with in a book he was writing, which he was discussing with all the white Souls on the high front veranda of his big white house, by the sound of music coming faintly from the building where the girls were housed. The sound was faint indeed, unheard by the others till Mr Hollower drew attention to it. "Listen!" he said, holding up a long index finger. "What is that?"

Silence, while the tide lisped to the beach and the wind whispered to the coconuts.

"Music," said Mr Hollower. "An harmonicon. It must be those new girls. It must be stopped."

He rose, and with the sisters descended from the house and went into the brilliant moonlight and down a path of crushed white coral flowing like a stream of milk through the black and silver palms. His face and those of his companions were grave at first, but softened as their owners neared the dormitory and heard the music more distinctly. It was that old rollicking hymn *Roll the Chariot,* a great favourite with the Gospellers. Subdued voices were singing and feet lightly thumping. With one accord the feet of Hollower and the sisters trod less heavily. The refrain danced through their minds:

If the Devil's in the way we will roll it over him;
If the Devil's in the way we will roll it over him;
If the Devil's in the way we will roll it over him;

As we all go marching on.
Oh roll the Old Chariot along!
Yes, roll the Old Chariot along —

Mr Hollower chuckled, snapped his fingers, said, "The young villains! But of course we must stop it."

They reached the gate. Now their faces were grim. The tune was the same — but not the words! Mr. Hollower hissed, "Open the gate — open the gate! Don't make a noise. We must see who's at the bottom of this. Give me your torch."

The sister who had the key dropped it in long grass. All bent to search for it, while blasphemy and insult smote their ears. But oh how the singers were enjoying it! The composition was the work of Christobel, who had a gift for such a thing.

Oh roll the Ol' Chariot along;
Yes, roll the Ol' Chariot along;
And fill the air with laughter and with song,
As we all go down to Hell.

If Ol' Hollower's in the way we will roll it over him;
If Ol' Hollower's in the way we will roll it over him;
And then we'll sin and sin and sin and sin,
And we'll all go straight to Hell.

But when Hollower meets Ol' Lucifer face to face;
Yes, when Hollower meets Ol' Lucifer face to face;
Oh Ol' Lucifer's sure to offer him his place!
So we won't stop long in Hell.

Oh roll the Ol' Chariot along;
Yes, roll the Ol' Chariot along;
Who cares a damn for what is right or wrong?
Hurrah for good Ol' Hell!

The door burst open. The torch-light blazed. The voice of Mr Hollower thundered, "What is the meaning of —" The thunder fell flat. For the light revealed a group of yellow and black girls, most of them naked as usual in that stifling dormitory, the others in the long red nightgowns they were forbidden to remove, squatting on the floor between the rows of beds about Christobel and Tocky, the first half-clad, the other stark naked and holding to her mouth a mouth-organ.

"W-w-what —" gasped Mr Hollower. He doused the light and hissed in the darkness, "Heavens!"

For a second the place was in an uproar. Then silence fell, silence perfect but for the quiet breathing of a score of sleeping innocents.

LET OUR GRACE BE A PRAYER FOR FORGIVENESS

NORMAN arrived at Red Ochre just in time to see the last of the great activity of the passing season of prosperity. Just then the non-native staff numbered seven, who were old Sam Snigger of the Caroline, who had been working there as foreman ever since Burywell's death, and Charles Ket, a young man of peculiar breed, who had been there for six or seven months, and Frank McLash, who was out of his natural job again and working for Oscar temporarily, and two halfcastes, Dingo Joe and Peter Pan, and Cho Sek Ching the Chinese cook. Cho Sek Ching, as Oscar had only lately been rather shocked to learn from Frank McLash, who had it from his mother, was a brother of the late Cho See Kee, Mark's victim; but apparently, since he had been serving Oscar cheerfully and well for the past three months, indeed had been cooking him the best food he had ever tasted, he was not antagonistic to the Shillingsworth family as Oscar at first had thought he must be. Norman made the acquaintance of Cho at once upon arrival, though without knowing who he was. He met the others on the following day, when he went out with Oscar, dressed as a thorough-going stockrider, in bright blue shirt and white moleskin riding-slacks and neckerchief and wideawake and short topboots and spurs, in imitation of cattlemen he had seen in the town, but sitting his horse very badly, to take part in the last big branding-muster of the season. Oscar, stout and brown-faced and white-moustached, clad in an expensive tusser-silk suit and wideawake and tan elastic-sides, looked the beef-baron that Marigold now made him pose as. They rode quietly, talking, glancing at each other's face, black-brown eyes into faded blue, while their horses, aware of the sound of the mustering far away, champed on bits and tugged at reins and tossed their heads and whinnied, chafing at the slowness of the pace.

The locality of the muster was a place called Culabindi, in the foothills of the Lonely Ranges, about ten miles from the homestead. Oscar and Norman, approaching it through the hills, came upon it suddenly. It was a sort of circus, a wide stretch of open ground, bare and grey, half surrounded on one side by the hill in which they rode, on the other by a heavily-timbered creek. In the middle, directly below them, veiled in a haze of chalky dust, churning and roaring like a maelstrom, was a mob of cattle of about a thousand head, perhaps a tenth of the herd of the station, held in check by a dozen or so horsemen, who galloped about at breakneck speed, charging with crashing stockwhips points at which the whirlpool would have burst its banks, flying after drops that spilt, riding like demons, round and round, one dozen dominating a thousand.

Oscar and Norman rode down the hill. Then Norman's horse rushed off in pursuit of an escaping calf, overtook it, wheeled it, ran it back, regardless of his rider's struggling to restrain him, then raced to a bellying point in the mob, reared within a yard of a phalanx of horns, then sped after a steer that broke away, and in wheeling to head the creature off, spilled his terrified rider. Norman fell flat on his back. The steer jumped over him.

Norman was rising, dazed, when a horse, reined to haunches, stopped beside him, smothered him with dust. He found someone helping him up. A voice bellowed in his ear, "Y' hurt?" He saw an unshaven dust-grey face. It was Frank McLash's. Frank bellowed again. Norman grinned feebly.

Then Oscar came up, dismounted with a rush, seized Norman, crying, "Y' hurt?"

"All right," gasped Norman. "Bit of a bump, that's all. Where's the horse?"

Norman's horse had caught the steer and was driving it back. Frank saw it, leapt into his saddle and sped after the runaway, brought it back, dismounted and bawled at Norman, "I'll ride him. You take mine. He's tired. He won't give you no trouble."

"Sure you're all right?" asked Oscar.

"Sure," said Norman with a grin, and took the reins Frank handed to him. Frank helped him into the saddle, then mounted the fresh horse and dashed away. When Norman gathered his wits he went after him, and stayed near him throughout the drafting.

Soon the mob tired, ceased its wild gyrating, gave up

trying to break free. Then the drafting, or Cutting Out, began. Oscar and Sam Snigger and Charles Ket forced a wedge in the mob, and rode in looking for Clean Skins, or unbranded beasts, and for Hornies, or beasts with ingrowing horns, and for such beasts as were maimed or diseased and must be destroyed. The chosen, most of which were very young calves attended by their mothers, or at least by cows to which they had attached themselves, having most likely lost their true mothers in the crush, were quietly extracted, passed out to blackboys, who drove them off to form the Cut, an evergrowing mob nearby, which was guarded by Peter Pan and Dingo Joe. Norman and Frank patrolled the ground between, occasionally driving back distracted cows of the mob that thought they saw lost calves in the Cut, and interfering in scuffles between amorous bulls that threatened to disturb the peace. Norman, at first too much afraid of horns to approach within a dozen yards of the mob, found courage as the beasts quieted, and soon came close enough to break in his new twelve-foot whip. Frank showed him how to use it.

Norman asked Frank who the men with Oscar were. He would have liked to ask Frank who he was, too, but was afraid, since Frank seemed to take the fact that he must know him for granted. Already Frank had asked him how he had enjoyed the voyage, how he liked Fitting, how things were in the South, and had told him that he was himself a locomotive-man.

Frank said, "That's Sam Snigger, the lanky old coot with the ginger mo. Remember him? Lives down our way, across the bridge."

Norman nodded, though he did not remember.

"He's the foreman," Frank continued. "Sarcastic old cow. You look out for him. He's sure to try to take a rise out of you. That other feller's Charlie Ket — or Charles, he calls himself." Frank chuckled. "For gawdsake don't call him Charlie to his face. It goes right up his nazzle." He chuckled again. "Old Sam calls him Charlie. You oughter hear him. Charlie aint spoke to him for weeks —"

"Why don't he like being called Charlie?" asked Norman.

"Sounds too darn familiar like. Sorter name you call Chows and Binghis by. He's a kinda halfcaste —"

Frank lashed at a bull that tossed its head at him, bawling, "Barsted — do that to me I'll chop your horns off!"

"Halfcaste?" murmured Norman, staring at the pasty-faced Ket.

"Yeah — his gran'pa was a Chow, and his gran'ma a lubra. Queer sorter bird. There was a lot of trouble about him a while back. He got jailed. He come here just after he come out —"

Frank's horse, ever watchful, shot away to head off a wandering steer. As Frank came back, Norman lunged at a young bull that broke and headed for the Cut. Frank yelled at him, "Lennim go lennim go! He's a clean-skin."

"How d'you know?" asked Norman.

"No ear-mark," said Frank. "All them's branded's ear-marked too." He spat and added, "Chit of a game this for blokes like us, aint it! Drivin' blunny cows when we oughter be drivin' injins." After a moment he added, "But I'll soon be back at the old game again. Got promise of a job drivin' on the noo Transcontinental. Start in Noo Year with the construction. When the track's through I'm pretty sure to be put on permanent." He went off after another steer. When he came back he continued, "You oughter put in for a job on the Transcon too, Norm. They'll be needin' fitters. On the construction you could make a pot of hoot in no time. You oughter be able to get two or three quid a day when things is busy."

Norman's attention was withdrawn by the crack of a revolver. Sam Snigger had shot a diseased beast, which charged wildly through the mob for several yards, then fell with a moan. Beasts around it drew back, stared at it with seeming amazement. One or two stole up and sniffed at it, drew back hastily when they scented death, causing a great crowd to move with a sudden sound like the pattering of rain. Blackboys darted up and checked the rush. Again and again the revolver cracked. Slowly the mob was moving towards the creek, leaving the carcasses. High in the air a flock of kite-hawks wheeled and whistled. Crows kahed in the timber of the hills.

The drafting occupied about an hour, during which about a hundred clean-skin beasts were segregated. The Cut now stood at the foot of the hills, the mob quite close to the creek. Then Sam Snigger and Oscar rode up to Frank and Norman.

"Getting along all right?" asked Oscar of Norman. Norman grinned. Sam ran an eye over him and said, "Goodday — howzit?" then turned to Frank and said, "Poke 'em over the creek, Frank, and run 'em round the bend."

"Good-o," said Frank, loosing his whip, and turned to

Norman and said, "You comin' too? I'm gunner run the
mob off."

"Good-o," said Norman, moving after him.

Sam bawled after them, "Come back to camp for dinner."

Norman and Frank and a couple of blackboys flogged
the mob across the creek. At first it was not an easy task,
because an extensive love-match had begun in which there
were involved several full-grown bulls that resented interference. Norman it was who first interfered. He got the
shock of his life when a huge roan beast turned and
rushed him. He was saved by the swiftness of his knowing
horse. Thereafter he used his whip on cows and calves
and steers. Unhappy steers! The other beasts seemed to
know that they were eunuchs and to despise them. Goggle-
eyed and gaping, looking like great clowns, they blundered
into the scuffles where mating was going on, to be butted
by the bulls and cows alike, and sometimes even by the
calves, and often to be subjected by the bulls to gross
indignity.

While they were returning from having dispersed the
mob, riding up the creek to the dinner-camp, Frank related
to Norman what he knew of the history of Charlie Ket.

Ket was a native of the West Coast, from whence he
had come during the recent boom. He arrived in Port
Zodiac on a cattle-boat, unknown to anyone, and introduced
himself as Harold Carlton of the West Coast town of
Dampier. He came into prominence through his proficiency
in sport, which he had acquired, as it was subsequently
learnt, by contesting with natives and halfcastes, first in
the Marist Mission at Anchor Bay, where he was reared,
then in the Aboriginal Prison Settlement on Buccaneer
Island, where he had served a sentence of three years. Before long he became captain of the Meatworks Football
Team. Then he was made secretary of the Sports Club, in
which capacity he was just as strict about the colour-bar,
the most important principle of the Club, according to
Frank, as had been any of his pure-white predecessors;
and it was said that during this time he treated all coloured people with great arrogance. Frank said that the
Sports Club was so particular about the whiteness of members that it even barred such swarthy types as Italians and
Greeks — Dagoes, that is — who were not considered
whitemen in Capricornia. He spoke quite frankly, giving
no thought to whether the subject might embarrass his

hearer, as it did to a slight extent. Norman was feeling vaguely humiliated.

Thus Charles Ket, or Charlie as Frank called him, or Harold Carlton as he was calling himself at the time, was lucky to be a member of the Sports Club, let alone its leading light. He was at the peak of popularity when someone came from Anchor Bay, recognized him, denounced him as Charlie Ket, illegitimate son of Johnnie Ket the baker of that settlement, by a whitish woman of some doubtful breed, grandson on his father's side of a Chinaman and a full-blooded lubra, and a fellow well known on the West Coast for offensive presumptuousness and bad character. He had been jailed several times for theft and violence. Finally he had battered and robbed an aged Japanese, for which he had been sent for three years to Buccaneer Island. He had not been long released when he came to Port Zodiac. Members of the Club were naturally staggered to learn that they had given their money and business into the keeping of one who was a convicted thief and was denied fellowship by their very precious principle. This tickled Frank, who roared over it. Laughing, he went on to say that Ket, after an attempt to deny the denunciation, defied the executive of the Club to depose him till his term of office was concluded. But they deposed him by the simple means of electing another secretary without consulting him. They had to do so in the billiard-room of the First and Last, being unable to use the clubrooms because he refused to surrender the keys. Then he destroyed the club-books and trophies, drew the club-funds, which amounted to something like £100, from the bank, and stowed away aboard the *S.S. Cucaracha*. He was found as the steamer was departing, put ashore, arrested. In court he raved at first, saying that he had been persecuted all his life by whitemen, that he was white, as white as anyone, as white as the Judge, and a damned sight whiter than the Prosecutor, then wept and begged for mercy. He was sent to the Calaboose for a year. At once upon release he left the town, shunning everyone.

It was a chance meeting with Oscar that brought Ket to Red Ochre, Frank said. Oscar met him at Black Adder Creek one day in the middle of the last Wet Season when he went across with Sam Snigger to examine the place with a view to taking it over as an out-station. Oscar and Sam knew that Ket was at Black Adder, camped in the old Garrison, having been told by the people of the Caroline a few days before that he had been seen there by the fettlers. Previously he had been seen at Red Coffin Ridge, from which he had retreated, evidently with intent to return to Town — as Frank said, to swallow his pride with a decent feed. Just then the weather was very wet; and the fellow had no possessions but the rags he wore, and was evidently unused to living in the bush. When Sam and Oscar found him, as they did when they went to the old house to shelter from the rain, he was squatting over a fire stewing cape-gooseberries in a rusty jam tin. He ignored their greeting, and when Oscar persisted in addressing him, turned and abused him. Among many things he called Oscar a White Bastard. Oscar and Sam left him, while they examined the homestead. Later Oscar returned and told him that unless he wished to die or go mad he must go find human food and company, and that if he were worried about anything or afraid of his fellow men, he might come over to Red Ochre and work a while; and he told him how to get to the station by following the pad through the ranges. Ket ignored him. When Sam and Oscar departed they left behind a gunny-sack containing half their dinner, a tin of tobacco, a tin of matches, and a couple of packets of cigarette-papers. Three days later Ket was seen at Red Ochre, drinking from a trough connected with the stock-tanks behind the homestead, slinking like a dingo. Some hours after he was seen he came to Oscar, scowling, and asked for a chance to earn a meal and a cigarette. Oscar handed him over to Sam, from whom Frank had got his information.

The last of the tale was told at the camp in sight of Ket, while Frank was unsaddling and hobbling his horse and helping Norman with his. Ket was watching them while he ate. As Norman approached him he felt guilty; but apparently not so Frank, who bawled, "What-o Charl — howzit?" Ket grimaced in a friendly way, then nodded to Norman, who smirked and murmured, "Goodday."

Oscar, who was sitting with Sam, a little apart from Ket, said to Norman, "How'd you get on?"

"Good-o," said Norman grinning. "Bit sore round the seat, though."

"You'll be eating your supper off the mantelpiece tonight," said Oscar.

Frank and Ket chuckled.

Then Oscar glanced at Sam, who was squinting at

Norman, and said, "My nephew, Sam. Norm — this's Mister Snigger, the foreman."

"Pleezter meetyuz," grunted Sam.

Norman said the same and held out his hand, which Sam took limply and without rising.

Then Oscar glanced at Ket and said, "And this's Mister Ket — and this's Mister Frank McLash — but I suppose you know him pretty well already."

Ket set down his plate and rose to take Norman's hand, which he shook warmly, saying, "Ow are ya? Mighty pleezta. Have a good trip up?" And he eyed him closely with peculiar narrow black eyes. His hair and eyes betrayed his Chinese heritage, if nothing else did; but the only evidence of the black was the swarthiness of his skin, which was, in fact, little more noticeable than Frank's.

Frank did not shake hands. He saluted with a finger, saying, "Howzit?"

Norman sat down to eat, watched intently by Dingo Joe and Peter Pan, who sat well apart with the blackboys, eating with fingers off tin plates, as the blackboys did. Norman, eating off enamel with knife and fork, scarcely saw them.

While Norman and Frank were driving the unwanted beasts away, the Cut had been placed in a wire-fenced branding-yard near the hills. Thither all went after dinner. Blackboys were already there, with the brands hot and the fittings of the ramp set up. And the kites and crows were perched on posts, waiting for the pickings. Work was begun at once.

The first beasts dealt with were tiny inquisitive calves, which, ignoring frantic efforts of their mothers to restrain them, came to stare and sniff at the strange bipeds that climbed through the fence. The older beasts shrank away from the monstrosities. Rarely did they ever see a man on foot. The inquisitive ones were pounced on, seized by the legs, flung bawling on the right side, and held by strong hands while other hands maimed and marked them. The right ear was slit with a knife from base to apex; into the left cheek was burnt the figure 30, to record the year of the creature's birth, and into the left flank the figure IS, the brand of the station; and in the case of males the testes were removed by rapid slitting and slicing with a razor-edged knife in the hands of old Sam Snigger. Kites hovered over Sam, crealing and fighting, ready to snap the testes as they left his hand. Sam did not throw all the glands away. Some of a certain size he placed in a clean tin box for cooking and eating later, believing that as food the substance was rejuvenating.

When no more calves could be caught by hand, Frank McLash mounted a big strong horse named The Policeman, to whom was attached by a stout leather surcingle a hide lasso. By now the cattle were aware that something devilish was afoot. They fled from Frank, bellowing, to be stopped in a second by the fence, jammed and helpless. He lassoed a young heifer, and towed her, bucking frantically and uttering a continuous heart-rending half-strangled Blah-a-aha-a-aha! to the ramp, which was a double gatelike apparatus of stout rails set up near the back of the yard. The two sections of the ramp were separated by a gap about three inches wide; and the top rail of the lefthand side sloped slightly outward; thus when The Policeman passed the ramp on the left side and turned to round it, as he did of his own accord, being a knowing fellow and having an eye on what was going on behind, the taut lasso slid up to the gap and slipped into it; and thus the beast was drawn to the middle of the ramp with head jammed hard against the rails.

As soon as the head touched the ramp, the two leg-rope men, Ket and Dingo Joe, leapt out from behind, snared the right fore and hind legs with their rawhide nooses, threw the ropes over non-reversing pulleys on each side of the ramp, and yelled to The Policeman, "Easer!" Finding its head free, the heifer heaved away from the ramp. The legropes jerked. She fell on her right side — thud! Peter Pan, the head-man, was waiting. He grabbed the horns, turned the head round and back till the neck cracked. Bulging bloody eyes and lolling dripping tongue and laboured breathing. Meanwhile the leg-rope men had cast the ropes and seized the legs and bent them. The fore-leg-man simply bent the left leg double from the knee, and held it so with his crouching body, standing on the right leg, while he slit the right ear. The hindleg-man dragged the left leg back with both hands, while he forced the right forward with his feet. Then came the brands, borne by a blackboy. A hiss — a gasp — a shudder. Then smoke and stench of burning hair and flesh.

The brand-man skipped away. The hindleg-man yelled "Leggo head!" Simultaneously three pairs of hands let go their holds. The three men leapt up and darted to the cover of the ramp. A moment of heaving for breath. Then the heifer leapt up, staggered, glared, charged the nearest enemy, the ramp, then bellowed distractedly and fled.

Frank had another beast before the heifer was up. It was a hefty young bull of at least two years. He did not waste breath on bellowing. Used to having his own way, finding himself ensnared, he tried to remove the lasso by violent tossing of his head. The Policeman waited for a favourable moment to pull. He pulled. The bull staggered after him for a few yards, then stopped, heaved away, strained till it dawned on him that the statuesque Police-man had something to do with it, then snorted and charged the glossy bay rump. The Policeman had suffered many a wound in learning his trade. He heaved aside suddenly, lashed out with a huge hind hoof as the bull went by, then braced for the shock. The bull was astride his tether when he reached the end of it. His head was pulled under him. He turned a somersault. The Policeman shot to the ramp and had the rope in the gap before the bull regained his feet. Then began a tug-o'-war, with the bull still a good six yards from the ramp. The bull drew back with all his fine young strength. The Policeman turned sideways, leant to the right till Frank's foot was on the ground. He grunted, heaved. The bull still stood. Then The Policeman straight-ened up. The bull sat down hard. The Policeman heaved again, and pulled the bull a yard. Again he grunted, leant. Again he straightened, baffled the bull, and gained another yard. No-one spoke. Meanwhile the bull was choking. Suddenly he collapsed. The Policeman had him up to the ramp in a trice. The humans piled on him. Sam's knife came into play again. The kite-hawks fought and snatched. In this case the operation was performed principally to prevent inbreeding.

The brands brought the bull back to life. When he was released he lay for a while goggling and groaning, then struggled to his feet and staggered away. Then suddenly he remembered, wheeled, and rushed, still in his heart a bull. Ket was nearest. He yelled and ran. So did Norman who was next. These and some blackboys fell over the fence. Old Sam was left. He was whetting his knife. The bull was a yard off, galloping, head down. Sam kicked dust in its face, skipped aside, went on whetting. The bull crashed into the fence, broke the wire, fell blaring, and lay, defeated, spunkless, a eunuch. The brand-man rushed at it and placed a gratuitous 30 on its rump. The creature heaved up, fled blaring and dripping blood. Perhaps some-

day someone would say Grace over his flesh, thanking God
for the kindness of creating him.

Next some easily-handled calves. Then a full-grown
cow with an in-growing horn. She went mad, jumped her
own height a dozen times, fell every time as she landed,
jerked The Policeman all over the yard, at length broke a
leg, but went on plunging, Blah-a-aha-ahaing frightfully,
till at last she broke her neck. And added to the confusion
was a tussle between Sam and Ket. Once when the cow
went down near the ramp, old Sam rushed out to deal
with her in the open, calling on the others to follow. All
but Ket, who was hindleg-man, obeyed. Without Ket's
aid the assault was futile, more, dangerous, since it was
attempted in belief that he was at his post. The cow kicked,
tearing Sam's shirt wide open on the left side, and faintly
scratching his skin. Instead of thanking God for his luck,
he flew at Ket as he fled from the cow, and aimed a blow
at him with the horn-stick. Ket dodged, roared, grappled
with him.

"Slant-eyed lousy cowardly Chinee barsted!" bellowed
Sam.

"I'll murder you!" roared Ket. His peculiar eyes twitched violently; but for the rest his face was calm.

Oscar rushed up, shouting, "Here — cut that out!"

"Dirty jiggerin' son of a halfbred blunny —"

"You rintin' dirty old dog — by God I'll —"

"Cut it out!" roared Oscar, parting them.

"He's always pickin' on me," roared Ket. "Never lets
me alone. If he don't leave here, then I will —"

"Now, now!"

"I mean it. The dirty lousebound old skut! You dunno
what I gotter put up with from him. I tell you I'll pull out
if he stays here —"

"You slant-eyed yeller-bellied pong, you —"

"Here — for godsake!" cried Oscar.

Then the cow broke its neck. Sam had to go and free the
lasso.

Soon a horny steer was caught, a full-grown beast in
good condition, weighing a good half-ton. The horn had
penetrated its skull just above the left eye and already
blinded it. Frank rescued it from a group of young mickey
bulls that were tormenting it after the indecent manner
of their kind. But it was far from grateful. Its plunging
and bellowing was even worse than that of the cow. Perhaps in its poor mad eunuch's head there was a hazy

memory of the horrors of the branding-ramp. The Policeman had to use all his cunning to keep his feet. Clever fellow that he was, though a man-made eunuch like his victim, at length he worked it to the ramp. The great beast
crashed to earth. It lay sobbing like a human, while its
tongue, torn by teeth in its struggles, lolled bleeding in the
dust, and its mad eyes rolled. "Oh! Oh!" it sobbed distinctly. "Oh — have mercy on me masters!"

Sam thrust his stick through the loop the horn made,
heaved, with the base against the cheek, heaved again, again
— *crack!* — and the horn broke off at the skull. He jerked
the horn off. It came away scraping, revealing red-raw
nerve-laced bone. Blood spurted. Sam skipped back. Ket
yelled "Leggo head!" The monsters scuttled into safety.
But the bullock did not rise till the brandman placed a 30
on its rump. It started up, stumbled, smothered its bloody
horn in dust, gained its legs, and tottered away sobbing,
as Frank came up with one of the mickey bulls.

The job was finished. Smoke-o was called. The billy was
boiling, tucker out of pack-bags and spread on a ground-
sheet just outside the fence. Norman ate with the whitemen. So did The Policeman, who hung over the fence while
Frank fed him huge chunks of buttered and sugared
brownie. Ket ate at a little distance as before, and again
on Oscar's side of Sam; and the halfcastes ate with the
natives; but whereas Ket drank from a pannikin out of
the whitemen's pack, the halfcastes drank from those they
always carried on their saddles, as the natives did, it being
a custom of the land to give such creatures utensils for
permanent use, as one gives a dish to a dog. Oscar, watching Norman, and noting how well he was treated by Frank
and Ket, was reminded for a moment of Peter Differ, who
had once said, "Teach him to be a whiteman and as such
he will be received." Then he remembered the unhappy
Ket, whom he disliked, as everyone seemed to do, but for
whom he sometimes felt compassion and whom he often
took the trouble to please. He looked at the man, found him
watching him, and smiled. Ket's eyes lit up, though the
smile he returned was wooden, Chinese.

Ket loved Oscar, considering him the most kindly and
cultured man alive. Oscar always called him Charles, had
done so from the moment he had heard that he disliked the
diminutive, and lent him books and newspapers, though
he knew that he could scarcely read, and sometimes had
him in the house and discussed with him other subjects than

CAPRICORNIA

those of the cattle-run, and encouraged him to bank the little money he earned (Oscar paid him much less than the union-wage to balance up for the compassion), in order to go South someday and begin his life anew. Though Ket banked the money he had no intention of leaving Oscar. He hoped to become his right-hand man some day, soon, if a bull would gore old Sam, as he often prayed with fervour that one would; and more, he even dreamt of becoming his son-in-law. Marigold was also kind to him, though unconsciously, not deliberately as Oscar was. She did not know much about him, since Oscar had told her little and she never mixed with people interested in the cases of such as he; and then she found him useful for getting her good horses to ride and acting the lackey to her, and particularly for catching pythons for her, and curing the skins for material to make fine shoes for herself and a crowd of friends. Ket misunderstood. The primary cause of his misunderstanding was the knowledge, gleaned first from Sam Snigger, who had spoken of it with jocular contempt, and then from the McLashes, who were his only white friends besides the Shillingsworths, that Marigold had lived as the sister of a halfcaste. If she could do that, was it absurd to think that she might be brought to marry a white quadroon? Ket despised halfcastes, hated them in fact, as he hated the natives and all other things that reminded him of the enormous shame that all his life he had been trying to hide, the shame of his coloured blood; but he did not hate Norman, his possible relative; in fact he had been looking forward eagerly to his coming ever since he heard of it from Mrs McLash, who, having handled the telegrams, had known of it even before Oscar.

§

Back at the homestead that night, Ket was sitting in his hut, which was an old refitted harness-shed laboriously reading an old primer of Norman's he had found there, when he heard footsteps approaching. He glanced under the canted iron shutter that served as a window and saw white-clad legs in the moonlight, which he recognized as Oscar's. He hid the primer hastily under the pillow of his stretcher.

Oscar stamped over the veranda, crying, "You in, Charles?" It was necessary to give warning of one's approach to the men's quarters if one did not wish to catch them with their lubras.

"Yes, Mister Shillingsworth," Ket said. "Come on in."
Oscar, clean and rosy of face, clad in spotless white shirt
and pants, stood smiling at the door. He had in hand a
cheque. Ket glanced, guessed it was payday.

"Your cheque," said Oscar.

"Thanks," said Ket, taking it apologetically.

"It'll be a bit more next time," Oscar went on. "You're
promoted." He smiled.

Ket's eyes lit up. Oscar stroked his moustache, looked at
the floor, said, "I've put Sam off."

Ket's heart bounded.

"He's finished up now," continued Oscar, glancing at the
wooden face. "He'll be off tomorrow — and Frank too."

Ket drew a deep breath.

"So you'll carry on as foreman from now," said Oscar.
"There won't be much to do now, of course — bit more
branding, then water-shifting. You can take young Norman
with you and break him in. We can do without Dingo
and Peter too. I've paid 'em off. See they clear out. Get
rid of 'em before they can bring grog into the camp."

Ket tried to answer.

Then Oscar said, "That all right?"

Ket swallowed, mumbled, "Aw — yes. Aw — thanks
Mister Shillingsworth — I — I — thanks very much."

"Good-o," said Oscar. "Well — goodnight son." He went
out.

Son! thought Ket, watching him go. Son — aw gawd!
Then he turned round slowly, and with fists clenched and
banging his thighs and eyes wide and blazing, paced the
room, breathing, "Aw gawd — aw gawd — I'm foreman!"

He stopped before a mirror hanging on the wall, stared
into his eyes for seconds. At length he went to the door,
and stared at Sam's quarters, Differ's old house, where
Sam sat in the doorway talking to Frank McLash. Ket
could not hear what they said, but guessed, and smirked
with malicious pleasure. He believed that Oscar had dismissed old Sam on account of the incident at the branding-
yard that afternoon, when he himself had threatened to
leave if Sam remained, and supposed that Sam was venting
his chagrin. He stood smirking till reminded of the halfcastes and the new authority he was itching to exercise,
by the rising sound of corroboree in the native camp. He
went out, past Sam's house strutting and smirking, and
down towards the river. He was wrong in believing what
he did. Oscar had long intended to dispense with Sam's

services if trade did not improve, and had given Sam some warning. Sam's services cost £5 a week and keep, and Frank's £3, whereas Ket's cost only £1. Sam knew that Oscar had little use for him now, but believed that the main reason for his dismissal was that Oscar feared he would not tolerate Norman as an equal. He had been present when Oscar paid the halfcastes off. That had happened soon after the return of the mustering-plant. At the time Charles Ket was superintending the stowing of the gear. Though he seemed to take his dismissal cheerfully, Sam was really mortified, being greatly in need of his pay because he was deep in debt. Hence he was pleased to make a mountain out of a molehill-idea. He told Frank that he was dismissed because he was considered too superior to associate with an up-jumped yeller-feller, that the half-castes were dismissed because they were too low and might presume, that Ket was retained as the happy medium, that for his part he was glad to go. Frank, with human love for a mountain made from a molehill, believed him. Sam was not wholly wrong. It was a fact that the likelihood of his and the halfcastes' giving Norman offence had moved Oscar to act upon his intention to economize. However, Oscar would not have been so scrupulous about Norman's welfare had he needed the men. He had come to consider it inevitable that Norman would soon learn all there was to know about himself, and was in a way desirous that he should, while never doubting but that he could save him from humiliation in the process.

Ket's smiles faded as he neared the uproarious camp, where, round a blazing fire, a dozen blackmen, naked and ochred and plumed and armed, were performing a furious dance to celebrate the victory over the cattle. In unison they stamped and lunged, telling the tale of their adventures, each in turn, in a rapid high-pitched sentence snatched from each other's lips — A black bull charged me — he was a monster — a great black devil — he killed my horse — the blood of my horse — swept over me reeking — I flew at the devil — mad with rage — because he killed my brother the horse — and grasped his horns — and flung him to the earth — and in a storm of dust and blood — broke his neck — accompanied by the compelling staccato click of the music-sticks and the reverberating bellow of the great pipes called didjeridoo and the intermittent rising and falling chanting of the squatting crowd — Eeyah-eeyah,

eeyah-eeyah, ee-mungallini kurri-tai, ee-minni kinni tulli-
yai, eeyah-eeyah-eeyah —

The corroboree stopped dead when Ket appeared. He was
well known as a bully. He snapped at the gathering, "Shut
y' blunny row. If you want for c'roboree, get over the other
side the river. I'll belt you s'posim I hearim you again. I'm
boss here now, you lousy cows. Sam Snigger finish. Kick
out. Me gettim kick out. And now I'm foreman. You savvy? Foreman long Red Ochre. Boss next to Mister Shillingsworth. And don't none you forget it. Here — you yeller
barsteds — pack your traps and get ready to hook it first
thing mornin' time. D'you hear? If I find you on the run
tomorrer mornin' I'll belt you off with a stockwhip."

For a moment he glared at the sullen faces of Dingo and
Peter Pan. Then he spat, looked over the gathering, and
said, "I'm boss — boss — see? Mister Ket the foreman.
Anyone't calls me Charlie again, I'll kill him." He turned
away, went back to the homestead and to the quarters of
Cho Sek Ching, to whom he boasted about his promotion
and hinted, for an hour or more, about his prospects of becoming a member of the Shillingsworth family. Back in his
house, singing softly all the while, he worked till late preparing a snake-skin from which to make a tobacco-pouch
for Oscar.

SON OF A GIN

NORMAN had been at Red Ochre about a month, when one
train-day he went in to the Siding with the buckboard to
meet Marigold returning from a trip to Town. He was
accompanied by Ket, who invited himself, saying that he
wished to go in on business, when in fact he went simply
for the pleasure of sitting with Marigold during the homeward drive, taking advantage of the fact that Oscar was
kept at home by slight illness. This was Ket's first trip to
the Siding since Norman came, though not the first time
he had wished to go. Twice he had laid himself out to be
invited to join the family in train-day excursions, only to
be ignored, as he would have been this time but for inviting himself. So far he had made no headway in his aim to

become intimate with the family, for which he blamed
Norman, the very one through influencing whom he had
planned to work his way. Norman had proved to be not only
unresponsive but tacitly averse. Ket's early attempts to win
his regard by truckling to him had only caused him to become condescending, with the result that Ket often found
himself struggling to hide fierce resentment. In fact he had
found that since Norman came, Oscar took less notice of
him than formerly. Thus he had come to feel jealous of
Norman and to look forward to his departure. That he
would not be staying long he was sure, having satisfied
himself on that score by talking to Oscar, and once having
overheard an argument between Norman and Oscar in
which Norman talked of getting an extension of leave in
order to work for a while on the railway-construction and
Oscar had said that under no circumstances would he allow
him to neglect his job in Batman. So Ket dealt with Norman
patiently, even during this drive to the Siding, when he was
chafing over having had to invite himself and having had
his company accepted with indifference.

The train was very late that day, as the result of a break-
down in the Caroline Hills. It arrived at the Siding at
three in the afternoon instead of midday. The engine was
positively limping, and panting painfully, and advancing in
jerks, because only one piston was working. Part of the
off-side driving-gear had come adrift.

Norman and Frank McLash, who had been together
talking locomotives all the while, ran to inspect the damage. They were on their knees beside the engine, prying
and touching, when the engineer descended. Frank rose and
said, "Hello Barney — spragged well and truly, eh?"

"Yes," said the engineer. "What d'you think of it?"

"Pretty crook. Done in the bearing of the steam-chest
valve too, eh?"

"Yes — rod buckled before the connector broke. I could-
n't do nuthen but dismantle and bring her in on one leg.
And old Ruggerlugs on the train too!"

Frank grimaced, and looked down the train to the crowd
coming up, at the head of which he saw the fat, waddling,
khaki-clad and topee'd figure of Mr Ian Norse, the Railway Superintendent, who was the person to whom the engineer referred.

Looking at the engineer, Frank said, "Have to get
another injin up, eh?"

The engineer grimaced, answered, "They haven't got one that'll hold steam. We'll have to get the fitter up."

Frank said quickly, "We got a fitter right here," and nodded to Norman, who was still on his knees, but now looking at the crowd, among whom he saw Marigold with Stanley Steggles.

"Eh?" murmured the engineer, eyeing Norman's soft brown profile. Frank touched Norman's shoulder. He was feeling very friendly towards him at the moment, having not long before borrowed £3 from him.

"This's Norm Shillingsworth," said Frank. "Old Oscar's nephew. He's a qualified fitter. Works in the loco in Batman."

The engineer stared incredulously.

"Think you can fix her, Norm?" asked Frank when Norman turned.

"Easy — if we got the tools," said Norman.

Then the crowd came up. Mr Norse blinked small pouchy eyes at the engineer, and puffing, said, "Well — Barney — what're you going to do?"

"Can't do nuthen, Mister Norse," said the engineer. "It's a fitter's job."

"Tut tut! And you say they haven't got an engine fit for the road? Dammit — we'll be stuck here till to-morrow!"

Eager to attract the attention of the Superintendent in these days of hope of a job ahead, Frank said, "Scuse me Mister Norse — we got a fitter on the job already."

"Eh — eh?" said Norse, blinking. "Oh it's you McLash. A fitter you say — where?"

"That young feller," said Frank, pointing to Norman, who had risen and gone to Steggles and Marigold. "He's a qualified fitter. Works in the big Batman loco."

"What — but he's a halfcaste, isn't he?" said Norse; then seeing Norman kiss Marigold and shake hands with Steggles he added, "What — that's that Shillingsworth boy, isn't it?"

"Yes," said Frank. "He's been brought up like he's white. Acts like it too."

Steggles pushed through to the Superintendent and said, "What's going to happen, Mister Norse?"

"Fraid we're going to be hung up for the night and half tomorrow," said Norse. "They haven't got an engine to send down. We'll have to wait for the fitter."

Noticing that Norse was eyeing Norman, Steggles said,

"Why — we have a fitter here. This young man's a fitter, Mister Norse. I say Norm — perhaps you can help us, eh? This's Mister Ian Norse, the Superintendent. Mister Norse, this's Mister Shillingsworth's nephew, you know."

Norman grinned and thrust out his dark hand. Norse took the hand hesitantly, watched by the crowd, and blinked and puffed in confusion.

"Please to meet you," said Norman loudly. "Like me to fix her up?"

"Eh — eh — well —" puffed Norse.

"Put her right in a couple of hours if I've got everything't's needed," said Norman; and he turned to the engineer and asked, "You got white metal for the bearing?"

The engineer blinked.

"There's white metal over the pump-house," said Frank.

"And a forge?" asked Norman.

"Fettlers got one," said Frank.

Norman looked at Norse and said, "Do it easy then."

"Mister Shillingsworth works for the Hume Railways, Mister Norse," said Steggles. "He's up on holidays. I'm sure he could do the job and save us a long wait."

"Well —" said Norse slowly. "Well — if you think he can —"

"Course I can," said Norman. "I'll get to it right away, eh?"

Frank, behind him, prodded him and whispered, "Ask him to let me be your labourer. I wanter get right with him."

"I'd like to have Mister McLash to help me," said Norman. "He's clever with tools."

"Well — er — a — all right," puffed Norse, and mopped his round red face.

People had been staring and whispering. Marigold had seen and heard, and had withdrawn, ashamed. And Ket had seen her, and had come, bright-eyed, eagerly but slowly, to greet her. She passed him unseeing. He turned after her. He was nearly up to her, when Steggles came running and joined her saying, "They've given Norman the job of fixing the engine. Isn't that fine?"

After a moment Steggles said, "Well how're we going to put in the time? You won't be able to run away just yet. I wish your place was nearer. We could go out there, eh?"

"We'd better have something to eat first," she said. "Then let's have a walk down to the bridge."

"Bridge!" cried Steggles. "Don't you think I have enough of bridges?" He laughed.

She smiled and said, "But the river's lovely. You needn't look at the bridge."

"Nor at the river either, eh?" said Steggles, chuckling.

Ket at their heels clenched his teeth.

They were opposite the house. Steggles touched her plump brown arm and turned her, saying, "Let's get in for a feed before the rush."

As they turned, Ket raised his hat and smiled. Marigold glanced at him under her wide straw hat, nodded slightly, passed on. Ket bit his lip.

While Marigold and Steggles were down at the bridge, and Norman, watched by half the people about, was working on the engine, Ket talked to Mrs McLash, while helping her to unpack goods in her store. In the course of the conversation Mrs McLash learnt what Ket believed regarding the dismissal of Sam Snigger. She believed the same as Sam. So she disillusioned him, gently but thoroughly, and knew she did, in spite of his fierce arguing that he was right. After a while he left her. Later she saw him squattting on the veranda near the post-office, staring fixedly at the train.

Ket was still squatting there when Norman, smeared from head to foot with grease and grime, with black curly hair hanging wet over sweaty face, came strutting up to find the engineer. Seeing Ket, Norman went up to him, and impolitely asked him within hearing of a group of loungers, "Where's Miss Marry?"

Ket's eyes twitched at him.

"Eh?" demanded Norman.

Ket looked away and spat.

Norman realized that he had been rude. He swallowed, said amiably, "Will you run her home, Charl? It'll be dark before I can get away."

Ket looked up quickly. "What — aint you comin'?" he asked.

"This job'll take me another couple of hours at least," said Norman. "No good yous two waiting. We can't go home in the dark. I'll camp here tonight, and borrow a horse to go home on in the morning. Where is she?"

"Down the bridge," said Ket, and added with a smirk, "With a feller — a wonk with a topee."

Norman grinned and said, "That's Mister Steggles the engineer. Will you go and get her?"

"Good-o," said Ket, and moved off, elated by the prospect of having Marigold to himself for two or three hours. The elation lasted till he reached the cattle-trap, when it was douched by a rush of memory of what Mrs McLash had said. His brisk gait slackened to dawdling. Once he stopped, and with hands clenched and eyes twitching, stared at the bridge, for a moment contemplating having done with the Shillingsworths forthwith. He went on slowly, alternately fuming in the humiliation that belief in Mrs McLash's ideas caused him and floundering in doubt.

He found Steggles and Marigold sitting side by side in shade of a tree at the top of the flood-bank of the river near the railway. He paused on the track and watched them. Steggles, a tall, thin, brown, wiry fellow, with high-browed narrow head, was talking animatedly and smiling, while pitching pebbles down the bank. Both had their hats off. Marigold's silky brown bobbed hair was flying sideways in the wind, exposing a pearly ear. She was giggling. Ket eyed her beautiful throat and neat arms and legs and feet. She was not lovely, but comely enough, and strong and attractive of face.

Ket sauntered towards them. They heard him, turned and regarded him with enquiring blue eyes. Steggles, who did not know him, said in surprise, "Hello?" Ket glanced at him in a manner meant to express contempt, then turned to Marigold and said gruffly, but with the nervous care he always exercised when addressing her, "Your cousin told me to tell you Miss, he can't come home tonight. If you wanter go I'll take ya."

"Oh — all right," she said. "But why isn't he coming?"

"Says he can't get away 'fore dark. Says he'll camp here and come home in the mornin'."

Marigold took up her hat and moved to rise. Just as Ket was moving awkwardly to assist her, Steggles bounded up and took her hand. Ket looked at him. Steggles nodded and smiled. Ket turned his back. Marigold moved off, putting on her hat, while Steggles walked behind with Ket, dusting his bright tan shoes.

"You work at Red Ochre?" asked Steggles after a moment.

Ket did not answer at once; he grunted without looking, "I'm the foreman."

"Oh are you?" said Steggles with interest, looking at him. "D'you know, I'd like to take a run out there one of these days to see what the place is like."

Ket sniffed. Then Steggles bounded ahead to help Marigold up the embankment of the railway. Thus Ket fell to the rear, where he stayed, although while they walked to the Siding Steggles looked back several times at his wooden face as though inviting him to catch up.

Marigold could not bring herself to go to Norman while he was surrounded by a crowd, though she tried hard to do so. She particularly feared that he would kiss her as he did when greeting her. So she went straight to the buckboard. But Norman saw her, dropped his work, and watched by the crowd, went to her, and kissed her. She and Ket were silent for a mile or more.

It was Ket who broke the silence. While letting the horses drink at a creek, he turned to her suddenly and asked a question he had had on his tongue from the moment they set out: "D'you reckon me as a coloured man — Miss?"

She was startled out of mean thoughts of Norman. She gaped. For a moment he held her eyes, then asked rather sharply, "Do ya?"

"I — I don't understand," she murmured.

He was at a loss to say more. He turned to the horses, set them going. After a while, keeping his eyes ahead, he told her in snatches what he had learnt from Mrs McLash. She made no comment. After some minutes of silence, while he drove at a furious pace, he asked, still looking ahead, "D'you think that's right?"

Though she did think so, she answered indistinctly, "I — I don't know."

He looked at her and snapped, "Eh? — but you must."

She coloured, and said with a weak attempt at haughtiness, "Really — I don't, Mister Ket."

"Mister Ket!" he sneered at the horses.

After a while he turned to her and demanded, "Don't your father talk to you?"

She was dumb, clutching the rail of the seat of the lurching vehicle and staring ahead.

Again he fell silent. Then he looked at her quickly and asked, "What's your father's opinion of me, anyway?"

"I — I can't say. He's never discussed you."

Ket let the horses slow down to a walk. Minutes passed. Then, without looking, he asked breathlessly, "Well — what's your opinion of me?"

She looked at him surprised. He turned and asked, "Eh?" She answered stiffly, "I don't understand you."

His eyes twitched. He asked harshly, "Have you got any at all?"

"Don't be foolish," she snapped, and looked away.

"I aint bein' foolish at all," he said. "I'm haskin' you a plain simple question, Miss."

"Well kindly don't," she snapped. "And please drive on quickly. I want to get home."

He drew a deep breath. For a moment he regarded her woodenly, then turned to the horses, lashed them into a gallop.

Meanwhile Norman was completing his job. The Superintendent, who had come and eyed his operations dubiously several times, at length came and said, "Good lad — good lad — you're a wonder!" and patted his shoulder. Norman grinned, and breathed on him the reek of beer with which several appreciative passengers had been plying him.

The job was finished by the light of kerosene-flares, in which Norman looked as black as a Binghi. At last he crawled from under the engine, spanner in hand, and dashing sweat from his forehead, said to the gathering, "That's the lot. She's right."

"Good lad — good lad!" cried a dozen voices.

"Here — have a drink son," said someone, thrusting a bottle of beer into his hands. Norman showed his fine teeth in a grin, and raising the bottle said, "Here's fun!" and drank half the contents in a breath.

While sitting on the veranda of the Siding House that night with the McLashes and Joe Steen, Norman learnt what they thought about the dismissal of Sam Snigger and the halfcastes and the retention of Ket. But the significance of the subject as it concerned himself was lost on him. In fact he took little notice of what they said at first, being preoccupied with controlling amusement caused him by Mrs McLash's frequent angry asides to old Joe, with whom she had been bickering all the evening. The pair sat side by side in deck-chairs, while Frank and Norman squatted together at the edge of the veranda leaning against a post. Light from the sitting-room fell on Mrs McLash's pudding-bag figure and round red blotchy face and untidy mop of grey bobbed hair, and on old Joe, long and stringy and grey bearded, who frequently interrupted her, and when attacked, strove to assert his right to speak.

Talk of the staff of Red Ochre at last included Cho Sek Ching the cook. And talk of him naturally led to the subject of the murder of his brother, which Mrs McLash found mighty pleasant when she learnt that Norman knew nothing about it. Norman was interested enough in that. Before long he knew practically all there was to know about his father, except that he was the father of a halfcaste Aboriginal son, which his informants supposed he was well aware of and refrained from mentioning because of his generosity to Frank. But it was with no ulterior motive that they thought the most disgraceful feature in his father's history not the fact of his having robbed and murdered a Chinaman but that of his having been outlawed for doing so; for that was their honest opinion; and he might have shared it had he been inextricably in debt to Chinese storekeepers and moneylenders as they were. As it was he was rather shocked. However, he did not feel at all humiliated by what he learnt. As soon as he got home he passed the information on to Marigold, guessing that she would be interested.

§

Marigold was prompted by what she learnt about Uncle Mark from Norman to go seek the wisdom of the Sibyl McLash in regard to her mysterious mother. As it was she was secretly shocked by what Norman told her, but quite unprepared for what the Sibyl had to say. Mrs McLash, having been till then practically ignored by the proud Marigold, considered that she had a score to settle with her. She settled it gently but thoroughly by relating to her the history of the Shillingsworths to its last unsavoury detail, at the same time settling old scores with the proud Jasmine and Oscar too, and even with Heather, to whom she owed a grudge. Thus Marigold learnt that there was a barmaid in the family too. Or was she merely a barmaid? Mrs McLash dealt with Heather in a manner that left much to be inferred. And she learnt that her mother was a wanton whose paramour was the grubby drunken old wretch from the cattle-boat whom people called Greasy S'mellio, that her cousin, whom she had described to everyone as a highcaste halfcaste Javanese, was a Yeller-Feller, that her uncle was a low waster and a hunted murderer, and that her aunt on that side was — a lubra! What a history was the Shillingsworths' — the Shillingsworths what a clan!

She was urged by no reciprocal sisterly desire to acquaint Norman with her knowledge. Indeed for a while she avoided him, and her father too; not that she loathed either, but was reminded by their presence of the loathsomeness concerning them. In fact, during the worst of her humiliation she would have fled from them had there been any place to flee to but the town where she would meet her friends. Her friends? Of course they must have known the truth about the family all along. What did they think? How they must have laughed about the strutting of her whose mother was a wanton and aunt a gin!

She sought consolation in the Rubaiyat of Omar Khayyam, a volume of which Steggles had given her. But she found none, nor anything, indeed, but advice about the Riddle of the Universe, which seemed inconsiderable compared with this complicated business of her own. Deciding that Omar made mountains out of molehills and then procrastinated over shifting them, she gave him up in disgust.

Just prior to unearthing the family skeleton she had learnt that Steggles would be going to a Government billet in Singapore when his work in Capricornia was done. The news had piqued her pride a little, because Steggles had imparted it without a sign of the distress that the prospect of being separated from her should have caused him. As a matter of fact he had seemed quite pleased. But beyond slight pique she had not been much concerned, supposing, she the potential beef-baroness, that if she had set her cap at him in earnest he would not be so pleased to leave her side. But the beef-baroness was dead — long live the niece of a blackgin! The proud heiress to broad acres had suddenly become heiress to the Shillingsworths' dirty past, and a very ordinary and lonely little girl. And the scorned Stanley Steggles, who had doubtless been aware of the value of the heirloom all along and had perhaps been dallying not dallied with, had suddenly become her heart's desire.

Her desire to win Steggles increased, and obsessed her. When she heard that he was back in Town and found the courage to face again the people she had so ludicrously disdained, she sought him. Then her suspicion that he had been dallying was confirmed. She gave him every opportunity to suggest that Singapore would be a better place to live in if she were by his side. He took none. She was distracted, convinced that the cause of her failure was the history of the family.

Steggles had often hinted that he would like to visit Red Ochre; but as his company had previously been useful only in Town to Marigold, his hints had been practically ignored. To her Red Ochre had been merely a cattle-run, a place unsightly when comfortable to live on and uncomfortable when pleasant to see. She had long since grown tired of doing the things that guests like Steggles would want to do. The place had become simply her means of support, the means by which she had been able to act as the beef-baron's daughter; and because she had less interest in the means than in the acting and practically none in station-life, she had spent much of her time in Town. So it had been. But Marigold the niece of a lubra had come to see the Station as her very necessary dowry, not only of broad acres and multitudinous beeves, but one in which was expressed that which was now her sole prestige, that counter-blast against the infamy of the rest of the Shillingsworth family, the respectability of her father and herself. She wished Steggles to see it, and also wished to remove him from the distracting influences of his multitude of friends for a while in order to get him under her own. Therefore she prompted him to hint again. He did so. Then it was agreed that he should come down home for Christmas and New Year.

Marigold worked cunningly. Studying her man, she con-cluded that two weeks of undiluted Marigold and station-life would be more likely to bore than charm him, that he would appreciate her company more if he had to seek it sometimes, and that he would seek it more eagerly and make better use of it if seeking ladies' company were part of the general entertainment. Therefore she decided to make a party.

She invited five people, who were Sister Nan Pannel of the hospital-staff, a plain but sensible young woman beside whom Marigold was a beauty, and Rhoda Norse, daughter of the Railway Supertintendent, who was dazzlingly pretty and whose chief occupation was exercising what she called her Sex Appeal, beside whom Marigold's moderateness was beautiful, and Courtney Fish, the Taxation Officer, who appeared to be in love with Nan, and Sidney Gigney, the engineer in charge of the construction of the new railway, who lived on Rhoda's doorstep, both of whom could be expected to introduce courting into the party, and Rhoda's father, who could hobnob with Oscar. No provision was made for Norman in her plans. Indeed she could have made none. But she saw no reason to consider him, since she believed that he would be leaving by the mid-December boat.

She had good reason to believe that Norman would be gone before Christmas, having, as Ket had, overheard Oscar tell Norman that he must not stay longer than originally intended. But Oscar was not as scrupulous about Norman's career as an employee of the Government of Hume as she believed. He had not wished Norman to go to work on the Melisande because he feared that he would be exposed to humiliation there. It had been shown pretty clearly lately that Norman was regarded by most people as a superior young man and also that he was quite capable of maintaining his dignity. First there was that public demonstration of his ability as a mechanic, which Oscar knew had become a topic of the gossip-area; then there was the calmness with which he had taken the truth about his father, which he had related to Oscar as though he were talking of someone who did not concern him; and then there was his subjection of Peter Pan and Dingo Joe, who had returned to the homestead and boldly demanded equality of him, only to be flogged by him, and set to work carrying water from the river to the stock-tanks for wages of sixpence a day, and made to call him Mister.

The effrontery of Peter and Dingo Joe was not nearly so brazen as it seemed. They had come at what they believed was Oscar's invitation, having been told by Ket, who had gone to the Caroline to find them, that Oscar wished them to take their place in his house with his nephew, and having been advised to demand equality of the nephew because the fellow was a prig and not likely to give it freely. Ket, now consumed with hatred for the family, had also vainly tried to stir up trouble with Cho Sek Ching and the natives. Finally he had to resort to such poor acts of spite as running stock to death and off the Station, torturing horses, falsifying reports, damaging equipment, wasting rations, and polluting water. But poor as were these acts, he derived fierce pleasure from committing them, and did them stealthily, wishing to have the pleasure last till he could consummate it in a law-suit he planned to bring against Oscar for not having paid him according to Award. For that reason alone he stayed, awaiting the advice for which he had sent to the Labour Council in Port Zodiac. Oscar and Norman were ignorant of these intrigues; indeed they did not even realize that Ket was ill-disposed to them.

But chiefly what influenced Oscar to regard postponement of Norman's departure with favour was his usefulness, his genius indeed, since genius was what Oscar thought it was and what he described it as when proudly discussing it with the many people whom it interested. The genius of Young Yeller Shillingsworth, as Norman was now being called abroad, soon became famous, and was the cause of the coming of many people to the Station to see the evidence of it, which was a permanent water-supply he had set up at negligible cost on the driest part of the run. His work could scarcely have attracted more interest from local graziers had it been a process for converting Dry-Season carcasses into gold, as in a sense it was, being a means whereby many beasts were saved from becoming carcasses.

This contrivance of Norman's was very simple, one about which the most remarkable thing was the fact that no-one had thought of it before. Near the southern boundary of the run lay a chain of great flat porous rocks some two miles long, round which, covering an area of two or three square miles, grew the best of the Station's permanent grazing, in spite of the fact that no part was further removed from permanent water. The earth owed its fertility to the rocks, which gave off moisture, or sweated. The chain was but the exposed backbone of a great expanse of rock that underlay the grass. The hidden expanse apparently sweated all the time; hence the permanent verdure; but the backbone did not, or rather did not appear to do so, except for a couple of hours before sunrise, when it would be found to be literally dripping. The reason for this state of things was that the backbone was hot all day and night except during a couple of hours before the dawn, and that its moisture was for the most part given off in vapour. This had been known for long. It remained for Norman to make use of it.

One day Norman built a shed of boughs over a portion of the backbone, and on the following morning had the satisfaction of showing his sneering companion Ket a fairly large expanse of wet rock in the broad hot glare of day; not a dripping rock but a wet one nevertheless; the dripping came when the roof was thickened and the shed extended. It was then found that the water oozed from a myriad tiny springs, quickly and abundantly, but in such a way as to be unable to gather and run before it was evaporated.

Norman next scored the rock with a vein-like system of channels, innumerable tiny ones running obliquely, converging, and joining large perpendiculars, and so on, down to the base, where it concluded in a trough cut out of the rock itself and concreted. He soon had the pleasure of

giving a pannikinful of cool sweet water to his uncle, who
came to him doubting one day at noon.

This water-supply was invaluable. The only permanent
water on the Station, except that in two or three billabongs
whose contents at the height of Dry Season could be dipped
out with a bucket, was the Caroline River, which became
towards the end of the Dry a mere chain of muddy holes
whose fertile precincts had long been denuded of grazing.
Hence the stock must constantly be driven back and forth
from southern grazing to northern water in Dry Season,
which was more than their strength was equal to. And not
infrequently if the blasting Trade blew overlong or the
Wet was late in setting in, even the pools of the river dried.
Then the stock, the best of it that is, had to be watered
meagrely at the homestead from the stock-tanks. On account
of the floods of the Wet it would have cost an enormous
sum of money to dam the river; and even if a dam were
built, it would still be necessary to water-shift the stock.
The fine grazing about the chain of rocks had therefore
previously been of little use in Dry Season; for it was
fifteen miles from the river, a good day's journey for
healthy cattle, a two or three days' for cattle weak with
thirst, for a number of which it would mean a journey to
the bovine Styx, in crossing which they would in spirit
surely enter upon no worse existence than that they had
endured in the flesh in Capricornia.

That was Norman's masterpiece. But it was by no means
his only valuable service to the Station. In a few weeks he
had effected many improvements that no-one had thought
of in all the years the place had been established, indeed
that no-one not a trained or born mechanic would have
thought of. Nor was he useful only as a mechanic. He
turned out to be a far better rider even than his tutor Ket,
being pleased to take risks that in his thoughtless confidence
he overcame. And in a remarkably short time he learnt
much about the cattle. When he again asked Oscar if he
might apply for a further three months' leave, promising,
in return for permission, to scour the Lonely River country
for strayed stock and to draw up plans for a part-hydraulic-
part-steam electric power-plant before going to the Melisande, Oscar agreed, not readily as he had it in his heart
to do, but with a show of reluctance to save his face for
having formerly disagreed.

Such was the state of things at Red Ochre when Marigold came home from Town on the Second of December,

bringing Norman the shipping agent's latest news of the movements of the south-bound steamer. As a matter of fact such had been the state of things there for a fortnight. Oscar and Norman had come to the agreement a day or two after Marigold went away. That was her third trip to Town since Norman came, her second since deciding to hold the party. In fact it was expressly to complete arrangements for the party that she had made it. She knew all about the masterpiece, having watched Norman working on it and having heard about it from graziers she met in Town. Seeing and hearing such things had pleased her, but had not in the least affected her desire to see Norman gone, nor given her any cause to think his going would be postponed. But just as she was ignorant of Norman's and Oscar's doings during her absence, so were they of hers; for though she had had the party in mind for several weeks, she had not mentioned it to them, being reluctant, she told herself, to have Norman think he was missing something pleasant, but being in fact loath to utter what her guilty conscience realized would amount to a confession of her shame of him. She had planned to tell her father about it as soon as Norman went, to tell him casually, as though it had just occurred to her.

When she told Norman that the steamer was at Batavia, he smilingly answered that he would not have to think of steamers for another three months, and seeing her face change, but not realizing why it did, laughingly asked her if she were sorry. She was not merely sorry; she was stunned; but she weakly smiled and said that she was glad.

Later, after spending a night in miserable cogitation, after indulging in much weeping and reviling and self-pitying and self-reproach, she told Norman and Oscar about the party, intending not merely to give them pleasant news, but to make a clean breast of her difficulty and seek their aid. But they accepted it merely as pleasant news, giving her no chance to mention difficulties while she had the courage to do so, and accepted so innocently, apparently in belief that she had decided on the party in the last few hours for Norman's benefit, and showed such eagerness to take part in it, that the courage to tell them the truth was lost to her for ever. So she had to leave the matter at that and be resigned. And so successful was she in her resignation, that before long she came to feel almost proud of the magnanimous attitude towards Norman that was forced on her.

§

Marigold's guests left Town by the usual Christmas train in the morning of the day before Christmas Eve. Oscar and Marigold went in to meet them, leaving Norman behind to muster some docile horses for the guests' convenience. There were no docile horses on the Station just then. Ket and Peter Pan and Dingo Joe had been chasing the station-prads for days, roping them, flogging them, scaring them with guns, till they had worked them into such a state of fright that it was impossible to get near them. Ket knew that the guests were coming. He had been asked to get the horses.

Norman eventually caught six weary beasts and yarded them, and with the aid of Ket, who seemed as much concerned about their condition as he was and as puzzled about the cause of it, did what he could to make them fit for the services required of them next day. But when after break-fast on Christmas Eve he went with Gigney and Fish and Steggles to saddle up, the rails of the yard were down and the horses gone. So were the three horses always kept for service in the small yard near the house, and with them their harness. He supposed that the horses from the big yard had escaped of their own accord, freed perhaps by a knowing one of them; and he supposed that Ket, who he found was absent, had taken the service-horses and gone in pursuit of the others with blackboys; so he and his companions went back to the house to await the return of Ket.

The guests might have been kept waiting all day in their spurs had not Norman chanced to mention the loss of the horses to Cho Sek Ching at morning-tea-time, when he learnt that Cho had heard horses galloping just before dawn, which went to disprove the supposition that the horses had freed themselves, because a horse, as Norman knew, is at its sleepiest during the last hour or so of night; and in any case, a horse that has freed itself would hardly be likely to gallop. Cho also said that he had heard Peter Pan and Dingo talking in Ket's house in the night. This struck Norman as suspicious; for he had forbidden the halfcastes to come near the house; and it caused him to look further into the matter of the vanished horses.

A blackboy was sent out to see whether the tracks of the saddled horses followed those of the others. He returned after about an hour's absence, mounted on The Policeman and driving the other docile horses, to say that the saddled ones had followed the others only as far as the southern gate of the home-paddock, through which they had gone, and then had turned eastward, following the fence, presumably heading for the Siding; he had found the others grazing.

Tracks about the yards were examined by another boy, who told Oscar and Norman that the rails of the big yard had been dropped by Peter Pan and the horses driven out by Dingo, that the naked feet of these same two had trodden the earth of the small yard, and that the booted Ket had accompanied them. One of Peter's lubras said that Peter had told her that he and Dingo were going in to the Siding to get drunk for Christmas with Ket. And before the day was out the investigators discovered for themselves that the stirrups had been cut from every saddle in the harness-shed and taken away by Ket. Fortunately for the guests, who might never have been able to stain their brand-new spurs, before sundown the tracking blackboy found the stirrups in a bag hidden in a broken stock-tank. Thus Oscar and Norman discovered that Ket was ill-disposed to them. They were surprised. They concluded that he had left them.

But Ket was not done with them yet. He and the half-castes returned to the homestead that night at ten o'clock, and after spending a riotous hour or so in the native camp, came up to Ket's quarters with lubras and began a Christmas party of their own, one calculated to interrupt the party in the house, if not by outvying it in noise, then by outraging it with unseemly language.

It would have taken much to outvie in noise the party in the house at that hour, and more to distract the attention of the revellers than Ket's playing his consumptive concertina and the Dingo's banging a kerosene-can and the shouting of a mere six voices. For Marigold was banging the piano, Steggles twanging a banjo and Rhoda a ukelele, Norman and Gigney ringing horse-bells, everyone stamping feet and singing lustily. And the eyes of everyone were bright with happiness, and every face but Norman's flushed with wine. Ket's party had been in progress for an hour before the others realized that he was in the neighbourhood.

At midnight Norman and Rhoda slipped out of the dining-room. The others went on singing. Norman and Rhoda returned disguised, she as Santa Claus, sitting on a queer extemporized vehicle with a mail-bag full of presents, he as a reindeer. Rhoda looked merely lovely. Norman was a joke. The banging and singing gave way to shouts of laughter. Even Gigney laughed, in spite of being angry in his heart with Rhoda, not believing as the others did that her choice of Norman as her partner in this hitherto secret pantomime was simply a *beau geste,* but suspecting that it might be an experiment with her Sex Appeal; he had in fact expected to see Norman come disguised as a Sheik or some such erotic character; the sight of him in a ridiculous state was a relief. But the sight of Rhoda's cherry mouth surrounded by whiskers soon drew the male eyes from Norman. She halted her cart beneath a bunch of scarlet mistletoe. Even Oscar kissed her.

Preparatory to Rhoda's distributing the presents a hush fell, the first for an hour or more. Then it was that Ket and his companions were heard. They were singing *Show Me The Way To Go Home,* bellowing it, but apparently not so much for the sake of singing as of uttering the indecent expletives with which they crowded the normal wording. At first the people in the house were surprised, then shocked.

But the bad language that was sung, since most of it was unintelligible, was nothing compared to that shouted at Oscar and Norman when they went to remonstrate. Oscar was given a second lesson in vituperation by Ket. While this went on, Norman ramped about Ket's quarters, trying to get in, and Oscar hammered on the door. Ket's was the only other voice to be heard just then. It was enough.

Then suddenly the front shutter was flung up, striking Norman and hurling him off the veranda. Ket's black head and sweaty naked trunk appeared. He was looking at Oscar hammering at the door, and did not see Norman. And as he looked he pushed the shutter further out with left hand and with right produced a bottle.

"Dad — look out!" yelled Norman.

Fortunately for Oscar, Norman yelled as the bottle left Ket's hand, so that when it burst through striking the saddle-rack between the shutter and the door, the flying glass did none of the harm it might have if the warning had been given sooner and Oscar had had time to turn.

"Murderous swine," roared Norman, rushing at the shutter.

Ket let the shutter fall.

"Come away," cried Oscar.

The shutter was shot up again and Norman sent flying.

And Ket appeared with another bottle, yelling, "You dirty yeller snat of a thing —"

Norman skipped out of range.

"Let him go," cried Oscar. "The fool's gone mad. His brain's turned or something. We'll get the police."

"Get 'em!" shouted Ket. "It'll take you a week, you lousy sweatin' old shyster you, you dirty blunny —" He went on with extravagance. Norman and Oscar went back to the house and slammed the door.

But no door of that house, nor wall, was impervious to the voice of the victorious Ket. He cursed till he was hoarse, then got his companions to shout for him. Rhoda went on with the interrupted distribution of the presents, trying to make the witty comments she had planned. And afterwards everybody tried to sing and laugh; but it was evident that their desire was only to make a noise to hide their embarrassment and to drown the cause of it. Their voices were harsh and strained, their eyes, so lately dancing, clouded and preoccupied. Tension! Every lip was tight, every ear listening. Then Marigold brought relief to all by rising suddenly and flying from the room with hands to ears. The shouting of the rivals burst in upon the pause she left. But above the din the company heard her stumbling and sobbing in the hall.

A moment. Then Steggles rose with working face and cried, "My God! Can't the fiends be stopped?"

A pause. Then Norman flung down his horse-bell, and rising said, "I'll stop 'em."

All looked at him.

"Don't do anything rash," said Oscar. "The man's gone mad or something. He always was peculiar. I'm sorry I ever had dealings with him. I — I — lord I'm sorry you people've had to —"

"That's all right," said the guests hastily.

"In my own house too!" muttered Oscar. "Like a nightmare."

"I'll stop 'em," repeated Norman. "Once we can get those gins and yeller-fellers away from him he can't carry on. He's drunk, that's all."

The guests had heard him use the expression Yeller-Feller before and thought it strange; but now they did not notice it; he was their champion.

"The problem's how to get at them," said Oscar.

"Bash in the door," said Norman. "No good talkin' to

'em. Bash in the door and windows at the same time. You fellers on? Good-o then — come on."

As he opened the door a great yell rang out, as though the enemy sensed his brave intention and defied it. But the thing was as simply done as said. Simultaneously the young men attacked the windows and the door with mattocks and axes, while the old men and Rhoda and Cho Sek Ching stood off with stockwhips. Nan stayed behind to comfort Marigold.

And the thing was done almost as quickly as it was said. Norman, bursting through the back window, had the good luck to find Ket grappling with Steggles at the shattered door, and sprang on him and knocked him senseless with a well-placed rabbit-punch. The halfcastes and lubras, using his entrance as an exit, fled before he could turn.

Norman knocked down the remains of the door and dragged Ket out by the arms. Then he revived him by douching him with water, and gave him a stiff dose of bromide, and with a great show of strength carried him back and dumped him on his bed. While telling him what he would do to him if he continued his rioting and ordering him to leave the place next day, he packed up his liquor for removal. Ket was too dazed to reply.

Thus Norman retained with ease the role of champion he had easily assumed. The company paid him full honours. For the rest of the night his masculine vanity was in paradise. The party went on till three o'clock, when the revellers, laughing and yawning, retired.

Norman was soon brought back to earth, and by him at whose expense he was exalted, by the inextinguishable Ket, to whom a remarkable opportunity occurred at once to take revenge for the rabbit-punch and to effect the *coup de grace* he had long dreamt of.

On Christmas morning at about eleven, while the Shillingsworths and their guests were lounging on the front veranda considering what they should do to occupy themselves till dinner-time, Ket suddenly appeared among them, having marched boldly through the house, carrying a stockwhip. Though his face was haggard and his eyes were red and hands shaky, he bore himself jauntily. If his design in appearing thus suddenly was to shock, it was successful. Nearly every face of the gathering paled. He walked up to Oscar, who was leaning against the rail, and said at once, "Where's that grog of mine?"

The blood swept back to Oscar's face. He stood erect,

fingering his moustache, and after a moment's struggle with Ket's narrow eyes, said huskily, "Ah! — I thought you'd come to apologize."

But for a slight quivering of lips and dilating of eyes, Ket's face remained unchanged; but his voice was intense when he said, "You did, eh? And what I gotter pologize to you for?"

Oscar swallowed, said with difficulty, "Well — of course if you don't realize — I wasn't aware I'd done anything but give you a square deal always —"

Ket smirked in his wooden way, and trembling visibly, said through his teeth, "Hell of a lot of square deal I've had from you! But wait'll I get you in a court of law."

Oscar looked amused, and said, "You're talking nonsense. Have you gone mad or what?"

"You muster thought I was."

"I've certainly come to that conclusion lately. But I'm hanged if I can see what I've done to you to make you come here bouncing. I've treated you —"

"Like a nigger," cried Ket. "Like a blunny nigger —"

"Here — moderate! There's ladies present."

The ladies could not go, since Ket stood between them and the door.

"Like a blunny nigger," Ket went on. "That's how you've treated me, Shillingsworth, you dirty old swine —"

"Enough of that!" cried Oscar angrily. "What d'you mean treated you like a nigger, you fool? I found you living like one —"

"Like a nigger," Ket cried passionately, and turned and pointed a trembling finger at Norman, adding, "By chuckin' that dirty yeller-feller at me."

There was a pause, while Ket glared at Norman and Norman stared at Ket. Then Ket turned back to Oscar, and in a voice now trembling, but no less passionate and loud, went on, "I know why you sooled Sam Snigger and the yeller-fellers, Shillingsworth. Damn you, I know. Cos they was either too high or too low to be fit 'sociates for your lousy up-jumped yeller nephew. That's why. And you picked on me as the sorter happy meejum, a poor cow what was neither white nor yeller and didn't have no say in the matter of bein' 'sociated with the dirty up-jumped son of a murderer and a gin —"

"Get out of here!" roared Oscar.

"Stand back," cried Ket, loosing the whip. "Stand back or I'll chop sumpen off your smug white dial. I'll have me say. I aint frighten of you and your blunny jiggerin' yeller-fellers and flash wonks."

All gaped.

Then Norman stepped up and roared, "Get out of here!"

"Get back or I'll chop your ears off," cried Ket. He could not have wielded the long lash with much certainty in that confinement; nevertheless his threat stopped Norman. "You flash hoon," he went on. "Kiddin' you're white, eh? But you aint no whiter than Peter Pan, and no better. You only had the luck to be taken out of a niggers' camp, you son of a gin —"

"You slant-eyed cow!" roared Norman. "I'm not the son of a gin."

"You are. Your mother was a lousy camp-gin. The way you kid y'self anybody'd think she was a duchess."

"My mother was a Javanese. You shut your trap —"

"Javanese!" cried Ket contemptuously.

"Yes," cried Norman. "And a high-caste one at that. You've got nothing to mag about, anyway — your grand-mother was a lubra and your grandfather a Pong."

"Gawd!" cried Ket, staring at him. "You been kiddin' 'em your mother was a Javanese?" Then he turned to the guests and laughed and said, "Don't you b'lieve him, Wonks — she was a blackgin. His old man had so many yeller kids he had to give 'em away and lose 'em — like pups." He laughed again, and turning to Oscar, said, "That's how old Oscar got this one, the one't's name was No-Name. His old man put him in a bag and tried to lose him. Oscar picked him up and took him home. Aint that so, Mister Shillingsworth?" Again he laughed and said to the guests, "And his old man murdered an inoffensive old Chow for thirty quid — Oh the high and mighty Shillingsworths!"

Norman rushed at him and struck him on the jaw. He fell in a heap, senseless.

A moment of silence. Norman looked from Ket to his fist, then at the guests, and said with a grin, "That's the only way to deal with that pest."

They merely stared. Norman's grin faded. He looked at his fist again, shook it, then at the guests and said, "He's a liar. My mother was a Javanese."

Steggles grinned foolishly and nodded. Norman, dis-satisfied with the air of his audience, turned to Oscar and said, "That's so isn't it, Dad." It was not a question, but a mere request for corroboration.

Oscar swallowed, nodded, but looked at the others, not at Norman, red of face.

Norman looked surprised. He turned to the others, in time to see Marigold, red face bent, sidle towards the door. Steggles grinned again. The others shuffled. He turned back to Oscar quickly, with widening eyes, and this time asked a question: "That's — that's right, isn't it, Dad?"

Oscar blinked, rubbed his chin, said lamely, "Of course — of course — But the thing is what're we going to do with him?" He nodded to Ket.

Norman bit his lip.

Steggles said with a grin, "Why not truss him up and take him somewhere in the buckboard?"

"Good idea," said Oscar. "Put him on the road to the Siding. How's that, Norm?"

Norman grinned falsely. For a moment he looked at Ket, who was stirring, then turned to the door and walked off.

"Norm!" said Oscar. He did not heed. Oscar called louder, and went after him. Norman entered the hall. "Wait on — wait on!" cried Oscar. He caught up with him at the dining-room door and said, "Wait on sonny. Now have a bit of sense."

Norman turned and demanded sharply, "Is that right what that cow said?"

"Shh!" hissed Oscar. "I'll explain. Go and get the buck-board."

"Damn the buckboard! I'm off."

"Where?"

"To hell and gone if what he said was true. Is it? Have you been kiddin' me about my mother?"

"For godsake have a bit of sense, Norm. It's Christmas. You're upset and everything."

"Afraid to tell me," cried Norman, shrugging off Oscar's hand. "I ought've known. Gawd I ought've known! Tell me, Dad, dinkum — is it true?"

Oscar said desperately, "There's people outside Norm —"

"Is it true, I said!"

Oscar's face quivered. After a moment he said, "Yes — but —"

Norman flung the door open, narrowly missing Marigold who was behind. He stopped, stared at her, snarled into her drawn white face, "Listening!"

"What's wrong?" she gasped, clutching at him as he

passed. "Oh don't go away, Norm. Please. It'll spoil everything."

"Can I stay here with these people when —"

"They know. They know all about it. Please don't go."

"What d'you mean?"

"They — they've always known. Everybody. It doesn't
matter."

He stared at her, then asked, "You too?"

She nodded.

"God!" he muttered. "Everyone but me. Made a fool
of me. Hell — let me go!" He wrenched away and went.

As the fly-wire door leading to the back veranda slammed,
Oscar hissed at Marigold, "Go after him." She obeyed.

§

Ket had a rough trip to the Siding. He made the first
six miles of it lying on his back in the carrier of the buckboard, unable to move, because he was trussed, unable to
express himself, because his captors were eager to use the
whip. And in addition he was ill, having aching bruises
on the neck and chin, a tongue like that of a mildewed boot,
a cess-pool for a stomach, two hot coals for eyes, a bag of
broken glass for brains. The rest of the way he made on
foot beside the river, the lukewarm muddy waters of which
he drank at every hundred yards and vomited at every fifty.
An utterly miserable day it would have been had his lacerated brains not had just the power to think occasionally of
the *coup de grace*. For that the *coup* had been successful
he was sure, knowing that Norman, who otherwise would
surely have superintended his eviction, was not among the
crew of the buckboard nor apparently about the homestead
when the eviction began. Convinced that he had cooked
the Shillingsworth's goose, he could find it in his heart,
when his stomach was not master of that organ, to chuckle.

Ket was delighting himself with an illusion. While he
was vomiting and chuckling on his way, the Shillingsworths
were sitting with their guests at Christmas Dinner and enjoying themselves almost as much as they had hoped to do
before Ket struck at them. For since they had not been de-
ceiving the guests about Norman's breed as Ket supposed,
it was easy for Oscar to explain the situation. The guests
replied that the exposure was regrettable. And it was a
fairly simple matter to induce Norman to return to the
house when his case was explained and he made to realize
that as the guests had known about his caste all along and

yet respected him they were not likely to begin to disrespect him now that he had learnt of it himself.

So tactful were the guests in their relations with Norman that during the rest of the time they were available to him he even sought their company to escape his own. When alone he did too much thinking. It was significant that he did not go down to the native camp to punish the half-castes as he had said he would. Yet in the presence of the guests he behaved as arrogantly with the natives working about the homestead as ever.

So tactful were the guests, indeed, that in their desire for comfort they led him to suppose that they even admired him. Thus he came to love them all, even Gigney, who was sometimes brusque with him. So a pleasant week passed.

On New Year's Eve there was another party. Rhoda staged another pantomime, one in which Norman appeared with Steggles as a Rajah. She would have dressed poor Gigney, who did not understand *beaux gestes*, as a Eunuch to attend to this pair, and herself and Marigold, who were dressed as Rahnees. Gigney dressed himself rather poorly as a Sheik, and chided Rhoda for showing too much of her Sex Appeal by wearing breeches of mosquito-netting over naked legs.

The hilarity outlasted the Old Year, but by barely half an hour. While the company was re-entering the house, coming back from a fireworks-display to which Cho had treated them, Norman kissed Rhoda and caused trouble. He had been wishing to kiss her for days, and trying to do so all night. He was encouraged at last by seeing Steggles, who was walking ahead of him and Rhoda, kiss Marigold as he led her into the hall. Norman and Rhoda were on the veranda at the moment. Gigney was coming up the steps. Oscar and old Norse, the first carrying a bright benzine-lantern, were well in the rear.

Rhoda had known all night that Norman was trying to kiss her, and was prepared to stop him gently. But he took her unawares, kissed her swiftly and hungrily, rendering her powerless with the pressure of his arms and the surprise. So Gigney saw her clasped as he came to the level of the dark veranda.

Rhoda broke free, and when Norman tried to draw her back, cried in a frightened voice, "Oh don't — don't!" She tugged rather sharply, collided with the iron wall.

"What's up?" cried Gigney, leaping across the veranda. "Hey — what're you doing?"

"It's all right," said Norman, chuckling. "She only slipped."

"It aint all right," snapped Gigney. "Mauling the girl. You oughter have more sense — and her too."

"What's up with you?" asked Norman in surprise.

Rhoda tried to slip into the hall, but was driven back by Steggles and Marigold coming out to see.

"Don't be silly," Gigney said, trying to control himself.

"Silly yourself," snapped Norman. "What's it got to do with you what she and I do?"

"What's wrong?" asked Steggles.

"Gigney's jealous," sneered Norman.

"Oh don't be mad," snapped Gigney. "I only wanted you to stop making a fool of yourself."

"What's up?" asked Steggles. "What's wrong?"

"He was mauling Rhoda and I —"

Oscar and Norse came up. "Hello — what's up?" asked Oscar.

"Nothing," said Steggles hastily. "It's all right. Come on inside."

"It aint all right," cried Norman. "He insulted me. Where's Rhoda?"

She was standing blinking in the glare of Oscar's lamp. "Did I maul you?" Norman asked.

As she opened her mouth to speak, Oscar asked Norman sharply, "What've you done?"

"It wasn't me; it was him."

"It was nothing," said Gigney. "As much her fault as his, I suppose. But nothing. I'm sorry."

"So you damn well oughter be," cried Norman. "What do you mean by saying I was makin' a fool of myself?" Gigney was going in. Norman caught him by an arm and said, "Wait on. Let's have this out."

"Now don't be a fool Norman," said Oscar sharply.

"Mind your own business," snapped Norman. "Now then — what'd you mean?"

"I simply meant that you shouldn't have done it."

"Why shouldn't I've done it?"

"Oh don't be mad."

"Come on. I know what's in your mind. Say it!"

"Come on you goats!" cried Steggles, trying to part them.

"He meant I'm a halfcaste," cried Norman.

"Godstruth I didn't!" cried Gigney.

"You did."

"Let me go."

Norman gave him a push that sent him back to the steps. He stood for a second on the edge of the veranda clutching for his balance, then toppled back and fell. He landed on the ground with a shriek.

A pause, while all eyes stared at Norman. Then Gigney attracted them by crying, "My arm — oh my arm!" A rush to the steps. Gigney got up, and clutching his left elbow like a wounded schoolboy, goggled at the crowd.

"What's up?" cried Oscar.

"Broke my arm," croaked Gigney.

"Break your blunny neck you insult me," cried Norman.

"Oh I never," croaked Gigney. "I never had any intention —"

"Well what'd you say —"

"Shut up!" cried Oscar. "Have you gone mad, boy?"

"Ask Rhoda what happened," cried Norman.

Rhoda shrank away.

Norman looked from her to the others. Their faces were dead white in the glare. He saw his own dark hand as it stretched out in expostulation. He dropped his hand. Even Steggles' face looked hard.

Gigney began to clump up the steps. The other men went down to help him. Norman stood for a moment, then wheeled about and hastened into the blackness of the hall. At the dining-room door he paused and looked back. White faces staring at the panting white-faced Gigney. He flung the door open and marched through the room and out.

Four hours later, still dressed as a Rajah, Norman crept in from the yard, and after standing breathless for a moment in the dining-room, listening to the moans of Gigney that came from the side-veranda, stole to his own room, found an electric torch, and as silently as possible began to collect a few of his belongings. Half an hour later, dressed in grey moleskin pants, khaki shirt, and wideawake, and carrying other things rolled up in a blanket and ground-sheet, he crept out of the house to the kitchen, and having deposited his burdens there, donned his riding-boots and went to the harness-shed. Later he roused Cho and got the key of the storeroom. At dawn, driving The Policeman and another docile horse named Juggler, whom he packed, and riding his own lively chestnut, False, he set out southward. At the stock-tanks he stopped and looked back at the dim white house. He stared for seconds. Then suddenly he spurred and rode away.

IT was shame of his folly that drove Norman from home.
He dared not face those who had witnessed it. But he did
not admit as much. He went angrily, insisting that he had
been wronged. He intended to ride to the Melisande. Thus
he would avoid having to meet the guests again, and Oscar
and Marigold, who would surely be angry, and also the
people of the Siding, who would surely know all about the
affair with Ket and want to know more; and by travelling
thus he would be occupied during the couple of weeks for
which he must wait for the opening of the Construction.
So actually he chose the precipitate mode of departure for
very practical reasons, though he preferred to consider it
dramatic. That New Year's Day he travelled twenty-seven
miles, first stopping at his water-works on the southern
boundary, where he had dinner and slept for several hours,
then at Purruwunni Creek near the railway, where he
pitched his camp for the night. The day was calm and
dry, as had been every day for a week past. As yet Wet
Season had been mild.

Darkness put an end to his conceit. Never before had
night found him out of earshot of his kind. It was long
before he slept. He heaped up the fire, heaped it up, not
for warmth nor for illumination, since the night was hot
and the blaze roused sinister shadows, but for companionship. Squatting — no, crouching — at the bottom of a grey-
and green-walled well of light, he sensed the Spirit of the
Land to the full. Phantoms came crowding, wailing afar
off, whispering as they neared, treading with tiny sounds,
flitting like shadows. He felt afraid. His scalp crept. His
black eyes rolled.

A golden beetle shot into the firelight, for a while dashed blindly round, then settled in a bush, began to sing:
Whirrrree - whirrrree - whirrrreeyung - eeyung - eeyung -
eeyong - eeyung - eeyahng - eeyah - eeyah - eeyahn, eeyung -
eeyong - eeyong - eeyong - eeyah - eeyah - eeyah- eeyah —
reverberating droning rising rising in compelling volume
into miniature boom of didjeridoo diminishing to momentary pause then rising rising waxing waxing seizing mind compelling limb — eeyung - eeyung - eeyong - eeyong - eeyah -
eeyah - eeyah — voice of the spirit of Terra Australis —
eeyah-eeyah-eeyah — and Norman, wrapt, with eyes on

Southern Cross, took up a stick and beat upon a log —
click-click — clickaclick-click — click-click — clickaclick-
click — eeyung-eeyung-eeyong-eeyahng-eeyah-eeyah-eeyah
— O mungallini kurritai, ee-tukka wunni wurri-gai, ee-
minni kinni tulli-yai — ee-yah-eeyah-eeyah!

He dropped the stick. His skin was tingling. He looked
at his hand, ashamed. Then he snatched up the stick and
hurled it at the beetle. The beetle fled. But for long its
song went on.

He sought companionship of stars that formerly had
been as familiar as street-lamps, to find them strange, utterly strange, vastly remote, infinite, arranged now to form
mysterious designs of frightening significance. The cry
of the kwiluk — Kwee-luk! — Kwee-luk! — Kweeee-luk! —
which he had heard every night since coming home but
scarcely heeded, became the lamenting of the wandering
Devils of the Dead. He heaped up the fire, heaped it up,
poked it to make it blaze and crackle, tried by staring into
it to burn from his mind his tingling fears. But the higher
the fire blazed the greater grew his own black shadow,
which he knew without turning round to see was reared
above him, menacing. He had to restrain himself from
seeking relief in the Song of the Golden Beetle. Then for
the first time he realized his Aboriginal heritage. He was
mighty pleased to hear occasionally the clink of hobbles and
the clank of the bell and the clump of the horses' hoofs.
When the horses came to the smoke of the fire to rid
themselves of flies he was delighted. He hailed them as
fellows, rose, went to them, fondled them and talked to
them for hours. It was past midnight when he fell asleep.
He slept badly, dreaming that he was lost with some sort
of silent nomadic tribe among moving shadows in a valley
of mountainous walls.

He woke at dawn to see through his mosquito-net a pair
of red-eyed crows making furtive examination of the pack-
bags. He stared at the familiar surroundings in surprise.
He rose and went down to the creek to drink and bathe.
By the time he returned he had abandoned all thought of
riding to the Melisande.

But much as loneliness had increased his love of kind and
home, it had not engendered any illusions in him about the
reception awaiting at Red Ochre. Undecided what to do,
he set off up the creek towards the Lonely Ranges. By
noon he had stifled the inclination to return. After dinner
he set out with purpose to find the pad to Tatlock's Pool.

having decided to spend a day or two there with Joe Back-house and Bill Donniken, who lived on the late Pat O'Hay's property, and whom he had met at the Siding, to spend another day or two in hunting cattle along the Lonely River, and then to go home with a handful of beasts with which to appease Oscar. But though he had, as he supposed, arranged matters satisfactorily, he was far from happy. Throughout the afternoon he was haunted by thoughts of his debasement, and that night was more sensitive to the Spirit of the Land than ever.

On the third day he became quite cheerful, as the result of discovering for the first time in his life that he was thinking deeply. This he did through solving with a minute's thought a problem in mechanics that had been puzzling him for weeks. Encouraged to ponder other problems with what he thought remarkable success, he began to feel for the first time in his life that he was clever. Soon he forgot his debasement. And he found himself marvelling at the phenomenon of his existence as a creature, of the existence of Mankind, and of nature's contrariety to Man that made Man's ingenuity essential. And for the first time in his life he began consciously to doubt the existence of the conventional Divinity in which he had been trained to believe, and to wonder about the Something he could see in the stars. So he came to marvel at Infinity instead of fearing it. That third night he forgot the phantoms roused by his fire in pondering over the phenomenon of combustion.

He retained this pleasant state of mind till he reached Tatlock's Pool. He arrived there at noon on the fifth day, loving all Mankind. He departed two hours later cursing the Universe. For Backhouse and Donniken received him as they might any wandering yeller-feller, questioned him as rudely as they might a nigger, and as though he were a nigger did not ask him in to dinner but sent a portion out to him on a tin plate to eat on the veranda. He was amazed at first. For a while he sat staring at the nigger's dollop, then rose and went away. Backhouse and Donniken were surprised to find him gone, then annoyed to find his food aswarm with ants.

He rode eastward blindly. Natives in a camp he passed rose up and shouted. He did not heed. Blindly he went on, following a pad to the Lonely River. So he came to a crossing, wide and turbulent, over which the yellow water boomed as rage was booming in his heart. He did not halt. He wished to put a barrier between himself and the hated world. Barrier! He shouted the word through yellow spray while flogging the horses over. Barrier! Barrier! The river boomed the word. Jabiroo and ibis swept up croaking it. Barrier! Barrier! As though he were not barriered off already!

Loving the river because its violence suited his mood, he rode up its grassy western bank till sundown, camped beside it, and slept soundly with its booming in his ears. Night held no terrors for him now; and loneliness no longer troubled him. He spent the hours between sundown and ten o'clock in working out a problem in mechanics and studying his map.

Having in the last few hours lost all desire to go home, he was reconsidering the idea of riding to the Melisande, this time by following a route that appeared on the map to be much shorter than the railway, that is, the course of the Lonely River, of which the Melisande River was a tributary. According to the map the Melisande joined the Lonely at a point about fifty miles above Tatlock's, and the railway bridge was no more than thirty miles above this point. Thus he was now but eighty miles from the construction-camp, a three or four days' quiet ride, whereas at Purruwunni Creek, which now lay forty miles to east of him, he had been one hundred and sixteen miles from it.

Scanning the map, he observed that the railway ran through what appeared to be a chain of hills. This was the backbone of the Willnot Plateau. He wondered why it had not been built along the Lonely River, knowing enough about the country to suppose that little difference would be made to the cattle-industry, the country's only staple one, if the road ran anywhere to east or west within fifty miles of the position chosen. What he did not know was that the Plateau was about the only part of Capricornia of much extent within three hundred miles of the sea that was not completely flooded in Wet Season. The Plateau extended from Port Zodiac to the Leichhardt Tableland, a distance of three hundred miles, and was, on average, some thirty-five miles wide. He had descended from it when he rode away from the settlement at Tatlock's.

He had often been told that it was impossible to travel in low country during the Wet. Not knowing exactly what low country was and having forgotten how violent the Wet was when it set in properly, he had never appreciated the information.

Next morning he had to hunt far for his horses. He

found them back at the crossing trying to cross. The river was there quite shallow, and the strength of it not great for all the turbulence. But the horses were short-hobbled and unable to negotiate the rocks and holes. Never in his experience with them had they wandered more than a hundred yards or so from camp. The fact that they went as far as possible on this occasion might have struck one more conversant with the whims of horses and the ways of Capricornia as significant, especially as the air was heavy with humidity and dark with clouds. He merely thought that they had gone back with intent to join the horses at Tatlock's.

Above the crossing, as far as he had seen as yet, the river was about a chain in width, not half as wide as at the crossing, though obviously much deeper. That it was swollen much above Dry-Season volume was apparent, as also that the volume had increased through comparatively light showers that had fallen in the last two days. This much he realized. What he did not realize was the river's capability of swelling rapidly and mightily. He could not have realized the rapidity without seeing it for himself; but he might have understood its potentiality for rising mightily if he had studied the scored and snag-littered bed of the grassy spaces flanking it. The space on his side was a good six chains wide near the crossing, bound by a ridge a good thirty feet above the level of the river, which meant that the river was capable of spreading to a width of at least twelve chains and rising thirty feet. The grassy space was actually the river's flood-bed. The western flood-bank was the distant bush-grown ridge.

The vegetation hedging the river's normal bed comprised such semi-aquatic growths as banyan, swamp-mahogany, leichhardt, paper-bark, bamboo, and pandanus palms. A cataclysm could not uproot such growths. But for all their sturdiness they never could have lived a week in earth so dry as that in which the common gum-trees grew in the Dry Season. The grassy spaces flanking the river were strips of no-tree's land, being too wet in the Wet for eucalypts, too dry in the Dry for aquatics. The fact that they were treeless was significant. Norman considered it merely fortunate, since it made travelling easy. The fact that he saw no kangaroos in the vicinity, whereas he had seen hundreds on the banks of watercourses on The Plateau, was also significant and also lost on him. There was no sign even of the almost amphibious buffalo.

He might also have realized how mightily the river swelled by simply looking into trees and noting the old flood-debris thirty feet above, instead of noting only cocka- toos and nuttagul geese and cranes. Thus, though lately he had become well-skilled in the art of using his eyes, all un- conscious of the river's dangerous potentialities, he rode up the grassy flood-bank, under a rain-filled sky, towards a destination that to him was only an inscription on a map, as careless as he would have been if riding to Red Ochre from the rail. During that day's march he came upon another crossing, but ignored it, preferring the western bank because the map described the eastern further up as swampy. He thought the western would be easy all the way, since it was dealt with on the map with much less detail. The country eastward of the river, that is on The Plateau-side, was fully detailed on the map, while that to the westward was for the most part marked *Not Sur- veyed*.

He noticed as he went along that the grassy space he rode in widened gradually, that the ridge that bounded it de- clined, and that the vegetation there grew denser. Thus till noon, when he crossed a tributary creek, which brawled through tangled growths like those along the river, and came upon a very different scene. The ridge had dis- appeared; the vegetation on the right, or west, had, as it were, closed in; the river had become much wider; and the grass that grew in the now restricted space was six feet high instead of three or four as it had been. The vegetation on the right was now of the aquatic type, composed mainly of paper-barks so closely crowded that their trunks looked from a distance like palings of a huge white fence. And the grassy space was only three chains wide instead of six, and the earth of it moist and steaming. He stopped on the further side of the creek and pitched his dinner-camp beneath a shady tree. Though he had ridden neither far nor fast his clothes were soaked with sweat and he was weary. The heat was overpowering. One-third of the sky was packed with voluminous black and woolly-white clouds, the rest of it blazing blue. Sunbeams peeping through the leaves stung him like rays from a burning- glass, forcing him to rig his ground-sheet as an additional shelter and stifle himself still more. After a meal of tinned peaches and biscuit and tea he covered himself with the mosquito-net and fell asleep.

He was wakened by the sound of crashing foliage. He

jumped up, thinking of buffaloes. Soon he heard a horsey
snort and clink of hobbles. He found The Policeman in
the middle of the creek, caught by the pack-saddle in bamboos. Later he found Juggler and False on the other side,
waiting for The Policeman to come. Still the fact that
there was significance to be found in their attempted desertion was lost on him. He made haste to be on his way,
annoyed to find that he had slept for more than two hours.
Now the sky was pitchy black behind him. Thunder was
rumbling far away. Wind was moaning in the jungle to the
right. Obviously a storm was brewing. But he went on
fearlessly, not realizing how violent a Capricornian storm
could be, since the few he had experienced so far had been
moderate.

That storm was a cockeye bob. It was not long in coming. It began with a gust of wind that smote him like a
club and sent him and horse staggering into the scrub beside the river, that for a moment crushed the tall grass flat,
that filled the sky with leaves. Then lightning streamed
down the black wall in the north like water down the face
of a bursting dam. Then a mighty cannonade. Then bursting of the dam. He leant upon his horse's neck, helpless
while the deluge flogged him.

The squall blew itself out in a minute or two. But the
rain did not stop; indeed, as with the falling of the wind
it descended perpendicularly, it seemed to increase in volume, and with a roar as steady as that of a waterfall poured down for half an hour. Norman soon dismounted and
sought the shelter of a tree. He was troubled about the
pack-horses, afraid that they might have bolted. He could
not see a yard ahead for rain, could not even see his top-
boots for water racing to the river. Then the rain stopped
dead. The surroundings were revealed as though by the
drawing of a silver curtain. He saw The Policeman and
Juggler at once. And they saw him and whinnied. For all
their powers of prescience they evidently lacked the sense
to hate him for his folly in frustrating their wise endeav-
ours.

He mounted, and in bright sunshine went on his way,
intending before night to cross another fair-sized creek that
was, according to the map, some eight miles distant. Now
a great cascade was flowing from the jungle to the river.
And the river had begun to race and murmur. By nightfall
the river was spilling over its banks and surging. Norman
crossed the creek. It was worthy of the name of river, so

big and strong was it. He took care to camp well away from its spreading waters, and from those of the river too, though he was not yet aware of danger. And he hobbled the horses fore and hind.

Being unable to make a fire on the streaming ground, he went to bed early, to lie on a stretcher rigged with saplings, pack-saddles, and the ground-sheet. Sleep did not come to him till the accustomed hour of ten, though not so much because he was troubled by the custom as by scores of tiny frogs that set up an ear-piercing chorus as soon as the sun went down, and by swarms of mosquitoes and fireflies that whined and flashed about his net, and by the din of running water. He was proof against the insects, but not against the frogs, which burrowed under the net and crawled on him. The frogs were not so friendly as they were cunning. They were seeking insects, not his company. Scores climbed the net like sailors climbing rigging, piping as though they .were all bosuns.

Though the sky was starry, the early moon he had expected did not appear; so he supposed that the eastern sky, hidden from him by the river-trees, was clouded, and feared that another cockeye bob might come and blow his bed away. This fear helped to keep him wakeful too, and persisted even when at last he slept, so much so that he woke with starts from dreaming of thunder. The rainstorm that came down in the small hours of the morning and raged till nearly dawn crept on him silently and dumped the net and canvas shelter over him before he woke. He did not sleep again till dawn.

He rose at eight, tired and sodden and stiff, to eat a breakfast of mouldy damper and butter sprinkled fluid from the tin. He had tinned meat and preserved potato-starch, but did not fancy them. For a moment he thought of going out to shoot one of a flock of nuttaguls that were yelling in the river-trees near by. But he could not see the tops of the trees for a mist of steam; and then he could not make a fire. Everything was sodden except his waterproof wax matches and tobacco in its rubber pouch. And mildew had set in, growing in patches on his clothes and boots and saddles. The heat was stifling.

When he went to the river to drink and bathe he found to his surprise that he had much less distance to go to it than he expected. It was gushing through the grass within six yards of the camp, having increased by a good ten yards in width since last he saw it, or rather, since it must have spread an equal distance on the other side as well, by a good twenty. And it was spreading still. But he did not realize his danger. He bathed while the river spread by inches. He struck camp at ten, and with his sleeping-nap spread out to dry on The Policeman's saddle and wood and grass for a fire on Juggler's, went squelching on his way up stream.

The jungle on the right was described but briefly on the map, set down as a line of dots running parallel with the river for thirty miles or so, behind which were the words *Dense Jungle*. Norman calculated, making allowance for the increased bogginess and height of grass and the fact that seven creeks lay in his path, that he would pass the jungle before sundown of next day. He rode easily, letting the horses pick their way, thinking more about the past than of the future. He rode easily only for a while. Two hours after setting out he stopped to cook a meal and rest the horses. By then the fuel was dry and the horses tired out. He had covered about five miles, only half the distance he had reckoned, and had done so with difficulty, finding the earth boggier and the grass taller and tougher as he went, and that there were six times as many creeks to cross as the map-makers predicted. He reckoned he had gone five miles because the first creek marked on the map was about that distance from the one from which he had set out, and since this creek was much bigger than the five unmapped ones he had crossed, which was saying a good deal for its size, and was, unlike the others, screened by trees, he supposed it was the mapped one. Evidently, he decided, that part of the country was surveyed in the Dry, when the smaller creeks did not exist. He never thought that the surveyors would not expect to have to serve Wet-Season travellers. Then he began to wish that he had crossed the river when he might have done so. Still he was not alarmed, thinking that he had merely come upon an inordinately well-watered stretch that he would soon put behind.

It took him long to cross this creek, so deep was it and vigorous and cluttered with snags and beset with tangled vegetation. In the middle, which was shoulder-deep, False fell and spilled his rider twice, and the second time, becoming entangled in the sword-sharp leaves of a low clump of pandanus palms, sustained deep cuts about the neck. It took them all a good half-hour to recover normal breathing. Norman patched up False's wounds as best he could, and made a pack-horse of him. When he went on he rode Juggler. Progress became even slower. The horses were tired and dejected. Covering the six miles to the next big creek took a good four hours.

Norman had decided that if the second creek should appear to be as difficult to cross as the other was, he would follow it into the jungle till he came, as he thought he would come without having far to go, to a point where crossing would be easier. And this he did, finding the creek all he had feared and more. But he did not find the easy-crossing point, though doubtless he would have had he gone on far enough. He gave up the search when it occurred to him that it was harder to enter the jungle than to cross the creek. He turned back on his tracks. It might have been easier to cross at the point he reached; but had he crossed there he would have had the difficulty of breaking another track through the jungle on the other side. As it was, his clothes and flesh were torn through his having to ride ahead and hack a path for the widely-saddled pack-horses. The horses were torn and tired too, and obviously glad to have done with what to them must have seemed sheer madness. Their legs and bellies were chafed raw by grass before they entered the jungle. They had gone in with great reluctance. They almost trotted out. The creek was crossed, with a great struggle, near the river. Camp was made in twilight. An hour after darkness fell a cockeye bob roared down.

Norman was not prepared for the prodigious display he saw in the storm that night. The fulminations of the other cockeye were rendered mild by the light of day and the sense of security engendered by that blessing. This one had the pitch-black night to blast and blaze in. Norman was badly scared, not only by the blasting and the blazing but by the sheeting rain and surging water at his feet. While blasting and blazing was at its height he crouched beneath the ground-sheet, waiting to be shattered. And while the deluge was at its worst he staggered about calf-deep in water, blinded, fighting for his breath. He staggered into the river, yelled when he felt it pulling at his legs, ran from it, staggered into it again. He splashed about madly, sliding, falling, till at length he crashed into a tree and nearly brained himself. Thus by sheer luck he reached the jungle. Lucky for him that he did not reach it earlier. He discovered in the morning that lightning had struck close

to where he stood. He spent the night squatting with back
to trees, and even slept a little.

At dawn he was relieved to see the horses in the jungle.
He had feared that the booming river had engulfed them,
hobbled as they were. And he was relieved to find that the
river had not risen nearly as high as he expected, had not
even reached his camp. But not all his discoveries were
relieving. The creek he crossed the night before had swelled enormously, which made him fear that those ahead
might be impassable. And he found that though the river
had not yet filled the entire grassy space it soon would do
so, and not only that, would flood the jungle, submerge it.
He saw the debris in the trees.

He thought of turning back, but after consideration decided that, since he would have to cover at least fifteen
miles in that direction before he would regain high ground,
he might as well cover the fifteen miles ahead. He had no
map to help him now. That, together with many other
things in the pack-bag with it, razor, nap, clothing, his hat,
net, and some food, had been washed into the river. The
loss caused him no dismay. He was thankful he had not
been lost with it. After a breakfast of biscuits and tinned
meat, eaten in drizzling rain, he saddled up and went his
way.

To his great delight he found that the third big creek,
which he reached after three or four hours of laborious
travelling, was not impassable. But his delight soon passed.
Crossing the river cost him False, his favourite, who, while
plunging wildly, scared of pandanus palms and floating logs,
tripped over a snag and broke a leg. Norman shot him. It
was a miserable cavalcade that carried on. Norman was
troubled by the memory of False's eyes, Juggler and The
Policeman by the memory of screaming and the consciousness of False's absence.

Before he reached that creek the rain had stopped and
the sky had cleared. He had believed as he crossed that
the journey ahead would be less arduous. But everything
was changed with the death of False. Clouds swept up and
blotted out the sun; rain poured down again; Norman felt
that he was doomed. And soon he had good cause to feel
so. The fourth big creek, which he reached at two o'clock,
proved to be impassable, to be so big, indeed, that at first
he thought it was a sudden bend of the river. It required
no trial to prove it was impassable. That was proclaimed in
the creek's own booming voice. The horses would not go

near it. Norman went to it on foot, and stared at it long, seeing little more through silver mist of rain than blackish water surging over flattened grass. He turned from it shuddering, splashed back to the horses, led them into the jungle.

Now he must travel up the creek if need be to the source to cross it. And he must do so quickly. But first he must eat and rest and shelter for a while from the incessant rain. He was ravenous, tired to the point of falling when he walked, and sodden to the bone. He stopped beneath a paper-bark where the earth was not awash, and took the pack off The Policeman, saddle and all, intending, after he had rested, to arrange the pack so as to make it as narrow as possible in preparation for the struggle through the jungle. He did not unsaddle Juggler, nor hobble either horse. They were as tired as he was.

He made himself a gunyah by first cutting a strip of bark from the tree with the tommy-axe and stripping it to the base in such a way as to leave the bottom still attached, then by pegging out the free ends and propping up the middle with the rifle. He threw in a few loose sheets of bark and the pack-bags to make a floor, then stripped himself and wrung his clothes and put them on again, then crawled into the gunyah to eat. He had scarcely done eating when he fell asleep.

He woke with a start to find the moon staring in his face. He sat up blinking, absently striking at mosquitoes. Then he leapt up. Water was winking at him from the grassy corridor crushed by his horses in entering the jungle. He rushed to see. The river was in the jungle!

He looked for the horses. No sign of them or of their having gone further into the jungle. He shouted. Bursting foliage and hasty flap of wings replied. He listened long, unconscious of the boom of the creek and river, but well aware of the chuckling of water in the grass. He shouted again. A kwiluk answered — Kwee-luk! — Kwee-luk! — Kweeee-luk!

His clothes were dry. He looked at the moon. It was nearly overhead. He went to the gunyah, groped for his tobacco-pouch, found his watch. The time was half-past twelve.

After searching widely for the horses, he climbed a tree and looked out over the space he had ridden in. Except for the swaying tops of scrub and grass in the foreground and in the background a black line of half-submerged trees, there was nothing to be seen but water, water in a vast, booming, scintillating, silver flood. When he got back to the gunyah he found the water licking at his belongings. He snatched the things away as from a thief.

The horses were gone, perhaps back to look for False. At any rate, there was no time to look for them. Thus Norman reasoned while he packed a few things and watched the advancing water. But he did not hurry. For much as he feared the chuckling assassin before him he was wondering about the wilderness behind. What if he should get lost in the jungle? What if he should struggle through to meet with the assassin on the other side? What if he should escape a death by drowning in low country to meet one by starvation in high? He did not leave till he saw the bark flooring float out of the gunyah. Then he took up the rifle, shouldered the pack-bag, and fled.

He travelled till the moon went down behind the trees and left him in pitch darkness. For three hours or more, sunk to the tops of boots in foetid mud and with the same filth plastered over hands and face and places where his ragged clothes exposed his flesh to protect him from mosquitoes, he squatted waiting for the dawn, fearful not so much of the creeping waters now as of the Devils of the Dead. Time and again he broke into the Song of the Golden Beetle.

He resumed his painful way with dawn of day and travelled till the night. The jungle grew thicker and boggier as he went; but because the roar of the river was decreasing and no roar rose ahead to second it, he was grateful, and grateful also because the sky was clear and because he found dry wood with which to make a fire. The second night he camped on a bed of leaves beside a roaring fire and sang himself to sleep with the Beetle's Song before the moon rose. Next day was also fine, and made more pleasant by the fact that the jungle was becoming thinner and less boggy. The third day was wet, but was made the best of all those countless days of wandering because it was the day of his deliverance, of his deliverance not only from the jungle and the fear of death, but from unutterable loneliness.

Soon after nightfall of the third day, six or seven hours after leaving the jungle, he was squatting by a fire under a gum-tree in a pleasantly sterile spot, grilling a turkey he had shot, when he heard a sound behind, and turned to behold a savage.

He dropped the turkey in the fire, leapt up with a startled cry.

The savage was tall, broad, bearded, naked but for a belt of human hair, painted hideously, white from head to foot, and striped with red and yellow, and armed with a handful of spears. Norman was terrified, open-mouthed, breathless, crouched.

For a moment the savage eyed him, then shocked him more by saying mildly, "Goodday."

Norman exhaled, gaping at the death's-head face.

Then the savage smiled eagerly and said, "By cripes — Norman!"

Norman gaped. He caught sight of other savages stealing up. The first, looking him over, noting burst boots and rags and beard and matted hair, said, "Wha' name — you go walkabout?"

Norman swallowed.

"Me Bootpolish," replied the savage. "You no savvy?"

"Bootpolish?" breathed Norman. "W-what — old Bootpolish work longa Red Ochre?"

"Yu-i," said the savage, and skipped to the fire and retrieved the burning bird.

Norman caught him by a shoulder, and looking wide-eyed at his death's-head face, cried, "Bootpolish — Bootpolish — what you doing here?"

Bootpolish grinned and answered, "Belong me country. Me go walkabout. Me fella bin hearim rifle, come look see."

"Oh God!" cried Norman. "Ol' Bootpolish — ol' cobber! Well I'll be damned!"

"What you doin' here, Norman?"

"Me? God — I been through hell!"

When Bootpolish heard the tale he said, "Too bad! Yeah — him proper cheeky bukka dat one chungle. No good. Dibil-dibil country — Aint it?" he asked of his friends. They nodded gravely.

"Now I wanter get back home," said Norman.

"Carn do it," said Bootpolish. "Big-fella Wet come properly."

"Eh — can't I get round somewhere?"

"Too muchee water."

"But I gotter get home," cried Norman.

"Carn do it," said Bootpolish. "Dis one wet-time. Can't go nowhere. You askim Muttonhead. Him ol' man boss belonga me-fella. Him savvy."

Norman's old friend Muttonhead grinned at him and told

him that he could not hope to reach home for four or
five more moons.

"But — but I gotter get back South," gasped Norman.
"Or I'll lose me job."

Muttonhead picked up the rifle and eyeing it said, "More
better you stop long me-fella."

"But I can't —"

"More better stop. You harcarse. Plenty harcarse stop
longa bush longa blackfella."

"I — I mean I gotter —"

"Proper good country dis one. Plenty kangaroo, plenty
buffalo, plenty bandicoot, plenty yam, plenty goose, plenty
duck, plenty lubra, plenty corroboree, plenty fun, plenty
ebrytings. Number-one good country. More better you sit
down all-same blackfella — eh Norman? Dat lo—ng
lo—ng time you gotter wait — You gottim plenty baccy?"

THE GOSSIPS HAVE BEEN BUSY

WET Season was passed, but the Dry not yet begun. The
land was drowsing, while it drained and dried, in the hal-
cyon days preceding the boisterous period called by the
Aborigines the Breaking of the Grass, which would begin
with the rising of the Trade Wind. It was the afternoon of
Tuesday, the Twentieth of April. On the veranda of the
Siding House at Soda Springs sat Mrs Violet Blaize and
Trooper Dan O'Crimnell and Ganger Cockerell, chatting,
while idly watching the antics of a band of bush-natives
who had just appeared from the scrub behind the fettlers'
camp and were most of them now scuttling off, evidently
scared by having caught sight of one of those debil-debils
incarnate — the police.

Trooper O'Crimnell was in full uniform, having but an
hour or so before returned from the Caroline, where he
had gone, summoned by Mrs McLash, to settle a violent
dispute in the native camp; or perhaps more truly, since it
was impossible for one such as he to get near enough to
bush-natives to parley with them, he had gone to scatter the
disputants by simply appearing in their neighbourhood; one
such as he was able simply by showing himself to scatter

a tribe for weeks. He wore a silk khaki tunic-shirt with silver buttons, and a highly-polished revolver-belt and holster, and corded khaki riding-slacks tucked into short tan top-boots, and a wideawake with brown and white pleated puggaree band and a large silver and blue-enamel badge in front. He eyed the startled natives as disinterestedly as his companions did till he noticed that one was not running off but coming towards the house, a tall broad-shouldered fellow who wore a ragged khaki shirt and grey trousers tattered to the knees and carried a gun. It was the gun that caught the trooper's eye. Possession of firearms by Aborigines was an offence against the law, a very serious one in the eyes of policemen, who seemed to fear that the humble creatures whom it was an important part of their duty to protect might do them injury.

O'Crimnell had been chuckling over a tale that Mrs Blaize was telling. At sight of the gun his broad strong-featured face set grim. He heaved his big body up from the depths of his deck-chair, and interrupted Mrs Blaize by snapping, "Well I ask ya! Look — here's a nigger comin' here bold as brass with firearms."

"It's a yeller-feller," said Cockerell.

"Same thing," said O'Crimnell, rising. "Yeller-feller livin' with niggers is a nigger." For a moment, standing clasping a veranda-post with a large brown hand, he quizzed the approaching figure under heavy sandy brows, then spat, and said in a rumbling voice, "I do b'lieve it's that young Yeller Shillingsworth."

All stared hard at the ragged figure. They had never seen Norman, but had heard much about him, especially since his disappearance, or rather, since Trooper O'Crimnell had gone out in search of him. O'Crimnell, whose district included Red Ochre, had been asked to make the search by Oscar about a month after Norman left home. By capturing some of the natives of the camp at Tatlock's Pool, who had seen Norman cross the river and had subsequently read the import of the smoke-signals of their brethren wandering in the bush to westward, he had learnt enough to surmise that Norman was taking a holiday, or Walkabout, with his poor relations. And this idea of O'Crimnell's had been spread far and wide, slowly at first by common gossips, then rapidly by that chief gossip of the land, THE TRUE COMMONWEALTH, to which Charles Ket had imparted it after having been defeated in the legal action he had brought against Oscar on account of wages he claimed as due to him. Ket had been backed in his action by the Labour Council, which was the power behind THE TRUE COMMONWEALTH, and which, having boasted of intent to make an example of Oscar for ignoring its mandates, had been enraged by his easy victory. Hence the paper had been glad to listen to Ket and give the world a witty account of how the grand Christmas party had come off and how the elegant halfcaste nephew and heir had gone a walkabout with the Old People.

Sure enough it was Norman. He came up grinning through a curly wisp of beard, eager to look upon what he still regarded as his kind and bursting to tell the tale of his adventures. First, he was dismayed by the rating the trooper gave him for being in possession of firearms while associating with natives, next by the reception given to his tale. The fact that he had spent four months in the bush with natives, living in native style, which he spoke of as though it were a remarkable achievement, left his audience cold.

Still, he was treated by these people far better than any ordinary halfcaste would have been. Cockerell offered to take him up the line on the trolley next morning, when he would be going to run the length before the mail-train, and to hand him over to Jake Ledder, whom they would meet at the 90-Mile, and who would take him to the Caroline, where he would most likely meet his uncle. He declined, not wishing to meet Oscar in public since having learnt that he believed in common with everyone that he had gone a walkabout. He asked O'Crimnell if he would lend him a horse for the journey home. O'Crimnell readily agreed. And Mrs Blaize agreed to give him credit for an outfit of clothes for himself and tobacco and flour and calico for his late companions, and of her own accord offered to give him a meal and let him sleep the night in her wash-house. Then when he hinted that he would like to have a shave and a hair-cut, O'Crimnell took him over to the police-station and set his tracker-boy to work on him. And after he had been trimmed and shaved, O'Crimnell gave him soap and a ragged towel and let him use his shower-bath. When he returned to the Siding House, clean and spruce, he was so cheerful that he ignored the fact that Mrs Blaize gave him his meal on tin-ware out on the back veranda.

Mrs Blaize talked to him while he ate, and drew from him the facts of the trouble that had caused him to leave home, concerning which the gossips had so far been able

to learn but little. He told her quite simply, believing that
she knew all about it, as she pretended to do. She also
discussed Ket with him, and many other subjects. He learnt
from her that he had lost his billet in Batman, that Oscar
was greatly worried about his future, that Marigold was to
be married to Steggles in November and was going to live
in Singapore, that Gigney had only lately regained the use
of his arm, that Ket was now working at the Melisande as
fireman with Frank McLash on construction trains. She
was very affable. He asked her to let Mrs McLash know
that he had returned, so that Oscar might hear of it when
he went to the Caroline next day. She had done that while
he was away with the trooper. The news of his return was
known from end to end of the railway. As soon as he went
off to his bed of sacks in the wash-house, she telephoned
Mrs McLash again, and passed on to all the eager ears the
facts of what had happened at Red Ochre on New Year's
Eve.

Next morning Norman had breakfast with Mrs Blaize
in her kitchen. He set out for home on the trooper's horse
at eight o'clock, rode up the railway as far as Purruwunni
Creek, then cut across country by the track he had taken
when he left home. He had about forty miles to travel.
When he reached home it was dark.

Oscar was at home, sitting in the dining-room, reading the
papers that had come that day. He heard Norman go to
the kitchen and hail Cho. He set down his paper and waited.

Norman opened the fly-door, looked in, grinning sheepishly, and said, "Hello!"

Oscar stared at him.

He entered slowly. "Know I was coming?" he asked
breathlessly.

"Yes," said Oscar stiffly. "Where've you been?" He rose.

Norman stopped before him. "I've been out the other
side of the Lonely," he said. "I got cut off by floods. Didn't
Ma McLash tell you?"

"She said you'd turned up with a mob of niggers you'd
been living with. Explain yourself."

Norman did so, while Oscar eyed him closely. When he
had done, Oscar asked, "D'you know that people're saying
you went a walkabout?"

"It's a lie," said Norman. "I've been trying to get back
home all the while."

"Well, you've set them talking. It was even in the paper."

"What's it matter what they say?"

"A lot, my boy. D'you want people to regard you as a nigger?"

Norman was silent.

"You realize you've lost your job, I suppose?" asked Oscar in the same stiff tone.

"Ma Blaize told me," murmured Norman to the floor; then he looked up with pleading eyes and asked, "You're not wild with me, are you Dad?"

"Not if it's true you didn't go a walkabout —"

"I never, Dad — dinkum. The niggers'll tell you. If you like I'll go and bring 'em in. Or you can send for 'em yourself."

"All right," said Oscar. "I'll be glad enough to have you stay for good if it's true. But if it's not, Norm, back South you go, job or no. This's no place for you if you're going to get the walkabout habit."

"Aw Dad!" gasped Norman, seizing Oscar's arm and looking at him miserably. "Aw Dad — dinkum I never!"

Oscar saw tears in his rolling black eyes. "All right, Sonny, all right," he said, and drew him close and kissed his cheek. "Now then — what about some supper?"

OH DON'T YOU REMEMBER BLACK ALICE?

NORMAN came home just in time to take charge of the mustering of cattle for shipment to the Philippines. He did more than muster them. To save the expense of railing them, he walked the first draft, a mob of three hundred steers, valued at £3 a head, all the way to Port Zodiac. He reached Port Zodiac on the last day of May. He left for home on the Fourteenth of June, bringing the cattle back with him. For the S.S. Cucaracha, while coming through the Karrikitta Reefs, struck a rock, ripped out her bottom, and sank. Captain Gomez came to Port in a lifeboat, clad only in a singlet and a towel, drunk, and weeping bitterly. Oscar could claim no compensation from the shipping-agents. When he learnt that it was not likely that the vessel would be replaced for some time, he sent word to Norman, telling him to bring the beasts back, thankful for having him to do it. With Norman as drover, the cost of

moving the cattle was negligible. He was assisted only by
blackboys. Peter Pan and Dingo Joe had gone to the Melisande.

It looked as though the grazing industry were in for
another period of slump. But the prospect was not so de-
pressing now that the country was in process of being linked to the markets of the South by rail. Norman set to work
to raise fat beasts for Southern butchers' shops.

As yet but one station was benefiting by the Transcontinental Railway. That was Gunamiah, on the Melisande, the
place founded by the late Jock Driver, who, had he lived
and stayed there, might one day have seen the transcontinental trains, with their loads of holidaying Senators, pass
by his homestead. It was said that a branch-line would
eventually be built from Gunamiah to the Billow Hills
Country, and that most likely a township would spring up
there, in the very home-paddock, which would be of great
advantage to the man who held the ground on a ninety-nine
years' lease as Jock had. The present lessee was the man
who bought Jock out, Andy McRandy, who was driving a
roaring trade in butchered beef consumed by the six or
seven hundred men employed in the locality. McRandy
said that whenever he got a cheque these days, Jock's devil
could be heard howling at night down in the river timber.

Norman made the acquaintance of Andy McRandy in
August, when he came out to Red Ochre to see the famous
water-works. Not from all the outsiders put together who
had yet seen his masterpiece did Norman get as much praise
as from old Andy. Though everyone had admired the
work itself, few had praised him personally, and these
had not done so lavishly. Old Andy was positively embar-
rassing with praise. He called him a genius, pounded him
on the back, hugged him, told him that he would become
the leading man of the country, and kept on doing so
throughout his three-days' stay, right up to the moment of
his climbing into the brakevan of the goods-train on which
he went home. He was not only liberal with his praise.
For ten fine young bulls that Norman had lately brought in
from beyond the boundaries, he offered £100. Nor was he
insincere in his behaviour, as it was proved to Norman
when he drove the bulls down to Gunamiah in September.
Old Andy welcomed him as warmly as he had taken leave
of him, took him into his house, treated him as though he
were already the country's leading man.

Thus Norman completed the journey on which, clad in

spotted blue print pants, he had set out seventeen years before. His host reminded him of the fact, chuckling over the change that had been wrought in his condition during the interruption, and took him round and showed him those relics of his father's deal with Jock, the decayed remains of the electric-power plant. Norman was intensely interested. Andy, who had known Jock well, told him some amusing tales about the fellow; and he told him some about his father too; but these were only tales of hearsay; for he had not known Mark at all.

§

The first meal Norman ate in the house at Gunamiah was supper. He and his host ate alone in the comfortable dining-room, seated at a table laden with the best of food and drink, attended by a smiling young lubra who was neatly clad in an expensive green satin dress and adorned with good jewellery. As the lubra went off after her first appearance, old Andy, tall and lean and stooped, and silvery of long moustache and scanty hair, winked a twinkling eye at Norman, and hissed behind a leathery hand, "My missus!"

Norman, guessing that a compliment was sought, looked after the girl, who glanced back as she entered the kitchen, and giggled prettily into a slim black hand. He turned back to the eager Andy grinning, and said, "You've got a peach all right."

"Plum!" hissed Andy. "Sugary black plum. A damson — Ha!" He attacked his food with zest.

He ate swiftly for a while, then looked up and said, "I call her Velvet. Lovely name, aint it. I call 'em all that. Lovely creatures." He returned to his plate.

"What — you got a harem?" asked Norman cautiously.

"Eh — harem?" asked Andy, gaping. Then he laughed, and said, "No-more! I mean I call 'em all that in rotation. Harem? Ha! Ha! Ha! Gawd — I'm nearly sixty!"

After eating for a while he continued, "Course an old feller like me can't keep 'em long. Just a few months. They're just gettin' nice and fat and cheeky, when their bucks come round and sneak 'em back. But it never worries me. I soon get another. Not like some old coots I can name — old Alfie Alcock over Bonnidinka for one — when they find they been jilted, go mad as snakes, get out the gun, saddle up — and a-huntin' we will go. Ho! Ho! You'd think old Alfie was goin' an explorin' trip the plant he takes with him when he goes out huntin' for his elopin' light o' love."

"What's he do when he catches her?" asked Norman.

"Her? Them, you mean. Course he don't never catch none of 'em. He takes boys with him to do the trackin'; but course they just lead him a dance. Ha! Ha! Ha! Comicalest thing you ever seen. The whole darn country laughin' at him; and him trackin' up and down lookin' as sour as a bluegum buggoo. Ha! Ha! Wow!"

Norman choked over his food.

After a while old Andy went on, "There's sumpen terrible fascinatin' about a lubra all right. I dare say you find that yourself, eh?"

Norman grinned slyly.

"I reckon it's because you can't get to understand what's goin' on inside their pretty 'eads," said Andy. "Men always goes rampin' about a woman that's got 'em beat in the way of bein' incomprehensible. See what I mean? In the case of lubras it certainly aint a matter of mere taste that sends the boys after 'em. I reckon any normal healthy man'll fall for 'em if he'll expose himself to the risk. I don't care what anybody says. Even parsons have done it; and they aint what you'd call normal and healthy. I've seen comboes of all sorts — as smart fellers as you'd wish to find, and dunces, and fine lookin' fellers and others with faces like fried grummets, and even married men. They're all the same. It's only a question of gettin' used to the colour and the different kind of countenance. They say a feller aint been in this country unless he's tried the Black Velvet. And that's a fact. Some of these here newchums workin' on the railway here — they come here stickin' up their noses at the ladies, sayin' they can't see what you see in 'em — but by golly it don't take 'em long to see it for 'emselves, I can assure you. Even that Chief Engineer feller — what's his name? — Sid Gigney — know him? But o' course you do. Aint that the feller you broke his arm —"

Norman blinked, muttered, "How'd you know that?"

"Eh? Course — don't everybody know it! Well I was sayin' — When Sid Gigney come out here last year while they was surveyin' the track, he rousted hell out of the surveyor fellers for keepin' lubras in their camp. Well, he was out here again a fortnight back. And what d'you think? Ha! Ha! I put him up for the night, y'see. Just after supper he says he wants to go over and see the contractor fellers on the line. I says I'll go with him for a bit of a stroll. Oh no, he says, not to bother, and goes for the lick of his

life. I had me suspicions. And I was right. About twenty
minutes later I caught him at the kitchen door, whisperin'
sweet nuthens to my little Velvet there. Ha! Ha! Ha! I
catches him behind all of a sudden, and asks proper sharp
and nasty, 'What's the game, Mister?' He jumps and dith-
ers. Ow! — it was worth a tenner to see him — Ha! Ha!
Ha! — 'I — I — I lost me bearin's', he blithers. 'Well go
and get one out of the camp,' I growls, 'stead of pinchin'
other men's,' I says. And off he pithers. Did he stop the
night? Not him! He snuck right off. And I aint seen the
poor simple feller since — Ow! Wow!"

After a while Andy asked, "You heard that yarn about
Con the Greek and old Paddy Larsney and the lubra?"

"No."

"Well you know Con the Greek, o' course —"

"Can't say I do."

"What — dunno Con the Greek?"

Norman shook his head.

"He works for your Auntie Heather."

Norman looked puzzled.

"Heather Shay. He's doin' her cookin'."

"She's not my Auntie," said Norman.

"Well — sort of. She's Oscar's sister-in-law. And she
was your Dad's best girl. Might easy've been your Ma."

"Is that a fact?" asked Norman.

"Course it is. Didn't you know?"

Norman shook his head. Andy explained. "A great girl,"
he said in conclusion. "She's got a grog-shanty up the
depot now — the Transcontinental Hotel —you know?"

"Yes — I heard she had," said Norman. "How's she
doing?"

"Well she oughter be doin' pretty good. There's only her
and Jerry Rotgutt got the monop'ly of fillin' six or seven
hundred bellies. She needs to do well, anyway. Time the
cattle-boom, her and old Ma Shay put most of their profits
into a store up Town that turned out a failure. And they
had a feller bookkeepin' for 'em at the pub that did a bunk
with all the rest of their cash. This shanty's a sort of root
put out to keep the old Princess Alice from fallin' down,
it seems. They reckon Heather wangled things so's the
Government wouldn't give no-one else a licence to sell
liquor in the camp. Course Jerry Rotgutt was there from
the start. He had a shanty in old Melisande when I first
come here. That was when the head of the road was at
Copper Creek."

Andy was behind with his meal. For a while he applied himself to it vigorously. Then he went on, "But I was tellin' you about Con the Greek. You dunno him, eh? Con Constantinopolis or sumpen is his name. He use to be the cook up the orspidal in Town. Now he's workin' for Heather, and in his spare time runnin' a gamblin' school out the back of her place. He must've cleaned up a terrible lot of money since he started. Course, like all Greeks with money, he kids poor. You never see a Greek actin' flash unless he's broke. And you never see one puttin' his money in the bank, neither. You see 'em up in Town gettin' round in rags like Binghis, while they've got four or five hundred quid stowed away at home, in the fowl-house under the broody chooks, or in the stuffin' of the bed, or somewheres. Queer breed. They reckon this here Con carries his roll round stuffed inside his clothes, which's why he's got so fat since the construction started."

Another pause to eat.

Andy went on, "But I was tellin' you a yarn about old Paddy Larsney, the magistrate, and Con and a lubra. It happened durin' the boom, when Con was workin' at the Meatworks. He was livin' in a humpy down Mylunga Beach and had his bit of Velvet keepin' house for him. Course it's hard to do that sort of thing up Town. I suppose Con thought he could get away with it cos there was a big crowd about. Anyway, a sneakin' coot of a police-boy stationed at the Compound got to hear of it and told the jonnops. You see, at the Compound, they was callin' this lubra Missus Constantinople, same's they do when a lubra's got a whiteman playin' round with her, y' know. Well the jonnops come along and found the lubra with Con and grabbed 'em both. They brought Con up on a charge of consortin' with a female Aborigine. Seems they was after Con for some knifin' business at the Meatworks that he'd bluffed himself out of. Certainly they couldn't't've brought him up simply because of the consortin' business, seein' they couldn't't've been too innocent on that score 'emselves. Anyway, there he was in court before old Paddy Larsney, with things lookin' pretty black for him, seein' they had that sneakin' police boy to say the lubra'd been called Missus Constantinople for a month past. It just looks like old-man Larsney's goin' to send him up, when Con gets a brainwave. You see, this lubra'd been workin' as a servant in Paddy's house not long before. Well Con knew a thing or two. Just at the crucible moment he ups and says that he can name other fellers that ought to be up in the dock with him. 'Go ahead,' says Paddy. So Con turns to the police-boy and says, 'What name they bin call this one lubra before they call him Missus Constantinople?' The police-boy looks a bit sick. He won't say nuthen, but keeps lookin' at Paddy cross-eyed. Old Paddy gets wild and bawls, 'Answer up, dern ya!' So the police-boy does, and he says, 'Before they bin callim Missus Larsney' — Ha! Ha! Ho! — The police-boy was discharged as an unreliable witness — and Con got off — Ha! Ha! Wow!"

"Yes," said Andy after a while, "Con's makin' a mint of money these days. Looks like he's gettin' most of what's bein' paid out in wages here. Yes — and be cripes — he's gettin' a lot that aint bein' paid out in wages and ought to be." He nodded to the open door that led to the front veranda and added, "A lot of these here contractors they got doin' the work now aint payin' their men properly. There's a camp just over the way there — you can see the fire through the trees. That's run by two fellers, Jack Ramble and Joe Mooch. They only pay their men when they have a win with Con. And they do much the same with me too, dern 'em! There's more like 'em, too. I can assure you, as one that has to rely on their luck to get my money, that they don't have much of it."

"Why do the men stand it?" asked Norman.

"Can't do nuthen else. You see, when the job first started the Government was boss. Then the local lads had a grand time strikin' and generally friggin' about. So the Government imported a lot of Pommies and Greeks and things that wouldn't give trouble, and let the work out to contractors. Labour-conditions is rotten at present. The Labour Council can't do nuthen with them poor crawlin' Pommies and things. Even though they don't get paid, they're afraid to kick up much of a shine case they lose their jobs and have to go and live on police-rations down the river. There's a good two hundred fellers camped on the river down the depot now, out of work and likely to stop out. There'll be a bust-up soon, mark my words. Things can't go on as they are. And when the bust-up comes the job will close down for good."

"What — the construction?"

"The whole box and dice. There's talk already of only takin' the line as far as Bukkajinjin, on the Tableland. I heard it from Gigney himself. That means this new National Government that's just got in don't want to build the

line at all. They're sure to want to undo all the other
Government done. I'll bet you that all's needed for 'em to
call a halt any time now is a bit of a bust-up. And that I
bet you comes with the Wet, when either the whole blasted
show'll wash away — as is pretty likely, seein' the slipshod
way these here contractors are buildin' it — or the men,
Pommies and Dagoes and all, will get the Wet-Season
feelin' and down tools. Nuthen ever sees the Wet through.
This aint goin' to be no exception."

"But what about the Transcontinental Railway?"

"What about it? I'm sure I don't want to see it built. It
won't do no good. If it does anything at all it'll spoil this
lovely country."

"Eh? But I understand it'll be the makings of it."

"How?"

"Well — we can send our stock down South if we've
got a railway. And then other industries'd be encouraged.
The old place would hum."

"Go on! Can't they produce more stock and more everything down South than they can consume and export? And
how much do you reckon it'd cost to send a bullock two
thousand miles by rail?"

"They reckon we'll be able to send our stock at very low
rates."

"Don't you believe it. Do you think the Southern graziers'll stand bein' taxed to bring down beasts to cruel the
market for 'em? They've got to pay heavy to rail their own
stock to market. They'll see that we do the same. And
there's another point they'll bring up. We don't pay income-
tax at all up here, and, with the Binghis, we've got cheap
labour. Graziers down South have to pay State and National Taxes and have to employ their men at union-rates."

Norman was silent.

"No Sonny," said Andy, "There aint no need for this
here railway at all. If there was you'd find more than one
ship a month callin' at Port Zodiac. And that one only calls
cos it gets a huge sum of money for carryin' the mail. There's
plenty of empty space to fill up down South yet. This railway's only the whim of a few transplanted cocknies that
hate to see places without tram-lines in 'em, and of engineers that want jobs, and of manufacturers that want to sell
things to the men employed on the buildin', and a few newspaper editors and other blowbags that dunno what they're
talkin' about and don't care so long's they can talk. Listen
— this country's been settled donkey's years, and has had

all the chances of development that the rest has. Yet today there's less people here and less business doin' than there was fifty years ago. Why's that? I'll tell you. It's because it's an utterly useless land. You can't grow nuthen properly on account of the climate. Dry Season it's a desert. Wet Season it's a lake. A fair indication of what this country's like for growin' things is the fact that all the vegetables used in Town are imported from the South. I've paid a shilling a pound for potatoes there. And green stuff costs as much as tobacco nearly. If you could grow them things here in marketable quantities, don't you think that someone'd try? And if you can't — aint there sumpen darn well wrong?"

"What about tropical produce?" asked Norman.

"What'd you do with that? They don't want it down South. They can grow it 'emselves in the subtropical parts as well and better than we can — yes, and can grow more than they want, too, as you can see by the fact that they've got to limit production. And they can't export it, because, Australia bein' a workin' man's paradise, which is better than it bein' a paradise for Plutes, their cost of production is too high for competition with countries where labour is sweated. Anyway, they're too far from the rest of the world. Yes, producers in the South'd go mad if we started sendin' 'em tropical produce. So they would if we started sendin' 'em beef. They're all mixed up financially as it is on account of overproduction. Well, where else'd we sell? To the East? Course we couldn't. They can produce anything we can at a hundredth the cost. And they don't eat beef. There's loonies suggest we ought to grow sheep. I've seen it in the Southern papers. Amazin' madness! And at the same time I see that they're killin' off their sheep down there so's to stop a glut in the mutton-market. Anyway a jumbuck aint tall enough to keep his head above water here when it rains good and earnest. Aint it a significant fact that rabbits don't live here? Why don't they? Cos the blunny place is always either a desert or a lake. Rabbits've got more sense than them blowbags that write in the Southern papers."

"But what's goin' to happen to the place if we don't do something with it?" asked Norman.

"It'll look after itself, Sonny, till it's really needed. It's been here a hundred million years or so without evaporatin' for the want of bein' cleared and fenced."

"But the Japs," said Norman. "If we don't do sumpen with it the Japs'll take it."

"You been listenin' to Billy Hughes?"

"Well — aint that right?" demanded Norman.

"Don't you think the Japs'd take it a dern sight quicker if we was to clear and cultivate it a bit for 'em first?"

Norman was silent.

Andy chuckled, and went on, "I said just now, Sonny, that the land has been here a hundred million years or so. The Japs've been livin' not far away a good while too. And the Chows and all the other teemin' hordes of Asia. But they never thought of comin'. I'm nearly sixty; and I've been hearin' about the Japs comin' all me life. You'll be hearin' it when you're eighty, I dare say."

"But the Japs are gettin' terrible strong."

"Might be they are."

"Look what they done in China."

"Ah! But they can chuck a brick at China. And then, the Chows are their special meat. No-one can interfere with 'em there. But we're not their special meat; and we live a month's journey away from 'em. If they was to attack us they'd have to fight their way with rations and reinforcements through the navies of the world."

"What say the navies of the world was mixed up in a fight of their own at the time, and couldn't help us?"

"What say an earthquake come and wiped us out? Or, what's more likely, what say one come and crippled the Japs while they was doin' their stuff?"

Norman was silent.

Andy chuckled again, and said, "If the Japs come here they'd have a terrible time gettin' the land settled to support 'emselves. It'd take 'em years and years and years. They'd have to come in hundreds of thousands to hold it. They'd have to be fed from outside for years. And all for what? For a tract of country that's a desert in the Dry and a lake in the Wet, and that'd be fenced round the coast by battleships of all the navies in the world, and across the back by six million people who'd never cease to fight. I give the Japs credit for havin' more sense than to do that. Not that I don't want the Japs to invade us. I do. It'd be the makin's of us. We need sumpen like that to bring out our character, to make a real true nation of us. We're a great people, we Australians. There's nuthen to touch us in the World. Course every race says that about 'emselves. But there is something special about us. And what's given it to us is our freedom from slavery to industry and our sunshine and our elbow-room. For them three things no race of people on earth comes near us. Now we only want sumpen to wake us up to ourselves. An invasion by the Japs'd do that. I have a lot of time for the little Jap. I reckon he could give any nation on the earth a good go in a scrap. He could wipe us off the face of the earth if he tackled us alone. But he'd get terrible knocked about in the process."

For a while there was silence. Then Andy said, "This talk of invasion by the Japs is all plain bulsh. Damn me if I can see any reason for it, except that it might be got up by military men who want jobs fixin' up a defence policy. You'll find there's ulterior motives like that behind most things. And what catches the public mind in the matter, I dare say, is the exciting possibility, the unconscious desire to have this scrap that'll form our national character. Don't you think?"

Norman was silent.

"There was thousands and thousands of Asiatics in this country long before the White Australia Policy came in," said Andy. "They were in their hordes on the Copper Creek and Republic Goldfields. They built the railway. They set up hundreds of little farms. But where are they today? They weren't kicked out. They couldn't drift overland to the South in them days. There was a good thirty thousand, I'll be bound. But I doubt if you'll find three thousand now. They must've gone home. Now if they didn't dig 'emselves in with that special bent for diggin' in they're supposed to have when they could have done so legally, are they likely to try to do it when it aint? No, Sonny, there's no fear of any sort of invasion here, except in the way of a politician now and then and a few of them newspaper blowbags and an occasional gang of starvin' Pommies or Dagoes to break a whiteman's strike?"

He was silent for a while. Then he said, "D'you know, Sonny, I like to think that the Great Bunyip, the Spirit of this Southern Land of ours, the Lord of your Aboriginal forefathers from the beginnin' of time, and now the Lord of us who's growin' up in your forefathers' place and goin' the same old manly carefree way, wants to keep a bit of the place in its aboriginal glorious wild state, and has chosen this here Capricornia for it. If that's so, good luck to Him, says I. And who but a blunny spit of a cockney'd say otherwise? Isn't elbow-room sumpen to thank God

for? Course it is! Well we have it here. Let's keep it. To
hell with the Transcontinental Railway. And speakin' of
elbows, what say we adjourn to the front veranda and take
a bottle of whiskey with us?"

They had been sitting on the front veranda, talking and
drinking, for about half an hour, when from the firelit construction-camp, which lay about two hundred yards away,
there came the sound of a concertina.

"That's Joe Mooch," said Andy. "He can make that dern
thing talk."

The musician was playing *The Red Flag*.

Andy chuckled and said, "Muster been trouble in the
camp. Luck out with Con the Greek most likely. Joe always plays tunes like that when there's been a barney with
the men."

"He's one of the bosses, isn't he?" asked Norman.

"Yes — him and Jack Ramble."

"Queer sort of tune for a boss to be playin', aint it?"

"Oh he's a character, that Joe Mooch. He kids to stir
the men up when they growl. Him and Jack know how to
handle that bunch all right. They've got it all over 'em.
Hear him singin'."

On a gust of wind came the words distinctly:
        Though cowards cringe and traitors sneer,
        We'll keep the Red Flag flying —

"Care for music?" asked Andy.

"Love it," said Norman.

"Well come on over to the camp. We'll take a couple of
bottles with us. Joe's a champion booze-artist."

They found only two men by the fire, the musician, who
was sitting on a kerosene-case, playing, and a tall, lean,
black-bearded fellow in khaki shirt and trousers, who was
reclining in a deck-chair, with hands behind his head and
bare feet jigging to the music. The musician was short
and stout, and round and red of face; and he was bearded
too; but his whiskers were grey and stubbly and unkempt;
and he wore khaki trousers and a sleeveless grey flannel
shirt. The tall fellow was aged about forty-five, the other
a good ten years more.

Andy and Norman were close before they were seen. The
tall man sat up, nodded to Andy, and scrutinized Norman
with a swift curious glance. The musician stopped playing,
blinked bleary eyes at them, and cleared his throat and said,
"Uzzit?"

"What-o!" said Andy. "How's things?"

"Mustn't grumble," said the tall man, stretching.

"Heard you callin' on the boneheads to rise and fight for their rights," said Andy. "So we come along case might be they took you at your word, bringin' a bit of sumpen for fortification purposes." He produced the bottles.

"Well," he went on, "this here's a young friend of mine — Mister Norman Shillingsworth, of Red Ochre, up the Caroline. Norm — this's Mister Jack Ramble —" he indicated the tall man "— and this's his partner, Mister Joe Mooch."

Both men stared, looked at Norman wide-eyed.

"Ow d'you do?" said Norman, smiling at Ramble and holding out his hand.

Ramble raised his hand slowly, took Norman's mechanically. Norman turned to Mooch and said, "Pleased to meet ya." Mooch fairly goggled at him, and gasped fumes of alcohol in his face.

For a moment there was an awkward pause, which caused Norman to feel that he was not wanted. His smile faded. His black eyes rolled. Then Mooch returned the greeting, saying huskily, "Pleased to meet ya too, Sonny."

Ramble swallowed, said almost inaudibly, "Very pleased."

"Not intrudin' are we?" asked Andy, looking from one to the other.

"Not at all," said Ramble quickly. "Not at all. Take a seat. Take this one." He waved Norman to the deck-chair.

Norman was relieved. He smiled and said, "No thanks. The old haunches'll do me. You sit there Andy."

Ramble snatched up a box and placed it for him. Norman sat down.

"Glasses," said Mooch, and set his concertina down and hurried away to a tent.

Andy exchanged a few words with Ramble about the construction. Ramble, standing by the fire, with hands tucked in the waist of his trousers, answered absently, while eyeing Norman, who was looking about the camp. Then Mooch returned with glasses and a water-bag. Norman was gratified to see the contractors raise their first glasses to him. After drinking, Ramble spoke to him for the first time since answering his greeting, asking, "What you doing out this way?"

Norman explained.

Andy broke in with a glowing exposition of Norman's cleverness, which he delivered while bending forward and patting his shoulder, and which he ended by saying, "And he aint a prig with it. That's what I admire about him. He aint forgot his Old People as you might expect. On the contrairy, right from doin' all them things he went a walkabout, stayed away all the Wet with a mob of Binghis, livin' as one of 'em, then come back and got straight to work managin' Red Ochre for his uncle again."

Norman was appalled.

"Aint that so?" asked Andy cheerfully.

After a moment Norman gasped, "No!"

"Eh?" asked Andy, surprised.

Norman turned on him wide-eyed, and gasped, "I never went a walkabout. I got lost."

Andy blinked at him and said, "Eh? But they all reckon —"

"It's a lie!" cried Norman. And he turned to the others and went on, "I got trapped by floods. I couldn't get back. I — it was an accident."

He dropped his eyes before the stare of Ramble, looked at the fire for a moment, then turned to Andy again and said, "It's a blunny lie!"

"What?" asked Andy, staring at him fixedly. "Are you ashamed of the Old People after all then?"

Norman dropped his eyes.

"Eh?" persisted Andy.

Norman looked up and cried angrily, "I tell you it's a blunny lie! And anyone I hear sayin' it again I'll take to court for slander."

"Tut! tut!" said Andy. "Don't get wild, Sonny. I aint sayin' nuthen the contrairy. That's just what I heard. And I believed it, and thought all the more of you for it. So you are ashamed of the Old People, eh?"

Norman was staring at the fire. His hands were clenched, his nostrils quivering.

"Why, Sonny?" asked Andy gently. "What you got to be ashamed of 'em about?"

Norman gulped.

After a moment Andy put his hand on Norman's head, and went on in the same gentle tone, "Let's consider the Old People for a jiffy, and see what's wrong with 'em. Forget the ones that live in civilization. They're starved and sickened and kicked and stupefied and generally jiggered out of all recognition. Let's consider 'em in their natural state. How do we find 'em? Big, strong, broad-browed, keen-eyed, laughing fellows. Consider their manner of livin'. Their tribes are families, in which no-one is boss, in which no-one is entitled by any sort of right to bully and grab. Then there's their laws regardin' Supply and Demand. They have a certain area stocked with game and vegetables. It's their farm. People accuse 'em of bein' too stupid to practise husbandry. Quite to the contrairy. They practise it in the most amazin'ly clever fashion. They simply preserve their game and fruits and things, by drawin' on 'em carefully, and so save 'emselves the labour of havin' to till and sow and the trouble of gettin' all mixed up financially over their stock as we do. You might call that Primitive. But lookin' at it closely and comparin' it with our system of sweat and worry and sinfulness, I dunno but what it aint quite as good. The point to look at is, what are we livin' for? Is it to create intricate systems that all become obsolete after a while and have to be changed with painful reconstruction? Or just to enjoy in the simplest way possible the breath of life that's in us? What is the perfect state of society? Aint it the one in which everyone's equally happy and well fed? If it is, then Brother Binghi has it. And as to the Primitive business — well, they've had the mighty good sense to limit their population to suit the natural food supply. That idea is only just occurrin' to us. It seems to me that all our intricate system of society has only been brought about by the fact that we've overstocked our paddicks with the human herd. If we'd thought of birth-control a thousand years ago, providin' we hadn't allowed a few greedy hounds to rule and rob us, today we might've been livin' as simply as the Binghis 'emselves. Do you think a Binghi livin' out in the bush in his own style would swap his lot for ours, if he knew the full strength of it?"

Old Andy looked round his audience.

He answered himself. "He'd be a blunny fool if he did,' he said. "Look 'ere — most of us aint a scrap higher animals than the Binghis — and there's a lot of us a dern sight lower. Find me a whiteman in all this continent that's capable of inventin' a steam-injin — not makin' it, but inventin' it, not knowing that it was ever thought of before. You'd have to look a dern long way. Cos only one whiteman out of millions of 'em in thousands of years was capable of that. Are we a scrap more intelligent than the Ancient Greeks? Well it's three thousand years or sumpen since their time. Why didn't someone invent a steam-injin till lately? That's got you thinkin', I see. Well, only one man invented it, after thousands of years of idleness in that direction. Then several pretty smart fellers got the guts of the invention and improved on it. So they made a machine that'd do all sorts of things that was impossible before. Well a lot more smart fellers gathered up all the thinkin' that'd been done durin' the three thousand years, and turned it upon this here machine, and made a lot of things. All these new things was needed on account of the overstockin' of the paddicks. And the more they made the more the paddicks got overstocked for some reason or other. More machines had to be made. One led to another. But they was all mothered by the steam-injin, without which there wouldn't've been any at all, and the white race'd still be livin' in much the same way as it was when it believed in witches and the Divine Right of Kings. Now our machine-worked system is very clever. But we ordinary sorts of fellers aint no right kiddin' ourselves up on the strength of it. Give you an example of what I mean. Remember that aeroplane from England that flew over here a couple of months back? Well I was down in a contractor's camp at Bamboo Creek at the time. When the machine flew over, course we all jumped up and had a pike at it. As it was passin' out of sight, travellin' at about two hundred mile an hour, a blackfeller workin' there says dreamy-like, 'By cripes whiteman him clever too much!' And that's the way we felt about it. But he was wrong. None of us were a bit more cleverer than that poor half-starved Binghi before we learnt things out of books that had in 'em the learnin's of three thousand years or more. Only one whiteman in a million is any more clever when he's born than the average black piccanin. And you may bet your boots that some of the piccanins have genius too, or how come their people to possess such clever contraptions as the spear-thrower and the boomerang?"

Andy looked round again. "The Binghis have their arts," he went on, "their music, and story-tellin' and play-actin' and astronomizin' and such things, which are no doubt quite as good as those of the ancient people we come of not so long ago, and probably a dern sight better than what we could think up ourselves without assistance. We've been assisted in acquirin' our culture by all the races of the earth except the Binghi, which has been hid away from the rest of the world always. No tellin' what we could learn off him if we could get him to trust us with his knowledge. No tellin' what he would've become if he'd had the luck to pick up from other races as much as we. Is he any more primitive than an African Negro in the wild state? I don't think so. Well, look at the Negroes in America today!"

Again he paused. He went on, "There's no need to say any more. If you know anything about Binghis in their native state, you can't help but honour 'em, unless you're a fool. But I must say there's plenty of fools about. You've been listenin' to what those fools say, Sonny. You've been readin' newspapers, which from start to finish are only fit for the purpose we bushwhackers use 'em for when we've read 'em. Take my advice, Sonny, see for yourself and think for yourself. Learn all you can about your Old People, then go and tell the world about it. It's certainly nuthen to be ashamed of."

Norman was regarding him wide-eyed.

"I aint kiddin'," said Andy. "And it aint nuthen new. Plenty of people've discovered the worth of your Old People. And plenty more will. Listen Sonny, the day'll come in your own time when your Old People'll be recognized as our Old People too, as the Fathers of the Nation, and'll be raised to a place of honour. No exaggeration. There's signs of it now. Twenty years ago they was killin' off the Binghis round here like they was dingoes. The Government didn't mind at all. But the Government'd come down heavy on you if you did it now. It's a long while since anyone made war on 'em on the grand scale of the old days. I'm referrin' to private individuals, of course. The police are still pretty handy at shootin' 'em up if they get the chance. Course you can't class a policeman as a normal citizen. It takes abnormal men to catch abnormal men, you know. But even the jonnops don't treat the Binghis anything like they used to. Last big shoot-up of niggers by jonnops was in 1928 on the West Coast. Last big one that was made public, I mean. No tellin' what they get up to on the sly. And it's likely to remain the last. There was a row about it. The people of the South wanted to know What For. Time will come when jonnops'll go to jail for knockin' Binghis about, I'll bet me boots. The people of Australia are wakin' up to the fact that they've got a responsibility in Brother Binghi. That'll lead 'em to gettin' to know him. And gettin' to know him will lead to gettin' to honour him, givin' him the citizenship that it's to the everlastin' disgrace of the country he's been denied so long, and education, rights as a human bein', and the chance to learn this new system of society that's been dumped down in his country and so far done nuthen but wipe him out. The blackfeller aint a Negroid type. His colour's only skin-deep. Three cross-breedin's and you'll get the colour right out,

M

with never the risk of a throw-back. You're an example of
what can be done with the crossin', Sonny. And you aint
unique. I've seen hundreds of halfcastes just as fine of
face and form as you. And I reckon they'd've all been as
smart in the 'ead if they hadn't been treated like they was
half-bred dingoes. Look — down Anchor Bay there was a
full-blooded Binghi workin' as a missionary. He was a
parson, a full-blown one with a B.A. and all. And there's
another in Bulimba is a lawyer's clerk. Yes — and there's
a halfcaste boy what someone took out of a camp in Cooksland, got the Rhodes Scholarship, went to Oxford, come
back a full-blown engineer. His mother was a lubra same
as yours. No doubt there's more examples. If there aint —
well it's the fault not of the blackman but of the mean-
hearted white. Don't be ashamed of your Old People, Sonny.
Be proud. Boast of 'em. Take their case to the humane
people that'll help 'em. Be their spokesman. Be their lead-
er. Lead 'em to honour. Sit in parliament as their representative in the days that are soon to come. See? Well, put that
in your pipe and smoke it. Give's a drink Joe — I've rasped
me old throat raw."

Silence reigned for seconds. Old Andy drank, sighed,
set down his glass, smacked his lips.

Then Jack Ramble said quietly, "By cripes, Andy, that
was a great wongi."

"Hear him!" said old Andy with a laugh. "Speakin' the
Aboriginal tongue!"

They laughed. Norman looked at Ramble with shining
eyes.

Another silence, while Ramble with eager blue eyes and
Mooch with meaty red ones and Andy with misty grey
ones looked at Norman. Then Andy said, "Give's a good
Australian tune, Joe — one't expresses the Spirit of the
Land."

Mooch took up his concertina, fingered it for a moment,
then played a few bars, then, with a swing, began, singing
in a husky contralto:

> Oh when I'm dead don't bury me at all,
> But pickle my bones in alcohawl;
> Place a bottle of grog each end of me,
> And be assured I'll R.I.P.

They laughed heartily. Andy said, "That only expresses
the spirit that you live in the land in, Joe. Give's another
— one for the boy here."

Mooch glanced at Norman's spurred top-boots, fingered
for a moment, then set off again:

> Wrap me up in my stockwhip and blanket,
> And bury me deep down below,
> Where the dingoes and crows won't molest me,
> Way down where the coolibahs grow —

They laughed again. "Nix on your chyackin'," said Andy.
"Give's *Waltzin' Matilda.*"

Mooch drank first. Then he set the echoes ringing:

> Once a jolly swagman camped beside a billabong,
> Under the shade of a coolibah tree;
> And he sang as he sat and waited while his billy boiled,
> 'Who'll come a-waltin' Matilda with me?
> Waltzin' Matilda, Waltzin' Matilda,
> Who'll come a-waltzin' Matilda with me?'
> And he sang as he sat and waited while his billy boiled.
> 'Who'll come a-waltzin' Matilda with me?'

> Up came a jumbuck to drink at the billabong;
> Up jumped the swagman and grabbed it with glee;
> And he sang as he shoved that jumbuck in his tucker-
>   bag,
> 'You'll come a-waltzin' Matilda with me.
> Waltzin' Matilda, waltzin' Matilda,
> You'll come a-waltzin' Matilda with me.'
> And he sang as he shoved that jumbuck in his tucker-
>   bag,
> 'You'll come a-waltzin' Matilda with me.'

> Up came the Squatter, mounted on his thoroughbred.
> Up came the Troopers — one, two, three!
> 'Where'd you get that jumbuck you've got in your
>   tucker-bag?
> You'll come a-waltzin' Matilda with we.
> Waltzin' Matilda, waltzin' Matilda,
> You'll come a-waltzin' Matilda with we.
> Where'd you get that jumbuck you've got in your
>   tucker-bag?
> You'll come a-waltzin' Matilda with we.'

> Up jumped the swagman and dived into the billabong.
> 'You'll never take me alive!' cried he.
> And his ghost may be heard if you camp beside the
>   billabong,
> Singing, 'Who'll come a-waltzin' Matilda with me?

Diminuendo.

> Waltzin' Matilda, waltzin' Matilda,
> Who'll come a-waltzin' Matilda with me?'
> And his voice may be heard if you camp beside the
>   billabong,
> Singing — 'Who'll come a-waltzin' Matilda with —
>   me?'

Silence. The men were staring at the fire. Then Mooch reached for the glasses and in silence filled them. Then old Andy looked at Mooch and said, "Eh Joe — tell the boy what that musician feller told you about that song."

Mooch looked at him, then turned to Norman, cleared his throat, and said, "Aw — one time when I was at Southern Cross Island I run into an English musical coot, sorter perfessor of music. He heard me playin' *Waltzin' Matilda* in a pub. He said he'd heard it in the bush in various parts. He reckons it's a genuine folk-song. That's a song peculiar to a tribe of people y'know, one't expresses their feelin's. He says that this here Spirit of the Land that Andy mentioned is in it, both in the music and the words. You notice the two minutes' silence after it? Well, accordin' to this perfessor feller, and I can vouch for it meself, that's always observed by born Australians, because we sort of look on the Jolly Swagman as a cobber that's been martyred. Accordin' to the perfessor feller, we look on stray things knockin' round, such as sheep drinkin' at a billabong, or anybody else's chooks, and things like that, as public property, or rather property of the tribe, same's the Binghis do things that's knockin' round the bush. So the Jolly Swagman's the typical Australian, doin' just what he thinks is right, like a Binghi spearin' a kangaroo or somebody's bullock. And the Squatter and the Troopers are the outsiders, the imported people, the foreigners, what have a strong sense of property and a different way of looking at things. See?"

"There you are!" cried Andy, thumping Norman on the back. "What'd I tell you about the Great Bunyip gettin' us all down, eh?"

Norman laughed.

After a pause, Ramble said to Norman. "You stoppin' round here long?"

"No," said Norman. "I think I'll be gettin' away tomorrow."

"What's the hurry?"

"Well — I got a lot of work to do at home."

"Important man, eh?"

"As a matter of fact I want to finish up everything for the year before my cousin gets married."

"Cousin — what, Oscar's girl?"

"Yes. D'you know my uncle?"

Ramble looked down, blinking. After a while he answered, "Yes — but I haven't seen him for years. How is he?"

"Oh pretty good. Haven't you seen him since he came back?"

"No. I've been away myself. But I will go and see him one of these days. I must."

"What — you know him well, then?"

"Oh yes. I've intended going to see him for a long while. Never get the chance."

"I'll tell him," said Norman.

Ramble smiled slightly, and murmured, glancing at Mooch, "Yes."

After a moment Norman asked, "Did you know my father too?"

Ramble looked at him quickly, and after a slight hesitation answered, "Yes."

Norman felt slightly embarrassed. He looked down. After a moment Ramble asked. "D'you know where he is now?"

Norman looked up quickly and said, "Oh he's dead."

Ramble looked startled. "Dead?" he murmured.

"Yes," said Norman rather hesitantly, "he was killed at the war."

A pause. Then Mooch drew out his concertina and played very softly:

O let me like a soldier fall,
Upon some open plain —

They looked at him in surprise. He chuckled, reached for the bottle, poured himself a drink.

Then Andy yawned, and said to Norman, "Well Sonny — gettin' late."

Norman rose. The others did the same. Ramble shook hands with him warmly, saying, "Well — don't forget if you're out this way again, drop in. We'll be shiftin' out further all the time. But Andy'll tell you where to find us."

"Thanks," said Norman. "But I might be seein' you up home sometime, eh?"

"Most likely."

Norman then shook hands with Mooch, who blinked at
him as though he were in tears. As he was turning away,
Ramble, eyeing him closely, asked, "What d'you weigh,
Son?"

Norman looked surprised. After a moment he answered,
"Aw — somewhere about twelve-eight."

Ramble's eyes widened. Norman grinned, nodded, said,
"Mummuk," and went off after Andy.

Ramble stood staring after him. He was still staring,
now into darkness, when Mooch's concertina sighed heavily,
then began to play very softly:

> Oh don't you remember Black Alice, Ben Bolt,
> Black Alice so dusky and dark,
> That Warrego gin with a stick through her nose,
> And teeth like a Moreton Bay shark —

SPINNING OF FATE THE SPIDER

NORMAN remained proud of his Aboriginal heritage for
several weeks, during which he spent much breath in boasting about it to Oscar and Marigold and Steggles and the
people of the Siding and Cho Sek Ching and the natives.
Only Marigold and the people of the Siding seemed not to
understand him. The latter were merely amused. The former was bewildered at first, then rather impatient, then finally quite definitely impatient. It was Marigold who shattered his pride. She did so a few days before the departure
to Town for the wedding, when she suddenly found courage to tell him frankly what she had been trying with hints
to tell him for weeks, namely that she did not want him at
the wedding. She tried to tell him gently, pretending that
she considered him ineligible on account of the affair of
New Year's Eve. He said at once that she was lying, that
her reason was shame of his breed. He stormed. Oscar in-
tervened, at first in support of him, then in support of both,
finally in support of Marigold, to defend her from Norman's
fury. It all happened in an hour on a Tuesday night. They
were to catch the train to Town on the Friday. The wedding, which was to be a very elegant affair, was to take
place on the Monday, the Fifth of November, the day of

the departure of the ship that was to take the couple to Singapore. Next morning at breakfast, Oscar was informed by Cho Sek Ching that Norman had come to him at dawn and borrowed £10 from him and said that he was riding in to catch the train to the Melisande, where he would try to get work on the construction.

Norman did as he had said. That day he travelled to Copper Creek, where the train camped for the night as usual, then on to the Melisande next morning, Thursday, where he arrived at ten o'clock. Leaving his swag at the station, he went straight to the Loco-Shops to ask for a job as a fitter. He saw the Loco-Foreman, who received him brusquely, heard his preliminary statements while rudely eyeing him from head to foot, then, as he was producing his certificates, snappishly informed him that he had no place for a coloured-man, and walked away. Norman retired fuming, to idle about the railway-yards, debating what he had best do next, till he noticed that the train by which he had come was on the point of starting on the return journey. He lounged back to the station.

The station was merely an iron shed, fronted with a veranda and floored with cinders. A crowd was gathered in the shed and about the three passenger-cars. Norman stood watching from a distance, most of the time thinking glumly of Oscar and Marigold, who would board the train next day.

The bell rang. Passengers climbed aboard. The guard, clad in black shirt and khaki trousers and a wide puggaree'd hat like a trooper's, came out of the office bawling, "Carm on now there — get a move on. All aboard!"

Then Norman saw Heather. She was standing on the platform of a car nearly opposite him, talking to someone on the ground. She was clad in white, with a wide floppy straw hat, and carried a suitcase and a sunshade. For a moment he stared at her bright flushed face, then pushed through the crowd to her. "Hello Heather!" he cried.

She looked. "Why — Norman!" she cried, and stepped down to take his hand.

"Where you off — Town?" he asked.

"Yes. What you doing here?"

He hesitated. "Come to look for a job," he answered.

"Why?" she asked, with grey eyes looking into his. "What's wrong at home?"

The guard whistled, raised his green flag. Norman looked towards the engine.

"Come on up," said Heather. "They stop the other side of the bridge. You can get off there and walk back. It's not far. I want to talk to you."

When he reached her side he said, "I was down here about six weeks ago — out Gunamiah. I passed through on the way back, and dropped in to see you, but you were up in Town."

The engine whistled. The train began to move.

"Yes," she said. "I heard you were down. You met — Jack Ramble, didn't you?"

"Yes. You know him?"

She was looking into his eyes again. "Yes — well," she answered, then added, "He likes you."

Norman smiled and said, "I like him too. Most prob'ly I'll see him again now."

After a pause she asked, "What's the trouble at home?" Hesitantly he told her.

"Tcht! Tcht! What paltriness!" she said.

"They've left you out of the wedding too," he said. "Old Andy McRandy told me about you being our auntie."

She grimaced and nodded. Looking out on the vista of humpies and tents and tree-stumps, she said, "Oscar's a fool." She looked back at him and added, "But it'll be better with Marigold gone. You and Oscar'll be happier."

The train was on the bridge, clanging through the girders.

Heather shouted to Norman, "Where are you going to camp?"

"Down the river here, with the mob," he answered. "I spent the night here when I was down this way before."

"You got a tent?"

"Don't need one."

"You will soon. The Wet'll soon be here. Look — I'll be back next train. If you haven't got fixed up then, I'll give you a shakedown at my place. What sort of job're you after?"

He told her of his interview with the Loco-Foreman.

"The pig!" she cried. "That's Bill Wrench. I'll have a word with him about that. Go over his head. Go to Joe Pointer, the Works Manager. Tell him who you are and all about yourself. I'll bet none of the men they've got in the Loco've got certificates like you have. Demand a job. Tell him you'll go to the Engineer if he don't give you satisfaction. Tell him you'll write South and make a barney."

The train stopped amid the ruins of what had been the

old settlement of Melisande River. Two old men and a herd of goats were waiting.

"Thanks Heather," said Norman. "You're a great sport. If you see Dad and Marigold, don't tell 'em anything I've told you about not getting a job."

"I'll give 'em a piece of my mind about the wedding, anyway. Now look after yourself. If things go wrong, go out to — to Jack Ramble. He'll help you."

The engine whistled. Norman took Heather's hand. "Goodbye, Heather," he said warmly. "See you when you come back."

"Goodbye, Norman. Now go straight and see Joe Pointer."

The train was moving. Norman alighted, and stood and waved her out of sight. Then he returned to the construction-camp, and went to a Chinese eating-house for dinner. From there he went to the office of the Works Manager. He got a very different reception from Mr Pointer, but no more satisfaction, than he did from Bill Wrench, the Loco-Foreman. Mr Pointer received him with courtesy, and listened politely to all he had to say, even to his threats to complain to the Engineer and to the authorities in the South if a place were not found for him, then begged him to be patient, saying that to dismiss a whiteman for a coloured-man, no matter how superior the latter might be in the matter of competence, would only cause trouble, then went on to talk vaguely about openings that would occur with the establishment of a new depot down the road. Obviously he was a temporizer. But Norman was well pleased simply with the treatment he got. He went away thinking Mr Pointer a fine fellow, got his swag from the station, and went on down to the river to find a camping-place.

He returned to the railway-yards at half-past five to meet Frank McLash, who, as he had learnt from the station-master, was expected to return with his ballast-train at about that time. He had a parcel for Frank from his mother.

Frank brought his train in at six. Ket was with him on the engine, black of face and arms, clad in dungarees, and filthy singlet, with a sweat-rag round his neck. He it was whom Norman saw first as he approached the engine. And Ket saw him, and stared from the cab with white-ringed eyes. Norman's feet faltered. He had no wish to come in contact with Ket again. He turned aside, and

watching from the corner of his eye, began to walk down
the train. Then Frank looked out, gaped, waved a hand.
Norman turned, raised the parcel, and cried, "Something
for you. See you after." Frank nodded.

They met in the twilight outside the Loco-Foreman's office as Frank came out from signing off.

"What-o," said Frank, shaking hands with him, "What
you doin' down this way?"

"Lookin' for a job," said Norman. "Here's a parcel from
your Ma."

"Thanks," said Frank; and feeling the parcel he added
with a sooty grin, "You needn't've troubled bringin' it. It's
only epsom salts and socks and singlets.   She's always
sendin' 'em."

Norman chuckled.

"Well where you off to now?" asked Frank.

"Nowhere partic'lar — only over to get tea at the
Chow's."

"I'll come with you. Come on over home first, and have
a drink. I wanter wash up. What you say — yous lookin'
for a job?"

Norman avoided explaining why he had come down,
though he knew Frank would soon learn the reason from
his mother, who he guessed had divined it. He merely told
how he had been treated by the men to whom he had
applied for work.

"Garn!" said Frank, upon hearing what Joe Pointer had
said. "That's all bulsh about trouble if he takes on a
coloured-man. What about Charlie Ket? Aint he coloured?
He got the job of a whiteman — feller't was put off for
boozin' heavy on the job. And what'd he know about injins?"

"How'd he get the job?" asked Norman.

"I got it for him. He was workin' as a labourer in the
yard here. He wanted to come with me from the start.
Said he'd make it worth me while. So when Jack Bender
was put off — that's the fireman I had before — terrible
booze-hound — I fixed it for him with Bill Wrench, who's
a good cobber of mine. You went the wrong way about it,
anyway, Norm. You can't get any sorter job down here
without payin' for it. You oughter started negotiations with
Bill be offerin' a bit of a present."

"Is that a fact?"

"Too right. Everybody wants their cut. Charlie paid Bill
ten quid down for his job, and gives him a quid a week

out of his pay. And he give me another tenner for helpin'
him, and gives me a quid a week too — just friendly, like,
o' course."

"Can't have much left for himself," said Norman.

"Don't you b'lieve it. He knocks up an average of eight
quid a week."

Norman whistled.

"I get twelve," said Frank. "You oughter get even more
as a fitter, with your ticket. And be cripes they need a
decent fitter on the job, I can tell you. These blunny old
injins want rubbin' out and buildin' all over again. The
bosses oughter jump at you. They got three fitters on the
job now; but none of 'em's properly qualified. I could do
a better job meself — and often have to, too. And soon
they'll be wantin' more men for the noo depot they're goin'
to put up at Bonnidinka. Did you tell Bill about the way
you fixed the mail-train injin that time?"

"No," said Norman. "The cow wouldn't even look at me
ticket. He just said he didn't want coloured-men."

"Don't you b'lieve it. Look 'ere. I know what. I know for
a fact they'd dump one feller they got workin' in the Loco
if they could find someone good to take his place. That's
Greasy Grimes.   He's a cleaner.   Terrible booze-hound.
Drinks the blunny methylated. You oughter be able to get
his job all right. That'd be the start. You'd soon show 'em
what yous worth as a fitter, and be boss of the shop in no
time. Course it's night work. D'you mind that?"

"Oh I'll take on anything," said Norman.

They were at Frank's house, which was one of a group of
iron huts that served as barracks for railway-men. Now it
was dark. There was a light in the house, and, as Norman
saw as he stepped on to the veranda, a person — Ket.
Norman halted.

"Come on in," said Frank.

"No," said Norman. "Ket's in there. I don't want to meet
that slant-eyed barsted."

Frank grinned and said in the same tone, "He don't
wanter meet you neither. Most prob'ly he'll walk out if you
come in."

"No — I'll wait for you," said Norman, drawing back.

Frank went in chuckling. While he was washing he told
Ket that Norman was outside. Ket's queer eyes twitched.
Frank saw, and grinned to himself, knowing how furiously
Ket hated Norman.

After a while Ket growled accusingly, "What you cobberin' up with that yeller shisser for?"

"I aint cobberin' up with him," said Frank through suds. "He's after a job. I think I can see a chance of makin' a bit of money be gettin' him one."

"What — in the Loco?" asked Ket in evident alarm.

"Yes — but'd be night-work. You wouldn't have to meet him."

"Oh I aint frighten' that yeller barsted," snapped Ket.

Frank grinned into the towel and said, "Oh I know that. But I can see a chance of makin' a tenner out of him. And be jees I need it pretty floppin' bad! I owe that lousy barsted Con the Greek forty quid now. And I aint got a chance to win it back with all these jiggering' damn dunns and blunny graspin' shysterin' barsteds grabbin' me pay soon's I blunny well get it."

Frank said to Norman as soon as he rejoined him, "Yeah, Norm — I think I can work the horrickle for you all right. You don't mind payin' for it, do you?"

"Oh no," said Norman. "I don't mind. How much d'you reckon it'll be?"

"Well, course a tenner down. Then there'll be sumpen a week to Bill. I won't take nuthen till you get fixed up as a fitter. I owe you four or five quid as it is. You can sling us a few quid when you get set."

"Good-o," said Norman.

"Well when can you let's have the tenner? I'll make sure of the job by plankin' it right down in front of Bill."

"Matter of fact," said Norman. "I've only got nine quid to me name. I only brought a tenner. And I'll want a bit to live on."

"Oh you can get credit easy enough if yous got a job. Well give's eight quid. I'll put in the rest. You can square up with me later."

"Want it right away?"

"Just as well. I'll go'n see Bill first thing the mornin'."

Norman parted with the money without a thought that the deal might be a bad one. In fact, so pleased was he with Frank that he scarcely noticed the way in which he wormed out of paying for his share of the cost of the meal they ate at Charlie Wing Song's, nor the way in which he dodged away when Charlie tried to discuss the matter of a debt with him. Nor did he find cause for mistrust in the fact that during the half-hour or so they spent together after leaving the eating-house, while lounging together under the

trees outside Jerry Rotgutt's shanty, Frank talked most of
the time with evident envy and admiration of a certain
criminal of the City of Batman whose recent successful exploits in grand-scale robbery had become notorious even in
Capricornia. But then Frank had often talked admiringly
of criminals to him before.

At eight o'clock Frank said that he had to meet a man
at Heather's place, the Transcontinental Hotel, and cunningly reminded Norman that he was prevented by law from
accompanying him. Norman strolled that far with him, then,
having arranged to meet him at the station at seven next
evening, left him, and thinking him the best of fellows, went
down to his camp. Frank slipped through the shanty, past
several men to whom he owed money, to the bakery at the
rear, in which rambling building Con the Greek ran a
Crown-and-Anchor game. He lost Norman's £8 to Con in
as many minutes.

Frank's intentions were not wholly dishonest. Knowing
how badly a competent fitter was needed in the Loco, and
having great respect for Norman's competence in that direction, he believed when he took the money that he could
get Norman a job on his bare merits. He thought he would
only have to tell the foreman how Norman had repaired the
engine of the mail-train to interest him. Thus he regarded
the money as his own, and suffered no qualms of conscience
when he lost it, nor indeed when subsequently he was
brought to book for having done so. His conscience was not
highly developed. When next morning he learnt that the
Loco-Foreman would not take on a yeller-feller of any sort
at any price, all he gathered from the situation was that his
luck was out. He was not at the station to meet Norman
that night, nor at home when Norman went there later. He
was dodging about waiting for his luck to turn.

Norman was waiting for the ballast-train when it came
in at one o'clock on Saturday afternoon. But he missed
Frank, because his attention was distracted by Jack Ramble
and Joe Mooch, who climbed down from the engine as he
approached it and greeted him heartily and took him away
to have dinner at the Transcontinental Hotel. He did not
see Frank again till next morning, when he went to his
house and caught him in bed. Frank was very affable. He
leapt out of bed and fetched a bottle of whiskey, and while
pouring it said that the job was secured but that the man
whose place Norman was to take had yet to be got rid of
in some cunning way. He asked Norman to be patient, and

advised him not to come to the Loco again till the foreman should send for him, lest the victim of their machinations or his friends should divine their intent and forestall it. Norman was reassured. He left in good spirits, prepared to wait for more definite news till Thursday, which was pay-day, when, according to Frank, Greasy Grimes would most likely be paid off. They were to meet on Thursday at the station.

That night Wet Season opened with a thunderstorm. Norman spent several miserable hours with about a hundred other men, lying on wet bark under a rake of flat-top waggons that stood on a siding near the bridge. It was not only the rain that made the situation miserable for him. Several men near him who had laughed and jested with him as with each other at first, practically ignored him after his face was revealed to them by the light of a match.

Monday and Tuesday passed slowly and for the most part miserably for Norman. He spent most of his time alone, occupied either with fishing or bathing in the river, or with browsing over several books he had brought with him, amongst which was the Rubaiyat cast aside by Marigold, which pleased him greatly, or with walking in the bush, practising what he had learnt of bushcraft during his sojourn with the Mullanmullaks, which also gave him much pleasure. Not that he wished to be alone. He feared to make advances to men of superior type lest he should be rebuffed, and most of the time preferred to stand aloof from the inferior ones who made advances to him. During that time he saw Frank but twice, when he was rushing somewhere in a great hurry. On Tuesday night it rained again. On Wednesday night he spent his last shilling. He was looking forward to Thursday with impatience, but not so much because it was to be the day of definite news from Frank as because it was to be that of the return of Heather, for whom he found himself almost yearning.

On Thursday morning he went to the station at nine o'clock. He lounged about alone till the smoke of the train appeared above the bush beyond the river, when, while he was gazing absently in that direction, he was accosted by a Greek, a short podgy fellow, clad in a dirty brightly-striped silk shirt and greasy blue Oxford bags and sand-shoes, out of which his grimy great toes peeped, and a threadbare black velour hat, who came up to him smiling brightly and with hand outstretched, saying, "Ello — ello! Ow are ya Norm?"

Norman stared.

"My name's Con," said the Greek, still with hand out-stretched. "I use be workin' up de orspidals."

Norman realized that it was the famous Con the Greek; but he merely grunted, "Uh?"

Still Con held his fat hand out. "You dunno me," he said chuckling. "But I knows you all right. An' you knows some-ones us both knows — young Tocky an' young Christobel — eh?"

Norman gaped.

"Put it dere!" cried Con, thrusting the hand right at him. He took it limply.

"Dem two kidses got sent away, y' know," said Con. "Got copped out wid boys same nights dat yous seen 'em down de beach."

Norman cleared his throat and asked, "How d'you mean?"

Con evidently thought that Norman's dealings with the girls were confined to that one meeting on the beach. He explained how they had been caught as they came home from the party and what had happened to them subsequent-ly. Then he went on to suggest, speaking as though he had known Norman for years, that he should go to the Pro-tector and offer to marry one of the girls, preferably Christobel, who was the elder, and thus effect her release from exile. Norman, feeling greatly alarmed, kept his counsel. Con was still extolling the virtues of the girls as likely wives when the train came in. Norman left him abruptly to go to Heather, with whom he went home.

When Heather heard about Norman's dealings with Frank she cried out in amazement, called him a fool, told him that Frank was an out-and-out rogue, advised him to go to Bill Wrench at once and find out what had been done. He was alarmed; but he would not follow her advice; he said that he would wait and see what Frank had to say when they met in the evening. This he did. He waited for Frank for an hour, then went to his house, then hunted the settle-ment for him. Frank was not to be found.

Next morning he went to Bill Wrench and learnt what Frank had learnt a week before, namely that the man would not take on any sort of yeller-feller at any price. Wrench was even ruder than before. He cut Norman's talk about Frank short by saying that it was no business of his, and walked away. Norman had to restrain himself from rush-ing after him and teaching him better manners with his fists.

Heather now advised him to go to the police. Furious as he was, he could not bring himself to do that. He decided to deal with Frank privately that evening. He spent the rest of the day in the abandoned settlement across the river, expressing his feelings with a hammer on building-material that he was collecting for the purpose of adding a wing to Heather's shanty. At five o'clock he returned to the camp, but not to the Transcontinental. He lounged about the railway yards till the ballast-train appeared, then took up a position near the Loco so that he might be able to confront Frank as he came from the office after signing off.

Frank came out of the office with Ket. Norman slipped up and appeared beside him suddenly. He and Ket turned and gaped. Norman's face was expressionless.

"Er — ello!" gasped Frank, grinning feebly. "W-where'd you spring from?"

"I want a word with you," said Norman icily.

"Er — what's wrong?" asked Frank.

"You know blunny well what's wrong."

"Eh?" asked Frank, blinking at him. Then he looked about, nervously, like a trapped thief looking for a chance to escape. Several men were near, some, among whom was a policeman, standing in a group within a few yards of them. Ket moved slowly on.

"I said you know blunny well what's wrong," snapped Norman. "Where's my eight quid?"

"What — don't you want the job?" asked Frank, still blinking.

"You know damn well I can't get it. I want my money back."

"Why — what's bitin' you?" asked Frank, a trifle impatiently.

"Don't frig about. Give's my money or there'll be trouble."

"I don't get you," said Frank, shooting a glance at the policeman, who was idly eyeing them. "You give me the money to pay for a job for you —"

"And you couldn't get me the job."

Frank looked at him, then at the buckle of his belt, and said, "Who says I can't?"

"Bill Wrench."

Frank blinked rapidly at the buckle, then looked up and asked, "You — been to him?"

"Course. Think I'm soft?"

"What?" asked Frank with a weak show of indignation. "You distrusted a feller?"

"I wouldn't trust you with a thrip'ny-bit."

"Eh — eh — easy!" snapped Frank. "Careful what you're sayin', young feller."

"Aw for gawdsake!" cried Norman. "Don't futt about. I want my money — or by cripes I'll make a row. Cough up!"

For a moment Frank was silent. Then he looked after Ket, who was lounging near, and cried, "Eh Charl — come 'ere."

"We don't want him," snapped Norman.

"Yes we do," said Frank. "By cripes we do. You aint gunner put nuthen over me, boy. Eh Charl — just a minute — this's important."

"What you mean put nuthen over you?" demanded Norman.

Ket came lounging back, eyeing Norman slantwise.

"Just what I say," said Frank loudly and cheerfully. Then he turned to the policeman and shouted, "Eh Barney — Barney McCrook — just a tick."

Norman looked surprised. Turning from eyeing the approaching policeman, he demanded, "What's your game?"

"You don't come the blunny bounce on me," said Frank. "No — by cripes you don't."

"Eh?" demanded Norman. "By cripes, McLash, if you don't pay up that money —"

"What's the trouble?" asked Trooper McCrook.

"Feller comin' the bounce," said Frank, and turned to Ket and added, "He's come dunnin' me already for that eight lousy quid I borrowed off of him only a week ago —"

"Borrowed!" hooted Norman. "Why you lyin' dirty sod, I give it to you to get me a job!"

"Aw be jiggered!" snapped Frank. "You lent it to me." He moved as though to depart in disgust.

"Well if you aint a low-down lyin' spit of a thing!" howled Norman.

Frank swung round and bellowed, "Say that again!"

"Go easy!" snapped McCrook. "Now come on, what's the strength of this?"

Frank cried, "This feller 'ere — a week ago he lent me eight quid —"

"I didn't!" roared Norman. "I give it to him to get me a job —"

Frank roared louder, "I asked him for the lend of it —

and the sod said he would if I'd try to get him a job —
no question of givin' at all —"

"You dirty blunny floppin' liar —"

"Cut that out!" bawled McCrook.

"Ask Charl Ket," said Frank. "Ask him. He's a witness.
He heard what was said."

McCrook turned to Ket, who answered readily, "That's
right. Last Thursd'y it was. Frank put it on him for the
lend of a tenner —"

"By jees —" began Norman.

"Shut up!" roared McCrook.

"Frank put it on him for a tenner," continued Ket. "He
asked Frank if he'd put in a word for him with Bill Wrench
to get him a job in the Loco. Frank said he would, seein'
they was old cobbers. Then the yeller-feller —"

"Don't you call me a yeller-feller, you slant-eyed runt,"
roared Norman, lunging forward.

"Shut up!" bawled McCrook, and hurled him back.

Ket went on, "Then the yeller-feller lent him eight quid,
and said it didn't matter when he paid up, seein' they was
old cobbers. And Frank tried all roads to get him a job.
He's still tryin'. Ask Bill Wrench. The yeller-feller's been
quite satisfied till tonight —"

"It's a lie!" roared Norman. "He deliberately asked me
for the money to pay for the job. He's been swingin' me
off for a week. It's only when I asked Bill Wrench that I
got the strong of the sod —"

"Aw spit!" snapped Frank.

"If you don't pay up I'll give you in charge," roared
Norman.

"And if you don't shut up I'll fill your blunny eye," roared Frank.

"Shut up! Shut up! Both of you," bawled McCrook.

"Take him in charge," roared Norman.

"What for?" asked McCrook.

"For robbin' me. It was barefaced blunny robbery. I asked him if he could get me a job — No I never — it was him
suggested everything — I give him eight pound —"

"I can't do anything," said McCrook.

"But I want my blunny money!" howled Norman.

"You'll have to take him to court then," said McCrook.
"It's a private matter."

"But the barsted robbed me —"

"Call me a barsted?" hooted Frank.

"Yes — and I'll call you a dirty, thievin', sneakin', lyin'

dingo-barsted too!" howled Norman. "And by cripes, if you don't pay me back that money I'll just about blunny well murder you —"

"Ere!" bawled McCrook, getting between them.

"I will!" howled Norman, struggling. "I'll blunny well kill the cow —"

McCrook swung him round and shoved him hard, yelling, "Get off home —".

Norman turned and yelled, "By golly —"

"Get off home — go on, I tell you — nick off — both you! If there's any more trouble I'll run you both in."

Norman went home ramping.

Next day Jack Ramble and Joe Mooch came up to spend the week-end. When Ramble heard Norman's tale he told him to leave dealing with Frank to him, saying that he was on very friendly terms with the fellow and was sure that he could induce him to return the money. Then he offered to take him back to the head of the road with him on Monday and place him in his gang. Later in the day Norman learnt that Ramble and Mooch and Frank intended to start a gambling-school at the head of the road, a dinner-hour affair that was to be conducted aboard Frank's train, which would make a special trip to pick up clients from among the large number of men at work on the last two or three miles of the road. He learnt that from Mooch. Not long after he did so, he came upon Ramble and Heather in Heather's private sitting-room, arguing, and heard enough of what they said to gather that Heather was averse to Ramble's gambling and that Ramble was hopelessly in debt. He was not surprised to find them thus intimate. On Thursday night he had learnt from Con the Greek, who had sought him out again, that they were lovers.

That night at about eight o'clock, Norman was setting out for a stroll, when he came face to face with Frank on the cinder-strewn footpath under the veranda of the store next to the Transcontinental. They nearly collided. Frank was with Ket and two other young men. Though Norman's blood began to boil at once, he turned aside, and would have ignored Frank utterly, since he had decided to leave dealing with him to Ramble. But as he turned he heard someone snicker in the group. He looked round quickly, to find Frank and Ket looking back at him and leering. He lost his temper, wheeled about, stepped up to Frank, and demanded through his teeth, "What's the matter with you?"

Frank eyed him defensively for a moment, then sniffed and turned away.

"Ere — wait on!" snarled Norman, and seized his arm.

Frank turned on him with dilated eyes, then glanced at the black hand on his khaki sleeve, then freed himself with a wrench.

For a moment they glared at each other. Then Frank turned away again. Norman grabbed him by a shoulder, spun him round. Frank snorted, struck out. Norman dodged, struck back, hit Frank in the ribs, hard. Frank gasped, staggered back. For a moment he stood off, glaring; then he snarled, "You up-jumped yeller-bellied spit — you would, wouldjer!" He flew at Norman and struck him a terrific blow in the chest. Simultaneously Norman smote him in the mouth. Frank bellowed, dropped his hard blue chin to shoulder, spat out blood, and charged. Norman went back to the iron wall of the store before a hurricane of blows. Men rushed out of the store. Men came flying up the road. The cry went up, "A fight — a fight!" Dogs could not have responded quicker.

Norman, breathless, spattered with blood, was buffeted against the wall for seconds. At last he smothered head in arms, sagged at the knees as though falling. The fists of lusting Frank crashed like bricks against the iron. Then up came Norman like a spring, caught Frank a terrific uppercut. Frank shot back. The crowd howled its appreciation.

Norman rushed after his advantage, pounded Frank out to the road. They splashed and slithered in the mud. Hiss and biff and thud and crack! While the crowd rocked round them. Under his guard, Frank, under his guard! That's the stuff boy! Use y'left, Darkey, use y'left! Don't be afraid the big bull-barsted! Belt blue hell out of him! Ere — you — push me again I'll dong ya! Y' would? Be jees I would! Rock it into him Darkey — you got him now!

Frank was falling back. He fetched up against the fence of the railway-yards, crying for breath. Then he rallied, struck with desperate purpose, fought his way back to the road. Norman barged into Ket, who was waiting for him. Ket kicked him in the right leg behind the knee, shot his leg forward. He lost his balance, staggered against Frank, who struck him on the jaw and knocked him flat. Frank blundered over him, fell on hands and knees, rose and turned in time to knock him down again. Norman lay on his back, heaving, goggling, while Frank reeled above him,

slavering, dripping sweat and mud and blood. The crowd
was in ecstasy, heaving, hoarse.

A moment. Then Norman drew in his legs, heaved up
to haunches, and snarling, shot up and smashed Frank in
the face. Frank staggered back. Norman flew after him,
pounding furiously. Frank reeled about, smothering. Again
he rallied, bellowed hoarsely, struck out. But his strength
was gone. He staggered after his blows, struck blindly, neglected guard. Norman struck him in the face — Thud!
— and again — Thud! — while the man-pack roared and
heaved — and again — Thud!

Frank was tottering, sobbing. He fell back cowering into
the crowd, who flung him back to Norman, to whom he clung,
hissing bloody spittal in his bloody black face. Distorted face
to distorted face they heaved about, tearing each other's
flesh with nails. Then Frank brought up his knee. Norman
gasped, heaved out of his clutches, doubled up. Frank
caught him a blow on the side of the head, sent him face
down to the mud.

A moment — while Frank staggered, sobbing, with brok-
en bloody hands hanging paralysed before him — while the
man-pack crouched, goggling and clawing — while Norman
lay convulsing in the mud.

Then someone yelled, "Foul! — Barsted knee'd him!"

Babble of voices.

"Down him!" screeched a voice.

There was a movement. Frank croaked, turned, butted
into the crowd with his bullet head, and fled.

Norman was raised, borne to the footpath, half-stripped,
massaged. Chief among his attendants were Ramble and
Mooch, who, when he could stand, took him home between
them. Heather found him on the back veranda washing,
stripped to the waist. She came rushing from the bar, having just heard the news. At first she was horrified by the
sight of him, could only stare, while silently he laved in
bloody water. Then she began to scold him weakly. Finally,
when he looked at her dully from out of the towel, she
turned away, dropped face to hands and burst into tears.

§

Monday dawned dripping and steamy from a night of
torrential rain. At seven o'clock the lengthsman set out
from the depot on his motor-trolley as usual to inspect the
new road. He got no further than the 223-Mile, where he
found the rails hanging in the air over a swirling yellow

stream about two chains wide that filled a depression once
bridged by a tall embankment. He was glad, being loath
to go further, because the road got bumpier as one went
along, and he was suffering a recovery from a week-end
jag. He took a long pole from his machine, fixed a red
flag to it, then strode back the number of paces prescribed
by *Rules and Regulations,* and set up the pole on the track.
Then he staggered back, took a long pull from his bottle,
and sat down to wait for the train.

The first train left the depot at half-past seven. Frank
McLash, swollen and bruised of face and touchy of temper,
was driving. Ket was feeding the fire, and annoying Frank
by singing merrily in the joy of having won something like
£200 from Con during the week-end. Jack Ramble and
Joe Mooch were lounging, one on his haunches, the other
on a stool, against the tender behind Frank, watching him
with expressionless faces, thinking their own thoughts about
him, while he from time to time turned round and bawled
at them something concerning the plans for their gambling-
school. And sitting up on the tender on the coal on the
other side of the cab was Paddy Pickandle, the Roadmaster,
scowling because Frank, whom he had rather bluntly asked
to settle a long-standing loan, had insulted him. Paddy had
been caused to fear that Frank might not honour his obligation by hearing of the way in which he had dealt with
Norman. And the success of the way in which he had
dealt with Norman was just what caused Frank to decide
to deal with all his creditors similarly. Paddy was sitting
in discomfort on the coal because Frank, whose authority
on the footplate was like that of a captain on the bridge
of a ship, had ordered him to go there and hold his blunny
tongue.

The engine was at the rear of the train, pushing it. This
was usual with trains running on the new road, because, un-
settled as the road was yet, derailments were frequent, and
it was simpler to rectify the derailment of a waggon or
two than of a locomotive. The train consisted of a rake of
about twelve long bogey-wheeled flat-top waggons, which
were loaded with rails and steel sleepers. On top of the
load sat upwards of a hundred men who were returning to
work, most of them on the foremost waggons. Norman,
also swollen and bruised of face, was aboard, riding on the
second waggon from the engine, taking care of the belongings of Ramble and Mooch, who had only gone to the engine when called by Frank. The shunter was at the further

end of the leading waggon, from where he watched the road ahead, and, when necessary, signalled directions to the engine with flags.

Creature of her puffed-eyed captain's wilful mood, the train came bowling along at dangerous speed. The shunter saw the lengthsman's flag while it was still a long way off. He rose and raised his own red flag. According to *Rules and Regulations,* Frank, who ought to have been watching the road, either through his own eyes or those of his fireman, should have responded to the signal with a whistle, then slowed down. Frank did not see the signal. At the moment, like a mariner looking ior his latitude, he was taking a sight of the sun along an inclined bottle of beer. And his fireman and prospective business-partners were watching him, awaiting a turn with his instrument; and Paddy Pickandle, whose mouth was full of soot and cinders, was watching with hopeless envy.

The shunter became anxious, leapt up on a stack of rails, lost his balance, fell overboard. Passengers who saw the shunter or the danger also leapt up. Then everyone on the first four waggons leapt up, saw what lay ahead, and turned to the engine and roared like a sudden storm.

Frank heard the roar, and glancing through the bull's-eye down the train, saw the gesticulating crowd, but not the danger, because the crowd was obstructing his view. He supposed that a gang who had neglected to tell the shunter, or about whom the shunter had neglected to tell him, wished to alight. Much he cared about that. It was the shunter's business. And the shunter was no friend of his. That it was nothing serious he was convinced because he could not see the shunter's flag.

Then Ramble saw the shunter flash past splashing in a muddy pool, and yelled and pointed. Frank looked back, peering over the tender, saw, chuckled. Much he cared. That was also the shunter's business.

Then, like rats from a sinking ship, half the passengers of that ill-fated vessel whose captain spotted latitude while breakers lay ahead, leapt overboard. Ket saw them from the bull's-eye on his side, yelled, then saw the danger ahead, gaped at it for a moment, then shrieked and leapt at the throttle. Frank only saw Ket's action. Being ever jealous of command, he caught the wrist of the grimy hand that would have shut off steam, and flung it away.

Paddy Pickandle had seen everything. He had been sitting transfixed. Then he leapt from the coal bawling. Ket was howling. Frank looked ahead again, saw, yelped as though kicked, seized throttle in one hand and handle of the air-brake in the other, and stopped his pounding drivers dead.

Even had Frank taken the utmost care in stopping, he could not have saved the leading waggons from destruction. But had he taken a little more than he did he might not have lost any of the lives for which he was responsible. For all the passengers on the leading waggons had jumped, to sustain no worse injuries than broken ribs and limbs. As it was, the couplings of the waggons near the engine could not stand the sudden strain imposed by rushing heavy-laden brethren ahead and locked-wheeled engine at the rear. The couplings linking the second and third waggons snapped under Norman's nose. The rest of the train, with its tons of iron and steel and flesh and blood and bone, rushed on to destruction. Few of the remaining passengers had time or wits to realize their peril. The first waggon brought down the hanging rails, plunged head-first into the stream, upended with the second heaving over it. The rest piled up on them — *crash!* — *crash!* — *crash!* — Terrific din! — As though they played a giant's game of hi-cockalorum-jig.

§

In the 223-Mile Smash eight men were killed and sixteen badly injured. Fortunately — that is in the opinion of the majority left to discuss it — six of the dead were only Greeks, and most of the injured were the same. Frank and Ket and Paddy Pickandle and Jack Ramble and Joe Mooch and the shunter were taken to the police-station and questioned and detained for several hours while communication was made with Town. Paddy Pickandle was in a highly excited state. He told the truth and more. The shunter also had much to say, though he was feeling very depressed, having sustained in his fall a broken wrist, a sprained ankle, a gash in the head, and a fractured rib. Ramble and Mooch said very little, and nothing to incriminate the crew. Ket flew into a violent rage when Paddy spoke out. He had to be restrained. Frank, dazed throughout the journey back from the scene of the disaster, when questioned broke down and wept. Shattered was his precious dream of driving transcontinental trains. Gone for ever was all the hope of his ever standing again on a footplate: Of a certainty he would be occupied for the next year or two or more behind prison-walls. And it was likely that Ket, who shared his responsibility for the lives lost, would bear him company. At last they were all released, with instructions to report at the police-station daily till the inquest.

The Greeks of the settlement were infuriated. They talked of lynching the murderers of their brothers, but not loudly, lest the brothers of the murderers should hear. If there had been a lynching of Frank and Ket at the hands of the Greek community, there certainly would have been another of Ramble and Mooch at the hands of their hungry gang. For as no attempt was being made to repair the damaged road so that trains might pass and the construction be resumed, it was being said definitely that the work had stopped for good, as it had been rumoured it might for weeks past.

If Ramble and Mooch had not paid their men, they had fed them, and had kept them hoping. But their rations had been scattered in the train-smash. Their hopes were dashed when they trudged up starving to the depot to see what had gone wrong and learnt what was being said. They sought out their masters and demanded some sort of security for the future. Their masters had already been sought by demanding store-keepers. And soon they were being sought by officers of the Labour Council, who, having no fear that they might lose something by speaking out, spoke out in no uncertain terms. These miserable workmen, who had previously been regarded as blacklegs by the Council, suddenly became its darlings. Ramble and Mooch at length became so embarrassed that they hid. Nor were they alone in their condition. Nor were their workmen alone in theirs. A week after the disaster, one hundred and twenty-seven men informed the Council that they were owed by seven contracting firms the sum of £14,000. A day or two later the Council summoned the seven firms to court.

But taking the community generally, the rumour that work had ceased completely caused small regret. The depraving influences of the Wet were at work. Most men had come to think that it would be a shame to open that happy land to fizzling tourists and touts for real-estate.

While this was going on, Norman was earning his board and lodging and a little money by building the new wing to Heather's shanty. He spent the money with Con the Greek. He still did not wish to go home, though he had received a humble letter from Oscar asking him to do so. He decided to wait till Christmas.

Ramble and Mooch came out of hiding on Tuesday, the Twenty-seventh of November, and said that they were going up to Town to consult a lawyer with respect to the impending case with the Labour Council. Norman knew that Ramble had had a long talk with Heather about whatever he had in mind. And it was easy to see that she was worried about him. Ramble and Mooch were going up by the goods-train. Norman accompanied them to the station, and learnt on the way that Ramble intended to drop off at the Caroline, where the goods would meet the down-coming mail, and where he would most likely meet Oscar, with whom he would stay till the mail returned. Norman was surprised. This was the first time that Ramble had mentioned Oscar to him since the meeting at Gunamiah. He himself had refrained from making mention of his uncle, because, when he had spoken about Ramble to Oscar after coming home from meeting him, Oscar had said that he had never heard of the man. Thus he regarded the matter of Ramble's knowing Oscar as a delicate one. He had spoken to Heather about it. She had told him that most likely Oscar's memory was failing him. But now that his curiosity was roused again, he told Ramble what Oscar had said. Ramble smiled with his fine blue eyes, leaned towards him, and told him in a disarming way that Oscar had known him under another name. He had no chance to ask questions. Ramble had scarcely told him this when Frank McLash appeared, slinking round a stack of construction materials near the station and beckoned Ramble to him. The pair disappeared. Ramble came back alone, and said in an absent way that Frank had given him a message to take back to his mother. Then he asked Norman what message he would take from him to Oscar. Norman told him to say that he would not come home till Christmas. Then both Ramble and Mooch took leave of him, but with such an air of parting with him for good that he, knowing that they must come back next week to attend the inquest, was surprised. As the train steamed out he saw Ramble waving to Heather, who was standing on the shanty veranda. She went inside before he returned, and stayed in her room all morning. When he met her at dinner she was very merry. But he guessed that she had been weeping.

§

Five quiet days passed, while the people of the Melisande recovered from the excitements of the past fortnight.

Then, on Sunday morning, the community was overwhelmed with the news that Con the Greek had been robbed and done to death.

It was Norman who made the discovery. When Con did not come in to cook the breakfast, thinking that he must be oversleeping, Norman went to his den in the bakery to rouse him. He found him alive, naked, weakly grovelling on the floor in a welter of blood. Con had been stabbed, frightfully. And his den was wrecked. The door had been battered in with an axe. But no-one had heard the din that must have resulted. And small wonder. For between the hours of two and four all mundane sounds had been obliterated by a thunder-storm in which a siege-gun might have been discharged and all the Greeks in Capricornia blown to bits without anyone's being aware of it but Greeks and gunners. Norman rushed for the police.

Con was still alive when the police arrived. He said that he had been attacked by Frank and Ket. They had entered masked with neckerchiefs. But they had lost these in the struggle. One lay on the floor. And Con had had his electric torch. Frank had set upon him with a sand-bag. There it lay on the floor, burst, broken on his wooden head, said Con with a dying smile. Roused by the breaking in, he had been standing ready with his torch and knife. He knew what they were after. He had been waiting for such an attack all along. But he had not bargained for a storm to drown his yells. It was big Frank who struck him with the bag. Who stabbed him he did not know. That had happened after he had lost the torch and his wits. He only remembered a desperate struggle in which he had struck to kill till the knife was wrested from him. Then he had fought with nails and teeth till he dropped. He did not remember having his clothes ripped off him. His money was in his clothes, sewn into them like padding. The sum was something like £3,000. He had recovered consciousness at dawn. But he could not move, because his limbs were dead, nor cry out, because his lungs were choked with blood. Whispering and smiling he died. It was found that his spinal cord had been severed.

Meanwhile the tracker-boys were busy. Their task was not an easy one. Since the Wet had begun, a broad path of cinders, with branches going to the showers and latrines and wood-shed, had been laid across the muddy yard from the shanty to the bakery. And this had been well-trodden since the rain. The first strong scent the boys picked up led them to a tent by the river in which were two surprised and bleary-eyed old fellows who had paid an early morning visit to the back of the shanty for hair-of-the-dog. The next strong scent, the strongest they ever found, led them from the latrines down the corduroy right-of-way between the shanty and Ho Quang Hing's restaurant and across the cindered footpath to fresh cart-tracks in the muddy road. They followed the cart-tracks nearly to the sanitary depot before it dawned on the trooper in charge of them that they were following the nightmen.

The search for tracks about the shanty was soon abandoned. The trackers spread out. By noon they were in the bush, searching every foot of ground over a mighty circle. Now their task was still more difficult. The dry grass and scrub had been trampled down by hundreds of feet that recently had borne their owners out in search of firewood and hunting. Slowly the circle widened.

Meanwhile the troopers had learnt that no horses were missing from the settlement. What they learnt was correct. But four horses were missing from the camp of old Gabe Angel at the 213-Mile, together with riding-gear and packs and compass and maps and burning-glass and everything else that travellers would need for a lengthy journey through the bush. That the police did not know, and never knew. Though old Gabe Angel drank so much on the strength of his loss that he died in the horrors before Christmas, he never breathed a word about it to a soul. He had been keeping those four horses in readiness for days, waiting for the coming of the robbers down the railway on a tricycle that now lay at the bottom of a creek. He knew the robbers well. Many a time he had swapped yarns about crime and the insides of prisons with them. He alone of all those left behind knew how they had trodden cinders and corduroy all the way across to the spot in the railway yards where they had kept the tricycle hidden. He had chuckled over the plan to rob the Greek, had said that he wished he were young enough to take an active part in it. But he was deeply shocked to learn that they had killed their man. And so were they when they cooled down. They believed he was dead when they left him. Ket was the assassin. In the excitement he lost his head.

The general public envied the robbers their spoils, but not the task of earning them, which still remained to be accomplished. Where would they go? They had choice of many roads, and several millions of square miles of wilder-

ness to wander in safety. But what a safety! To reach
civilization and the chance to enjoy their spoils they must
travel in a straight line for at least a thousand miles. That
straight line was now a trooper's beat. To reach civilization unmolested they must travel many thousand miles. By
the time they made the journey their spoils would be out
of currency and their bodies worn of the desire to enjoy.
But they would never make it. They would struggle on till
the wilderness beat them. Then they would struggle back,
praying to be caught and rescued from their plight, till they
dropped in their tracks for the crows and dingoes. Or the
myall niggers would get them before they had covered a
hundred miles. Fools! As if Con the Greek — and
the stores and the shanties and the post-office and the
pay-train — would not have been robbed long ago if it
were possible to make a get-away! And double fools! What
road but a railroad had either of them the wits to follow?

Their critics did not know that they had had the wits
to start their journey by following the railroad, nor fully
realize that they were desperate men who already had
punishment to face and nothing much to live for after they
had faced it.

The inquest on the victims of the 223-Mile Smash should
have opened on Thursday, the Seventh of December. It
was adjourned *sine die*. Not only were the principals in
the case, Frank and Ket, unavailable, but all four witnesses. Paddy Pickandle had drunk himself into the horrors in his excitement. The shunter had gone up to Town
to hospital with pleurisy brought about by the injury to his
rib. Ramble and Mooch had disappeared.

Norman learnt of the disappearance of Ramble and
Mooch on Thursday afternoon, when, while he was sitting
with Heather discussing with her a letter he had that morning received from Oscar asking him to come because he
was ill, Trooper McCrook came to Heather and asked if
she knew where the men had gone. It appeared that Mooch
had been in Town since last Wednesday, and that Ramble
had joined him on Friday night, when they were last seen.
McCrook said that after the murder of Con the Greek the
police had sought Ramble on account of having heard that
on the way up to Town he had dropped off to stay with
Mrs McLash, to whom they thought he may have borne
some message that might have given them an idea of where
Frank was making for. Heather said she knew nothing,

and by her manner gave Norman the hint to hold his
tongue.

Apparently the police did not know that Ramble had
gone to Red Ochre. But had he? That was what Norman
was asking after McCrook had left them, when Heather,
who had been staring dully before her while he talked,
suddenly dropped her head to the arm of the cane lounge
on which she sat and sobbed convulsively.

Norman was sitting in a deck-chair. He stared at her.
She had been upset ever since the murder. Several times
she had asked him to leave her alone when he came to talk,
saying that she was ill. But he had never suspected that
Jack Ramble might have anything to do with her condition,
as now he did at once.

"What's up, Heather?" he said after a while.

She continued to sob.

He rose and went and sat beside her and took the limp
hand from her lap. She looked at him with tear-filled eyes.
Tears sparkled on her lashes, coursed down her powdered
cheeks, splashed on her quivering breast. She clenched
her teeth. Her lips and nostrils quivered violently. She
hurriedly took a tiny handkerchief from her bosom and
dabbed at eyes and nose.

"What's up, Heather?" he asked. "What's gone and upset you so bad?"

"Oh — Oh — I c-can't tell you!" she quavered.

"Why? I might be able to help."

"Oh — no — you can't."

She dropped her tawny scented head to his shoulder and
sobbed afresh.

He placed an arm round her shoulders. "There — there!"
he whispered, patting her arm.

After a while he asked, "Is it about Jack Ramble?"

She quivered.

"Tell me," he whispered, "I might be able to help."

"Oh — Oh — he's not Jack Ramble," she sobbed.

"I know — I know," he whispered. He had already told
her what Ramble had confided to him.

"He's — Oh — Oh — he's your father!"

Norman stiffened, gasped, "Eh?"

"He's Mark — my Mark — Oh God — and he's gone!"

Norman gaped. After a while he muttered, "Where's
he gone?"

"Run away — be-because he was afraid they'd find out
who he is — at the inquest — old Larsney'll be coroner —

he knew him well — and the police-captain too — and if he got through that all right — then if he was sent to jail on account of — of the wages business — they'd shave him —and Paddy Keyes at the Calaboose knew him well — too well!"

"But how's it no-one else's spotted him yet?"

"He kept clear of — old-timers."

She sobbed again.

After a while he asked, "Why didn't you tell me before?"

"I would have," she quavered. "But you've been so mean about him when I've talked. I've hinted. Several times you said he — he hasn't been much of a father to you. And — and one time you said he was a murderer. He didn't kill that Chow. It was an accident. He didn't even know he was dead till I told him. Do — do you think he would have come back if — if he'd been guilty? He — he only knocked him out. And the money he took was — was what the Chow had robbed him of. It's true. I know it's true. You ought to have seen his f-face when I told him — Oh — Oh — Oh!"

After a while he asked, "Is he mixed up in this — this business of murdering Con?"

"Oh no — oh no! How could you say such a thing?"

"I didn't mean anything. I only mean did he know anything about it. I saw him talking on the sly to Frank the day he left."

"You're talking about your father, Norman!"

He was silent.

After a while she said, "What he did — he fixed up with them — with Frank and Ket — to pick them up some place down the coast — the Jinjin River — in his boat, and take them over to the Dutch East Indies. They wanted to get away so's to get out of trouble. So did Mark and Chook. Through talking about their troubles together they found out each other wanted to go. And when the others found out Mark had a boat, they asked him to take them with him."

"Who's Chook?"

"Joe Mooch. His proper name's Chook Henn."

"Was it fixed up to rob Con?"

"Between him and them? No — I'm sure it wasn't — be-because if Mark had been going to get something out of the robbery he wouldn't have worried so much about getting a bit of money to go with. I gave him some. It was only Frank and Ket. And perhaps they didn't think of

it till after he had gone — because they wanted to go to
the boat with Mark. But he said that it'd only draw suspicion. No-one'd notice he'd gone. It was better for them
to wait for wet weather and make across country. They
told him they had a couple of hundred pounds. Ket had it.
They were going to give him half to take them out of the
country. If Mark had known of the robbery he wouldn't
have asked me for the little bit I was able to give him. And
do you think he'd risk waiting for robbers? If they'd only
run away because of the smash-business the police wouldn't
have bothered looking far for them. Now they'll comb the
country for them. That's why I'm afraid. And Mark doesn't
know what they've done."

"Do they know who he is?"

"No."

"What'd he want the money for?"

"The money to go away? Why — for food and things to
stock his boat. He might have to wait months for them
— for Frank and Ket."

"Where was the boat?"

"Somewhere near Zodiac. He and Chook Henn have
been roaming round in it for years. That old boat's the
curse of Mark's life — and that old spaniel Chook, too.
He's been in trouble ever since he took up with them. He
always will till he gets rid of them. I can't do anything
with him with Chook about."

"How'd they get to Zodiac in the first place?"

"An army could land there and no-one'd be any the
wiser. They left the boat in a salt-arm somewhere outside.
This's the second time they've been here. They came first
when the Meatworks was open. They heard about it in
Timor when they were broke and in debt. They worked in
the Meatworks four months."

"Did you see him then?"

"No. He was afraid to come to me. I suppose that old
Chook thing stopped him. You see he owed a terrible lot
of money when he ran away. He was scared he'd get put
in jail — not for the Chow-business — he thought that'd
blown over — but the debts."

"Where's he been all the while?"

"When he first went away he went to Papua. He and
Chook sold the boat there and went down to Bullimba and
enlisted and went to the war. After the war they came
back up North. Mark tried to find Oscar in Batman, but
couldn't. You'd shifted or something. He found Maud's

husband, but didn't like the look of him, and didn't tell him anything but that he was just a friend. They're not much alike. And Maud's husband didn't know where you lived, on account of a row you had, or something. They came up to Southern Cross Island. And there they found their old boat lying on a beach, abandoned. They fixed her up and went to the Indies."

"Do you think he went out to Red Ochre?"

"Yes. He wanted to see Oscar again. He didn't want anything off of him. He just wanted to see him. He probably never will again. When he went away he said he was going to Papua after he got rid of those two, and he'd send for me later on. Oh I tried to stop him from having anything to do with them. But he's so obstinate. It's all because of that old Chook. I could handle him but for Chook. I wish that old thing would die. I'll never see Mark again unless the police catch him — Oh my God!" Her mouth opened suddenly. She thrust her handkerchief into it, bit hard, closed her eyes tight. But the tears burst through her lids. Norman gently fingered her hair, whispering, "Heather — Heather dear!"

"Oh — Oh — a-Oh!"

Then she drew away from him, dashed her face into the pillow at the head of the lounge, wept her heart out. He slid up to her, tried to comfort her with caresses. "Do you like him such a lot, dear Heather?" he asked.

"Oh!" she sobbed. " I — I — I love him with all my life!"

She sobbed brokenly for a while, then quavered, "I've loved him always. But — but something always comes and — and takes him away from me. I — I was a fool at first. When I heard he was a — a combo — I — I ran away from him. But all men are comboes one way or — another. What's difference black lubra or white? Oh, I thought I had him this time. After all the years — he walked into the bar here — my Mark — my own dear Mark — and looked at me so old-fashioned — and asked me for a drink — I knew him — Oh — Oh — Oh — I knew him at once — I thought I would've died!"

Norman was blinking back tears, fighting to control his jerking features.

"And — and — and," she sobbed, "I thought that when — the — the road was built — I'd get him away from Chook — take him away somewhere. I — I — I've been slaving to get the money. But — but before I could get

N

out of debt — this happened — and now — Oh God! Oh
God! — he's gone!"

DEATH CORROBOREE

ON Friday the Seventh of December the rumour that work
on the Transcontinental Railway had ceased for good and
all became a statement of fact, which was issued in a type-
written circular by the Chief Engineer, Mr Sidney Gigney
That night Mr Gigney was waited upon by an angry deputation who wanted to know why they had been kept waiting for the news so long and whether they were going to
receive compensation for having been dealt with as they
had. They interrupted a game of bridge that he was playing
with some gentleman friends. He received them brusquely.
As they waxed angrier he waxed sarcastic. Finally he
slammed the door in their faces. After stripping his pawpaw
trees and upsetting his privy they departed.

Early next morning another deputation waited on Gigney to ask him if he would arrange for the running of a
special train to Town so that the men who were going
South might catch the mail-boat, which would be leaving
next day at sundown. He agreed. Then he telephoned to
Town for formal permission, then gave orders for the
marshalling of a train.

There was just then but one engine in the local Loco fit
for service; and there were only eight waggons of various
kinds and two cattle-cars in the yards, the rest of the
rolling-stock being either piled up in the mud at the 223-
Mile or standing stranded on sidings further down. From
these available units the train was made up.

Gigney was sitting in his bungalow reading, when at
about ten o'clock, Trooper Robbrey called on him, looking
flushed and worried, and said that the whole six or seven
hundred men in the camp were trying to board the train.
Trooper Robbrey was the only policeman left on the Melisande. The rest of the local force were far away in the bush
hunting for the murderers of Con. And he was young and
inexperienced, and rather too human for his job. He explained that when he had tried to keep order at the station
he had been rough-housed.

Gigney took up his topee at once and went off to settle things. He found the precincts of the station alive with men, who were swarming over and around the train like ants over the carcass of a snake. The roofs of the two cattle-cars were packed with them, jostling, shouting, heaving their swags about. There was a crowd even on the coal of the engine. Among these last was Norman, who was going home. Gigney, glancing up, saw him, recognized him, and, as he always did when nowadays they met, looked away.

A meeting was in progress before the station-building, addressed by an impish little fellow, standing high on something, whom Gigney recognized as the most abusive of the deputation of the night before. When the speaker sighted Gigney he pointed at him and yelled, "Ere he is — ere he is — ere's the sod himself!" The meeting turned to look.

Gigney was not liked by the men. He was a supercilious little fellow. "What's the trouble?" he asked in a superior tone. He was answered by the crowd. He waved impatiently, then pointed to the imp and cried, "You!"

"There's too blunny many of us for the train," yelled the imp.

"That's obvious," cried Gigney.

The crowd laughed, at him, not at what he said. He took it as a compliment to his wittiness, smiled slightly.

"But the blunny thing aint goin' without all of us," yelled the imp.

"That's illogical," cried Gigney.

"I don't give a monkey's jigger what it is," yelled the imp. "But it aint floppin' well goin' without all of us, unless —" He paused, looking at Gigney with popping black eyes.

"Unless what?" cried Gigney, amused.

"Unless we get it in writin' that us't's left behind gets paid for the time we gotter waste waitin' here a blunny month for the next blunny steamer. See?"

Gigney blinked, looked annoyed, cried, "Nonsense!"

"Not nonsense at all," yelled the imp. "It's a hultimatum from me an' me feller-workers."

"Well the sooner you scrap it the better," cried Gigney angrily. "It's preposterous!"

"Not so pre-blunny-posterous as what yous mob puts over us," yelled the imp. "Me'n me feller-workers is stickin' up for our blunny rights. And be jees we'll get 'em! What you think we are, a lotter floppin' coolies or what? Sackin' us at a moment's notice — keepin' us waitin' close on three weeks to know what's doin' — and then calmly tellin' us we can go home — walk home, I s'pose you blunny well mean, eh? — a mere coupler blunny thousand floppin' miles or so — or do you 'tend us to pawn our swags and raise the hoot to pay for a first-class cabin-de-luxe passage like you'll go y' soddin' self, y' barsted, eh?"

The crowd roared approval.

Gigney, now red in the face, shouted, "You came up here of your own accord. You were taken on and employed by the hour —"

The crowd drowned him. Now he was surrounded. Men from up near the engine had come along to hear. Norman was among them.

When he got a hearing Gigney shouted, "Another train'll be sent down for the rest of you —"

"We've give you our hultimatum," yelled the imp.

"Well you can damned well take it back!" shouted Gigney, and turned to the guard, who was standing near him, and cried, "Go on — off you go!"

The guard grimaced, said, "They've got the hand-brakes down on all the waggons. They're sittin' on 'em."

"Kick 'em off!" cried Gigney.

"Have a go at 'em y'self," grunted the guard.

Gigney turned and spoke to Robbrey. Meanwhile the imp went on addressing his fellows.

Then Gigney pushed through the crowd to a flat-top waggon, climbed on to it, forced standing-room for himself among its crowded complement, and turned and faced the imp. The trooper climbed up after him.

"Men!" shouted Gigney, high and clear, raising one hand and placing the other on his hip.

The crowd guffawed.

"Men!" he cried. "Men — stop this silly nonsense!"

The crowd roared with laughter.

The imp mocked Gigney, placed a hand on a hip, put a finger to cheek, and cried out in a piping voice, "Girls, girls, toss yer curls — boys, boys, stop yer silly nonsense!"

The crowd rocked.

Gigney flushed crimson, put his offending hand in his pocket. A giant behind him took off his topee and sent it sailing across to the imp, who caught it and put it on, then resumed his pose and screamed, "Bumps to the wall, Bertie!"

"Look here!" cried Gigney.

The imp became serious, yelled, "You gunner give us what we want?"

"I certainly am not."

"Well shut up!"

"I'll send for the police."

"Yeah — you're just the sorter sod that would. You're the sorter bonehead barsted that looks on fellers like us what have a different kinder philosophy to you as blunny criminals, aint you? Well we look on misanthropical sods like y'self what thinks a workin' man's only put on earth as a convenience like a gelded horse the same, see? You're workin' for the Government same as us, and contributin' to your own pay with taxes same as us, but you're a Capitalist, which's a misanthropical sod. I tell you this train don't go without all of us unless we get what we want. And no other train will neither. Bring your blunny basher-gang down. That's all right. Then we'll have to go quietly. But be jees, Mister Stinkin' Chief Engineer, there'll be a blunny great row when we get down South, and you won't get another gang of men to work under you in this God's free country as long as you blunny well live. See? Now — do we get what we want?"

"I'll see you in hell first!" shouted Gigney.

"Fellers like us don't go to hell," cried the imp. "We do our penance on earth, working under spits like you."

The crowd cheered.

The giant placed his hands under Gigney's armpits and raised him high. He yelled in alarm. Someone grabbed his legs. Robbrey tried to interfere. Someone pulled his hat down over his head.

The giant slipped a hand down to Gigney's belt, stepped to the edge of the waggon with him, and dangled him, struggling wildly, above the crowd. Someone pushed Robbrey overboard.

"Now get ready," cried the giant in a rumbling voice. "Get ready, Mister, cos I'm gunner drop ya." He had to give many warnings before his yelling victim would gather in feet and hands. "One — two — three!" boomed the giant. Gigney dropped through the air, to land on hands and knees, and subside to belly. When someone made a grab at him he leapt up with a yell and fled. Robbrey went with him.

The crowd chased them, those in front whooping and prancing, those behind, among whom was Norman, running only to see what would be the end of the fun. The pair leapt the railway fence, fell in a deep muddy drain, got up, ran for their lives to the police-station, rushed in with the crowd roaring at their heels, and slammed and barred the door. Then they barred all the doors, then armed themselves with pistols, and crouched in a corner, panting and goggling, prepared to fight to the death. The crowd piled up at the windows and added insult to injury by laughing at them. At length the crowd filed back to the station, to find to their astonishment that the train was gone. The wise fellows who had stayed behind numbered less than two hundred.

The crowd turned to the shanties. Never had Heather or Jerry Rotgutt been patronized in such force before. And they were not prepared for such patronage, having let their stocks dwindle without the customary replenishment since it had begun to seem likely that the work would not go on. Not everyone in the crowd had money. A good fourth had been living for months on police-rations. But all who wanted it had drink that day. When things had warmed up and attention was drawn to the envious hundred or so, a whip-round was organized. Heather was drunk dry by four in the afternoon. Jerry Rotgutt would have been drunk dry even sooner but for his resourcefulness. He had had plenty of experience in the matter of making his stocks last out when in the old days his shanty stood on a goldfield fifty miles from the head of a railway on which ran but two trains a month. He put it to use now. At the first opportunity he slipped away to a Chinese store and bought eight gallons of methylated spirit and eight pounds of black treacle and five pounds of tea, which he had brought to his shanty by the back way by blackboys. He made a strong infusion of the tea in a kerosene-can, strained it into a beer-cask, added the bulk of the spirit and treacle, and filled up with water. This he sold as bulk rum. The remainder of the spirit he diluted and used to fill up half-empty bottles of anything on his shelves. Customers who complained he told to go to hell. Those who asked politely what was wrong with the liquor he told that it had been standing a long while in the cask. Everyone seemed satisfied. The stuff certainly had the desired effect. At nightfall his shanty was as crowded as a beehive. He had to set up a special bar on the front veranda.

All went well till somewhere about nine o'clock, when a group of fellows coming from the latrine caught Rotgutt stealing in by the back way with another can of spirit he

had had to buy. He was carrying this one himself. He tried
to pretend that it was kerosene for the lamps. But it was
labelled in large letters. So after some argument the fellows
dragged him into the bar and denounced him before the
crowd. He tried to point out that since he had saved the
men from a dull evening he was actually doing a public
service. The crowd could not see it. They stripped him,
douched him with his own liquor, tossed him into the road,
chased him, pelting him with mud, to the river. Unfortunately for him it was moonlight and he was a very big fellow and lily-white of skin. He plunged into the river and
swam across under a shower of mud, and followed by a
storm of yelling and a horde of mosquitoes, clambered up
the further bank and fled sobbing towards Copper Creek.

The more cunning, the more thirsty, and the less fastid-
ious drinkers, did not take part in the chase, but stayed and
turned the barmen out and helped themselves to anything
in the place that took their fancy. When the mob came back
from the river they tore the shanty to pieces and scattered
it to the winds. Trooper Robbrey and Mr Gigney and several other fellows who were not good mixers maintained
law and order among themselves in the police-station,
watching what little they could safely see of the scene, and
continually reporting to Town over the telephone.

Pandemonium raged all night. The settling of the Rotgutt affair started the settling of affairs between factions.
The factions split up into pairs. There was enormous energy in that eight gallons of methylated spirit. When day
dawned there was not a grievance left.

At nine o'clock in the morning a lengthy train, drawn by
two engines and composed of every type of vehicle in the
service, arrived from Town, after a furious journey through
the night, bringing eight uniformed troopers and their
horses and arms, and twenty young Government Officers
who had been enrolled as special police. The entire populace was then fast asleep. Nothing untoward happened
when the rioters awoke to find the settlement policed, except a quiet rolling in the mud of two of the Government
Officers when it was learnt why they were come. Mr Gigney marched bravely forth with four armed troopers at his
back and called a meeting at the station, where he informed
the men that a large cargo-steamer had been called to
port to take them down South at the State's expense. The
imp, who had his head bandaged with a shirt-sleeve and

his left arm in a sling, could do no more than lead the crowd
off in a farewell chorus of unseemly sounds.

The train departed. Norman rode with a crowd of
Greeks on a flat-top waggon, lying on his back on his un-
rolled swag, listening to the chatter and strange singing of
his neighbours, watching the smoke rush across the azure
sky, watching the red walls leap at him and the trees go
spinning by, and sometimes studying the Rubaiyat.

The train travelled that day as far as Republic Reef,
where it camped for the night. The crowd amused itself
by scaring the little community of Chinese who dwelt there.
The journey was resumed at dawn. Caroline River was
reached at ten o'clock. Norman alighted, and while walking
to the Siding House, saw a group of passengers, easily fifty
strong, dart into the bush to eastward, heading for the
native camp and a last indulgence in Black Velvet. He
chuckled. Those lusty fellows, product of two thousand
years of Constituted Authority and Christian Virtue! That
was the last he saw of them. While he was in the house
vainly trying to rouse Mrs McLash from a drunken stupor,
the train departed, with engines whistling — whistling to
call the lusty fellows back.

Norman had expected to find the buckboard waiting for
him. He had sent a telegram to Oscar saying that he was
coming home, and had paid porterage to ensure its delivery
to the Station. No-one was at the Siding but the fettlers.
Though he did not know it, he delivered the telegram to
Mrs McLash himself, in a long official envelope given him
by the guard, who had got it from the postmaster at Copper
Creek. The envelope contained, besides a copy of his telegram, an inquiry regarding Mrs McLash's failure to answer
the telephone for dictation. He tried to convey to her the
impression that it must contain something of importance
by showing her the letters O.H.M.S. with which it was inscribed. She merely blinked at it. What affair of His
Majesty's could compare with the monstrous one that filled
her drunken mind? The man might have a son; his son
might be his Pride and Joy; but was he flying for his life
through an unknown wilderness as robber and murderer
doomed to die by starvation, drowning, thirst, madness,
spears of savages, or hangman's noose?

Norman went to Joe Steen's place, found old Joe moping
over Frank's trouble, talked to him for a while, had a bite
to eat with him, then borrowed a horse from him and went
home. He arrived home late in the afternoon. He was hail-

ed from the native camp as he came through the slip-rails by the river, but not from the house. The house looked dead. He yarded the horse and came in. The grass had sprung, but was not yet high enough to hide the stones and rubble of the Dry. The homestead looked ragged. Whitewash had been scoured from the roofs by rain. Paint was peeling. Though he had been gone little more than a month, he felt as though the time were years.

He looked into the kitchen, found it deserted. He crossed to the stove and touched it, to find it warm. As he was emerging he ran into Cho, who had come from his quarters to see who was clomping about the kitchen.

"Ho-ay — ho-ay!" cried Cho in surprise. "Nlorman — good-o! Howzit?" He seized Norman's hand.

"Where's Dad?" asked Norman.

"Him dere," said Cho, nodding to the house. "Him sick. Plopper no good."

"Yes? I had a letter from him; but he didn't say what's the matter with him. What is it?"

"Him hurt himself longa hinside guts time him get chuckim off longa holse."

"Chucked off a horse? Hell! How'd that happen?"

"Time him mustlim up bullamacow."

"Musterin'? What's he musterin' for?"

"Stock him clear out too muchee far time Wet come."

"But he could've sent boys."

"Him wantl lookee see himself."

"Tcht! Tcht! Who's lookin' after the stock now?"

"Allabout boy. Sometimes Hi go lookee see."

"You? What — ridin' your old donkey?"

"Yeah. Ol' donkey good for mustlim up young-fella calfees. Dem calfees tink donkey belong him mumma — come lunnin' longside."

Norman chuckled, asked, "And what do they think you are?"

"Might be tink me belong him papa ol' bull, eh?"

Norman laughed and turned away. Then he turned back and asked, "Eh Cho — you bin see one fella whiteman came here last week?"

"No-more," said Cho.

"What — no-one come?"

"Ho yeah. One fella whiteman him come train-day week before. Hi no see. Boy bin tellim me. Dat time Hi way longa south-side lookee see mustlim-up."

Norman nodded, went off. He found Oscar lying, clad

in pyjamas, on top of his bed on the east-side veranda, asleep, and sickly yellow and drawn of white-whiskered face. He was shocked by the sight of him. He woke him. Oscar started up, regarded him for a moment stupidly with haggard red eyes, then cried out joyfully, clutched at him, kissed him.

Oscar did not remain joyful for long. Soon he sagged back to the bed and began to complain in a whining voice of a multitude of woes. He blamed Norman for his injury, saying that he should not have sustained it had he not deserted him. He complained about the cattle and the horses and the dingoes and the natives and the fact that the Transcontinental Railway had shut down and the fact that he had to finance Marigold and Steggles. It was hard, he said, after all he had done for his children, to be deserted by them in his age and insecurity. His day was done. He felt he would not see the Wet out. So he had made his will, dividing the little he had saved with so much difficulty equally between Norman and Marigold. The Station, for all it was worth now that hope of securing a reliable market was gone, and a portion of the money, would be Norman's, the rest of the money Marigold's. Not that either had done much to deserve it. All this and more, to which Norman listened patiently and without much concern, but never a word on the subject he was bursting to discuss — his father. That Oscar was filled with that subject too, he felt sure; for whenever he tried to lead to it, as several times he did when the Transcontinental was mentioned, Oscar became agitated and talked rapidly and often foolishly of other things He was thus discouraged from broaching it. He was discouraged similarly for two days.

In the middle of the afternoon of his second day at home, Norman came into the dining-room, where Oscar was dozing in an arm chair, and woke him to ask what had happened to a certain rifle.

Oscar pondered half vacantly.

"The buffalo-rifle," said Norman. "The three-o-three Stan gave me. Quick. There's a buffalo down the river."

Oscar slowly coloured. He said hesitantly, "Oh — yes — er — it's gone."

"Eh — gone — where?"

"I — I gave it away — I mean to say —"

"Eh?" demanded Norman, astonished. "Gave it away?"

Oscar was silent, looking at his fiddling hands.

"Who to?" asked Norman.

"A — a man."

"A man! Who?"

"Oh — I — I forget his name. Stranger. Came here last week."

"Ah!" breathed Norman.

Oscar looked at him.

"I know who it was," said Norman brightly.

"Oh no you don't," said Oscar promptly.

"Yes I do — it was —"

"You don't!" cried Oscar, heaving himself up. "And I don't want to hear about it. Get to your work. You've plenty to do without shooting buffaloes."

"It was —"

"Hold your tongue boy. Leave the room."

"Oh blast it!" cried Norman. "I know who it was. Don't be so —"

"You don't — you don't. Silence! Not another word."

"It was —"

"Go!" shouted Oscar, purple of face.

Norman glared at him for a moment, then wheeled about and went. He realized that Oscar supposed he did not know Ramble's true identity, but not that Oscar was hiding the truth from him for fear of shocking him, nor that Oscar was greatly shocked by the truth himself; hence he did not give him due credit for his behaviour; in fact, on account of that incident he avoided him for the rest of the day; and Oscar helped him to do so.

Next afternoon Oscar came hobbling out of the house on his stick to see what was the cause of scraping and thumping on the roof, and found Norman and several blackboys at work whitewashing. Norman grinned and came down and talked whitewash to him for a while, then led him round to the front veranda and sat with him to take smoke-o. Norman then found an opportunity to broach the troublesome subject.

"Dad," he said earnestly. "You don't need to get upset about that business, cos I know all about it, see?"

Oscar eyed him mildly and asked, "What business is that, Norm?"

"About my father coming here."

Oscar started.

"It's all right," said Norman. "You thought I didn't know, eh? Heather told me."

Oscar gaped.

"She told me just before I left," Norman went on. "I

ought've guessed it myself, though. Things he and Heather used to say. And he's something like you about the head and eyes, too. I wish I'd found out sooner."

Oscar gasped, wriggled, and clutching at his tufty white beard cried, "Don't believe a word she says. She's a bitch!"

"Who — Heather? Go on — she's a real good sort."

"Bitch!" cried Oscar. "He told her not to tell you."

"Oh but I'm glad."

"Like all the rest of her blasted family! What the hell's she want to mag to you for?"

"What's the harm?"

"Fool!" cried Oscar. "Interfering damned woman — spoiling everything —"

"Steady Dad, steady. I'd like to talk about him —"

"I won't hear a word."

"But —"

"Stop! I'm sick. This's upset me already enough. Oh the fool to come back! And then that bitch to go upsetting you by magging!"

"Steady Dad. I'm not upset. Not a bit. Don't get yourself worked up. I know all about him. He's not a bad sort. But he means nothing to me. You're my Dad, you know — my dear old Dad."

Oscar clutched the yellow-brown hand that soothed him, and muttered, "Good boy — good boy — I always knew you would be — dear boy." Then he sighed, and staring at the river added, "He came to see me — just to see me — I thought he was after something — but he wasn't. Just to see me. As you say, he's not a bad sort. Just a fool. But I wish he hadn't come. It's so dangerous. People might guess if they knew he came here. He said he told Ma Mc-Lash he was coming out with a message from McRandy. He said she was too upset about the train-smash to notice much. But that old woman wouldn't miss much if she was lying in her coffin. And he's not gone right away. That's the trouble. He's gone to meet those murderers. He told me he was only going to get them away from the trouble about the smash. That was before the murder, of course. It never dawned on me then that they might be planning something big. Oh the fool to get mixed up in a thing like that!"

"He wasn't mixed up in it," said Norman, and explained as Heather had to him.

Oscar looked relieved at once. "Well —" he said. "Well if that's true — but even if it is, he's mixed up with them. And ten to one the police'll catch him now. He went away that Friday night. That's why I gave him that rifle and a few other things he wanted, so's he needn't have to buy them and attract attention. He won't know anything about the murder. So he won't think that the police will send out an expedition after those men —"

"They've got a good chance of getting away," said Norman. "The jonns haven't got on their track yet. When they pick it up, if they ever do, the Wet'll have set in strong. Then they won't be able to follow. And afterwards they'll never find the track. They reckon down the Melisande that they'll probably give up huntin' for 'em soon and just wait on 'em at all the places they're likely to come out at."

"Oh don't let's talk about it, Norm. He's my brother, you know. We never seemed to get along together, ever. I don't know why. I tried to pull him up several times. He had better chances than me, too. But he's got a kink in him somewhere. Still we're brothers after all. But don't let's talk about him, Norm. I'm too sick."

"Good-o, Dad. Now look here, you'll have to let me take you up to Town to see the Doctor. It's no good goin' on like this."

"No — I won't go. I might get right myself. If I went to the doctor he'd only put me in the hospital and want to operate on me."

"Well why not, if it's best?"

"No fear. They always think it's best to go chopping you about. They love it. It's all right for them. If they make a good job of it they get a feather in their cap. If they don't, they've only got to tell your relations some yarn about you being too weak to stand it, and go looking for someone else to try again on. I've heard too much about 'em. They killed poor Peter Differ. They treated him for years for something he had wrong inside. Then they operated on him. After that they couldn't treat him any more. Why? Because they'd made such a mess of him, you can bet. They tried to get rid of him down South — sort of pass him on to someone else. He wanted to go. He would've if I'd given him and his daughter the fare. I wish I had. It's often troubled me. It's been troubling me a lot since I've been lying here sick. The other night I dreamt about Conny and that feller Lace —" He wandered on and told the story of the adventures of Constance Differ and her child as he had heard it from Mrs McLash, who knew the details pretty thoroughly. He added that he had it in mind to locate the child someday and do something for her. Norman did not say that he knew where Tocky could be found, nor reveal the fact that he had heard of her. What he had learnt from Con of the Protector's efforts to bring to book the youths who had been in the company of her and Christobel that night had scared him badly. He did nothing more than listen.

Oscar tired at last. Then Norman said, "Now have a bit of a snooze. Better stay here where you can't hear us on the roof. You must go up and see the doctor, Dad. This's no damn good, you know. You might get worse. What say we go up for Christmas, eh? You can go and see him then, and when you're better take a run up to see Marry and Stan, eh?"

"You're a good boy, Norm," said Oscar wearily. "All right, we'll see. Yes — I think I'll run up and see them when I get better — if I ever do. This pain in my side is killing. All right. I'll have a bit of a snooze now. Always snoozin' — and the precious hours flyin' — still, I can't help it — fetch the net, Norm — flies are bad."

§

Oscar returned from the hospital in the middle of February, worse than when he went away. He came home with a steamer-ticket to Singapore. Having been practically turned out of the hospital because he had worn the patience of the doctor almost to anger by persistently refusing to undergo an operation that the doctor considered urgent, he had decided to take his illness to Singapore to have it healed by more civilized physicians and nursed for love, not money, by his daughter.

He had been at home but three days and had got together no more of his luggage than the linen Cho had prepared for him, when he collapsed. Cho found him looking as though he were dead, and rushed off to bring Norman from the run. Norman came as fast as his swift horse could carry him. Oscar was unconscious. Norman rushed out shouting for the buckboard and a pair of stout horses and for a courier to ride like hell to the Siding and tell Jake Ledder to have his trolley ready to take Oscar up to Town. When the buckboard was ready he carried Oscar out to it in his strong young arms, kicked a blackboy into the driving seat, climbed up with his burden, assisted by many anxious hands, and held it, whimpering over it, throughout the two hours' furious drive.

The haste was vain. Oscar died on the Siding House veranda a minute or so after arrival, with Mrs McLash's red arms round him and her rummy exhalations fanning his cooling cheek and her honest tears wetting those eyes that would weep no more. They laid him on a mattress on a flat-top trolley, which they towed with the motor up to Town.

Norman was crazed. A fettler had to sit with him on the flat-top with the corpse to prevent him from falling off. On and on through the hot afternoon they raced, pop-pop-pop-popping through the wilderness, while red walls leapt at them clanging and trees in a wild corroboree-dance went spinning by.

The funeral took place next morning. Norman, blind and stupefied, saw nothing of the grand affair, though it was he who would have to pay for it. Throughout the journey to the grave he sat in a hooded car with head buried in Heather's breast. And the burial was nothing to him but a blur. He spent the rest of the day weeping in Heather's darkened room. Heather could not comfort him now. For old Mrs Shay, who had been ill for some time, had taken bad upon hearing of the death of Oscar. And that night old Mrs Shay gave up her devil.

Norman did not see the second funeral. When next morning he heard of the death he snatched up his hat and ran to catch the mail-train home. The train was very late that day. He did not reach home till after dark, when he found the natives in the midst of a great Death Corroboree and Cho and a crowd of Chinese friends he had summoned from Republic Reef and elsewhere sitting out in the yard near the kitchen chanting dolefully over joss-sticks and paper-streamers and a huge roast pig.

O mungallini kurri-tai, ee-tukkawunni wurri-gai, ee-Mister Chilnsik tulli-yai, ee-Oscar munalunga-wai — ee-yung ee-yung ee-yah!

The devil of the departed master was everywhere. It stood in empty boots, in hanging clothes, sat in the armchair in the dining-room, stood beside the ashy pipe and dusty pouch and misty spectacles, stole among the shadows, moaned in the nor'east wind, flew with ragged clouds across the moon's dead face, wailed in the timber of the river — Kwee-luk! — Kwee-luk! — Kweeee—luk! — I am lost!

No incantation in the Rubaiyat for this.

O mungallini kurri-tai! O Great Bunyip! Most Puissant Joss! Almighty God of Abraham! Rest him — rest him!

At dawn on Friday Norman called for the buckboard, packed his bags, gave the keys of the place to Cho, put Oscar's steamer-ticket in his pocket, and left to catch the train. On Monday he sailed for Singapore.

SINGING IN THE WILDERNESS

NORMAN returned to Capricornia in August. He had not stayed long with his cousins, not having been encouraged to do so and not having himself felt much inclined. Mr and Mrs Steggles had become Tuans — Malayan Lords. The grandeur in which they lived was great. They had received him well enough, and when alone had treated him with affection. Trouble was they had rarely ever been alone. For they were friends of a multitude of pompous people who seemed to love their company, and masters of a number of coloured slaves who seemed to be omnipresent. And evidently they feared the criticism of both in the matter of their possessing a coloured relative. He was glad to leave them. They told him to go home. He said he would, and did, by way of Burma, and Cochin China, and the Treaty Ports, and the Philippines, and Borneo, and the Celebes, and Java. While he spent freely he did not want for friends, most of whom he found among genteel half-breeds. So what with one thing and another, his trip cost him something like £500. He could ill afford such extravagance. He had often to make reference to the Rubaiyat to throttle down regret. He tried quoting the Rubaiyat to Heather to stop her scolding him for having been a fool. She said by imbibing such stuff after such behaviour he was doing nothing more wise than dose himself with hair-of-the-dog.

He spent three weeks in Town, the first rather miserably at the Princess Alice, trying to act the Eurasian Gentleman before a crowd that refused to regard him as anything but an unusual kind of yeller-feller. His failure with *savoir vivre* drove him to The Paddock, where he spent the second week so riotously that he was arrested for drunkenness and disorderly conduct. The third he spent in the Calaboose, spoiling the nails he had lately trained to elegance, with a spalling-hammer and a heap of stones.

When released he acted on the advice of the police and went home.

He found the Station none the worse for his having neglected it so long, thanks to the diligence of Cho, and well enough dispossessed of the influence of the devil of the departed master, thanks to the work of Time, to allow of his installing a comely young lubra as his mistress without feeling much queaziness. He had little to do. The cattle-market was dead. And thanks to his water-works, the stock would require no attention till the Wet set in. He spent most of his time at home, occupied either with a crate of second-hand books he had had sent up from South, or with an old steam-engine and dynamo he had brought from Singapore, or with his lubra, Opal, of whom he tried to make a lady. Trooper Dan O'Crimnell dropped in on him one time while passing. Soon afterwards the gossips were nodding and saying that the state of things at Red Ochre was just what they had expected all along. They should know. Most of them had been lying on their backs and playing with lubras for years.

Six weeks of idleness were enough for Norman. At the end of that time, intending to put into effect an idea he had had in mind for some time past, he set out to visit his birth-place by travelling overland. When people heard of this they said he had gone another walkabout. They heard it from Mrs McLash, from whom he bought his provisions.

He took with him two natives of the Murrukaburra tribe, a few survivors of which dwelt in the camp at the Siding. It was through their country that he would first have to pass. That region was deserted nowadays. The Murruka-burras had been practically exterminated by a company of whitemen who had attempted to set up a cattle-station in their much-too-fertile territory and whose stock they had slain. And he took equipment for shooting and skinning buffaloes, for the hides of which there was just then a very good market. His armoury consisted of a powerful new .44 repeating-rifle, a shotgun, and an automatic pistol, his plant a riding-horse and two packs.

The first two days out from home were spent in following the Caroline down to a point where the salinity of the water gave the hint that it was time to turn eastward to avoid the maritime marshes that the map indicated thereabout. During those two days the blackboys followed submissively on foot. They were far from young, and were out of condition through having lived long in idleness and want. When camp was made on the second night they were tired out. But Norman gave them no consideration. He told them before they went to sleep that because he wished to travel a certain distance next day he expected them to have the horses in and harnessed and the fire lit and the billy on the boil before the sun rose. It was broad daylight when they woke. It was Norman's stockwhip that woke them. They leapt up, fled yelling into the bush, and never came back. Norman was occupied till noon with bringing in the horses and breaking camp.

He was not much upset by the desertion. The boys had begun their acquaintance with him by being unduly familiar, and upon being put in their proper place became sullen. Towards the end he had found their company positively irritating. The only thing that troubled him was that now he would have to spend much of his time tailing the horses. He went his way. Loneliness did not trouble him. He had a swag of books with him to absorb that imaginativeness which was worked upon at night by the Devils of the Dead, and a mouth-organ upon which to spend the impulse to sing the Song of the Golden Beetle.

On the seventh day the first rain of the season fell, light rain that scarcely left a trace of its having fallen. It rained again soon after he passed the Lungahole River, and then more heavily, but not so much as to give rise to fear of floods. These rains were abnormally early. It would be long before the Wet asserted itself. He reckoned that by travelling quietly as he was he should come to Flying Fox on the nineteenth or twentieth day, should be able to spend a few days there if he found the place interesting and make the return journey in comfort. Should there appear to be any danger of floods, he could make the return journey in half the time he was taking to go out. He did not know that Flying Fox was now the mission called the Copra Co. of which Con the Greek had spoken. His map described the place as a trepang-camp.

After crossing the wide delta of the Madman River, he passed out of marshy country and was able to take a course more northerly. So he came on the fifteenth day to the Smoky Ranges, which he crossed and skirted on the northern side in search of the Jinjin River, which he would follow to the sea. He caught his first glimpse of the sea early in the morning of the sixteenth day, and soon afterwards came to the Jinjin, which he found flowing through a deep ravine. He followed the river, or stream as it appeared to be, through foothills all that morning, and came, soon after noon, into sight of the level country of the coast. The silver bar of sea was now sunk out of sight. He stopped his horse and, letting it graze, rolled a cigarette and studied the land-scape.

As he was about to take out matches, the horse raised its head and snorted and flicked ears towards the jungle into which the river disappeared.

"What's up?" he asked, bending to look between the ears. But he saw nothing unusual nor heard anything but the murmur of water and the sigh of the sea-breeze in the trees and the far-off shouting of cockatoos.

The horse snorted again. One of the packs behind echoed it. Then Norman heard for an instant what sounded like a wailing human voice far distant. Bending again, he saw a faint haze of smoke above the jungle at a point half a mile away. Binghis, he thought, and rose.

He rode on and entered the jungle, leaving it to the horse to guide him to the source of the sound, but stopping occasionally to listen for himself. That it was not a black-fellow's chant he heard he was soon convinced, and being so, began to think with a twinge of apprehension of Mark and Chook and Frank and Ket; for this was the country in which they had arranged to meet; and though he realized that they were not likely to be still there, he had lately thought much about what he should do were he to meet them.

He did not hear the sound again for many minutes. When next he heard it, it was much louder, and was clearly discernible as a single voice, that of a woman.

He left the river behind him when he entered the jungle, being led to do so by his knowing horse, which evidently wished to avoid a tramp round a bend. When he came to the river again the singer was so close that he could hear her words and the splashing of water that accompanied. She was singing a hymn, or rather, since she sang the same verse over, a part of one:

> Till we mee-ee-eet, till we mee-ee-eet,
> Till we meet at Jee-ee-ee-zuz feet;
> Till we mee-ee-eet, till we mee-ee-eet,
> God be with you till we meet again.

He assumed that he had come upon a party or mission-natives. His horses did not neigh as they would have done if other horses had been about. And surely there would have been horses about if there were whites in the party. He had been waiting for the horses to neigh, for a moment more afraid than ever that he was about to meet the murderers. He was relieved to find that the song was not one that murderers would sing.

Keeping away from the river to avoid its tangled growths, he rode on, and came at length to a clearing where the river, which had been deep and quiet further back, ran shallow and murmuring. On the further bank he saw a camp-fire, behind which stood a very rough gunyah of boughs and bark set up under the hanging roots of a big fig-tree. No-one was to be seen, nor just then to be heard. Not only did the sight of the gunyah convince him that he had come upon a party of natives, but that of the prints of naked feet about.

Then the song burst forth again. He looked to the left and saw the singer just below the camp, sitting on a lumpy snag in the middle of a deeper part of the river. A white woman. A girl. She sat sideways to him, looking downstream, and sang lustily while splashing under water with extended legs and dashing it over her light brown nakedness with her hands.

He stopped dead, astounded, stared for seconds, unable to believe his eyes. Then he grinned. Then, afraid of shocking the girl by coming suddenly into her sight, he uncoiled his whip and cracked it.

The singing stopped abruptly. The girl looked at her camp, then at the tree-tops, gaping. When he cracked again she turned to him, stared at him for a moment wide-eyed, then, with swiftness and smoothness of a startled crocodile, slipped into the water. He saw her black head pop up again under the high grassy bank. Without looking back she struggled up the bank, sprawled there, leapt up, flew into the jungle.

He chuckled. Still standing as he was, some seconds later he chuckled again to see her pass like a flash from the jungle to the gunyah. But in spite of chuckling he was afraid to advance; indeed he even avoided staring at the gunyah; and though the desire to play the faun to this nymph was in his heart, thought of flight was uppermost in his mind.

At length he turned to his pack-horses, which appeared to be as astonished as himself, and with a loud whip-cracking drove them ahead of him towards the camp. The horses crossed the shallows and stopped before the gunyah to stare and sniff at things that lay about. He followed slowly.

The camp might easily be taken for a native's. The only
articles lying about that were not of native-make were a
ragged blanket and a fishing-line and billy-can. The rest
were a fish-spear, a kylie, a yam-stick, a dilly-bag, and a
tikki fire-lighting set.

Without dismounting or looking directly at the gunyah,
he said, "Hello — anybody home?" He looked directly
when he heard the rustling of leaves. No other answer. He
said again, this time with the thought of flight clamouring,
"Hello — all out or what?"

Again a rustling, which ended in a crackling. To his
momentary alarm a small swarthy white face popped out
and stared at him from a leafy wall. After regarding a pair
of bright blue eyes for a moment he exclaimed, "Well I'll
be hanged!"

The swarthy face brightened; the eyes blinked rapidly:
the mouth extended in a smile.

"You!" he cried. "Little Tocky from the hospital, aint
you?"

The smile became a grin. Then the face withdrew, to
reappear a moment later with the body of Tocky O'Cannon
coming on hands and knees from the low entrance. She
was now dressed in a short ragged smock of what appeared
to be coarse tanned calico. He chuckled. She cut a quaint
figure. As she rose he dismounted, to stand looking down
into her shyly smiling face. "Hello Tocky!" he said.

"Hello Norman!"

"Anybody else here?"

"No-more."

"What — not on your own, surely?"

"Yu-i."

"Where'd you come from?"

"Dere," she answered, pointing down the river with her
lips. "Mission."

"Ah! I heard you was there. And where's Christobel?"

"Stop longa Mission. Gottim lil beby."

He was alarmed. He swallowed, said hesitantly, "A —
a baby?"

"Yu-i. Belong to one blackboy."

Norman sighed his relief. "What you doin' here?" he
asked.

"Oh I runned away."

"What — from the Mission?"

"Yu-i."

"On your own?"

"No-more. Me an' t'ree udder girl — Rosalind, Honey-suckle, an' Diana. Dey wanner go look for Japs in lugger for takim way. I leave 'em, cos wanner go home."

"Where — the Compound?"

"Oh no-more! Black Adder Creek. Dat my mumma an' papa live long time before. Dat my home."

"Tim O'Cannon's place, eh? But that's a hell of a long way from here. And you're not Tim O'Cannon's daughter, you know. You're Humbolt Lace's."

She eyed him without comprehension. Then she looked at his packs and said shyly, while drawing lines in the earth with a toe. "You gottim plenty tucker?"

"Sure. We'll have some dinner right away. What you been livin' on?"

She swallowed, licked lips, said with a shy smile, "Oh yams an' lily-roots — an' fresh-water tuttles an' fish an' stick-eggs — and poor lil frogs and birdses — an' sometime nussing."

He laughed. When he had unpacked he made a huge loaf of damper and set it in his camp-oven, and while it cooked, lay out a meal of cold roast bustard, chutney, tinned peaches, condensed milk, butter, sugar, jam. Tocky squatted beside the fire watching eagerly, sniffing the steam from the damper, salivating. And when the meal was ready she attacked it ravenously; and when it was ended she leant against a pack-saddle and fell asleep while he was rolling her a cigarette.

He did not rig his fly as he had intended before sitting down to dinner, because in the meantime he had decided to build a more substantial gunyah for Tocky and camp with her for a while, having abandoned the idea of going on to Flying Fox since learning from her that it was the site of the Mission. A storm was brewing. So he took up his tommy-axe and went off to cut bamboos and bark while Tocky slept.

§

Tocky asked Norman to take her to Black Adder, and after going to some length to prove that there was no danger of her being found by the missionaries and so involving him in trouble, succeeded in getting him to agree. But she could not make him take her there at once. He was set on the idea of playing the faun in Arcady. Their difference of opinion on that score brought about their first quarrel. The second was brought about by Tocky's inability to appreciate the beauty and wisdom of stanzas quoted from the Rubaiyat, and Norman's inability to stop quoting them. Peace was established on each occasion by the production of the mouth-organ.

That night, reclining in Norman's arms beside the fire, still clutching the rifle with which she had spent most of of the afternoon in joyous hunting while Norman built the gunyah, Tocky recounted her recent adventures.

The three girls with whom she had escaped from the Mission were two of them halfcastes and one a black quadroon; and there were as well four black youths, back-sliding converts, whose cunning had made escape possible. It was the third time she had escaped, and the only time she had remained at liberty for more than a few hours. Now she had been away more days than she could count. The escape was made in the mission-schooner's dinghy, in which she and her seven companions had sailed far to westward. They had landed in the mangroves of a salt-arm, hidden the dinghy, and come to the bush without leaving a trace behind. It had been the intention of the party to travel westward circuitously to a part of the coast where the crews of Japanese pearling-luggers came ashore to hunt and fish. These luggers sometimes called at the Mission to buy stores, the place from which they came originally being somewhere in the Indies apparently, or, as Tocky put it, Nudder Country Up North. The fugitives' vision of the future apparently had not gone beyond a meeting with the Japanese, whom they — the girls, that is — expected to take them away. Norman, bred as a whiteman, was rather shocked to think that they should think nothing of placing themselves in the hands of such low creatures. Then Tocky fairly horrified him by cheerfully confessing that the blackboys who had accompanied them had been their paramours.

She went on to say that after landing, the party had travelled inland for some distance, obliterating their tracks as they went, and then had turned westward, keeping well away from the coast during the first part of the journey for fear of meeting searchers from the Mission and during the latter part to avoid being seen by whitemen who lived on a little island called Tumbukka, which lay close to the mainland at a point not far to eastward of the Jinjin River.

Norman was startled at the mention of the whitemen. He asked about them. Tocky knew nothing about them beyond what the blackboys had said, which was that there were three or four of them, that one or two were old men, that they owned a lugger, that they wandered much about the bush as though looking for something, and that the young ones pestered the lubras of the tribe of the neighbourhood, the Mundikualas. It was mainly on account of this reputation for pestering women that she and her companions had taken pains to avoid them. Besides, they feared that these whitemen might betray them to Old Lucifer should he come that way in search of them.

After passing Tumbukka, the party had struck back to the sea, and at last had arrived at the mouth of this Jinjin River. There they had split up, as the result of Diana's — she was the black quadroon — wanting to go to the Mundikuala people with her boy. Tocky was never enthusiastic about going to the Japanese. All the while she had had the idea of persuading the others to come with her to Black Adder. Thus when a quarrel had arisen out of Diana's wanting to go to the Old People, she had sided with Diana and persuaded her to come to the railway. Rosalind and Honeysuckle, tired of their boys and having no further use for them, had crossed the river alone and gone westward. The rejected boys had turned back. Tocky and Diana and their lovers had travelled up the river for two days, during which Diana had assumed the humility of a lubra so completely that Tocky, seeing that she was expected to do the same, had quarrelled with her and the boys and left them. They had turned eastward, heading for the Mundikuala camp. She had come on up the river. She had been alone now for four days.

Norman then told her how her old friend Con had been done to death, and how the murderers had travelled across country to this very river to meet his own father who had killed a Chinaman. Tocky was shocked. She had begun to weep for Con; but the news that the place they were camped in was a murderers' meeting-place and that the island she had passed might be a murderers' kitchen, dried her eyes instantly and set them to watching shadows in the bush. Norman then horrified her by discussing murder generally, beginning with his father's crime and ending, after having dragged her mind through many a frightful scene, with those committed by the French Bluebeard, Landru. And after that he turned to the subject of the slaying of murderers by the law, for which, as in the former dissertation, he went beyond Australia for his many gruesome instances. Thus Tocky learnt that murderers were not only hanged by the neck till they were Daid, Daid, Daid, as she had often heard Mr Hollower say with great ferocity that they were, but sometimes garrotted and electrocuted and suffocated and guillotined. And she learnt that white people often killed their brethren and that Government put white murderers to death. She was astounded. Formerly she had thought that murder and capital punishment were things that concerned only coloured people, her knowledge having been gleaned solely from lectures Mr Hollower often delivered to his flock in order to teach them to obey the Ten Commandments. She had heard of any number of murders at the Mission, but of only one that was not a blackfellow's business, namely the Cain and Abel Case, in which each person concerned, according to the colouring of the Bible Pictures at the Mission, was a coloured-man of some kind, as was the only Person—He also was depicted on those scrolls—who had ever been put to death.

In punishing murderers the wrath of Government as described by Norman was comparable with that of God as lavishly described by Mr Hollower. Tocky was appalled. The fact that these Masters of Mankind were eager to put coloured murderers to death seemed natural enough; but their eagerness to slay their brothers, and to do so to avenge not only the murders of whitemen, but of humble Chinamen and Greeks, seemed monstrous. It took a good while, during which Norman argued like an utterly heartless State Prosecutor, to convince her that the thing was so.

The talk of murders and man-hunts and trials and executions spoiled Tocky's sleep that night, and also spoilt the hunting with the rifle that she set out to do next day. An O'Cannon bred if not so born, she loved a rifle for the sight and feel of it and the power to deal death it gave; but that day she could not concentrate her sighted eye upon a likely victim without thinking that she was doing murder. Indeed she shot but one small wallaby, although a crocodile, a buffalo, and two old-men kangaroos had come within her range. And with the blood of her one small victim she mingled tears of stricken conscience, and over its beautifully baked carcass, which she nevertheless partook of with appetite, told Norman she hoped she would not be seized in the night by the Wallaby Tribe and judged and gelatined.

THE joys of Arcady soon palled on Norman. His nymph, he found, was not the amusingly artless and sweetly amorous creature he had taken her for, but a shameless little fool. Poor Tocky! Her experiences in love, though by no means few, were all of necessity hasty, and hence were too brief and practical for her to learn from them much about the peculiarities of the male. Not knowing that men are prudes when not desiring, she did not realize that it was unseemly to behave at noon as she had done at midnight, or at sundown as she had in the middle of the afternoon; and not knowing that to hold the interest of an undesiring man a woman must listen, or at least pretend to listen, to his talk, she did not scruple to interrupt to say something for herself nor to yawn in the talker's face.

By the fifth day Norman desired nothing more than to be alone. He decided to go in search of the Mundikualas' camp in order to learn something more about the white men of Tumbukka Island. Guessing that Tocky would want to accompany him and most likely make trouble if refused, he kept his decision dark till it was revealed when he began to pack on the morning of the sixth day. Tocky joyfully supposed at first that he was preparing to go home. Thus the hurt of disillusionment was added to the insult of being left behind. She wept, cursed, flung things about, snatched up the automatic pistol, threatened to do murder, called him a snake and a dingo and a yeller barsted. All this did anything but make him change his mind.

He had to handle her roughly to silence her, and to convince her that he intended to return, as he honestly did intend, had to divide his pack and replace the hobbles on one of the horses. And to stop her clamouring to come, he had to sit down and tell her how the country into which he was going was now swarming with murderers and those debil-debils incarnate the police. By doing that he only succeeded in making her clamour for him to stay. He was forced at last to cuff her. That appeared to be the most effective way of dealing with her. He resorted to it several times during the rest of the argument. He told her that the reason he wished to learn whether the murderers were still about was that he should be rewarded by the police if he could say where they might be found. He explained, drawing solely

on imagination and merely to impress her with the importance of his errand, that the reward on the heads of Frank
and Ket was a thousand pounds.

Tocky was not so impressed by the magnitude of the reward, since money meant practically nothing to her, but by
the fact that such rewards were paid, it being another amazing instance of the horrible eagerness of the Masters of Mankind to put their brothers to death. She then began to clamour for the rifle, which she said she must have to defend
herself should any of the monsters with which the country
was swarming come her way, and continued to clamour for
it, in spite of his cuffs and roars, right up to the moment
of his departure, but not nearly so much because she wanted it for the purpose stated, which could be served quite
well with the shotgun she rejected, as because she loved it
for itself and wanted it for hunting. He wanted it for
shooting buffaloes. He flung the shotgun at her and poked
the rifle through the straps of his pack; then, taking up
the leading-rope of the pack-horse, he mounted the other
and went off.

At the moment of his departure Tocky was squatting on
haunches, hunched and moaning like a mourning lubra. He
left her thus, because he feared that conciliatory action
might spoil the good work he had done. As he slipped into
the saddle he looked at her and bade her a gruff farewell,
and did not look again. Thus he did not see her bright eye
kindle as he went, and having no cause to look back for
some time afterwards, did not see her rise and come slinking after him.

It was with intent to follow him all the way that she
went after him; but that intention did not take her far; for,
after spending a minute or so within reach of the darling
rifle, she wished for nothing more than to get possession of
that. She drew it from the pack with a single tug, rushed
back to the camp with it and in a panic hid it in the gunyah.
An hour or more passed while she sat waiting fearfully
for Norman. Then fear of him was forgotten when she
caught sight of an old-man kangaroo coming down the other
bank to drink. She darted into the gunyah. The magazine
of the rifle was full. She hugged the heavy oily thing,
gurgling for joy.

Norman did not discover his loss till he camped for dinner at noon. The thought that Tocky might have taken the
rifle never entered his head. He supposed that he had lost
it on the track, most likely in a certain lancewood thicket

some two or three miles back in which the pack-horse had several times become entangled.

After dinner he rode back on his tracks, and, having passed through the thicket and seen that it was difficult to find a rifle in the long dry grass, turned round, and, travelling this time on foot and searching carefully, passed through again. As that thicket was the only one he had encountered since leaving the jungle, he came to the conclusion that he must have lost the rifle near the camp. But for the fact that he had to return to the creek where he had had dinner and left his belongings, he would have gone back to the camp from the thicket. As it was he did not reach the creek till nightfall.

When he retired that night he intended to return to the camp next morning; but he did not rise with that intention; lying smoking under the Morning Star, delighting in the sweet virginity of dawn, he thought of that harlot Tocky and of the trouble of having to part with her a second time. So he decided that the finding of the rifle could wait till he returned from the Mundikualas, and that in the meantime he could make good use of the opportunity forced on him by necessity to learn, as he had long planned to learn, to become a dead-shot with the pistol. Soon after sunrise he went his way, riding towards a creek called Yalgah, up which, according to what Tocky had innocently told him, Diana and her black companions would have marched for some distance after having crossed from the Jinjin. He intended to find and follow their tracks.

Just before noon, while approaching a sunken line of trees that he supposed marked the course of the creek he was seeking, he came upon fresh tracks of a horse. His own horse saw the tracks before he did, and stopped and sniffed at them, then sniffed the air, then neighed. The pack-horse neighed also, and came trotting up. He took up the lead-rope again, thinking that they were about to meet a mob of brumbies that might lead the pack away. So he rode on, following the tracks, expecting to witness the usual scene of equine amazement enacted when wild horses caught sight of their slave-brothers at their labour.

But the amazement was his; for, come to the edge of the flood-bank of the creek, he saw below on a small green flat beside the stream no mob of wild-eyed brumbies poised for flight, but one lean drooping nag in saddle and bridle and hobbles; and near it was a fire and some camping-gear. He drew rein sharply, instantly afraid that he had blundered on the murderers' camp and half expecting to see the tall bearded figure of his father come strolling into view. But no-one appeared, though minutes passed while the bony horse whinnied and made enough noise with hobbles and hoofs to rouse a sleeper fifty yards away. He waited about five minutes, then slowly rode down to see. He was not afraid of meeting Mark or Chook, but of meeting the other fellows.

His fear left him as soon as he saw the camping-gear, which was so scanty that it could not have belonged to more than one man, and so poor that it was not likely that its owner was white. The nap, which lay on the grass as though someone had lately risen from it, consisted of two greasy bran-sacks, or, as bushmen call them, Wagga Rugs; and there were only three food utensils, an enamel plate and pannikin, both of them old and chipped, and a quart-pot that had once been a can containing engine-oil, the brand of which could still be seen. Rice was boiling in the pot; and beside it a split duck grilled on a fence-wire grid.

He dismounted, went to the creek to drink and look for the camper. He saw nothing but tracks in the mud, boot-tracks, presence of which disproved his notion that the camper was not white. Mud still oozed from tracks near the water. No tracks could be seen on the other side.

He returned to the fire. Though he wished to have dinner, he did not touch his pack, knowing that it was contrary to bush-convention for one to settle in a stranger's camp without invitation. He sat on haunches and gave some attention to the cooking food, at the same time keeping a look-out for the camper so that the man might not be shocked by coming on him unawares. But for knowing how eerie his voice would have sounded in his own ears he would have cooee'd.

His considerateness was being wasted. The camper was crouched in a bamboo-clump not a dozen yards away, watching him through the sights of a rifle and trying to command his trigger-finger to do what his mind had been urging it ever since Norman appeared. More than once when Norman's black eyes unconsciously found the black eye behind the sights the finger tightened to do the bidding of the mind and drew the span of his future to a very hair's breadth. But every time the finger loosened, balked in the task it was willing to do by the clamouring of the coward heart that stood between it and mind. And thus in the bamboo-

clump, while in the space where the fire burned, Norman
sat stirring the rice.

The hidden man was Charles Ket, murderer of Con the
Greek, and potential murderer of anyone whose existence
threatened him with the retribution of which he lived in
constant dread. He had thought that the approaching horse-
man was Frank McLash, but with customary caution had
dodged to cover. At first sight of Norman he had thought
that the troopers were come at last, because Norman was
clad in khaki. He had seen his colour at once, but thought
he was a tracker with the troopers at his heels, which was
why he had not shot him on sight. He wished he had done
so, wished with all his mind; for at that moment his heart
was hot with desire of the flesh to preserve itself; since
then it had grown cold with the fear of doing murder, and
colder and colder as time passed.

He recognized Norman when he reached the camp, and
knew that he would recognize him and betray his whereabouts if he got the chance, betray with eagerness, as he
would do in his place. And he wondered while he covered
the khaki breast whether a reward was out for the capture
of him and Frank and whether that and hatred had brought
this yeller-feller out there. He could see that Norman was
unarmed, and that apparently the only weapon he possessed
was the pistol in the holster on his saddle. He would rather
have seen him standing there armed and suspicious, since
killing him would then be easy.

But kill him he must, unarmed and unwary though he
might be. Cold Blood! What difference did that make to
murder? He clutched the rifle tight to still the trembling
of his hands. Cold Blood? Nonsense. Kill him. Bury his
body in the creek-bank. No-one would ever know. Kill him,
fool, and kill quickly. He is as much an enemy as a policeman!

Though Ket's hand stayed, his mind was made up to
kill. He even thought while watching Norman roll a cigarette that the joy of a smoke, so long denied him, would
soon be his again. In a few seconds' time, if only coward
heart would not freeze willing finger! Tobacco. And good
rich food in the pack. But would he be able to smoke over
the body of a man he had killed in cold blood? Bah — kill
him!

Norman took the well-grilled duck from the fire and placed it on top of the quart-pot, then looked about for a knife
he had seen lying near, intending to scrape the carcass clean

of charcoal. It was a bowie-knife. He picked it up, glanced at it, then uttered an exclamation, stared at the wooden handle hard. It bore the burnt inscription IS, the brand of Red Ochre. He rose, looked about for other things —

Bang!

The quart-pot burst and spattered him with scalding rice. He yelled, not because he felt the rice, but saw a cloud of smoke.

Ket, now in a fury, snarled as he ejected the wasted cartridge. Norman heard the snarl and the click of the rifle-bolt. He yelled again, hopped.

Bang!

Wharng! A heavy bullet passed Norman's ear. He reeled. Then, catching a glimpse of a terrible figure, black-bearded and shock-haired, clad in a ragged black shirt and dungaree trousers, rising in the bamboo-clump, he screamed, dashed to the creek. The horses bolted after him.

Bang!

He heard that as, taking the longest leap of his life, he cleared the stream. He was halfway up the high flood-bank and climbing frantically when Ket caught sight of him again.

Ket, hot with the old hatred now, with all his criminal instincts in command, had run after him. At the edge of the stream he dropped to a knee, raised the rifle to a perfect target.

Click!

Norman knew nothing of his luck. A moment after it he was hurling himself at the horse that came thundering past him. He was struggling to lift himself into the saddle when Ket jerked the bolt.

The magazine was exhausted. The rest of the ammunition was with Frank.

Ket could not hear the thunder of hoofs for the thundering of his own heart. As he rose he passed his left hand over brow and drew great gulps of air. Then he began to tremble violently, so that the rifle fell from his right hand into the stream and splashed him. He dropped to the ground again, this time on both knees, and dipped burning face into muddy water.

Norman, who while handling the automatic pistol had often visualized scenes in which he fought gun-battles with the thin-lipped nonchalance of the honourable murderers of the screen, gave no thought to battle as he rode away, but rode as fast as his horse would carry him, thinking of

nought but getting out of the enemy's range. When at
length he stopped, the horses were exhausted. But it was
far more fear of danger ahead than thought for the horses
that stopped him. After a lengthy hesitation he decided to
turn back, certainly not on his tracks nor anywhere near
them, but in a direction that would bring him back to the
creek well above the scene of the encounter.

He remembered the would-be assassin only as a
beard and a mop of hair and a black shirt and a rifle, but
was certain that it was Ket. The branded knife was proof
of that. Either Ket had had it in his belongings when he
left Red Ochre or it had been given to Mark by Oscar with
other things and Ket had got it from Mark. No doubt, he
thought the rifle that had nearly killed him was his own
.303. He rode warily with pistol drawn, though perhaps
with not much certainty that he would use it if the need
arose. His wariness, like his earlier considerateness, was
wasted. Ket was heading for home.

Ket was galloping back to Tumbukka to warn his comrades of the peril started by himself. While Norman in
fancy saw him creeping through bush with murderous intent, he saw Norman racing for the troopers. Fool, he
shouted. Unutterable hell-damned bloody fool! Fool who
had so hellishly bungled the simple act of securing himself
from discovery that he had advertised his hiding to the
world. Oh monster fool!

§

While Ket and Norman were flying from each other,
Frank McLash was riding quietly up the Jinjin towards
Tocky's camp, unaware of the existence of the camp itself,
but well aware of the fact that Arcady was near at hand,
since it was the little footprints of a dryad he was following.

Frank had not merely happened on the dryad's track.
The blackboys who had turned back eastward when rejected by Rosalind and Honeysuckle, had met him and Mark
and Ket near Tumbukka, and, being careless of what might
happen to their late companions now, had, with some slight
hope of being rewarded by these notoriously amorous fellows, said that four parti-coloured girls were wandering
unprotected in the bush. Their hope was slight, because
they knew that the whitemen were stingy, or rather thought
so, not understanding that poverty was responsible for the
fact that they sought to win the favours of the Mundikuala

women for nothing, and believing that all whitemen were
supplied with their wants and more by that chieftain of
theirs the Government. The men of Tumbukka were actually
poorer than themselves.

Halfcaste damsels wandering in the bush! How Frank
and Ket had chuckled! Not Mark, however, who, though
he found life at Tumbukka as dull and wretched as his
comrades did, yearned after no woman but one. Now that
old Chook Henn was dead he wished he had not gone away
without that woman.

The young men, speaking at first in jest and then in
anger, told Mark that he was growing old when he refused
to let them set out in the *Spirit of the Land* in search of
the two girls whom they thought it would be easier to find,
that is of Rosalind and Honeysuckle, who had gone up the
beach to the luggers. Old and prudish, they cried. And indeed it seemed to them that they were right in saying so,
since his objection to their having dealings with the girls
was fear that the story that they did so would be spread
through the bush by blacks till it reached the Mission and
betrayed their whereabouts to the police, which seemed a
needless one to the young men, seeing that they were about
to set sail for the Indies. They had already been to the
Indies and stayed away long enough to be careless of pursuit by the police. They had returned in the middle of the
year to find the packs they had lost during the journey
from the Melisande. How could there be any danger of
betraying their whereabouts, they demanded, when the task
of getting the girls would be simply one of going ashore for
them in the dinghy? Then they could set sail for the
Indies at once.

Mark argued that it was certain that if they were to set
out in the lugger the story that they had gone in search of
the girls would be spread by the blackboys who gave the
information; and, having reached the Mission, as it must
do when search-parties came from there, the story would
be passed on to the police, who would at once want to
know who were the whitemen with the lugger and would
pass a description on to the police of the Indies. He said
that Frank and Ket had given him quite enough trouble as
it was; he had promised to see them through their troubles,
and even though the venture had proved a costly one to
him, seeing that he had spent every penny he possessed on
it and now had no hope of being reimbursed by them since
they had been fool enough to lose their money, he would do

o

so, but not in any way that would get him into trouble; the
halfcaste girls must not come near his ship.

That was not the first time Frank and Ket had been told
what they might or might not do since falling in with this
man they knew as Jack Ramble. Since the return to search
for the lost packs they had been told so many times that
they had been tempted to stain their hands with blood again,
and might have done so quickly had they known how to sail
a ship. So they had been forced to abandon the happy plan
of going into exile with brides, to take up the one to which
the autocratic Ramble might object but could not prevent
them from carrying out, namely, the plan to run the other
girls to earth and possess them temporarily. They set out
to effect this without confiding in the autocrat. They pretended that they were going out to make a last search for
their precious packs.

They set out on horseback, rode to the mouth of the Jinjin and found the tracks of four pairs of feet leading up
the right bank. They followed the tracks together till they
reached the point where Tocky left the others. Her small
footprints were obviously a girl's. So they parted, Ket
going on towards the Mundikuala camp, Frank after Tocky.
They arranged to meet again on the beach.

§

Frank arrived at the arcadian camp late in the afternoon
of the day of Norman's encounter with Ket. He might
easily have passed it. Supposing that he still had far to go
before he should come upon his quarry, and being intent
on travelling as fast and as far as possible before nightfall
and the bursting of the great storm that was brewing, he
was not taking particular notice of the track nor surroundings. Tocky was bathing at the time, but not singing as
when Norman found her. Hearing the crashing progress of
Frank and thinking it was Norman returning, she cooee'd
loudly, swam ashore, and, naked as she was, ran out to
meet him. Frank was as much shocked by the sight of her
as she was by the sight of him. And his horse stopped
dead, amazed. Tocky was stopped by paralysis. She stood
with one hand to a breast, the other to her mouth.

Frank was not a pretty sight. He wore a curly black
beard; and his hair was so voluminous that it peeped
through the crown of his battered hat. Besides the hat he
wore but two garments, a holey cotton singlet that exposed
his great brown hairy arms to the shoulders and much of

his hairy belly, and tattered khaki trousers that exposed a
good deal of his legs. His large dirty hairy toes cocked
up inquisitively and stared at Tocky from the stirrups.

A moment of staring. Then Frank's beard parted, revealing black and gold teeth. He said, as one would to a
pleasant friend one suddenly meets while seeking him, "So
here you are, eh? Where'd you spring from?"

Tocky gasped, wheeled, tripped over a tussock of grass,
fell with a yell. But she was up in an instant, and in another
was in the gunyah. Frank laughed heartily.

He rode to the camp and dismounted, looked in some
surprise at the pack-saddle and other gear that had led him
to suppose she had a horse, then saw her calico dress lying
spread on rushes where she had dropped it. He got the
dress and brought it to the gunyah, saying, "Hey — here's
your dress, kiddo."

Tocky did not answer. Below the ragged blanket screen-
ing the doorway she could see his feet. "I aint gunner hurt
you," he said. "Here's your dress to put on."

She was not to be drawn. She stood against the further
wall, wrapped in Norman's blanket. Thus she stood still
till she saw a foot move forward and the ragged blanket
bulge; then she reached for the rifle, which leant against
the wall near by, and snatched it up. She had been wishing
to do that for several minutes. When Frank poked his
smiling face round the screen he looked into a ring of
steel. He withdrew with haste. But he did not leave the
doorway, though he now stood aside. "Don't you want your
dress?" he asked uncertainly. She did not answer. After
a lengthy pause he asked cheerily, "You camped on your
own, kid?"

"Go way," muttered Tocky.

"Garn! I wanner be friends. Here's your dress. Don't
you want it?"

"Go way," she said, with a little more strength.

"Listen, love —"

"I aint you love!" she cried. "G'wan away — or I'll
shoot you daid."

"Well, you're a nasty little bitch, anyway."

"Go way I tell you!"

He grunted and withdrew.

After standing long in the same position, she found courage to creep to the screen and look out. He was unsaddling
his horse.

With sunken heart she watched him hobble the horse

then unroll a small bundle then break and set up bamboo sticks and rig a filthy little sand-fly net and a shelter of paper-bark, then take a bag of food to her fire. She watched till her back ached from stooping and her eyes from the strain of staring through a hole. She saw him make tea, in her billy with her tea, and roll a fat cigarette of her tobacco. He appeared to enjoy the tea greatly. The cigarette made him cough at first, then spit profusely, then retch. He flung it away. She did not understand that he had not smoked for weeks. She knew, however, and with anything but joy, that he was one of the murderers. She felt doomed.

Having recovered from sickness, Frank looked at the gunyah, looked right into Tocky's eye, she thought. She shrank away. After a while he rose, picked up the dress and came back. As soon as she saw his feet she squeaked, "Go way!"

"All right, all right," he said testily. "Only wanner give you your dress." He touched the screen.

"I kill you!" she cried.

He jumped back.

After a while he said, "Garn — you aint game to shoot. Gimme that gun here."

"Aint I game!" she cried.

"What's wrong with you? I aint gunner hurt you, blast you. I only wanner help you. You run away from the Mission, and I —"

"Go way!"

"Do be different!"

No response.

After a while he asked, "There any crocodiles in the river here?"

No response.

"I asked you's there any crocodiles in the river here. You might answer."

"Go way!" she cried. "Big ting! I know what you after. You go way an' stop way — or I shoot you daid — dere!"

"Garn — you couldn't shoot pussy!"

"Couldn't I? Don't you worry. I'm too good. Don't you try or you see pretty quick. Go way — go way — go way!"

He grunted and withdrew. She crept to the screen in time to see him, stripped of his ragged singlet, as though he feared that contact with water would do it harm, but clad in trousers, no doubt out of modesty, plunge into the river. She hoped fervently that a crocodile might be there.

She watched him eat his supper of yams and rice and dried fish. Though his fare did not appeal to her, the fact that he was eating made her salivate. All her food was with her in the gunyah, but consisted of flour and stuff in tins that she dared not set aside the rifle to deal with. She watched him thicken the roof of his shelter when a flurry of heavy rain-drops fell, and watched him crawl into it at dusk, and watched till all was hidden in darkness. Then she retired to the middle of the gunyah, doubled the blanket and spread it on the ground, let the mosquito net down from the roof, and sat down to watch the faintly luminous space below the screen. It was her intention to steal away to the bush. She watched for a long while, till, without knowing it, she fell asleep.

She was wakened by the din of a storm. Thunder was crashing. Wind was roaring in the trees. She started up. The ragged screen was flying in the wind, so that the clearing was revealed to her by a flash of lightning. She saw everything as she had seen it at dusk, except that the earth appeared in the rain to be bubbling. Darkness crashed down. Water poured through the flimsy roof of the gunyah. Wind tore at the net. Again the lightning blazed. Then she saw what she had been expecting from the moment of waking — Frank. He was running from his shelter to the gunyah. It was only for an instant that she saw him; but the sight was plain enough; he was dressed as when she saw him last, clad only in his trousers. She did not hear him burst through the screen; for all small sound was drowned in an avalanche of thunder; but she felt him do so; and as she did her hand closed on the cool stock of the rifle.

The thunder ceased. She heard him panting. Then she heard him roar, " 'S rainin' like hell!"

Then a flash of lightning revealed him as a black giant leaning over her.

"Go way!" she screamed. Her little voice was lost in thunder.

She felt the net being dragged from under her knees, felt hot breath in her face. Then when the lightning flashed again she saw him looking down at her with the net caught up in a mighty hand. In the chaotic darkness she shot him. She heard him yell. In the flash that followed she saw him go reeling through the door with shaggy head flung back and clutched in hands.

Still on her heels she squatted, still with rifle gripped in iron hands, sweating in the humid heat, breathing the fumes of cordite, staring before her into a great irregular fire-rimmed patch of darkness, the hole in the net burnt out by the rifle's flash.

She saw nothing, heard nothing, scarcely thought, her mind and body lying crouched in terror of that leaning form. The fire in the net had almost died out, the devils had driven the storm a long way off, the frogs in the river were singing the begging song she used to love to join them in — Give money, give money, two bob, two bob, give money, give money, come on — when she collapsed with a sigh and buried her face in the blanket and fell asleep.

In the early dawn she stirred, feeling cold, and feeling the stings of a swarm of mosquitoes. A mosquito stung her nose. She slapped and woke. She sat up wearily, stiff and sore, rubbing the great weal the rifle had cut across her back through her lying on it.

With a start she remembered. She listened. No sound but the flutter and cheep of stirring birds and the gurgle of the river. She crawled out blinking, went to the door. There was just enough light for her to see. Frank's shelter was lying flat, and moving, moving, as she discovered after staring at it for a while, because there was water under it. The river, low as its banks were there, had over-flowed.

The sight and sound of water made her lick her lips, which were as hard and smooth as leather. So she stood for many minutes, while daylight waxed and spread. Soon she was able to see Frank's footprints, faint flat footprints coming from the shelter, deep ones of ball and toes leaving her door and disappearing into the scrub and grass a few yards away. Her eyes, given to looking for such things, since such things were always eyed with interest by those with whom for years she had been forced to associate, look-ed at the tracks once more. There was no sign of their own-er. Then she looked at the water, which she saw was steadily creeping in, then at the sodden fireplace. She thought of food. The thought was put out of mind by sight of her dress lying where Frank had left it. She stared at the dress till she found courage to dash out, clad in the blanket, and retrieve it.

Back in the gunyah she opened a tin of beef, but found she could not eat it when she tried. She returned to the door to watch the river and to desire to fling her hot body into it and drink it dry. At last thirst gave her courage to dash out again. Dressed now, and carrying the rifle, she ran to

the fireplace, snatched up the billy, and went on blindly
to the river, ignoring the water through which she had to
run for yards, because that was filthy. The river was filthy
too; but that did not trouble her; she scooped up a quart of
it, and turning to eye the camp, drank of it greedily. Where
was he? Where was he? Where was he? She had been
asking herself that ever since she woke. Had she killed
him? Had she wounded him? Had she scared him away?
She was almost convinced that he was sitting somewhere
in the scrub watching. She saw his bay horse standing in
the jungle not far away with Norman's black.

She did not see Frank till she reached the fireplace on
the much less hasty journey back. The sight of him caused
her to drop the billy. Water shot up into her face and blinded her. He was in the scrub a few yards from the gunyah
door.

She blinked back her sight. Her hands were paralysed.
It was only his feet she saw, his large white feet standing
side by side on heels, with toes pointing to the bright blue
sky.

She heard the hum of blow-flies. Blackfellow that she
was, she knew what that sound meant. Trackers look for
dead men in the bush by climbing trees and listening on the
wind. She rushed to the gunyah.

She sat for hours. She watched the heavens darken and
another storm sweep down, watched the clouds roll by and
the sun retake possession, watched the coming of the birds,
the big black crows, the feathery-legged kites, the ibises,
heard them fluttering furtively in the trees above, squabbling
softly in the scrub. But she saw nothing consciously, and
heeded not what she heard. For she was thinking, thinking
of blow-flies, thinking of death, thinking of murder, thinking of the lust of the Masters of Mankind for revenge—
thinking of the silhouetted form, of the crash of the rifle,
of the yell, of the acrid smoke, of Norman, of Mr Hollower, of Satan, of God — of God, Old God, Mr Hollower's
Boss, who, Mr Hollower let it be known, was more terrible
than himself, more powerful and vindictive than Government, more savage than police, whiter than any whiteman,
furious hater of sin, for ever hanging out of clouds and
thundering down at wicked old earth — Thou shalt not this,
thou shalt not that, but above all Thou Shalt Not Kill!

She thought of Norman, but not as one to whom to turn
for help. He was a friend of hangmen, of electric-lighters.
of the fiends that operated the gelatine. He was gone off

to catch three murderers now, one of whom was his own
father. His father and that remaining murderer of poor
dear Con would be strapped up and dragged screaming, as
Norman said, to a Thing that would hang them by the necks
till they were Daid — Daid — Daid! If Government would
act like that in respect of a Dago and a Chow, what would
it not do in respect of one of the Anointed? And what reward would Norman get for capturing the murderer of
such a one?

Then it occurred to her that Frank might only be wounded — or even asleep. She rose and went out slowly. No —
he was dead. He was dead! The flies were raging over him.
The air was thick with them. And the birds were perched
on him. They swept up in a body when she appeared.

Pains in her belly. With a gasp she turned. Back in the
gunyah her flesh burned till it was scarlet, then burst out
sweating, then turned ice-cold. She thought she was dying,
smitten by Old God. She wondered what she would say at
The Judgement. She saw Old God. But for his long white
beard and nightshirt, he closely resembled Dr Aintee.

At length she felt better, and forgot God in desiring to
drink. Soon she took up the rifle and stole back to the
river.

Again she thought that Frank might only be wounded.
She stared at his bluish feet. She jumped when a crow
kahed hoarsely.

Wounded, and tired out through having spent the night
out in the rain. Poor fellow! She might make him a billy
of tea.

She coughed — Oh her cough was more terrifying than
the croak of the crow! She said "Hey!" and made her flesh
creep. She tried to whistle. She raised her voice to cry
out "Hey!" with all her might, but only squeaked.

Desiring to drink again, she filled the billy from the water
dragging at her feet. As she rose a Thing dropped out of
Heaven and smote her. She staggered, shocked to the heart,
dropped the rifle in the river. A jabiroo was sweeping lazily
downstream on great swishing, creaking wings.

Recovered from the shock, she searched for the rifle,
first with feet and then with hands, while fearfully watching the feet. She could not find it. She stood bewildered,
feeling helpless. Then slowly she came ashore. Loss of
the rifle enabled her to do something possession of it had
restrained her from doing. She crept up to look.

Frank was grinning at the sky. Meat-ants were swarm-

ing over him, making him appear to be woolly with red
hair. The birds had pecked out his eyes, torn off his ears,
stripped his nose. Still she thought he might be alive. She
picked up a stick and threw it towards him gently. The ants
swarmed madly. The flies shot up in an angry crowd and
hurled their tainted bodies in her face. Pain in the belly
again. She turned and fled to the gunyah.

She saw Frank's shelter float away, saw his saddle rocking, saw the filthy water come within a yard of her. Then,
acting on a sudden thought, she rose, with frantic fingers
filled a pack-bag with anything lying near to hand, then with
the bag and the blanket and the shotgun stole out of the
gunyah and fled.

§

Norman was driven far out of his way by fear of Ket
and further by fear of floods. Returned to the creek that
he had jumped the day before, he found a swollen river.
Remembering that a tract of marshy land that must have
been flooded by the deluge of the night lay between him and
the Jinjin, he did not cross the creek, but followed it up to
high ground. The map gave him a fair idea of where he
was going. Thus, after travelling through the foothills of
the Smoky Ranges for a day, he came to the head waters
of the Jinjin, down which he went with intent to rejoin
her whom he was again regarding as desirable. He was
still in the hills when night of the second day's flight from
Ket descended on him.

He was still in the hills when after three hours' travelling
next morning he came upon his nymph; and having supposed that the arcadian camp must be flooded out, because
more heavy rain had fallen since the deluge, he was not surprised. The nymph herself was more than surprised. She
was asleep when he found her, lying on a blanket under
a shelter of boughs set up against a wall of rock beside the
stream, and sleeping so soundly that she did not waken
even when he came and knelt beside her. Delighted by her
beauty, her virgin-like tranquility, her full lips, her thick
black lashes lying on her now quite pallid cheeks, he bent
and kissed her.

She opened her eyes. She screamed and heaved away.
Then she recognized him, and after a second of wide-eyed
staring, flung herself into his arms. With surprise and no
small satisfaction he found her weeping. "Well now — well
now!" he crooned over her glossy head. "Did poor lil ting
tink I was a debil-debil?"

At length he asked, "Did you get flooded out down there?"

She nodded against his breast.

"This all the gear you saved?"

Another nod.

"Didn't lose the horse too, did you?"

Nod.

"Oh hell! And he was hobbled. If he got caught he'd get drowned. Couldn't you catch him?"

Shake of the head.

After a pause he asked, "I say — you never saw a rifle lyin' about anywhere, did you?"

Stillness.

"Eh? I lost it. Haven't been out east of the camp, have you?"

Shake.

"I lost it somewhere out there just after I left you. Wish I'd give it to you now. Won't be much chance findin' it after this rain. Still I might. It must be somewhere in the jungle."

Stillness.

He suddenly drew her back from his breast and looked at her and asked, "What's up?"

She dropped her head.

"Face all white and wet. Not sick, are you?"

Shake.

He placed a finger under her chin and raised her face. She lowered her eyes. "Sick?" he repeated.

She nodded.

"Love me?" he asked.

Nod.

"What — you been lonely, eh? Aw, well, it's all right now. Here I am."

After looking at her for a while he said, "You look sick, too. Not short of tucker, are you?"

"No-more," she muttered.

"Moping," he said. "Poor kid. I'll cook you a feed right away."

He kissed her and rose, and rising said, "I intended to look for the rifle coming back, but couldn't come back same way. Wait till I tell you what happened to me — Hey — don't cry honey! Here I am again. And I'm gunner take you home. Lie down — go on — lie down while I get you some tucker."

Within an hour of the reunion he mounted and rode

down the river to the old camp to look for the horse and the rifle and whatever might be found of the things that Tocky had left behind. She would not accompany him. She sat in her gunyah like a mourning lubra, watching with haggard eyes. He was not displeased to go alone nor curious about her behaviour, since he believed from what she had told him that she was ill.

He returned at midday bringing the one pack-bag she had left behind and a few small articles he had found in the gunyah. He told her that the whole clearing was under water. He asked her if she had burnt the mosquito-net while smoking in bed. She nodded. He had left the net behind. She made no comment on anything he said about his experiences down there beyond an occasional husky Yes or No when he asked a question. He left after dinner and went back to make another search for the horse.

He told her at breakfast and dinner what had happened to him since he left her, but very sketchily, because she had seemed in no mood to hear. He reserved the telling of the tale in full till the night, when she seemed more cheerful. He made a good job of it, describing his meeting with Ket more as he would wish it to be than it actually was, that is, as an adventure in which he behaved aggressively. But he made himself only a hero in his own eyes. Tocky was deeply preoccupied at first with the awful notion that the black-bearded man he had put to flight was the same as she had murdered, and then with fearing the loud-voiced hero himself, because he had begun to talk heartily about blood-money. He was at length silenced by her failure to laugh when he said, "Vengeance is mine, saith the Law; I will reward. Ha! Ha! Ha! How's that for a pun? Ha! Ha! Ho!"

During the silence — lull in a storm it was to her — she reasoned that since Norman had fought and beaten his black-bearded foe at much about the same time as she had set eyes on hers many miles away, the adversaries could not have been one and the same man. This relieved her a little. She snuggled up to him and asked in a tiny voice, "S'pose pleeceman catch dat man — will day h-h-h—"

"Hang him?" cried Norman. "Course they will. And serve the dirty murderin' sod right. By cripes I'll get even with him. I'll go to the jonns soon's I get back and tell 'em where he is."

Tocky was lost for answer. She desired nothing more than to confess her own piece of murder — Oh, but not to

such a rabid advocate of the merciless law as this! He
terrified her. There throughout the waking hours of the
night he sat beside the fire, vociferating about murder,
gloating over frightful retributions, looking all brown and
red and evil, like Mr Hollower's Beelzebub himself.

Usually Norman delighted in talk of murder and man-
hunt and execution no more than any normal civilized person does. But that night, being in a peculiar mood through
having been badly scared by Ket, he fairly revelled in it.
Tocky shrank from him.

Next morning, urged more by his own fears than by
the pleas of Tocky, he strapped a blanket on the pack-
saddle, lifted her on to it, and, followed by her timid grateful smiles, led the way home through the ranges.

§

Tumbukka Island was about twenty miles to the east of
the mouth of the Jinjin, one of a group of low sandy isles
that lay so close to the mainland that some of them, including Tumbukka itself, were part of it at low water in
spring-tide times. Such a tide was running when Ket came
up the beach from the mouth of Yalgah Creek on his way
home from his encounter with Norman; but it was running
in. There was no sign of life on the island nor indeed of
human habitation. The houses were built on the ocean side
and the lugger kept there in a bay. The fact that it was
inhabited was concealed deliberately.

Ket shouted to Mark to come and get him with the
dinghy. He shouted himself hoarse. Then he made a fire
and piled it high with green-stuff till he was blinded and
choked by the smoke. At length he flung himself down in
the shade and cursed Mark while the sun-spots and ants
and sand-flies worried him.

Mark was at home, lying brooding in the humpy. He
did not know that Ket was there, or, dislike him though he
usually did, he would have gone in for him at once and welcomed him. He was just then unutterably lonely, lonely
as he had never been before, and aware as never before of
the fact that he had made of life a failure. So he had been
feeling with increasing intensity ever since Chook Henn
had died. Chook had been dead three months. He had been
poisoned by spirits he had distilled from a brew of unknown but pleasant-looking palm-nuts. Mark owed his escape from a similar death to the fact that his thirst was
more easily satisfied. Chook died at a time when Frank

and Ket were away in the bush making one of their many searches for the pack they had lost when a horse of theirs was swept away by a flooded river. Mark and Chook had not been told how precious that pack really was. They thought it contained a mere two or three hundred pounds. So Chook had died alone with Mark, suddenly stricken with paralysis while trying to help Mark, who had first shown signs of distress. No doubt it was the sort of death he would wish for. And he died as he had chosen to live for fourteen years, a voluntary exile, a martyr to his affection for Mark. Mark had buried him with his own half-paralysed hands, weeping into his shallow sandy grave the first tears his eyes had shed for years.. And over the grave he had rigged with wire and kerosene-cans an ingenious device that would save it from desecration by crocodiles, and from the side of the humpy had removed a sheet of bark so as to keep the grave in constant view. He was staring at the grave while Ket was cursing on the beach.

At last Ket was able to walk home. He came straight to Mark, and, before Mark had time to exercise the tolerance he felt, told him what had happened. He knew that Mark was friendly with Norman, and believed from what he had said in accounting for articles he possessed that bore the brand of Red Ochre that he was friendly with Oscar. They had often quarrelled about the Shillingsworths. Mark had learnt from him all he knew about that notorious one of them, himself.

Mark was infuriated when he heard what had happened. "You blithering fool!" he roared. "Shot at him? What the hell for?"

Ket could not answer that.

"He wasn't doing you any harm," roared Mark. "Most likely he was coming out here to Tumbukka."

Ket said quickly, "What's he want to come out here for if he aint lookin' for me and Frank?"

Mark was lost for an answer now. He had decided at once upon hearing what Ket had to say, that Norman was come in search of himself, having learnt where he was from Oscar or Heather. A pleasant thought. At the back of it was an idea that either Heather or Oscar had sent for him to come back to their much desired company, possibly because they had found some way in which to get him out of his trouble.

"Comin' here to put the mocks on us," said Ket. "Might be there's a reward."

Mark rose from his neat bed and said, "I'm going after him."

"What?" cried Ket.

"I'm goin' after him. He must've come here after me."

Ket stared for a moment, then cried, "You're mad."

"It's you that's mad," shouted Mark. "You homicidal blunny maniac — shootin' at the boy like that. By cripes if you'd've shot him I'd've shot you, too."

"He'll shoot you, you aint careful."

"Aw, shut up! You're mad. What's he want to shoot me for? I'm his — his cobber."

"But the jonns," cried Ket desperately. "What if he's gone for the jonns, and you run into 'em?"

"Jonns? Bah! He wouldn't tell the jonns!"

"But if he rekernized me —"

"What if he did? Only make him know I'm round. Which way'd he go, you idiot?"

"I dunno. He was headin' straight for the Mundikuala camp when he bolted."

"And where's Frank?"

"Gone up the Jinjin."

"Might be the boy'll meet him."

"If he does he might shoot him."

"Who shoot who? Frank shoot Norman? Frank's not a blunny lunatic like you."

"I mean he'll shoot Frank. Frank hasn't got the gun."

"Bosh! You've got the rifle, have you? Well, give it here. I want it."

"I've run out of ammunition."

"Eh? You haven't shot it all out, surely?"

"No — Frank had the bag. I forgot to get it off of him when I left him."

"Now we're in a pretty fix. How we goin' to get tucker without a gun, you blunny fool?"

"'Ere!" cried Ket. "You mind what you say —"

"Eh?"

"Mind what you blunny well say. I've stood just about enough off of you, Jack Ramble. Don't you bawl at me."

"Bawl at you! I-I-I oughter dash your blasted little bit of brains in."

For a moment there was murder in Ket's twitching narrow eyes. For a moment he looked into the fiery eyes of Mark. Then he spat an obscene word at him and walked away.

NORMAN's talk of intent to betray the murderers was only blather. He had no illusions about the kind of fame he would win among his fellow citizens by doing so, nor so much love for the man-trackers that he would help them in their wretched business even for reward. Moreover, there was the safety of Mark to consider, which, though he realized that he was beholden to him for nothing but the not-always-pleasant fact that he was a halfcaste, he would not have jeopardized for anything.

But, being the type of youth he was, he was bursting to tell someone what he knew. He told it to the one person in the world who could be trusted to keep it secret — Mrs McLash. He told her when he called on her to buy tobacco and a dress for Tocky at once upon arrival at the railway. It was not the truth he told her, nor a lie exactly, since it was told with as much desire to gladden the wretched old woman's heart as to gratify himself by making the best of a good story. Indeed he quite believed what he told as he told it, and half believed it ever after; and indeed it was not so far from being true; and some credit was due to him for having for the sake of pleasing her sacrificed the chance to boast of the manner in which he had dealt with Ket. He told her that he had seen Frank.

He told her that while out in the Mundikuala Country he had come upon a camp in which two men were sleeping — Ket and her Pride and Joy, the latter looking (this in answer to her instant question) a little out of elbows and unkempt perhaps, but otherwise quite well. He had not disturbed them for obvious reasons. He might have stopped at that if given the chance. But Mrs McLash wanted every detail. He went on to say that later he had met a camp of blacks who had told him that four whitemen were camped at a certain place on the coast with a lugger. He had gone to this place, and without letting himself be seen had discovered that it was Frank's base and that the other two men were Jack Ramble and Joe Mooch. All had looked quite happy and well. He could not think why they had not yet gone away. Much of the latter part of the story, being forced from him by questions, was rather lame. But Mrs McLash, who in another matter might have doubted an Archangel's words, believed it all, as she showed by presenting him with a pound of the best tobacco and the best dress in her store. Then she asked him to go back to Frank with food and clothes and a letter to ask him if he would let her join him. He saw his mistake. He said that it would be impossible to make the journey till after the Wet. Leaving her snivelling, he went off kicking himself for a fool. He had intended to drop a note to Heather telling her the news. After his experience with Mrs McLash he decided to wait till he should see her.

He took Tocky home with him, but not with intent to keep her; for though he thought much more of her since secret troubles had made her less affectionate, now that he was reminded of the Masters of Mankind by sight of civilization, he feared he might get into trouble for consorting with her. She was greatly pleased with Red Ochre, which was a palace compared with any place she had ever dwelt in, not excepting her old home at Black Adder Creek, pleasant memories of which were responsible for her not objecting to his proposal to take her over there and leave her. A couple of days after coming home he took her over by the pack-track through the hills, and, promising to pay her a visit before long, left her there with a rifle and a mouth-organ and some food and clothing.

Tocky's first and only night's residence among the creaking ruins of the Garrison was made hideous by a thunderstorm. She was driven from the house by rain and vicious shadows that the lightning startled out of corners, to spend the night in a barrel on what was left of the back veranda, kept awake and terrified by the elemental raging and the memory of a dead man staring eyeless at a fly-filled sky. Until that night the memory had lain for a week or more in a faded and still fading state, like that of a nightmare. No doubt she inherited a faculty for disposing of unpleasant burdens, and for keeping their existence secret too, from her father. But that night her memory was vivid enough. In the dripping dawn she found the pack-track, and, whimpering and bedraggled, trudged back to Red Ochre like a homing outcast cat.

There was no getting rid of her a second time. Norman stormed at her, even threatened to hand her over to the police. Finally he ignored her, and ordered Cho and the natives to do the same.

She lived like an outcast cat for days in the shed in which Ket had lived. Then she began to assert herself, slowly at first, and carefully for fear of Norman, then, when Norman went off to work on some distant part of the run, swiftly and drastically. Her first move was to secure Cho's sympathy, her last to depose Norman's scoffing mistress, Opal.

Cho's sympathy was not secured easily, since, while he did not know whence Tocky came, he knew enough about her from what Norman had told him to understand that there might be trouble if police should come and find her in the house. But she secured it, and having done so, found deposing Opal easy. At her suggestion Cho stopped Opal's rations; and when he learnt that other members of the native staff were feeding her, as he did soon enough from watchful Tocky, he stopped all rations but Tocky's, and told the staff that he did so because he could not bear the sight of Opal.

Opal was forced to retire to the camp. Tocky ruled the house thereafter. When Norman returned and Opal rushed back to claim her rights, Tocky was standing guard with a stockwhip. Opal armed herself similarly, and, being more used to handling whips than Tocky, succeeded in forcing her way into the kitchen; but she came out of it following the hair of her head, and was so badly beaten in the tooth-and-claw encounter that took place in the yard, that, observing that Norman did nothing in the matter but laugh, she resigned her rights and fled.

Norman was too busy just then to bother about the affairs of the homestead. He suffered Tocky's usurpation with intent to wrest it from her later on, and suffered it so long that at length he came to see that it was valuable. With Tocky in the house he could take Cho away to help him with the branding without fear that the store might be raided in his absence, as it surely would be if left unguarded or guarded by some such loyal sister to her people as Black Opal.

He observed before long that Tocky not only refused to give food to natives who did not work, but made a practice of putting phenyle in the garbage-cans, and that through her mistress-ship the interior of the house was bright as never since Marigold went away, and that now when he came home weary and sodden from days of working in the rain, there was not even need to ask for his wants, because there were intelligent eyes to see them and eager hands to get them — good food, hot water, fleecy towels, dry clothes, a snowy-sheeted bed, and a soft companionship that was not mercenary, that did not remind him of his unhappy heritage, and that above all did not stink of the native camp. Hence his harsh intentions dwindled, so much so that for Tocky's sake he spent Christmas at home instead of in Town as he had planned. Tocky had at last learnt something of a man's peculiarities.

§

That was a very different Christmas from the last one celebrated at Red Ochre, but one no less happy and hearty. Cho, who at one time had been chef at the Residency in Town, cooked the dinner, which was one such as Norman, who could boast of having dined well in great hotels and aboard great ships, and Tocky, who boasted of half-for-gotten banquets at the O'Cannon Garrison, had to admit was unsurpassable. And it was as strange a dinner as it was excellent, being half-Anglo-Saxon and half-Chinese — a halfcaste dinner, as Cho called it — for the convenience of the mixed company that ate it. And it was prepared with so much cunning that the borderline between the tastes of Orient and Occident was not perceivable, so that Orientals and Occidentals were able with relish to make inroads into one another's fare; and thus the twain were brought together for once at least.

The Occidental guests were Norman and Tocky. The host was Cho. The others were Chinese friends of Cho's who brought much of the stuff for making the Oriental dishes. They were Quong Ho Ling, a peanut-planter, of the Skinny River, and the Low Fat family, of Republic Reef, who were supposed to live by fossicking for gold in the abandoned workings round their home and by selling opium to the natives. Quong Ho Ling came up to the Caroline by train and out to Red Ochre on his blackboy's back. The Low Fats, who comprised old Johnny and his wife and two elder-ly sons and a young daughter and her husband, came across country riding donkeys and driving a fine team of horses with packs. Their mode of travelling, the converse of that generally adopted by people of the land who owned both horses and donkeys, was the one invariably adopted by Chinamen, even by Cho, who of late affected in every detail of his dress the style of a white stockrider. No doubt it was Chinese cautiousness that was responsible for the mode, there being little to fear from equine perfidy when one's feet are on the ground. During the party Cho wore nation-al costume, as did his friends.

Such people were the guests. Between the two sections communion was mostly restricted to nods and smiles unless Cho stood by to interpret. He was usually too busy for that. Still, all thoroughly enjoyed themselves, kept too busy by the busy Cho to bother much with interchange of views. For, besides vast quantities of food and drink, partaking of which, by virtue of the ease with which Chinese food may be digested, went on for hours when once begun, there was the gramophone blaring always for the guests to sing or dance to. Cho had shown the same cunning in the mixing up of music as in the mixing of the food, having sent up to Town for as many Chinese records as there were American ones in the house, thus effecting, since one kind of din was rarely distinguishable from the other, another shrewd mingling of tastes.

Then an Uninvited Guest arrived. He came out of drizzling rain late on Boxing Day, when the feast was at its height. He came not hurriedly as another might have come; for, being about as sodden as one could be from having spent days in rain, he thought nothing of a little extra wetting; besides, he was afraid of the other guests. For several minutes he stood at the edge of the back veranda trying to see the noisy ones through the moisture-laden wire of the fly-door. Seen in a market-garden standing as he stood there, he might easily have passed for a scarecrow. His only garments were a khaki shirt and pants. They were in tatters. His hair and beard were tangled like old unravelled rope. The skin of his hands and naked feet looked like that of a drowned man, bluish white and deeply creased, in a state he himself described, when showing it later to Norman, as the Washerwoman's Pip. He was Mark.

Clatter of falling pots drew his eyes to the kitchen, at which he stared while sniffing the savour of rich hot food that had been teasing his nostrils ever since his arrival and while letting his mind indulge in a vision of the flaming stove. Two lubras at work in the kitchen were dripping sweat, as were the people in the house, because the atmosphere was humid to supersaturation and as hot as the humidity would allow; but Mark was cold and shivering.

He had not been dry for a moment during the past five days. During that time the sun had been hid, and the clouds, when not occupied in drenching the earth, were resting their clammy substance on it. His belt was so thickly mildewed that it looked like a rich green suede. He had discarded his boots because they had begun to poison his feet. And during that time he had eaten nothing but raw and unsustaining fruits and roots that he had gathered

as he walked. He had lost his horse and all he possessed
in the saddle-bags while crossing the Madman River.

He turned back to the fly-door, and after some more
peeping, approached it cautiously and knocked. He had to
knock loudly. A Chinese voice in the flesh was screeching
to make itself heard above the voice of an American singing on the gramophone. He had to thump. Then the Chinese voice stopped dead, and the American's subsided into
a sonorous rasping.

"Hello!" cried the voice of Norman.

Mark did not answer.

Norman came to the door and opened it a little.

"Hello!" croaked Mark.

Norman blinked.

Mark grinned faintly and said, "Dunno me, eh?"

Norman gaped for a moment, then emerged, letting the
door bang to in the faces of Tocky and Cho.

"Where's Oscar?" asked Mark, in a whisper. "He
there?"

"No —" said Norman, slowly. "Oh — he's — he's dead."

Mark's jaw fell.

"You — you came to see him?" asked Norman.

"I — I came after you really. When did he die?"

"Oh, nearly a year ago."

"Is that why you came down the coast — to tell me?"

"No — not exactly. But how'd you know I was down
there?"

"One of the boys with me saw you — Ket."

Norman blinked and rubbed his chin, and after a pause
said, "I really went out there only for a trip. I thought
you'd gone away long ago."

"Oscar told you, eh?"

"Yes."

"Did he tell you everything — about me?' '

Norman looked down; then, after a glance at Tocky and
Cho, who were peeping through the wire, he looked un-
easily at Mark and answered, "Yes — but I knew before
— Heather told me — just after you left."

Mark looked down. Then he said, "Got a party on, eh?"

"Yes," said Norman, and seeing Mark shiver, added,
"You're wet through. Come inside."

Mark looked at him with bloodshot baggy eyes and asked, "They're Chows you got in there, aint they?"

"Yes — just some friends. Come on in and get a change
and a drink of whiskey."

Mark shivered again, and whispered, "I — I can't if they're Chows."

Norman eyed him with understanding.

"Can I go into the kitchen?" whispered Mark. "I'd like a warm up and a feed. I — I been eatin' grass for days."

Norman led the way. After giving Mark dry towels and a change of clothes, he sat him down to a huge hot meal and sat with him while he ate. Mark ate ravenously, saying nothing for himself, listening to Norman's story of his adventures since their parting and his description of Oscar's death. Norman talked to him as he had to Jack Ramble, though his mind, rather muddled with drink as it was, was regarding him as a creature of legend come to life. To him his father was a man of many characters, at one time the unknown honourable fellow of long ago, at another the loose adventurer of whom he had conjured up a vision from the tales he had heard, at another a mixture of these two, or a mixture of one or both with the stranger, Jack Ramble. But the man who sat before him bore no resemblance to any of those fathers. In spite of his black hairs he looked an old man, a wretched old man, whose resemblance to Oscar made his state touching. It was the wretchedness of him that put Norman at ease with him.

Having eaten, Mark stated briefly while Norman rolled him a cigarette why he had not left the country for good and why he was come there. Then Norman, making an effort to remember, told him fairly truthfully about his encounter with Ket. While lighting the cigarette for him he concluded, saying, "But I had no intention of sayin' a word to the jonns. I wouldn't do that. Course I had to think of you."

Mark inhaled deeply and said, "Oh I know you wouldn't, even if you hadn't known I was your dad."

The ease with which he said that gave Norman rather a shock. Evidently the subject of their relationship did not worry the father nearly as much as it did the son. Norman turned the delicate subject off by saying, with reference to Frank and Ket, "So they lost the money, eh? That'll be a find for someone some day. I reckon I'll go out and have a look for it myself when they're gone. They pinched something like three thousand."

Owing to the effects of the tobacco, Mark's hand was shaking and his face, lately flushed again, gone pale. He said with an effort, "Pinched — what mean?"

"What — didn't you find out they robbed Con the Greek before they left the depot?"

Mark gaped.

"Didn't you know?"

"No."

"It's a fact. And murdered him, too. Chopped him to pieces with a knife."

"Good God!" gasped Mark.

He sat up straight and stared with rolling eyes. Then he began to gurgle. His head began to roll. In that state he dropped his head in his plate. He had fainted. He was pinched back to life by Cho, whom Norman called, and by Cho and Norman carried through the house and put to bed on the side veranda.

§

The intrusion of the Uninvited Guest put an end to the Christmas party. Not that the others found his company obnoxious. It was he who found theirs so. By his behaviour he gave it to be understood that either they or he must go. As he had nowhere to go and was sick and a whiteman, it was obvious that the choice would not be his. That they were not wanted they were told by Cho, who was the first to realize that their presence, and his own as well, was regarded as obnoxious. He had gone to Mark with cake and whiskey and cigarettes with intent to sit with him and cheer him with a little chatter, only to have a back turned on him. He thought that the newcomer was colour-proud, not, as he was, afraid. That the guests must go they learnt on Boxing Night from Cho again, who had it from Norman, who had been conferring with the Uninvited One to the long neglect of the others. Cho laughed when Norman gave him the news, and said in what Norman thought a sneering tone, "Woffall all-same? First-time you talk makim party go longa Noo Year. Thatl one whiteman quick-time makee plenty tloub, eh?"

"Oh, no," said Norman. "It's just — well — you see it's about time to wind up, I reckon. Too muchee long time eatin' and drinkin' and kickin' up hell's delight no good."

"Gwan you!" said Cho with another laugh, and went off to spread the news. Norman listened from the side veranda. Cho spoke his own tongue, but laughed in a peculiar manner several times, which made Norman think that he was scoffing. When he rejoined the company, Norman felt sure that everyone but the drunken blithering Tocky was sneering at him.

Early next morning the Low Fat family set out for home with all the Chinese food and Quong Ho Ling to help them eat it. Norman had offered to give them a quantity of liquor too, and to lend them the buckboard and the gramophone. They would accept nothing, not even his apologetic thanks for their company. They took leave of him with dignified politeness, then went off on their donkeys, Quong Ho mounted on a tiny roan behind old Johnny, all looking so quaint that Norman felt a pang in the loss of them.

Norman said to Cho who stood beside him watching the departing ones, "Me sorry too much for losim. Him altogether properly good friend."

Cho smirked and said, "Ho yeah? S'pose you likim allsame, woffall you sendim way?"

Norman grimaced and said, "Can't be helped. Gotter get rid of 'em sometime."

"Gwan you!" said Cho. "You no-more sendim way. Thatl one whiteman him come the bounce on you. Him no flully good thatl one whiteman. Me savvy. Him lunaway man I betcha."

Norman started slightly.

"Aw, me savvy," said Cho with a smirk.

"What the hell you talkin' about?" muttered Norman.

Cho jerked his head towards the house and said cheerfully, "Him lunaway from pleeceeman."

Norman said with difficulty, "No-more — He's — he's Mister Burns — come up from the Melisande — I — I used to know him there."

"Ho? All-i — s'pose him come longa Melsing, woffall him no-more gottim boot?"

Norman swallowed.

"That's gotcher thinkin'," said Cho with a smirk.

"Garn!" grunted Norman. Filled with alarm he turned to the house. He had not yet told Mark who Cho was for fear of broaching the delicate subject of the murder of Cho See Kee. As he walked off he wondered whether he should do so now. Cho went into the kitchen.

As Norman stepped on to the back veranda Mark came out of the house and asked, "Got rid of 'em?"

Norman nodded.

"Good-o," said Mark. "You can't trust them slant-eyed jiggers. They miss nothing. They're as cunning as dunnikan rats."

Cho showed himself at the kitchen door and cried out, "Ho! Woffall you talk all-same, Mistel Whiteman?"

Mark gaped.

"Woffall you talk bad longa Chineeman? Me savvy you talk all-i. Chineeman him no-more jiggel — him no-more lat belonga dunny. You jigglin' flully lat yourself."

Still Mark gaped.

"Woffall you come here makim humbug?" continued Cho, furious, no doubt, but looking as calm as usual. "Colour-man makee lil bit fun longa Clissmus. Thisl one fun no-more belonga whiteman. Thisl one belonga Nlorman an' Tocky an' me. Woffall you come buttinski?"

"Aw shut up," growled Mark, and turned to Norman and asked, "Thought you said the cows'd gone?"

"He works here," said Norman. "He's the cook."

"We don't want a cook. Tell him to nick off."

"Woffall —" began Cho.

"Shut up!" roared Mark.

"No-more, no-more!" cried Cho. "You can't talk bigfella whiteman longa me. Might be longa Town you can sing out Chineeman all-same dog, all-same you pig — but no can do it here. Whiteman him nussing here. Thisl station belong colour-man. Me — Hi'm partnel longa boss. Thatl one dere him boss — harlcarse. Me Austlalian — gottim all-same light sit-down this one countly same's you. Papa belong me Chineeman. Papa belonga you English. All-same. Folliner. All-i — more bettel you nick off yourself, you big fella bulsh — gwan — hoppit!"

"You talkin' to me, you slant-eyed barsted?" roared Mark.

"By clikely I am!" cried Cho.

"I'll kick your guts in!"

"Don't you tly, Mistel. Me gottim gun longa hinside here. I shoot you quick you come the bounce longa me. Gwan — hoppit!"

"Get to hell out of it!" roared Mark.

"You get to hellee you flully dammee self!"

Mark turned to Norman and gasped, "Get rid of him — boot him out."

Norman said nothing. Cho looked at him and said mildly, apparently chiding him for not taking his part, "Wha's mattel you?"

Norman was biting his lip. After a moment he said. "Better go, Cho. Come back after the Wet."

"Carn do it," said Cho.

"Why? I'll give you a good swag of tucker and a cheque. You can go stop longa Johnny Low Fat."

"Carn do it. Hi wannel stay. Thisl one belong me home
— good home long time. Hi work long Hoscal, long you.
Cookim tucker all-same no man can beatim. Washim clothes
lika hell. Mustlim up bullamacow all-same whiteman. Good
man me — plopper handy."

Norman turned to Mark and winked in vain hope of
warning him of the need for caution, and said, "He's all
right. Been here for years. Like one the family."

"No — get rid of him," said Mark, turning to go into
the house. "Cheeky cow! I never heard anything like it in
my life. For two pins I'd give him a damn good hiding."

Norman spat. When Mark was gone he went to Cho
and said, "Look — I think you'd better go, Cho. Business
pretty bad just now, you know. I really can't afford to
keep you on —"

"Hi no wannim pay. Hi wannel stay longa thisl one belong me good home."

Norman smiled and said, "Oh, that's all right. You can
come back soon's the Wet's finished. No-more losim good
home. Just go longa Johnny for a month or two and have
a spell. I'm your cobber you know —"

"Ho yeah?" asked Cho, eyeing him mildly.

Norman eyed the ground for a while, then sighed and
said, "All right, I'll try and fix it. Just a tick. I might
be able to work things." He turned and went into the
house.

Cho stood in the kitchen doorway for a few seconds
after Norman disappeared, then skipped across the yard,
stole to the fly-door and listened for a moment, then backed to the window of the room where Tocky, still drunk, lay
sleeping, then darted to the fly-door again, slipped into the
dining-room and across to the fly-door that communicated
with the side veranda, and stood there listening to the talk
of Norman and Mark.

Norman was saying, "He's been here for years. He thinks
he's a sort of partner."

"No — get rid of him," said Mark; and after a pause
he added, "I suppose you know why I've got to steer clear
of Chows?"

After another pause Norman said, "Yes — but — but —
well I thought it'd be better if this one stayed. You see,
he's a brother of that Cho See Kee."

After another pause Mark exclaimed, "Godstruth!"

"So I thought it'd be better to keep sweet with him. He

said just before you came out that he reckoned you were runnin' away from the jonns —"

"Eh? Hell's bells! And you want him to stay!"

"Oh, he doesn't know who you are —"

"But he'll soon find out. And he said that? What'd he say?"

"Only something about you not havin' boots when I said you were a cobber of mine from the Melisande. If we keep sweet with him I think he'll be all right."

"Oh, for the love of Mike get rid of him — or I'll have to go. Give him a big cheque and a lot of blarney."

"But —"

"Oh hell, my boy — can't you see it's impossible havin' him here while I'm here?"

"But you look another man even from when I saw you last."

"What about when I get better? All that Cho See mob knew me well. And all Chows've got eyes like bromley kites."

After a lengthy pause Norman said, "Good-o then," and rose and went into the dining-room, which he found deserted, and sat down to write a cheque.

When Norman went to the kitchen he found Cho there swatting flies. "Here you are, Cho," he said, handing him the cheque. "Now you can go smokim opium and catchim plenty young fella lubra. Twenty-five pound. That enough?"

Cho folded the cheque up very carefully.

"You takim spell longa Johnny," said Norman. "Do you good. Come back in about two months' time."

"No-more come back," said Cho, placing the cheque in one of the pouches of his stockrider's belt.

"Eh? Garn you! Don't be silly, Cho. You'n me's still good cobbers. You still belong me partner. Make it six weeks."

"Carn do it," said Cho, picking up the swatter.

"Why?" asked Norman, feeling uneasy. "What's wrong?"

Cho swatted, then said, without looking, "Hi tink you too muchee whiteman all-same."

That was a compliment to Norman, and more, a relief. He slapped Cho on the back, and said, "Garn! You'll be back." With that he walked away.

Thus the Uninvited Guest dislodged the host as well.

§

Six quiet days passed while Mark rested and with the

help of Tocky's good cooking and Norman's attention re-
cuperated much of the flesh and strength he had lost of
late. He and Norman spent most of the time together on
the front veranda talking roving and engineering and
Omar Khayyam and developing a strong attachment.

Tocky was ignored, and, annoyed at being so, but not
alarmed for her future, since she believed from the little
Norman told her that the Uninvited Guest would not be
staying long. She would have been greatly alarmed, however, if during the last day or two of that quiet period
she had understood the talk that went on between Norman
and the guest; for it was talk of plans for the future in
which she was not included, plans for the selling of Red
Ochre and the fitting out of the *Spirit of the Land*, the
making of a voyage with Heather to Papua, the trying of
luck on the goldfields there, and the subsequent founding
there of a cattle and copra station, on which the three of
them would settle down; had she understood as much and
guessed the identity of the Uninvited One and been in a
position to betray him, she might have taken such steps to
punish the man for robbing her of a good home as those
that were taken by Cho.

Six quiet days passed. The seventh, which was the third
of the New Year for which Mark and Norman had so
often wished themselves good luck while drinking, was
passed as quietly till noon.

A few minutes after noon that day, Norman was walking up the hill, returning to the house from the native camp
to which he had gone to bully life into one of his stockboys
who was supposed to be dying from having been wished
mortal evil by an enemy. He had covered about a third of
the distance when he heard a subdued commotion in the
camp, and glancing back saw the natives, among them the
dying man, plunging in a body into the jungle. It was an
unusual sight to see at Red Ochre, though not an unfam-
iliar one to Norman, who had seen the like of it many
times in his travels. It was the flight of timid or cowed
people at the approach of an unpleasant stranger.

Norman thought of police at once, and looked towards
the river-track leading to the Siding to see who might be
coming; and through the trees beyond the home-paddock
rails he saw a mounted trooper and a tracker-boy. Their
buttons and badges flashed. He started. He had a guilty
enough conscience. He was harbouring a wanted murderer
and detaining a Ward of the State. It was the Ward he

thought of instantly, having many times in early days of association with her feared the coming of police on her account. He had a plan to meet such an emergency. He rushed to the house to effect it.

He rushed into the kitchen, where Tocky, red and wet of face, was singing and salivating over three great slabs of fillet steak that sizzled on the red-hot stove-top. Her singing stopped.

"The jonns!" cried Norman. "Quick — nick over to the tank!"

His plan was that she should hide in one of the iron stock-tanks, one that was broken and out of use.

Jonns — Oh fearful name! She dropped her fork and squealed and dashed about like a lantern-baffled possum. He seized her, told her in hisses to be calm. "Out the window," he said. "And go for your life. Wait! Wait! What'd I tell you about trickin' the tracker? Put on my shoes." He released her and bent and tore off his sandshoes and slipped them on to her little feet. "Run through the horse-yards and keep low — bent like this — all the way. And before you climb the ladder of the tank, have a look to see if anyone's spotted you. If they have, go like hell to the river and after the Bings. Oh shut yer blunny wingein'! Now don't come back till I come for you. Now listen to what I say. Cos if they catch you I'll tell 'em you tacked on to me, which's the truth. Let me lift you out. There! Now go for your life."

He saw her dive through the rails of the nearer horse-yard; then he rushed from the kitchen into the house. Mark was sitting in the dining-room, clad in a suit of Oscar's pyjamas, reading a book of Norman's entitled *Dynamos and Steam.*

"Here comes a jonn!" cried Norman.

Mark leapt up.

"Out to Cho's hut — quick!" cried Norman.

"Jonn!" gasped Mark, looking bewildered.

"All right — only after Tocky. Quick. Go to Cho's, and crib yourself in that big camphor-wood box if they come near there. Don't worry. I'll get rid of 'em. They won't find Tocky, either. Quick. I want to put away her things."

Mark dropped the book and fled. Norman rushed into the back room that Tocky used and gathered up her few belongings and brought them into the dining-room to stow them in the sideboard. Then he ran to the front and looked out, to see the policemen coming up the mango-grove, still a long way off. He flew to the back, snatched up a broom from the back veranda, and with a few strokes erased Mark's tracks for several yards; then he rushed into the kitchen to clear the table of its setting for three.

He had scarcely done clearing the table, when through the window of the kitchen facing the house he saw Trooper Dan O'Crimnell saunter from the house. He was astounded. O'Crimnell had come to the homestead by a little-used track that led from eastward, and had examined the house while passing through. He came to the kitchen, looked in, said cheerily, "Good-day — howzit?"

Norman gaped.

O'Crimnell glanced at the stove and sniffed, and said, "That steak smells good"; and sauntering in he added, "Hotting up three plates, eh? Got company?"

Norman gasped.

Then O'Crimnell grabbed him, placed a hand on his chest, and after a moment said, "Been rushin' about, eh?"

Norman swallowed.

O'Crimnell released him and asked, "Who's stayin' with you, Norm?"

After a moment Norman gasped, "No-one."

"Well, what's the three plates and the big feed for?"

After a moment Norman answered, "Me 'n a lubra."

O'Crimnell grinned and said, "Do the lubra's cookin', do you? And why the three plates? Haven't raised a piccanin already, have you?"

"One's — one's to put the meat on."

O'Crimnell cocked an eye and said, "Well said! But are you sure you aint got a little family party on?"

"W-what d'you mean?"

"Not a gatherin' of the Shillingsworth clan?"

"I — I don't get you," mumbled Norman. But he did. Understanding was turning him sick.

After a pause O'Crimnell asked, "Where's Cho Sek Ching?"

"He — he's gone."

"Why'd he go?"

Norman could not answer.

Cocking his eye still more and looking comical, O'Crimnell said, "D'you know it's an offence to keep information back from the p'lice?"

"W-what you mean?"

"What you're doin' now. I asked you why Cho left."

"I — I give him the push. C-couldn't afford to keep him."

"Not with certain people about the place, eh?"

No answer.

O'Crimnell chuckled. Then hearing his mounted comrades arrive, he glanced through the door. Then to Norman he said, "Better take that steak off before it burns.
And if you don't mind, put on a couple more chunks for
me and Barney."

Norman moved weakly to obey.

O'Crimnell went out to his comrades, the white one of
whom, and doubtless the only one he recognized as a comrade, was Trooper Barney McCrook, of Port Zodiac, lately
stationed at the Melisande. O'Crimnell was in charge. He
said to McCrook as he dismounted, "He's here all right —
cribbed, I think"; then to the tracker he said, "Ginger —
lookim track."

Ginger took the merest glance at the earth, then said
pointing with his lips to Cho's quarters, "Some fella go
dat way. Some fella been try for hidim track longa broom."

"Follerim up," said O'Crimnell.

Norman, still at the stove, saw the three move off. He
stood still till they passed the window on the southern side
of the kitchen, then rushed out and after them. When he
saw them again they were at Cho's door. "Hey!" he gasped. "What's the strong of you?"

They all turned. O'Crimnell said, "Oh, just havin' a pike
round."

"W-what for?"

"For the rest of the Shillingsworth family," said O'Crimnell, taking hold of the door-knob with one hand and withdrawing his revolver with the other. McCrook chuckled.

"This — this's private property," gasped Norman. "You
can't—"

"Oh yes we can," said O'Crimnell and flung open the
door.

There was no-one to be seen within. But it was not on
sight alone that O'Crimnell relied for evidence of the presence of malefactors. He said to black Ginger, "He here?"

Ginger had been sniffing. "Yu-i," he said. "Smellim whiteman. Might be him sit down longa big fella box."

O'Crimnell went to the camphor-wood box and flung up
the lid, smiled at poor prostrate shrinking Mark, and said,
"Good-day — howzit?"

Mark gasped.

"Come on," said O'Crimnell, giving his left hand to assist

him, when he saw that Mark was incapable of rising unaided. "Wonder you didn't suffocate in there."

Then McCrook gasped, and cried, "Jack Ramble!"

"What?" demanded O'Crimnell.

"It's Jack Ramble — you know — Ramble and Mooch."

"Well, strike me!" said O'Crimnell.

Both policemen stared at Mark, who eyed them miserably. Norman was trembling at the door.

"You Jack Ramble?" asked O'Crimnell.

"Yes," breathed Mark. He swayed. O'Crimnell put his
gun away and gave both hands to helping him to the bunk.
He muttered, passing a hand over ashen brow, "Bit crook."

He looked so weak and shrunken that Norman, who came
pushing in, was smitten to the heart. "Leave him alone, you
lousy cows," he muttered.

"He's all right," said O'Crimnell. "Ere — don't get
funny. We aint hurtin' him." He pushed Norman away,
saying, "Go'n get him a nip of something — go on —
whiskey!"

Norman went out slowly.

McCrook said, "I'll go with him, Dan. He's a hot-headed
young cow. He might come back with a gun."

Mark soon revived after drinking a stiff peg of whiskey.
Then he recognized McCrook and said to him, "Hello,
Barney — howzit?"

"Mustn't grumble," said McCrook. "Jiggerin' hot, aint
it?"

"Better'n rain," said Mark, and shuddered.

"Oh, well," said O'Crimnell, breaking the pause that followed these friendly remarks. "Let's get this bit of business over. I been informed you're Mark Shillingsworth,
Jack. Is that right?"

Mark swallowed.

O'Crimnell had been thinking that a mistake had been
made. Mark's face assured him that it had not. He said
gently, "Come on. Best speak up. Plenty of people to
'dentify you. But first, of course I gotter warn you that
anything you say might be used in evidence against you."

Mark nodded, as if to signify that he thought that reasonable.

"Well — what about it? Are you Mark Shillingsworth?"

After a moment Mark breathed, "Yes."

"Then, Mark Shillingsworth, I've a warrant for your
arrest on a charge of murder."

Mark regarded him dully.

"Want to make a statement?"

"Statement?" murmured Mark.

"Want to tell us anything about the business?"

"Well — I know you've got the murder of a Chow against me. But you've got it all wrong. I didn't do it. As a matter of fact —"

O'Crimnell waited.

"I run away that time to dodge my creditors," said Mark. "I've heard all about what they put up against me after I'd gone."

"And when'd you first learn of the charge against you?"

"Well — not till I came to work on the construction about eighteen months back. I got a shock, I can tell you. I was here before when the Meatworks was open —"

"You were?"

"Yes. But I didn't meet anyone I'd known before then. I didn't hear of it till I came back to work on the Melisande."

"If what you say's correct — why didn't you come forward and deny the charge?"

Mark looked down for a moment, then said, "Well — if you don't mind, I'd rather get legal advice before I say anything more."

"Better make a clean breast of it old man."

"P'raps so. But I'll hang on to it if you don't mind. It's a bit complicated."

"Please yourself. But a straight-out statement always stands to your credit in court."

"No — I'll wait."

"Good-o then. Well, can we have a bit of dinner now, Jack? We want to get to the rail before dark. We'll be goin' up to Town by trolley."

"Good-o," said Mark. "But have a drink." And for all the trembling of the hand he put to the bottle, he smiled.

IN DEFENCE OF A PRODIGAL FATHER

MARK and his captors had dinner together, waited on by Norman, whom they all ignored. Mark was pre-occupied with reviewing his misfortune, though not so much as he might have been had there not been liquor to drink and had his captors not gone out of their way to cheer him. Norman was glad to be ignored.

After dinner Mark and Norman were allowed to talk in private while watched at a distance. Then Mark learnt that Norman would do his utmost to assist him. And it was then discovered how strongly they had become attached; for when they wrung each other's hands over Norman's pledge of faith, they were swept with gusts of feeling, Mark through hearing himself called Dad for the first time in his life, and called it by a husky voice, Norman through hearing himself called earnestly, My Son. And it was then they really parted; for though Norman saddled two beasts when he went to get a horse for Mark, he brought only one, and stayed in the house while the party set out. Mark went off looking spick and span in Oscar's clothes. Norman spent an hour on the front veranda staring into the bush, much to the discomfort of fearful hungry Tocky in the tank. And much to her further discomfort, after releasing her, he went to the Siding to telephone Heather, remained away till midnight, and returned with a trooper's tread.

Meanwhile Mark and his captors were rushing through the moonlit night. And pleasant it was on a night so cool and bright and sweet with the scents of the bush. Pleasant even to preoccupied Mark, who realized that for him the trolley might be nothing less than a clattering gallows-tumbril.

They reached Port Zodiac at two in the morning. A policeman was waiting for them in a car. And Heather was waiting too, hidden behind a water-tank. They did not see her. At the police station they found Captain Settaroge asleep with feet on his desk and head hanging gaping and gurgling in most unofficerlike style over the padded back of his chair. He woke boorishly, but remained boorish for only so long as it took him to gather his wits. Then he smiled at the prisoner and said, "Hello, Mark — howzit?"

"Hello, Jerry," said Mark. "You're a big man now, eh?"

They almost shook hands.

Settaroge was astounded to learn that Mark was Ramble. For a moment he did not know whether to charge him as Shillingsworth alias Ramble, who was wanted on a charge of Contempt of Court for having failed to attend the inquest on the 223-Mile Smash, or Ramble alias Shillingsworth. Mark was frank about his doings as Ramble as they concerned all people but Frank McLash and Ket, but no

more so about himself in his true identity than he had
been with the troopers. To Settaroge he merely said in
reference to the charge on which he was arrested that he
thought the man would have known better than to suspect
him of doing murder. Then Settaroge charged him apologetically, expressed sympathy on account of his obvious ill-
health and the loss of his brother and of his old friend
Henn, then personally conducted him to a cell, told him to
call if he should want anything, bade him a cheery goodnight, and spoilt everything by locking him in.

The news of Mark's arrest, started by gossiping troopers,
flashed through the town with the rays of the rising sun,
causing great excitement, since practically everyone had
heard of Jack Ramble and not a few had known Mark
Shillingsworth. Thus when the Police Court opened at ten,
a huge crowd was waiting for admittance, and when proceedings were begun, the principals in the list of small
cases wondered what element had crept into their affairs
to attract such public interest, and endeavoured to justify
the interest by putting up much more spirited defences
than they had planned, thereby oniy succeeding in crossing
Stipendiary Larsney, who also wished to show his worth,
and led him to increase their penalties.

If the number of men in the audience who had worked
for Mark on the Melisande were come in the hope of seeing him suffer for his sins they were disappointed. For
Mark, having for the past two hours been closeted with a
woman who loved his body and a lawyer who desired his
case, than whom no man in trouble could find more eager
liars to encourage him, came into court feeling far more
hopeful about the future than he had felt for many a day.
He was not pale, nor bent, nor downcast of eye, nor falter-
ing of step, as those and other enemies of his might have
expected, but rather flushed, and as straight as ever, and
even inclined to smile. If he faltered in his step while
climbing to the witness-stand the cause was far less fear
than natural confusion. When he looked at Heather seated
at the lawyers' bench he smiled like a schoolboy waiting
for a prize. And when he got his bearings and found that
the human mass beyond the rails consisted of individuals
some of whom he knew, he smiled again, and being nodded
to, nodded in return. Captain Settaroge nodded, though not
till he had nodded first, as did the troopers. But Stipendiary Larsney, whom he had known as a Government clerk
in the old days, answered his nod with a blink. Uppish,

thought Mark, or else, for all his authority, afraid of breaking some mean convention.

He stood on the stand for an hour or more, but was required to say very little. Most of the talking was done by Larsney and his minions, and mostly done in whispers, as though they feared to let the public know their business. And because while whispering they cast many a sidelong glance at Mark, it looked as though they were debating whether or not they had at last found work for that still-inoperative gallows at Red Turtle Bay. If such indeed were their occupation, the Noes in the debate won the day. Stipendiary Larsney, taking his first frank look at this prisoner whom pride of place or fear of conventions prevented him from remembering as a friend of old, told him, as the lawyer had predicted he would, that he was committed for trial on a charge of Feloniously Slaying.

§

Justice in Capricornia, though still incapable of punishing murderers as drastically as it still pretended it could do, was not nearly so incapable generally as formerly. It had fallen into the hands of one, Judge Pondrosass, who made up for irremediable deficiencies in one direction — that is, direction of the gallows — by applying harshly efficient measures in another — direction of the Calaboose. Or rather, he applied measures that were harshly efficient in comparison with the slipshod ones of old. He was not a Jeffries; in fact, he was less harsh than most judges are even in these times when striking malefactors with the iron punishments of Israel must be done with velvet gloves; he was merely too efficient for Capricornia. People were talking of seizing him, together with his right-hand man, the State Prosecutor, and several other recently-appointed officers of the Government whose new-broom sweeping was raising an irritating dust, and bundling them out on some passing steamer. Public pests had been got rid of in that way before.

The day when the rule of the Criminal Court was *The Graver the Charge the Less Chance of Conviction* passed when Judge Pondrosass came. He had changed the legal system greatly, and perhaps not unnecessarily. He had assumed the right to try without jury all criminal cases but those in which the charge was Wilful Murder. The exceptions never came before him. Charges of Murder were always commuted to Felonious Slaying. He had effected this

by having a special Act passed in the Capitol, three thous-
and miles away. And he had dismissed the humane State
Attorney who had been bungling the office of Prosecutor
for years. This he had effected by having the two Government doctors, one of whom was a new-broomer, the other
no friend of the humane man, declare the fellow insane.
Small wonder that the public called him Judge Jeffries.

But no doubt his purposes were honest and his decisions
wise. At any rate they were unimpeachable. Certainly it
must appear to the Rulers at the Capitol that justice could
not be done by juries in a court where jurors called prisoners by Christian name and drank with them after acquittal.
And certainly it must seem that a State Attorney, who on
one occasion gave free legal advice to a party of rioters
whom he afterwards unsuccessfully prosecuted, and on
another set free all the rats trapped in the Government Offices over Christmas, must be mad.   How could anyone
understand the ways. of Capricornia unless he lived there?

When State Attorney Easycomb was put away the public roared.   A Petition to the President was made out. An
Enquiry was held.   Then the man himself ruined everything
by writing a letter to Judge Pondrosass in which he said
that for peace and happiness and intelligent society give
him the interior of a madhouse every time.

Easycomb prosecuting in the Criminal Court had rarely
ever won a case for the State. Or rather, to put it as he did
himself, he had rarely ever done so for the Police, whom
he considered in their present condition a Bureaucracy
inimical to the State, which was the People, to whom those
he prosecuted belonged. He said that the only way in which
to deal with crime effectively was not, as the Police did, to
look for the bits of bad that are in everyone and punish
for them and so cause their magnification, but to look for the
lots of good and play upon them so as to cause genuine shame
of the bits of bad. Clearly he was not the man for the job
he had held. But new State Attorney Thumscrough rarely
ever lost a case. It was into the hands of this Thumscrough
then, and unto the mercy of Judge Jeffries Pondrosass, that
Stipendiary Larsney committed Mark.

Mark had heard much about Judge Jeffries and his crew
from Frank and Ket, who trembled when they spoke their
names, believing that they would use the gallows if they
chose. Therefore, until convinced that the charge against
him would be commuted to one for which the penalty was
not supreme, he had greatly feared to face them.   Imprison-

ment he did not mind so much, knowing how homely the Calaboose was and believing Lawyer Nawratt's boasts of ability to get him off with a very light sentence if not scot-free. He had not heard of the recent case of Baldy Masse. That took place while he was away with Frank and Ket and while Norman, who might have told him about it, was in the East.

Baldy Masse was a pearling-master, a big man and proud of his strength. He shot and killed a midget Japanese who had driven him to despair by overcoming easily with jiu-jitsu his attempts to punish him for some small misdemeanour. A case of whiteman killing coloured-man, a similar one to Mark's, one that in the opinion of the general public should never have come to trial. But Masse, tried on a charge of Felonious Slaying, defended by Nawratt at his best, with an excellent case of self-defence backed up by many European witnesses, a blood-stained knife, and a wound in the thigh that no-one could prove was self-inflicted, was hounded into making damning admissions by Prosecutor Thumscrough, and by Judge Pondrosass found guilty and sent to Calaboose for fifteen years.

That was the worst of several bad recent cases. The worst, and yet the case in which acquittal had seemed surest. Far from things' legal being what they were in Capricornia, the rule of the Criminal Court seemed nowadays to be *The Better the Defence the Heavier the Sentence.* Fifteen years in the Calaboose! What home from home could seem pleasantly homely day in day out for fifteen years? If Mark had not had a lawyer and a loving woman to lie to him, he who had no blood-stained knife and plea of self-defence to help him, must have wished he had surrendered years before. But having such people to encourage him, and loaded with comforts the woman prepared, he went out to the Calaboose smiling, to that home from home which perhaps he would not leave till the undertaker called for him, to await his trial.

Oh, what is there more valuable to Man than Woman whom he mostly values little? Heather realized Mark's danger. And she made Norman realize it too, and with him, on whom she must rely for ready money, set about finding a way to save her man.

There were two lawyers in Port Zodiac, Mr Alexander Nawratt, who was a powerful advocate but a lazy, vain, and drunken fellow, and Mr Hannibal Nibblesom, a man of strong moral character and diligence, but of a personality that would have been laughed at in a Sunday-school. Nibblesom was so feeble as an advocate that parties in private cases who failed to secure Nawratt's counsel fought against Nawratt themselves. Nibblesome made a comfortable living as a solicitor, or as counsel when Nawratt was drunk.

Heather knew Nawratt well. She engaged him as a bad best temporarily. Her idea was to send down South for a criminal lawyer of Flinders, about whom she had often read in Southern papers, the famous Cæsar Bightit. She sent a wire to Mr Bightit inviting him to consider Mark's case and to give an estimate of the costs he would require should he come to take it up.

Many wires were subsequently sent on account of Mark, not only by Heather and Norman and Bightit himself, but by Nibblesom, to whom Bightit sent of his own accord to learn what the case was worth. When Nibblesom had worked out the values of Red Ochre and the Princess Alice and assessed the worth of the owners' credit with the banks and judged the depth of their affection for the principal in the case and sent word to Bightit and received word back, he called on Norman and told him that Bightit would require to have a substantial sum of money deposited in a bank, say £500, which could be easily got by mortgaging Red Ochre, before he would commit himself to agreement. Norman was shocked by the mention of so large a sum, then relieved by being told what would have shocked him just as much had Nibblesom not been a cunning fellow, namely, that the great man's fees, about which nothing definite could be said just yet, would surely not exceed £250. Norman suggested that the depositing of the £250, which sum he had in cash, would be enough. Nibblesom said that Bightit would not come unless special security of £500 were made. He offered to bet Norman £100 to £10 that Bightit would get Mark off scot-free. Norman would not bet, for one thing being scared to do so with a man who might argue himself out of paying, for another wishing to see his father freed, for a third feeling that, as one about to become a mortgagor, he must be careful of his money. In fact he became so worried about money that he refrained from talking to Nibblesom for fear of incurring extra costs; but since he was unable to make Nibblesom refrain, his caution served little purpose.

The trial was postponed for Mr Bightit's coming. Six weeks elapsed, half of which time Norman spent at home worrying Tocky with pessimistic talk of the future of the

mortgaged station, and half at either the Princess Alice or
the Calaboose cheering Heather and Mark with optimistic
talk of the impending trial. He had to bear all the expense.
Heather was reserving her financial forces for the more
costly task of settling Mark's debts if he were acquitted.

Then the great man came. He came on the first steamer
he could catch. He was a man of extraordinary appearance, tall and heavy and stout, looking as clumsy as an ele-
phant, but acting as nimbly as a crab. In fact, he was crab-
like in many ways, having popping pale eyes that seemed to
see all round, and bright red colouring, and a peculiar manner of edging about and waving his arms. And certainly
he had a faculty for getting a grip of things. He learnt all
there was to know about the case and legal conditions in
Capricornia after talking to Nibblesom for barely half an
hour. But he was not wholly crab-like. It was possible in
an hour to see him looking bull-like, lamb-like, toad-like,
dove-like, turkey-cock-like, shark-like. So Norman saw him.
And he had an extraordinary loud voice, on account of
which Norman and Heather at once dubbed him The Shouter. Yet he could coo like a dove when he chose. He brought
his wife with him; or rather, since it was obvious that she
ruled him, he came with her. She, with all her power over
this extraordinary man, was only a wisp, a pretty, shallow, little woman, whose chief interest appeared to be dress.
Her dresses caused a stir in Town that rippled from the
Residency to the Compound. And he brought with him a
trunk of fine white clothes and topees, brand-new habili-
ments that Norman despairingly supposed were bought with
some of the £7-a-day expenses he had to pay him. These
expenses alone he learnt would cost him something like
£240. Nibblesom said that they were surprisingly light.

Norman also learnt that extra costs would be incurred
by the employment of the feeble Nibblesom to do the Shouter's dirty work — all his work, it seemed — while the great
man spent his costly time in talking small-talk and dining
and motoring and playing bridge with the crowd of superior people he and his wife soon joined. He realized that
the £250 would be the bare cost of the Shouter's work in
Court, and understood why he was required to have a special security of £500 behind him, and began to wish that
he had never become entangled in Mark's affairs. And he
soon began to see Bightit as yet another creature — a spider,
a huge, red, cunning, spinning spider.

A spider indeed the Shouter proved to be. During six

days in which he appeared to do nothing at all he spun a web that emmeshed Judge Jeffries' justice. He walked empty-handed into court on the day the trial began and stopped it by demanding withdrawal of the charge of Felonious Slaying and renewal of the one of Murder. The Court was astounded, from Back-door to Bench. Unprecedented! But could they show why precedent should not be established? He became a bull, a toad, a crab, a crocodile. He argued for half an hour, then left the court to go out fishing, in preparation for which he had come in his oldest clothes. What fool was this, the Back-door wondered, who preferred to stand his client on a charge for which the penalty was death? And then it dawned on them, as it had from the start on scowling Jeffries and his crew. The idea was to secure the certain benefits of trial by Capricornian jury!

At first it seemed as though the trial for Murder would never be begun, so hard to please in the matter of selecting jurors were both Prosecution and Defence, and so unwilling for selection were the townsmen. Half the white population was challenged. Half the franchised coloured would have been as well had Prosecution got their way and brought them into Court. It was nine at night of the second day before the jury were empanelled. The twelve were locked up at once in the police-station, where they spent the first half of the night in arguing about Capital Punishment, over which they could not agree, the rest in finding certain members guilty of inciting others to commit a felony, to wit, murder, with a view to silencing unseemly snores.

The third and fourth days were spent in presenting the case for Prosecution, a task not difficult in itself, and one that, since its materials were merely a handful of Chinese witnesses and a stack of yellowed papers, should have been disposed of in an hour or two. It was rendered difficult and long by the Shouter, who, assuming the character of an obstinate toad, croaked objections to nearly every point of it. Objections! Had Judge Pondrosass been the man of strength he posed as, he would have brained the Shouter with his gavel.

Prosecution presented their evidence. Then Defence's witnesses, those people who had supported Oscar's evidence at the Inquest, gave theirs. Then examination of Prosecution's evidence began. The Shouter assumed the character of a raging bull, trampled down every Chinese witness,

charged two policeman who made him see red, tossed the
yellowed papers into ridicule. Then he became a crocodile
and attacked and devoured Mrs Cho See Kee and her father, Ching Ling Soo. Then, being assailed by Prosecutor
Thumscrough, he turned on that man in the character of
a shark and snapped out of him all hope of a conviction.
Then he became a turkey-cock and strutted with many an
oosht! of spreading tail till the judge rebuked him. Then
he became a cooing dove. The audience was delighted. The
Warden found difficulty in keeping order.

The Addresses began. When the Shouter's turn came he
faced the Jury as a composite creature, part ass to please
a set of fools, part siren to win their minds, part crab to
seize and hold their sympathy and never let it go.

He delineated the character of Prisoner. Was it one of
a murderer and thief? Would the murderer come back and
mix with people who almost certainly would recognize him?
Prosecution stated that Prisoner came back disguised. Stuff
and nonsense! Scores of people recognized him, both in
Port Zodiac during the Meatworks boom and on the Melisande. Did the man known as Jack Ramble slink about?
Scores of people recognized him as Mark Shillingsworth
at once. They did not come forward at the time because
they were not inclined to be informers. They dared not
come forward now for fear of being charged as his abet-
tors.

Prosecution suggested than an innocent man upon returning to a place to find that a serious charge had been laid
against him in his absence would at once take steps to clear
himself. Assuredly — if to do so would be to his advantage. Would it have been to the advantage of Prisoner,
who was in debt to the tune of £700? The price of re-
establishing his good name would have been huge legal costs
and unlimited imprisonment as an absconding debtor. Prisoner had said of his own volition that the position he found
himself in shocked him terribly, but that being a man of
sense he had not rushed to clear himself, but had given
some thought to what doing so would avail him. What
would it avail him? As he was placed it would have avail-
ed him nothing but misery. Why did he work so hard on
the Melisande, why gamble so recklessly, if it were not true,
as he had stated, that he wanted money — heaps of money
— so that he might clear himself with ease?

Money! The Gentlemen of the Jury knew what Prisoner's character was in regard to money. A hundred pounds

to him was nothing. Now consider the case in hand. Of how much was the victim robbed? Of a mere thirty pounds or so. Poor compensation to a man like Prisoner for committing a murder — eh? Very very poor compared with the sum of money inherited by the victim's heirs.

Who were those heirs? Why, none other than our excitable old friend, Mrs Cho See Kee, and her ancient father and the bulk of the Prosecution's witnesses. Did those persons hate their benefactor in the flesh? The evidence showed that at least they did not love him. Was it unreasonable to suppose that they might have felt rather obliged to the murderer?

Who was the murderer?

The Shouter looked all round the court and set many a timid heart thumping with his wild accusing glare.

Listen to a little story, gentlemen. Let's call it a plot for a novel. We have a woman of a race that to us might seem non-moral. We know that the race is renowned for its ability to do dark deeds with ease. This woman is cunning, avaricious. She is married to a man much older than herself, a rich man, who, after the custom of their race, bought her. Does she love the man? Far from it! There has been trouble between them on account of a suspicion that she has been been allowing a youth of the breed to pay her secret court. On account of that trouble he has beaten her severely, not once but many times, and has forced her to keep to the house and away from her relatives. He does not like her relatives, nor they him, there having been a quarrel over money between him and them, between him who is rich and stingy and them who are poor and importunate. What a life for a woman young and handsome and avaricious! What a relief to her if the old man died! She would be free, and more, rich. And the cast-off relatives would share her fortune. Is it any wonder we find our plot taking a turn towards evil? The miserable young woman at last steals away to her relatives and with them plots to kill her husband, to do so in a way such as to let it seem that the guilty hands were others than theirs. How can it be done? Ah — there is a carpenter among them. Who better than he to juggle plans and build a scaffold for another? Besides, he knows something most opportune. He knows a whiteman who lives near by who is known to be poor and desperate and to have quarrelled with the old man over money. The very man upon whom to fix the guilt! For he is about to leave the neighbourhood in guilty style with intention never to return. The carpenter knows all this because he has been approached by this poor whiteman and asked to do repairs to the fellow's boat and has put two and two together. The very man! He can be watched. The crime can be committed at the very hour of his departure!

Merely a plot for a novel, gentlemen, fantastic perhaps, but not impossible; fantastic perhaps, but no more so than is the suggestion that a woman stepping half-asleep from darkness into a lighted room can honestly swear to the identity of a man of another race whom she has seen momentarily perhaps half a dozen times before and whom, on the occasion she has sworn to, saw for just two seconds; fantastic perhaps, but no more so than the suggestion that an old man who at the time could not read even large-size Chinese characters without the aid of spectacles should be able to swear to the identity of a man who collided with him in the bush late at night with such force as to knock him down, which are the principal suggestions on which Prosecution base their case; fantastic perhaps, but not nearly so much so as the suggestion that Mark Shillingsworth is a murderer.

Gentlemen of the Jury!

Needless to call their attention. They were enthralled.

Gentlemen of the Jury, it is not for me to warn you of the gravity of the task that it will soon be your duty to perform, task that has fallen to the lot of so few men in this happy community of brothers; but it is my right to tell you that this man is innocent, my right — aye! — and my duty to a fellow man. He is innocent. Therefore he must not — he must not — he must not die!

I thank you.

The Judge in summing up found fault with much of the Shouter's reasoning. But whether he succeeded in showing the faults to the Jury it was difficult to say. The Jury retired, to return after an absence of fifteen minutes, which they mostly spent in eulogizing Counsel for Defence, with a verdict of Not Guilty.

Uproar! People in the benches clapped and stamped. Those near the doors and on the verandas cheered and whistled. But it was not half so much on account of Mark's deliverance as on that of the conquest of Jeffries and his crew.

§

When Mark and Norman recovered from the effects of the party Heather gave to celebrate the victory, Nibblesom came to them to say that the Labour Council intended to bring an action against Mark on behalf of a number of men who had worked for him on the Melisande. Nibblesom said that he had known this for a good while, having been apprised of it by the Secretary of the Council, who had come to him for advice on the matter while Nawratt was engaged on the murder case. Immediately after the trial he had gone to the Secretary to learn whether anything further might be done, hoping that the case, in spite of its being one in which he would be opposed to a man on whose behalf he had lately worked — all's fair in love and law, he said — should be given to him. He had gone with no sly intentions, but had come away with many. Having been rather rudely dealt with by the Secretary for having lately worked on behalf of the man he now offered to oppose, he had talked at some length in order to prove the truth of the adage about love and law, and by doing so had learnt enough to make him feel sure that the Council intended to take action as soon as Mr Bightit left the country. Evidently they were afraid that Mr Bightit would be called to defend.

Mark and Norman and Nibblesom went to Bightit, who said that he would not mind missing the next steamer, since he was enjoying himself and would like to spend a week or two out at Red Ochre shooting buffaloes and studying their ways, and that he would be glad to take up the case, if only to try his hand again in civil action, though of course he could also do with the fee. When he had heard the details of the Melisande business he thought for about two minutes. Then he said he had the idea. He had dealt with a similar case years ago in Dirrinjinbanji. He took Nibblesom aside and talked to him for about five minutes, then went away to fish.

Nibblesom put a notice in THE TRUE COMMONWEALTH calling upon all persons who had just monetary claims to make against Mark Anthony Shillingsworth, otherwise known as John Ramble, to make them before the Twenty-first Instant, after which they would be ignored. The response was overwhelming. Within three days Mark Anthony was apprised of the fact that he was in debt to the tune of £1,953 15s. 8d. of which £1,331 10s. 6d. was the amount claimed by the Council, £120 what he owed storekeepers in the name of Ramble, the rest what was remembered of the seven hundred-odd pounds that had been owing for fourteen years. The six hundred-odd pounds to which the second and third debts amounted must sooner or later be paid to save him from going to jail. He paid it at once with money that Heather raised.

Then Mark, accompanied by Norman and Nibblesom, called on the Council Secretary at a time when he knew the man was not alone, and told him that he was not aware of the fact that he owed any money to the Council or anyone connected with it, and challenged him to contest that statement in court. Knowing that Bightit was at the back of the business, the Secretary was too wise to accept the challenge, but not wise enough to keep his mouth shut tight. He told Mark that he certainly did owe the men the money, and went so far as to call him a Bloody Shyster. That was what the Shouter wanted, even without the insult, as an alternative to an acceptance of the challenge. Mark issued a writ against the Secretary and the dozen or so men for whom he spoke for publishing a libel. Thus the Council were forced into court as defendants in the case Mark brought and as plaintiffs in the case they needs must state to defend themselves.

The Shouter came back from fishing. He had the libel case passed over. But he won the other for Mark with costs. His defence was that the men represented by the Council, having agreed to share with Mark out of his ultimate reward and to do so without respect to the Award-rate of pay and to be kept by him in the meantime in food and clothing and comforts, were not his employees but his partners, who must suffer through the collapse of his hopes the same as he. And while he said as much he flew at the Secretary like an angel-fish and chopped him to pieces, and while repeating it turned stingaree and stung Lawyer Nawratt stupid. The victory was celebrated with another party.

Nor was that the last of Cæsar Bightit's victories in Capricornia. When he returned from Red Ochre, where he and his wife had spent two weeks as guests of Norman and Heather and Mark, who hoped he might not forget their hospitality when he presented his as-yet-unmentioned bill, he defended the case of the Kai Yoh Chinese Society against Nawratt suing on behalf of Cho Sek Ching for the hundred-pounds' reward that had been offered for Mark's arrest. Kai Yoh Tang were already half beaten when the Shouter took over the case from Nibblesom; for there had been no mention made of conviction in the statement they had made when offering the reward; nor was there strength in their lawyer.

Norman and Mark, puffed with victory and none too sober at the time, hearing of the case and remembering that they had a score to settle with Cho, asked Bightit to go in and settle it for them, thinking that, since their champion was invincible, his work would cost them nothing. Indeed he was invincible. He ran Cho down like a buffalo-bull, choked Nawratt with a python-hold, won the case hands-down, but not with costs. Thus the Shillingsworths, or rather that one of them who had the money, sunk forty pounds deeper into the Shouter's debt. But it was worth it. A few days after the victory, the Kai Yoh Tang showed their gratitude by inviting the Shouter and the Shillingsworths to a banquet, at which the guests, responding to the many toasts drunk in their honour, boasted each in turn that they were dangeroush fellowsh to cross swordssh-hic-with.

Then one day the Shouter came to Norman in the character of cooing dove and presented him with a bill for £766 13s. 4d. Norman was staggered. Then the Shouter assumed the composite-creature character and held it till he saw he had Norman feeling ashamed of his ingratitude. Having heard his apology, he returned to the dove-state and cooed, "It don't matter about the fourpence, Norm," and went on to say that if Norman wished he would take over the mortgage from the bank so as to save him the pain of having to write so large a cheque. Norman agreed. Then the Shouter went home, shouting for joy, no doubt, for having spent a holiday so profitably.

Then Mark and Heather were married. There was another party, the best held in Town for many a year. When sobriety was regained, Norman suggested to Mark that he should begin to square accounts with him by giving him the *Spirit of the Land*. Trouble arose. For just like Norman, Mark had heard that a company of Japanese wished to buy an auxiliary lugger for shark-fishing; and just like Norman, he considered that the *Spirit of the Land* would fetch about £500. After some mild but stubborn argument, Mark rather angrily asked Norman if he were afraid he would not be repaid. Norman replied that he was beginning to feel that way since observing Mark's reluctance to settle up. Mark said that he had to think of the debt he owed Heather as well. Heather joined in and made matters worse. Norman learnt that far from having been imposed on, as he meanly insisted he had been, he had been honoured by being allowed to help his father, and that the honour ceased forthwith, and that the moment his damned money could be scraped together it would be flung in his greedy face. Most of what was said was instantly regretted by the lips it left. But retaliation blew too hard for the hoisting of apologies. Everyone was storm-torn and hurt. Norman left at the height of the storm and went back to Red Ochre in a rage.

THE DEVIL RIDES HORSEBACK

WHEN Mark left Tumbukka he had done so without a word to Ket. With a gunny-bag of sun-cured fish and rice and yams and a few utensils, he went ashore and took Ket's horse and made straight for the Mundikualas' camp in search of Norman. From there he crossed to Yalgah Creek and found the track that Ket had left when coming home, which led him to the scene of the shooting. Soon he found the broad track of Norman's two horses, which he followed over a devious route to the spot where Norman had found Tocky the second time, and ultimately to Red Ochre. He had no idea that he would have to travel so far when he set out.

Ket spent a lonely night at Tumbukka, then set out eastward up the beach on foot in the hope of meeting Frank. He went no further than the mouth of the Jinjin, where he camped for two days. Then thinking that Frank might have come to the beach at a point somewhere to eastward of him, he wandered back, and eventually returned to Tumbukka. He waited there for a week. By then the vision of Frank camped in some Arcady with a brown dryad had been ousted by another of Frank in handcuffs being dragged away by the police. This caused him to study the rigging and the charts and instruments of the lugger. He thought of sailing to the Indies alone. The idea frightened him. He knew nothing about the sea except that it was deep and dangerous. But any idea, whether promising of action or not, was something to keep his mind free of terrifying visions.

Then it occurred to him that if Frank had been captured,

so should he be by now, since it was certain that even if Frank were fool enough to shield him, the police would want to find him and would do so simply by following Frank's tracks back to Tumbukka. The vision of dryad and hairy faun held sway again. Thus till one day he roused himself, gathered together the few things worth removing from the camp, took them aboard the *Spirit of the Land*, hove up the anchor, and with a steady following wind in the skimpy bit of sail he dared to show, steered an unsteady course along the coast to the mouth of the Jinjin. He was going after Frank, with intent to take him and his dryad to the Indies. To hell with Jack Ramble!

He anchored the lugger in fairly deep water, made up a swag with a small roll of canvas, a gunny-bag, a billy, a knife, a burning-glass, an enamel plate, five or six pounds of rice, and two or three pounds of dried fish, and put ashore in the dinghy. He left the heavy rifle behind. Within a few minutes of landing, having dragged the dinghy high up the beach and fixed it firmly, he set out up the river.

He found conditions on the Jinjin greatly changed. The peacefulness was gone. The jungle, formerly soundless but for tinkle of the river at crossings and sighing of sea-breeze in the trees, was clamourous now with a multitude of birds; and the trees roared as lusty gusts of north-wind smote them; and the river was booming. He was pleased at first, having lately had enough of silence. Without scaring those ears that listened always for the approach of Nemesis he could laugh and sing. Show me the way to go home — I'm tired and I want to go to bed — I had a little drink about an hour ago — It went right to my head. Cockatoos and parrots answered. The pleasure passed when he found himself forced away by the swollen river from the horse-track he was following to towering grass that obstructed his view of things ahead. Fear of blundering into troopers seized him, besides that of treading on a crocodile or a snake. Many a time the sudden sight of a young palm standing in his path turned him sick. Many a time a rotten log or wriggling vine or wisp of bark stopped him dead. He was on the point of turning back when he came upon the track of a herd of buffaloes. He was relieved of the fear of blundering into snakes and other reptiles only to be forced to watch with anxiety for horns. Aboriginal blood flowed in his veins, but much more of that of the town-harlot. The bush frightened him.

So he went on. He found the arcadian camp through

picking up tracks that Norman had left when searching for his pack-horse and following them to the river. He saw the gunyah. He was approaching it, wading knee-deep in brawling water, when his nostrils were assailed by the stench of the very object of his search, which hung floating in scrub within a yard of where he stopped. He turned away, spitting and grimacing, thinking that the stench came from a dead beast and that the gunyah had belonged to natives.

He came to the camp in the foothills. He guessed at once that this had been Norman's from seeing matches and empty tins about. But for matches and tins he had no eyes when he saw fresh prints of horses' hoofs and freshly broken grass beside the stream, and, most pleasant sight of all, remains of fish and grains of rice beside the fire-place.

He jumped to the conclusion that the scraps and the tracks were Frank's. His error was easily made. But for the presence of the fresh horse-tracks he might have guessed the truth at once, which was that the scraps were Mark's. As it was, confronted with incoming tracks of which the freshness was indubitable — rain had not touched those tracks, though scarcely forty hours had elapsed since the rain last fell — he did not think of Mark. He crossed the stream and examined the tracks beyond, then returned, convinced that Frank had travelled in from the west and was at that moment cutting across country to Tumbukka. He was delighted. Had the hour not been sundown he would have rushed off in pursuit at once. Before the sun went down he was still more delighted to find by the gunyah in sheltered sandy soil beneath the wall of rock small fresh-looking prints of human feet that he rightly guessed were made by a girl but wrongly supposed a girl in Frank's possession. Then in the gunyah he found long hairs, and after groping among the leaves and bark that formed the flooring, found an unopened tin of beef and an open tin containing tobacco and cigarette papers. A few live wax vestas lay about. He gathered them. He smoked himself sick.

That night he ate hot beef and roasted yams. He intended to eat only a third of the beef that night. But the savour proved too much for him. It was as insidious as sin. It rose from the tin like a Bottle-Imp and crept through nostrils into mind and strangled his intentions. Bit by bit he ate it all. Afterwards he lay on his back and blew smoke at the mildly disapproving stars. Before long he was groaning with the colic.

He was up before the dawn next day examining the horse-tracks. It had occurred to him that they might be tracks of troopers' horses. The friendly light of day convinced him that they were made by but one horse and one not shod. Soon after dawn he set out to follow them.

Throughout the day his mind played with lascivious visions of the halfcaste girl whom he was sure Frank had found. Perhaps it was due to the beef. But it was soon scoured out of him. That night he was startled from sleep by a terrific explosion. He opened his eyes to behold the most hideous sight of his life. A huge ball of light was tearing through the bush. It was gone in an instant, obliterated by a crash as shocking as the sight itself. He was paralysed. If Satan or God or even Con the Greek had suddenly appeared he could not have been more terrified. Rain and a hail of smoking debris smote him. He did not know. Then his checked heart bounded, stilled lungs gasped, knotted limbs loosened with a jerk. He fell to the ground, panting, trembling, pouring sweat.

When he recovered and saw the vicious lightning slashing the black belly of the night and heard the crash of stricken trees, he left the shelter of his own great tree in haste and took what seemed a safer refuge in the tossing grass of the clearing. He stood in the rain till the fireworks stopped, then groped to the tree and sat till daylight listening to the tumult of water and thinking fearfully of floods. Dawn showed him a scene much less terrible than he was prepared for.

He could not light a fire for want of fuel. He took to the track without breakfast, chewing juicy grass-stalks to appease his hunger, ignoring tempting fruits on trees he passed in fear of meeting with the same fate as Joe Mooch. So he went on that day in a different mood, mainly hoping that the track would not lead him into swampy country, desiring nothing more than to reach the sea. Indeed he paid more attention to the lowering sky than to the track, and thus missed what with the eager scrutiny of the day before he surely would have noticed, namely, that the track had become wider and more distinct.

In the middle of the afternoon, having collected enough dry fuel to start a fire with a match, he made camp and cooked a miserable meal, and afterwards lay down on the canvas and slept. He woke in pelting rain and darkness. He cursed himself for the folly of having slept by day and so brought it on himself to spend a night in wretched idleness. He cursed for an hour, then saw to his great joy that day was near. He rose at once and busied himself with making up a fire with fuel he had kept under cover. Then he cooked a meal more miserable even than the last. He cooked in semi-darkness and therefore did not see that the fish was mouldy nor understand why it tasted as though it had been boiled with a musty dish-cloth. Wretched in stomach as well as in mind, he went his way as the sun rose.

In mid-morning he found to his great surprise that he was walking in his own tracks beside the Jinjin. He had been doing so for an hour or more before he became aware of it, thinking nothing of the fact that he was treading a buffalo-track again, since such tracks were common enough, and supposing that the river was a flooded creek. It was the finding of one of his own camps that told him where he was. For all he knew of direction during the past two sunless days, he could have been led anywhere.

He sat down to rest and try to remember whether the camp was the first or second he had made after leaving the beach, that is, whether the beach was a one or two days' march away. And while he thought, it struck him as strange that Frank should swing back to the river when there was apparently nothing to prevent his going straight on to Tumbukka; as mighty strange when it was considered that Yalgah Creek would be easier to cross high up since the rain than it would be at the mouth. Surely Frank, who boasted of his bushmanship, would not overlook a point like that? Then it struck him that Frank was baffled because he could not see the sun. Exciting thought! For if Frank were troubled by the sunlessness he could not be far ahead.

He jumped up and set out at a vigorous pace. If he had stopped to think, it might have dawned on him that Frank's homing horse would not need the sun to guide it. And careful study of ordure and broken grass should have told him that the tracks were made before the last big storm, that is, that the horse he was following had passed that way at least two days before, when the sun was shining. He was not stupid. Far from it. He was a much more than ordinarily thoughtful man. But he was impatient. He had never, unless forced to do so, looked at the fundamental points of a subject in his life. Hence the fact that he was trudging through the wilderness, ragged, starved, utterly debased

and alone, when his was a nature that craved comfort and
a place of respect in ordered civilization. As he followed
that devil's horse-track, he had followed the path of life,
concentrated only on overtaking desires, heeding not the
warning signs that showed what they were worth. The
solution of the one great problem of his life was admission
of his caste to himself and carelessness of what others
thought of it. He had been hounded because he had pro-
voked. He never knew it.

He went on briskly, thinking of the dryad again.

At length he came to a deposit of horse-dung that was
quite fresh. He whooped for joy. He came to another
presently. On he went with increased vigour, giving, in his
impatience to catch a glimpse of what he pursued, attention mostly to the distance. Had he given more attention to
the track he might have noticed signs not in agreement with
his expectation to see one man and one girl and one horse.
The second deposit of dung was within five minutes' walk
of the first and was trampled. Obviously there was another
horse on the track. He did not realize it.

He came upon the horses at midday. There were three
of them, Frank's bay, Cuthbert, Ket's own bay, Barnacle
Bill, and a black stranger, camped beneath a large fig tree,
Cuthbert standing, the others lying, all apparently asleep.
He first saw only Cuthbert.

He was within a few yards of them when they heard
him. With an accompanying clatter of broken hobbles Cuthbert wheeled about, stared, snorted, and, giving no heed to
Ket's calling him by name, tossed up his tail and bolted.
The others sprang up. Barnacle Bill wore a reinless bridle
and a stirrupless mud-caked saddle. It was Barnacle Bill,
coming home from the Madman River where he had lost
Mark, that Ket had followed from the hills. He had been
heading for Tumbukka till he winded the other horses on
the Jinjin. He and the stranger stared at Ket, then bolted
after Cuthbert, the stranger with broken hobbles clashing
about his hoofs. The stranger was Norman's pack-horse.

Ket rushed after them, calling his own horse by name.
But Barnacle Bill wanted nothing to do with him. He was
wild. He galloped all the harder for being shouted at. Soon
Ket was left standing with no sound in his ears but the
thumping of his own unhappy heart. He knew that the
horses were running wild. He pursued them only with intent to catch one and ride it home. Again he had spoiled

a chance with a hasty action. Disappointment smote him down. He flopped to the sodden ground and wept.

He fought his way back to the river through blinding rain, and made a wet camp under the horse-smelling fig-tree. So desperate was he then that he sampled the figs. Finding the taste no worse than peppery papier maché and feeling no ill-effects after having let four or five lie in his stomach for an hour, he made a meal of them. In mid-afternoon he went on down to the river, hastening still, but now because dread was at his heels.

In spite of what he remembered having seen at the camp in the hills, he had come to the conclusion that at least two of the horses had crossed the river there and that whatever had happened to set them free had happened in the bush to westward. What had happened? Had his comrades fall-en foul of troopers, or had they been trapped by floods, or merely fallen victim to equine perfidy? But it was not likely that both horses, docile as dogs as they usually were, should decide to give trouble at one and the same time, nor that both riders should be drowned. Was it not poss-ible that troopers had caught Frank while he was camped, and that his horse, frightened by shooting, had bolted? Ramble might have been drowned or unhorsed by a buffalo, but not Frank whose horse was hobbled. No — Frank must have been taken by the police.

He made camp at nightfall, and for want of fire, having exhausted the matches and neglected to use his glass when the sun shone, ate the last of his mouldy fish raw, wrap-ping each bite in grass to disguise the filthy taste of it. He did not sleep, but lay on a strip of paper-bark beneath the sodden canvas, twisting and turning and longing for bis-muth for indigestion and citronella for the mosquitoes At dawn he rose, shivering and cramped, made a meal of grass-roots and water, and went on his way in sunshine.

He had not gone far that morning when he began to smell the sea. Soon he came upon maritime vegetation and sandy soil. He was drooping with exhaustion; but on he went as fast as possible, urged by sights and smell to hurry lest the dread at his heels should materialize into iron hands that would clutch and hold him back from that which he now desired with every cell of his wretched body — the *Spirit of the Land,* the good ship that was waiting to bear him away from that accursed shore. He saw himself heav-ing up the anchor, setting the sails, skimming across the smiling sea to Kakkibalaka in the Indies, then on to some more civilized place — Batavia, Sourabaya, Singapore — where he would live for ever as a whiteman among cringing coloured slaves, full of food and happiness and grandeur. A mere matter of hours, sixteen, or twenty at the most, and he would be treading earth of a foreign country, safe for ever under a foreign flag.

He reached the beach at noon. There lay the smiling sea — but where the good ship?

He soon knew. She lay in fragments on the beach, wrecked at the moment when he was staring horrified at that chariot of fire in the bush. He goggled at the largest piece of her, which was her stem and a few plankless ribs buried deep in the sand, a perch for seven cormorants. Sure enough the Devil had ridden ahead.

WRATH OF THE MASTERS OF MANKIND

ABOUT a week after Norman returned in a rage to Red Ochre, the Rev. Theodore Hollower came to Town in the schooner *Alice Carstairs* to report to the police the disappearance and supposed abduction by Japanese pearlers of four coloured girls from his mission.

Mr Hollower could not have come at a time more favourable to the success, or the partial success at least, of his purpose; for the entire pearling-fleet was in for the annual lay-up just then, and its crews were ashore, and Cho Sek Ching, who could give the whereabouts of at least one of the girls, was working as cook for a Chinaman who kept a boarding-house for resting divers. Thus when the police came to question the divers about what they had heard from Hollower, Cho heard repeated in full the story Norman had only half told about Tocky. If the police had come but one day later Cho would not have heard, because he was on the eve of going bush to evade the consequences of not having paid Lawyer Nawratt his dues for conducting the case against the Kai Yoh. Cho was penniless, and exceedingly bitter in being so, knowing that he had all but got possession of a hundred pounds. He felt that he had been robbed, robbed not only of a hundred pounds, but, including the amount for which the lawyer was threatening to sue him, of one hundred and forty-six pounds six and eightpence, and robbed deliberately and for spite by the Shillingsworths. Hence he was glad to hear the story. He went at once to the police-station and told what he knew. He was disappointed to find that there was no reward, but well pleased to see how eagerly his information was snapped up. He went back to his kitchen chuckling.

Four days after Mr Hollower's arrival, Trooper O'Crimnell and Tracker-boy Ginger again visited Red Ochre, both of them coming with stealth this time, and disclosing their presence to the native-camp not till they had effected their purpose. As before, they came at noon.

Without being seen or heard by Tocky and Norman within, O'Crimnell stood at the eastern window of the kitchen for many seconds. Nor was he seen when he crept to the door and exposed himself frankly; for Tocky and Norman were busy at table, she with eyes on her piled-up plate, he with his on a book. O'Crimnell had to cough.

Norman glanced and gaped. Tocky turned and gasped. O'Crimnell grinned and said, "Goodday — howzit? Pair of dark horses, aint you?"

Tocky shrieked, rose, rushed to the open western window. O'Crimnell caught her as she was tumbling out.

"No you don't," said O'Crimnell, chuckling. "You can't go nowhere without me. Hereinafter I'm your chaperone."

He meant to make his deep voice sound good-natured. To Tocky it sounded like the Crack o' Doom. She shrieked. She wriggled free and rushed again to the window, and this time got through. O'Crimnell was too big to follow. He shouted to Ginger.

Tocky was halfway down to the native-camp before Ginger caught her. He could not hold her. She scratched and kicked and bit furiously. She was off again when O'Crimnell dashed up. He had to throw her and handcuff her and get Ginger's belt to strap her legs, all with great difficulty, not only by reason of the captive's violence, but by that of the velvet-handedness that officers of modern law must exercise when taking people into hard old iron custody, and by that of the fact that Norman was dancing about and shouting and looking dangerous.

"Blasted little fool!" panted O'Crimnell. "What's matter with you? Keep still. And you shut up, Shillingsworth, or I'll dong you. Watch that yeller cow, Ginger. Trip him! Oh damn you, you little bitch — bite me, would ya! Aw for gawdsake shut your yowlin'!"

He had to carry her to the house, and, in the buckboard in which he made Norman drive them to the Siding, had to hold her, trussed as she was, all the way. And he had to sit in a corner of a dirty cattle-car and be jolted about for hours on the journey up to Town; for Tocky, though she had exhausted strength of limb, was capable of shrieking no less loudly when the spirit moved her; so O'Crimnell could not travel in a passenger-car for fear that unseeing and unthinking and prejudiced passengers might think he was torturing her. The spirit that moved her was one conjured up by flashing visions of some such diabolic thing as a gallows, a gelatine, or an electric-chair. When it was still she lay against her fellow prisoner half swooning with exhaustion and fear. Norman sat sullen, staring. Her frantic behaviour astonished him too, but not as it did the trooper, since he knew how she feared old Hollower and detested the thought of being returned to him.

Norman truly loved Tocky during that dismal ride, understanding as never before her frightful destitution and poignant need of himself. Whenever the spirit moved her another moved him to fling himself on O'Crimnell and set her free. He had been loving her rather much for a week past, having been forced by the storm of rage against the world of whitemen set raging in him by the quarrel with Heather and Mark to take her as his single comrade in a battle. During that ride the storm of hate raged fiercer, not only because he and his comrade had fallen captive to one of the enemy, but because he believed that the principal enemy, Mark, had betrayed him, since he was the only person to his knowledge capable of betraying him who knew whence Tocky had come.

Late that night Tocky was charged at the police-station with being an Aboriginal State Ward Unlawfully Escaped from Custody; and, apparently to put an end to her committing the offence, she was taken at once to the Compound. She went in a dazed state, supposing that she was being taken to the Calaboose for execution. Norman was charged with having Abducted and Unlawfully Detained the said State Ward, and was released on his own recognizance pending his appearance in court.

Norman went straight to the Princess Alice to ask Mark if he had betrayed him. However, being still in a stormy mood, he did not merely ask, but forthwith accused. Mark, who at the moment was in the office working overtime at his job of bookkeeper, replied at first with a mild surprised denial; then, finding that he was being bullied, he jumped up and roared. Heather came running.

"What's the matter?" asked Heather; then, seeing Norman, she added, "So you're back again — eh? What's he saying, dear?"

Mark and Norman roared together, "He's been —"

"What?" asked Heather of Mark.

"He reckons —"

"He put the mocks on me," roared Norman.

"I didn't —"

"You did. No-one else knew but you, you damned old —"

"Here!" cried Heather. "Cut that out or get out."

"Who wants to stay in your lousy hole? I came here to tell that rotten old —"

"Don't you come here shouting, young man. I won't stand it. And just look here — Mark's your father and I'm your step-mother now, and —"

"Yet you treat me like a dog."

She turned to Mark and asked, "What's he saying, dear?"

"He — he reckons I told the police on him."

"What for?"

"For having that little girl Tocky out there."

Heather looked at Norman. While out at Red Ochre she had been told that Tocky belonged to the native-camp.

"And what about it?" she asked.

"She's one of those mission-girls they're hunting for," said Mark. "He reckons I pimped on him — and that's how the jonns went out and grabbed 'em both."

"Well how the hell d'you know they're huntin' for 'em?" demanded Norman. "It's more'n I do."

"Everybody knows it," snapped Heather; and to Mark she said, "Did you know Tocky was one of them?"

"Yes. He asked me to keep it dark. I did — dinkum. He's accusing me of putting the mocks on him —"

"Well who the hell else could've?" yelled Norman.

"Not me!" bellowed Mark, red in the face. "Damn you — ask the jonns."

"Blast you, I asked 'em. Course they wouldn't tell. You did it just to nark me for what I said last week, you rotten lousy old —"

"You pig!" cried Heather. "To talk to your father like that! Get out of my house."

For a moment Norman glared at them, then snorted,

wheeled about, and went off to get a room at the First &
Last.

§

Having of late learnt much about the law in very expensive lessons, Norman decided to conduct his own defence,
deeming it cheaper to be jailed than freed by a lawyer.
When his case began, he assumed the character of obstinate brown toad and grunted objections. At first it looked
as though Stipendiary Larsney would brain him with the
water-carafe.

Most important of his objections were the facts that
Tocky was classed as a halfcaste when in reality she was a
white quadroon, and that she was forced to be dependent
on the State when her father was likely to be living and in
a position to make the provision to which she was entitled.
His considered plan was to prove Tocky's custody unlawful
and hence that abducting her was no offence. This caused
a stir, not because the Court took the objections seriously
— quadroon or no, poor Tocky was still Aboriginal in the
eyes of the State —, but because of the references to Humbolt Lace.

He convinced them that there was something wrong by
assuming the character of determined parrot and silencing
preliminary pooh-poohs with repeated assertions that reput-
able people could be found to bear out what he said. Having done that much, which was something to boast of, seeing that the Court was disposed to regard him as Aboriginal too, he assumed the character of a wise old owl, and
while allowed to do so, wigged the Government for its ignorance of what it ought to know. His case might ordinarily
have been disposed of in a matter of minutes. As it was,
two hours were spent in listening to what he had to say and
in discussing it with the police and Dr Aintee. The result
was an adjournment pending further investigation.

Norman left the court like a turkey-cock, and for the
dual purpose of spreading himself before an appreciative
audience and righting what a talk with the police had convinced him was a wrong he had done his father, went
straight to the Princess Alice to apologise. His apology
was graciously received.

That was the day before paper-day.   Next day THE
TRUE COMMONWEALTH came out with a full account of the
proceedings. Norman was pleased to read that in the opinion of the editor there was more brains in his stern than in

all the heads employed in the Government Service. The report of the case was headed in typical blunt TRUE COMMONWEALTH style:

HALFCASTE ABO. GUNS GOV'T.
BRAINY AINTEE STONKERED
ABDUCTION CASE ADJOURNED

One result of this publicity was that Norman was told by many people that he ought to have been a lawyer. He strutted for days. Another result was that the previously uninterested Rev. Mr Hollower, who, having been led by Dr Aintee to believe that Norman would make an excellent husband for Tocky, had agreed to let the case be settled with a wedding, was moved to inquire about Norman for himself and ultimately to question him, with the result that he was brought to reconsider the agreement. Yet another result was that a clerk in the Taxation Office was reminded of a comically-worded letter in which Tim O'Cannon had confessed many years before to having stolen from the Compound a child named Tocky on whose account a claim for tax-reduction had been queried. The letter was found on a dusty file and brought to light. Thus Mr. Hollower came to consider that Norman was not a fit person to marry his charge, and the Aborigines Department to learn that Tocky was the halfcaste daughter of halfcastes Peter and Constance Pan.

A week later in court again, a moment before the trial was resumed, Dr Aintee told Norman to plead Guilty and have done with causing trouble. Norman smiled like a shark and said he liked trouble and stood up and pleaded Not Guilty. Paddy Larsney pushed the carafe out of reach.

Larsney was determined to be wigged no more. Dr Aintee had told him that the simplest way out of the difficulty was to marry the culprits and acquit them; therefore, not knowing what it was that Mr Hollower and Dr Aintee were at the moment arguing fiercely about at the back of the court (arguing over the head of timid Tocky and terrifying her), he silenced the argumentative defendant with a gesture, and barked at him, "You're going to marry the girl." That took the wind completely out of Norman's sails. He gaped.

Then Mr Hollower, tall and gaunt and hollow-voiced, came forward and said that as the actual guardian of the girl, who he considered should be kept strictly disciplined for a year or two, he wished to object to the marriage on the ground of Defendant's not being a fit and proper person to take care of her. He spoke of the well-known immorality of the married halfcastes of the town, the cause of which, in his opinion, was injudicious mating, the loosing among immoral people of girls who had not acquired moral-sense. Marriage did not make women moral. Defendant was a youth of remarkably good fortune, one to whom he would be glad to marry a charge of his if the same as could be said for his fortune could be said for his morality. At present he seemed to be something of a wastrel, though there was nothing to show that he might not make better use of his fortune later on. However, apart from that, there was another condition that disqualified him as a fit and proper person, and that the main one — his superiority to the girl. In his opinion, which he had formed during a long conversation with Defendant, it would be only a matter of months before the girl, if married to him, would be turned out of his house to live in a native-camp, as much through her own fault as the youth's. They were quite unsuited. Defendant posed as a man of the world. He boasted that he was an atheist, hinted that he was a libertine. Of course as yet he was irresponsible. And the girl as yet was no more moral than a savage. It would be better — from a moral point of view it was imperative — to send the girl back to the Mission to complete the course of discipline to which she was beginning to respond when she escaped.

Here Dr Aintee chuckled audibly. Mr Hollower broke off to stare at him.

Mr Hollower went on to say that perhaps in a year or two the marriage might be contracted with success. For that time Defendant might be bound over. At any rate, the girl was too young to marry yet. With all due respect to the good work done among the halfcastes by Dr Aintee, it must be said that the Aborigines Department was careless of many points in the case of these helpless people, particularly of the moral points, without attention to which they could never become truly civilized; and never to become that meant that they should always be, as unfortunately they were at present, out-casts as well as halfcastes. There were two solutions to the so-called Halfcaste Problem, one being to teach white people that halfcastes were intelligent human creatures like themselves and able to take an honourable place in society if given a chance, the other to teach the halfcastes that *they* were intelligent humans, not animals of a sort as most of them seemed to think they were, and to implant in them the wisdom that would win them any worthy place in life — yes, and after life —, the mighty wisdom of the man who knows he can rely on that Chiefest of Protectors the Lord God. Strange as it might seem, the latter solution was the easier to arrive at. Therefore His Worship might understand what was desired in the case of the girl Tocky. She must be disciplined, which she certainly would not be by a foolish youth like defendant, in order that she might grow up to be —

"What — blast ya?" roared the foolish youth, enraged to the limit by the disparaging references to himself, which were the more cutting because he had believed he had lately made a great impression on Mr Hollower with his man-of-the-world behaviour.

Tocky jumped as though she had been struck. The whole Court, shocked out of the dreamy state of a congregation listening to a sermon, roused and gaped.

"Grows up to what?" roared Norman. "Grows up to what? — you horse-faced bible-puncher — And what the hell d'you mean by calling me a wastrel? If I'm a wastrel, what the flaming hell are you?"

"Silence!" barked the warden.

"You long-jawed poler," Norman roared. "Living on the fat of the land, while your poor damn flock feeds on soup and coconuts and what they can root out of the bush. I know all about your blasted Mission. Discipline! Bible-belting and starvation for the flock — unlimited limelight and blather and plenty of good tucker for you."

"Silence!" cried Larsney and the warden together.

Mr Hollower's face turned yellow. Dr Aintee, previously frowning darkly, raised a hand to his mouth to hide a grin. Norman, an inflamed orator now, a Shouter with a grievance not faked up for a fee, leaned over the Court and bellowed, "Discipline! Why, you blithering idiot, your flock calls you Lucifer — Old Lucifer!"

Mr Hollower's face turned purple. He gasped. The rest of the Court echoed him.

"Old Lucifer — the Devil — the name of your own pet imaginary enemy — that's what they call you for your pains. And what do you do for them? Precious little — and all of it for your own lunatic ends. Call me a wastrel, would ya? You — why, you're poling on Jesus Christ!"

The warden was on the steps of the witness-stand. Mr Hollower joined in the shout of Silence!

"Precious Blood!" hooted Norman, now trembling and hoarse.

"Silence!" bellowed the warden in his ear. He flung off the hand that seized his arm, so that the warden lost his balance and fell down the steps. Two more policemen came running.

"Precious to you — my oath it is! Good tucker, money, power, slaves to wait on you — Dammit I'll have my say! Everyone can talk but me. Old Lucifer —"

"Silence him!" shouted Hollower.

Dr Aintee roared with laughter.

"What's she got to grow up to?" panted Norman. "I'll tell you — all of you, you pale-faced cows — to be a coloured slave to high and mighty whites — to the likes of you that can be masters just because your faces are damn well white — to be humble — to keep her place — to — to —"

"Silence! — Silence! — Silence in the court!" bawled Larsney.

As the policemen laid hands on him, Norman thrust out his neck and delivered himself of a hoarse conclusion: "To hell with your blasted court!"

Larsney, purple of face and panting, gurgled, "Remove him — take him away!"

When Norman was gone, the dazed Court breathed a sigh and took out handkerchiefs. Mr Hollower was the first to move his feet. He moved them to the table where his great white topee lay, then to the door, then out and up the street. A gigantic struggle raged within him. Human Anger was rioting and Christian Virtue reading out the Riot Act, while above it all an insidious voice was crying, "Old Lucifer — Old Lucifer — Ha! Ha! Ha!" Again and again he muttered as he went, "G-get thee behind me!"

Next day, in the presence of a strong body of police and before a packed and chuckling Court, Norman was sentenced to three months' imprisonment on three charges, one being that of Abducting and Detaining, the others Disorderly Conduct and Contempt of Court, the period to be whiled away with hard labour. He was relieved, having spent the night in a cell thinking that he would be jailed for years. Tocky was not tried at all. She was in court only as a witness, but did not know it. In the same motor-truck in which Norman was taken to the Calaboose she was taken to the Compound, where she was put to washing clothes for

the matron to while away her waiting for the departure of
the *Alice Carstairs.* Mr Hollower had had his way.

While Norman was breaking stones next day THE TRUE
COMMONWEALTH featured him again, under the heading:

JAIL FOR TELLING TRUTH.

HALFCASTE SHILLINGSWORTH GOES COPRA CO. SCONE-HOT!

"OLD LUCIFER!"

§

The *Alice Carstairs* sailed without Tocky after all, it
having been found that she was with child and it having
been decided that the marriage was unavoidable.

The fuss the discovery caused! To judge by the conduct
of Aintee and the matron, it would seem that it was they
who were pregnant, not Tocky, and theirs the discomfort
and shame. She did not mind herself, having been aware
of her condition for some weeks, and having been in a way
rather proud of her proven womanhood. Norman was
aware of it too, though quite without pride. He had telegraphed to Mr Bortells, his pharmacist friend of the
steamer, asking for his help.

Although considered a sort of monster now, Tocky continued to wash for the matron, but instead of sleeping with
the hundred bastards in the Halfcastes' Home was locked
up at night in the maternity section of the Compound. She
remained at the Compound for two full months, occupied
mainly with laundry-work and with pondering over the
change in her body and with brooding on lurking fears. As
no-one had told her why she was confined, she believed it
was on account of her crime and supposed that she would
be executed some day. By questioning comrades she convinced herself that they knew little about her crime. That
seemed natural enough. They knew little about anything
but poverty and humiliation. However, she had not found
the matron so ignorant. One day while ironing in that lady's
presence she made bold to ask whether They were going to
Kill her. The lady, engrossed in her own thoughts at first,
then alarmed for the safety of her clothing, replied sharply, "It wouldn't be much loss if they did — Ow! And I'll
kill you too if you burn those things — you little fool —
watch what your doing!"

To Tocky's mind the conditions of her imprisonment were
at variance with those of the condemned murderers of
Norman's tales only in two respects, that she was not re-

strained with stones and bars and certainly not well fed. The advantage to be taken of the lack of bars occurred to her one Saturday afternoon while the attention of the white superintendents was concentrated on a game of bridge and that of all the humbler residents on a rowdy game of football. She left her prison forthwith.

She ran to the beach and into the water, and after assuring herself that she had not been seen, walked to the rocks of Fathead Point, keeping to the water all the way for fear of leaving tracks for traitors. At the Point she was forced by the depth of water to come ashore, and forced to struggle for half a mile or more over and under and between and around huge rocks that looked as though they had been flung there in some gigantic battle between the wrathful gods of old. Wrath of the Gods! Poor midget pregnant semi-savage Tocky knew nothing of the gods of old, nor knowing would have. thought of such small fry, being as she was engrossed in the seemingly impossible task of escaping from the Masters of Mankind.

At last she reached Mailunga Beach, but for over an hour was denied the long-awaited joy of steeping bleeding feet in silky sands by a crowd of people lounging in the grove of coconuts beyond the little creek she first must cross. It was a crowd of whites, mostly children, a picnic of the sunday-school she guessed at once, recognizing the silk-clad figure of a rotund red-faced man as that of the Rev. Finchley Randter, who sometimes came to the Compound to teach his gospel of humility.

Sunday-school picnic! Cakes and fruit and lollies and sweety drinks galore. Although Tocky had never taken part in a sunday-school picnic, the Rev. Mr Randter never having introduced that part of his ritual into the Compound, she knew all there was to know about such functions, having spent many a stolen afternoon with coloured comrades watching the rich ones from the scrub and waiting to pounce on their leavings. The knowledge made confinement to the rocks less irksome. She settled herself, and smirking in anticipation of the feast that would be hers if she beat the ants to the leavings, watched Mr Randter beating time while his food-proud flock sang an invitation to Almighty God to join them in their feasting.

The shadows of the coconuts crept far; gold came flowing from the harbour up the creek; the Christians, having packed their bellies full and sung thanksgiving unto Him

who dealt so well with them, packed up their bags and
went off laughing.

Tocky came out of the rocks, plunged into the golden
creek, ran up the silky beach. There were scraps galore,
delicious scraps, corned-beef sandwiches with mustard and
pastry with cream, a little gritty with sand perhaps, but not
anty with ants as they should have been but for the Great
Bunyip's good sense in sending ants home at sundown. She
wrapped up some of the leavings in a piece of paper, and
munching went her way through the coconut-grove towards
the Meatworks.

It was dark when she reached the Tikka Point road. She
followed the road that left it for the 2-Mile where most
of the railway-workers lived. She passed through the settlement of 2-Mile like a wraith, unseen but seeing all, watching verandas and lighted windows, listening to the clatter
of dishes and the clack of tongues. Some little distance
past the last house she dived into the scrub, climbed the
railway-embankment, continued on her way down the road
of still-warm steel.

She walked for hours in the easy-going native style, with
body loose and drooping forward, hands clasped behind the
back, heels raised, toes turned in, the converse of the whiteman's style, but no less effective as an easy mode of going
far and fast for all that. The sleepers, buried to the tops
in gravel and overgrown with couch, were good to tread
on after rutty stony roads, and more, were spaced as though
to suit her paces. Little paces. About three thousand to
the mile, three-quarters of a million to the journey. Not
that Tocky calculated so. She knew Red Ochre was a hundred miles away, but realized what distance was no more
than most folks do. She was, however, not afraid of distance as most folks are. She would have walked to Batman had it suited her; even though she knew she might
be occupied in travelling unto the third and fourth generation.

The waning moon peeped over the bush, saw that the
coast was clear, and slowly climbed the sky. A silver road
for Tocky now. On she went, and on and on, till her feet
began to miss the sleepers, tangle in the grass, stub toes on
bolts of fish-plates, stagger off the road. One silver creek
she crossed, another, and another, all singing sirens' songs
to tired feet. At length the feet succumbed, defied their
captain, the fearful mind, and staggered down to drown
themselves in sweetness. She bathed, drank, stretched full-

Q

length on dewy grass to rest a while and listen to her friends
the frogs and watch her friends the stars till — Lo! the
stars were gone and the white-hot sun was hanging in the
trees and the froggy chorus drowned in the pop-pop-pop-
popping of a fettlers' trolley. She just had time to hide.

Tocky loved frogs for their sparkling eyes and merry
songs and friendly ways, but did not scruple eating them
if need be. There was need that morning. Apologetically
she slaughtered five and ate their delicate legs with dainty
bamboo-shoots, concluding her meal with native goose-
berries, a stick-load of sugar-bag honey drawn from a hollow tree, and crystal water.

She went her way. Just before noon she was scared off
the track by the returning trolley. In mid-afternoon she
was scared again when, coming from out of a reedy swamp
from hunting for roots and duck-eggs, she saw a bull-
buffalo on the railway not twenty yards away. She fell on
her face. The beast did not see her. He was looking eastward, with great head drooping, snuffling. So he stood for
several minutes, while a swarm of flies buzzed round his
scaly pig-like hide, and while marsh-flies and mosquitoes
and leeches dealt with Tocky; then he left the road and
wandered into the bush. Tocky did not move till she could
stand the draining of her blood no longer.

On she went and on and on. Early next morning she
came upon a gang of fettlers at work; or rather at rest,
because they were squatting on haunches among their tools,
talking and smoking. Their voices in the windless golden
air murmured like music; and their smoke rose high like
incense.

At noon that day the mail-train passed on its way to the
Melisande, passed in a cloud of dust and smoke, and passed
in a moment, leaving Tocky with a little more understanding
of distance and the slowness of her feet.

At midday on the fourth day she was delighted to see
the familiar ruins of the Garrison suddenly appear as she
rounded a pandanus thicket. She left the road at the little
shed where he whom she still regarded as her father used
to keep his tricycle, and walked up the clinker path towards the house. No talk of Norman's or Aintee's could
ever convince her that she was not an O'Cannon born. She
thought of old Tim as she climbed the hill, and halfway
up turned off to look at his grave. It was easy to find, being the one bare patch on the hillside. The fettlers who
fashioned it had sterilized the site in railway-style with

weed-poison. In fact they had made a railway job of it in
every detail. The mound was gravelled and shelved at the
edges; the fence was of forty-five pound rails; the cross
at the head of it was a steel sleeper to which was bolted an
iron plate in which some patient and bitter fellow had inscribed with a drill the epitaph:

TIM O'CANNON
FETTLER
BUCHERD BY TRAFFIC DEPT
XMAS DAY 1927
R. I. P.

Tocky's attention was suddenly drawn by the bray of a
donkey. On the brow of the hill she saw two donkeys grazing, a white one and a roan, which she instantly recognized
as Cho Sek Ching's inseparable Lidjin and Poltix. She did
not know that Cho was the cause of her recent misery, nor
much about that which he had caused Norman and Mark,
but was well aware that he was one of the lowest old
blackguards on the face of the earth, having lately heard
Norman often say so. Therefore she did not go near the
house, guessing that Cho was camped there, but, skirting it
warily, made for the pack-track, and went on to Red Ochre.

§

Before Norman heard of Tocky's disappearance she had
been gone a week or more. He first heard of it from a new
arrival at the Calaboose, a halfcaste youth who told him
she had been eaten by a crocodile. He was shocked. Next
he heard of it from one of his guards, who told him that
she had crossed to the other side of the harbour in a canoe
and that the police had gone in search of her. He did not
know what to believe nor what he wished to believe. Lately,
since having learnt from Aintee that the marriage was unavoidable, he had been cursing the day he met her. Then
Mark came to visit him and said that she had been drowned
and that the Town was saying that she had drowned herself
because the matron of the Compound and Dr Aintee had
ill-treated her. He began to believe it and to mourn her.
A few days later Aintee told him that she had been drowned while swimming, and said of the talk that he wished
the people of the town would pay as much attention to the
welfare of the coloured people they employed and used
as they did to those that didn't concern them, and said of

Tocky that he thought she was not quite sane. Norman was
convinced, and stricken with grief. He told Aintee that he
was a cruel liar and a hard-hearted hound; and that night
he wept a little. He heard of it again when on the day of his
release he went to the hospital for treatment for a rash with
which his close-cropped head was affected. There he met
Margaret O'Cannon, who could scarcely tell it for weeping.
Then the rest of the coloured staff told him and wept, then
the Lazaret girls, who bawled it and fairly wailed. It seemed
as though the whole world were mourning her. He did not
think it strange. By then he was loving her dearly.

He did not go straight in to Town, but, finding himself
drawn to Margaret, either by common grief or physical
charm, went down to her hut in Hospital Gully to stay till
his head healed and his hair was grown long enough for
presentation at the Princess Alice.

A reminder of the dear departed was the *Alice Carstairs,*
lying at anchor in Hospital Bay. Norman watched the ship
for hours on end, delighting in her beauty and that of her
surroundings and that of his own mournful thoughts. He
told himself that he had never known such peace, either on
earth or within himself. The Peace of God, he called it,
speaking to the wooden lady (an effigy of Miss Alice Carstairs herself, no doubt) who looked out from the bow of
that seemingly painted ship across the seemingly painted
ocean. And feeling so, he thought with charity of all the
world, even of Mr Hollower and Cho Sek Ching.

Just then the slopes of the gully were clothed with tall
grass, green and russet and still. A tiny stream ran murmuring in a mossy bed where a week before a torrent roared. When the sun went down it went like a town-bred pic-
nicker, leaving the west sky littered with flaky clouds of
many hues. It was autumn, Capricornia's autumn, the period of which was but a few short gorgeous hours.

Next day the trade wind sighed across the sea, breathing
life into the painting. Then the grass shivered, whispered
of death. The murmur of the streamlet died. The evening
sky became a fleckless field of saffron yellow-brown that
lay between a scarlet sea and a star-studded indigo zenith.
Next day the grass was crackling; the mossy growths were
dead. No clouds on horizons now but those of smoke that
told of the starting of natural fires that soon would sweep
the bush. For the Trade Wind was freshening, freshening
every hour, hurling the grass down, sawing tree against

tree, freshening, freshening, rising to blast the land with the long harsh drought of Dry Season.

Norman stayed a week with Margaret, another with Heather and Mark, then went off home, where, first to his horror, next to his amazement, and subsequently to his annoyance, he found his dear beloved awaiting him. She was not in the house when he arrived, but in the native-camp, where she had been living all the while. The house was locked.

"But what'd you run away from the Compound for?" he asked her. She hung her head.

He was going to say that it had been arranged that he should marry her, but thought better and said, "But the jonnops came out here once, didn't they? Aintee told me. How'd you dodge 'em?"

She smiled and said, "I runned away with the binghis. We bin hidim track."

"But what about the tracks round the house?"

"Oh I not come up much often. Den I wear old boots I bin findim. Dat nigger Ginger got no head for trackin'. I can beat him meself."

"Aint you goin' back to the Compound to tell 'em you're alive?"

Her eyes widened. She breathed, "N—o-more!"

"But what about the baby?"

"Aint you gunner gimme no more med'cine for killim?"

"Might be too late now. What'll you do if it is?"

"Go longa ol' Black Angel longa Lonely River. She proper doctor for madernty."

"And get me into a row for concealin' a birth? Abductin' waifs and concealin' births and deaths. Gawd — you'll get me hung yet. Aw now — don't start to howl. It's all right love. I'm only playin'. Come on. I don't mean nuthen. I won't say a word. You can stop long's you like. All right now?"

"Y-y-yu-i."

IF troopers had come during the first few hours that Ket spent on the wreck-strewn beach he would have surrendered with a grateful heart. But the weak mood passed at length, leaving him fearfully considering the challenge of Fate he saw expressed in the existence of the undamaged dinghy and the bits of canvas, rope, and spar that lay about, the challenge to do or die on the smiling sea.

He took it up. Next day he spent in stepping a mast in the dinghy and bending a sail, filling his gunny-bag with figs and roots and stalks of grass, cleaning a tin to fill with water, and studying a sodden chart. Next morning, with a light wind behind, he set out to do or die.

He did nothing good and many times nearly died of fright. The land-wind grew in strength as the sun rose up, and taunted the sea till the sea quit smiling and joined the malicious play. The dinghy sped with the speed of a flying-fish, stem hanging in a rainbow of spray, stern sunk in a foaming welter. He crouched in the bottom, clinging with one hand to the gunwale, with the other to the steering-oar. Steering-oar? But a name. The dinghy would not steer. She was bent on racing the roaring waves. She would have capsized had he baffled her. Nor would she brook interference with the sail, but would bury her head were it drawn an inch, and were it drawn more would snatch it from the lubberly hand and fling it *crack!* on the other side. She became personified in truth in the lubber's mind. He hated her, feared her, but coaxed her with tender names. And the wind and the sea became personified. But they were monsters, terrible, vast. He dared not speak to them. He felt like a fly, a fly with bulging eyes and standing hair and trembling bony knees, a fly caught in a vast green heaving web, trapped by Fate the Spider. He prayed to God to still the sea. The wind roared at him. The green sea spat and hissed.

What he thought was a hurricane was nothing but a lusty morning breeze, blown from the cooler land across the luke-warm sea in order to replace the rising warmer airs. It slackened as the land grew warmer, till at noon, when equilibrium between the temperatures of land and sea was reached, it fell, leaving Ket on a sea of glass. At first he was grateful, thinking his prayer was answered. Soon he began to curse the calm and heat.

An hour or so later a breeze sprang up from the opposite quarter and turned the dinghy round. Ket tried to beat to the wind for a while, then gave it up in a rage. This breeze was no mere vacuum-filler, but preliminary breath of a gale that soon came roaring down, driving before it all the clouds it had gathered out of Java and all the rollers in the Silver Sea. He who had set out for distant lands came back with hair and beard salt-rimed and flying in the wind, with face ash-grey and hands ice-cold, devouring with smarting eyes every glimpse of that best of good earth, Australia, that the hills of the sea allowed, praying with heart and mind and tongue for deliverance up to any fate but that of floundering in that seething jade-green web.

God cast him ashore at midnight. Without a word of thanks he dragged his numbed frame up the beach and flung it down in warm dry sand beneath a tree. Nor did he utter nor think thanks when in the morning he found that God had landed him within two miles of Tumbukka. He rowed home cursing the lack of wind.

He stayed a few days at Tumbukka. Driven out by fear of imaginary danger, he went to a remoter island of the group and there set up a camp from which he might watch both land and sea for approaching Nemesis. What he should do if she should come he did not know. After some days of living on shell-fish and crabs and grass, he returned to the mainland, and camped on a billabong near the sea, where, but for sickness and unceasing yearning for civilized food, he might have lived quite well. As the result of living in poverty for many months, he had contracted beri-beri. He did not know it. He thought his complaint was caused by certain fruits and eggs he had been eating lately, really wholesome foods that would have cured him had he not dropped them from his diet. His body swelled. His legs became so weak that he often had to crawl to move about. He thought he was dying. Wishing to die in human company, if only of the kind he had cursed and despised and hated all his life — his poorest of poor relations — he made a terrible journey to the Mundikualas.

The Mundikualas were barely civil to him, but took him in, believing he was pure white and fearing that trouble would come if they should deal harshly with him. The camp as he found it was peopled only with the aged and infirm and infantile. The young and vigorous were away in the bush driving game to convenient places for the season. Although he could not understand their speech, he knew quite well that they did not want him; still he stayed, alternately sneaking and bullying; and by virtue of the food they gave him, which at first he gorged then picked contemptuously, he made a great recovery. He lived on their grudging charity for eighteen days.

Then the young ones returned, among them the girl Diana, whom Ket hailed as a fellow creature and subsequently tried to woo. He tried to induce her to come to Tumbukka and from there to Kakkibalaka, to live in ease and luxury with him as her willing slave. She listened politely. And her husband behaved with forbearance. Then Ket raped her. He was set upon, beaten, thrown out of the camp. But for the fact that the Tribe was aware of the whiteman's law of a tribe of blacks' lives for a whiteman's life, they would have slain him. The momentary discomfort of a lubra was not worth avenging at the risk of extermination. In fact, when their anger cooled, the Tribe regretted even the little they had done, became alarmed, demolished their camp, and wiping their tracks out as they went, fled to the hills, sure that the wrath of the Masters of Mankind would soon come down on them.

§

Ket returned to the sea. He set out in the dinghy to work his way to Papua, not across the Silver Sea, a journey of about six hundred miles by way of scattered islands, but round the coast, eastward to Cape Nordoster, then southward and eastward and northward round the Gulf of Capricornia to Southern Cross Island, and then across the Coral Sea by way of multitudinous islands to his goal, a journey of at least two thousand miles. A brave one — if he made it! His conscience knew that he was simply bent on going to Flying Fox to beg a bit of civilized comfort and a passage to Kakkibalaka.

His conscience was right. One bright morning in the middle of April — it might have been August for all he knew — he rounded a cape and sighted Flying Fox. No — it was not Flying Fox he saw; that, a mere pearl-rimmed emerald in a silver-splashed turquoise setting, was a sight far too common to be noticed by his nature-weary eyes; he saw the Mission Station, that cosy hamlet, that abode of civilized men. He ran the dinghy into hiding in the mangroves of the mainland.

He hid in the mangroves for an hour or more, gorging the sight. Roofs, a winding windmill, gardens, ordered grove of palms, smoke from a chimney, spire of a church, a flock of goats, a mob of grazing bullocks. He crept out of hiding and stole across the dancing water to the jetty. He landed, stood in the chuckling shallows staring. Glint of a window, clothes on a line, pawpaws on a laden tree, a rooster on a fence.

Natives in the sugar-cane that grew between the houses and the palm-grove stopped their work to stare. They had seen him round the cape and creep into hiding, had watched him watching, in glimpses stolen while the back of David, the Solomon-Island overseer, was turned. David had told them to keep their eyes on their work and their thoughts on Things Above and leave the watching to him.

Who was this? they whispered. Certainly not a China-man or Japanese or Malay. Surely a whiteman could not become so wretched as this man seemed to be. Who was he?

Then someone unable to contain himself cried out in the native tongue, "It's Lazarus, the poor man number one!"

"No!" cried another, "It's Esau the hairy man."

Esau come to sell his freedom for a meal.

"Sinners!" cried David. "Silence! Get to your work!"

Over the mat-screened railing of the veranda of the great white house, to which led the coral path, a neat-trimmed greying head appeared, and gold-rimmed glasses winked in the morning sun. This was Brother Simon Bleeter. He stared at the ragged visitor. He himself wore pants and shirt and shoes of spotless white. As Ket, who had not seen him, reached the veranda steps, he closed the large black gilt-edged book he held and went to the head of the steps on noiseless rubber soles.

Ket was taken by surprise. For a moment he gaped. Then he said in a rusty voice, "Goodday."

Brother Bleeter did not speak at once, but stroked his trim black greying beard and quizzed the scarecrow visitor with eyes that were almost shut. At last he said in a very quiet voice, "Good morning — and who might you be?"

"Me?" gasped Ket, "Aw I — I —" he cleared his throat, "Aw I been shipwrecked."

After an unpleasantly protracted pause, Bleeter said as quietly as before, "Indeed? — Come up."

Was that the way to greet a man who had been ship-wrecked? Ket began to feel alarmed. He stammered, "Aw — but — but I'm so terrible dirty."

"Come up," said Bleeter firmly.

"Thanks," breathed Ket, and obeyed.

Bleeter, scrutinizing him closely, murmured, "Ship-wrecked?"

Ket made a bold attempt to meet and hold the puckered slits of eyes. He cleared his throat and answered as stoutly as he could, "Yes."

Incredulity was stamped on Bleeter's face. Ket saw it and began to hate the man. Brother Bleeter was a man incredulous by nature of anything not concerned with Holy Writ; but just then he was not so merely by strength of disposition, but by knowledge; for he had heard from searchers come from scouring the bush for the truant half-caste girls that whitemen noted for their raggedness and hairiness were camped on the coast not far away, and had supposed it likely that the men were those who had committed the murder at the Melisande of which he had heard.

"Shipwrecked?" he murmured again. "And might I ask where?"

Ket had an answer, long prepared; but he could not find it; for it was lost in the panic caused by the quizzing eyes. He groped frantically. At last he answered breathlessly, "Aw — way down the coast — back along — Aw I dunno this coast too well."

"Where do you come from?"

"Kakkibalaka."

"Ah!"

Ket planned to pose as having come from the Indies, his idea being at once to make his plight appear more desperate, to save himself from being questioned about Australian States or Towns, to account for his presence on a coast about which he must know something had he sailed it as an honest man, and to induce the missionaries, by saying that his wealthy father in Singapore would reward them for their kindness, to take him to Kakkibalaka in their schooner. If they should want to take him to Port Zodiac, he could slip away in the dinghy. He planned to say that his ship had been blown to the coast by a storm.

"Are you alone?" asked Brother Bleeter.

"Yes — all hands were lost."

"Whitemen?"

"No — all natives."

"Are you a whiteman?"

Ket blinked and swallowed. After a moment he answered in a strained voice, "Yes — course I am."

"Yes? But your face is peculiar — especially your eyes."

Ket dropped his eyes and shuffled.

"Are you an Australian?"

"N—o," muttered Ket.

"Where were you born?"

"In the East."

"Ah! Where?"

"Singapore."

"Indeed! I know it well. We must have a talk about it."

Silence, while Ket sat like a stone and Bleeter quizzed him.

At length Bleeter said, "But please sit down — and give me the details of your experiences. You came in a dinghy, I see."

Ket sat down. He wished to say that he had not sat on a chair for eighteen months, but could only say that it was good to see a chair again. Bleeter nodded knowingly, and laid his book on the rattan table beside which Ket sat. Ket glanced at the book. It was inscribed, in large gold letters, *Quiet Talks About The Tempter*.

Ket told his tale of the wreck of the good ship *Maskee*, the name of which he found it hard to recall at first, and which, in spite of having told it to the wind and sea a thousand times, he pronounced not always as *Mahs-kee*, but at times as *Meski*, short. That was the name of a ship he had often heard Mark speak of, and a Malayan word meaning No Matter. The trouble was that he had heard Mark pronounce it short when speaking of the ship and long when using is as an expletive.

At first he stumbled badly. His face burned; his eyes grew hot; but his discomfort was not apparent in anything but his speech. He explained that it was weakness due to suffering that tied his tongue; and then he switched from the difficult subject of the wreck to a description of his sufferings, which, being true, was easy. At length he remembered that he had a wreck to show to doubters, and said so, and offered to go get a few bits of wreckage from the dinghy. Bleeter's answer that it did not matter gave him heart. He grew bold, looked Bleeter in the face and returned to the wreck of the *Maskee*. Then mid-morning refreshments arrived in the hands of matronly Christobel, and saved him from wrecking himself.

He ate a great meal of buttery toast, not cold and in thin-cut slices as Bleeter did, but in huge hot slabs that Bleeter sent Christobel to prepare for him. Ket ate toast till his beard was streaked with butter, then ate a large pawpaw, then swallowed two cups of tea. When he had done, he asked for a cigarette. For an instant Bleeter's slits of eyes opened, disclosing colourless hard eyes. Bleeter answered softly, "I do not smoke; nor do I approve of the habit in others." Ket looked out to sea and belched.

After a protracted pause Brother Bleeter said, "You've certainly been having a rough time of it."

Ket turned to him and said gravely, "Thanks to God I got through. I prayed."

Bleeter answered gently, nodding, "There are much worse ways of gaining one's ends."

Ket did not like the tone. He turned away blinking. After a nerve-wracking pause he turned back and asked, "Are you the head of this Mission, sir?"

"No. The Reverend Mister Hollower is the head."

"Is he 'ere?"

"No — away in Port Zodiac. But how did you know that this was a Mission, Mister — er — Mister?"

"Melville's me name — Harold Melville."

"Ah — quite a book-name! And how did you know?"

"Saw it on the chart."

"Indeed! Have you the chart with you?"

"No. I did get it from the wreck; but it was all pulped up; so I threw it away."

"A pity. I'd've liked to see it. Do you remember the date on it?"

Ket moved uneasily, answered slowly, "Well — can't say I do."

"Was it an old one?"

Ket felt trapped. He answered breathlessly, "Well — not so old."

"But not new — eh?"

"I — I couldn't say. I — it was on the schooner when I bought it."

"Ah! And was the vessel old."

"Well — fairly."

"How long had you had it?"

"A — about six years."

"That's strange. Your chart must have been issued a good while ago. Our latest chart of this part of the coast, issued two years ago, described this island as Flying Fox, a trepang-fishers' camp. That's how it is marked on every chart I've seen. The chartographers appear to ignore our existence."

Ket swallowed, remembered that Mark had pointed out his old home as the site of the Mission. Because Bleeter left breaking the silence to him, he was forced to say, "P'raps — p'raps it was really a new one."

"It couldn't have been a newer one than ours," answered Bleeter.

After another long pause Bleeter said, "From what you tell me about the place where you were wrecked — the Jinjin River, I guess —, you were as near Sunday Cape as you were to us — nearer in fact, because if you'd gone that way you'd've had the Trade behind you. It's a wonder you didn't go."

"I — I dunno this coast too well," Ket muttered.

"But surely you'd know Sunday Cape!"

"Can't say I do. So many capes and bays, you know."

"But only one on all this long long coast like Sunday Cape. You must have seen it on your chart — eh?"

Ket clenched his hands, fighting against a rising surge of fury. He muttered, "No — I never."

The purring voice went on, "Then your chart must have been much older than ours after all. Sunday Cape is marked most conspicuously in red and yellow — big yellow circle with red inside. Of course you know what that means."

Ket was forced to answer. He breathed, "N—o."

"Oh come! — Captain of a schooner for six years and don't know how a lighthouse is shown on a chart?"

Ket was dumb.

The silence was left for Bleeter to break. He shattered it. In his softest tone he asked, "Are you sure you didn't come overland from the Melisande River?"

Ket started, so that he kicked the grass mat from under his feet, sent it spinning down the polished veranda. He looked with expressionless face at the expressionless face of Bleeter.

Breaking the next spell was likewise left to Bleeter; he shattered that too, saying as softly, "Are you not one of the men who murdered the Greek gambler?"

Ket gasped. Seconds passed. Then he cried above the storm within him, "I — I dunno what you mean."

Bleeter, quizzing him, murmured, "No?"

Ket's nostrils were quivering, his queer eyes jerking, his brown hands showing white on the arms of the chair. A moment. Then he leapt to his feet. Bleeter shot from his seat to the rail and shouted, "David!"

Ket did not move. Bleeter turned to him, quizzing. David rushed up with a crowd of natives, crying, "Master!" A moment of quizzing; then Bleeter turned to David and

said, "All right, thank you. I thought I might need you.
You may go."

David and the natives retired gaping. For a minute Ket
stood alone with Bleeter, staring at him, blinking; then he
dropped his eyes to the steps, drew a deep breath, and
shuffled away. Through slits of eyes, stroking his greying
black beard, Bleeter watched the scarecrow figure shuffle
to the Beach.

§

Ket returned to the dinghy and sat there for hours, staring sometimes at the mangroves of the mainland, sometimes at the horizon of the sea, sometimes at the laughing
water under him, sometimes at that cosy hamlet of men. At
length he rose, took up his gunny-bag, stole up to the grove,
and gathered a bag of coconuts, provision for the voyage
he had made up his mind to begin forthwith. When he returned to the dinghy he found that the wind was not in
favour and the remaining hours of day too few to allow
of his setting out at once. Jibed at by his conscience, he
dragged the dinghy out of the sight of the houses, beached
it, and lay down to watch the sunset. That night he slept
in the coconut grove.

At noon next day he went to the house again, this time
to the back door, and knocked and scared Christobel. Soon
Bleeter came.

"Good morning," said Ket humbly.

Bleeter nodded.

After a pause Ket said, "Can I have something to eat,
please. I'll do anything to earn it. I'm starvin'."

Quizzing him, Bleeter asked, "Are you going to stay
here?"

"I — I'm sick," said Ket miserably. "I'm weak. If — if
only you'd be so kind, sir —"

Bleeter stroked his beard for a while, then said, "I should
think you'd prefer to go away."

"Aw I can't!" moaned Ket. "If only you knew what it's
like to go day after day, day after day, in storms and rain
and heat — alone like a dog — no, dogs get good food —
like a — like a —"

"A dingo?" murmured Bleeter.

"Aw it's terrible!"

"The way of the transgressor is always hard."

"Aw gawd — it's more'n I can stand!" cried Ket, and
dropped his head to his hands and wept.

When he looked up, sniffling and blinking, he whispered to the never-changing face of Bleeter, "Aint you got no mercy? Aw gawd I've suffered enough!"

"Do you intend to wait for Mister Hollower?"

Ket's throat was full.

"Do you intend to give yourself up?"

Ket struggled for speech. At length he said brokenly, "Give me a rifle and I'll go."

Bleeter did not reply.

"A rifle — and a handful of cartridges — any old one. I can't kill with my bare hands."

"No?" murmured Bleeter.

"Aw please, sir, gimme a rifle and let me go. I gotter have a gun to get tucker. I've tried huntin' like a nigger till I've nearly gone mad with hunger. Please gimme a rifle, good sir. I'll work for it. I'll do anything for it. Look — I'm big and strong — and I got brains too. I'll live decent if I can get away. I never was bad. Dinkum, I never was. The world's been against me. What I've done was only mistakes — bad luck — and I was driven to it. Aw I'm starvin'. I'm weak. I can't go on. Oh! Ah!"

Bleeter waited.

"Aw holy man — holy father — in the name of the God that made us both, do be kind to me — no one ever was kind to me — so do be kind, father — Aw do be kind!"

"You can get a meal in the natives' dining-room," said Bleeter, and pointed.

Ket looked through his tears, then turned back to Bleeter, and, still panting from weeping, said, "God bless you!" He staggered away. Bleeter closed the fly-door very gently.

No buttered toast in the natives' dining-room. Ket dined that day on a sort of gruel made from flour and kangaroo's bones, which he enjoyed so much that he begged more from a hoary old fellow who sat beside him. Next course he ignored, that being coconut-meat, of which he had lately eaten so much that copra-bugs followed him. Next course he enjoyed as much as the first, it being musty black tea boiled with sugar-cane. He tried to beg tobacco; there was none about; for it was regarded there as an evil thing, at least by the superintendents.

He ate with the natives again that night, when the food was cold sweet-potatoes and tea, as it was next morning at breakfast. At noon that next day there was hot roasted kangaroo and hot sweet-potatoes and more tea. Tea was always on, and more often than not the gruel; but there

was sometimes hot roast nuttagul, baked pumpkin, boiled
fish. Ket relished it all, but complained of the quantity.
Soon he made trouble among the natives. Bleeter asked
him to eat in a shed.

The Nuttagul Days were Sundays, of which Ket spent
two at the Mission. He went to Church and sat on the floor
with the natives. There were no pews but two rows that
stood in the chancel on either side of the pulpit, one for
the white missionaries, the other for the coloured assistants.
Natives and halfcastes sat in order on the antbed floor, or
rather did so when allowed a spell from kneeling to sing
or pray. The pulpit was occupied night and morning by
Brother Bleeter, in the afternoon by David; but what they
said, important though it must have been, since it always
took them long to say and worked them into states of great
vehemence, was lost on Ket, the only person present who
did not understand the Yurracumbunga tongue; and it was
also lost on many of the flock, to judge by covert yawning.
Christobel led the female choir, sang hymns in solo, and
sometimes led a prayer.

Eleven days elapsed, each dawn of which saw Ket break
the resolution he made each night in his palm-leaf gunyah
to sail away. In the heat of the twelfth day, while Ket was
asleep in his shelter, the *Alice Carstairs* arrived, bringing
Mr Hollower home and Trooper Robbrey who was come
out to search for the girls.

Half an hour after the schooner's arrival, Ket was awak-
ened by a touch on the breast. He opened his eyes to see a
friendly young brown face beneath a badged and puggaree'd
hat. He gasped.

Trooper Robbrey smiled and said, "Hello Charlie —
howzit?"

Ket choked.

"Where's Frank?" asked Robbrey.

Ket goggled. He was waiting for awakening from a
nightmare. At length he gasped, "Frank?"

"Yeah — Frank McLash. Aint he with you?"

Ket struggled up. Still the vision persisted.

"What's — Frank left you?" asked the trooper.

Ket gasped, "Didn't — you — catch him?"

Robbrey smiled and said, "No — we aint seen him.
Where's he gone?"

"I — I dunno. I — I aint seen him for months."

Robbrey took a tobacco-pouch from a pocket of his shirt
and said, "Have a smoke?"

Ket took the tobacco and papers in shaky hands. After a moment the trooper said, "Better let me roll it — eh?"

§

Ket submitted quietly. Failure to resist was not a matter of cowardice but decency. Trooper Robbrey captured him with courtesy. He even cut his hair for him and allowed him to use his razor, when he might have left all that to his tracker-boys. It was his first arrest.

It was while cutting his hair that Robbrey actually arrested him. Thus any embarrassment felt in saying and hearing what must be said — and embarrassment there must have been, since the formal declaration must have struck terror into the heart of Ket and half choked the young self-conscious trooper — remained the secret of him who felt it, the speaker being concentrated at the moment on the hair of the hearer's nape, the hearer on the raven curls that glistened on his sheeted knees. Silence. Then Snip! Snip! Snip! Then, replying to the formal and courteous warning, Ket murmured, "Thanks." And in reply to that the trooper murmured, "Good-o — bit closer on the neck, eh?" "Close as you like," breathed Ket. Then Snip! Snip! Snip! again.

They left for Town as soon as Mr Hollower had questioned a number of his flock and learnt to his dismay that it was a fact that he was known among them as Old Lucifer. They sailed in the *Alice Carstairs*, coasting all the way to Sunday Cape, calling at Tumbukka and the Jinjin on the way in the hope of seeing Frank or trace of him. That hope was solely Robbrey's, if Hollower did not share it. Certainly it was not Charles Ket's. Frank, the world's one witness to the murder of Con the Greek, was the last person in the world Ket wished to see; but very cunningly he pretended that he shared the hope, pretended more and more as with the declining of Robbrey's hope his own hope rose, his hope that Frank was dead, killed by his horse, or by a buffalo, or by a crocodile, or by a snake, or by the blacks, or by any other of the thousand evil things that lurked in that hell of a wilderness.

If Frank were dead his shoes were Ket's. Surely they could not hang Frank if it were he who was arrested and Ket the one who was dead? And what could Frank say to prove his innocence that Ket could not? Lucky for Ket that Robbrey had asked him where Frank was. Lucky for him to be arrested at all, since surely there could be no hanging or life-imprisonment now. Prison for robbery no doubt; but better a term of years in jail than another week of frightful liberty in the wilderness. And what was this about Jack Ramble? Robbrey had asked if he had seen Ramble on the coast. He had answered No, not for the sake of Ramble, but for fear of doing himself harm by telling the truth. And then he had learnt that Ramble was Mark Shillingsworth. Small wonder the fellow had been so scared of betraying his whereabouts! Arrested for murder, tried by that terrible judge on the capital charge — and acquitted! Why not Ket acquitted too? The nearer Ket got to the gallows he had feared so long the higher rose his hopes of cheating it. He could have killed Robbrey and Hollower in their sleep; he could have taken possession of Robbrey's arms and forced the Malayan captain and the crew to take him anywhere he wished; but no; for he wished no more than to live for a while well fed in a cosy prison.

Port Zodiac at last. The schooner arrived at sunset. Ket saw the many roofs, the gilded windows, the mail-boat at the jetty, the white-clad crowd. Civilization. Then darkness, and electric lights, and a bright-eyed motor on a man-made road. Ket spent an hour staring at the lamp-lit shore while a tracker went to the station with a message from Robbrey. Then a ride in a motor. Headlights glaring through red dust of roads, illuminating fences, lampposts, houses, men, a cat, a dog, an old boot, a bottle, a gutter running suds. And bright shop-windows packed like the mouths of treasure-caves. How good to be back again, how good, how grand, if only as a captive of the System!

MURDER WILL OUT

FOR once the police did not gossip about their business. To have done so with regard to the arrest of Ket would have cost the gossiper his job. Captain Settaroge feared that Frank, who he believed was hiding somewhere along the railway, might be scared away if news of Ket's arrest was broadcast. No-one but the police knew that Ket was in Town, not even Mark, who, having been asked by Settaroge if he had seen anything of anyone when travelling from

Tumbukka to the railway or when lately he went out to Tumbukka by sea to get the *Spirit of the Land* guessed that the police were on the track of Frank and Ket. Setta· roge had learnt from Ket of Mark's association with the murderers, but said nothing about it to Mark himself, only wishing to learn from him if he had seen Frank after Ket had.

Mark said nothing about the murderers to anyone. He supposed that they had betrayed themselves in the manner he had predicted and had gone to the Indies or to the bottom of the sea in the ship that he had been on the point of selling for the much-needed sum of £700. Even so, he did not think of them without compassion, well knowing what it felt like to be flying from the law. He did not tell even Heather what he guessed, for fear that she might want to betray the men if she thought as he did that they had run off with the means of making £700. Quite without realizing that he spoke the truth, he had told her when he returned from Tumbukka that the lugger had been piled up by a storm.

For a week or more, while troopers searched along the railway, Ket lived quietly at the police-station, taking his exercise by night in Settaroge's yard and in remote places to which Settaroge took him in his car, and spending the rest of his time in his cell, reading and sleeping and eating good food. He did likewise for another week while Settaroge sent messages to the Dutch East Indies in the hope that Frank could be located there. Settaroge's new theory, founded on knowledge of the pursuit of the halfcaste girls, was that Frank had struck back to the sea and found the girls who were making for the pearling-fleet and had gone to the Indies with them. Ket suffered much through this waiting, his own belief that Frank was dead having been weakened by Settaroge's that he was not, and his opinion that civilized comforts were worth any price having changed now that he had them at the cost of his liberty. As a matter of fact Settaroge was not so sure that Frank was alive; he only hoped he was, knowing that the case against Ket would be weak if Frank could not be produced; and he also hoped that Ket would be worn down by waiting to confess his true part in the crime, to which end he questioned him daily. However, at length these hopes collapsed. Ket learnt to his great relief that he would be required to join an expedition to the Jinjin to search for Frank's remains.

The expedition set out in the *Alice Carstairs* in the last

week of May, going without betraying the fact that Ket was a member and as though merely bent on settling some trouble between Mr Hollower and the natives. The personnel comprised Trooper Robbrey and two other policemen, and Ket, and four trackers who would carry out the detective work and carry the dunnage and perhaps their masters as well when swamps and creeks were to be crossed. They called first at Tumbukka, and finding the place as Ket and Robbrey had left it, went back to the wreck of the *Spirit of the Land*, then up the Jinjin to the arcadian camp, then stopped, having found the object of their quest.

Although the river was now returned to its bed of Dry Season, the party might easily have passed the camp without realizing that they did so; for as Ket believed (and he had led his companions to believe the same) that the last trace of Frank would be found in the camp in the foothills, he did not remember the lower camp, and the flood had demolished the gunyah there and had with the help of new-sprung grass long since wiped out all tracks. What led to the discovery was the label of a fruit-tin hanging in a tree, spotted at twenty yards' distance by a tracker. A few minutes after the party arrived in the clearing, indeed while the troopers were lifting the top-most sheets of the bark of the fallen gunyah, the same sharp-eyed tracker, turning from a momentary rooting about in the scrub to the right, cried out and held up to show a human femur and a plaited leather belt that he had found. The troopers and Ket had barely gathered the import of this find when their attention was drawn to the river by the cry of another boy, one who had gone to the water to fill the billy, who held up to show a rusty weedy rifle.

The finds were examined. Ket declared on sight that the belt was Frank's, and recollected having come to a camp thereabouts and been driven away by a stench. He was telling the troopers that Frank was unarmed, when a brand on the butt of the rifle was revealed. He gaped at it. It was the brand of Red Ochre. Then one of the boys dragged a burnt mosquito-net from the ruins of the gunyah and showed a similar brand in marking-ink on the canopy. Then another boy said that the brand was Red Ochre's. Ket said nothing, mindful of his attempt to kill Norman on Yalgah Creek. However, the troopers were reminded of the fact that Norman had been roaming thereabouts when he abducted Tocky. Ket had not heard of what they knew before. He kept silent till the finding of a human skull that had been pierced by a bullet, when, fearing that he might be suspected of having been concerned in another murder he told what he knew. He did not confess to having shot at Norman with intent to harm him, but said he had scared him away by shooting above him, afraid that he would betray him should he see him. The troopers listened eagerly. Far from regarding Ket with suspicion, they were pleased with him for his help, and more so when he identified the skull as Frank's by its three gold teeth.

The party searched the river and surroundings for several days, by the end of which they were convinced that everything it was possible to find was found. Most of the things were bones. The troopers were excited and delighted, as was only natural in creatures of their kind. Clues! A bag of human bones, a skull pierced by a bullet, several other things of which the ownership was proved. The skull belonged to a man who had been searching for a girl who had been found in the house of the owner of the rifle who hated the owner of the skull; and there stood a man who had seen the owner of the rifle within a few hours of having parted with the owner of the skull. A murder! Oh lord, a murder! What joy to a policeman!

§

The time for Tocky's accouchement was near at hand, but exactly how near she did not know, having, through being forced to go to Town that time, mislaid the notched stick with which she had begun in the native style to keep a reckoning; it was, however, near enough to make her life a misery, though not perhaps so bad a misery as it made of the life of her slave Norman. As he often told her, though never to convince her, her suffering was purely physical, while his was mental, and worse, because from physical suffering one might gain a little pleasure either in realizing one's ability to suffer in silence (pity not all folks had the ability!) or in indulging in unrestrained animal howls, while mental suffering, especially of the kind caused by sight and sound of physical suffering for which one was made to think oneself responsible, was — blast it! — simply suffering.

He often said that he wished he had sent her back to the Compound while he had the chance to do so without getting into trouble again, more often that he wished he had never set eyes on her, and still more often that he wished he had been born a bull. Cows, said he, suffered travail in silence, not because they suffered less than womankind (Tocky should think herself lucky that he was no bull or faun or devil or some such father that endowed its calves with hoofs), but had no-one to complain to of their suffering. Perhaps, said he, if men had the courage to be as callous as bulls, women might be as patient as cows. Tocky refused to believe it. Although capable of suffering as quietly as any cow with calf if need be, being a protected mother now, she behaved like a princess carrying a prince. There was but one way to silence her, and that by supplying her liberally with gin and aspirins.

It was to buy gin and aspirins from Mrs McLash that early in the afternoon of the Seventeenth of July, which was the day before train-day, Norman set out from home for the Siding, going thus late in the day because he had been delayed for several hours, first by the bungling by natives of the selection of a bullock for slaughter and next by a false alarm in respect of Tocky's deliverance.

Norman carried before him on the saddle a bag containing thirty pounds of beef, twenty of which was for Mrs McLash, the rest for the fettlers; ten of the twenty for Mrs McLash would buy the aspirins. Mrs McLash's aspirins were really not expensive; the beef he exchanged was but a portion of what Norman, who must kill a beast at least once a week to feed his staff, would give away to his staff's relations. The price at which Mrs McLash valued twenty pounds of beef was five shillings, but half the price at which the same quantity would be sold retail by the butcher in Town, and but a third of what Norman could get at the time for a whole live bullock. Hence she did not really deal as meanly with him as he insisted she did to everyone but her. She knew what he insisted. The fettlers often told her. She often talked about him behind his back, and with much more bitterness, because she hated him now that through his shillyshallying so long she knew he had no intention of going back to her Pride and Joy. And he knew she hated him and why. She made it plain enough when there was no-one but old Joe Steen about to hear. It was only fear on her part and necessity on his that kept them doing business. She could have bought her beef as cheaply from any of the impoverished graziers on the railway, but feared that Norman might revenge himself by betraying her Pride and Joy; and he was forced to be her butcher, since it was solely out of this mean trade in meat in a bag that nowadays he paid expenses.

Economy was the order of the day at Red Ochre, economy in all consumable things that had to be bought but gin and aspirins. Norman was penniless. He could have raised money by mortgage, but found one mortgage more than he could bear, from a financial as well as a moral view-point. He had had to borrow the first quarter's interest on the sum he owed Mr Bightit from Heather who was finding it hard to meet payments herself. The wreck of the *Spirit of the Land*, as reported by Mark who had promised to share the £700 with him, was to him the wreck of his hope of ever regaining solvency.

Norman thought of the Shouter as listlessly he rode down the river that day, thought of him not as a friend, not as a spider nor a crab nor any other of the tricky animals in the character of which he had seen him, but as an octopus that had him in a strangle-hold. Thus, when not far from the home-paddock rails he passed one of his bulls lying quietly ruminating in shade with the group over which it lorded, he envied it not only its callousness in conjugal matters but its freedom from care.

He was topping the crest of a hill about five miles from home when a snort from his horse roused him from his listlessness. The horse stopped and flicked its ears forward. Norman looked into the gully ahead, then up the next hill, but saw nothing but the smoky bush and yellow grass. "What's up?" he asked. The horse raised its head to neigh. Norman silenced it sharply, having glimpsed what it saw.

Unconsciously he had become almost as sensitive to the sight of khaki and bright leather and silver buttons as a native in a camp. That was the sight he saw. He stood in the stirrups. A moment, and he saw the sight again. Police! Two troopers and a tracker, distant about half a mile.

Instantly he thought of Tocky, whose whereabouts — whose very existence, indeed — he supposed only to be known to himself and the Mullanmullaks. He thought quickly. He had kept her hidden so long at first in hope that the reason for which he would be forced to marry her might be aborted with the help of Mr Bortells, the chemist, and, when that hope had faded, had kept her in compliance with her pathetic wish to stay. He had little fear of getting into trouble for kidnapping her, because, in the event of her being discovered, he had carefully planned that she and himself and the natives would say that, unknown to him, she had been living in some distant camp of the tribe all along; or rather he had feared it little till he set eyes on those policemen, who were, as he supposed, coming after her, while she was lying wingeing in the house. She must be got rid of.

He wheeled about and started for home at a gallop, sure that his going would not be noticed, because a harsh wind blew from the east and raised much dust. He did not draw rein till he had covered a couple of miles, when he stopped at a creek that ran into the river. He listened a while. No sound of pursuit. So he crossed the creek. Some yards beyond the creek he stopped again, this time to place the bag of beef in a fork of a big leafy tree.

He reached the home-paddock, jumped the rails, raced up the hill, drew rein in a cloud of dust at the side veranda, and bawled, "Hey!"

"Wassup?" asked a sleepy voice.

"Jonns comin'."

No sound.

"I said jonns're comin'!" he bawled.

He was answered with a squeak and the creaking of a bedstead.

"Crib your things," he bawled. "Put 'em bottom the sideboard like I told you. Then put on my shoes and go out and lock up the house and put the key with the key of the kitchen. Then go for your life. There's plenty of time, but none to waste. I seen 'em a long way back. But get a move on in case the Binghis see 'em comin' and do a bunk without you. If you can't catch the Binghis you'd better go to the tank again — but catch 'em if you can, cos the jonns might camp here. Can you do it?"

He was answered with a gasp.

"Can you do it, I said!"

"Oo — yis."

"Well shake it up. I'm off. I won't come home till late. Mightn't come home till mornin'. I'm gunner cut straight over east and double round the cows. You all right?"

"Y-y-yis."

"Good-o then. Be careful. Don't knock yourself up; and don't get panicky. They're still a long way off. Use as much savvy as you did when you first come here. Mind you, if you get caught I'll say you battened on to me — and so you did. Get away with the Binghis and go to Black Angel — and don't come back till I come for you. Got that?"

"Y-y-yis."

"Good-o then — I'm off — use your head and you'll beat 'em — hooray!"

Meanwhile, riding quietly along the river-track, came Troopers O'Crimnell and McCrook and Tracker-boy Ginger. The troopers were discussing Walter Lindrum, while Ginger behind them listened to their talk and wondered about the frequent word Billiards and tried in vain to pronounce it. But while Ginger's tongue was busy too, his eyes were not as idle as his masters'; thus when he came to the place where Norman turned, he saw the prints of hoofs and made deductions; but realizing nothing of immediate importance in the sight and knowing that a word uncalled-for might move his masters to rebuke him, he kept it to himself. He rode on quietly, muttering, "Peeyuss, pilluss, wallalintrum, nussrykennons", till his masters were within a few yards of the creek where Norman had stopped to listen, when he spurred ahead to see what might be seen.

"What's matter you?" snapped O'Crimnell.

Ginger's usually alert respectfulness was absent for a moment while he studied the muddy bank. O'Crimnell repeated the question in a voice that made him jump. He looked up meekly and answered, pointing to the ground, "Some fella bin ridim 'orse."

"What fella?"

Ginger pointed with his lips in the direction of their coming and answered, "Me bin lookim 'orse-track more far behind. Some fella bin stop, bin look-out you two fella (he excluded himself from the party), bin run away quick-fella." He swept his hand from the point indicated to the creek.

The troopers regarded him with interest. A nigger, they knew, was capable of seeing things that the most observant whiteman would miss. It was for that reason they employed their trackers. But they granted the fact of the capability as contemptuously as one does the fact that a dog has a keener sense of smell than a man; and this they did deliberately, realizing that they should have to accept their base servants as equals if they were to recognize their prowess in tracking as an art, and preferring to keep them as base servants. Ginger was O'Crimnell's boy. He did all his master's detective work, and cleaned his boots, and cooked his food, and tailed his horses, for which he was paid ten shillings a month by the Government, with scraps of food and a bit of niki-niki and an annual allowance of one pair of pants and a shirt and O'Crimnell's cast-off hats.

O'Crimnell was paid £32 a month and given furnished quarters and granted for each three years' of service a quarter's holiday on full pay with a first-class steamer-passage South. Ginger lived under O'Crimnell's house on a couple of bran-sacks. His own people would have nothing to do with him; for he was a policeman-born and, like his master — indeed like all his brethren of the man-catching profession —, of strange unloving and unlovable nature — actually that of a rogue set to catch rogues.

"How long before you bin lookim track back there?" asked O'Crimnell.

"Might be two mile."

"Well why the hell didn't you tell me?"

Ginger blinked.

"It new track?" asked McCrook.

"Yu-i — look-see, grass him come up." Ginger pointed to a tussock slowly rising from having been struck down by Norman's horse. All three dismounted.

Ginger knew every type of grass that grew in the country and understood the facts about its flexibility according to the season, the hour of the day, the temperature and humidity of the atmosphere. Thus he was able to explain to his masters that the horse that crushed the tussock had done so not half an hour before. But for his inability to express himself properly in the language he was required to speak but never taught, he might have been able to tell the time to the minute.

The troopers studied the unshod hoof-prints that still oozed muddy water. McCrook looked at O'Crimnell and said, "Mighter been a brumby — eh?"

Ginger interposed in an apologetic tone, "No-more brumby, Boss."

"How d'you know?"

"First time me lookim back dere me talk long inside me 'ead, 'Might be brumby bin makim dis one track. S'pose him 'orse belong station, him no fright for seeim man ridim longa nother-one 'orse — all right, him sing out. (Ginger simulated neighing.) Him sing out you two fella 'orse; and might him stop for lookim close-up. All right, s'pose him brumby, him no-more sing out — him run away, come dis creek, drink lil bits, look behin', runaway some more —"

"Dammit! Don't go on for ever," snapped O'Crimnell.

"All right," said Ginger, pointing to the creek, "s'pose him brumby, him drink lil bits — dry time brumby all-time drink —; all right, dat one 'orse (pointing to the tracks before him), time he try for drink, dat man bin pullim longa reins."

"How you savvy man?"

"Dis one 'orse bin walk up for drink — see track. Den him bin come back dissa way." Ginger backed like a horse.

"Well?"

"Brumby no-more back, Boss. 'Orse no-more back s'pose he can turnim round. Time 'orse back, man pullim — see?"

"Ah!"

Ginger waved a lean arm and said, "Plenty room for 'orse turn round 'ere. I tink dat man bin pullim up 'orse time him wanter drink, cos might be him bin wanter listen longa wind for some fella come behin'."

"Ah!" said O'Crimnell. "And you think he didn't neigh back there because man bin pullim?"

"Yu-i. Might be man frighten longa jonnop."

The troopers looked at each other. O'Crimnell said, "Looks like someone doin' a bunk from us."

"The yeller-feller," said McCrook. "Gunner give us a run for it."

"Come on," said O'Crimnell, and sprang to his horse.

Across the creek Ginger said, "Hey Boss!"

"There's the old gramophone again," said O'Crimnell crossly. "What's up now?"

"Cockatoo sing out," said Ginger, pointing with lips into the bush to the left.

"What about it?"

"Some fella man go ridim longa top-side, I tink."

"Ah!" said O'Crimnell. "Come on then — into it."

Norman, riding quietly through the bush along the brow of the hill above the river, stopped suddenly upon hearing the crash of foliage and the clump of hoofs. He wheeled his mount and applied his spurs; but before he had gone a score of yards he heard a shout, "Stop there — stop!" He obeyed, and turned to see O'Crimnell.

"Goodday," cried O'Crimnell, halting beside him. "Howz-it?"

Norman gaped.

"What you ridin' round in rings for?"

"Me?" murmured Norman.

"Yeah — you were down the river a while back. Where you goin'?"

Norman swallowed and said, "Just — just lookin' round for stock."

"You been lookin' pretty hard," said O'Crimnell, eyeing

the sweat-soaked heaving horse. "Bad weather for hard ridin', son."

Norman was silent.

"But what about that bag of beef?" asked O'Crimnell, cocking an eye.

"W-what?" gasped Norman.

"Bag of beef you's takin' to Ma McLash?"

Norman gaped.

"Well?"

No answer.

"If you was takin' a bag of beef to Ma McLash, how come you're quietly lookin' round for stock?"

Norman swallowed and said, "I—I heard a calf sing out up here."

"Sure you didn't hear an angel voice a-callin'?"

Norman swallowed again.

"Bad weather to leave beef about in trees, son — the flies is bad. You forgot 'em. You could hear 'em a dozen yards away. Oh well, let's get goin'. I want to have a bit of a wongi with you. Come on back to the homestead."

"But — but I want to get the bag of beef."

"Beef's all right. My nigger's got it."

"But — but Ma's waitin' for it."

"Oh no she aint."

"But — but — yes she is. I always take a bag in every Tuesday."

"I say she aint. She's gone up to Town on the trolley."

Norman gaped for a moment, then asked, "W-what you want me for? I aint done nuthen wrong."

"Never said y'ad. But wait'll we get up to the house. Not cribbin' anyone there again, are you?"

"No," breathed Norman, relieved to learn that the presence of Tocky was evidently not suspected.

"Good-o then, you won't mind our company for a bit. So let's get goin'. You lead the way — up to them rails this side. Don't try to do a bunk — or you'll be sorry."

Norman was pleased to find that he could go as slowly as he wished.

At once upon entering the kitchen, O'Crimnell went to the corner near the dresser and took up a rifle leaning there. He looked up from studying the brand on the butt and said to Norman, "Sit down." Norman obeyed.

O'Crimnell came to the table and showed the rifle to McCrook, then turned to Norman and said, "New — eh? What'd you buy this one for?"

Norman scowled and answered, "To light the fire with."

"Don't be funny, son. I want to know what you bought it for."

"What the hell d'you think?"

"That's what I'm askin' you. Haven't you got another?"

"Think I'm startin' a blunny armoury?"

"You'll get too funny d'reckly — and then I'll get mad. Cut it out. You're wastin' my time."

"What about you wastin' my time? What the hell's wrong? If you think I pinched it, you're wrong. I've still got the receipt."

"Well where's the other rifle you had?"

"What rifle?"

"The one you bought at G.P.'s on the Ninth of September last year."

Norman gaped.

"Well?"

Norman was beginning to feel afraid. "Why — what's wrong?" he muttered.

"I asked you a question — where's that other rifle?"

"I — I lost it."

"Oh you did? Where?"

"How the hell do I know? If I knew where it was, would it be lost?"

"People sometimes lose things on purpose."

"Not me."

O'Crimnell set down the rifle and sat down. McCrook also sat down, and took out a note-book and pencil. O'Crimnell exhaled impressively, put his large brown hands together as though about to pray, studied them for a while, then parted them suddenly and thrust a long fore-finger at Norman and asked, "Now where'd you lose that rifle?"

Norman, thoroughly scared, swallowed and blinked.

"Come on now," said O'Crimnell. "Where?"

"Down the coast somewhere," muttered Norman.

McCrook took down his words.

"Whereabout down the coast?" asked O'Crimnell.

"Jinjin River."

"Ah! And who'd you meet down there?"

Norman hesitated.

"Come on — no good keepin' anything back."

"Young Tocky."

"We know that. Who else?"

"No-one."

"Think again."

"I tell you I saw no-one."

"Don't get off your bike, son. I know you're tellin' lies."

Norman was thinking of Ket. He swallowed painfully.

"Now think, and answer truthfully," said O'Crimnell. "Didn't you see a man?"

Norman licked his lips. His throat was too dry for speech.

"Come on son. Who'd you see?"

"No-one," muttered Norman.

After a moment O'Crimnell asked, "Didn't you see Frank McLash?"

Norman answered chokingly, "No."

"But you told his Ma you did."

Norman gasped.

"Well?"

Norman licked his lips again, answered with difficulty, "I didn't."

"Didn't what?"

"Didn't see him."

"Then you admit you told his Ma you did?"

Silence.

"Come on."

"I didn't see him."

"Don't beat about the bush. I asked you a question. Did you or did you not tell his Ma you seen him?"

After a painful silence Norman answered weakly, "Yes."

"And you did see him, didn't you?"

"No, I never."

"Well what'd you tell her you did for?"

After another distressing pause Norman answered breathlessly, "I — I was only kiddin' her."

"Go on with you!"

"Dinkum," said Norman, wide-eyed and trembling slightly.

"But you knew Frank was down there somewhere, eh?"

"Yes — I — I mean I suppose so."

"What makes you suppose so?"

No answer.

"Well?"

Norman stirred and muttered, "What's the strong of you? What's the questioning for? I've done nuthen."

"Never said you had. Just want to ask a few things."

"Why pick me?"

"Cos you might know more about 'em than anyone else."

"What things?"

"What I'm patiently tryin' to get you to tell me — Where you seen Frank McLash and what happened when you did."

"I didn't see him, I tell you."

"You told his Ma you did."

"That was only kidstakes."

"But you admit you know where he was. How'd you know if you never seen him?"

Silence.

"Did you see Charlie Ket down there?"

Norman swallowed and stared at his fiddling hands. He was thinking that the murderers had been traced and that he was about to be charged with aiding and abetting them by failing to betray their whereabouts.

"Well?"

"No."

"Are you sure?"

"I am."

"But he says he seen you."

Norman started.

"Well?"

"Ket says?"

"He does. Well?"

After a moment's hesitation Norman muttered, "I'm not a pimp."

"What you mean pimp?"

"I'm not a police-informer. Go and get a crook — one of your own breed out of uniform — to do your dirty work — or do it your blunny self."

"The law demands co-operation."

"Jigger the law."

"The law'll most likely jigger you, if you aint careful, son. Now answer these questions and give no trouble. We've all gotter get up to Town tonight."

"Eh? Not me."

"Yes — you."

"To hell with you!" cried Norman. "I've got work to do. I can't leave this place —"

"You can and you will. Come on—let's get on with it."

ONCE again the citizens of Port Zodiac heard of a murder in their midst. They were delighted, but dared not show it for fear that the handful of bloodless mystogogues and pedants watching over them might call them Morbid.

The tongues of the police were now free to wag. Thus the citizens learnt why Mrs McLash had come up on a trolley, why she had spent hours at the police station, and why she had been lying ever since in a darkened room at the First & Last weeping. Why? Because the police had wished her to identify a bag of bones that were bone of her own bone. And thus the citizens learnt why Young Yeller Shillingsworth had come up under escort and been at the police-station ever since. Why? Because it was suspected that it was an act of his that had reduced the bone of the good lady's bone to an envelope of sacking.

A bag of bones! Musty relic of a victim of murder! Who killed Cock Robin? What joy to a normal-minded public!

The news came to the Princess Alice. Heather heard it, rushed with it to Mark. "Norman's been arrested for murder!" she cried.

"Eh?" he demanded.

"Arrested for murder."

"What're you talking about?"

"Young Robbrey just told me. Frank McLash has been murdered; and Norman's arrested for it."

"Are you serious girl?"

"Yes — As if I'd —"

"Frank McLash murdered, you say?"

"Yes."

"Well that's wrong for a start. Frank McLash's in the Indies or somewhere."

"He's not. Robbrey said —"

"Robbrey knows nothing about it. I know for a positive fact that Frank and Ket got away."

"But Ket's arrested. He's here — in Town. They've had him for weeks. And they've got Frank's bones."

"Frank's bones?"

"Yes — in a bag!"

"Godstruth!"

"And that's why the old lady's crying."

"My God! But — but — when'd it happen — the murder?"

"While you were down the coast. Just before you came in to Red Ochre."

"Aw they're mad! There was some trouble down there between Norm and Ket — Ket tried to shoot Norm — Lord, that must be it! And where's Norm now?"

"At the police-station. They've had him there all night, questioning him. He was arrested yesterday."

"Well I'll be damned! It must be all about that Ketbusiness — that shooting —"

"No — it's about Frank McLash. I tell you they've got his bones."

"Then Ket must've murdered him. He's a homicidal maniac, that thing. I'll go round and see about it. I'll go now."

As Mark took up his stick and topee and moved off, Heather said rather sharply, "Wait — what about your coat?"

"Aw it don't matter about a coat —"

"Oh don't it? Come and put it on. Come on now. And hold your back up. And don't go making a fool of yourself with Settaroge. You know that pimping crowd'd like to get even with you. Be careful what you say. They might try to drag you into it."

"All right, m'dear — all right."

At the station Mark found that he was already dragged in. Settaroge handed him a summons as soon as he set eyes on him.

"What's this?" Mark asked.

"Subpoena. We'll be wanting you at the inquest."

"Eh — what for?"

"Give evidence, of course. You know Frank McLash's dead?"

"Yes — that's what I've come about. I hear you've got my boy locked up?"

"Yes. Inquest's Monday."

"But you can't lock him up. What's the idea?"

"He's not exactly locked up. We're only asking him a few questions. He'll be free to go soon."

"But you've had him here all night You wouldn't do that to a whiteman."

"I dunno so much. Anyway, we're within our rights. Inquest's on Monday."

"Damn your inquest. Think I'm goin' to give evidence against my own son?"

"We're not asking you to give evidence against anyone. It's just an inquiry into the circumstances responsible for a man's death. The boy's just a witness like yourself."

"Well I want to see him."

"Just wait a while. We'll let him go directly. Here — hang on to this summons."

"Blast your flamin' summons! I'm not going to any inquest till I know what it's all about."

"The inquest's to find out what it's all about. Now look here, old man, don't give us any trouble. We happen to know that you were aiding and abetting two wanted men —"

"I didn't know that they were wanted men."

"You knew all about the accident business — and you're guilty of contempt of court on that count yourself. But we're not saying anything about it. Only don't give any trouble, old man. We just expect you to come and tell what you know."

"What about?"

"Your association with Ket and McLash and a few other things."

"I can tell you right off that Ket tried to shoot my boy."

"So the boy told us. You can tell what you know at the inquest."

§

On the morning the inquest began the public section of the court was so tightly packed that Coroner Larsney, grimacing with disgust, had the punkah set going to clear the air. Then, like all good ponderous justices, he delivered a scathing speech on Morbid Curiosity. The public dropped their eyes, but did not budge an inch, determined not to turn their backs on a real-life drama for the sake of a crabby old pedant who was sure of his own entertainment. Indeed, anyone in the public section of the court who wished to leave would have been put to a task to do so, so tightly packed were the door-ways with stubborn people come to see the bag of bones.

There were other stubborn people on the verandas, who, though they could not see what was going on inside, nor hear it unless it was related to them by people at the doors, were too strongly drawn by the spell of Morbid Curiosity to give way to anyone going back and forth but uniformed police. The relating by those at the doors to others behind caused Larsney to hammer with his gavel and ask sarcastically whether a court of law were a place of public entertainment. A wag replied by asking from concealment what the Public Section was for. Larsney threatened to clear the Court. Therefore the relating and asking had to be carried on in such low-spoken words as:

"Hey Bluey — who's maggin' now?"

"The old bird."

"What's he say?"

"Talkin' about a witness Yeller Shillingsworth says he's got. That little tart Tocky he was locked up for pinchin' from the Mission — one't drownded herself, y'know. Shillingsworth said a while back that she wasn't drownded at all."

"Go on! That a fact?"

"Dunno about fact. That's what the yeller-feller reckons. Says she's been at his place all the time, livin' with the niggers, and he only lately found it out and didn't like to put the mocks on her."

"And what's the old bird sayin' about it?"

"Shh — he's got me pipped — no he aint. He was sayin' just now that if the kid's alive she's a very important witness."

"Don't he believe she's alive?"

"Dunno. The jonnops don't seem to. It's fishy, be cripes. The jonns reckon for a start that the yeller-feller's told 'em three different yarns already about the kid bein' out there; and they reckon they went back to the Station to look for her. The yeller-feller says she done a bunk with the niggers. That's why the old bird's moanin'. He reckons the police must be a poor mob if they can't catch a few niggers. There — he's off on the moan again — says he can't accept the jonns' word against Shillingsworth's till they bring him in some of them Mullanmullak niggers to prove the little sheilah aint there. He says —"

"Yeah?"

"Ding it — he's lookin' right at me."

A long silence — then:

"Hey Bluey — who's maggin' now?"

"Old bird's at it again."

"What's he sayin'?"

"Bein' sarcastic — says if everyone't oughter be in the Calaboose was there, there'd be less crowdin' in the courts of justice."

"Must be havin' a dig at the jonnops, eh?"

"Shh! Gawd — here comes the bones!"

And through the throng the whisper ran, "The Bones! The Bones! The Bones!"

The Bones were removed from the bag, placed on a large lacquered tea-tray, and handed to the doctor by Captain Settaroge. What Settaroge then said sounded absurd, because the doctor was known to everyone in the country, and especially to Settaroge, who was a confirmed petty invalid.

"Your name is James Joseph Bianco Boyles?"

"It is," replied the doctor, bouncing a neat white hand on the edge of the witness-stand and smiling at the absurdity.

"You are a medical officer employed by the Government of Capricornia?"

"I am."

"And you have exhibited these examines — I mean you have exhabited these eximines —"

"Silence!" snapped Larsney. Tap! Tap! Tap!

"That is so."

"Eh — well then, Doctor, will you kindly tell the Court what you have learnt from your — er — ex-am-in-ation?"

"Good-o — Hurrumph! Hurrumph!"

The doctor said that the Bones were parts of a human skeleton that had been exposed for a period of from six to twelve months.

"Aw!" said Larsney, scratching dobey-itch on one of his legs and grimacing. "Cairn't y' give the peeriod more execkly, Doctor?"

"No Sir. Decay of the flesh in this case would not take place in the ordinary way. There would be water, insects, birds, beasts, all that."

"I don't think the period matters so much, Your Worship," said Settaroge. "The identification's pretty right."

"All right. Let the Doctor proceed."

The doctor went on to say that the skull was that of a whiteman aged between thirty and forty. He drew this conclusion from the formation of the skull. Three of the teeth were filled with gold. It was perforated in two places, in such a way as to suggest that the instrument responsible was a heavy rifle-bullet — Yes, perhaps such a bullet as would be projected from the exhibit. A bullet passing through such an object would do more damage at the point of exit than at that of entry, on account of its being enlarged by the first impact; therefore he concluded that the bullet entered the skull by piercing the frontal bone above the left eye-cavity, and left it by piercing the crown at a point distant in a straight line from that of entry of three and three-quarter inches, the perforation in the latter being bigger and more jagged than in the former. Undoubtedly the perforations were made before the skull was exposed. In his opinion death would be instantaneous.

Larsney asked if it were likely that the deceased had committed suicide.

The doctor replied that it certainly was not. If a man were to kill himself with a rifle he would do so either by shooting through the heart or through the throat upwards or through the mouth. According to his books, no known person had ever purposely shot himself with a rifle in any other way, no doubt because other ways would be too awkward for one who would certainly want to do the job as simply as possible.

Right-handed persons who shot themselves with pistols did so either by placing the weapon against the right ear, the right side of the head, the right temple, or the middle of the forehead just above the bridge of the nose, if they did not shoot as was first described with the rifle. Naturally in cases of suicide the weapon, rifle or pistol, was carefully placed, so that, though in most cases the bullet flew high owing to the kick of the weapon held in an intensely nervous hand, the perforation of entry was always low. However, in this case the perforation of entry was high, so high indeed, that had the weapon kicked, as it surely must do in the hands — two hands in this case — of a man whose muscles were tensed, the bullet must have skimmed over his scalp. Moreover, the perforation was on the left side of the head of a man who, if the identification were correct, was right-handed. Of course it was not impossible for a right-handed man to place a rifle-muzzle against his forehead on the left side; but it was so awkward as to be very unlikely when the man intended to take his life. From all these reasons he was convinced that it was not through suicide that the late owner of the skull had met his death. However, he might have died by his own hand through accident.

The next witness was Sergeant Tocatchwon, the criminologist of the force and Settaroge's righthand man. He was so expert in solving the puzzles presented to the community by criminal minds that it would almost seem he had a criminal mind himself. He said that as regarded the likelihood of Deceased's having met his death by accident it was his opinion that the evidence gave no reason for the entertainment of such a theory. That Deceased's own finger had accidently fired the shot was out of the question, since such a weapon would have to be held at full length to have caused such a wound and held in a very awkward way. An accident with a rifle would be almost certain to cause a wound, in the head in an upward direction, if not in the body. The idea that Deceased might have pulled the trigger accidentally while squinting down the barrel or otherwise examining the muzzle could not be entertained in view of the length of the weapon from muzzle to trigger, which exceeded that of the arm-length of even an abnormally big man.

That the weapon was fired through the trigger's having caught on a twig or some such thing was possible only if one were to consider it likely that a man trained to handle firearms should carry a loaded and cocked rifle in such a way as to allow the trigger to become fouled while the muzzle was pointing at his head. The idea that the trigger, which even when well-oiled required a strong pull to move, might have fouled some such thing as a very tough twig while Deceased was carrying it in the one way to cause him to present the muzzle to his head when attempting to free it — that is carrying it on his shoulder — was rendered unlikely by the reasonable supposition that in withdrawing it he would either stand very erect and so thrust the muzzle away in drawing it up, or stoop in order to draw it towards him, in either of which positions he would certainly not be likely to be struck by the bullet in the head. Then again, there was the very important fact that the rifle was found at considerable distance from the skull. Undoubtedly the shot was fired at very close range.

Sergeant Tocatchwon's reasoning made a deep impression, as always.

Next witness was Joseph Patrick Wrench, the dentist, who with the aid of his books identified the gold fillings in the teeth of the skull as work he had performed in the mouth of Francis Donald McLash. The Coroner had to bawl at this witness to make him speak so that his words could be heard by other ears than his own. Mr Wrench appeared to be drunk.

The dentist's place was taken by Mrs Pansy McLash. She also began to speak inaudibly, and incoherently by reason of her sniffs and sobs. Larsney did not bawl at her;

instead he nodded sympathetically and smiled and leaned towards her. The warden stood in the stand beside her, holding in one hand a bottle of smelling-salts, in the other a glass containing a straw-coloured liquid. It was not till helped to many sniffs and sips that she was able to give her evidence.

Mrs McLash said that she was sure the skull was that of her dear boy. She wished to God it were not. She knew he had a low declining forehead and an egg-shaped head and that he had gold-filled teeth; but how many teeth were filled she could not say, not having been able to take the interest in his mouth she would have liked since he had shed his milk-teeth. Her son, she sobbed, was a good boy, and anyone who called him a thief and a murderer was a dirty bloody liar. Larsney, who in effect had called Frank such names at the close of the inquest on Con the Greek, turned purple; but he did no more than scratch his itch vigorously and clear his throat and interrupt the witness's eulogy to tell her that she must pay attention to Settaroge's questions and not make statements of her own accord till asked; then he nodded and smiled to take the sting from his words.

After saying that she objected to her son's remains being hawked about in a bag like bones picked up by a bottle-o, and that she wished to have them decently interred as soon as possible, Mrs McLash allowed Captain Settaroge to question her. She said in reply that somewhere about the middle of October of the previous year she sold Norman Shillingsworth, halfcaste, a quantity of provisions, among which was tinned stuff of brands similar to those on the labels and tins produced. When he bought them he said he was making a journey to the coast somewhere east of the Caroline. Some little time before Christmas he called again and said he had just returned, and, without her asking him, went on to say that he had seen her son camped on a river, the name of which he did not give, and that subsequently, with the assistance of natives, he had located her son's permanent camp and had gone to it to spy.

He said that he had not spoken to her son, which, because she knew nothing at the time about the quarrel the pair had had on the Melisande, seemed rather strange to her. Naturally eager to send word to her son, she asked Shillingsworth to return to the coast. He promised to do so when the country dried up. He did not keep his word; and when she asked him again, as she did from time to time, he answered evasively, saying a couple of times, indeed, that he felt sure her son would be gone by then. He said as much just before he went to jail for abducting that quarter-caste girl of Lace's. She asked him only twice again after that, having by then concluded that he had no intention of going.

"The dog!" she cried suddenly, turning to Norman, who sat with Mark at the lawyers' bench, and shaking her fist at him. "The yeller dingo — the bastard thing — he had no intention — because he knoo — My God he knoo all the time my dear boy was gone — dead and gone — dead and gone — because — because he'd killed him! Oh you mongrel — let me get my hands on you — I'll — by Christ I'll —"

"Calm yourself, Madam," cried Larsney. "Pray calm yourself. Poor distracted soul! Dear me! But — but — Oh Warden, you'd better take her away — Careful! Careful! Keep hor away from him — keep her away!"

Norman was startled by the outburst, and again when, soon after Mrs McLash had been led away weeping wildly, he glanced round the Court and met many an accusing eye. For the first time he began to feel anxious. He glanced at Mark and found that he was apparently feeling anxious too; then he glanced at Nibbelsom, who was sitting near him taking notes, and found him apparently pleased. Nibblesom nodded, blinked as if to say, "There! I told you it was serious. Better engage me." Norman ignored him.

Evidence was given next by the troopers who had found the Bones; and next by O'Crimnell, who described how he had questioned Mrs McLash and Norman, and how he had arrested the latter while apparently running away; and next by Settaroge, who read the statements made by these two witnesses and said a little more about the search that had been made and was still being made for the Mullanmullak natives with whom it was said the drowned girl Tocky Pan had fled. The Court then adjourned for lunch with rumbling bellies.

While Norman was eating at the Princess Alice, Nibblesom came with his notes, which Norman then learnt had been taken not merely out of idle interest in the case but on his behalf. Nibblesom again offered his services, saying that his case looked very black, that in fact he was willing to bet that Larsney would commit him for trial. Again Norman declined, politely at first, then, annoyed by the dolorous warning, at the top of his voice. Nibblesom departed clicking his tongue; but when the Court sat again he was back at the bench with his notes and his nods and his blinking.

First witness of the afternoon was Charles Ket, who gave the details of the trouble that had caused Norman and Frank to fight on the Melisande and to hate each other ever after. He then described his experiences in the Jinjin country. The way in which he gave his evidence, or rather the way in which it was drawn from him, filled Norman with alarm again and set Nibblesom nodding and blinking as though taken with the palsy.

Mark was the next witness. He described Ket as a homicidal maniac and Frank as a moron and the police as a set of rogues. When he stood down he was panting and red, as were Settaroge and Larsney.

Norman was the last witness. He stood in the stand for nearly three hours, answering Settaroge's and Larsney's questions, and seeing with amazement the production seemingly out of nowhere of proofs of his movements long forgotten. He spoke the truth, but often wondered while he did so whether he was doing wisely, indeed often wondered whether it was really the truth, so untruthful even in his own ears did it often sound. Losing the rifle — fantastic tale! Hiding young Tocky — even more fantastic. Small wonder that Settaroge and Larsney looked impatient.

How he contradicted himself! The foolish things he said! Settaroge asked him how he accounted for the fact that the rifle was found in the river when he asserted that he had lost it in the bush. He answered that perhaps it had fallen on a piece of bark and been washed into the river when the flood rose. Absurd! He bit his tongue for having said it. Washed into the middle of the river from the very edge of the flood in a straight line? demanded Settaroge. Well, said he, the only other reason he could think of was that McLash had found and flung it in the river himself; Tocky had not found it; he had asked her; she knew nothing about it; and he had left her with a shotgun.

When at length he stepped down from the stand the court was gloomy, and bloody lights were pouring through the western windows and flickering on the eastern wall. On account of some trouble at the power-house, for want of light to see his notes, Larsney had to sit in gloom for twenty minutes, grunting and scratching his dobey-itch.

At half-past eight Larsney and his Associates retired to consider the verdict. At ten minutes to nine they returned.

After much unnecessary fiddling and settling himself, Larsney told the breathless sweating Court that he found that the Bag of Bones was the remains of Francis Donald McLash who had been wilfully done to death by Norman Shillingsworth.

Norman gasped. For a moment he stared; then he jumped up and cried, "You're wrong!"

"Proceedings are now at an end," said Larsney coldly. "The accused will be presented at the police-court tomorrow morning."

"But you're wrong," cried Norman. "I didn't do it. Dammit! You've got it all mixed up. You're wrong."

Nibblesom took his arm and hissed, "Steady, Norm."

Norman flung him off and fairly howled, "I didn't, I tell you — damn you — listen to me —"

"Silence," grunted Larsney, leaving his seat.

Mark then took an arm. Nibblesom slipped up again and whispered, "Don't Norm — won't do you any good. Sit down. We'll fix it all later."

Norman allowed Mark to seat him. "But — but —," he cried loudly, "I didn't do it. Godstruth I didn't. They're mad."

"Shh!" hissed Nibblesom. "Just leave it to me. Don't worry. There's many a flaw in the case."

"I don't want you," cried Norman.

"But you've got to have someone. This's only a taste of what's coming. They'll stack it up tenfold at the trial."

"I don't want anyone. They can't do anything to me. I didn't do it, I tell you."

"Many a man's gone to jail and the gallows for what he didn't do. Circumstantial evidence. The case looks very black —"

"Well I don't want you, you blithering four-eyed thing," cried Norman. "Go away. You're a pest." And he said to the policeman who came to arrest him, "Send that cow away. I hate the sight of him."

He was taken to a cell in the lock-up. Mark and Heather went with him. They had been sitting in silence for some minutes when Mark said, "I reckon you'd better send for Bightit."

Norman looked up and said, "And lose Red Ochre!"

"Better lose it than go to the Calaboose for fifteen years —"

"They can't send me there!" cried Norman.

"You dunno what that old cow Pondrosass can do. Better

let me send for the Shouter right away. It won't break you."

"I can't stand another mortgage."

"But the Station can. What if you got mortgaged up to a thousand. The Station's worth at least a couple of thousand even now that times are bad."

"But can't you see I can't pay anything off? Bightit'd get it in the end. Aw gawd, I always knew something like this'd happen when I got into debt."

"Go on! A boom might start at any time."

"Not it! Not my luck. Aw, one damned thing after another. Did you ever hear of anything like it? Gawd — sometimes I feel like I really did it, as if I must've been in a trance or sumpen — it's all so well stacked up against me."

"The Shouter'd get you out of it in two ups."

"And ruin me. Gawd — the barsteds'll get me back to the bush before they're done with me — because I'm a half-caste — and they think I oughter be a nigger."

"Don't talk like that, Norm," said Heather. "You know we'll stand by you."

"You? What can you do? You're pretty well bust your-selves."

"But we wouldn't let you down, Sonny."

"You told me a coupler months back you'd go to Papua if you went bust; but you never said nuthen about takin' me with you."

"No — because you've been making yourself a stranger. Look, Norm, we're a family, we three; try and remember that always."

"You've got your trade to fall back on, anyway," said Mark.

"What's the good of it here in this colour-mad hole? They'd never give me a job."

"I dunno so much. You're thought a good lot more of here than you realize. Anyway, if the worst came you could always go South again."

"I'd rather go back to the Old People than be a wage-plug in the South."

"Then send for the Shouter," said Heather. "It's obvious you got to have someone now."

For a while there was silence. Then Norman said, "No — I'll wait and see what happens to Ket. His case comes off in a couple of weeks. He's got Nawratt. Lord knows how he got him. Might be the State pays for a lawyer if you haven't the cash. If Nawratt can get him off, surely to God he can do it for me who's done nothing; and he'd do it for a tenth of what the Shouter would."

"Please yourself," said Mark; "but I reckon myself it's a case for the Shouter."

§

Indeed it was a case for the Shouter, as Norman was soon convinced. Ten days after he was committed for trial on a charge of Felonious Slaying, he learnt from Mark, who had it from Nibblesom, that two Mullanmullak blacks had been arrested who had denied that Tocky had been at the Station. He sent Mark off to tell the police that the boys were lying to shield him and Tocky, as he would prove to them if they would bring the boys to him. Mark returned to the Calaboose within an hour to say that the police had said that the proving could be done at the trial.

Then late in the afternoon of the fifteenth day, Ket came back from the police-station, where he had spent three days while being tried on the charge of Robbery Under Arms, to spend twelve years in the Calaboose. Norman saw him led staggering to his cell and was kept awake all that night by his weeping. First thing next morning he sent for Mark, who came with Nibblesom. They sent for the Shouter.

So the Shouter came back. He came overland in a car, having been prevented from catching the steamer through pressure of business. He came with his wife again, and with his two crab-like sons; and perhaps because he lent some of his power to the machine, he made the exceedingly rough journey of two thousand miles in a mere seven days, which was a record. Each day cost his client ten pounds.

He arrived looking redder than ever through exposure to the sun, and with voice even louder through shouting above the wind and engine and the silence of deserts, and with added to his character ways of fresh types of animals — camels and eagles and cattle-camp cooks.

At once on arrival he took up bridging and dining and fishing and left the preparation of the case to Nibblesom. Norman did not see him for several days, by which time, having been disappointed in his hopes that Tocky would be found and that the Shouter would secure him a trial by jury, he was in the depths of despair.

The trial began. This time the Shouter, not having simple jurymen to deal with but two Associates who would most likely be displeased with trouble-mongering, raised

not one Objection. Judge Pondrosass and Prosecutor
Thumscrough were obviously relieved. Nor were there
any challengings of Associates, nor any desire for such a
thing. These gentlemen were the Resident Commissioner,
Major Luffmey, and Malcome Whyres, the manager oť
the Cable Station, with both of whom the Shouter had
bridged and dined during his former visit. The Resident,
who invariably acted as associate to Judge Pondrosass, was
a State Magistrate. Whyres was a Justice of the Peace.

Norman found to his amazement that the existence of
Tocky was still in doubt. He soon found to his great concern that all doubt had been removed. By the end of the
first day of the trial it was pretty certain that everyone who
mattered in the Court was convinced that her existence
had ended soon after she was last seen at the Compound.

The whole of the first day was spent in dealing with the
disappearance of Tocky. Policemen said that they had
found her clothes in the house and ample evidence of her
presence there, but nothing to show positively that she had
lived there since she was arrested. Fresher traces, such as
prints of feet and hands, could easily have been left by
lubras. Positively, no-one had been near the place since
Accused's arrest. No importance could be attached to the
fact that aspirin and gin bottles were found there; for when
buying these things accused had told Mrs McLash that he
consumed them himself. It was impossible to track down
the tribe without the assistance of one of its members who
knew their particular tricks of erasing their tracks and
concealing themselves. Then the two captive natives were
placed in the stand. To all except Norman who questioned
them, including the Judge and the Shouter, they readily
said that they had not seen Tocky since the day she was
taken away by O'Crimnell. To Norman they replied in
various ways, saying at one time that Tocky had hidden in
a camp in the bush for weeks unbeknown to him, at another
that she had fled with them when he was arrested recently,
at another that they had not seen her since then; quite obviously they were baffled and willing to say anything they
thought he wished. Settaroge said that he had questioned
the natives for days, and that though he had got little out
of them and feared he could get no more unless he tortured them, he had got enough evidence to convince him
that the tribe had fled at the approach of the police on
account of some guilt of their own and had not taken
Tocky nor seen her. Norman tried to explain why natives

ran away from policemen. He was stared at. Then Prosecutor Thumscrough submitted that the captives were unreliable witnesses. After some discussion on the point, the
boys were dismissed. Not understanding that they were at
liberty, they lounged about the yard near the cells, waiting
for transportation to the Calaboose, till discovered by policemen and driven away at the point of the boot.

Next day the subject of Tocky was raised again. The
Court sat only so long as it took to agree to adjourn for
five days at the almost humble request of the Shouter,
who said he would like to have time to examine the matter
from a different angle. His request was granted graciously.

§

The trial was resumed. The evidence produced at the
inquest was brought out again, in a state more refined and
devilish for having been stored. Prosecution made out their
case with a will. Norman did not sleep that night of the
day of resumption. Next morning he was examined. In
the afternoon his cross-examination was begun. He slept
that night only because he was exhausted. He came into
court to face Thumscrough again convinced that he would
be convicted. He had lost all faith in the Shouter. At the
time of adjournment the Shouter had raised his hopes very
high by asserting, after having questioned him closely about
his dealings with Tocky, that he thought he saw ways to
prove that the girl was still alive and to get him acquitted.
Since then the man had seemed to avoid him.

Indeed it seemed as though the Shouter were at a loss.
He did little more in court than truckle to the Bench. He
was now but a purring cat. Many times rage swept over
Norman while he watched the man dully examining and
cross-examining, so that he had to restrain himself from
jumping up and hurling invective at him. "Why don't you
do something?" he asked a score of times. The man merely
asked him what there was to do but have faith and patience.
In the afternoon of the third day Thumscrough began his
Address. Norman did not sleep that night. Next morning
he came dazed and red-eyed to hear that mouth-piece of
constitutional revenge continue his misanthropy, resolved to
conduct his defence for himself.

Then halfway through that morning the Shouter set to
work. He took the skull and placed it on top of a pile
of books that stood on a chair on the lawyers' table at about
the same height from floor as it would have sat if on the

late owner's shoulders, and placed it so that its pose was what it would be if its owner were standing erect; then he took a long thin stick and thrust it through the bullet-holes, so that it slanted downward, clearly showing that the track of the bullet was something like thirty degrees from the perpendicular, supposing that at the time the skull was pierced it stood as then; then he took the rifle and handed it to Norman, whom he requested to place himself in any position that would bring the rifle into line with the stick while yet he held it so as to be able to pull the trigger. Tall Norman braced himself in many positions, all awkward, many fantastic, none suggestive of the fact that he had fired the shot that had caused the holes. The Shouter chose several other poises for the skull and placed it at various heights for attitudes of stooping he wished to show; and he invited Thumscrough to try his hand at the game. The results of the experiments were all the same. Therefore, he said, if Accused had fired the shot deliberately he must have crouched or lain in an extremely awkward position, which was not likely unless he were suddenly attacked by Deceased, in which case he would have shot in self-defence and could admit it.

Now let other things be considered. Take the fact that the rifle was found in the river, on account of which Prosecution had wasted much breath in harrying Accused. Was it reasonable to suppose that a man who committed a murder in the wilderness would bother to dispose of the instrument? Prosecution said it was, suggesting that such a man might do so in unreasoning terror. Perhaps they were right; but would not such terror induce him to dispose of the corpse as well? If the corpse had been flung into the river the bones would not have been found where they were; and if Accused was so fearfully guilty as to dispose of the rifle while loth to touch his victim, would he not have demolished his camp, if not at the time of the crime, then a week or a month later? And would such a fearfully guilty man go straight and tell his victim's mother that he had seen her son? Consider that most damning piece of evidence in the case, that Accused went to Mrs McLash and told her he had seen her son. Understanding of human nature was required to consider it wisely.

Now the most truthful of us are the dullest, the most untruthful the most imaginative. While harrying Accused just now, Prosecution reminded us of the fact when considering the boy's character. Let us consider it. His father

and step-mother and other witnesses have all unconsciously
in innumerable small statements borne witness to the fact
he is to some extent what is called a Romantic Liar. And
he is inclined to boast and strut; and he has written what
he calls poetry, reads a great deal, spends much of his time
in dreaming. This is Aboriginal. Now any normal innocent
man who has seen so startling a thing as a hunted criminal
would want to tell someone he had, to tell it to the first
person he met. A romantic liar would dramatize the tale
he told, that is would add or subtract details to balance the
whole so as to rouse the greatest possible interest.

The first person Accused met after his encounter with
Ket, not counting Tocky, was Mrs McLash, whose interest would be roused at once by mention of her son. Accused knew that Frank would not be far from Ket, and so
would suppose his tale not far from truth. Then what more
natural than that such a man should tell the mother such
a tale? Why should he tell it? Simply to rouse interest, at
once to gratify his desire for creating drama and his desire
to attract attention to himself. He did not tell his father
that tale, as was quite evident from the cross-examination
of the elder Shillingsworth. He might easily have told him
without fear of betrayal. Why did not he do so? Because
there was no such gratification in that case. There he got
his gratification by describing his encounter with Ket em-
bellished for his own glorification. A simple matter, but
one requiring understanding of human nature.

All this the Shouter said in the character of dove, cooing
logic, cooing reason and persuasion. Then he became quietly
bull-like, and tossing his head and stamping lightly, said
he was now about to deal with the strangest and most important part of the case, that troublesome disappearance of
Tocky. He did not assume the character with a view to
terrifying, but to impressing with his strength.

He took from his pocket three sheets of paper, which,
he asserted, with a challenging glare at Thumscrough, constituted evidence that Tocky was still alive and living at
Red Ochre after she was last seen at the Compound. Then,
seeing that the Judge was beginning to glare and the Associates to shift irritably, he quickly apologized to the Bench
for producing this evidence so late, saying that his doing
so was not a trick, the fact of the matter being that it was
not till the adjournment that he had discovered that such
evidence was procurable, and that the procuring, seeing that
part of it had to be fetched from Batman, was not easy; in

fact he had not been sure of the value of the evidence till that very morning.

The papers were a telegram and two letters. The former was obtained for him very kindly by the police from the local post-office, into which it had been handed by Accused some weeks before Tocky's arrest. It was a message to a certain pharmaceutical chemist in Batman, asking cryptically for advice on the matter of aborting a certain condition that it was known Tocky was then in. One of the letters was one that Accused had sent to the chemist after Tocky was last seen at the Compound. It bore the chemist's rubber stamp and the word Received and a date. It had been obtained from the chemist with difficulty, had been sent by air-mail to Bullimba, from there to Carrawilla by special aeroplane, and the rest of the way overland by car. It had only just arrived. It stated that the patient, who had been forced to relinquish the treatment sent in answer to the telegram, was now in a position to resume it, but that the writer thought that now the patient's condition was advanced so much further (the state of advancement described tallied with what that of Tocky's condition would be soon after Accused returned home from jail) a more potent kind of treatment would be necessary. The other letter was one sent by the chemist in reply, saying that it was now too late to procure the desired event with safety. It had been in the possession of Accused, who had not realized its value; in fact he had thought it destroyed; it was found at Red Ochre by Mr Nibblesom. Hence the delay. Their Honours must accept this evidence as honest, even though perhaps there was little more to prove it was than the presence of the chemist's stamp, otherwise the case must be stopped in order that the chemist might be subpoenaed.

After examining the evidence and discussing it at length and listening to some brave but hopeless wrangling on the part of Thumscrough in the face of the mild but menacing glaring of the Shouter, Their Honours decided to accept it.

Norman became excited. Now he was looking at the Shouter as a saviour. The man became a turkey-cock, strutted for a moment before Thumscrough, then relapsed into the state of dove.

The Shouter said that now the case had taken a new turn, no objection could be raised to his calling several new witnesses, although Proceedings were so far advanced. He

would call several people who had known the girl Tocky
fairly well and who would describe her as being very cunning and close-lipped on occasions. To that end he would
call the matron and one sister from the hospital, and Dr
Aintee, and the matron of the Compound, and two or three
girls from the Halfcastes' Home; then he would call Ganger
Jacob Ledder to describe the life of the children of the
O'Cannon Family, then Trooper O'Crimnell to describe
the unreasonable terror of Tocky at the time of her arrest;
finally he would place Accused in the stand again and in-
struct him to tell in his own simple way what Tocky had
said and done on the Jinjin, and would allow his Learned
Friend to cross-examine him scone-hot.

All this the Shouter did after lunch. The stir it caused!
People on the verandas had thrice to be driven back from
doors and windows by the police. The matron of the Compound stated under questioning that Tocky had once asked
her if she were going to be killed. The halfcaste girls told
of similar utterances. Ganger Ledder stated that Tocky
had been reared with a rifle in her hands. Trooper O'Crimnell admitted that she could not have shown more panic at
the time of her arrest if she had thought she was being
dragged to the gallows.

Then Norman went into the stand and told how Tocky
loved hunting with a rifle, how she had striven to get his
rifle when he left her on the Jinjin, how queerly she had
behaved when he returned, and how queerly at times ever
after. It was obvious that he was telling the truth. His
eyes were shining, his voice quick, his brown hands eager.
Oh it was quite obvious that he was telling the truth.
Every now and then he would stop to say that he had
thought of none of this before. Prosecutor Thumscrough
turned bulldog and tried to worry him into contradictions,
but without success.

Then the Shouter assumed every character he possessed
but that of the shark, and enthralled the court with a reconstruction of the crime as it was committed in his opinion.
Much had been said, he shouted, about the likelihood of
the fighting to death of two men for a girl they wished to
possess, but nothing about that of the girl's killing one of
the men to protect herself from him. Yet what more likely?
McLash found the girl alone. She shot him to protect herself. Now let us see how she did it.

He had erected the skull again and rigged up the burnt

mosquito-net on sticks. Hastily he bundled one of his half-caste girls into the net and gave her the rifle.

Tocky was in bed at the time, he said, and shot McLash while squatting on haunches thus and he bent over her thus. See how easy it was for a little girl to shoot from that position! Note the hole in the net!

How did Tocky come by the rifle? Impossible to say. But that she had come by it they might be sure. Possessed as she was of the shot-gun, what more natural than that she should fling the bloody rifle away. Accused had left her with a head packed full of tales of the punishments that murderers suffered, and came back talking of betraying the murderers of Con the Greek. What more natural than that a child of her character should hold her tongue forever? There was no fear in her when Accused left her. When he returned he found her utterly changed. She was described as the Deepest girl in the Compound. Consider her character. It was supposed that she had drowned herself. Was it not likely that the cunning little minx had pretended to do so? Where was she now? Perhaps she had truly drowned herself at last.

"Unhappy child!" shouted the Shouter, glaring round the Court. "Unhappy waif! So much suffering for nothing. No court of law would condemn her for what she did. A woman has every right to kill to defend herself from a ravisher. None but a court of monsters would condemn the child. Oh unhappy waif!"

His voice sank to softness as he turned to the Bench; but all heard what he said and were thrilled by it. "Your Honours," he said, "if that child is living and is captured and brought up for trial and condemned as the result of what I have said, I swear by the Almighty that I shall return to this court at my own expense and free her. I have betrayed her, poor miserable outcast waif that she is, only for the sake of this innocent man. This is a case of circumstantial evidence. Accused is not guilty. I thank you."

Judge Jeffries summed up so meanly; he said so much in support of his Thumscrough and so little in that of the Shouter that not only one heart quailed but a hundred. He said this, he said that, and all so coldly. He was a judge of men, a man himself, yet did not seem to realize how men feel. He said this, he said that, so reasonably, so precisely, as though dealing with a piece of logic and not with the liberty of a man. Why did he not throw his gavel at Thumscrough and rise and say with a smile, *He's Not Guilty*?

No — he said this, he said that, and all so coldly, and so much in support of the misanthrope Thumscrough and so little in that of the champion of fallen men, the Shouter.

Their Honours retired to consider.

Oh they were so long away! Not only one heart ached with anxiety, but a hundred. Oh but how that one heart ached! How those brown hands clasped and clutched to still their trembling!

Their Honours returned. Oh how slow they were in taking their places! Ponderous asses, pompous dogs! Why could not one of them have shouted the verdict from the retiring-room door as soon as it was decided? No — they settled themselves as though they were come in to a formal banquet. Convention. Unavoidable, perhaps, like many things in the world, but contrary to humanity no less.

After many minutes of cruel delay Judge Pondrosass fixed trembling Norman with hard eyes and told him he was judged Not Guilty.

Uproar! Policemen had to fight to clear the court.

The Shouter went off shouting till he met his wife, who silenced him.

BACK TO EARTH

THE Shouter turned shark when he presented his bill to Norman. The sum was £496. 6s. 8d. Huge expenses had been incurred, he said, in procuring the letter from Bortells; for since the man, through fear of getting into trouble for having dabbled in illegal trade, had refused to give assistance, it had been necessary to hire a burglar to steal the letter; and then there was the cost of having it sent up. In presenting the bill on this occasion he lost no time. He did it on the day of acquittal. Nor did he bother to be diplomatic, but bluntly asked Norman if he would sell him Red Ochre for £1,122 7s.4d., and forthwith produced a document that plainly showed that that was exactly what the place was then worth to Norman.

Norman was rather shocked by the proposal, but not dismayed, because, having been greatly worried by the thought of eventually losing the station through the mortgages, it struck him as a profitable way out of difficulty.

He said he was agreeable, but would like to think about the matter and talk it over with his parents. The Shouter said he wanted a prompt decision, and left him, arranging to meet him after dinner. Mark and Heather also agreed to the proposal, saying that Norman could invest the money in the Princess Alice if he wished, or if not in that, in some sort of business in Papua, to which the three of them would go.

The meeting with the Shouter was timed for eight o'clock. At seven Norman happened to meet Nibblesom in the street and tell of him of the proposal. At quarter to eight, while Norman and Heather and Mark were waiting in the office for the Shouter, Nibblesom rushed in and without wasting time on greetings cried, "Don't agree tò that proposal. I smell a rat."

They stared.

"Bightit's bought two stations already," panted Nibblesom. "Andy McRandy's place and Kumma-Kumma. I just met old Andy. He told me Bightit's bought him out for someone down South. The bloke from Kumma-Kumma came to me for advice about debts about a week ago and told me he was selling out. He didn't say who to; and I never thought at the time to ask; but I remember seeing him with Bightit several times."

Still they stared.

"And Bightit's been nosing round the Meatworks. I know that for sure. He asked me a lot of questions about it. And he's been sending loads of wires South that had nothing to do with the case."

"Well?" asked Norman. "Where's the rat?"

"I don't know. But I'll soon find out — if you'll make it worth my while."

They eyed each other.

Nibblesom stepped back and looked into the hall for the Shouter, then returned and went on quickly, "Look — that feller wouldn't take an interest in cattle-stations for nothing — especially with trade in the state it is. And what's he nosing round the Meatworks for? You bet if he's willing to pay you a thousand in hard cash for Red Ochre when he could get it for nix in time, he's only doing it because he'll get ten thousand back before long and has to act quick."

Still they stared.

"If you'll promise me you'll make it worth my while, Norm. I'll look into the matter. Is it a go?"

After a moment Norman replied, "Sure — but what're you gunner do?"

"I know someone down South knows all about the cattle-markets of the world. I'll wire him right away and ask a few questions."

"But I don't see what there is to suspect," said Mark. "The trade's as dead as wood."

"But Bightit's not. Trade's as dead as wood; and yet he offers you hard cash for Red Ochre."

Nibblesom, as though prompted by some sense, skipped to the door again, and bounded back, making for the back door, and hissing, "Here he comes. Say nothing. Make out you haven't decided yet. He's terrible shrewd; so be careful. I'm off. See you tomorrow with the goods."

At halfpast three next afternoon Nibblesom rushed into the hotel, and finding Mark in the office, sent him off to get Norman. Mark came back with Heather as well.

"Well?" asked Norman.

"Great news," said Nibblesom. "I really ought to ask you to sign an agreement first about making it worth my while; but I know I can trust you. Look — if you can make a clear thousand profit in the next six months on the strength of what I tell you, will you give me a hundred pounds?"

Norman looked wide-eyed at Heather, who, after a moment said, "Why — sure!"

"Give me your word," said Nibblesom.

Norman gave it.

"Well," said Nibblesom, "Bightit's formed a company down South to open the Meatworks here!"

A pause. Then Norman asked, "But what's he gunner do with the meat?"

Nibblesom smacked his bony hands, smirked, stood on his toes, adjusted his spectacles, and said, "Through the National Meat-market's Board, Australia has just secured a five-years' contract to supply canned and frozen meat to the French Army and Navy at home and in the Colonies. The business is to be given to the graziers of the North. That happened — or rather it was published in the Southern Press — the day before Bightit left for here. He must-'ve come up with it in his head. He'd be interested, seeing he has an interest in Red Ochre; and he'd keep it to himself for the same reason. We won't hear of it till the mail-boat comes. And next, but by no means least, since it means the recovery of the Philippines market, and more, there've been — Ha! Ha! Ha! — there've been terrible earthquakes in Argostinia. The country's all upside down, and burning with ashes chucked out by a volcano. Cattle have perished in hundreds of thousands. That happened while Bightit was getting the burglar to pinch the letter. His partner must've sent up word with it. You can bet he knows it. He knows everything. Well, what's it all mean?"

"A boom!" cried Heather.

"Oh gosh!" cried Norman. "A boom!"

"A boom!" cried Heather again. "Oh no credit to booze-artists this time — and no thieving bookkeepers." She turned shining eyes on Mark and cried, "You wouldn't do a bunk with the cash, would you, dear?"

"Me?" laughed Mark. "And leave a treasure like you behind?"

She took his arm, then Norman's, and drew them to her.

Nibblesom coughed gently behind his hand, then said, "Er — Norm — er — just as well to put that promise in writing, eh? D'you mind?"

§

Norman returned to Red Ochre to find Cho Sek Ching in possession. Cho had been there for a fortnight. He said he had come back to look after the station because he had heard that Norman had been sent to jail. Norman was grateful.

Cho had a new donkey, a big stubborn white beast he called Cullapride, which he was vainly trying to break in. Norman went up to the big horse-yard one afternoon soon after his return to watch him make a last despairing bid for mastery. Although Cho had the animal saddled with a huge stock-saddle and rode it with spurs locked beneath its belly, he could not keep his seat. At last Cullapride bucked him clean over the gate. He fell on his face in the dust. Norman and the blackboys ran laughing to pick him up. He sat up, dazed, staring at the stupid white face that was staring at him through the rails; then suddenly he snatched up a handful of dust and flung it at the face, yelling, "Yah-a — you blunny myall! Nobody can teachee you nussing. Me finish. Gwan to hellee!"

Norman, spluttering with laughter, went across to the stock-tanks to drink. He was drinking from a trough, when he was startled by the sudden appearance of two crows that swept up from out the broken tank. Then he noticed fluttering from the rim of the tank a piece of dusty blue cloth. He stared. The cloth fell limp, fluttered, fell again. Dry grass rattled against the iron. Dry wind moaned through rust-eaten holes. He stepped up to the tank and peeped through a hole. Nothing to see but the rusty wall beyond. He climbed the ladder, looked inside, saw a skull and a litter of bones. He gasped. A human skull — no — two — a small one and a tiny one. And human hair and rags of clothes and a pair of bone-filled boots. Two skulls, a small one and tiny one. Tocky and her baby!

The crows alighted in a gnarled dead coolibah near by and cried dismally, "Kah! — Kah! — Kaaaaah!"

COONARDOO
KATHARINE SUSANNAH PRICHARD

When *Coonardoo* was published in 1929 it was greeted with considerable controversy. It tells the story of Coonardoo, a young Aboriginal woman, who is trained from childhood to be the housekeeper at Wytaliba station, and, as such, is destined to look after its owner, Hugh Watt. The love between Coonardoo and Hugh, which so shocked the audience of 1929, is never acknowledged and so, degraded and twisted in on itself, destroys not only Coonardoo, but also a community which was once peaceful.

Introduced by Drusilla Modjeska, this tough, uncompromising novel, daring for its time and set on the edge of the desert, still raises difficult questions about the history of contact between black and white, and its representation in Australian writing.

MY BROTHER JACK
GEORGE JOHNSTON

'My brother Jack does not come into the story straight away. Nobody ever does, of course, because a person doesn't begin to exist without parents and an environment...'

In *My Brother Jack*, George Johnston traces the lives of brothers David and Jack Meredith. He focuses on their childhood during the First World War, growing up in a patriotic, suburban Melbourne household, and describes the events that help shape their very different lives. Through David and Jack, Johnston explores two Australian myths: that of the man who loses his soul as he gains worldly success, and that of the tough, honest, 'Aussie' battler, who sees the justification of his life in the realization of his ambition - to serve his country during the war.

My Brother Jack is a deeply satisfying, complex and moving novel. It is an Australian literary masterpiece in the true classic mould.

THE TIMELESS LAND
ELEANOR DARK

First published in 1941, Eleanor Dark's classic novel of the early settlement of Australia is a story of hardship, cruelty and danger. Above all it is the story of conflict: between the Aborigines and the white settlers.

In this dramatic novel, introduced here by Humphrey McQueen, a large cast of characters, historical and fictional, black and white, convict and settler, brings alive those bitter years with moments of tenderness and conciliation amid the brutality and hostility. All the while, behind the veneer of British civilisation, lies the baffling presence of Australia, a timeless land that shares with England 'not even its seasons or its stars'.

WATERWAY
ELEANOR DARK

This sparkling novel, set on the edge of Sydney harbour, follows a small group of people through the intricacies of a single day; a day that reaches its climax on the harbour when the ferry bound for Watson's Bay collides with a liner and sinks.

How will the accident change the life of Winifred, married to vindictive Arthur and in love with Ian? Will the events of the day alter the resentments of Jack Saunders or the vanities of Lorna Sellman? Is there any reason or morality when it comes to accident and death?

First published in 1938 when Eleanor Dark was at the heart of her powers, and reprinted here with an introduction by Drusilla Modjeska, *Waterway* is as brightly patterned as the harbour and as full of life as the people it describes.

ALIEN SON
JUDAH WATEN

'As soon as they saw me they burst out laughing and pointed to my buttoned-up shoes and white silk socks. I was overcome with shame and ran back into the house where I removed my shoes and socks and threw them away. I would walk barefooted like the other boys.' With such a gesture a child can adapt himself to a new country and new people, even though for some time he may not 'know a word of what they were saying'. For the older generation, however, things may not be so easy...

Judah Waten's classic story of a Russian family settling in Australia in the years before the First World War is published here with an introduction by David Carter.

'*Alien Son* is a real contribution to Australian literature...It even has some of the descriptive simplicity of Chekhov and Katherine Mansfield.'
SYDNEY MORNING HERALD

'This book pioneers a rich field for the fuller imaginative interpretation of Australian life. *Alien Son*, sympathetic, penetrating, shows us many possibilities...'
THE AUSTRALIAN

'In *Alien Son* the child, the parents are two additions to the short list of characters in Australian fiction who deserve permanent life in our imagination...They are fully, grubbily alive. Mr Waten's ruthlessly realistic picture of them is nevertheless wonderfully tender.'
THE AGE

MY BRILLIANT CAREER
MY CAREER GOES BUNG
MILES FRANKLIN

'I am given to something which a man never pardons in a woman. You will draw away as though I were a snake when you hear.'

With this warning, Sybylla confesses to her rich and handsome suitor that she is *given to writing stories* , and bound, therefore, on a brilliant career.

In this ironically titled and exuberant first novel by Miles Franklin, originally published in 1901, Sybylla tells the story of growing up passionate and rebellious in rural New South Wales, where the most girls could hope for was to marry or to teach. Sybylla will do neither, but that doesn't stop her from falling in love, and it doesn't make the choices any easier.

For the first time ever, *My Brilliant Career* is published with its sequel, *My Career Goes Bung*. It is introduced by Elizabeth Webby.